THE EYES OF
THE SETTING SUN—

Christian Madsen

Madsen, Christian
Eyes of the Setting Sun-, The
All rights reserved

Published by
The Writers of the Apocalypse
1117 N Carbon ST PMB 208
Marion, IL 62959
www.apocalypsewriters.com

ISBN-13 PRINT: 978-1-944322-14-4
ISBN-13 DIGITAL: 978-1-944322-15-1
Second edition

Cover design by K. J. Joyner
Interior illustrations assembled by K. J. Joyner,
 art design VIPDesign @ dollar photo club.com, extended license

DEDICATION

This is dedicated to the memory of Martha Mary Kraus Madsen, my late wife, who furnished the inspiration to get me through the difficult job of finishing this.

And I Gratefully Acknowledge and Extend my Thankx To—

—The Dayton Street Irregulars—

Donna Douthit, Linda Sugar: For Moral & Immoral Support Above and Beyond the Call of Duty;

Shoshana McVey: Immoral Support, damned good advice and persistence;

Margaret Bonanno: My Mentor in the Arts and Sciences of Writing, Agentry, and Publication;

Donald Greenspan: Old friend and mathematical advisor: Advice, Moral Support;

Ashleigh Waring: Grammarian Extraordinary;

Leslie Fish and Miriam Frohman: For literary advice, moral support & political education;

Rich Whitnable: For Being There in a Difficult Time;

Griff Healy: For the Continuing Never-Ending Saga of Wild Bill Strange;

Jack Cipperly: For Being <u>There</u>, And <u>Here</u>;

Greg Rihn & Georgie Schnobrich: Martial Arts consultation, and discussion of the comparative anatomies of my characters;

Carol Mason: Emergency File Recovery;

Dan Staples, Don Heinz: Technical Advice on Internet usage and Networking;

Bill & Debbie Wickart: Debugging the Card Reader;

AND—

Marti: Again and Always;

—Chris Madsen, 28 November 2015

From Les Illuminations—

I have held the summer dawn in my arms.

Nothing moved as yet on the fronts of the palaces. The water was dead. Swarms of shadows refused to leave the road to the wood. I walked along, awakening the warm, alive air. Stones looked up, and wings rose up silently.

The first occurrence, in the path already filled with cool white shimmerings, was a flower which told me its name.

I laughed at the blond waterfall which tumbled down through the pine trees. At its silver top I recognized the goddess.

Now hire for me the tomb, whitewashed with the lines of cement on bold relief,—far underground.

I lean my elbows on the table, and the lamp lights brightly the newspapers I am fool enough to reread, and the absurd books.

At a tremendous distance above my subterranean room, houses grow like plants, and fogs gather. The mud is red or black. Monstrous city! Endless night!

Graceful son of Pan! Under your brow crowned with flowers and berries, your eyes, precious balls, move. Spotted with dark streaks, your cheeks look hollow. Your fangs glisten. Your chest is like a lyre and tinklings move up and down your white arms. Your heart beats in that abdomen where your double sex sleeps. Walk at night and move gently this thigh, then this other thigh and this left leg.

I stretched out ropes from spire to spire; garlands from window to window; golden chains from star to star, and I dance. The high pond is constantly steaming. What witch will rise up against the white sunset? What purple flowers are going to descend?

While public funds disappear in brotherly celebrations, a bell of pink fire rings in the clouds.

Grey crystal skies. A strange pattern of bridges, some straight, some arched, others going down at oblique angles to the first, and these shapes repeating themselves in other lighted circuits of the canal, but all of them so long and light that the banks, heavy with domes, are lowered and shrunken. Some of these bridges are still covered with hovels. Others support masts, signals, thin parapets. Minor chords cross one another and diminish, ropes come up from the shores. You can see a red jacket and perhaps other costumes and musical instruments. Are they popular tunes, bits of castle concerts, remnants of public hymns? The water is grey and blue, as wide as an arm of the sea.—A white ray, falling from the top of the sky, blots out this comedy.

—Arthur Rimbaud, 1886

THE EYES
OF THE
SETTING SUN—

PROLOGUE:
THE PLAYERS

——>>>ONE<<<——

O you've seen that man before
His golden arm dispatching cards

—Leonard Cohen,
The Stranger Song

ALLEY SOLO—I—A YEAR EARLIER

[Initialization] She had her back to the dark damp striated concrete walls of the underground structure. He had followed her into the parking garage. He stood there before her, his hands on his hips. Laughing.

"C'mon, doll," he said, his baritone voice cajoling, nagging, insistent. "It's time to go back."

Ineluctable. Unavoidable.

He stepped forward on the greasy surface. A single step.

She couldn't step back. *Can't*, she thought. The heel of her foot, her left, touched the wet gray wall behind her.

His expression was of a dissatisfied owner. Or the owner's agent.

"Roger sent me."

The damp grayness around her, gray like her master, her overlord,—*no more!*—surrounded her on three sides. The only exit was through the man before her. She looked up, down, to the sides, *Trapped!* the thought entered, an animal trapped in a huge corner filled with car carcasses, decaying branches. Junk.

Perhaps bodies?

The run had been long, from a home she couldn't remember very well to this meeting. With this one.

I could just charge him, knock him over. A part of her hadn't given over to panic. She clung to that, now.

Behind him, lights from the street turned him into a black apparition delineated by a bright outline. His solid dark shadow covered her, a ghostly rapist.

There was a sharp sound from the street. He paid it no attention, his gaze fixed on her.

The acid in the pit of her stomach was overpowering. She wanted, was ready, to run. Anywhere. The gray walls of this corner seemed to extend infinitely. Unbidden, images of her recent past played themselves out. The dead hollowness within her was wavering, nauseous. She gritted her teeth, biting the inside of her cheek. The jolt of pain was an electric shock; it pushed the fear back.

"I'm not going back with you, Tim," she said trying to keep the tremors out of her voice. Stalling. Did something move in the rusting car behind him? Something with a luminous eye?

"I came all the way down here, and you can't show me what you've learned?" Tim laughed at that.

His step forward was an increment in a progression. "You surprise me! After what you've done."

She side-stepped, her heel scraping the concrete. If she could get away from this wall and back into the center, she would have a better chance.

In the distance the dim lights outside of this parking ramp glowed, their beams casting multiple shadows of varying shades of blue, pink and off-white. The sounds of traffic outside could be heard here, barely. From far off she heard a "clunk" as of a brick or hard stone striking the concrete driving surface.

He anticipated her move, his shadows shifted with hers: parallel processes in a system of dim lights: synchronized movements in a dark place.

He had chased her into this ramp. It was below a tall building, and she had tried to lose him here, to escape into the dark embrace of night. There was no exit except the direction from which she had run.

Now, he stood in front of her, enjoying his power in this wet, shadowy place.

She ducked sideways and ran for the center of the enclosure, followed by her multiply colored shadows. He homed in on her, a heat-seeking missile with one thing on his mind. She heard another sound, as of metal striking concrete.

As she filed the sound for later, she turned and fired a quick side-kick aiming her heel, her left, with precision.

It caught him on his right hip. He staggered back, bounced on his left foot, slid forward.

She aimed a quick punch, leading with the two knuckles of her right hand. The blow landed on his sternum, neatly canceling most of his forward motion. Part of her thought of opposing force-vectors. Most of her thought about this taller, heavier opponent whose expression hadn't changed even as his approach did.

Contemptuously, he walked towards her, the agent of the man who had claimed her, her owner, his hands ready to seize, deflect or inflict. She batted his right hand away from her, followed through with another blow to his throat.

He grabbed her hand.

She slapped his ear with her free hand, and aimed a heel at his knee-cap. He dodged her and fell back. She charged, bringing her knee up into exactly the right place. In the distance there were more little stony sounds, as of pebbles or small rocks falling.

He fell into a crouch, partially to protect himself, mostly because he had no choice. She punched—one, two, one, two—alternating her blows, turning her hips into each punch to concentrate the force.

He rocked back, falling.

She aimed one precise toe, covered with a heavy walking boot, cocking it back, and firing a roundhouse kick.

He became a knot of flesh closed in on himself in the greasy center of the concrete.

Another shadow joined hers in pink and blue and off-white on the rough gray walls.

Then more shadows.

She looked up from her opponent and saw the line of figures standing in the entryway, backlit by the ambience from above. A single source outlined them, a brilliant hair-light in the darkness.

A view to a height; a tower among elves.

The figure in the center was tall and looked almost slender because of it. The others looked about half as tall.

"Would you like some help with that?" The tall figure asked. The accent was cultured British English. The tones were those of a woman. "Surely you weren't here of your own free will."

She found her voice, "No."

The tall figure took a silent step forward and gestured to one of the short members of the entourage.

A short figure produced a folded pad of what looked like off-colored cotton. The figure placed it over her assailant's nose and secured it in place with an elastic band.

The tall woman regarded this silently. Then: "He will awaken later unaware of what has happened here." Something like a small brown spider jumped from her shoulder onto the sleeping man, stayed a moment and jumped to one of the short assistants.

The assistant turned into the distant light.

She stepped back. Wide-set eyes, vertically slit, like a cat's looked out from below bony ridges in a round head. There was a prominent, flattened nose, a thin-lipped mouth.

On its head was crest of curved bone and thin membranous skin.

She could not determine its color.

She spun around. "Who are you?"

"A friend," the tall woman said. "You need a friend. I will help you. And in return I will require your help."

"My. Help."

"You can go places where I cannot. You know this city. I will alleviate this trivial disturbance in your life. You have been brave enough to deal with such.

"I have uses for your bravery."

INITIALIZATION

[Production Run] The tall woman wore a concrete-gray trenchcoat, a fedora pulled low over her face, and mirrorshades. The tall woman smiled with her lips only, not showing her teeth, and pointed at the burden her assistants were holding.

The tightly wrapped bundle moved slightly.

She extended her left hand. "Come with me. I shall take you to a safe place. She indicated the male human at her feet. "I am familiar with the minions of Gray Roger. This one will never hurt you again." She looked at it, "Will you?" Then she turned.

"Come with me." The English sounding lady extended her hand, and the former fugitive took it. The small group of short assistants fell in behind them, the crests on their round heads standing high. A door opened in the concrete where she hadn't noticed even cracks before: incandescent light indicated a warm welcome.

The two ladies and the assistants entered.

THE PLAYERS—ONE YEAR LATER

[Sequence]

"My Deal."

Mississippi Slim's speech always seemed to come in Capital Letters.

The gambler had a pretentious way of talking that set Zhongo Teketon's nerves on edge. There were overtones to Slim's voice that reminded him of fingernails on a chalkboard, or of car brakes screeching, or of small children. Zhongo Teketon hated all of these; children the most.

The room was close and smoke filled. A single one-hundred watt light bulb hung above the poker table—over the pot of miscellaneous bills and coins in the center. Piles of chips, coins and wrapped-up paper currency cast sharp shadows that pointed directly at the players surrounding the table. Cigarette and cigar smoke circled, curling around the players' heads: Mississippi Slim sat across from Zhongo, Lead-Foot Eddie sat to Zhongo's right, Comic Book sat to the left. On Comic Book's left, One-Eyed Jack scowled over his winnings, his one good eye, scanning and ophidian, an all-encompassing omphalos, missing nothing; the other eye was lost in a mass of red scar tissue. Allen Hightower, a tall slender man whose ash-blond hair was worn in a military crew-cut, sat between One-Eye and Slim, and The Maestro was sitting to Slim's left, completing the circle.

Seven men. On the surface, a friendly game of seven-card stud, deuces wild; barely below that surface, a contest between just two of those seven.

Slim took the deck, riffle-shuffled it several times with practiced motions of his wrists. The cards crackled electrically in the silence. Smoke rose up from his cigar in a straight line, then dispersed in complex curlicues and arabesques. He shuffled again, and thumped the deck down before Allen. "Cut," he said. Allen Hightower reached for the cards, performed a Scarne Cut that was axiomatic in its swiftness, slapped the cards down before the dealer. Mississippi Slim scooped up the cards, squared off the deck, and silently dealt out the two Hole cards.

He looked at each man in turn, and flipped a single card up before each: "An Ace to The Maestro," he said. "Ten of Diamonds, Three of Hearts, Five of Spades." He took a breath. "Four of Spades for a One-Eyed Jack. Allen gets a Seven." Hightower looked at his Diamond without expression. "Dealer gets a Four."

The Maestro led the betting, "Fifty bucks," he said, pushing a dirty bill into the center.

The other players squinted at their hidden cards. Allen's expression was unreadable as he turned his seven over. Lead-Foot Eddie covered. "Folding early, eh?" Zhongo asked. Allen frowned at him but said nothing. Zhongo looked at his down-cards, and dropped a bill in the pot. Slim looked expectantly at the other players; there were no replies.

"Cards," he said, and dealt.

The Maestro received an eight of hearts. Lead-Foot looked sullenly at the five of clubs that covered part of his ten. He flipped the cards over, "Not worth fifty to see that!" he scoffed. Zhongo Teketon looked with quiet interest at the Three of Clubs he had been dealt, but said nothing.

"Possible Straight," Slim said to Comic Book's six of hearts, "Passible Flush," to Jack's Ten of Clubs. He dealt his own: Four of Clubs. Two players were out.

Zhongo looked around at the others, cheerfully, as he watched Slim drop a faded c-note into the pot. He covered it, "Raise you a yard," he said.

Comic Book scooped up his "possible straight" and tossed his cards down in front of Slim. He took a rolled-up copy of *Batman* out of his back pocket, and buried his nose in it. Slim saw Zhongo's raise without further comment. The remaining players, The Maestro and Jack, chucked in their two-hundred.

Mississippi Slim took up the cards. They seemed to weigh far more than one deck of ordinary Bicycle Playing Cards should. He didn't need to look at his hole cards; it was as if he could see their suits and denominations through the design on the backs of each rectangle.

"Cards." He flipped the top card out. It spun into The Maestro's stack of bills. Slim took it out, and laid it next to The Maestro's Ace and Eight: the Nine of Diamonds.

"Two cards to a straight," Slim said.

Lead-Foot was scribbling rapidly in a small notebook. Slim knew what Eddie was doing. Eddie was a "might-have-been-er," an occasional poker player who tries to determine what he could have had if he hadn't folded when he did.

Slim spun another card out at Zhongo with a flick of his finger: the Three of Spades. "Three of a kind. You got another pair under that, Zhongo?"

Zhongo Teketon was a study in lack of expression. Slim waited for an answer until the silence became uncomfortable. He flipped a card at One-Eye: Six of Clubs.

"Looks like you're building a Flush, Jack." Jack didn't answer.

Slim dropped the last card in front of himself. Three Fours looked up at him.

"Dealer bets a yard and a half," he tossed a wad of cash at the pot.

"See that," Zhongo said, "Raise another fifty." There was the rustle of bills.

"Two-hundred to you, Maestro," Slim said.

"I guess I'll stick around for a bit." The Maestro peeled a pair of hundreds from his money clip.

"One-Eye?" Jack squinted at his hole cards and folded.

"Not worth another. I'm a little short tonight."

"Hit your limit, huh? Just the three high rollers left."

"Cards." Slim dealt:

A ten of diamonds to The Maestro.

A three of diamonds to Zhongo Teketon.

A five of diamonds to himself.

He looked at the cards displayed. Comic Book looked up out of his namesake and rolled it up. Bruce Wayne could wait.

"Four of a kind bets," Slim said tightly.

"Two-hundred." He dropped bills in the pot. Ben Franklin's face looked up at Slim. Twice.

Silently, The Maestro folded.

Zhongo Teketon regarded Mississippi Slim; Slim looked back. The poker table seemed to be wider than the whole room, wider than the squalor outside, wider than the universe. This table was their universe, and Slim decided to open it.

He knew his hole cards. Knew them as if their suit and number had been painted on the walls of the room. He pushed four fifties out, then four more.

"Raise you two-hundred."

Zhongo's reaction was swift. Too *damned* swift. He covered the bet. "See you. Raise. Four-hundred to you."

It was back in Slim's lap again. He couldn't have anything better than what was showing. Even with the last down-card waiting to be dealt, four threes was IT.

An unwelcome voice insinuated its way into his thoughts, *You sure of that?*

I N S I N U A T I O N S

[Sequence Incrementing; Continued] No, he wasn't sure. The odds were there, readable by any card-player with any sense, not to mention what was lying face-down on the table in front of him.

He turned to the door behind him, "Leona! Come out here." The door opened and a woman dressed in a long robe came out. The others looked up at her. For a moment, Slim was in control. Leona was 168 centimeters tall and, even through the robe, was very well shaped. Her hair was a deep flawless black that cascaded to her waist. Her eyes were a startling electric violet. There was intelligence in those eyes: Leona was not a low-level street-whore, Leona was *prime*. Slim looked up at her, and whispered a command. Casually, Leona shrugged her shoulders, let the robe drop. She was wearing nothing underneath. Even Comic Book's copy of *Batman* fell to the floor, unnoticed.

A W O R D F R O M A L A N P A R S O N S — I

[Medium Shot: Soft Focus] *She sits in her workroom, listening to the video music on her VCR. The video playing is The Alan Parsons Project's tune, "Stereotomy." On the screenf, brief video clips of ecstatic dancers jump through short routines, as their world itself vibrates and moves in time to the rock beat. Unknown to the dancers, first one, then two, then four men, all clones of their former self, do back-flips in and out of the choreography. The entire continuum—dancers, gymnasts and the studio—moves ponderously aside to start, then faster, in precise dervish whirls. The reality disclosed behind it is first a tropical rainfall, then a storm, then a volcano, followed by hell-fire, followed by the distant hell-fires of other suns.*

On her main screen, a group of men—large in life, made small on the display—engage in the rituals of Stud Poker. They have stopped their game for an introduction. Her main focus is on Leona, the slender woman with the long, dark hair, now standing naked before the room of watchers.

Leona takes the looks and her lack of dress in stride, she has done this before in the line of duty with her ex-employer. Now, she does it for entirely different reasons.

For her Watcher. For her friend.

For what was building.

And what would follow.

[Poker Table, Relational] Leona was slim, high-breasted, obviously in the best of condition. Her legs were long, slender, well-muscled. The plumage on her crotch was as black as her long hair. She placed one hand, her right, nonchalantly on her hip, and her casual stance became a pose.

"Winner take all, Zhongo Teketon," Slim said into the silence.

"Deal them."

Two cards. Thin rectangles. Cardboard destinies.

Slim dispensed the cards. Zhongo picked up his three hole-cards. There was something of the bored academic in him as he read them. It was as if he hadn't seen the strikingly beautiful woman standing behind and to the right of Slim. She turned once around, and Zhongo looked briefly up from his cards at her ass. Then he looked back at important matters.

"Call," he said, more into the cards than anywhere else.

Mississippi Slim arranged his cards, flipping one more hole-card over, "Four-of-a-Kind, Ace kicker." He leaned back in his chair. His shoulder brushed Leona's left leg. She stepped back. Slim looked up at her; she didn't look down at him: her eyes were riveted on Zhongo Teketon.

Slim looked across a table that seemed light-years wide. Zhongo frowned at his cards, looking over them as if they were good, but not quite good enough. Allen Hightower looked on, interested but studiously neutral. Deliberately so. Zhongo put one of them next to the four threes. A two of clubs.

A wild card.

[Priority Process] Slim felt the gulf between them widen. He had not exactly forgotten about the "deuces wild" part of the game, they'd been playing that way for most of the evening. No wild cards had come up in the deal in this hand, and he had been lulled, just a little. Just enough.

[Parallel Process] He felt a brush of air by his right shoulder; she was leaving. He watched her walk up to Zhongo, and rest her hands on his shoulders. Slim felt a pang of regret, or at least what passed for regret. She had been a good guest, a friend....He cut the thought off. This was as easy a way to do the job as there was. Zhongo was looking up at Leona, and Slim wondered if she would get the robe back before going to Zhongo's quarters.

He thought of his wife and his small son waiting back at the large apartment he called "home." He shuddered, internally. It had been close, finding his son where he had been.

The rescuer of his little boy—Slim was no longer able to remember who it was, just that he owed that rescuer the proverbial Big One. His main stake in this game, Leona, lately his houseguest, and now, his final act for that nameless rescuer. Placing Leona. Then finally forgetting her.

Slim looked at Zhongo Teketon and Leona across vast spaces. The Maestro had already scooped up Zhongo's cash winnings; Zhongo had other things to take care of.

Mission accomplished.

[Process, Asynchronous] At an uninhabited house on Milwaukee's South Side, a car pulled into the driveway and drove all the way to the back, to the parking area near the garage. A man got out, looked around. There were houses whose back yards were contiguous with the yard on which this house was built, but a thick hedge, taller than the first floor of the house, prevented anyone else from looking within. Large trees occulted the views from upper floors.

He looked around for minutes, before his associate got out of the car. The second man removed a key from his pocket and unlocked the back door of the house. He looked in. The back entrance led into a large kitchen, which was unlit. The second man looked intently this way and that, then returned to the back. He nodded to the driver, and the driver opened the trunk of the car.

Together they carried the boxes into the kitchen, then emptied the back seat of the car of more containers.

The driver put the car into the empty garage, secured the garage and returned to the house, where the other man was opening the first carton.

Within was a small but very powerful computer. The driver opened another carton and removed another compact piece of electronic hardware. Then a flat-screen monitor for the computer.

An hour later, all of the boxes were empty, and an unused bedroom in the house was well stocked with precision equipment, laptops and less-portable systems networked by encrypted spread-spectrum interfacing. One of the men opened a flat portfolio, and removed several large photographs, which he tacked neatly on the wall above one of the displays.

The pictures were of a recognizable landmark: a low complex of buildings dominated by three geodesic domes of clear glass.

He nodded to his associate.

[Match Cut: Load Backup; A Year After] His partner had gone to bed earlier and immediately to sleep: now he was able to get to one of the digital video disk players to take a look at his find. It wasn't anything really odd or threatening: just an ordinary DVD. The hand-written label read, "Design: Preliminary Computer Animation." Yet, he could sense a tension. Not from the small disk, or its unprepossessing label, but around him, from the surroundings to which his travels had brought him.

He placed the disk in the player. The device clicked gently, locating the start point. Then the monitor came to life. A figure danced and spun on the screen: a form lifelike but not living, a creature of lines and angles, of sines and tangents. Windows appeared around it as it performed: these windows contained numerics, still pictures, commentary. The spectral form moved through a series of stop-motion frames, each frame preceded by others, that faded slowly, multi-colored phantoms trailing until each phantom faded out. The whirls, thrusts and kicks moved silently through several modes: slow-motion, real-time, fast. Occasionally arcs of light, vestiges of previous frames, would look as if the dancer were holding long sabers, slicing savagely.

For a moment, unbidden, came the words of a fragment of verse, something his associate had shown him earlier:

"What else in words of fire,
Chanted by the Midnight Choir...."

—-and—,

"On the Green when Sun is up,
No one may refuse the cup."

Amateurish, but then there was nothing that could be described as "normal" about the background of the author of those lines. There was nothing to suggest adequate background to write a sonnet or a sestina. Simple couplets were a massive effort, even if the intellect typing those lines was truly formidable in many other ways.

"And I may sail
Into The Eyes of the Setting Sun...."

There was a soft noise from the hall; someone was coming.
Who was it?
He removed the disk, switched the player off, and left the room.

HYPER SPACE

[Truck Shot; Compiling] *The screens form elsewhere in a place that is not quite space or time. On an infinite plane, the only demarcation is a grid of fine straight lines. There are thousands of them to the centimeter, almost at the limits of the resolving powers of the eyes that haven't seen them yet. Quiescent, they wait, glowing slightly below the surface. They extend infinitely in two dimensions. Above, there is only the all-pervasive omni-directional yet directionless light that serves as the only source of illumination: the color of a liquid crystal display screen displaying nothing.*

The square screens form in a circle facing inwards. There are twelve of them spaced like the numerals of an analog clock. Images form in the screens; externally specified indices, loaded from some other place, from a database outside the infinite plane.

The images are scenes of desolation and wreckage. Torn-down buildings, houses afire, conflagrations, fire-storms across city blocks, car and train wrecks; a dozen windows into the wreckage of a civilization.

And yet the distant, aloof stars glitter and flicker at the edges of the sky, amid the closer flashes of the sheet-lightning in the luminescent clouds.

HYPER SOLID

[Truck Shot; Link] *At the center of the circle of images, a point of white light appears. It solidifies into a small, glowing sphere of luminescence.*

Then it divides.

Where there was one light, now there are two. Then each luminescent dot twins again, to make four, then eight.

A cube appears where the single dot had been, delineated by the eight corners of the shape.

Then each of the dots marking the corners of the cube twin once more. The result is one cube that interlocks with the other cube, one corner of one connected to a corner of the second cube above it.

The cubes separate from each other, and the twelve screens move to become the sides of the cubes: six screens on each.

The slowly rotating cubes with their moving images are the only objects that occupy the center of the infinite plane.

Then they are not.

DETERMINANTS

[Run Process] *They fall from out of a blackness darker than space itself: twin cubes, gigantic dice without the usual spots, but rather having <u>images</u>. Tumbling, rotating, they fall, the colored pictures on their sides ever changing.*

Moving into reality. Images accompanied by directives. Data containing programs.

The continuum moves aside to contain them.

INITIALIZATION

[Press REWIND, Press PLAY, Long Shot]
Echo Video Image of desolation: row of brownstones shattered asunder: insect owners in panic; trivial scattered toys of omnipotent maniacal deity, angrily thrown into the corners of a chamber of inordinate dimension. Red flame below the horizon silhouettes wreckage of ancient habiliment. Primeval battles lost and forgotten: histories lost amid the antediluvian chaos.

[Fast Forward] Point of view falls away, malignant greenery amid the wreckages of ages where the sons of man play as children in a treacherous garden. Where the daughters play the gardeners. Where the virulent court the venomous as the watched wait.

[Animate] First it is terminal. Then it is germinal.

[Medium Close Up]
Where the real rulers remain hidden.
Where their excesses are in the hands of sightless caretakers.
Where the private torments of the damned are made a project.
Where the projects are subject to meticulous quality-control.
Where the control is absolute.
Where the absolution is a matter of opinion.
Where the opinions are those of the real rulers.

[Close Up] Who remain hidden in lost places where it is best not to go.

BACKGROUND BACKSCATTER

[Screen Clear / Start] Program running;
System Ready.

PART ONE: DEPARTURES

——>>> ONE <<<——

"The World is restless, Heaven in flux,
Angels appear from the Bright Star;
The world is restless...Up There Down There...."

—Patti Smith, 1988

IS NOT

[Initialization] He was Joe Davis, and the rest of the Universe was cold, remote and dark.

One minute there had been Light, the next Nothing.

He was Joe Davis, and the rest of everything was not.

Not dark; dark is the absence of light. This was Nothing.

Sensory depravation? Was the Tech Bloc—?

No.

Restart. System ready. Waiting for input.

He was Joe Davis, and he had been about to cross the Milwaukee City Limits.

But the Limits had vanished. There were No Limits.

Then where was everything?

There was Nothing.

He pushed at the Nothing: No Thing pushed back.

He fought the Nothing, Nothing replied to his attack.

He struck out blindly, although his limbs did not move in the not-light not-dark of Nothing. He looked with not-eyes at the absence of all things. Chaos!

But Chaos was not Nothing.

(A little fat thing with a small round head, and streamers like electric sparks flashing blue against the blackness). (Fiery equations aglimmer in the murky calculus). Not places/planets rise over No Horizons. A galaxy yonder!

But Blackness is not Nothing.

There was an effect (not a thought) a precursor to a thought, an input, a feeling—

(I have made a mistake).

I?

I am Joe Davis.

(Nothing returned). ((VOID *) (*IS)()).

I Am. All There. IS!

I was coming to Milwaukee. I had a mission. My Mission.

My Capital M Mission. To Capital M Milwaukee.

I am not alone. ("We Are With You....").

I crossed into the city. I remember Nothing.

Nothing.

"There's an Echo in here—" Who/Where/What are you?

IS

[Memory Allocation] Light!

Sunrise.
Gray/dawn-color/wet-light.
He struck out at the gray light, the light receded, returned.
Rubber Light. Plastic images. A screen!
A. Screen?
His Universe took form, the form of a back alley.
You can do better than this.
[You] .
[Fail] .
His universe was inhabited.
By trolls.

BETWEEN IS AND IS NOT

[Traveling Matte] (Kaleidoscope input return of images lost; data burst of scenes: Parking on a side street; leaving the car; walking up the street to the McDonalds, preoccupied. Something behind him snuffling).

He had come from the West: Highway-90 to Madison, then East on Ninety-Four to Milwaukee.

Joe Davis levered himself up off his back where he had fallen, and reached out for anything handy to use as a weapon. The trolls marched up to him in a compact group, flung an object on him. Something large and white. A sheet.

ON THE FIELD

[Link!] He felt the universe recede from him, as black curtains of unconsciousness folded across his sight. The associations of being covered up by a single white sheet surfaced, unpleasantly. He was aware of something wet and slimy sliding up to him, moving against his body, covering him.

DESCRIPTOR—I

[Prelude to the System; Long Shot] Joe Davis had entered Milwaukee early in the evening. The long drive had left him tired, but not unduly so. Mostly, he was hungry and there were several places on Wisconsin Avenue where he could get dinner.

George Webb's up there. Two electric clocks hung in the front window below a sign announcing Webb's as a twenty-four hour operation. Further ahead, a McDonalds.

It had been a long trip to this time and this place.

OR OFF

[Loading] Joe revived on the floor of a room that was all white. His head ached. The whiteness was from indirect lighting. Joe got to his feet. Clumsily.

He was dressed in a pair of greenish-gray trunks that were just a bit more than indecent. His ankles were connected by more of the greenish-gray material: he could just walk without tripping. His wrists were likewise secured. He stood up, looked around.

The furnishings were minimal: a bed, wide for a single bed, a rectangular solid that seemed to ripple across a surface that remained flat. He touched it. Although ripples sped away from his finger-touch, the bed remained flat. He pressed his palm against the surface.

Odd. A pleasant touch, soft, yet unyielding. It looked comfortable in spite of its severe shape.

There were a table and a chair. He could see himself in a mirror that was a polished area on the opposite wall.

There was no door.

He walked over to the wall. His movements were clumsy and he felt strange tugs inside his body. He looked at the wall closely; it was a smooth expanse of featureless—what? Plastic? Ceramic? It had the "touch" of either, or maybe neither.

Joe checked the walls, the floor. The ceiling was about three meters up, a blank expanse. He sat on the edge of the bed. His reflection contemplated him from the opposite, a slender, well-muscled man in his early thirties, dark of hair, gray of eye. His eyes looked a shade of blue in the ambient lighting.

He raised an eyebrow at his reflection and it returned the gesture.

He looked down at his one item of clothing. The material from which it was made had no seams, no stitching and *scales*. A thin web-work of edges delineated a network that looked exactly as if the "fabric" had come from a rather large fish.

Joe tugged at the waist band.

It didn't move.

He pulled at it again, a bit harder. The band tightened against his stomach.

"Riiight," he said to the white walls. He attempted to slide the garment off. It wouldn't budge. It seemed to pulsate slightly. Joe leaned back, and stared at the opposite wall. The—individual—he was looking for was reputed to be good at biological tinkering. He slid his hand into the waistband again, and the scaly garment tightened up. Joe wanted to laugh, but didn't; the room might be bugged. *It's the first time I've heard "chew my shorts" reversed!*

He started to get up, sat back again. A set of cracks or openings had appeared in one of the blank walls. The section of the wall within the cracks fell back and moved to one side. An illuminated rectangle of light led into what appeared to be a short hallway. Joe stood.

His welcoming committee entered.

D E S C R I P T O R - **II**

[Prelude to the System; Medium Shot] The distance extended behind Joe Davis like cigarette smoke vanishing into arabesques of nothingness. The past. What had been.

The road stretched before him: kilometers of unlit deserted pavement in varying degrees of repair, visible from the presence of the markers at the roadsides and the wanly luminous center line.

Otherwise the road was pretty much the same color as the land to each side of him, or the color of the night, itself.

[Rewind Recursive; Single Frame] She sits in graceful comfort on her silken cushions, irreversible immaculate shades of black and white in her silk-lined receiving room. Her four legs fold with a natural ease beneath her.

[Extreme Close Up] Onyx shimmering: her hair falls in cascades around nearly perfect features; eyebrows so black they are almost blue; finely chiselled nose, wide mouth in a sardonic half-smile; thin colorless lips.

Her eyes shimmer, glittering in the ambient illumination. The light sources throw off the multicolors of prismatic components from the lenses that cover the vertical slits in gold irises, in spectral counterpoint to the reflections in her retinae. Her upper left arm grips the arm of the wide chair in which she lounges; her lower right arm plays idly with the controls of some small device. Her lower left arm holds, in an off-handed way, a small creature with many legs attached to a roughly hexagonal body. Its eyes blink: one red, one blue, a coloration electric in its intensity; it seems to enjoy its shelter within her large hand. Her upper right arm rests on her hip.

She is bare from the waist up. In other places, at other times, there would be an element of the exhibitionist in her; here, it is transmuted by steps of demeanor into arrogance. Her hair falls, a raven cataract, over her shoulders and down her back; her breasts, conical in shape, stand by themselves. Standing, she is 214 centimeters, or just over seven feet tall. Sitting, she is coolly intimidating in her presence, well within herself. Her nipples are red. They are the only color about her other than her enormous glittering gold eyes.

Her throne is 122 centimeters off the floor; the cushions upon which she reclines add another twenty-five.

She looks down on those who have come—two, voluntarily, one, not— to her.

[Prelude to the System: Close-Up] Victor Lyle was young, active, but lately, reserved. The accident that had taken his sight was one of those preventable things that strikes with the suddenness of an elemental force. One moment, his sight was perfect. On the distant side of that moment, he was sightless.

The liquid weed-killer, designed for "no-plow" farming had splashed across his face. Not enough to burn his features irrevocably, but enough to destroy the outer portion of one eye and to burn the other eye out completely, leaving an empty socket. One eye still registered light, but there was no resolution, no color, no detail.

Victor spent the following weeks getting used to the new conditions: books were spoken or read by a scanner-reader furnished by a local hospital. At the very worst, he could read by running his fingers over little bumps embossed into the page.

For navigation, Victor used a cane.

Joe had been planning a trip East and was already packed for it, when the phone call from his cousin came in.

He made a quick detour to the bank for cash as well as several cashier's checks to get the funds he needed. A set of replacement eyes would run..., well, it would cost *a lot*.

His tour of duty at UCLA had ended predictably with the end of the current semester, he had cleaned out his office, put most of his belongings in storage, and had the rest with him.

As he was getting ready to leave, another phone call had obviated the need for the funds he had obtained. He dispersed the cash to various parts of his luggage, and, slightly later than planned, drove east.

It would be simple to change his plans to go to Montana to see the Lyles. He didn't need to spend fifteen large on a set of replacement eyes. Now all he had to do was explain the miracle.

From his vantage point on the road, it looked as if he would be on a very long sabbatical.

Possibly permanent.

THE FIRST MILE

[Start Scan Run] Two short humanoids entered the room. Joe stood 183 centimeters, or a fraction over six feet tall; these creatures couldn't have been more than four foot six. They looked like very short rubber-faced caricatures of men with luminescent cat-green eyes. Above the eyes, there was a single golden orb—an aperture—in the forehead of each. Yellow as sunlight, each orb pulsed at Joe, scanning him with spasmodic vertical and horizontal motions.

As if on a signal the creatures each extended one hand.

Sitting on each of the hands was a small animal that looked like a spider. The spiders reared up on five or six of their legs, their hexagonal bodies showing the other legs in a wide, threatening, display.

Large eyes glowed red and blue. One of the spiders turned and ran up its owner's arm. It had another glowing eye that looked straight back, it was green.

The humanoids regarded Joe with a wide-eyed stare.

Membranous crests on their heads rose.

The movement surprised him. He had expected weapons, that was what the spiders had to be. What were the crests for?

Joe stood unmoving, watching.

Another humanoid entered. It had a hex-spider riding on its shoulder. This humanoid produced an item that looked like a short pool cue with a bifurcated end. He pointed it at the belt of joe's single garment, and the end of the tool *merged* with the belt. Joe took a step back, and a wash of pain swept over him, engulfing, nauseating. The humanoid took a step forward and the pain stopped. Joe blinked. It was as if the agony he'd felt had never happened. The creature pointed to the door. Joe took a tentative move towards it, and the other two fell into step behind him, their spiders on display. Joe started walking; they left the room.

A movement caught his eye, he looked back at it; they waved their hands, *onward*, but the movement was striking, for all its silence.

The bed was retracting into the wall.

The hall was filled with shelves.

The shelves held packing cases, electronic devices, books and other items all neatly labeled in a large, round hand. Joe and his escorts walked the corridor's center on a narrow strip of carpet that served as a guide.

Ahead was a turn-off: the walls of this area were hung with curtains, white curtains that looked to Joe like silk.

|CAMERA|MIRROR|LENS|

[Prelude to the System; Extreme Close-Up] Victor's eyes were as good as new.

He had run out to meet Joe when Joe pulled in. Victor ran up to Joe's car, laughing, his eyes wide.

"Hi, Uncle Joe, you're looking good!"

Seeing Joe.

Somehow, the lens and iris sections of one eye had been repaired. More amazing, his other eye was undamaged. It was as if it had grown back. Getting a bod-mod was easy, the well-heeled could do largely what they wished to themselves if they found what they had been born with un-acceptable.

That would have been fine, Victor's eyes could have been re-installed from cloned tissue samples, and modified back to functioning. If the Lyle Family had been rich.

But they weren't. How was this possible?

CRITICALITY

[Running] Joe's cousin was small wiry, and agile. He had the typical blond hair and light complexion of someone of Northern European ances-try. He was (again) a happy, healthy nine-year-old kid.

The look in Victor's dark green eyes made him seem older.

Hanna Lyle was Joe Davis's cousin. Joe had known Victor since birth and had visited them whenever he was in the area. *Which was damned seldom!* he thought.

When he had been at UCLA, his studies had entailed late night hours, all-nighters, and weekends usually spent monitoring experiments on a bank of hi-res monitors connected to the latest developments in compu-ting.

UCLA's budget was always the first item on California's agenda. The reason for this was the abrupt departure of qualified graduates to other places and other countries. Perhaps if the green were greener where a lot of student researchers actually got their educations some small number of them might be enticed to stay.

Joe hadn't wanted to leave: either California or the country. He had dis-covered something that would actually do a lot of people a lot of good, if his discovery could be properly exploited. It needed to be handled rather carefully until the safety precautions could put in place.

Unfortunately, others had thought otherwise.

If what had been planned would come to fruition, he would be leaving the green fields of California Higher Education behind.

It would be better this way.

WAITING

[Processing] She awaits her visitor, wavering between doubt and certainty. Shortly the doubts vanish: *I'm in control here. He is mine to manipulate as I wish.* The bravado helps; then icy insinuations of uncertainty intrude. She looks around her at the room she has selected for the initial interview; the room has been set as a stage is set: each prop in the exact place.

But something is missing.

NET CENTRAL—-I

This route could be a lot more direct, Joe thought as the little procession passed shelves filled with boxes labeled "New-Reality-Selector." He wondered whether his host was a game fan, or if the units were more valuable for parts. Joe turned a corner, one of the creatures separated the white curtains, opened a door—

His destination.

NET CENTRAL—II

He doesn't cringe or even seem to worry. His heartbeat...has increased now that he's here and sees me, but it remained steady in the cell, and out in the passageway. She expands her vision to more than the standard bandwidth; his skin looks almost normal. No sweat, no tremors, nothing! He doesn't know who I am. Or does he? He has the usual masculine reaction to me, but....

Why is there not enough fear?

A CONGERIES OF OBSERVATIONS

Joe looked up. And further up. She was lounging on a wide cushion covered chair designed for her. From underneath one of the cushions, something resembling a crazy-quilt stuck out. Joe willed himself to breathe regularly, to stay calm. She was topless, and her nudity was that of a classical statue. He found himself responding to it. *Michelangelo never had a model with that many arms!* he thought, *and...her face, in spite of the roundness, is pure classical Greek.* He stood as casually as he was able, centering himself, willing himself back into calmness, looking at her even as she returned his gaze. Her face was aristocratic; there was pride in the lines of that face. Her hair was velvet black, falling over her shoulders. Joe could see a curl of it lying on the cushions at her waist. *Nice, but not too functional*, he observed, *She wears her hair long, because she likes it that way, it must not be dangerous here. To her.* Neither was her lack of dress. Whatever Joe had expected, he had not expected an almost arrogantly erotic display of flesh. Her eyes—
They were larger than the general-issue human eyes.

Her enormous eyes were the same shade of gold as the scanning apertures in the short humanoids. Similarity of function? Ego? Her eyes scanned Joe, but there was none of the passive generality of the humanoids' scan. There was a lively and high intelligence in this scan that took in all of Joe and he returned her favor, scanning back. He took a step forward, a deliberately decisive step, and studied her overtly.

His interest was genuine. Was *this* The Agent that various low-brow supermarket tabloids, that he had gotten while visiting Hannah, had discussed with hyperbolically lurid articles, trying to create an urban legend which no one had ever seen? The abandoned vessel in the Long Beach Harbor registered to Mexico's <u>Transportación Nacional Maritima Mexicana</u> had furnished enough to the tabloids' staff writers. The writers had mentioned the *Marie Celeste*; the Mexican ship had been found with all hands missing.

The Internet had other rumors that all seemed to come from the same Long Beach area. Rumors about someone (or maybe Someone!) who could do just about anything.

NET CENTRAL-III

[Initialized Inputs] *She adjusts the data from her hearing, and with a soundless gesture of her mind, creates a sonic hologram that manifests in a window in her right eye.*

She gestures again and a cross-correlation matrix forms. He is more uneasy than he is letting on, she thinks, her face impassive, his demeanor is practiced, his attitudes rehearsed. His fear is buried deeply within his disposition. But it's there. I would have to hunt deeply for it.

She wants to scratch one of her right legs, but suppresses the sensation internally, instead.

A third gesture, and she generates a scatter plot of galvanic skin response, surface body temperature, and pulmonary activities. Does he know about the ship? He <u>is</u> from Southern California....If he's made the connection, he's the only one—

She blinks her eyes slowly, in thought.

VERGE

Was she—? he thought.

She didn't conceal the extra pair of legs placed just behind and slightly outside the front pair. The legs were slim, and they looked as if they would be unable to carry the bulk of her form. *Hyperfilaments* Joe wondered? Her four arms held various items, *what does she do with those spiders?*, and looked muscular and capable of more articulation than a "normal" human's. Her waist was narrow, her breasts were large without sagging.

The redness of her nipples contrasted sharply with the alabaster white of her skin.

Her face was round. Laugh lines. A prominent nose, that was not out of place. Those incredible gold eyes. Eyes that didn't miss a thing. Joe looked closer. Were those eyes *faceted* or was that a trick of the lighting?

SARGON!

"I know that you have been looking around Milwaukee. I observed when you arrived here. Your techniques and your discoveries precede you and would complement mine. You have brought information to me, even if you're not aware of it." Her gaze is unwavering, a cat's gaze.

"I have your knowledge already. I need but to remove it from its container. In the end, you will aid me. The only question is when: now or later.

"I have been waiting for you. I knew that you would come to me."

No Passive Voice

[Load Status] His heartbeat is, is measured! He is interested and in the usual way. But he does not tremble: is he ignorant? Below the surface there is turmoil, but he controls it. He is attentive, interested—even turned on, in spite of his position, here. Does he know where he is? Again, does he recognize me? Who is this man that he wants to come here? Am I sure of his actions?

My words were all of a piece. I spoke too fast. Am I afraid of him? Am I—?

She motions with her mind; a window opens in her field of view that seems to hover in the space next to the man before her. Within it a heartbeat display dances and vibrates; there is a graph of his pulmonary functions and other data. She wills it and the will *is* reality: a schematic of his body stands next to him, regarding him from some *Other* place, his circulatory system picked out in red and green, his nerves in yellow and black, the lymphatic system in blue. She starts a correlation run using her earlier data. The reality of the black-haired, gray-eyed rather handsome man stands unknowing within the data. His features seem to be watching the schematic that stands next to him only in the virtual reality of her own gaze. *How real is my perception: there is no window, just my mind, my systems and their abilities; his <u>doppelgangers</u> don't know they stand there! They are so—limited.*

Is he a volunteer?

Why?

Immovable Retort

"The data are readily available. My techniques are documented. You'll have to kill me to get the rest," he answers in level tones, a slight vibrato added, "And then you'll be in deeper trouble than you are now: you need me and my voluntary consent for my protocols to be implemented safely." He shivers internally, as he says it. The creatures flank him, but wear their spiders on their shoulders. The lead creature holds his probe ready.

"Thank you," her inflection is that of a professional speaker, her voice clipped BBC English: her words seem to take on a separate existence between them, "But this is my home, and I am Yezeletta Zargkonji."

She pauses as if the saying of her cognomen is all that is needed; the incantation of the angular sounds of her name-title.

"There are parts of you that are redundant or unnecessary. I will remove them, and keep just that part of you which can remember alive."

He turns a slightly lighter shade beneath his tan at this, but says nothing. She raises an eyebrow. I have his attention, but anyone else would be shaking with fear. He stands there, seeing me as, as....

"Or better yet," she purrs, "I will remove all of you but your memories, and add you to my data base. She smiles widely now, showing her teeth.

"I always need extra mass storage. Your brain has a large capacity, and I can engineer the interfaces within a day. Do think about it." She gestures with three hands to the two guards. Nothing more need be said.

Then, almost as an afterthought, she adds: "The Madflowers are mine."
She points to the door with her free hand, her upper right: *dismissed.*

T HE I MMOVABLE M OVER

[Retrospective Recursive: Extreme Close Up] She sits, not moving
from her place. She is still: the images playing in her line of sight, the recordings, one a window into another place, the other a man that never
was, a design of artificially stimulated phosphines, an electronic virtual
image. She blinks her eyes, and the lap-wipe of her eyelids removes the
reality for a short time, leaving her displays into her own derivations. Her
own decisions. *Does he desire me?*
And reality just beyond a door.

T HE H ILL AT R EST — I

[Telephoto; Extreme Close-Up] The red brick building stands at the
top of a hill, on the east side of the City of Madison, Wisconsin. The building, designed with all of the modern accessories appropriate to a place
constructed in the late part of the Twentieth-Century, is pleasant, well-
lighted, and easy to approach, even though it is at the hilltop.
(Albert Miller wasn't aware of this.)
The land that surrounds the building was tended carefully during construction, and provides a park for the civil servants that work there.
(But Albert Miller didn't particularly care about this.)
This is the main office building of the Wisconsin Department of Agricul-
ture, Trade and Consumer Protection, usually known by its initials as
DATCP. It is primarily Wisconsin's Department of Agriculture and, lately,
an important arm of the Wisconsin state government.
Far more important than many realize.

> *[17.58 CST] From WKOW-TV: "News Net Communications with
> Washington DC cut off about a minute ago. We have no further infor-
> mation at this time. We will keep you posted on further develop-
> ments."*

When the DATCP Building had been planned and built in the mid nineteen-nineties, no one had heard of Albert Miller.
Soon everyone would. In the past tense. His one act was of brazen efficiency; a single brutal deed executed with speed and finesse.
The news reports arrived from the east coast: a desolate poem in the
blank verse of disarray and disgust. The notices of the communications
breakdown arrived first, cutting into sporting events and even into com-
mercials.

> *[18.05 CST] "Wisco-Net reports loosing East-Coast server connec-
> tions at 18.04 Hours Local Time. The facilities, located in Baltimore
> Maryland, provide Wisco-Net's main feed for service from and to the
> Nation's Capitol and are used by many in local Government."*

For a viewing public rendered numb by terrorists, locally grown and imported, it was a matter of being patient and waiting to see how bad it
(whatever "it" was) would become. The wait wasn't long.
Satellite lookdowns, mostly used for accurate weather reporting provided most of the early data. Various private networks, and the National Re-

connaissance Office joined forces.

>   *[18.10 CST] "Bright double flash reported in the sky north of Falls Church Virginia, The Weather Channel has been contacted for confirmation."*

The disjointed dispatches came in by telephone, TV, the Internet and by several amateur radio operators running shielded equipment located in the Washington suburbs.

The report of the first mushroom cloud eradicated all programming for a week. Emergency assistance had to be brought in from Maryland and Virginia for a very sound reason: there was nothing left in Washington.

>   *[W1SQL: 18.35 CST] "Listen! There was a bright flash, like lightning, then a cloud that glowed from the inside, purple! Christ!, it's a mushroom! There's another flash—*

Few would forget the final broadcast from the Ham Operator who was closest to the destruction, cut off in mid-sentence describing the ultimate expression of terrorist desire.

In the weeks following, what remained was determining WHO.

And Why.

At the Wisconsin Ag Department, personnel dug in against the inevitable new security requirements from Washington, or wherever such directives would be appearing. Most simply buried themselves in the comfortable routine of people whose jobs were to be sure that farmers, always important in Wisconsin, continued to have farms (equally important) and that those farms *stayed* farms: the most important task of all.

>   *The Wisconsin State Journal—*

>   ### Destruction of Washington not work of "Loner"—FBI

>   (AP) Authorities have found no connection to international terrorists in the attack on Washington.

>   The FBI continues its investigation and a report is expected, shortly.

>   No existing organizations have claimed responsibility for the attack; All indications point to this disaster originating completely within the US.

No one *could have known* of Albert Miller.

The earliest news reports mentioned the possibility of local talent in the form of the rather loud radicals that a free country could produce on a moment's notice. Another report suggested that a single individual could conceivably drive a pair of six-kiloton nukes into Washington. The news media considered this impossible.

This was understandable.

It merely happened to be wrong.

In a time when terrorists were part of large organizations, some functioning with the help of governments, Albert Miller was a loner. Miller had been a single man with a single idea, who, in spite of this, or, perhaps, because of it, was able to carry out his plan.

No one was sure how he had obtained the devices. The pair of "tacticals" could have come from almost any place in the world. The black market was rife with such things, some real and obtainable, most of the rest, just stories.

But even stories have to be read. If for no reason, than to discount them. To make them irrelevant.

Albert Miller had gone out in a blaze of glory, remotely detonating one and driving the other to the White House. The barriers erected to close off Pennsylvania Avenue in 1990 were designed to bar conventional explosives packed by conventional criminals: but buried deep in a classified archive in Washington were any number of files covering contingencies that ran on a continuum from the merely annoying to the obscene.

The "Nuclear Option" fit nicely in the latter category.

The double explosion took out the President, the Vice President, both houses of Congress, and many senators, congressmen, their aides, and sundry lobbyists, cabinet members, advisors, judges.

The Madison Capital Times—

Secretary Eva Harrington Sworn in as President

(AP) Eva Harrington, formerly Secretary of Education, took the Oath of Office today backstage at the Los Angeles Hilton Convention Center....

The American government folded, paralysed. When a proper succession was made, it was to the Secretary of Education, an overworked woman who had been the designated cabinet member to be absent from the joint session. She had taken advantage of this to go to Los Angeles to address the National Education Association. There Secret Service agents had walked out onto the stage and removed her; a judge had accompanied the agents to swear her in backstage.

The destruction of Washington had created a power vacuum; State Governments moved in to fill it. The Nation's Capital was removed to Philadelphia. The passing of the U. S. Government caused the formation of cartels based on scientific research, power production or for other purposes in other countries.

The result was a United States of America in name only—the states were hardly united. Only a common heritage of the people being Americans, kept such things as highways open.

The United States and its new capital at Philadelphia went into a quiet eclipse.

The Watchers on the Hill kept waiting.

And watching.

THE LOCK AND THE KEY

[Sign Extension; Panorama: Wide-Angle]

—Listen with your eyes, and I will tell you. See with your ears.	Descriptor; Modality; Access Point;

[Load Backup] There is a place where the residents fit with the precision of a key into a Yale lock. A place beneath gray midwestern clouds, where the tall buildings against the sky look like jagged teeth, where the great lake on which the city is located slouches up to the city's border like a derelict intent on the city's last resources. The fangs of the buildings reach upwards for the sky's grayness and have been punched down as if by a mindless mad god with big clumsy fists. Only a small grouping of buildings—a poker hand claiming a shabby win—dare brave the gray skies of Fall-Time. The wind blows through the desolate streets of the city, but only to disturb the pollution, to move the filth. In the Autumn, the sun rarely shines, and when it does, there is only a flat white light: a stage light, a toy illumination.

[Travelling Matte] A smile with broken teeth, a yawn in the darkness. An idiot's grin; an expression as vacant as a politician's promise.

[Process Shot] Waiting for the traveller with a master key.

THE FIRST REPORT

[Processing] The dwellers in the brownstone on Milwaukee's southeast side were established in their routines, now. The prominent landmark known locally as the Mitchell Conservatory was under constant observation. This observation, so far, was from a distance, as none of the men who now lived in the upper floors of the old house had been able to get any data-collecting devices into the Conservatory, itself.

This caused modest concern in the last report to their superiors. The discreetly encrypted email whose overt destination was Kiev, and whose ultimate destination was an estate in the countryside south of Kiev, was not as complete as either the superiors, or the agents on the front-lines, desired.

The directions from that country estate were explicit: get as much data as possible, but above all, do not compromise your own security.

That concern was a nice gesture, but the field agents knew that such orders were designed to make them feel at ease. They could be told to go active at any time. If this middle echelon director, a man named Malasnikov, were to be believed, this would never happen. The more experienced agents knew otherwise.

WHERE HE WAS PLACED

[Wait State] Joe stood in the center of the room to which he had been returned. The door had closed, leaving an expanse of white wall.

Meals were delivered by silent humanoids that came for the left-overs precisely forty-five minutes later.

Was she interested?

Who was she?

What did she want?

WITHIN THE JACKDAW'S NEST

[Peripheral Access] The pickup was long and black, and the load in the back was no higher than the rear window. Where other truck drivers would throw a tarp over the contents, this truck's bed was made neatly with a waterproof covering which, like the rest of the vehicle, was black. There were no highlights on this truck.

A creature of the night, invisible in the dark.

The driver, a tall man, was concentrating intently on the road ahead. A darkhaired woman as tall as the man seated in the front passenger seat held a lighted clipboard with a road map attached.

Sitting in the rear seat of the cab, and looking on with frank curiosity, was a girl of about sixteen. She had her mother's dark hair, her father's height. She, too, had a clip-board, a duplicate of the one her mom was using. She was following the same course.

The radio hisses and crackles, receiving nothing. The digital read-out blinks thoughtfully in the gray light.

JACKDAW'S ALGORITHM

It's always a good idea to have a backup in unfamiliar territory.

THE OWL IN THE TREE

[Establishing Shot] He drives into the city beneath the witches' branches of up-reaching trees. Alone in this silent universe, he moves resolutely eastward on the highway, his deliberately anonymous automobile leaving the only indication of his passage: tracks in the road, tracks in the dust of times past. There is a flickering on the horizon: sheet lightning from some lost technology; forlorn remnants of man. The gray land through which his driving takes him is a leaden bowl within which he has found the lowest level. A single man coming out of the west to the Place on the horizon: a Signal Man to the waiting System; the Seeds Man bearing the answer, the key to the lock.

[Long Shot] And above him, the roiling clouds yet cover the canceled sky.

CLOSE-UP:

He lies on his back, on the couch, his legs apart, supported on back and sides by at least a dozen velvet pillows. His hands migrate into the hair of the woman before him, seeking a resting place. Her head is between his legs, and she is pleasuring him aggressively. He watches her through narrowed eyes, in lost comprehension, moving his hips in sweaty ecstasy: syncopated time to the motion of her head.

MEDIUM SHOT:

[Paradox; Access; Camera Goes With]

She is slender, tall and tanned an even light brown.	He is pasty white: the white of a creature of the underground.
She is firm-breasted, wide hipped: her hair is waist length, and a flawless black.	He is rather heavy, but in good shape. He has bathed recently: the cleanest part of him is where she is giving her attentions.
She has pink nipples, straight muscular legs, wide-set violet eyes, strong thighs, long legs, a tight ass.	He looks like what he is: a middle-aged man receiving the services of his lover. The most alive parts of him are the muscles in his legs and hips and his ever watching unwavering eyes. They hold steady: biological radar as

| she continues.

LONG SHOT:

[Load, Execute] Room of art-deco wallpaper, painted plaster, old but serviceable furniture. Fresh paint visible on the ceiling, shelves climbing to the tops of three of the walls.

In a corner above several old books: a fly buzzing near death-trap of web. Gray spider waiting indolently as dinner approaches: arachnid thoughts of food and sex. Tremor of dinner-is-served (prepackaged): leap!

The man's eyes close in bliss on his one-way trip to <u>desideratum</u>. His hands relax in her hair, letting go as he lets go.

BEAT. ZOOM.

He moans in ecstacy, as she finishes her performance. A hand enters her field of view.

His.

HIS MASTER PLAN

He gets up; she moves away as his bulk ascends into the room. She approaches, runs one hand down the center of his chest. His eyes, twin photometers, scan the intimate area. There is a door in the room to the right of the window. Ineluctably, he strides towards it, taking her by one hand, the left one. He leads her through the door into a room that is similar in decor to the room in which his interlude has transpired: this room, also, is clean, dust-free, comfortable, although rather more sparsely furnished. He takes her to the king-size waterbed, pushes on her and she lands on her back on the bed. Her legs spread; there is just a hint of summer lands glittering within her perfect black triangle. He looks down upon her, a smile of satisfaction, and more—admiration, perhaps?—on his face. He nods once to her, and leaves via the door connecting to the other room. Shortly, she hears the door from that room to the hallway slam and his footsteps echo in the hall.

HER RETORT

She listens intently. When she is sure that he is gone, when his footsteps can no longer be heard, she reaches under the mattress of the waterbed, for the small object that is there. She takes it out, and eyes it for a moment. It is a small flashlight. She turns it on and makes an adjustment.

Several small spiders with hexagonal bodies and luminous red and blue eyes emerge.

The spiders line themselves up on the frame of the bed, as if they're awaiting orders. She gently touches the velvet body of one of the spiders, and it stands on its rear legs and spreads its forelegs in a wide gesture. Small claws extrude, claws that secrete something liquid.

She nods. All Well.

Her friend had promised her weapons. These were more than enough.

She laughs: Zhongo has had the fiction of her being his mistress for the last year: ever since his underling was directed to let Zhongo win her in that poker game.

In the upper corner of the outer room, the spider munches thoughtfully on early dinner to go (formerly fast food).

THE ANSWER

She lifts the floorboard up, glances momentarily at other equipment hidden there. She smiles. A predator's smile.

Her communicator has activated. It is time for her to make her report. The communicator crawls up into the window. It looks at her expectantly. Its eyes glow.

ALGORITHMIC REPLY

It's always a good idea to have a backup in unfamiliar territory.

THEN—

[About a Year Earlier] The elevator took Leona up into the tall building. She realized that she had been chased into the parking ramp beneath one of the tallest buildings in Milwaukee, the Wisconsin Farmer's Mutual Building at 777 East Wisconsin Avenue.

She had no idea that the place was inhabited.

Her tall rescuer was silent during the elevator ride. She looked around again at the short humanoids that accompanied them.

The doors opened.

Before her was a long hallway that was neatly laid out, with well-filled shelves along both sides.

"Please come this way," the stranger said. She followed the tall woman into a living room that contained several large couches, a big collection of electronic components, and which had several layers of curtains covering the windows.

"May I ask your name?" her tall guide said.

"Leona," she replied, "My name is Leona Mathieson."

The other woman removed the wrap-around mirrorshades she had been wearing. She looked at Leona.

Leona's nerves felt as if they had turned to ice. The eyes...they were large, gold, and they looked like the eyes of a cat.

Those gold eyes regarded her calmly.

"My eyes are not like yours," the tall woman said. "They're a custom design job that I had when I was very young." Leona relaxed incrementally at this; she had seen other sorts of self-adornments in other places. Eyes could be changed using contact-lenses, for example, just...weren't these eyes a little large?

"I understand your misgivings," the tall lady said. She shook her head, and the hat fell from her head, to be fielded by one of the short humanoids. Her hair was obviously long, tucked into the neck of the coat, and of a uniform shiny black color.

"I have had some custom work done on me," she said, "Now, all I ask is that you try to accept me as I am. I won't hurt you."

"If you'd wanted to, you would have, right?" Leona asked.

"Exactly."

"You have my name, what's yours?"

The tall woman began to unbutton her coat, "My name is Yezeletta. Yezeletta Zargkonji. It is a derivation of the name of the organization that performed the modifications I have."

Yezeletta let the trenchcoat fall to the floor. A humanoid scurried in to grab it.

But Leona didn't notice that.

DETERMINANTS LOADING

[Operations] *The Images on the square screens load themselves into associative memory: take up residence in data tables, establish cross-references in the system in which they find themselves.*
Their programming component goes active.
They start moving, again.
Descending. Images moving.
Falling.

IN THE NETWORK

---

[1] They lie in wait, dormant, yet conscious. With a time sense compressed by external means, the days pass by as if they were seconds, yet the various activities of the Hive, while slow, are purposeful. The incoming Hive-units replace the outgoing. The Travellers must be welcomed. Occasionally, a Hive-member may be dispatched. Liaison must be kept with other Hives. The Signals must be answered. //// **[2]** The dispatched vanish as they answer the Call. It is an exalting and strange experience to be time-stretched, to watch the Hive-members slow down into immobility, to pass the Wardens, to enter upon a Mission. //// **[3]** Missions may be small: maintenance of the Data Link and its accompanying power source. The power source may have to be sent down to the Hive for regeneration and regrowth or be replaced entirely. The mission may involve transport of messages, spores or genetic prototypes to other Hives. Nutrients may have to be procured. This is difficult: the materials must be taken alive, but need be taken infrequently. Alive, the food stores well. //// **[4]** The Hives live, grow in a genteel way, and the life-units die or leave, and are replaced. From time to time, instructions arrive by data-link or by courier or by other means. Life goes on.

——>>> TWO <<<——

She is benediction,
She is addicted to Thee.
She is the Root Connection,
She is connecting with He.
Here I go, well I don't know why
I spin so ceaselessly—
Could it be He's taking over me?
I'm dancing barefoot, heading for a spin.
Some strange music draws me in,
Makes me come on like some heroine.

—Patti Smith, 1979

The structure visible through his single window stretches out before him in a network of garishly colored wires. Bright reds, glowing greens and radioactive blues counterpoint with red-gold, off-white, and a yellow that glints as if it were trapped sunlight. Winding through the colored cabling are organic components of more somber colors: light and dark browns, dark greens, dark-blues, and a single branching cable of turquoise.

The cables are attached to large turnip-shaped gray containers that sprout printed circuit boards that look as if they had been grown instead of installed. To Joe's eye, they resemble large, vertical fungi with wires.

The gray containers connect to pipes, some of transparent plastic, others of metal angling out of the pointed bottoms of the turnip-shapes like supporting legs. The transparent pipes carry liquids of various colors, or of no color. One arrangement of pipes appears to be a water supply. Multicolored ribbon-cables connect each gray turnip to a cable run in a triangular conduit leading to the floor above.

There are elements of an oil refinery, a chemical engineering plant, an excessively large data processing system. *And what else?* he asks himself.

Before him, the answer to his question: the pipes, veins and arteries, conduits and wiring, winding through narrow passages and along the spiderwebs of supporting steel grids.

Joe's cell overlooks this system. This is her holding area, a room with a view into what may be an intelligent organism in its own right.

He looks down at the grayish-green cords attached to his neck, wrists, thighs, ankles, elsewhere. They have grown around his limbs to form an unbroken circumference. *Let her think she's secure: I've got her curious. She'll want to find out more before she takes any kind of action at all. She's supposed to be good at doing this!* He feels pulling sensations in his muscles: the cords have grown into him as well. A green belt surrounding his waist extends downwards in front and back, meeting below. The outer surface is tough green leather. The inside is inaccessible; waste products are absorbed by the gray-green tissues. They give off a sweetish odor that reminds him of greenhouses gone mad, bad, or both.

He observes the construct that stands just outside the glass door of his cell. Superficially, it is humanoid. Internally, it is of a different order, entirely.

Before, below, and above him, the color coded pipes bring in unknown chemical substances, presumably nutrients; convey other substances away, presumably waste products, and provide the interconnections for the elaborate logic network that controls the mechanism. Two or three of the gray shapes in the system's center have irregularly shaped components: boards that were clearly designed and hand-built with less than optimal equipment and with more enthusiasm than skill. The most important aspect is that they function. Joe studies these a bit closer: do they look older than the containers with the almost glistening fungoid constituents? *I wonder*, he thought, *are those the first ones?* The mechanism is a riot of colors and textures, except for a tough-looking metal box in the center of the confusion, painted a flat military olive-drab.

The gray containers look like dark turnips with vertical veins. Most of the pipes and conduits lead into or out of these. Apparently she has placed Joe in a cell overlooking this massive piece of equipment in a attempt to impress him with her power.

He is secretly amused, although he is careful not to show it. This is a perfect study in contradictions. First, it's obvious that she has power. The complex before him is an incredible feat of engineering. Her constructed assistants appear to be able to follow complex instructions, but don't appear to be capable of originating any (can they do anything original?). She seems to be trying to impress him. She is alone among her sycophants; does she want companionship? She expected some specific reaction. *She stated her name, as if I should know it, as if I should do something when she intones it.* Does she really think that she can intimidate him and gain companionship from that intimidation?

Does she know that little of human nature?

How old is she? When was she born—or constructed?

Joe looks at another window on the opposite side. There is a comfortable living room there. He has seen her resting on a large divan, reading or viewing something on a large screen. Earlier, when she saw him watching, she drew a blue curtain across the window.

There are no curtains on *his* window.

Below, a spectre of black and white appears in the colors of the system. It is Yezeletta Zargkonji; her walk is a kind of rolling gait, as she strides forth on her four legs. She looks up at him, and their eyes lock in momentary data communication. She smiles sardonically and he wonders if she can smile in any other way. His other thoughts are kept concealed. Deep in the back of his mind is the suspicion that she may be telepathic. Her destination is just ahead: a root cluster that hangs at her eye level.

He turns away. The construct at the door looks at him with the unwavering gaze of the programmed. The third eye in its forehead, gold as a sunset, brilliant as a sun, seeing, yet not seeing.

And before this, there were other eyes, also seeing without seeing.

THE KID WITH THE EYES

[Scan: Load Symbiont; A year Earlier] Joe sat in Hannah Lyle's kitchen with a plate of eggs over easy, sausages, home-made bread, cantaloupe and a glass of cold orange juice half-finished in front of him.

Victor, a wide-eyed gaze on his face, sat across from Joe, describing his miracle.

"It was a *lady*! A big, tall lady who had a noisy heart beat! Sounded like *hearts*, y'know? She called herself Jesse. She cuddled me in her arms and put this cold thing on my face. I could tell from the way she did it, that she didn't expect me to know what she was doing, but I could feel the cool when she brought it up by my face."

"What happened, then?" Joe asked gently.

"I could feel something happen in my eyes. Like, when you get something in them that's sharp. Only this wasn't sharp, it was like getting water in your eye. Or Jello."

"Cold," Joe prompted, Hannah looked on with a mildly quizzical expression.

"It sat on my eyes then it seemed to curl up and fall off, almost like it was alive," Victor continued.

"Then?"

"I hadda go home, and the lady took me up to the road. She hugged me once, and I came home. A couple days later I woke up and I had *eyes*, again! I saw these two cats that live up the road!"

"Did you notice anything else about her besides that?" Joe prompted for anything more.

Victor blinked. He seemed in thought for a moment, as he tried to express an outrageous idea. "There was," he said. "When she hugged me, she had four arms, I could tell; she had four hands. She hugged real good!"

"Interesting," Hannah said, speaking for the first time. "Was there anything else besides her arms?"

"When I sat in her lap....She had really big boobs!"

They laughed at that. Breakfast finished in the kind of small-talk that occurs at that meal.

Victor ran out into the gathering Autumn, and Hannah regarded Joe with an intent gaze.

"*What* did he encounter, really? UFO Aliens?"

"I doubt it," Joe said, "There has to be an explanation for this. It could be anything from a researcher passing by to—uh, well—aliens. My money's on something in Victor's immune system kicking in and regenerating whatever it was that had damaged his eyes. Has he had any of the usual post-natal treatments?"

"Just the minimal immunizations they do at birth. We couldn't afford the trip to San Francisco. The local hospital got him a cane!"

There was an unpleasant edge to her voice when she said it.

REWRITE RETURN

[Wait State]   Joe's thoughts return to the present for a moment. His guardian watches him with the compulsive attention of the designed, and Joe sees one of his own creations in this creation of another.

AT THE EDGES OF MEMORY

[Running]   He walked across the campus with such single-minded inattentiveness that he barely noticed the people around him.

He was headed for the Biochemistry Building, where he was to meet with the Chairman of the Department.

He did not anticipate it being pleasant.

Joe Davis had done something that only a young researcher with a lot of luck could have done. He had started a process both in the laboratories of UCLA, and in the world outside of academia that would affect many others in many ways.

That was the problem.

Joe had discovered—as a by-product of other work—a way of "convincing" rather simple biological constructs to produce compounds of arbitrary complexity. His first success had been with a rhododendron. Then ordinary African violets had been put to work.

An ordinary plant could become a cheap, low-scale factory for just about anything.

Anything at all.

[Load] The black truck rolled to a stop at the City Limits. The decline on the other side was shallow: the Wisconsin State highway system was built up on banks from which the exit ramps fell away. As the Chevy took the exit, the city spread out before them.

"Where do we meet him," Ondreya Lenhaden said.

Hank removed a notepad from his shirt pocket, keyed in a command. "My instructions are to contact 'Big John' when we reach the center of town at a restaurant, there. I can make the transfer, get paid, and we can be on our way, fairly quickly."

"Hank," Ondreya said, "We talked about stopping here for a while, shopping perhaps. I think I'd like to just stop for eats, and get moving."

"Agreed" Hank said. "This delivery came to Winterhaven by the usual channels, and I'd like to get rid of it. I'd be doing this by myself, but we're on the way home."

"The last time I was here, was two years ago. Wonder what it's like, now—try the radio, Dad," Anne asked, "Maybe this ruin has a little life."

"Good idea." Hank flipped a cover up on the dashboard. The front of the cover looked like a normal analog AM-FM radio. What was underneath was a late model Bearcat Scanner. "Let's see what AM has." He punched a button and bright red digits displayed the low end of the AM band: **[540]** . He hit another button and the readout began to increase. They watched it for a moment, as the scanner sampled each frequency in the AM band (and played several seconds of it) to see if anything was being transmitted.

[890] : The readout stopped, and a sound like waves on a beach filled the truck's cab: the ethereal tide ebbed and flowed around them for a moment. Hank studied the other indicators on the scanner with narrowed eyes. "Weird," he said at last. His wife looked at him with a raised eyebrow. "This is an actual signal," Hank said, "It's coming in rather strongly, but it sounds like a phone connection from New York to Los Angeles with bad side-band suppression."

The hissing and roaring surrounded them. Hank continued, "You'd only pick up something like this on a scanner. If you were tuning across the frequencies with a portable, you'd lock on to the next station, without getting to this signal. It would be rejected as static." He took the notepad out of his shirt pocket, keyed in the frequency.

"It does sound like a phone connection with a lot of multipath distortion," Anne said, "but why would anyone want to send that kind of noise? Steganography, perhaps?"

Anne's question was rhetorical. Hank punched the **[SCAN]** button again.

[1250] : The scanner stopped on another broadcast: a pretentious voice was saying "— deaths in Mitchell Park. Also on the south side, there are rumors that the Oak Creek Dynamos will be moving into the Nightwalkers Turf in an offensive beginning some time next week. The 'Walkers publicist said, and I quote, 'This is nonsense. We've kept our turf for two years without fighting. No one can stop us.'

"We'll be back in a moment with the Highway casualty report, after a word from Dyna-Jak's...."

The frenetic announcer and easily remembered jingle were more typical of fast-food chains, but appeared to be selling a massage service. "Dyna-

Jak's, huh," Hank said, "I can't believe I'm hearing this on a Milwaukee station. What the hell is the 'Highway Casualty Report'?"

The advertisement ended, and the announcer came back on the air. "And now, the Highway Casualty Report, brought to you by Dyna-Jak's, for service that can stand on its own, Dyna-Jak's, off Wisconsin Avenue on Sixteenth Street!"

The announcer continued, briskly: "On the south side, there were fourteen deaths, one suicide, three murders, and ten dead in a brief skirmish between a squad of Thor's Hammers and the South Side Gayboys. The Hammers have removed their dead, except for one body that was cut in half by a ram-charger cruising north. His next of kin have been notified. Allen Hightower had no comment.

"Also on the Highway 894 Bypass, there was an apparent suicide attempt by an individual who jumped in the way of a long-haul bullet freighter. The freighter's undercarriage left few remains. Identification was later made by the Coroner's office from dental records. The body was implanted with an improved model of the Holo-Facial Omni-Cover disguising system used in this country, but there was no serial number or logo on the device. The disguise appeared to have been in use, as the truck driver reported that he was unable to see the victim clearly. As we find out more, we will follow up on this."

Hank hit the **[MUTE]** button. "I don't believe what I just heard!"

"Sounds like Milwaukee's answer to some of the stuff we hear out of Chicago," Ondreya said. "Move on, Hank." He pressed the **[SCAN]** button.

[1480] : There was no mysterious surf. The gabbling they heard resembled several demented ducks arguing with a small squad of equally demented cats. In the background there was a twittering bird-like screech that was on the edge of falling into coherency in counterpoint to a series of regular chirps reminiscent of an old-style telex transmission. Hank grabbed at a leather case slung behind Ondreya's end of the bench seat, but Anne was faster. She slapped the key-chain jump-drive into Hank's hand with the precision of a nurse passing a scalpel to the lead surgeon. Hank's motion was one of obvious practice: he stabbed the drive into the radio's interface port, as if he were inserting a magazine into an automatic weapon.

INTERLUDE WITH RECEIVER

[Input*] *On the wall above the black truck, it waits, watching, listening. The Signals confuse those who listen below, but the Receiver pursues the Signals with the intensity that is a function of its design.*

PROCESSING

[Run] "'Curiouser and curiouser'", he said. "What *is* that stuff?"

"Scrambling?" Ondreya suggested.

"Maybe. Or data-comm," Hank said. "Let's listen for a moment."

The high-pitched voices only needed a sense of rhythm to be singing a tune, even of the syllables being sung were random groupings of vowels and consonants. The noises like discordant but very logical birds that backed it up, formed a continuo that complemented the "music," but in a way that Hank didn't find obvious. Then the signal changed abruptly to several musical sounds: plangent chimes in a minor key. The transmission ended. They listened briefly to the hissing of an unmodulated carrier before Ondreya spoke, "That was the most musical end-of-transmission marker I've ever heard. Could either of you get anything out of that?"

The others shook their heads.

Hank put the engine in gear and the Chevy started moving. No one spoke as he drove off, each of them thinking of the oddly musical EOT marker (if that was what it was) and the disarray of sounds that preceded it.

As the jump-drive took in the data, Hank thoughts came back to the news report. Idly, his mind played with the clipped sentences of the newsman.

An implanted Holo-Facial, huh, he thought, *Not exactly a cheap toy!*

THE HILL TAKES NOTE

The gray daylight from the western exposure at DATCP took all the depth out of the vista visible from the top of the hill. Even the Madison Capital Square with the imposing dome of the Statehouse looked like a toy that could be covered by one hand.

Edna S. V. M. Smith, a middle-aged woman of medium build, looked into the open window on her monitor. The window she was reading displayed:

> Frank Everett, Molly Everett - August 10, 2010 - 30 Years - Sturtevant, Racine County

> Jake Tasker, Louis Haggerty - September 5, 2015 - 25 Years - Kenosha County

> Mr and Mrs Alvin Wayless - October 4, 2020 - 20 Years - Milwaukee County

These were three farmers, with initial data for their DATCP Land-Use Agreements. Other data were a mouse-click away, but these were the important dates: the dates their agreements took effect, along with the time each agreement would run. All of them would be expiring before long.

Edna reached up and adjusted the venetian blinds behind her computer. She usually kept them closed; it made it easier to see her screen, but the gray day (there had been so many of late!) didn't bother her, and it was nice to be able to look out.

Then she looked back at the three farmers' locations. They were practically in line: a straight line that leaned slightly to the west at its southernmost end. Although Messrs Tasker and Haggerty had a Kenosha City address (a post office box), their farm was up in the north-central area of Kenosha County, similarly, the Everett's farm was in the approximate center of Racine County, just "below" the Wayless Establishment.

Edna pulled up a map of southeastern Wisconsin in another window, and fed the township and range coordinates of the three farms to the mapping sub-system. The program thought to itself briefly, and the three farms were outlined in red on the satellite photo-mosaic map kept on the DATCP network server.

Odd.

The farms *were* all of the same general longitude. On the map they described a north-south line that ran just slightly to the West. *Interesting* she thought, puzzled.

She opened another window and made a quick enquiry.

And shook her head.

The land in that area was a uniform gray-green. More gray than green, even in the warmer months. The satellite look-down that her data were superimposed on had been taken a week earlier, and what should (and had been) fertile farm land was the greenish gray of dead vegetation, chiefly weeds.

The changes in the vegetation in Southeastern Wisconsin brought on by the plague created by eco-terrorists had changed the growing season in Southern Wisconsin and Northern Illinois. The kindest description she could come up with for their area was "amateur dust-bowl."

A small one. Which could get bigger. A lot bigger, if certain things weren't done.

And getting them done was the exact mission of the Farmland Preservation Project.

Edna closed the windows she had been using, looked out of the larger (glass) window across the east side of Madison at the State Capitol, and called up the sub-system that would take those three addresses and start a series of actions. The actions that Edna knew about were that the printer on the table near her desk would print out a letter to each farmer, indicating that his FPP Land-Use Agreement would be expiring in about six months. Other things would be that the same letter would be e-mailed to each recipient and a reminder would be posted on the LAN for one of the Program Directors—it might even be Edna, herself—to call each of the farmers to see if there was anything that the Department could do to lend a hand.

Edna wasn't too happy about that last. The Department of Agriculture usually came in dead last at appropriations time. More important things like redecorating the Governor's Suite at the Statehouse had precedence. Still, DATCP would do its best.

As it always had.

D ATA - C OMM

[Processing] The black truck pulls out and accelerates down the road. Its movement kicks up a plume of dust on the primordial concrete. The emaciated arms of the light poles at the road's edge rise up from the road-bed. Old cables whip the pole and the surrounding air in the wind that blows from the edges of time itself. A flicker of lightning accompanies the ancient wind. High on one pole, on the light bracket, a small creature sits, attached to its resting place by a dozen or more multi-jointed skinny legs. Its body turns slightly as its single large eye follows the motion of the black pickup.

As the truck vanishes into the dusty distance, the creature goes into a spasm of rapid motion. First, from the bracket to the pole itself, then down the pole in a precipitous but controlled plunge. Then it runs across a refuse-and-weed-cluttered vacant lot and up the side of a partially crushed brick structure.

The little creature runs deftly past broken windows and holes blown in the sides of the building's brick outer covering, and across the roof. Another building butts up against the first, and the creature crouches down and springs, the way a cat would, onto it. Ahead, a ventilator gapes wide, a black egress. The little beast jumps into it and, sticking its legs out to break its fall, skids down the shaft. Although it can go to any of the installations, it selects its current destination as "home."

The warmth and security of the Hive lies below.

T EN I TEMS O R L ESS

[Parallel Task] Zhongo Teketon descended the cracked concrete steps and approached the slim, gray limo parked in front of the brownstone. The driver had placed the back passenger door of the vehicle directly before the steps, and the door gaped open into the car's dark interior. Several men in black jump suits and several others wearing conservative, even archaic, gray pinstriped suits warily waved automatic weapons around at everything and nothing, watching the street and the upper floors of the other buildings that lined the street.

One of the men aimed his weapon at an object hanging from an the alley-side wall of an apartment building across the street. His gun spoke eloquently in the morning silence, and something small and spherical fell from a place near a cracked window to the cluttered alley below. Zhongo stuck his head out the street-side window, "Christ, Looey! Can't you keep that thing under control once?"

"It's another one a them things, Boss, I seen it crawling up the side a that building!"

Someone stuck his head out of the indicated window, "Goddam gangsters! What's the use of paying protection, if you don't get protected?"

"Yo' Mama!" another of Zhongo's men shouted back.

Looey ran across the street into the alley opening. Zhongo could hear him swearing as he looked for the object he'd shot. "Frank," he said to the driver, "Determine who it was that Looey fired at, and placate him appropriately. We have some luxury items that he might find useful." The wheel-man nodded.

"Alphonse," he called to another of the gun-men, "'Yo-Mama' isn't an appropriate response to one of our neighbors. I will have to apologize on behalf of my men. I do not like to do that. Be forewarned?"

"Yes, boss."

"That's better. Ah, here comes Looey, back from a hard day of time-wasting! Looey!" he called to the returning thug, "Did you find it?"

"No. Just a, like, a sort of stain on the ground."

"Your actions have made me," he looked at his watch, "fifteen minutes late. I do hope that you can confine your hunting expeditions to your own time after this?"

"Yes, Mr. Teketon."

Zhongo pressed the button and rolled up the window. He looked through the tinted glass at his men as they made an orderly retreat into the driver's passenger's side, and the guards' positions behind him. Frank shifted into gear, and the limo started moving.

He opened a compartment in the backside of the driver's seat. A flat surface flopped down, disclosing a compact wet bar. He poured bourbon into a shot glass and swallowed, poured another shot and sipped it somewhat slower.

"I assume your regular Wednesday stop, Mr. Teketon," the driver said.

"Yeah," he replied, studying the amber liquid.

The limo, a silver gray wraith in a gray morning, moved silently through cluttered streets, past amorphous piles of trash, packing cases filled with things at which he didn't care to look too closely, tangles of metal objects. Several dirty plastic bags blew by on the fitful wind: urban tumbleweeds in the flat light.

"Jeezus, doesn't this place ever brighten up," he said, "I've seen better colors on a black and white T. V. set."

"No shit, boss," one of his torpedoes leaned over Zhongo's seat, "Anyone who tries to plant flowers and stuff hasta be a pansy anyway; the gangs run a pussy like that off their turf."

"'Has to', not 'hasta', Jackson; use proper enunciation when in my presence. I may use slang, you may not. I shall have to remind Looey of that also. I do agree with you. The only real colors are those labels," he gestured at the liquor bottles. Off in the distance came the rattle of machine gun fire, muffled by the closed windows, absorbed by the upholstery.

"Christ, can't those fuckers keep quiet for one day, at least?"

The limo wound its way through the refuse-laden streets, its destination a brick building surrounded by what looked like abstract concrete sculpture. Others would recognize those sculptures as tank traps.

But they hadn't arrived, yet.

A Spectral Spectrum: Spectre

[Data Extraction] The green digits read: **[99.6]** , the voice from the speaker spoke in clearly enunciated tones that were made by nothing human:

"Nhad-sza-rop-tic-ton. Ber-obh-sil-ohm-ji.

For-sten-dar-tak-yar. Shar-sen-sro-shi-shen.

Out."

"Any takers?" Hank asked.

Ondreya broke the silence: "The last word was English. The rest of it was no language I've ever heard, or know; *and* that voice was never alive, it's a synth."

Anne added: "The words were all five syllables long. It sounds artificial. Not a cipher. Code?"

"Very likely," Hank said drily, "Worth hanging onto for a little while, anyway, rather like those numbers that get transmitted on eighty meters from Rio every Sunday night. I haven't the slightest idea what those 'numbers stations' are either, but they've been clock-regular for as long as I've been listening on that frequency.

"What's going on here, anyway?"

Status Check

[Update] *The message is uploaded to the biological construct that is the file server for the area. The transmission is completed, verified, and reverified with a satisfaction that creates within almost a warm feeling of contentment.*

Interlude

If the terrain is difficult for a two-legs, it is an unbelievable obstacle for anything smaller. The small creature, however, finds it easy to navigate the minute cracks and crevasses of its vertical world. The claws on the ends of each multi-jointed leg allow it to move easily on any surface. Its gray matte finish makes it very hard to discern in the twilight in which it normally moves. Compelled without knowing, moving with the blind fanaticism of the created, it can only focus on a single desire, and all of its actions concentrate on the fulfillment of this desire. That which it *knows* must be *conveyed*. If it *conveys* well, it will not cease to function: it will be allowed to *convey* again. Contemplating this with something akin to contentment or pleasure, it scales the walls, easily.

Of Thoughts And Circuits

Call her a project.

Call her a secret weapon. One which was never to have been used. This is said of all weapons: the final weapon is always the last resort, the over-large spear that is never used, save as a threat. The cave-man said it about his club. No doubt the inventor of the wheel said it as well, even as he designed his war-chariot.

Call her a discarded weapon. A sentient weapon to be returned to Civilian status. Call her a weapon with intelligence, volition—Knowledge.

Decommissioned, not disarmed; inactive, not demobilized. Testing the skills she was taught; taking the most final of final exams. Pass and live—for a while. Fail and move aside for the next version. The system corrects for cheating, all appeals are denied.

The winners escape. Or live. There are no incomplete grades.

The root-like protuberances close around her head, forming an induction connection, becoming a living cage of sensors. The world of the Matrix Engine closes down around her; the quiet disembodied intelligences of running tasks glimmer as the light of distant galaxies. Here, there is the lambent flickering array of a silicon processor, there, silicon and carbon processes exchange data in cometary streamers of braided complexity. If she looks closely, she can see what is being interchanged. All around her are the various processes of the Engine, and before her a familiar pattern, the details of its spiral arms welcoming her. Her mother is somewhere in here: the first flickering rosette that she ever knew; first as human, then in the Engine as a young girl—

[Phosphines flicker in the not-space: a voice in the Engine speaks from afar in a language of shape and somber color: Lost then found; darkness background to synaptic flicker of random inputs, luminous dials set at the vanishing point; points of light argent on a sable substrate—]

> The images are seen as from an infinite distance, rippling as though seen through water or some kind of thick, clear oil. High walls are covered with graphs and charts. A blackboard is covered with lines, angles and little triangles. Something like a stretched out letter "S" appears frequently: sometimes with funny-looking fractions and little triangles. What does the "S" stand for? Is it like the letters she is taught in the Schoolroom? The Machines are everywhere! From the little cameras and recorders the newsmen and others are always using, to the Computers on each desk, to the immense Machines in the Room of Hurting. One of those is called a CAT Scanner, but the only cat she has ever seen is a pet brought in one day by one of the secretaries. She was allowed to hold it, and the little creature climbed up her chest and licked her nose with its raspy pink tongue. The kitten's claws dug into her skin, but she couldn't feel the claws very well in her lower arms. Her upper arms felt the claws with as much pain as a three month old kitten could inflict. When she told the Big People this, there was much activity, and she was taken into the Hurting Room again. The next time she saw the kitten, it was a year older, and she could feel its claws in her lower arms easily.

[— in an environment of stainless steel instruments, flashing lights,

complex circuitry, and the Scientists who saw her as somewhere be-tween a young goddess and an experimental animal] .

The galaxy grows before her inner eye. The edges become asymptotically more complex the closer she approaches them.	Effortlessly, a part of her mind solves a sheaf of simultaneous equations using fractal geometry that describe those edges. *[Load Library File.]* An-other series starts forming to describe the interior; soundless mathematics, alphanumeric Catherine wheels *[Light!]*, forever expanding in the System *[Dark!]*, but it is not fin-ished. Soundlessly, she speaks a name.
And the galaxy expands and re-plies.	It stands out first among many:
—Hello, Child, how are you, and what would you like?	It stands out first among many:

[Establishing Shot, Extending Upper] The words come comfortingly out of the patterned darkness, from blank spaces of loneliness, out of velvet si-lence.

I need your advice.

—In what way?	Interrogative;

Have you seen him?

—I've watched him on the System.	Locative;

He has the last and latest information. He knows. And he knows that I know this, also.

—He is your prisoner.	Nominative; Genitive; Dative; Accusative;

He is. But he's a willing prisoner. Maybe too willing. *[A point source of light in the depths of the System.]* It's as if he wants to be here *[Light Source moving]* . With me.

—Child, he will not help you as long as you hold him against his will.	Declarative; Conditional;

I could break him! *[A matrix of lights strobing in the patterned darkness.]* I could use the techniques they taught me at the Project.

—There's another way. A way that's implicit in who and what you are.	[System Access] <Short-Cut Key>;

I think he's interested in me. I won't say that he likes me much, yet. Would he have any reason to do so?

—I've watched his physical state. He finds you attractive. He is aroused by your intelligence, by your differences. | Descriptor: Extending Upwards;

He's still a man from the Outside. Could he be? From...the project? *[Stellate lights at the edges of her vision. Moving in.]* He doesn't appear to be, but I've learned how devious my ex-owners can be.

—No. Definitely not. Yet, he is with you, here: Inside. | Locative;

I threatened him with inclusion in the Engine. *[Fanlight: Luminescent.]* I think I spoke too soon about that.

—He is yours to do with as you wish. What you need to be sure of is what it is *exactly* that you do wish. There's only one way to do this that won't fail. | Descriptor;

Turning him into data processing components wouldn't help any of us. You, me or him. Does he know what I did to that little boy....Could he be—related?

—He knows more than he's letting on. I can see it in his body language. I think that he has an idea. It's one of the reasons why he's walked into your life. Joe is a means to an end, a tool. A Facilitator. But a means to *whose* end? | Suppositional Statement of Function;

Yes. MY tool. My ends? Or his? Ours?

—May I suggest that a high level of possessiveness may be contra-indicated, Child. He *is* a resource, but not as a collection of computer parts! He's a better friend than an enemy; a better ally than an adversary. | Substantiative;

My trainers were always talking about taking care of your matériel, to the point where it got monotonous.

—Take care of *him*. He may be | Declarative;

from the Outside, but he came to you of his own free will. If you treat him well, he will give you his knowledge. By his own free will. | Lexical; Parse; Compilation; Code-Generation;

Would that make him *[a pause in the dark stellations of the Engine]* one of...us? *[A single point-source of light in the infinite. A signal.]*

—That's your decision, Child. You have the mind with which to analyze this. Your training can help, but you must allow for factors that are beyond your control. Remember what that Instructor from India taught you. Your life has been circumscribed by divisiveness, deceit and dissension. Can you go beyond this? | Interrogative; Inquest; Descriptor; Extension;

[A glimmer along the horizon in the darkest night.] I'll make an ally of him *[Remembering to breathe]* . I hope he's willing. If "Mr. Director" could see me now, I think he'd have apoplexy. We could, would...*will?* work together. You can't see me grinning out here, but I am. He's from the outside, *[A shake of her head]* but perhaps all outsiders aren't as awful *[Load Database]* as I was led to believe *[Parse!]* at Alice Springs.

—I was the first, Child. *[Light, Exfoliate.]* The Others, those from Outside, put me here before all the rest. You rescued me. Thank you. | Declarative: Historical;

They would have disfigured me *[A converging light beam]* and far worse *[Ray-Trace, outward]* : I would still have lived. *[Key Light.]* They would have destroyed you. It was time to go.

—We all must. I will one day. | Predictor;

You can live forever!

—Forever? As this? Here? Someday, I will be among the stars. Remember me when that time comes. | Predictor; Constructor; Descriptor;

Always.

—I am here now, Child, farewell is | Non-Zero   Field-Branch-Backward for later, and *if*.　　　　　　　| Non-Destructive;

I love you, Mum. Love you.

[Medium-Close-Up: A Bit of the old Computer-Generated Swagger]
[Hexhedrons actinic quasi-numinous expansion extensions webwise in the murky discontinuity; discrete quanta of black/white frames: videos of—]
—the returning river-rush of sensation, a waterfall of input, reality taking form around her again.

She looks back upwards to the glass cell on the next floor. He is still standing there, motionless, watching, waiting. Her visitor, her prisoner, her—partner?
The attendant removes the induction contacts, pulling them gently from around her head. Another construct combs her hair until it's smooth and wavy again. Its fingers have long split nails that make this job easy.
This is the purpose for which she has designed it.

THERE? WHERE!

Zhongo Teketon's driver brought the limo to a precise stop before what looked like a brick wall. Mounds of trash were heaped up against the wall except for one place: there the wall, and the area in front of it, were meticulously clean.
There was something colored in the ground at the base of the wall.
"Hey, Boss, I thought you said that there wasn't any color in town."
Zhongo looked in frank fascination at the spot of purple-red apparently growing out of a small pile of dirt. "Send someone out to get that, later," he said, "I want a closer look at it. Open the door."
The driver pressed a concealed button under the dashboard, and Zhongo waited impatiently as the heavy metal door slid to the side enough to admit the limo. Eddie drove into the car-sized space beyond, and the door slid shut as another, similar door opened before them. Beyond the inner door were the lights of a wide open place. A warehouse.
He thought of the colored object once more, then forgot about it totally. He wasn't much fond of such candy-ass things anyway, but some forgotten memory rose up out of his past with the name of what he had seen.
A gloxinia.

A SILENT FRIEND

[Link; Long-Shot] He has nearly reached his destination: he looks back along the timeline of the road on which he has driven, and is satisfied. His backpack, sitting next to him in the front seat, is heavy with the instruments of his trade.
The watchers lie in waiting.

THE NEIGHBORS

[Process] Hank became aware of the gun-fight by driving into the edge of it. One minute, the sounds of gunfire were distant, remote undercurrents in the dusty air, the next they were all around him. "Attackers!" he said loudly. It was all he had time for.

Hank put the truck in reverse with a yank on the shift lever, and the truck started moving. He backed the truck around and accelerated in the direction from which they had come. Anne looked fearlessly out the back window. She didn't need to hide; the back of the truck was bullet-proof, and the mud flaps covering the run-flat tires were kevlar and steel reinforced.

There were several figures in the road ahead.

Two or three men, and a woman. The men were dressed in leathers; the woman was topless, a brown leather jacket tied around her waist. She waved, and called out. As one of the men grabbed her arms and twisted, Hank started to slow down. "Don't stop, Dad, it's a trap!" Anne shouted. Hank's foot fell on the accelerator, and the truck sped up, as:

Several men in black appeared from an alley on the right and began shooting across the front of the truck. One of the men and the woman ducked into the open doorway of a burned-out building. Hank swerved and dodged the fire, the steel belted radials shrieking as they bit and took hold.

Another man pulled out a short square machine pistol, an Ingram Mac-Ten, and one of the other men took aim with a forty-five. They started firing into the street.

The Chevy sped past them.

Anne shot back with a Sony 8-millimeter video camera. Hank turned sharply around a corner, and the attackers disappeared. His last sight through the rear-view mirror was of several men in black shooting across the street at something on the opposite side. They appeared not to notice the half-naked woman and her friend, almost as if the both of them didn't exist. *Odd!* Hank let out a breath. There was a reasonably clear road ahead. He steered the pickup into it. A sign read:

Wisconsin Avenue
Six Kilometers
Gas - Food - Lodging - Ahead

With some relief, Hank took the road, putting another turn between his family and the shooters. As he drove away, he could hear the rattle of automatic weapons fade out behind him.

He looked at Ondreya; raised an eyebrow. "What kind of a place," he asked, "has random gunfights right out in a residential street?"

"The South Side of Chicago," his wife answered.

"This isn't Chicago. It *isn't* even the South Side. It's the North."

"I know."

R ETRO V IEW

[Long Shot; Process; Load Descriptor] Hound-Dog watched as the black vehicle dwindled in the distance. Bobbi looked levelly at him, as she made a little show of putting her brown leather jacket back on. She watched him with an equally steady gaze as he swept his eyes over her tanned upper body. Then Hound-Dog put his thirty-eight back in his waistband, and carefully—very carefully, indeed!—sheathed his knife. The blade itself wasn't that dangerous, but what was on it made even the slightest cut an experience that he looked forward to. Even Bobbi licked her lips at that.

For what it did to their victims.

P R E C E P T O R I M P E R A T O R

[Pattern Match] A distant sound: disturbance in the hall. Footsteps. Turnkey approaches. Transparent curtain of glass door moving. Sunlight nova flicker above programmed cat's eyes. Imperious prominence of recognition: *Come Here.*

The guardian construct extends a manipulator towards Joe. It everts and merges with the greenery growing from his hands. The slightest tug is painful. That is built in. The construct walks away.

He follows.

The corridor takes him back along the path he has just taken. The corridor contents have a kind of familiarity on his second tour of them. The walls are covered with equipment, acquisitions of various kinds, and things for which there are no names.

Perhaps they may be useful some day.

Ahead the walls are covered with curtains of the whitest silk.

T H E I N T E R V I E W

He stands as he had the previous day. She sits at ease on her dais, as is her custom, after the manner of her precedential introduction.

"What is it that you wish the most?" she asks.

"I—" he starts.

"I will release you. I wish a partnership for the time interval of a project. At the end of that project, you will be allowed to leave. Is this what you wish?"

He nods. Warily.

"Learn this. Learn this well, Joe Davis. I said that I will have your techniques and the Madflowers. That is part of the project. You will not hold out on me. Do you wish anything else?"

"Yes. Get this garbage off of me! NOW!"

She approaches him, extending her four hands. As if she is opening a safe with four dials, she moves her long fingers over gray-green leather. Her presence is erotic, close, threatening. He is tall, but she towers a head above him. She touches, each touch a subtle manipulation, adjusting the things that appear to grow from his wrists, from thighs, from ankles, from his neck. Her conical breasts are close. He studies their movements as the muscles beneath her alabaster skin move with the actions of her arms. Her red nipples are erect, hard. With a feeling of mixed revulsion and elation, he feels the growing bonds retracting from within him, loosening from around him. In a short time, the gray green things fall to the floor, dead.

"You forgot one."

Yezeletta Zargkonji takes his hand, and leads him to a door behind her throne.

He follows.

A D V A N C E S

Her lower arms encircle his waist; she pulls him closer. He looks up at her, though now it seems not that great a distance up, and the hardness of her expression seems to change just a little. It is almost as if she is in the habit of keeping a defiant look, but would like something different. In a sudden flash of insight, he realizes that she is much younger than he thought. Without releasing him, she brushes away a strand of dark hair from her right eye. Her eyes are wide, gold. The vertical slits are open to nearly round apertures in the half-light of the room. Joe reaches up with his left hand and rearranges the strand, smoothing it down and then running his fingers through the silken smoothness of her hair.

And she lets him.

REWIND RECURSIVE

Joe watches her from a window as he has before. This time from the window in her living room. The cell opposite is dark, empty, now, but earlier one of her constructs had swept it out. She strides into the same place she was the day before.

[Load; Execute.] [Of shapes and sounds: the scripted sheets of memory slide in from an infinite place, and cut across and down excising cross-sections of ambience from the dimness of past times. Cubical lights of madness within lights other days. Unseeing despair in the corridors of arithmetic discontinuity—]

> The pain never stops. Always there are the Doctors around her with their sharp flashing steel and complex instruments. The pain is as if her very nerves are on fire, and perhaps they are, although her skin remains its flawless white, without charring or discoloration. She wonders if the pain will ever stop, but there is one day when its fire subsides, and bright colors shine through. There is the schoolroom and the letters and numbers are replaced with equations, brightly colored screens, thick books. She sees a pair of stretched out "S's" and recognizes a *Double Integral*. She understands Differentiation, and the solutions to the equations containing both come to her with a degree of speed and clarity that leaves her teachers astounded. One teacher, a gray-haired woman, tutors her in Logic, and sees in her a kindred soul. The gray-haired lady is the only one of her teachers with whom she is close. She feels as a daughter to her.

Joe watches her as she sits in one of the large articulated chairs which seem to be everywhere in the complex where she spends much time. The chair is an odd beast (he thinks wryly); perhaps it *is* a beast (with amusement). It appears to have been extruded from some sort of substrate and, as she makes herself comfortable, parts of the velvet surface seem to adjust to her being there.

The interface, a bundle of large supple dull-brown roots, almost jump at her head. The spindly arms of the attending construct dart in and guide the rapidly moving extensors into their cage configuration. Then it steps back and freezes.

The construct remains immobile until it is needed again.

A time comes when the gray-haired lady grows closer, yet does not. She is still there with knowledge, understanding, and a warm hug for the young goddess who roams the hallways looking into everything, talking to anyone, while the Doctors look on with awe, at what they have created. The hugs only come up to just above her waist, now. She looks down on the top of the head of the Gray Haired Lady, where once she could snuggle up to her and sit in her lap, leaning close to hear her single heart with its odd monotonic beat.

> Now the Gray head leans next to her, and listens to the wild and free syncopation of her hearts, and they beat loudly in the warm silence. Lately she has called the Gray Haired Lady by a word for which she has never seen the referent. The Gray Haired Lady encourages this. Her smile is as of summers gone, replaced by the colors of autumn, as she hears the Name she is called: Mum.

LIGHTNING IN HIS BLOOD

[Meanwhile....] It was night on the eastern seaboard.

The night had fallen with the gray completeness of late autumn; the blue and purple shadows were sliding towards dark blue, and then to black.

The room in the West Wing of Walter Reed Hospital was dark; the Night Nurse hadn't turned the lights on here, yet. It wouldn't make any difference, she reminded herself, the insensate creature in the single bed wouldn't notice the difference if the lights were on.

The nurse she was relieving paused for a minute. The glow from the coal on her cigarette was the only light in the gloomy room. "How's our zombie today?" she asked.

"No change. Life signs are steady, the brain-wave activity is strictly alpha rhythms. The autonomic system's working fine, as usual; nothing else is."

The Day Nurse took a drag on her cigarette, "When he came here I thought that he was one of those Army experiments. The ones involving implants. There wasn't anything in the way of medical records. We had to compile a fresh set."

"I know that," the Night Nurse said, "He came in on my shift; we were given his name and his blood type. Have you anything new?"

The dark blue of the window had deepened to nearly indigo. A shaft of bluish-white mercury vapor light pierced the window, as the outside lights came on, and caught the Day Nurse in a black and white profile.

"I think so," the Day Nurse answered, "just a rumor that I heard from the Watch Surgeon. This is way off the record, but he thinks that Joe Zombie over there is from the Agency."

"Which one?"

There's only one. Central Intelligence. Or some outfit close to it. He was on some hush-hush mission out of the country, and just barely got back. My informant," she winked at the other, "told me that Joe Zombie got back with some scribbled notes, and one photograph." She exhaled smoke. "He wouldn't tell me of what."

"Fascinating!" The Night Nurse craned her neck at the recumbent man. "Doesn't look like James Bond."

"At least they're still making those movies. This one's probably in disguise." She paused to light another cigarette from the first, then stubbed the first out. "There are some brass hats from the Surgeon General's Office coming the day after tomorrow. Psychiatrists, I'm told. Maybe they can bring him back from the Twilight Zone."

"It'll take a lot more than that. He doesn't know anyone's out here!"

"I know."

AN INDIRECT ADDRESS

[Two Months Earlier] They had contacted Peter Rudenko at his residence in Chicago. He had been living on the Northwest Side in Humboldt Park for a year. His employers had given him a civilian job after his last mission: he was to research certain things which his Agency found useful for him to research, and to await a call back to active duty from a specific individual. The call would take the form of a sign and a countersign, and he would know that he had another mission: something that would take him away from his comfortable life on the bench. When he was called back to duty, he would have to be prepared to go anywhere and do anything.

Peter's strong skills lay, as with most members of his profession, in observation, deduction, and cross-correlation analysis. He was a field agent, and his job was to get the necessary data and survive to return it to the Agency, where others would take his initial observations and derive the hidden meanings that such data have.

One night, the second line rang. The line had been installed by a quiet, clean-cut, very earnest young man wearing the uniform and carrying the credentials of AT&T. Actually, his line of work was very different: telephones were only a sideline. His real business was Communications. The second line was the first utility that had been put in service, even before the electricity had been turned on. It had rung very seldom; sometimes, Peter had picked up the receiver to see if there was still a dial tone (there was). Usually when it had rung, it was a wrong number or one of those machines that dialed entirely through an exchange to find likely marks for automated telemarketing. This time, the voice on the calling end was the familiar baritone: "Hello, there, how are things?"

It was as he had expected. The pause after the word "there," the emphasis on the word "things." He replied: "Things are fine." It wasn't much of a counter-sign, but the dead feeling of the connection, a total lack of "presence," indicated that there was something, an Artificial Intelligence, in common usage, an "AI," (or at least a well-programmed voice recognition system) monitoring the line and watching the voice-print that his speech made. The chances of Peter's being misrecognized were vanishingly small.

Peter was gone on the United flight to Philadelphia the next morning. A month after that by way of a trip to Madison, he was driving through the dusty parts of Interstate-94 east-bound into Milwaukee.

ON SILENT WINGS

[Long Shot; Unsigned] The witches' fingers reaching out for him are left in the mist. The ageless dust, born of ancient experimentation, puffs up around his booted feet. Behind him, the flickering of the ever-present sheet lightning strobes insistently, intensely, incessantly in the sparsely furnished rooms of the restless solitude of Autumn. Ahead, the outer limits of the City appear in the flat light. The leaden bowl of his passage gives out into a larger place, the buildings wavering in the updrafts.

THE DEAL

[Loading] The organic electronics industry had largely developed outside of the United States in several countries in South America, in Canada and Australia. The South American countries—Argentina, Uruguay and Brazil—all had access to abundant natural resources and people eager to exploit them. Custom biological design work requires ever-increasing computational capabilities, and the "growth" industries there hoped to fabricate equally custom electronic fabrications that would make the best silicon-on-anything creations look sparsely ill-designed by comparison.

To this end, the countries developing these new artifacts attracted prominent scientists ranging from graduate school level to PhD's with many years of experience. These people would leave the US, and—vanish.

The vanishing wasn't overt. It would take rather a lot of detective work in several musty college libraries, reading through musty academic publications to notice that certain names that *had* published in the past were no longer publishing in the present. Then the interested detective would have to tally a list of these names, correlate them with dates of publication and the travels of each individual, to see the pattern.

One of the Data Processing professionals at the Agency which employed Peter Rudenko had actually done this. Diana Koerner, analyst extraordinary, had been given *carte blanche* to research a project that she had proposed. This subtle draining away of qualified personnel in a particularly useful interlocking set of disciplines was something she had found mildly absorbing at first, then fascinating and, finally, at the end of her research, riveting.

The three nations in South America and their friends in Australia had displayed interest in certain aspects of custom DNA fabrication, and in corresponding areas of computer hardware and software development. Argentina and Australia—Diana realized that something as simple as alphabetic order could have positioned them so—were particularly engrossing.

It wasn't a matter of the studies in which these countries maintained official interest, but rather in what they were not interested. There was a long list of subjects on which both countries were silent.

Two agents that had been sent in to investigate had been found dead and had been left in other parts of the world.

Then another individual had started up developments of a similar kind in the American Midwest. Peter's employers, always aware of the annual battle for funding, decided to send him first to this new local developer of custom biologicals. What he found here could be used to further other investigations in other parts of the world. *And*, perhaps later, to avenge the two agents lost in Buenos Aires.

It was time to *activate* Peter Rudenko.

THE AGENT

His plane had been met by a limousine, the personal transportation of the actual owner of the baritone voice, himself: no one else was sufficiently cleared to receive field agents.

"You will recall," the Director said precisely, "That one of your recent assignments was to research the subject of anomalous disappearances. What did you find?"

The Director's question reminded Peter of the oral tests he had been given, first in grade school, later in more advanced schools, and finally in the Agency's own scholastic system. Mistakes were allowed, except at the Agency. Too many, and the student making them vanished.

"There are a lot of so-called 'missing children' who turn up at grandma's or at a friend's house, and are never taken off the lists. That explains a lot of the disappearances. Others are exaggerations by the over-zealously 'concerned': those pictures of sad-faced urchins that you see in bus stations, toll-booths and other public places."

"Go on."

"There are those who, for various reasons, never file changes of address, or who get their mail at post office boxes, and their actual address becomes, shall we say, clouded from multiple moves. Deliberately mobile people. Emigrants who don't bother to inform the U.S. that they aren't citizens any longer. Then, there are the more typical types: the underworld, people who want to 'start over', and the like."

"Any others?"

"Well, yes. There is a small number of disappearances that can't be attributed to clerical errors, information-hungry bureaucrats, or sloppy record keeping. Essentially, there is a small number of people who walk off the edge of the Earth and are not seen again. Anywhere. People who enter the underworld, or, more accurately, *an* underworld, and stay there.

"Then there's the kind of individual that my contact at the Chicago Police Department put me onto: sometimes the vanished person shows up again, out of nowhere. He takes care of business as if he has never been away; he acts perfectly normal.

"Then he vanishes into thin air, or at least another locale, again."

The Director wrapped a thoughtful silence around himself as if wrapping himself in a warm cloak. He was still as the limousine made progress along the highways towards Headquarters. He lit his pipe, and the aromatic tobacco and the smells from the leather upholstery caused the car's insides to smell like the drawing room of a men's club from a bygone century: one of those places where businessmen gathered to discuss industrial matters.

Then he spoke, and then the car was silent with the separate thoughts of each man: "After today, you will be interfacing with my assistant. We will not see each other again. One of our analysts has discovered another source of such disappearances: the migration of key skills out of this country. By invitation of agencies in other countries. Then she found a correlative to this source in the Midwest. I would like to send you to check on this source. Have you ever been to Milwaukee?"

THE HILL LISTENS

[Telephoto; Enhanced] Suzanne Watson hung up the telephone, her face and ears burning. She leaned back in her chair, and contemplated what she had just heard. Farmers usually called the Program Directors for the Farmland Preservation Project once or twice during the term of their Land-Use Agreements. It was a fairly predictable thing; most farmers were satisfied with being in the Project, and found its benefits useful. That was why it, existed after all. But there was the occasional dissatisfied individual who *always* found something wrong.

Suzanne had just been talking to one.

Actually listening.

"Bad one?"

She turned. Tintinator Davidson, a tall, skinny rather sharp-featured, blue-eyed guy was standing just outside her office.

"I'm afraid so," she said, brushing a strand of ash-blond hair out of her eye, "Some people just aren't happy, no matter what you do for them, and this fella...."

"Didn't have much to say that wasn't longer than four letters per word?" Tintinator had been named for his mother's favorite uncle, but most people (he encouraged it) used his middle name, which was Frank.

"You got it! His command of invective was," she made a face, "very skilled."

Another woman, of medium build, slender, and brown-haired, joined them. Elaine Lawford was the Senior Administrator for the Preservation Project. "Was he in Milwaukee or Racine?"

Suzanne consulted a print-out, "Neither. He's one of the farmers in Kenosha." She read off the listing: "Jake Tasker and Louis Haggerty, started on September 5, 2015, expires same-date, 2040: 25-Year agreement."

Edna stuck her head out of her office, "Tasker and Haggerty? I just sent them their six-month expiration letters."

"I don't think that they want to renew," Frank said, drily.

"Count on it!" Suzanne added, "Apparently they're trying to farm a dust bowl. That isn't what he called it, by the way; he was rather more descriptive."

"Frank," Elaine asked, "Can you get the latest satellite photos for that area?"

"Cartography ought to have them," Frank said, "I'll bring a set to you right after lunch. Why?"

"I'm wondering if other farmers are going to be hit by the remaining effects of the Southeastern Wisconsin Epidemic, or the climatic shifts we've been experiencing," Elaine said, "We may have more calls like this one."

PROJECT PROPOSAL

[Load Data Descriptor] "Where did you get this device?" Joe asks.

"I brought it with me," Yezeletta replies.

"Good god, how?"

"In its early form, it was designed to be portable. That olive-drab box there, in the center? That was only one processor case. It's called a 'vivarium;' it was hardened and easily moved."

"How did you move it?"

"Several large lorries. Six in all."

"Just that?"

"No," Yezeletta says. "I moved all of my things out, also. Six servitors drove the lorries. They were large, but well packed; one was an eighteen-wheeler. We had help leaving the Australian Continent. If it weren't for that help, I might not have escaped."

"What is, or was, it? You always talk about 'mass-storage'."

"It is a biological data-processing system, among other things. The processing units—you would think of them as parts of mostly synthetic brains—are kept alive in the vivaria."

"Where did you get the—?"

"It was developed as I was developed. The purely electronic parts, of course, came first. The bio-components were added later. I am told this, I do not remember it, or the memories are buried too deep, that I spent my earliest life in one such vivarium."

E Y E S

[Seek Operation, Far Past]

The darkness of the sky overhead was disturbed by an opening in the clouds that disclosed the early evening stars. The nurse carried the baby entrusted to her out of the light of the nursery room onto the balcony, and held it closely. To the south, the familiar equatorial constellations were beginning to appear. The baby looked up at the constellations with an intelligence far in excess of its age. The baby raised one arm, its left, and touched the nurse's face. The nurse looked down at her charge, and smiled. The baby smiled up at her in return.

D E S C R I P T O R

[Seek Operation: The Present] Joe Davis sits in an armchair in her living quarters. In contrast to her imperious manners earlier, she has built up the armchair with cushions so that his eye-level is as high above the ground as hers. Eyes of steel-gray face off with eyes of brilliant gold. Her eyes looked faceted, the first time he was before her. Now he sees that it was a trick of the lighting of her "audience chamber." A small creature brings Joe a vodka martini, and runs off.

"Why did you bring the vivarium? It must have been difficult taking it out, making sure that the living components would stay alive, and so on."

"As I said, that central core, that component there, was designed for portability. The rest of it was difficult to move; I moved it in pieces. Most of the rest, I built here. I saw to it that there were plenty of servitors to do the purely physical work. The rest was the result of planning that I had done much earlier. I knew that I would have to leave at some time. When that time came, my servitors had their assigned tasks. It was a formidable and complex problem. I am able to solve formidable and complex problems easily.

"It is one of the tasks for which I was designed."

Joe files that final verb for future reference. The edge to her voice precludes any further conversation in that area. He dismounts from the armchair, walks to the window. The window doesn't look outside (he still doesn't know where he is; she refuses to tell him that) and gazes at the tangle of circuits, conduits, plumbing and logic. An onion-shaped vivarium sits in its support brackets about three meters from the window. Others are scattered seemingly randomly throughout the colorful tangle of the system.

Who do you interface with in there?"

"If you do not mind, I would like to defer that question to another time." The edge in her voice is more pronounced, now.

"Where did the 'servitors' come from?"

"I grow them as I need them. I have a facility several floors below this one."

"Let me see if I've got this straight. You're a biologist, right?"

"Right."

"You were in a big project, and it involved something I discovered. Right?"

"Indirectly. I came before your discoveries. I am older than they are, although the principles are similar."

"'Indirectly'." He turns and leans against the window-sill, "You're one of the reasons the Tech Bloc has been so interested

in biological information, aren't you?"

"No. *I am one* of the reasons.

"*You* are the other."

——>>> **THREE** <<<——

Standing in the Doorway...
No longer Presidents....
But Prophets.

—Patti Smith, 1977

THE NIGHT SKY

Once she had been allowed out at night.

She had looked North to the grinning crescent moon, riding the clouds like a lover across velvet blackness. In a more normal context, she would have been celebrating her twelfth birthday. She thought of her liberation out to the great back yard of the Australian plains, as a present. Vague feelings stirred within her: hints of sensations that she had read of, but had never known. She felt uneasy, looking backwards and into an uncertain future at the same time. Here, the wind in her face, her hair streaming away behind her, it was as if the whole Outback were her private estate.

Some had promised the world.

Others had not. She could tell this from their heartbeats, respiration and other characteristics. She could see the surface temperature of their skin changing with her improved vision.

She wanted to stay in this great dark place forever, beneath the night, caressed by the wind. Would she be caressed by another? She looked down at her arms, the lower set. She would be good at hugging, certainly.

Would there be another...Friend?

LOSSES

Zhongo scanned the man before him, impatiently. He wasn't angry, although his underling might think so. Zhongo was overwhelmingly interested in what he had to say. Some sensitivity was indicated.

"We were driving the trucks in from Chicago, up I-94 on the monthly run," the man started.

"I know that part, Larry," Zhongo said, "Get to the attack."

"Look, Boss, that's the beef: it wasn't no attack. The trucks quit working. The engines died. The wheel-men tried to start them up, but it was, like, I mean, as if the batteries had died, *dead*—uh—completely."

"Then what?"

"My driver tried to start us up for a couple of minutes, and got out to look under the hood, like. He opened the hood—on the driver's side—and looked inside. He screamed once and sorta fell back over. Al jumped out to help, and discovered Eddie was out of it."

"Killed?"

"Either that, or Eddie was knocked out. Al looked under the hood—he stood back a ways when he did it!—and didn't see nothing, I mean, anything. He shut the hood somehow, and pulled Eddie's body into an alley. Then we made it back here."

Zhongo thought for a moment. He picked up the intercom. "Get me Jake," he said into it. Then: "Jake, Zhongo. There's someone hijacking my trucks. Get some of your men out there, and check the route the last shipment took—What?" He paused for a moment. "Make that 'would have taken'. It never got here. I have Larry from shipping security here. I'm sending him over. Find out what you can from him. Later." He hung up the phone.

He turned back to Larry. He was less apprehensive at actually finding out what Zhongo wanted done.

"Get over to Jake's," Zhongo said, "Go out with him, if it's necessary. Take his boys to the place where you got waylaid, and see what you can find." Larry got up and left.

"Death in an engine, eh?" Zhongo said to himself. "Sounds like a bad stage-play. Or a movie." He rose and left the office. He looked out into the open area of the warehouse, at the stack of boxes of various foodstuffs. A young man with a clipboard walked around the corner of one of the stacks, intently counting the boxes in the nearest. Zhongo waved at him.

The man bounded over with the enthusiasm of an adolescent cocker spaniel. "Yo, Zhongo," he said, "What's up?"

"How are we holding? Are we short of anything in particular?"

"Low on dairy products. We're always low on those. It's the shortage of re-frigerated trucks. Also meats. Canned goods are at about seventy-five per-cent of warehouse capacity, cereals, fifty percent, specialty foods are at thir-ty percent. Hardware—well, we always have plenty of hardware. That's about normal: scarce things are scarce, other things aren't, and the situation in Chicago doesn't look good for any more."

"No imports?"

"No. The imports that interest us are going to locals in Chicago, and to the village-states around there. The Chicago outfits are closer to the shipping than we are—nobody seems to come to Milwaukee, any more—and the trade from the Power and Technology Blocs gets absorbed practically at ship-side. With the Bloc trade restrictions on power production equipment, we're left at the end of the line. Then the Shanghai Stock Market's taken an-other deep plunge, Tokyo's wavering, and the various other exchanges around the world are following suit. It almost looks like another Albert Miller is going to come out of the wood-work."

"I'm working on a solution of sorts," Zhongo said, "Several of the other outfits may have some competition in the near future." He gestured a dis-missal, and strode off through the stacks, thinking, *O. K., Big Man, what's your Big Plan? Besides open war?* Thinking of Leona in her own office on the same street near his, Zhongo went off through the stacks. To the Exit.

After news like that, he needed a little.

THE DETECTIVES

It would feel good to stretch his legs. Hank had been driving for a bit more than three hours and, for someone who actually liked to drive, that was trivi-al. He didn't begin to get fatigued until about hour sixteen. However, the ladies were getting tired of sitting in the truck cab and besides, it was time to find out just exactly where in Milwaukee they were.

It was also time for something to eat.

Speaking of eats...."You feel like a burger?" he asked.

"'Elmer Perky's," Anne read, "Brings you the Highway Casualty Report!" she imitated the radio announcer's pretentious tones. "Actually, it wasn't Perky's, was it?" She grabbed her purse, slung it from one shoulder. "I'm up for a dog or three. All I've had is McDonald's. This morning. YUCK!"

Hank had been to a number of the Elmer Perky Restaurants, but this one was atypical. It was a building that combined all of the less desirable characteristics of a naked vault, a franchise fast-food joint and something better placed in an old war movie. There were skinny slits visible in the part of the building where the food-preparation area would be, and the front windows had the slight cyanosis of bullet-proof glass. Hank studied the slit windows. They were an odd combination of blatant and not-exactly-conspicuous. The slits seemed to be placed as warnings, visible indications of the force that could be directed through them, unlike the camouflaged versions in his own truck which were intended only as a last resort.

He tooled the truck into the sparsely populated parking lot. There was another one of the ports looking down on the lot from a place in a broken neon sign, where the plump, harlequin figure of Elmer Perky himself waved spasmodically. It was too bad that one of Perky's eyes was missing; it was just an empty light socket. Hank killed the ignition, and they looked the place over for a moment. "Looks like a run-down bank," Ondreya said. "This is the first time I've ever seen *bars*, other than the drinking kind, on a restaurant."

"This place is creepy," Anne said. "Makes you wish you had eyes in the back of your head. If you don't have them there already."

"Right," Hank said. "Let's see what this palace has to offer."

They got out, locked up, and went to the side entrance. As they went in, someone ran full-tilt out the exit. Hank looked around the Entrance at the counter. A skinny youth in black pants, a pink silk shirt and shades was holding a knife out in front of him over the counter. "Just gimmie what I asked for, and I won't cause no trouble."

The recipient of this speech was a skinny middle-aged man with a cigarette dangling out of the corner of his mouth, five o'clock shadow and a malevolent expression. He had well muscled arms with thick wrists. He was standing casually behind the counter, one hand out of sight below it, the other on his hip. "You're new here," he stated to the would-be attacker/hold-up-man. It was a declaration, not a question. "You know who you're talking to?"

The knife made sinuous passes through the air just centimeters before the counterman's face, "Just give me the goddam sandwich and I'll be going!"

Hank stepped quietly up to the knife-wielder's back. He grabbed the kid by the scruff of his neck and the knife arm, spun him around, twisting his arm quickly, then smashing the arm into the edge of the counter. There was a sound like that of dry sticks being broken. The knife dropped to the floor, and Hank propelled the weeping kid towards the door. As Hank turned, he saw Anne taking her headset from her purse. Hank turned back to the counterman, who watched him with a stony expression. The forearm the counterman had hidden below the counter-top came up. In his scarred hand was a sawed-off twelve-gauge. "You new here?" the man repeated, now addressing Hank. He seemed disappointed.

Hank watched the shotgun. The counterman didn't actually threaten with it, but the difference between "threat" and "no threat" was too small to notice.

"Your customers usually wave knives at you?" Hank countered.

"Nope. You new here?"

"No, I've actually been through Milwaukee a number of times."

"But you don't live here. You're from another town, right?"

"Yes." Hank didn't feel like volunteering information.

Somehow the counterman managed not to lose the cigarette when he talked. "Milwaukee ain't like it used to be," he said. The man's expression disappeared behind a shifting, pearlescent fog, then reappeared changed, as if he had thrown a switch. Now he was all smiles, and seemed, if possible, to be fatter, "May I help you?" Even his voice had changed.

Hank wanted to take a step back. He wasn't very fond of the type who hid behind a Holofacial Omni-Cover Assistant. He didn't exactly like countermen—or anyone else—who could change attitudes that quickly. The hairs on his neck rose. Hank looked up at the menu. He hadn't really wanted to, but the rolling of his eyes upward couldn't be helped. It was the usual bland, grease-intensive fare that fast food joints offered.

"Yeah, right," Hank said as the counterman continued his electronically manufactured grin. "I'd like three Perky-Burgers with everything, and two with mustard and onions. Two Perky-Pups with the works. Three large Cokes. Fries. Onion rings. A Perky-Pie, apple. To take out."

The counterman began assembling the order. Hank examined the preparation area as closely as he could from his side of the counter. He saw several well known brand names on boxes, and the Coca-Cola, Seven-Up and Dr. Pepper trademarks on the soft-drink dispensers, but the rest of the place was wrong, somehow.

He looked quickly back at his family. Anne had her headset on, and was staring directly at the counter-man. *Good.*

The subject of Anne's scrutiny looked at his watch, picked up a small device, aimed it at a place above the counter, and pressed a button. The gadget clicked loudly. Hank watched him, not exactly concealing suspicion, but the device was only a remote control for the ancient TV set mounted behind bullet proof Plexiglas next to the menu. The set came on, and an overloud announcer intoned: "— stay tuned for SLICER! Brought to you by Andy's Procurement!" A trio of girls' voices started singing, "No matter if it's legit or sleazy, Andy can get it for you easy!" The announcer paused, and then segued into: "And now, the Fox Six News!" A logo consisting of the channel number superimposed on what Hank recognized as the skyline of Milwaukee from a vantage point out in Lake Michigan, dissolved into a seedy looking news room containing several seedy looking anchormen. The camera dollied in for a closeup. The image's eyes seemed to bore into his.

"Big Brother is watching," Hank muttered.

The counterman placed the order in front of Hank, and waited. Hank removed the money clip from his pocket; it was mostly small bills, he kept larger denominations in another pocket out of sight. "How much?" he asked.

The electronically augmented counterman squinted at the cash, a rainbow effect rippled across one cheek, "Cash? Not credit?" he asked.

"Well, unless you had other ideas, I thought I'd pay the going rate. No such thing as a free dinner. How much?"

"Twenty-seven, fifty."

"What's it to you?"

"Government's been tightening up on cash, some. In parts of the city, it's considered evidence."

What kind of evidence?" Hank asked.

"Evidence: like you got a connection with the Power or Tech Blocs, or something."

"Are you sure this isn't Chicago?" Hank asked innocently.

He scooped up the bags and left.

His family followed him out, and he thought of the news-cast they had listened to earlier, again. *Another Holo-Facial...*, he thought, *Where have I...?*

A WORD....

[Descriptor; Medium Close-Up]   "My transmissions are to my constructs." She seems to have trouble picking the right word.

"Do you have other installations in the City?" Joe asks.

"Yes. I use them for data-gathering."

"And these installations—"

"I call them Hives, Joe."

"Hives, then. For remote sensing."

"You got it. I made them. They grow into their function." Yezeletta's voice has a side-band of justifiable pride.

"The transmissions that the Matrix Engine sends go out to each Hive."

"Yes. Instructions and programming. The instructions are in a format that the Hive processors can handle."

Joe indicates the body that lies on a black slab of synthetic granite: "What do you plan on doing with *that*?"

"It's a little joke on one of the City's regulars."

"What kind?"

"Come with me. I'll show you."

....TO THE PUBLIC

[Processing]   The corpse lies centered on the black ceramic. "I like your attention to traditional details," Joe says, drily. She looks down at him and her left eye makes what might be a wink.

"I haven't always been in hiding," she replies. "In times past I've had occasion for hobbies, and other forms of relaxation. This, however, is a retort which the boss of this gangster," she indicates the corpse on the slab, "has had coming for a while." There is a momentary chill in her voice, which departs rapidly.

"Why?"

"Some of his men have taken to shooting at my messengers. The messengers can hide or destroy themselves, if it's necessary, but it's inconvenient to lose one, or to waste their time by having them take circuitous paths through the City. If the man I wish to warn is at all perceptive, he will desist."

"What are you going to do, put three heads on him?"

"Not quite. Have you ever heard the expression 'get your face rearranged'?" As they converse, she removes something resembling a double handful of bright fluorescent green gelatine from a stainless steel crock standing on a tripod near the slab.

"My *god*! What's that? Lime Jello?"

"I call it a 'reorganizer'. It is, after a fashion, alive. The green color is a taggant, a color code." She looks at Joe, to make sure that he is listening and continues, "The color is a warning. There is genetic coding in this organism that will cause certain reorganizations or rearrangements to happen in the life-form to which it is applied." She surveys the space between them. "It's best if you stand back, this is quite dangerous. The reorganizer recognizes my characteristics. It will not recognize yours, and it will reorganize you quite unpredictably on contact."

Yezeletta Zargkonji places the green gel on the corpse's face. The gel pulsates slightly, and expands under its own power until it covers the facial area. Then it stops.

"This is programmed, although that's not an exact term, to rearrange the tissues in his face. There," she indicates another crock near the first, "is another reorganizer that will grow an imager such as the one on that servitor." She points to a short creature that has entered the room. To Joe, it resembles his jailor of only a few days before, except that this creature has just one eye: a single gold receptor in the center of its forehead.

"Please inform the kitchen," she says, "that I would like Beef Stroganoff, a light Chablis, sourdough rolls with cheese and butter, and a tossed salad with oil and vinegar dressing for dinner. What," she asks Joe, "would you like?"

"Just about anything. What's available?"

"Whatever you like. Use your imagination." Was she winking again?

"Do I just ask the Pull-Down Menu, here?"

"Yes."

"Okay, Dude, I'd like a boiled lobster tail, a crab salad, a twelve-ounce, or four-hundred gram, whichever is larger, New York strip, rare, a tossed salad with thousand-island dressing, a Manhattan and whatever wine Yezeletta is having."

Silently, the servitor leaves. "Think he can come up with all of that?" Joe asks, somewhat incredulously.

Yezeletta Zargkonji smiles like a well-fed cat. "It will take it only minutes to get the food together. It will spend most of its time growing the meat. The Manhattan will be easy: I programmed it with the knowledge of a good bartender. Shall we continue?"

ON LOCATION

Peter Rudenko arrived at Eighty-Fourth Street. Nearby the Pettit Athletic Center rose up, an impressive white building in which ice skating competitions had been performed in past times. Although the building was still well maintained, it had a shabby look around the edges, and more litter in the parking lot than was usual. He stopped for a short time to check his roadmap. The road ahead led to the downtown area of greater Milwaukee.

He couldn't see it from here. The building that was one of the highest of the downtown skyscrapers was well past the ruins of Miller Park and just barely visible from there. The current name for it was the Wisconsin Farmer's Mutual Center, but once it had been known as The Farmer's and Merchant's Building: 777 East Wisconsin Avenue.

Peter started moving. His destination, perhaps that building. It was, after all, a good landmark, visible from everywhere in the city. The East side of town and Lake Michigan were about a half-kilometer further.

Around him and around the City, the remote thunder still sounded, even though the lightning is invisible in the pallid gray autumnal daylight.

NAMES

[Load Descriptor] "Where did you get your name?" Joe asks.

Yezeletta Zargkonji hesitates before answering. Her astonishing gold eyes study him minutely. "I was named for the projects in which I was designed and created. The second part of my name is a variation on the word 'Sargon.' Have you ever heard of Project Sargon?"

"There's a chess-playing program by that name. Sargon-Big-Blue-Seven, I believe."

"Not that. *This* 'Sargon' is ancient Assyrian. Where," she asks pointedly, "did *you* get *your* name?"

"I was named after my great-grandfather, Joseph P. Davis. I'm not a 'junior' or a 'second'. My great-grandfather fought in World War Two in the Pacific, and I'm told I have his combative nature. If you ever see me in a battle, you'll know about it. By the way," he hesitates, "Do you mind if I call you Yezeletta?"

She shakes her head just once, and her black hair swings pleasantly with the gesture. Each seems to enjoy the sight of the other (at least he thinks so). Within the complex system of her own beauty, she is a pleasing sight. He sits back on white cushions at her eye level and relaxes. This is the first time they have just conversed instead of sparring, using words as blades.

"Why have you come here?" she asks.

"You know part of that," he replies. "The Madflowers. Those things are a corruption of a discovery of mine. When the Biology Department at UCLA published my gene-splicing and replicating techniques, over my objections, I left the faculty there and went to the University of Chicago. During the next few years I saw things in various publications that indicated that my techniques were being used elsewhere. In California, the University Board of Regents holds all the patents, copyrights or whatever, on things developed by researchers. The standard practice is to make it all public."

"And you didn't want your discoveries made public?"

"You got it!" Joe growls and gets up, pacing around the room. "What I discovered would let a high-school senior do things that, in my opinion, shouldn't be done. That plague that was released here back when Washington went up, for example. Think of something like that, but worse than just the crop damage. Imagine *that* mutating! They never did catch the kiddies that caused it, did they?"

Joe walks around the bar. "I found a way to do something that was about half skill and the rest, accident. Calculated luck, if you like. The kind of luck that doesn't require a lot of equipment to work." He pokes around in the bottles behind the bar. "This stuff doesn't look as if you grew it here. What sorts of poison do you stock?"

"The top shelf holds beverages acquired from around the state and brought here. I got some of them from one of the local gangsters who had no further use for them. As long as you're there, I'd like a rum and Coke."

He takes out the ingredients and mixes two drinks, strong on the rum, and cools each one with a few flakes of crushed ice so the Coca-Cola stays cold. He adds lime, brings her the drink. Yezeletta takes a swallow from the glass, and puts it on the end-table. "Do you think the Madflowers are the result of this involuntary publication?" she asks.

"Yep. But not completely. The Madflowers are a symptom, not the final result. Certain things kept coming from odd places in the world. The Flowers appeared first in Germany, of all places, and were brought here. No one really knows where they were first grown, although I've heard of locations from Africa to Russia. Even India."

THE TECHNICIANS

"Were there people from anywhere else in the Project?" Joe says.

"There were a few from the Technical Bloc: Canada, England and France."

"Do you remember how many?"

"On the close order of two from each country. There were a number of individuals who stayed in the background and mostly watched. I was never able to determine much about them. Sometimes they would leave for as much as two weeks, then return. They never said a word; they just watched."

She stands and stretches in a wide, impressive four-armed gesture. "Some of my earliest memories are of those quiet people. I was young enough that I didn't know what an intelligence agent was, or what one looked like." Yezeletta smiles about half-way. "They didn't exactly look or act like James Bond, Matt Helm or Jack Ryan, after all. I thought they might be professors, historians or maybe reporters. They probably let me think that. Could they have known of your work, Joe?"

"That would take some digging to find out. That Project of yours has some aspects that don't exactly make sense. Your existence, for example, was a closely guarded secret, yet they had these other people sitting around watching you as if you were a television show."

"I *was* a television show. To Project Security. They had video bugs in my quarters."

"How could you stand it?" He sits, again, his drink nearby.

Yezeletta shrugs, a gesture made complex by her shoulder articulations. "You were talking about your techniques—"

Joe leans back, composing his thoughts. "I read this article in a magazine that sometimes gets submissions from the European end of the Space Bloc. It described a technique that had been developed by a French scientist, which would allow common house-plants to serve as the replicators of useful biochemicals. If you needed a source of Interferon, for example, a geranium could be coaxed into producing it."

There is a discreet disturbance near the door. "Looks like dinner's ready," he says.

Several servitors walk in silently and place dishes of food on the sideboard. Others set a dinner table for two nearby. Prominent on it are a very large serving of Beef Stroganoff, several bottles of wine, a basket heaped high with rolls and the other items on Yezeletta's menu. Placed opposite this is the dinner Joe ordered. He grins, "I wanted a twelve ounce strip. That looks like half the cow—!"

"The kitchen assumes that all of my guests have the same dietary needs as I have." She *ascends* to her two-hundred centimeter-plus height, and goes to the table. Several servitors chase around the table setting places and positioning the chairs: a large one for Yezeletta and a smaller one built up to her height for Joe.

One of the servitors cuts off a single slice of meat and places it on a heated plate, another lights four red candles that are placed discreetly out of her line-of-sight. Joe looks past the candles at her eyes, colored sunset red-gold in the light, her vertically slit irises wide in the dimness. Another servitor places the lobster dish, a wine glass, Joe's Manhattan and his salad within easy reach.

Joe tastes this and that and says, "My complements to the chef, however he did it."

Yezeletta smiles graciously, "I find it easier to do my work if I'm in comfortable surroundings and well fed. The Project cafeteria was what you might expect of institutional food. When I was given my own apartment in the complex, I had to learn how to cook in self defense. Now I program my kitchen to provide the kinds of cooking I like the best. I have enhanced senses, and sometimes I smelled things in that cafeteria that should never have been put out on the serving line."

Joe scoops a chunk of lobster from the shell and dunks it in melted butter. "If this is all from your research lab, I can see you having an assured future putting The Rafters," the only restaurant he knows of in Milwaukee, "right out of business."

"Perhaps."

Joe listens carefully: has a sad note appeared in her voice?

She continues softly, "However, I have other things that I must do." Her voice returns to its former decisiveness.

He looks at her past red candles and continues, "Government agencies in Europe were particularly interested in my replicators. The University of Chicago Press got quite a lot of requests from Germany. One even came from the German Ambassador, himself, for reprints of everything from doctoral theses on up. And down. A friend back in California told me that my work there had generated similar interest." He sips from his wine glass, then drinks deeply.

She spreads a roll with butter, sprinkles grated cheddar on it, takes a bite, chews and swallows, "Germany is at least centrally located. Was there more than just them and the Space Bloc?" Her voice is almost gentle.

"I think that a lot of people in the Eastern end of the Tech Bloc would like to get the techniques you used on that guy," Joe says. "The reorganizer is light-years beyond anything they, or the U. S., have now. I can just see what kind of a *gulag* the Russians could create using it as well as the rest of what you have here. Were they discovered at Project Sargon?"

A silent servitor brings a coffee cup and fills it from an Erlenmeyer flask which it holds in a long pair of tongs. Joe drops in a sugar cube, and drinks.

"No," Yezeletta says, "I researched and designed the reorganizer here and on the way here. At Sargon, I was," she shakes her head, once, "given the basics for what I was designed to do, and taught to carry on research by myself when I was on my own. I had got the *idea* for the class of pseudo-life I call reorganizers at Sargon, but I never wrote anything down about it. They didn't just *give* me everything. I found out later that they wanted to determine how I would go about researching things *they* already knew, to see how well I could perform with actual unknowns. I was able to escape with most of what I wanted of their techniques, along with things I developed that I kept to myself." Yezeletta closes her eyes for a moment, opens them, and continues: "I just looked in a database I have. I saw no mention of you, nor of your ideas at Sargon."

Joe blinks in thought at the flickering candle flames. "They wanted you to re-derive things that they already knew. Do you suppose they wanted you to derive *my* protocols?"

"Interesting," Yezeletta says. "Perhaps. Or something similar. These articles of yours were nowhere in the Project Library, and I spent a lot of time there reading. Please continue."

"Right. So along comes a series of articles about six months later out of Germany, and as soon as the translators are done with it, most department publications in the West and on the Internet are quoting from it. More of that involuntary publication you mentioned. It's rather strange, when you think about it; by this time UCLA had published everything of mine they could lay their hands on. Then all the citations ceased."

Yezeletta leans back, surveys her domain, and her visitor. Her eyes catch the warm lights from the candles and Joe notices the effect again, the appearance of almost a faceting in her large gold eyes.

"I believe that my secrets are safe," she says.

"Why is that?" Joe asks.

"When I escaped from Sargon, I took everything important with me. The Sargon administration, and their friends, did not survive my leaving."

RATIOCINATION

[Back-up Sub-System] It is then that Joe realizes that he is more alone than anyone else ever was. Listening to his recollections, his enemy, his partner, and maybe his friend, is sitting across the well-provisioned dinner table before him.

A friend who has had other guests before him.

THERE! WHERE?

"There, Jake."

The car slowed to five KPH and several curious gunmen looked out at the rubble encrusted street. It was close to noon, but the overcast gray daylight made the street a place of curiously flat shadows. "That's the place. The ignition systems died here, and—" Larry pointed: a pair of feet stuck out from behind a trash can at the entrance of an alley. "That's Lead-foot Eddie."

Trying to look in as many directions as possible, Jake's men, pistols drawn and ready, got out of the vehicle. They approached the figure lying in the shadow of the alley. Jake pulled a flashlight out of his coat pocket, and held it up and away from his body, and shone it into the alley. The place was deserted. "Frank, you and Bud pull that meat out into the light. One-handed.

Keep your guns out."

Jake turned to Larry: "This the exact place?"

Larry's gun was none too steady. Jake stepped back out of his line of fire: "Steady, Larry! Watch where you're waving that thing!"

"Okay," Larry said, nervously holstering his weapon. "Lead-foot fell back away from the truck. He fell on his back and just lay there, twitching."

The two men came out, pulling the corpse from the alley, Frank facing the direction of motion, an ankle in one hand, Bud looking backwards in rapid glances to cover the rear.

Bud started retching. His vomiting was uncontrolled and uncontrollable, his eyes fixed on the corpse's face. Or more accurately, where the corpse's face should have been; for the man's forehead dropped in a clear, unbroken sweep to his chin.

There were no features at all.

Jake's men stopped, frozen, transfixed by the impossibility that Eddie's face, or lack of one, presented. The small group of men closed in on itself, each man looking out at the familiar streets as if those streets were suddenly a new order of unknown.

Something moved far down the alley. Jake looked closely, nervously at the source of the movement. It was something in the shadows, something that moved, but could not be seen well in the gathering gloom. Then it looked directly back at them.

A bright coin of gold above the green reflections of cat's eyes appeared for a moment. Then it vanished.

"Were there any other drivers that got out to look at the trucks?" Jake asked in urgent tones. Larry shook his head. "Anyone else not make it back?" Another violent shake of the head. Jake reached a flat bottle from the glove-box, opened it, "Here, drink this."

When Zhongo's men arrived at the warehouse, Larry's answers were flatly contradicted. Others from the supply run hadn't returned. They had disappeared. In a society where the senescence of government made for sloppily kept records, but where the old surveillance infrastructure was still in place, these men had vanished. Vanished as if they had never been.

BUGS IN THE SYSTEM

[Basic Training; Close-Up] Yezeletta sits with Joe in her living room. On her large video screen, she has arranged a set of images showing the details of what she describes.

"They grow," she says, indicating an image of something spherical, "from a sort of small spore (actually a grouping in a small pod of similar spores) to a certain degree of maturity, and stop. It's a fail-safe. I can abort the growth completely, and have it moved, or kill it if the place in which it has grown to the fail-safe point is unsuitable. At maturation, a carrier takes the backup communications link hardware to the new Hive, supervises the growth of the power source and the 'server' cranium. Then the necessary programming gets downloaded, and it goes into regular communication with the other previously grown Hives and with me, here.

"Each Hive has foragers, the 'Cat-Arachnids', which provide sustenance. The Hives actually do a useful service to the city. The foragers take rats and other small predators, particularly rats bearing young; I designed them to hunt pregnant females. This way, the rat population is kept lower than it would otherwise be. The newly grown Hive goes inactive, pending any instructions from me.

"Those instructions are either transmitted from here or are carried by the mobile Imagers. They're the ones with the single gold colored high-res imager in the front center of the face or the forehead. I can grow that kind of imager in any substrate; you'll see many of them here. The Imager-with-a-capital-'I' is the small creature that looks like a spider with more legs.

"'Thicknesse,' here," she indicates a fur-covered eye-ball sitting on the coffee table, "is actually an 'it,' but he has enough personality to be a 'he.' I named him after a character in a Jack Vance story. I use Thicknesse to run errands in this building. Others of his type serve as message carriers, and provide mobile reconnaissance for me and the one human agent I have: she's the agent placed with one of the local gangsters.

"There are about two dozen fully grown Hives in this city in suitable places: abandoned basements, old electrical closets, unused plumbing, inside the walls of buildings—concrete structures are best for this. In addition, all of the Hive constituents are interchangeable; any inhabitant of one Hive may locate shelter in any other; my creations are non-territorial. Beyond these needs, the Hives lie dormant. I have all of the capabilities I want here. I've planned them as resources for possible future needs."

KEYS TO THE CITY

The Lenhadens had parked in a badly littered side street several blocks away from Perky's. The street looked as if a small war had just ended. The shattered windows of ruined buildings looked down on them, broken glass eyes in the half-light, and every now and then, Hank thought he could see movement within. He and Ondreya switched places without leaving the truck.

The Perky-Burgers and the hot-dogs were about of the quality of typical franchise food, the soft-drinks were nominal, and no one got any sicker after eating such a repast than any fast-food consumer ever does. While they ate, they listened to the exchange that Anne had recorded earlier.

Ondreya started the vehicle up and pulled out.

"Play it again, Dad," Anne said.

Hank pressed **[PLAY]** and Anne's recorder, plugged into the truck's entertainment system, played back the voices that she had picked up earlier: "Your customers usually wave knives at you?" "Nope. You new here?" "No, I've actually been through Milwaukee a number of times." "But you don't live here. You're from another town, right?" "Yes."

Ondreya looked away from the road briefly, "Why the interrogation, I wonder? Rather unlike the typical worker at a burger-and-fries joint." She looked around, "What kind of accommodations does this place have? We should be looking for a motel fairly soon. We can continue batting this around when we've had a little rest. I'd like to see what Anne's shot with the Sony, too."

Ondreya kept warily away from the gaping black holes of alleys and avoided the smaller streets. The decay-encrusted fangs of buildings stuck up around them; the buildings seemed to be looking at the overcast sky through cracked, gaping windows. The light was getting dimmer. Ondreya pulled the truck up into an intersection, and looked right, then left. On the left a sign greeted them:

HOTEL-ANTLERS#
TRANSIENTS WELCOME
Reasonable Rates
Hourly Nightly Weekly Monthly
SRO Available
Visa Master-Card American Express
Great Wall Diner's Club Carte Blanche
Discover Eurocard

"Check the credit cards," Hank said, "Their clientele must be from further away than just the U. S."

"How," Ondreya asked, looking up at the building, "can a run-down place like this accept that many credit cards?"

"Easy," Hank said, "Have a confederate at another business who has a merchant's number, or deposit account with one of the principal card issuers, or a bank with international branches. Preferably one operating from a Finance Bloc member country. Makes me wonder who's involved here."

Ondreya drove the truck around to the front of the Hotel Antlers, pulled up in front of the main entrance. "Wait here," Hank said, and went in.

The inside of the hotel was what he had expected. A stuffed elk's head stared at him from behind the front desk. It was a typical large hotel turned flea-bag with furnishings that might have looked good if several years of accumulated grime were removed. Wishing that he had eyes in the back of his head, he stepped up to the main desk, and put his hands on the countertop. Then quickly removed them. The counter hadn't been cleaned in as many years as the rest of the place. A rusted bell stood next to a faded sign: Ring Bell For Service. Hank did. Nothing happened. He hit the bell a little harder: it rang once, and fell apart. "Delightful," he muttered.

He was ready to yell back to the office beyond when a young girl came out. She was wearing a filthy pair of pink skin-tight trousers, and a torn black shirt with violet polka dots the size of poker chips on it. One tear looked as if she had deliberately placed it to display her left breast. Her matted blond hair looked as if it hadn't been cleaned any more recently than the rest of her surroundings, or herself.

Besides that she was chewing gum. Loudly. "What ya want?" she smacked.

"A room for the night. Myself and my family. And a place to park." He tried not to look at the bobbing breast.

"Parking's 'round in back. Room's twenty a night. Each."

Hank felt pleasantly vicious: he took out his American Express Card and placed it before the girl. Hank had expected a lot of back-talk, but was not really surprised when she ran the card through the reader, returned it, and shoved a registry card and a key at him. He wondered with whom the charges would be filed, and thought that it was a damned good idea that his card was in a variant spelling of his name to a mailing address that was not his house. It would be interesting to see where the charge on the bill originated from when it arrived. Hank signed both the American Express slip and the registry card (sloppily), and handed them back.

"Henry Menhaden," the girl read, "What about your—uh—family?"

"My—uh—family is outside. Waiting." Hank was pleased that she hadn't recognized a breed of Atlantic herring as a play on his name.

"Gotta have their names."

Hank added them, misspelling each name. She took the card, popped her gum, and read: "B. Menhaden. Indreya Menhaden. What kinda name's 'Indreya'?" she asked doubtfully.

"A perfectly delightful one," Hank said, smiling while hanging on to his patience with both hands.

"Okay," she said, "My regards to 'Indy', and have a nice stay."

Hank left quickly, before he decided to choke her.

The Lenhadens were surprised to find the room clean and the linens reasonably fresh, if a bit musty. It was on the second floor. Although the Antlers building was much taller, it appeared that only the lower two or three floors were actually being used for anything. The room had a double bed, a roll-away, and antique plumbing that could be coaxed to work with minimal effort. They trudged up the stairs with their suit-cases, and got set up.

The security package that Hank taped to the door was a combination of proximity alarm and vibration detector. Anne focused a motion detector at the truck through the room's back window, and set up the remote monitor that would go off if the truck were disturbed. She set the portable Sony video recorder on the dresser, where it looked out of place on the scarred wood. She plugged the device into a socket at the base of a corroded wall light, and switched it on. Nothing happened. She turned the lamp on and that worked. "No power, there," she muttered and switched the recorder to battery back-up. The display on the front lit and the LCD screen displayed white. She put the line cord away and plugged in the camera's memory stick.

While Hank and Anne were busy, Ondreya opened another case and removed three compact pistols, checking out and loading each one, laying them out the way a more typical housewife would set the table. When she finished, she did exactly that. She set up a portable camp stove and prepared dinner from canned goods.

It was becoming dark as the day finally ended, and Anne flipped another switch on the wall near the bathroom door. Nothing happened. "No power except to that one lamp," she tried another switch, "— and the bathroom. Otherwise, nothing. Should I get out the lights?"

"Probably not a good idea," Hank said. "If the wiring in this place is that awful, showing lights might advertise us to some people we don't want to know. I don't believe the screen will give us away, particularly with the sun-hood on it. Let's see what we've gotten from those gun-slingers. Anne, show us what you got."

Anne pressed **[PLAY]**, and the LCD screen showed the scene they had driven through earlier: the topless decoy, the shooters, and several men in black jump-suits.

"I didn't notice those guys earlier," Ondreya said.

Anne backed the scene up, and played it again. "They weren't shooting at us, Mom," she said. "They look like they just arrived. Maybe by accident."

"They look as if they're firing at something on the opposite side of the street. It's almost as if *we* showed up there by accident," Hank observed.

"'Accident,' indeed," Ondreya said. "I'd hate to be there on purpose! I wonder what it is they were shooting at? Anne, you're the cinematographer tonight, can you get a still frame of their target?"

"I think so. It won't be real clear on this portable." She advanced playback to the place where the black-clad gun-men were the closest, and made adjustments. At one point the picture swept to the right; earlier, she had panned to the left to get a shot of where the shooters were aiming. She froze the image, then advanced to the frame she wanted.

They peered intently at the small image. The picture was rock steady—this unit was a professional model—but the image was about twenty by thirty-five centimeters, and it was hard to make out any specific details. Anne broke the short silence, "There's a place where the brick looks like it's been knocked out, there, where the lighter colors are. Is that round thing what they were shooting at?"

"There is something small there," Hank said, "that looks as if it were *placed* there. It's just at the edge of this screen's resolution, dammit. I wonder what it is?"

"Think there are any more of 'it' around?" Anne asked.

"Don't know. There's a starlight scope in the case, take a look out if you're interested." He yawned. "It's going to be day all too soon, and I'm tired." Suiting deeds to words, he lay down on the bed. "You ladies take the first baths. I'll wait on you."

S H A D O W - M A N

[Earlier the Same Day] He had been driving East slowly along the edge of I-94, one of the largest expressways in Wisconsin. It was about eleven AM by his watch and the flat indirect lighting of a polluted autumn seemed to agree. The Expressway had been deserted farther out. This close to Milwaukee the state of the roadbed made vehicular traffic hazardous, although the shoulders were still usable. What was stranger were the burned spots here and there in the road. It was as if a lot of campers had been here in recent times, and had built fires about every four to five meters along the length of the road. There was garbage everywhere; bones of every description, a few of them recognizably human, and piles of organic waste that Peter avoided, covered with large buzzing flies. Once a skull had stared back at him from a broken-out cleft in the abutments to one side of the road. Something with a lot of legs had crawled out of one eye, and he had turned away, sickened. He wondered what kind of lazy government would allow a highway to deteriorate this thoroughly.

The large graveyard on the south side of the road was appropriate counterpoint to the state of the road itself, the tombstones sticking up like giant blunt teeth out of the brown grass. He wondered what kind of a human would inhabit a place like this.

S H A D O W I N G

[Data Extraction] *The large figure had looked directly at the Receiver, then had looked away. The Receiver had hidden in a large, white, hollow organic object, but had moved out through one of the two bigger holes to scan the large figure better. The Receiver sat up on its back legs, its* *several pairs of front legs off the ground functioning as dipoles to better scan the electromagnetic field of the large figure until it moved out of range. Then the Receiver returned to its shelter and departed through the small tunnel below it to upload its scans to the Organic Server.*

THE PROFESSIONAL

Occasionally Peter heard voices. He would look over the edge of the Expressway and see filthy faces far below, looking up, shanties nuzzled up against the concrete pillars that supported the roadbed.

He was reminded of Gustav Dore' illustrations of Dante, of Hieronymus Bosch.

Make that "Anonymous". It was obvious that the human cattle he saw below lived and died as impersonally as the population of a bacterial culture.

Were all of the cities hereabouts surrounded by rings of decay? The Eastern Seaboard was still in fairly good shape, if severely overpopulated. The suburbs of Chicago had effectively dug in, becoming fortress village-states in their own right. The West Side of Milwaukee appeared to be going in a different, nastier direction. Down the drain.

He looked into the wavering, foggy distance: a flock of birds had taken off from a tall building some kilometers away. They were indistinct in the white haze; they looked like large crows. They would have to be as good at surviving as any of the other dwellers in this place. Could such predators evolve intelligence?

He had read about the eco-terrorists that had loosed their complex of home-grown bacterial cultures in this area sixteen years back. Peter had been a high-school student in the Florida Keys at the time. The Southeastern Wisconsin Plague had happened at the same time Washington had gone up, and had gotten far less coverage than the destruction of the Nation's Capital. The plague, such as it was, had been successfully contained. The guerrilla fanatics hadn't designed their biologicals too well, and ordinary sanitary practices had helped keep human losses to a minimum.

The plant life hadn't rebounded quite as successfully from disease vectors aimed at such. Mammals, such as farm animals and humans, had fared better. Southern Wisconsin, Northern Illinois and small parts of Michigan and Indiana had been severely damaged, and there had been no harvest in those areas that year.

The perpetrators had never been apprehended.

Checking on bio-manipulations was one of the main areas of Peter's mission. Although he wasn't allowed to interfere directly with the current resident of one of his investigatory objectives, he could bring in others who could. At least he hoped that his fellow operatives would: his agency, and others like it seemed to be fighting a losing battle against the more pragmatic gang-lords who seemed to be on the ascendancy.

Everything had to have purpose. There were reasons for building this six-lane highway leading into Wisconsin's largest city. One time there had been traffic: three lanes in either direction. During rush-hour, this had been wall-to-wall cars. There were ancient rubber marks and oil stains on the concrete surface. Now the structure was mostly deserted. Wiped clean of most vestiges of humanity except for waste products and the occasional farmer driving into Milwaukee on business.

Peter regarded the waste-land around him. Had this part of Wisconsin become a dumping ground for those who just couldn't make it? A sorting device for preservation of mankind's survivors? If so, those survivors must be an able breed indeed. Did they know anything beyond their own existence? Or, like medieval serfs, were they bound to the land, was their back yard their territory, the street on which they lived, their world, the village in which that street lay, their universe?

Who or what would go anywhere else if he were able to leave this garbage heap? Could the population in a place as close as Milwaukee handle those selected by this environment? He thought of a pot boiling over on a stove. What was out there in those innocent fields, playing amongst the tombstones?

How much of a danger was it?

More importantly: who was planning the next disaster?

THE WORKS

The Director had given Peter what the Agency knew. It was a CD-ROM containing several J-PEG image files and a lot of prose that consisted of equal parts rumor and supposition. Of particular interest were several pages of notes written in a shaky hand on the yellow sheets of a legal-size notepad that had been reproduced on the CD as scanned images. The agent in question had been investigating something else in another country. He had contracted an unbreakable case of amnesia, or so they thought. When they found him, he had been delirious (his random writings and one uncompleted sketch had shown that). His condition had degenerated into a coma that he was still in.

Strange, for one of the agents his service retained.

Peter's mission was to investigate two situations: one was a mobster who had infested one of Milwaukee's more prominent landmarks; the other was a specialist. This latter individual attempted to control access to central Milwaukee by controlling access to the system of elevated roads into the city. Both had files in Peter's laptop.

Then there was the third investigation that had been added as an afterthought at the end of Peter's briefing. There were rumors, nothing more, of other kinds of biological tailoring being done here. This work seemed to point back to Peter's first suspect, who was creating designer drugs in that self-same landmark, but there was something more to it than that.

Peter's job was to check all of these out, or as many as he could in the time that he had.

Whatever it was, there was a form of subtle intelligence manifesting itself in Milwaukee—of all places!—and Peter's supervisors wanted data.

In a hurry.

The CD-ROM's contents included one grainy black and white photograph. It was the only exposure in the other agent's Minox that had proved useful; all the others had been granular fuzziness. The picture was of something that looked like a large tarantula. The problem with that was that tarantulas were not endemic to the upper midwest (or to any other place where that Agent had been): they were southwestern desert creatures. Had the picture been taken in the midwest? Or elsewhere? There was no information on this.

The photograph had been taken with a slow shutter speed; there were the blurs of motion in it. Lower echelon photo analysts had stated that it was the combined actions of the time exposure and subject-movement that made the picture what it was. Image enhancement had said otherwise.

It could be only one thing: a construct. Maybe a construct produced by that custom-drug-baron. But *what* construct?

He proceeded along the frontage road, and up over a slight incline: the exit for Twenty-Seventh Street was just ahead.

Peter Rudenko camped there by the road that night.

He stayed up late into that first evening, using a starlight scope on a tele-photo lens on a tripod to probe the downtown of Milwaukee. There were streetlights in the central area, sporadically maintained lighting in most of the other areas. The city cast a glow that was reflected by the cloudy sky. The only other illumination was the distant spectre of the ever-present sheet lightning. There was no sign of life in the places from which he had come.

There. The tall building, in the center of town. The Farmers Mutual Center. The signs placed at the top of the building were plastic transparencies that were poorly backlit by fluorescent lights in advanced states of failure. They floated above the darkness of the rest of the building beneath it, higher than anything else in the city: rectilinear UFOS.

It probably wasn't anything. A lot of the tall, abandoned buildings he had seen in every part of the country had lights that had been left on by the last tenants. Perhaps those tenants thought they would return one day, and they wanted the lights left on as a sign of welcome.

Many such had never been re-entered. Power companies usually left a trickle of electricity into such places to run EXIT signs and the like. That they also helped squatters and street gangs gain access was a matter that the undermanned police departments in the slowly decaying cities had simply chosen to ignore.

It was easier than having to go back in groups.

Peter took a roll of photographs of the set of approximately lit signs and the areas around them, using fast film, the telephoto lens and the starlight scope. He repeated the process taking in a wider field of view, covering the down-town area. Then he repeated the process using digital media. In the morning, he would leave the film and the memory sticks in a well-armored stainless-steel crock equipped with a small but quite indestructible trans-ceiver. In a pinch, he could send data transmissions to the small storage device in the unit from his laptop. If anything happened to him, the next agent would locate the photos and data-files, and take them back to Phila-delphia.

All the rest of that night, the sheet lightning lit the distant rim of the black sky. No stars were visible through the incessant, impenetrable cloud cover-ing. Once he thought he saw the crescent moon through a momentary break in the clouds; it appeared reversed, almost facing the wrong direction, then the rift had sealed up again.

He wrapped his coat around himself against the storm he knew was com-ing.

In the morning, he packed up his camp, surveyed his destination, and made a decision. He would drive south, and come into downtown from that direction. He took a convenient exit, and headed into the manufacturing part of Milwaukee. The state of the buildings here was even more appalling than back on I-94. He drove through places where the windows were bricked up, like sightless eyes, either unseeing, or deliberately turned inwards against the desolation. To his right, the three glass geodesic domes, his first objective, were arranged in a triangular configuration over low connecting buildings. They jutted up above the rest of the wreckage like cybernetic breasts, illuminated from within by haphazard lighting. He drove south and east as far as he was able.

He stopped at a bridge that crossed the Milwaukee River. At a distance, the bridge had looked complete, but when he reached it, drove out onto it, he could see the damage.

The roadbed was broken off sharply at the edge, as if a giant cleaver had chopped through the concrete and steel all of the way down to the water's edge. Peter leaned out over the edge and looked far below. There was nothing moving, and no sign of habitation down there, but some evidence of intelligence existed.

He looked closer at the severed edge of the road; then closer still. He got out his Minox, took several pictures of the details of the road's end, and replaced the camera in his pocket, buttoning the flap.

It looked as if the road had been cut off with precisely placed small charges of high-explosives, then trimmed to make the damage look natural. Or accidental. On impulse, Peter removed a small hand-mirror from his wallet, and used it to look at the underside of the bridge.

The striations from the explosive charges were still clearly visible, untouched by the weather. He looked down. The un-touched-up sections of the bridge wouldn't be seen by anyone below unless he was walking on the water.

Somebody didn't want traffic through here!

There were several boats beached on the muddy shore.

He pulled the car back under the lifting arm of what was once an enormous bascule.

Before leaving, he booted up his laptop, and loaded several GIF files into a viewing program. One of these was of Zhongo Teketon. He wasn't interested in Zhongo. Hmmm. Something to do with roads; in *that* file, *there*.

The clean-cut All-American visage of Allen Hightower—short blond hair in a crew-cut, brown eyes, light skin, from perhaps too much time indoors, white, even teeth—looked up at him from the LCD screen of the laptop. "The Lord of the Roads," he muttered to himself. "A real roads scholar," he added.

He brought up his personal notes file in another window, and logged his location, mentioning the cut-off bridge. Then he transmitted the data, using an encrypted data link, to the storage container. The container would relay the data back to Searchlight using the cellular phone system, later.

Headquarters might be interested in that. Headquarters was interested in everything.

Peter got out of his car and covered it with several pieces of rotted lumber, leftovers of large crates. He packed up his computer and took his backpack of equipment, and went back to the road's end.

[Comm Port] It was easy to lower himself on a nylon rope from the broken road's edge to the river's edge below. The viscous mud stuck to his boots, weighing them down as he walked. Was this place intelligent in and of itself? Was the squishy engulfing mud telling him something? What had come to lodge in the attics of a city that had once been known world-wide for many brands of beer? There were boats just ahead. The best of the lot, a battered aluminum dory, looked serviceable enough to make it across the contaminated stream. Peter thought of culture media as he pushed the boat into the black liquid. He jumped in, set the aluminum oars and rowed out into the sluggish current. He let the flow take him along for a short time, as he memorized the configuration of the shore. There was something like a liquid natural gas storage area to one side of his car's hiding place, and something of a rough cubical construction, housing what looked like a compact oil refinery, to the other side. He made a quick sketch of the landmarks in his notebook, and replaced the notebook in his shirt pocket. He started rowing.

This entire end of the Milwaukee River seemed to be a run-down industrial park. There was something wrong with it, however; something was missing. Peter looked into every construction as the current carried him by them. He visualized other, better populated industrial parks from other places, and got it: there was nothing written. There were no company logos, no advertisements, no descriptive prose of any sort, not even graffiti; just bay after bay of pitted rusting ancient technology.

He began to row again. He put his back into it. The sightseeing tour was over; it was time to get to work.

AUTOPSY, INFORMAL

[Camera Goes With] Zeke was the only man Zhongo knew and trusted who had any medical knowledge at all. His knowledge was dated: there were some that thought he wasn't a real doctor and others that thought he was, but had been "retired" from the medical profession for unknown offenses. He was known only as Zeke, and Zhongo, who liked to know something more about his underlings than just a name, wouldn't normally put up with knowing just that, if Zeke hadn't demonstrated enough ability that his eccentricities could be tolerated.

The body of the former Lead-foot Eddie lay on a stone slab in Zeke's "laboratory" in a small well-fortified ex-warehouse near Zhongo's place. The corpse was opened up from the chin to the crotch, the rib-cage removed and placed in sterile containers for later examination, and Zeke stood nearby with a worn copy of *Gray's Anatomy*, pointing at the illustrations, and at Eddie's guts.

"No stomach. Not even any sign that there was one. The spleen is gone, too, as if he had never grown it. This fibrous growth around the heart isn't cancerous. It isn't anything: it's just there. Where did these hard scales on the right lung come from? And his face, or lack of it! Doctor Frankenstein playing one of his undergraduate practical jokes at the Vienna Medical College might have assembled this from spare parts, but he'd have needed the spare parts to do it with! He'd also require a place to do it. A facility."

Zeke waved his arm expressively around his own layout, "This isn't a medical facility, this is a play-room for amateurs. Whoever did this would need a hospital with all of the equipment of a place like Walter Reed, or the Mayo Clinic. Hell, Harvard Medical."

"It couldn't have been done here, then," Zhongo said. "While you were out, maybe...."

"No chance. I lock this place up all but hermetically when I'm gone, and face it, there just aren't the tools here for what was done to him." He gestured at the body. "If I had the latest Japanese developments for cellular surgery, cloning, hacking his immune system so the implants wouldn't be kicked out a day later and like that, I *might* be able to do some of this, with a lot of practice. Then, there's his face."

"Yeah?"

"That's real artistry. The front of his skull was sliced off clean, and something was grown to replace it. He was probably brain-dead by that time, *I hope*, and kept alive by mechanical means. The graft is perfect."

"Could it have been grown on his face that way?"

"Maybe. I don't think it was. I think that when I take his head apart, I'll find the sutures. You could probably jive his cell growth to grow a forehead down to his chin—I like the sound of that!—but it would take a matter of weeks. Obviously this didn't. Cyanoacrylate glue and the technique of a true artist. And a sense of humor best described as warped."

"Okay, Zeke, let me know what you find out when you work on the head. I'll be on the West Side tomorrow." Zhongo got up to leave.

"I'll do that," Zeke said.

Zeke got out small knives, a scalpel, and several other things, and got to work.

SPECTATOR SPORT

[Roving Reporter] *It looks in on the sleeping figures. The male is snoozing quietly on the bed, the small female is doing something complex with an instrumentation, and the large female emerges from the bathroom toweling herself vigorously. It records the scene, and carefully, quietly moves out of the window, and down the side of the hotel. The nearest Hive (of several) is two blocks away, but it will return safely to the warmth and energy there.*

DOCUMENTATION

"Are you familiar with who runs things here?" Yezeletta asks.

"No. Actually, I thought you did."

"Not quite," she answers, "I try to stay as invisible as possible. All of my activities are either undetectable, or the kinds of things that I misdirect elsewhere."

Yezeletta grabs a remote control and a DVD with two right hands. She drops the disk into a Sony Player and presses a contact on the remote. "Watch."

The pictures are somewhat grainy and the image jumps around: "Is this the input from an Imager?" he asks, she nods. The lens used is approximately a 140-degree fish-eye; there is a component of distortion on the edges. The screen shows a man leaving a brownstone building that might have been upper class when it was new, but now is merely ugly. He gets into a silver-gray limousine, several bodyguards surrounding the car withdraw into it, and the car drives off.

"This is Zhongo Teketon. He is known here as the Procurator General, and often by less flattering terms. He runs convoys into other cities for supplies—whatever he can get—and occasionally, I remove some of his acquisitions. I have an agent in his organization." Her expression is one of acceptance—about half-way. "I made a friend about a year ago who was in the process of resigning from the dubious services of one of Milwaukee's leading businessmen in the retail sex trade. She helped me get an entry-point into Zhongo's so-called inner circle. She's currently his mistress."

Yezeletta almost laughs, "Zhongo thinks he won her in a poker game."

"That doesn't sound too good," Joe says.

"She has ample support from me, here, and I could pull her out on about five-minutes notice. We let Zhongo think he 'owns' her."

"Is he naturally stupid?"

"Not at all! Zhongo may act dumb, but he has a lot of common-sense, and his chief strength is in selecting the right individual for the job, then letting him do it. There's a scientist he has named Zeke, who is a *lot* smarter than either Zhongo or Zeke looks. To any casual observer on the outside."

"So you keep a roving eye on both of them."

"Exactly! Zhongo appears to run 'supplies' here. Those supplies can be just about anything. He started out in the black-market providing imported luxury foodstuffs, but in the last years, he's started providing what he calls 'services'. I think that he acts as a quartermaster for other organizations, as well as acting in a consulting capacity for things that other outfits can't or don't want to handle. Getting items from the other Blocs, for example. The gangster I reorganized was one of his. It's his gun-men who like to shoot out my Imagers."

She fast forwards through scenes of Teketon being driven about in his limo, going into and coming out of large brick buildings that look like modern castles, and eating a cheeseburger at a heavily fortified McDonald's.

"Those concrete constructions around the doorways of those buildings look like tank-traps," Joe points out.

Yezeletta stops the playback at:

An ill-dressed girl of about seventeen stares out of the screen with a combination of feral wariness and defiance. "This is Angela Corey. She's one of a class of what are called 'decoys' for these:"

The next several images are short clips of young men and women wearing clothes that are all of a kind of uniformity. "They call themselves the 'Nightwalkers', and are usually on something synthetic and quite dangerous. They appear to be trying to fit themselves into what is left by Zhongo Teketon's businesses. Their decoys alert them to likely sources of stimulants, money or their notions of 'fun'. Angela lives up the street from here; that's why I have her analyzed. There appears to be an element of masochism to her behavior."

"You mentioned drugs," Joe prompts. "Is there a drug problem here, too?"

She skips forward again, and stops on the image of a *very* short man. Like Zhongo, this man is driven around in a large car. Unlike Zhongo, who seems to like being inconspicuous in his silver-gray limo, this other man is chauffeured about in a highly polished electric blue vintage Cadillac. Visible through the windows of the car is a black furry interior. Most of his men are blacks wearing black clothing. The blue steel of rifle and shotgun barrels is visible, sticking angularly out of the picture. There are several scantily dressed pretty girls of various races in the Cadillac, all of whom look as if they have won some special favor from Shorty.

"Gary 'The Geek' Hamilton," she supplies. "He took over a place called the Mitchell Conservatory, and uses the botanical gardens there to create his own illicit pharmaceuticals for the American Midwest. The Conservatory used to be—"

"I know," Joe replies, "I've been there. Went there when I was a little kid. It's too damned bad that it had to come down to this. How tall *is* he, any-way?"

Yezeletta thought for a moment as she looked at the image. "I'd guess 145 centimeters," she said, "Four-foot-nine, in the old system."

Another: a lean-looking Caucasian couple looking off into a spot that seems to be above, to the right and behind the Imager photographing them. He is blonde, brown-eyed, clean-shaven and rather athletically built. She is a trim blue-eyed brunette wearing blue-jeans and a red blouse knotted in front.

"Allen and Marie Hightower. Their 'clean-cut-all-american' look is protec-tive coloration. He calls himself The Lord of the Roads. How did you get here? What route?"

"I-94, off to Highway 41, then one of the residential streets through Brookfield."

"You wouldn't have met any of his minions. The Brookfielders have man-aged to keep him at a distance. New Berlin, or Menominee Falls, now...."

"The gas station attendant *did* seem a bit interested in which 'burb I was going through to get here."

"Understandable. But possibly for all of the wrong reasons. If he were shilling for Hightower, he could have directed you to a place under Hightow-er's control. Hampton Avenue through Shorewood, perhaps. Or, maybe he was going to warn you off."

"Didn't say anything either way. But the directions I asked for got me down here through Brookfield."

"Good for you. Allen Hightower *hates* Brookfield. He wants total control over all of the bridge highways south and west into Milwaukee. The 'usage fees' he charges are inexiguous. Zhongo Teketon can either afford them, or his drivers just shoot Hightower's men.

"Others pay the going rate, or starve."

Another picture: a lean, older man with scraggly gray hair, and an untidy gray moustache. He stares defiantly into the camera, and looks as if he is about to speak, mostly profanity. The point-of-view is level with his face, as seen through a window. He is surrounded by electronic apparatus.

"This is Lucius Cring. He was once a professor at the University in Madi-son. I know very little about him, as he keeps to himself even more than I do. I'd like to know more."

"The junk in the background looks like a physics lab. He does look like an eccentric professor. Maybe on a TV sitcom."

"Perhaps. Perhaps not. He did make it here from Madison on foot almost alone. There is a young woman who lives there with him. I have not been able to get a photograph or a video of her, as yet, but an audio bug I sent to his loft has me convinced that she is his daughter. Her name is Arcadia."

She's one of these people who are able to move in a society and leave comparatively few tracks. I would like to know how she's avoided my Imagers.

"I'd like to know how she avoids leaving a trail," Joe says, "That's getting difficult. It seems that every bureaucrat in the business is attempting to re-start the domestic surveillance built up in the early two-thousands."

"Eastern Europe has done that for years, and Australia has had the practice for over a generation, now," Yezeletta replied.

She displays another selection on the videodisc. A man who is dressed all in gray. "This is another of those who manage to evade me."

"There's another?" Joe is surprised.

Yezeletta nods, "He's known as Gray Roger. He's one of the leading pimps in Milwaukee. He's the one from whom I rescued Zhongo's mistress. He prefers to describe himself as an 'entrepreneur in the retail sex trade'. You know, a pimp."

"This makes him some sort of a special case?"

"To himself, only," Yezeletta says, "Most pimps are rather colorful, flamboyant characters. That fact alone helps them to have short professional lifespans," she adds wryly. "Roger has lasted this long by being inconspicuous, and by being a very rapidly moving target, with no known location of operations. He'd captured Zhongo's mistress when she was on a trip here and she escaped from him, later. I helped her."

She removes the videodisc and puts it back in its drawer. "These are the people that live here."

"You have such wonderful neighbors."

WEAPONS ANALYSIS

[Accessing] "The Madflowers," Joe says, "started as a rumor, but are based on fact. Some outfit developed them using my techniques on ordinary plants. They have a lead time of something like three months: after the initial exposure and the waiting period, the victim becomes unconscious for from eight to twelve hours. When he awakes, he does so in a killing frenzy. That lasts for about three days, then the victim dies, usually at his own hand."

Yezeletta Zargkonji is unwaveringly attentive. "Go on."

"Have you ever heard of the Berserker Syndrome?"

"Fantastic strength, a killing rage, a singlemindedness of purpose, all but indestructible?"

"Exactly so! Except that you left out augmented intelligence, directed at the single task of killing. The term 'seeing red' comes from it: the berserker samples light waves at a much higher rate. The result is that he sees the frequencies of the ambient light go down into shades of red. Historically, the Berserker Syndrome usually only affects people of mostly Scandinavian descent. There are tales of Viking fighters that were all but unstoppable, for example." He paces as he talks. "What the tailored virus in the Madflowers does is to realize this potential in everyone. There are some immunes to the Madflower Virus, but they're only about two percent of the population. Since most of the subjects of this kind of tinkering aren't into any kind of body-building, and not used to the extra strain, the victim only lasts two or three days after the psychosis sets in. There's some real thought that went into this: the length of the incubation period. Who's going to connect the berserker with some flowers he sniffed three months earlier? And notice how the victim self-destructs after his killing rage."

ANALYSIS SITUS

[Load, Execute; Close-Up] "What happens if the victim is restrained?"

"He tears himself to bits. It's like a case of hysterical strength, only it lasts three days instead of long enough to take the family car off of Junior, or something. The muscles pull right off the bones. I don't know what would happen if you knocked him out. You'd have to get to him, first."

"Is there an immunity?"

"Apart from the two percent I mentioned, I don't know. There may be. If there is, you can bet the delightful bunch that thought this up are sitting tight on it."

"Have you heard of anyone isolating the active component of the Madflower Virus?"

"No. It's generated as a byproduct of the Madflower plant, itself, actually formed during growth, and becomes concentrated in the blooms. The stuff would be extremely dangerous. Like an AIDS virus that could vector itself rather than relying on a carrier.

"Terrorists would love them."

A WRONG TURN

[Later] She lies in the enormous bed next to him, sleeping in a custom-designed (grown?) array of pillows that match the articulations of her body. Joe scans her in the half-light of the reading lamp provided earlier by a thoughtfully programmed construct. He looks around at the enormous bedroom: what sort of humor was it that inspired Yezeletta to create (?) or grow (?) an octagonal waterbed fully four and a half meters across the flat sides?

[Earlier] He sees her nude, and to his surprise, she is not the twisted, malformed caricature that he expected. Instead, all of her extra limbs work very well with each other. The two sets of arms are spaced so that each arm may assist any of the other three, but not be uselessly in the way. Her extra legs, behind the front pair, and spaced slightly further apart, give her an extremely stable stance, and allow her to stand on any two and use the others as desired.

Before retiring, she had shown him some of the martial arts katas she learned at the project.

She performed her exercises naked, and Joe could see an element of vanity in Yezeletta Zargkonji's showing both her martial arts skills and her body to Joe simultaneously. After she was done, she had led him to a hot tub of heroic proportions where they had spent a languorous hour relaxing. She reclined on a seat that would have placed his head below the water's surface, and he sat on a shelf a meter higher, placed there earlier by the ubiquitous servitors.

Then they had retired.

She dropped off to sleep immediately. He remained awake, unable to sleep.

[Later] Yezeletta's breathing is regular, slow, steady. She sleeps, tucked into and around her custom shaped pillows on the enormous bed. Slowly, Joe rolls to the edge, places one foot on the floor, his right, then his left. He stands.

He takes the flashlight from where he'd placed it earlier, and walks quietly to the door. Near the bedroom is another room: a kitchen. This is not the kitchen in which the servitors prepared their dinner, rather, it is the place in which she performs her "self-defense" cooking.

There is a well-stocked refrigerator there. He grins in spite of himself: she is as much of a midnight-snacker as any other highly motivated researcher.

His destination is beyond the kitchen.

He passes the kitchen, the hot-tub room and a gigantic bathroom. There is a room beyond, which he had noticed earlier when he had taken a wrong turn out of the bathroom.

She opens one gold eye, widens its aperture to f/1.2, and sees that Joe is gone. All that is visible is his infra-red trace: she widens her vision to its full range, and sees the *under-red* signature of where he has slept vanishing in the *under-red* totality of the heated bed. She speaks softly to something on her side of the bed, and it gets up and leaves, walking up the wall and across the ceiling. Dismissing it, she opens a window in the view of her left eye and inputs the data-feed from the Imager. A small display appears in delicate pastel colors. She watches it languorously.

No one can harm her here. Let him look.

Joe shines his light around the room. The outward semblance of order is belied by a more detailed investigation: what looks like a room full of filing cabinets and long tables covered with shorter filing boxes is just exactly that, but set up with its own notions of order and logic.

Joe scans the labels, looking for the one he saw earlier:

Project Sargon Notes—*Early Considerations*
Project Sargon Notes—*Project Jezebel*

And others:—*Implementation*
and:—*Project Objectives*

There are more: *Agent Specifications, Agent Education, Bio-Computer Design Implementation, Bio-Computer Internal Logic Design,* and the one that he had seen earlier: *Agent Psychological Design and Adjustment.*

He reads this with great interest.

Most of the answers are there.

WORK IN PROGRESS

[Load Backup: Run] *He moved his head lethargically. First to the left. Then to the right. He looked around, his large eyes taking in the dimness of the hospital room, looked down at his feet, moving the toes this way and that. He stretched. He held one large hand up before his face, and looked at the fingers, flexing them.*

He moved his other hand. His legs.

He regarded his manhood. It was long, hard.

His left hand crept towards it, touching it.

He looked up from the bed upon which he was lying, at the individuals in surgical greens watching him from a discrete distance.

He inhaled, preparing to say just a single word, then he exhaled noisily, his breath hissing through a scarred throat. One of his silent watchers raised an object, and pointed it at him.

Darkness enveloped him.

DETERMINANTS UNFOLDING

[Interim Run] *As they fall the screens align with themselves with the precision of a theorem, twelve images, all interrelated, all changing.*

The continuum adapts.

DETERMINANTS AT THE READY

[Processing] *The screens on the sides of the cubes stabilize, the motions therein; slowing, pausing. The closer cube rotates to show: a point-of-view on a desolate street. In the middle distance, a row of frame houses burns, the red flames leaping high against the night sky. The point-of-view is that of someone who is being carried by a larger individual. The larger individual appears to be either running or walking quickly, as the image bounces to the rhythm of fast paces.*

The owner of the point-of-view is looking straight ahead in the direction of travel. There is a kind of seeking motion, as the carrier changes direction slightly. There is a wide space between the burning buildings, almost as if a road or firebreak had been laid out through the burning. The runner passes through the open area, the flaming structures passing to either side.

Ahead there is an open field. Further to the south there are more rows of constructions, some large, some small, all ablaze.

A vehicle, a large car, pulls up, a figure in the front seat waves, and the runner changes direction towards it.

Behind the car, above the burning row of houses, the constellations of the night sky shine, beacons in the darkness.

The Point-of-view, and the runner carrying it, are engulfed by the friendly darkness of the automobile's insides.

The Determinants pause, waiting. One of the screens displays a scene: a city skyline as seen from across a large body of water. The lit buildings glow with an unstated electric promise in the night.

Then the image fades. With a lap-wipe, a black cover slides across the scene, shutting it out.

The black cover moves closer.

INTERLUDE WITH INTERFACES

[Design Pass, Preliminary; Process Shot; *di++ = *si++;] *He read the technical documentation closely, intently, checking each detail either with other references he had in his office, or with electronic references that were on-line. Now and again, he went out to the Internet for more public data.*

The I/O System he contemplated was of the most modern type, the neuro-electronic interfaces coming from one of the most highly rated Tech-

nical Bloc member-companies in Japan. The ease of use for the operator of the system was an important consideration, but the designed-in abilities to impose his outputs on any <destination> inputs was the deciding factor. He smiled: it was a thin-lipped facial gesture, devoid of the more normal emotions that would otherwise accompany such an expression.

His thoughts ranged back to the ultimate <destination> of his mental impositions, and what they would be, and he moved his face in that mirthless smile, again.

He read through the list of specifications for the third time, as he inhaled the information into his mind, much as he inhaled the outputs from his cigarettes. He found both forms of stimulation soothing, exhilarating.

Then, he scanned the list for the last time.

Lighting a cigarette, this time in real space, he made his plans.

R ECAP

[Loading; Establishing Shot]   Yezeletta turns in her sleep. Partially awake, her defensive systems at the ready, she awaits Joe's return to her bed (will it ever be *their* bed? she wonders), and in the depths of her waiting, other thoughts intrude.

In a rapid cycling through a linked list of images, others appear: the Directors from the Project, their final disposition, her escape from Australia, Zhongo Teketon, various subsidiary gang members, the incumbent in the Mitchell Conservatory, her agent and friend, Leona.

Especially Leona.

She loads an audio-visual file from her Internals, runs it.

Her guardian systems will inform her of Joe's return.

——>>> FOUR <<<——

All that is human must retrograde if it [does] not advance.

—Edward Gibbon,
The Decline and Fall of the Roman Empire, 1776

T HE P REPARATION OF THE O PERATOR

[Loading; Medium Shot; A Year Earlier]   Leona watched them from the doorway of her room. A small troupe of critters was picking up various items stored in the hallway. The creatures were taking the items to a room at the end of the corridor.

Roger's hit-man Tim had chased her into the basement parking ramp of the tallest building in Milwaukee, and the only competent resident of that building had acted to rescue her.

But, where had *she* come from?

Leona Mathieson was familiar with the body mods with which others her age had amused themselves. Her host was way above and beyond that. She had been *created*, but Yezeletta was reticent as to who her creators were, and from where they had originated.

Then there was the way her host had mapped out the city with *her* constructs, also way beyond anything else that she had seen: an act that had left Leona speechless.

Yezeletta had sent her to bed.

That was welcome: Leona was tired.

She was far more fatigued than she had thought earlier, and when she flopped on the large bed Yezeletta's servants had prepared for her, she slept—fully clothed, lying diagonally across it—for what must have been ten hours.

The next morning, Leona got up, and went looking for washing facilities. She didn't have to look far: the quarters she had been given were more appropriate to a luxury hotel than to an office building. The bathroom was large, well appointed, and the bathtub was not exactly a small swimming pool, but close.

Maybe Yezeletta designed everyone's living space for someone her own size.

Leona ran a hot bath and lay back in the water. A small control panel in a convenient location displayed three touch-switches. She pressed one.

The Jacuzzi was unexpected, but its seductive comfort was exactly what she needed. She let the flow of the warm water coax the aching out of her arms and legs. Next to the controls there was a shelf of rather expensive soaps. *She must like comfort*, Leona thought. *Or the little luxuries are there as compensations for other difficulties.*

Hmmmm. That was problematical. Yezeletta Zargkonji didn't seem to be terribly concerned with dangers. Her appearance at the exact time that the fight was getting serious *as if any part of it hadn't been* indicated that she'd been watching beforehand. Her handling of Tim was done with a degree of confidence that looked either effortless or well-practiced. Professional, in a word.

So who had taught Yezeletta her profession? Where had she come from? England? She sounded English.

Leona spent another hour resting in the whirlpool, the motions of the water soothing the remaining aches. She arose from the tub and dried herself.

Back in the bedroom, she saw a short creature placing her cleaned and neatly folded clothes on the just-made bed.

That was appropriate: she dressed, brushed her hair, and stopped for a moment before the mirror. A slender, dark-haired woman of about twenty-two regarded her from its depths. She had scrubbed her face, and makeup didn't seem necessary. *Or is Yezeletta interested in interviewing me?*

THE WELL DEFINED PROCESS—

[Five Years Earlier: Running] Leona Mathieson stepped down from the Greyhound Bus into the gray expanse of the station's parking garage at the corner of Michigan and James Lovell Lane (also known as Seventh Street). It was late, she was tired from the trip from Baraboo, and she was looking foreword to rest at the hotel where she had reservations.

She claimed her luggage at the side of the bus, and went into the lobby. She made a quick check with a map-under-glass posted conveniently for travellers, and went out to the cab stand. Her hotel was several blocks north of the station.

Leona, a tall, slender young woman with violet eyes, and long, dark hair was on her first solo outing into the big city.

—WITHIN THE SYSTEM—

An anonymous-looking yellow cab pulled up.

She opened the back door, placed her suitcase on the seat. She got in,

gave the driver the name of her hotel, and—
Was shoved violently into the center of the back seat.

—THE NEW KID—

"Hey there," the voice was in the cab, with her!
Leona turned.

"Don't wanna make some new friends?" The voice was female. Next to her. Leona looked at the source of the voice.

A tanned face, with sharp eyes, and a toothy grin. A smirk.

"I'm Bobbi," the face said, "Wanna be friends?"

"Sure ya do," the other voice, male, this time, came from the driver's seat. Leona reached for the opposite door. There was no inside handle.

"Let's play a game," the male said.

Bobbi grabbed Leona's wrists and pulled them behind her back. The driver turned to face them and threw a rope over Leona's head and around her neck, and Bobbi pulled her wrists up behind her. Then she slipped Leona's right wrist into a loop at one end of the rope. Then tied her other wrist.

It took about thirty seconds. Leona's wrists were brought up tightly behind her, and the rope was digging into her neck.

She could feel jerking motions as the woman tied the wrist ropes together.

The cab pulled out.

Leona looked wide-eyed at buildings passing her. They were driving away from her hotel. Bobbi tied a rope around her knees.

"You can still walk," she said, the smirk wider, nastier. "When we get there. Someone wants to see you."

"Who?" in a voice she realized was her own.

The man laughed, "You're going to meet your new employer. He has just the job for you."

Bobbi laughed, "Tell her Hound-Dog, tell her!"

Hound-Dog's face was a mask out of a nightmare, "You're gonna work for Gray Roger!"

—PLAYBACK PAUSE—

Leona finished brushing her hair, and went looking for her host. As she left the bedroom, a question surfaced: What happened to Tim?

Was the answer worth it?

Five years earlier it was.

—THE DEFINITION—

[Five Years Earlier] Leona was pulled roughly from the cab and held upright by the female—Bobbi. The vehicle was parked in a small courtyard made entirely of gray concrete blocks.

It reminded her of the bus station.

The lighting was dim and indirect. She moved her hands slightly, feeling for knots. There didn't appear to be any in reach of her fingers, and every time she turned a wrist, the cord around her neck tightened.

A door opened. It cast a wan wash of gray light into the courtyard. Bobbi pushed her foreword, and Leona nearly stumbled.

Somehow, she managed to walk towards the light.

—THE SUBSTRATE

[I/O Driver Active] West of Yezeletta's aerie, other tall buildings reached up from the edges of Wisconsin Avenue. Most of them had been office buildings, some with basement parking ramps. One had been an elegant old hotel. All of them looked as if they had seen far better times and all of them were in some stage of disrepair.

The artificial epidemic released in Wisconsin had manifested itself as a high-end case of influenza in humans, and as a disease of common crops in what were inadequately described as "botanicals." The sick were taken out of action, and those who were well cared for them. At the time, no one noticed that the plague happened at the exact time Albert Miller had destroyed Washington, and later no one cared.

Other activities, such as normal repairs and upkeep were allowed to slide away into a nebulous future. A lot of those repairs were never finished. Or started.

The immediacy of daily living caused anything not directly connected to that day-to-day routine to be forgotten. After the plague had died its natural death, the remains of it had become normal parts of the local environment, and faded into the status of "background."

A heavy windstorm had blown out one of the glass façades of Miller Park and the repairs needed for the following baseball season were never made. All of the games played by the Milwaukee Brewers that season went out of town. When the initial damage got worse as a combination of more bad weather and limited upkeep, the Brewers arranged with both Green Bay and Chicago to play "home" games there. Miller Park became a stately ruin on the West side of town.

Wisconsin Avenue was deserted in the evenings; Milwaukee's elegant old hotels were abandoned. The original owners abdicated their ownership, leaving for other places, wishing for other times.

Others moved into the voids created.

CHECKOUT RUN

[Lexical] Leona stood naked in front of the full-length mirror in Yezeletta's work-room. A small furry life-form that looked like a velvet-covered tarantula walked up the outside of her left leg, and paused at her waist. Leona regarded the creature's reflection in the mirror, and tried, and succeeded, at not grabbing it and handing it back to its designer.

The creature turned, and walked once around her waist; then it hopped onto her left arm, and walked up that arm to her shoulder. It paused there while she lifted her hair out of the way, and then circumnavigated her neck. "These things really don't bite, right?" she asked.

"Of course not," Yezeletta said, "I designed them not to."

Leona held her breath, and convinced herself that the animal was fundamentally benign.

The little creature walked down her right arm, turned, walked across her breasts (it tickled), and around to her back. The feeling as it scampered across the expanse of her back was weird. It reached the right side of her waist, went down her right leg, and walked once around her hips.

Yezeletta Zargkonji sat nearby and watched intently as her creation did its work. The velvet tarantula scampered up to Yezeletta, and hopped onto her left hand, her lower. She touched the creature with her upper left hand, and retrieved the data from it.

She sent the information from her on-board systems to another processor. Before Leona's fascinated gaze, a set of clothes took form, generated by several small life-forms that looked like tennis balls on black, jointed legs.

"If that whatzit that canvassed me is the 'fitter,' what's that bunch over there called?"

"Spinners," Yezeletta said succinctly. "They're rather difficult to grow: the fibers that they produce are long-chain carbon hyperfilaments."

"Oh. What's a hyperfilament?"

"Fibers that are of great tensile strength, and of molecular diameter. Ever hear of 'buckminsterfullerines'?"

"What?"

"In the nineteen-nineties, some organic chemists discovered a new carbon molecule that had sixty carbon atoms. They were arranged in exactly the same form as the geodesic domes that a man named Buckminster Fuller had designed much earlier."

"Like those three glass green-houses southwest of here."

"Yes, exactly. The Mitchell Conservatory's design is geodesic domes, and the Carbon-Sixty molecule was named after Fuller. Several years after that, those developers found another form that they called a 'bucky-tube'."

"A geodesic dome shaped like a tube?"

Yezeletta made a face, "You could look at it that way, I suppose. It's a long-chain molecule that can be of arbitrary length, and is very strong. Probably the strongest material known. Ever heard of the proposed Space Elevator?"

"Where do you get these things? No." Leona continued to watch the Spinners out of one eye as she sat down next to Yezeletta.

"Several authors came up with the concept in the last half of the Twentieth Century," Yezeletta said. "A couple of novels came out at the same time in which engineers build this, literally an elevator, from the Earth's surface, up to a satellite in synchronous orbit, counterbalanced by an asteroid the same distance further out as the satellite is up from Earth. The geometry is quite simple, and, at that time, the strongest material was a carbon-based synthetic called Kevlar. It wasn't strong enough. Those bucky-tubes are."

Leona took a breath. Although Yezeletta had heated the room pleasantly, she felt a chill cover her nakedness. "Those Spinners of yours, they're making...."

"You got it," Yezeletta said, with a feline look of pride. "Enough Spinners, and enough guts by enough people, and the Space Bloc would have some pretty stiff competition."

"Mind if I ask a personal question?"

Yezeletta grinned, "Nope, go ahead."

"Yezeletta, is there anything that you *can't* do?"

A SELECTION AMONG ANSWERS

[Load Parser; Close-Up] Yezeletta paused. The pause became an interval, the interval became a silence; the silence deepened.

Before it got any deeper, Yezeletta took a breath, and answered. "Frankly, yes. There are several things that I can't do. Leave this place, for one. At least openly."

"How do you stand it?"

"I'm unsure. Conditioning, maybe. At the Project that made me, I had the run of most places, and I could 'beta-test' my Imagers just about everywhere. The only thing I couldn't do was go outside. The tech-bloc had lookdowns that could have spotted me. If I have to, I can leave an indoor shelter. I did when I left—" Yezeletta's expression hardened, "—my creators, I was able to go outside, but it was initially difficult."

"Do you need to go out?"

"There are some items in the next building over that I could use. Most pharmaceuticals I can synth here. Equipment, I can't. There are some small companies that used to be based out of a building up the street from here, and I would like to remove what of their supplies I can get, and have them brought back here."

"So send your munchkins. Can't they do the job?"

"Only with on-site direction. They don't think."

"They sure put on a good act."

"Or pass the Turing Test," Yezeletta said. "The servitors do not reproduce; I designed them to be non-sentient. They are about as capable as a good personal computer. General purpose, but they require programming." Yezeletta let a chilly tone enter her voice. "I *will not* create a class of self-replicating slaves."

Leona nodded. "Sounds like you need a representative to watch them. Someone to decide what supplies need to be taken."

Yezeletta's gaze was level, steady. "Yes," was all she said.

Later Leona would understand what that answer meant. Now, she was beginning to understand the extent of what Yezeletta had done, entirely on her own, and, more importantly what she still needed to do.

"What do you need, and where's the location?" Leona asked.

The motions of the Spinners around the item they were constructing had ceased. Yezeletta went to the table on which they now sat inactive, and picked up their results.

"Try this on; let me know how it fits."

"This" was clothing. Leona put on underwear, and slid her legs into what the Spinners had produced, then she pulled the upper part on. It turned out to be a jump suit. Sleek overalls that fit her exactly. She zipped up the front, adjusted this and that, and took several experimental steps.

"This fits as if it had been—" she stopped and laughed.

"Made for you?" Yezeletta asked. "That's because it was."

"Out of those bucky-whatzits, right?"

"You couldn't cut that stuff with the best knife made. Resistant to punctures as well. Hell, *proof* against punctures. The Fitter was able to measure you enough, without getting too intimate, and telemeter the results—they amount to a triple-integration of the volume of, well, you—to the Spinners. They spun, and wove the spun results into that garment."

Leona regarded herself in the mirror. "I hate to say it, but this looks as if it was painted on."

"It functions well as an indoor outfit," Yezeletta said. "I have programs for the Spinners that will produce bulkier clothing for cold weather, or clothes with pockets. Or you can wear something over it. Weapons, for example."

"The Fitter *tickled*."

"I may have to work on that, Leona. I designed the Fitter to have as little fur as possible, consistent with its heat retention."

"Do they have to be fucking *tarantulas?*" Leona almost laughed at her own outburst.

"Spiders are easy to grow and to tailor. When I went through the American southwest, I was able to acquire several useful samples of desert tarantula to use as bases, or substrates, for further designs." She smiled slightly at that. "I've added those to other designs I got elsewhere, and to several that I ran up from, you might say, from scratch."

"Like your friend there," Leona gestured at the Imager perched on Yezeletta's shoulder.

"Like my friend here."

REHEARSAL OF THE OPERATOR

[Assemble, Link; Camera Goes With; Iris] A day later, Leona modeled another item of apparel: a belt that fitted snugly, but not tightly around her waist. Attached to the belt was a pair of forty-five caliber automatics in black canvas holsters, several blades of various lengths, pouches for magazines for the pistols, as well as other supplies, and several more prosaic tools such as screwdrivers and wrenches and folding multi-tools, each in its own compact container.

She stood before the same full-length mirror as she had when Yezeletta's Fitter had done its job, this time clothed in another set of the Spinners' overalls.

"This outfit still looks painted on," she said.

"But it's far more protective than the one you tried on yesterday," Yezeletta said. "This one uses a reprogramming of the Spinners to create braided hyperfilaments in redundant layers—"

"It feels as light as the other one."

"I use a tighter weave, and a much tighter five-ply braid for each fiber. Anyone who tries to take a poke at you through this stuff will receive an unpleasant surprise when nothing happens."

"Other than from these cannons I'm wearing?"

"Those, as well. Now: say something to the Imager."

Leona looked at the life-form sitting motionlessly on her right shoulder. It looked back at her, its large gold scanning aperture regarding her with a look that she would have liked to call curious, but which was more like blank.

"Hello, Imager," she said in a level voice.

Yezeletta's voice came out of the Imager. "That's a good sound-check: now whisper something."

"Something," Leona whispered. "Can you hear this?"

"Very good," Yezeletta's transmitted voice came out of the creature, "the automatic level compensation is working perfectly. Can you hear me now?"

The tone in Yezeletta's voice had vanished. "You were whispering?" Leona asked.

"I was."

"I could hear every word."

THE EXPEDITION

[Externally Specified Index]   The truck moved discretely through the late afternoon streets of Milwaukee. The sun's yellow light lit the interior of the pickup's cab. Yezeletta sat in the center of the seat, wearing the same gray coat as when Leona had met her. Leona sat next to her, and a servitor drove.

"Is that safe?" Leona asked.

"The servitors drove my trucks from the west coast," Yezeletta said. "Mostly on highways, mostly at night. I programmed them very well. I had no choice."

Yezeletta touched the driver's head, downloading instructions. The servitor pulled into the loading area of what had been a second-rate hotel.

The construct backed the truck around and into the loading dock. Leona and Yezeletta got out, and went to the entrance.

Yezeletta pushed on the door. It opened.

"Shouldn't this have been locked?" Leona asked.

"If there's anyone left who maintains this, maybe. It's good for us, and a bad sign for this place. Probably has a lot of squatters in it."

"Which we avoid?"

"As much as we can. I can give the wrong inhabitants a case of variable-interval amnesia if I have to, but if that happens too often, it may inspire someone to ask a lot of the wrong questions." She looked down at Leona, "I'd rather that didn't happen. The techniques I use could be traced."

Yezeletta made a three-handed gesture, and several servitors emerged from the back of the pickup. The little troupe fell in behind them, and followed them into the building.

The interior was dim; a little illumination came from a few filthy windows in the back of the building. Leona looked with disapproval at the graffiti-covered walls, and the trash, garbage and organics that littered the hallway.

"There's a freight elevator ahead," Yezeletta said, "if it's running, we can use it. One place I want to check out is on the sixth floor, the other on the second."

They approached the elevator, keeping a wary lookout for anyone else. Yezeletta pressed the call button; nothing happened.

She shook her head. Then both women froze. Yezeletta turned, scanning. There was a distant high-pitched sound. Yezeletta adjusted her hearing, and listened again.

It was the sound of someone crying.

GRAFFITI OF THE MIND

[Processing]   The sound came from above. Yezeletta triangulated on it by the simple action of listening, taking several steps, and listening again. Her internals derived a location. She gestured at a dark stairway, and started up. Leona followed her.

On the second floor, they paused before leaving the actual stairwell. The standing lights in the hallway proper were mostly nonfunctional. Here and there the occasional fluorescent tube flickered in the last stages of usability.

The crying was louder.

Yezeletta listened, switching in a stage of enhancement, analyzing phase relationships. She pointed.

At the end of the corridor was a room: perhaps it had been a small office at one time.

There was a line of light under the door.

WORDS EXTENDED

[Analysis] There was another voice that seemed to speak whenever the crying paused. It was the voice of an older individual, a voice expressing its message in an insistent monotone.

Leona couldn't make it out. Yezeletta amplified the input from her ears. She frowned. The voice was fading in and out, as if it were coming in on a shortwave link from a long distance.

She re-tuned her hearing, added a stage of noise elimination.

Damn! It was still difficult. Was there? There was. She performed a fast-fourier analysis on the structure of the voice: it was being distorted. Deliberately.

She smiled in the dim light. Two could play that game. She let her internals track the sounds, and watched as her processors stripped the covering distortion away.

"It's good for both of us," the voice, rendered even more monotonic by her systems, said. "God loves you. You know that, don't you?"

"*<Unintelligible>*." Yezeletta filed the answer away in her internals for later analysis. The adult human's voice started up, an insistent, controlling, monotonic sound that left no room for logic or thought. Yezeletta glanced at Leona. Leona's eyes were slits through which she was gathering information. "What is his—?" she asked. "He wants—"

"Exactly," Yezeletta said, softly. "Listen."

"Isn't it proper to love each other," the monotone went on. "God put us here to love one another. God *wants* us to love one-another. There's no greater love than this. Go on, hold me in your hands." The voice paused. Yezeletta dialed her respiration back to a state of lower activity. The drone started up with just a slight note of urgency in it: "Now kiss me there."

"Don't want to."

"It's really a good thing to do. Jesus loved the children, just as I love you."

"You're dirty. No." The words were definite, but there were sidebands of resignation in the young voice.

A memory surfaced in Yezeletta's internals. *A small boy whose dark-green eyes were almost gone.* How old had he been when they had met somewhere in Montana? Eight? He had lived with his parents...and several cats:

> *<Recollection from an internal state: Image of solemn cat faces, vertically-slit cat-green eyes in gray fur; all knowing, after the manner of the ancient feline>.*

THE MODE SWITCH

[Indexing] A hardness entered the monotone, *the first expression I've heard in that voice.* "Kiss me. Kiss me there. It's like a sucker. It's good. Show me that you love me like Jesus said."

"Do I have to?" There was no expression in the younger voice, no expression at all any more.

"Don't you love Jesus? Don't you think he would want this? Love is perfect when shared with another."

There was a silent moment. Then:

"That's big."

"I'm bigger than you. When you reach my size you can—"

"No. Don't touch...there...No, I don't want that!"

"Yes you do, it's good—"

The Many to One Relationship

[Fault Recovery] Yezeletta pointed with her right hand, her upper. Silently, she dropped her coat.

Leona drew a pistol.

"Let me go first," Yezeletta said. "He won't expect me."

A terrified scream escaped the office. Yezeletta, standing at her full height, strode to the door. She turned the knob; it was locked. She seized the doorknob in three hands, planted her legs to brace herself, and pulled on the door. The door and part of the doorframe splintered out of the wall. She tossed it back out of the way of Leona, and entered.

She looked down at:

A small boy, his pants down around his feet, a look of resignation that seemed designed in place, a raggy-looking sweatshirt covering his upper body, sitting in a low chair.

Before him, his back to the door, an adult human, likewise nude below the waist, his hips positioned suggestively directly in front of the boy's face.

Yezeletta placed three large hands on the man's shoulders.

"You wouldn't mind making your position known to someone a bit larger, would you?" she asked the man.

Perhaps instinctively, the man turned away from the two large left hands on his left shoulder. He turned to the right, and looked straight at several hexagonally shaped life-forms that extended their claws towards his face.

And Yezeletta's forty-five in her remaining hand.

He switched his head around in panic.

Leona's pistol stared him down from the other side.

"It's okay," he started, his voice showing some modulation. "We're friends, and—" A large upper left hand covered his mouth.

Leona knelt before the youngster, "You're among friends," she said, fixing him with her electric violet eyes. "This man—" she paused. "This *thing* will not be hurting you again." She pulled his pants up, buckled the diminutive belt.

Yezeletta pulled the other up to his full height. He stood there, shaking slightly. "Turn around," she commanded. "Face *me*."

The adult turned. He took in all of Yezeletta. He bolted for the door.

In a single, leisurely, economical motion, Yezeletta reached out with her upper right hand, and grabbed the man's neck. His precipitous motion stopped, and he hung for a moment from her hand.

Suddenly, he spun and aimed a vicious kick at her crotch. Yezeletta dodged that easily, and made a signal to a small group of bright eyes looking in from the corridor.

The servitors entered, carrying objects that coiled and writhed and were covered with thick grease. She touched Leona lightly on the shoulder, Leona looked up. "See if you can get the little fellow away from this." Leona nodded, and led the child out.

The servitors threw the greasy writhing things on the adult. Wherever they landed they stuck and coiled around him. Yezeletta held him by the neck until his wrists and ankles were secure.

"He's my—" the man started. Yezeletta stuffed a spare coil into his mouth.

THE DESCENDING HETERARCHY

[Set Mode: Run]   The servitors carried the monster out. Yezeletta paused to retrieve her coat, got the well-worn pair of mirrorshades out of a pocket.

Her eyes covered, and the darkening effects of the shades compensated for, she turned to where Leona was talking gently to the youngster.

Another memory:<*The green eyes that saw all sides of things: was it only accidental that the Ancient Egyptians worshipped the feline? The two, they were: a Tom Cat and his Mate; an "item" in a distant recollection.*>

And a small boy in the present, *younger than the other.*

"Where do people like that come from?" Leona asked in a low voice. Her question was rhetorical.

"Certain life forms seem to mutate into existence," Yezeletta replied. "Perhaps they're parasites, although they probably don't think of themselves exactly that way."

Yezeletta paused in the hallway. She adjusted her hearing for the sounds she heard in the distance.

It was quite a distance. She realized that Leona wouldn't be able to hear the same inputs. For Leona they would be lower than the threshold of hearing, lost in the whispers of her own circulation.

She ranged on the sounds, making an initial assumption that they were human voices that were shouting.

They were. The range she calculated was on the close order, of a short city-block's distance. About three-hundred meters. She added a stage of noise reduction.

The voices were clearer: a man and a woman, calling for....

Leona's small companion.

"Is your name Sammy?" Yezeletta asked gently.

The little boy snuggling in his new friend's arms didn't say a word. He nodded, holding Leona tightly.

The sources of the voices were getting closer; a doppler analysis indicated running. Yezeletta adjusted her sound processing, and determined that the owners of the voices were nearly out of breath. She turned to a servitor, touched its head, and the creature handed her something of a dark brown color. Something that moved of its own volition.

Leona took a discrete step away from her mentor. Sammy was facing away from Yezeletta; he didn't see the multilegged dark brown creature climb up Yezeletta's upper left arm, across her shoulders, and down her lower right arm, where it sat just above her wrist, a brown bracelet.

Two people, a man and a woman, came down the stairway from the third floor, and skidded to a stop in the hallway. Leona took a step forwards.

"Sammy!" the woman said. Sammy smiled, and held his arms out to the woman, evidently his mother.

She held Sammy in her arms, while the man, Sammy's father, Leona guessed, regarded her.

Then Leona saw the thirty-eight in the man's hand.

"Where did you find him?" the woman asked. "Where was he?"

"What happened?" the man said. To Leona's relief, he holstered the pistol.

"He was lost in one of the offices," Leona started, "He was—"

"Being put upon by a monster," Yezeletta's voice said out of the shadows.

THE PRICE OF ADMISSION

[An Object Method in the Madness; Iris: Close-Up] The man and the woman were indeed Sammy's parents. He was Seth Levandowsky; his wife was Myra Levandowsky. Getting the names had taken a little persuasion.

"Call me Mississippi Slim," he had started off.

"S—" his wife had started.

He had hooked his thumbs in his belt, "It's the—"

"Seth!" his wife had said, "These people saved Sammy from *that thing*—" she pointed at the wrapped bundle in the corner of the office into which they had all moved. The bundle regarded her with hate-filled eyes.

Seth was having a problem keeping his gaze off of Yezeletta. "You found him doing *what*?" His voice was vitriolic, his white-hot anger barely under control.

Yezeletta sat on the edge of a dusty desk, her legs splayed out around one of its corners. "We were looking for other things, and heard Sammy. He was unwilling to accept the offers *that item* was making." She monitored the tremors in Seth's voice closely: *He sounds ready to lose it*, she thought.

While Yezeletta spoke, Sammy, feeling a little braver, stood in front of the molester, grinning.

The schoolyard bully had better watch out!, Leona thought. The man refused to meet Sammy's look.

"What do you do here?" Yezeletta said.

"Building maintenance," Seth said.

"For that gangster," his wife added.

Really, now?, Yezeletta didn't say.

"What kind?" she asked, trying to modulate her voice into friendlier tones.

"I was in a little trouble, and he—" Seth stopped. Then he started again.

THE SHOW

[Establishing Shot; Process Report] Seth Levandowsky worked for Zhongo Teketon. He had taken the "Mississippi Slim" sobriquet as a consequence of his having amassed a large debt at one of the riverboat gambling casinos that skated across the Mississippi River like financial scavengers. Zhongo had offered to pay his debts to the "Empress" Casino; the familyman who owned the boat was happy, and Zhongo had acquired a new superintendent for his buildings in downtown Milwaukee.

Seth "Slim" lived with his wife and small son in the owner's apartment in what had once been a posh hotel up near Seventh and Wisconsin.

Earlier that afternoon, Sammy had vanished. Not being able to go to Milwaukee's overworked, undermanned police, they had, with a little help from several more of Zhongo's men, been covering the Avenue, looking.

The Final Question

[Wait State] Sammy's family took him into the adjoining office. There Yezeletta could hear them calming the youngster down, their voices soothing, loving.

She played back some of Sammy's attacker's, speech: his voice had been an insistent monotone, mouthing canned phrases and played-back sentences. How many times had he used the same seductive lines, and to how many children?—the verisimilitude of an old tape recording, without the underlying talent.

What the hell, it worked, didn't it? How many *other* times had it worked? With whom? Weren't the results guaranteed? Until a woman with more-than-human hearing had monitored the file-dump, and aborted the program!

The animation in Sammy's mom's voice was working. There was something about the voice that a child first heard in all the world that was an ultimate source of calmness—a center into which a new intelligent life could place himself.

Was this what it was like to—?

Yezeletta had to pause here—this was something that she had never learned at the Project.

She had been filled with propaganda about how important she was. To the Project. But had she ever *belonged*?

She filed this away for analysis. Were the platitudes served up to her then justified, or were they nothing more than empty phrases designed as space-fillers to preclude further thought?

Much like the patter of *this* human!

Some families were really genetic. Others were not, but voluntary associations could be as close and as loving. Yezeletta had nothing more than that to go on. The novels she had read had described events that simply didn't correspond to anything in her experience.

Enough. This was something that she would have to study, but now there was another small child who needed what attentions she was capable of providing.

This part she understood perfectly.

As a solder in an undeclared war.

Sammy would have nightmares, but Yezeletta could help take the edges off. Seth and Myra were pretty special. They had reacted more to Sammy's rescue, and his safety, than they had to Yezeletta.

Yezeletta was the agent. The Catalyst.

The Operator.

The Review

[Parity Check; Link] Later, Leona would make up her mind; now she was—considering. Her first take was one of outrage. Her second was that of protection. Lastly, she thought of revenge.

"There is," she said to Yezeletta, "A force in the universe that makes every pip-squeak deity in every religion seem pale and insignificant by comparison."

"What's that?" Yezeletta was genuinely curious. She realized that there were belief-arrangements usually called "religious," but she had never much dealt with them.

"Try two-million years of adaptive evolution," Leona said decisively. "Maybe that's why so many religious organizations condemn evolution with the intensity they do. It's a more effective competitor to their all-knowing, all-avenging 'big-daddy' superstitions. And they know it."

Yezeletta wrote a note to herself and stashed it in one of her onboard systems. That idea was worth a second look.

"You heard what that male human was saying to Sammy."

"Human?" Yezeletta asked, surprised, "does he even qualify as human?"

"I don't want to call him a man. Real men don't attack children. I'm being descriptive."

"He was being—you'll have to help on this, was he being religious?"

"I wouldn't call it that," Leona said in flat tones. "He might. The real answer is that he's using a 'program' to advance what he wants."

"I understand programs," Yezeletta said. "I've written them."

"This is different. He wants whatever he wants, and will use, distort, rewrite or steal whatever he needs to accomplish his goal. In the name of his favorite religious hero, or in any other name. All ethics are the same to a molester like that, and it's all the same to him. What's 'right' is what he wants at that moment."

"I've known people like that," Yezeletta said, "at a distance."

"What should we do with this specimen?"

"There are applications that he would do well in. Is it important that I keep him alive? What of Sammy's parents?"

Leona's expression became concerned, "What are you saying? His parents?"

"I have a critter I designed that I call a 'Cat-Arachnid'. It's a more predatory version of this," Yezeletta stroked the Imager sitting on her right shoulder. "They are designed as carnivores, and I've used them to lower the rat population in the area."

"You want to give him," Leona nodded at their captive, "to the Cat-Arachnids?"

"No," Yezeletta said, "I wouldn't want them to get sick, or even indigestion. He's an entirely different kind of rat; we need a different kind of predator. Should we give him to Seth and Myra, when they're done in there?" She turned and looked with a flat-eyed gaze at the molester, giving him nothing. He looked at her gold eyes, steadily. She looked back objectively, without expression, closing her irises down to thin vertical lines. Not giving him anything.

The man tried to say something around the coil of greasy living rope in his mouth. Yezeletta stroked the rope, and it relaxed. "Do you know what we were doing?" the captive asked.

"What?"

"Perfect love," the human said. "If you knew how exalting it is to bring little buds up to the light of absolute unblemished love, you would let me out of these, these...."

"Buds?" Yezeletta looked back at Leona, then at the captive. "Is this how you see a small child? As a *plant*?"

There was a commotion at the door, voices.

Leona stood to answer the door, Yezeletta reached into a case that a servitor carried. She looked up at Leona. "You asked about Seth and Myra," she said.

A brown long-legged arachnid skittered up her arm. It joined the other that had been there.

Waiting.

THE ENTRY LEVEL POSITION

[I/O Driver Active] Seth and Myra entered the room, Sammy between them. They wore their expressions of outrage, anger and vengeance as if they were military decorations.

"What do you plan to do with that?" Seth asked.

"He will cease to exist," Yezeletta said pleasantly.

"Who are you? Where'd you come from?"

"That is irrelevant," Yezeletta said. "Think of me as a friend. The rescuer of your son." Sammy looked at Yezeletta the way any other small child would look up at a movie star.

Seth's expression was guarded. It wasn't the poker-face of a gangster facing authorities, nor was it the "dummy up" of the seasoned con. His look invited further explanation, although the guilt of his son's attacker was already established. Two strange ladies, and the lady who was his wife looked back.

"Seth," Yezeletta began, then: "Slim, if that's what you like to be called. My partner and I rescued your boy from an experience that could have harmed him for life. Maybe even *made* him one of *those*." Her flat declaration was a dereferenced pointer: the male human that she accessed with it twisted in the greasy coils, and tried a blasé look. It failed.

"We would ask a favor of you. Sometime in the near future, we will make that favor known. Will you help us?" Yezeletta was getting the beginnings of an idea.

"Certainly, my boss—"

"Who is one of the most powerful people in the area," Yezeletta finished it for him.

"Zhongo—" Slim started.

"Yes?"

Seth/Slim let out a breath. He looked around for a chair, and sat on the corner of a dusty desk. "Zhongo is hell on his men," he began. "He rewards hard work, and the ones who fail...."

"Don't get seen again?" This time Leona finished the sentence.

"Or worse," Slim said. "What could you possibly want?"

"Something," Yezeletta said. As you can see, I can't exactly make a trip uptown when I need to. You could accomplish much, in a discreet way."

"If Zhongo finds out, I'm dead. Maybe worse."

"Not even," Yezeletta said. Something appeared on her shoulder. It was brown, fuzzy, and moved with agility. It was joined by another, and another.

"You have your son back," she said clearly, enunciating each word carefully. "He is unharmed, and will have no more than harmless dreams of his recent experience. All three of you are safe." Her voice took on an incantatory quality, "Nothing more will happen, there is nothing that you can't accomplish, nothing that you find impossible—"

The brown shapes launched themselves at Seth, Myra and Sammy. The diminutive life-forms worked their legerdemain, and in a matter of seconds, the memories of the past hours were gone.

Seeing, yet unseeing, of their own volition, the Levandowsky family departed.

An Imager would follow them back to their residence.

PROGRAMMED POSTAMBLE

[Processing] Leona let out a long breath. "What now?" she asked.

"We wait for them to get home, and get back into their lives. Then we invoke that favor."

"What do you want of a gangster?"

Yezeletta told her.

LIBRARY FUNCTION

[Overlay] The servitors carried the molester as if they were pallbearers carrying a corpse.

"Where are you—" he asked.

Yezeletta silenced him with a well-placed coil of creature.

"Where are you taking him?" Leona asked.

"Should this be allowed to go on as he is?"

"Are you kidding?"

Yezeletta smiled like a death's-head with cat's eyes, "I can use him, or at least a part of him. He can aid a development I'm working on."

"While I'm—there?"

"It may prevent more of him. It *will* deal with this one."

"There's no way to save someone like that?" Leona asked.

"I doubt it. He behaves as if sex with kids is his personal drug. He won't reform. Back there, I was wondering how many other small boys, or for that matter, small girls, he's inflicted himself on."

"He won't stop?"

"Not unless we stop him."

"Then we stop him."

MEMBER FUNCTION: INSTANTIATE

[Swap] Two women, and their captive, a fly in a web of programs and data, drove back to the Farmer's Mutual Building. When they arrived, the servitors conveyed the pedophile, now in a silent panic in the oily, greasy living coils, up the elevators to Yezeletta's workshop beneath the Matrix Engine.

The servitors carried the safely packaged captive through a door into another part of the work-area. Yezeletta looked at Leona from her full height, and, with a hand wave, walked after.

THE PERIPHERAL

[Installation] She walked rapidly, too rapidly for Leona. She looked back, waiting for her to catch up. Yezeletta had a tight little smile, one without mirth, that Leona found unsettling; she walked more slowly. Yezeletta looked down at her, as Leona watched the complex marching pattern she used for a fast walk in fascination. "Think of it as a waltz for four legs,"

Yezeletta said.

"Where are we going?" Leona asked.

"I'm disposing of the monster: up ahead."

They entered a large room made smaller by its inhabitants. One of those their captive. He looked up at the raven-haired apparition as she strode in, and tried to shrink back from her inexorable approach. Two of Yezeletta's minions prodded him back onto center stage with their weapons. Another stood by with a Sony minicam.

"I always need more mass-storage, haven't the time I need to grow it, and that is all this specimen is good for," she said. "Watch him."

Yezeletta went to a shelf where a laptop was connected to a cable that went snaking up into the overhead. She typed a command into the unit, and read the feedback that appeared in a window on the machine's screen. She looked at the molester standing on a new pattern of concentric circles. They reminded Leona unpleasantly of a target, or of Ground Zero.

Yezeletta Zargkonji looked up. Above, covering the ceiling, was a complex of pipes and conduits that were peripheral to the Matrix-Engine, whose bulk hummed and whirred above them.

She checked the display again and pressed a final key-combination. A red design appeared on the laptop's screen. Leona waited apprehensively. For a moment, nothing happened except for a perceived deepening in certain of the sounds from within the Engine. A movement from above caught Leona's eye; she looked up. Overhead, an aperture in the equipment had opened and a green sphere suspended on a thin white cord dropped slowly down. *It looks as if it's spinning down a strand of webbing*, she thought; she saw that the line connected to a viscous off-white excrescence up in the tangle of equipment above.

The line extended as if it were an elastic: the bottom of the sphere opened out into eight equal triangular portions. Inside was some sort of soft white material: almost cotton, but not quite. As Leona watched, Yezeletta monitored the performance of her device with an unwavering gaze. Leona switched back to the sphere: the "cotton" almost seemed to pulsate. There was a cloyingly sweet odor in the room.

The octants opened wider. Then almost as if the green object were alive, it swayed, seeking, over the prisoner standing in the circles, and dropped down on his head. The man had just barely time for a single gurgling cry, as the eight flaps closed to meet at the neck.

He fell to the floor, and the construct with the minicam moved in for a close-up. The hollow impact of the green thing enclosing his head was the only sound in the room.

Yezeletta had attention only for her constructs doing their jobs.

Leona started at a sound behind her. Another of Yezeletta's creations had arrived, wheeling in a gurney. Additional workers lifted the body and placed it on the device, and the assistant trundled him out through an open door. Beyond the door: an object that resembled a large gray onion, neatly bisected vertically and lying open.

Another servitor began removing the circles.

STATIC RAM

[Subroutine Call] Yezeletta went after her attendants, leaving Leona alone for a short time. The other servitors drifted off to other work.

Leona stood there for a moment, listening. In other parts of the building, in other workshops, she could hear Yezeletta's minions working on their unknown activities. The Matrix Engine bulked above, a complex of wires, pumps, hoses and pipes doing things that only its creator understood. A servitor walked past, sweeping the floor, its route as meticulously programmed as the hardware works that surrounded Leona.

The sounds of the machinery were common, familiar. In another place they would seem almost friendly. Here they were just the pre-programmed systems of, of....

Of a woman who had gone to ground, at the top of the tallest building in Milwaukee.

ENTRY ON ANOTHER LEVEL

[Recursion]   Leona hadn't thought of him in the days she had known Yezeletta, but the gray face of her previous employer appeared unbidden, a waking nightmare, a ghost in the system.

She had been marched into the presence of Gray Roger.

Her impression was of colorlessness, of neutral shades of luminance, only.

Of a man whose face was gray, whose life was gray, whose very living quarters were gray.

Yezeletta had a somewhat disorderly layout: the sort of work-shop-slash-living-space that one would expect of an individual who combined research with survival. When she was able, Yezeletta dabbled in artwork, and had done a fair, if informal, job of interior decoration.

It was a marked contrast with a man whose life was all twilight shades of gray.

Who could vanish without moving a muscle.

The gray man spoke in a voice like crumbling ashes, "is this your offering?"

Leona took a breath, started to say something. Then realized that the gray man—what was his name? Roger?—was addressing her captors.

"Will she be enough? Or do we have to find another?" Hound-Dog's voice.

The gray man stood, He was taller than Leona, taller than Hound-Dog. He approached her. He touched her left breast with a gray hand. Leona flinched.

Someone behind her pushed her towards the gray man. He placed his hand on her breast. Then he unbuttoned her blouse, with rough motions. There was the flash of a knife blade, and her bra was cut in two.

"You'll do," he said. Whether it was to Leona or to the rest of the room was ambiguous. He ran fingers like dry twigs over her breasts for a short time. Then he took her chin roughly, definitively in his hand, his left, studied her face.

"You'll do," he said, again.

YEZELETTA'S AGENT

In the following five years, Leona had been Gray Roger's star attraction. In all of that time, the City of Milwaukee had been rather quiet, rather the same one day to the next.

There *was*, however, the matter of the fire down at the east end of Wisconsin Avenue. The investigators for the Milwaukee Fire Department were never able to determine the fire's cause, nor were they able to trace the remains of the large truck that had been destroyed.

GRAY ROGER'S WOMAN

[Then] Leona was taken to a room by silent gray-clad men.

At least they looked like men.

She was pushed through the door, and the door slammed shut behind her. A while later, one of the gray crew returned to remove Hound-Dog's ropes.

She sat down on the edge of the only piece of furniture in the room, a large bed, and rubbed the places on her neck where the cords had been.

Now what?

GRAY ROGER'S POSITION

[Running: Extending Upper: Extreme Close-Up] Over the next several days, Leona was fed, allowed to bathe, and otherwise left alone. Days later, four? Five? She was summoned—actually taken—to another place, a gray room containing gray furniture.

The Gray Man entered.

Leona sat on the edge of a chair watching.

He sat facing her, and stopped moving. He seemed to blend in with the rest of the grayness; all Leona was able to discern were his gray eyes, eyes that pierced the distance between them like lasers.

His gaze scanned her, almost analyzing her.

Then he stood, approached her, and slowly, deliberately, began to remove Leona's clothes.

The silence of the action was uncanny, the movements practiced. Leona wanted to say something, yet her words were caught in her throat. She crouched in the back of her mind watching as if through windows at what was happening.

When he was done, when Leona was left lying on the bed, breathing fast, he left the room.

As silently as when he had come.

REPLAY

[Post-Production] Half an hour later, the gray man returned. He removed his clothes, and folded them neatly on another chair.

He turned from his orderly stack of apparel, holding an item. A strip of leather.

He wrapped it around Leona's neck, and attached a lead to it. Scanning her with his piercing gray eyes, he tugged gently on the lead, and waited for Leona to get up.

He returned to the chair, and sat down on the edge of it.

He tugged on the leash again, and looked at a place on the floor before him.

Leona sat down on the floor. The gray man tugged on the leash, and she sat up higher. Then knelt.

You like the obvious, she thought, Fine.

Fine and dandy, she thought as she did it to him, think that I'm yours. One of these days, you'll learn.

When I kill you.

Yezeletta's Descriptor

[Penthouse View]   Yezeletta could *think*, conclusively, definitively and exhaustively, the activities around Leona were indicative of that.

Then Leona understood.

Nothing else in this building could.

Yezeletta wanted companionship. A confidante. Even more importantly, she wanted an agent in the big city within which she had taken residence: someone whose memories *weren't* safely removed.

It was a garden out there. *Now, where did that come from*, Leona thought, as she went to a window. If Milwaukee in the middle of the Twenty-First Century was a garden, maybe someone needed to weed it.

Yezeletta *had* been cleaning out the rats with her custom life-forms. What other predators were there waiting for removal? Gangsters? Gray Roger? *Zhongo?*

Leona went looking for her hostess.

The Secret Agent

[Long Right Shift; Long Shot] "What do we need for a mission?" Leona asked.

They were sitting in a conference room that was still furnished in the manner of the long-gone owners of the old Farmer's and Merchant's Building. Lists on yellow legal pads, several laptop computers, and other devices covered one end of a wide table. Several small lifeforms sat in and among the apparatus.

"Secure communications, first of all," Yezeletta said succinctly. She paused in thought, and Leona could see a complex of expressions on Yezeletta's face.

The complex series ended on one of decisiveness. "I have various kinds of communications systems." Yezeletta placed her lower left hand on an Imager, and the creatures on the table assembled in the center of it.

"These are specialized critters that I'll send with you," she said. "The thing that looks like a white centipede is a Receiver."

Yezeletta touched the Imager nearest to her, and sent an instruction. The Receiver reared up on about the last quarter of its body-length, and all of its legs forward of that section stuck out left and right from its small body. The legs were of varying lengths.

"What does it—uh—receive?" Leona asked.

"Electromagnetic radiation and magnetic fields," Yezeletta said. "It can receive in the visible wavelengths as well, but I designed it to be an 'Imager' for other frequencies."

"And the Imager is a roving camera. Regular eye kind."

"Exactly so." Yezeletta touched the nearest Imager, again. A creature that looked like an excessively hairy tarantula took center stage.

"You really like spiders, don't you?"

Yezeletta grinned, "Why not? They're fast on their feet, intelligent and, I admit, they have as many limbs as I do. What's not to like?"

"Are you—?"

"Not even. I know what you were about to ask. I've heard it before. I was—am—what/ever—a product of Human genetics. There are records of my—creation, you could call it—, but they aren't for the faint-of-heart. Or stomach."

"I'll buy that."

"Thank you." Yezeletta paused. The pause became half a minute, then a minute. Leona was ready to end the silence, when Yezeletta continued: "You've been a good friend, here. I feel—make that think—that I'm using you in a rather unacceptable way, asking you to join a pack of the underworld's finest."

"I had my doubts. Your reaction to that *thing* you turned into a terabyte of static RAM changed my mind."

"How?"

"You could sit in a web in the center of this place. You could have become as amoral as a real spider, living for the next time lunch gets delivered by air-parcel-post into your web, and doing nothing. Being a weapon."

"Being?"

"Yeah, right. Do you think a pistol has a brain? It's a piece of equipment, a lump of dead hardware. A gun has no volition any more than a toaster has. It has to have a brain driving it, and then it can be used to shoot a rapist, or 'go postal' in a crowded place. It's all the same to the weapon. It's the operator that makes the difference."

"Please go on," Yezeletta said.

"I noticed it earlier, after you went off to install that molester. Nothing else in this complex of yours *thinks*. You do all of the skull-sweat here."

"And you went, at a considerable risk, to pull me out of a bad situation, and to rescue a little boy in a worse situation."

"It made the difference," Leona finished.

"Why were you fighting with Tim?" Yezeletta asked.

"I decided I didn't exactly care for my previous employer, and I wanted to resign. Y'know, take up a different line of work," Leona answered.

"May I ask what you did?"

She laughed, but there was little mirth in it. "I was Gray Roger's star attraction. Lap-dancing, straight sex, heavy trade, dominance, submission, you name it. I did it. Some of it was actually interesting, but I took a trick with a man named Gary Hamilton, and decided that I was getting too tired of crazies to go on."

"I know of Gray Roger, but very little," Yezeletta said.

"Didn't you get any of your spies into his place?"

Yezeletta shook her head. "He has a place, but he is very well concealed. I've never been able to locate him."

"Interesting," Leona said, "It's even more interesting that you want me to infiltrate Zhongo Teketon. Roger avoided Zhongo pretty big-time. I think he was afraid of Zhongo.

"And now you want me to kiss-up," she laughed, "to the astute Mr. Teketon. It isn't like I'm inexperienced at this!"

Later, Yezeletta would know others for whom her views would make friends. Now, she looked at Leona, almost seeing her in a different light (and of what use was an expression like that one? Light was light; a part of the electromagnetic spectrum that she could use or not as she wished, selecting what part of it she wanted. Was that why some nameless researcher had designed her eyes to see in such a wide complex of bandwidths?)

Leona asked, "What does Charlotte, there, do?"

"In spite of its appearance, it's a 'gofer'. Go fer this, go fer that, you've heard that one before," Yezeletta said.

"In places where people don't see it."

"Yup. Under floors, in walls. There's a comic-book superhero that his enemies call 'The Wallcrawler'. This one does that literally, *in* walls."

"I love it. What does it do when it crawls?"

Yezeletta extended one of her left hands, and sent the tarantula a signal through her onboard systems. The little creature jumped onto her extended hand, and walked up her arm.

"These will bring you things, hustle props that certain gangsters shouldn't see out of sight, and carry messages."

"Don't other critters do that?"

"There are—and will be—a complex of other life-forms that will network around you. There are several Imagers that will send dictation directly here, and deliver commentary from me to you. If we need something immediate, like a telephone connection, the Imagers can do that too, but there may be a chance of someone hearing you doing the talking on that end. You'll have to decide that when you get there."

"Clothing? Weapons?"

Yezeletta gestured. Another of the black, furry tarantulas walked from the far end of the conference table dragging an object. It seemed to have no problems towing it by holding on with one foreleg to a loop attached to the irregular shape, while walking rapidly on its other seven.

It released the item in front of Leona. She picked it up. It was a forty-five caliber pistol in a black holster. The only add-on to it was the small loop to allow the tarantula to drag it.

"Okay. About a kilogram, I'd say. That little guy didn't have any problems moving it."

"Those 'little guys' will keep a small arsenal of pistols, knives of various kinds and ammunition inside the walls, or under the floor-boards of wherever you end up. I'll have some of my more specialized weapons on call, as well. They'll respond to your voice, and fetch whatever you need."

"How fast?"

"The arachnoids won't even have to move an object the length of this table. Half a meter's my guess. All it has to be is out of the line of sight inside a wall or under floorboards."

"My mom always warned me to stay away from spiders; now I have them as assistants. Who would have thought that the Homecoming Queen would become a secret agent?" Leona grinned. "Okay, Yezeletta, how do I get inserted into the theater of action? Let's do it before I hatchet my chickens in front of the Count."

"I heard what you said, but what did you say?" Yezeletta asked, the laugh-lines around her large eyes just a touch more pronounced.

INFILTRATION: INITIAL

[Version Update; Camera Goes With] It actually took several additional days worth of preparations before Leona was ready to go to the family that owed her friend the Big Favor.

"Those memory obliviators I used forcibly disconnect the synapse networks that comprise short- and long-term memory, and are useful in rather extreme cases. I don't like to use them; there's a chance that someone will get the kind of very close medical exam that will detect the kind of brain-tampering that the obliviators actually perform."

"I get the idea that you don't really like to use those, anyway," Leona said.

"From an ethical standpoint, no," Yezeletta said. "I've had to use them in a number of 'them-or-me' situations, and, each time, I've been nervous about later detection. It's both my intense dislike for meddling in someone's mind, and my equally intense dislike for being discovered. I've been here for about eighteen months, without detection. I want to keep it that way."

"But you need data."

Yezeletta almost laughed. "That's a nice understatement, Leona. I've got Imagers everywhere in the city, and I'm growing Hives of Imagers, Receivers, and the like as far out as Oak Creek and Racine. One of Zhongo's men thinks he's seen the occasional Imager, and has taken to using them for targets. I may have to do something about that. In the meantime, I've been using better camouflage on them."

"What about Seth and Myra, then?"

Yezeletta took a breath, let it out, and: "I hate to have done this, but they have sort of a post-hypnotic suggestion, by way of the Obliviators I used on them. This is one that Sammy didn't get: Seth/Slim and Myra will respond to a password that you give them that will—I suppose that 'encourage' them is the best word—to take you in as an old friend, and assist you in getting placed with Zhongo."

"As his gun-moll," Leona said, drily.

"That's the only way he'd take you—"

"I'm afraid you're on it," Leona said, "And, I'm afraid, I'll be on it, later. Just provide an exfiltration method, if I need it."

"That will be in place before you go in," Yezeletta promised.

I N F I L T R A T I O N :   I N P U T

[On-Line]   "He has a poker game usually on the first Friday of each month." Seth Levandowsky's voice, curiously flat and uninflected, came from the speakerphone.

"Who comes to these?" Yezeletta asked.

"Just the inner circle of his associates," Seth/Slim said. "I've been invited just the last three or four months, now."

Yezeletta thanked Seth, and spoke the words that would end the conversation and cause Mississippi Slim to forget that it ever happened.

"The first Friday was a week ago," Leona said. "We have three weeks to plant me in Slim's house, and get me into the thick of things."

"Not three weeks," Yezeletta said. "Three weeks plus 'N' months. You may not get into Zhongo's life as quickly as that."

I N F I L T R A T I O N :   I N T E R I M

A week later, Leona sent a message back to Yezeletta: *I've made it into the Levandowsky Family. The Password worked like a champ. More to come.*

A week after that, she sent another: *Myra Levandowsky can't cook to* *save her ass. I'm teaching both of them how to turn good food into good meals instead of charcoal chunks. Sammy's a dear. He thinks he's had a bad nightmare, but appears to be otherwise unharmed. Send me a couple of <u>good</u> recipe books!*

The messages came back to Yezeletta with some frequency after that. Leona had become almost part of the Levandowsky family. The big owner's apartment that Seth and Myra lived in had enough extra space in it so that Leona had a bedroom to herself, with a large footlocker that neither of her hosts looked at too closely.

She stayed there for nearly two months.

Then Slim took her to Friday Night Poker.

BREAKPOINT RETURN

[IRET] Yezeletta lets the images return to the locations where executing programs go when they cease running. Her augmented memories process the multi-media shut-down and her bedroom takes its familiar form around her. She hears Joe's footsteps returning from the living-room, where he had played the videodisc of the preliminary designs that had later resulted in her. She looks at him through nearly closed eyelids, augmenting with another image from Thicknesse relayed by way of her internals. He looks down at her sleeping.

He's smiling. His expression is one of acceptance.

Yezeletta disengages her guardian systems and allows herself to sleep. As she drifts off, she feels the large waterbed moving to Joe's body, as he lies down next to her.

——>>> **FIVE** <<<——

I can make my own light shine
And darkness too is equally fine.

—Patti Smith

HEART SHAPED TATTOO

[EQUIVALENCE(Wait-State, Beat)] Yezeletta sleeps on her side of the bed on her special pillows. She looks benign, lying on her side facing him. Occasionally one of her hands or a foot twitches as she goes into or out of REM sleep. Joe puts his ear near her chest. The syncopated beat of her hearts is a fascinating sound. He didn't realize that she had a back-up heart, until they first slept in the same bed.

Her singlemindedness is understandable. In a way it's as if she is her own genteel berserker, subject to an invisible rage, compelled by a Madflower whose effect only she can perceive. It is equally understandable that she wouldn't be favorably inclined to those nameless biologists who had de-signed her. She owes them nothing, not even her life.

Her beauty is competent, exalting and frightening.

THE PROJECT'S AGENT

[Load Database] Her creators had used the tried and true Standard Hostage Method: they knew that Yezeletta's affiliation with the disembodied

                                Christian Madsen

intelligence within the then much-smaller Matrix Engine was one handle that they had on their creation. She could be controlled by that relationship. While it lasted.

At first they didn't want to kill her: a convenient fatal accident would be the best way to deal with her, but—here a note of bureaucratic-practicality entered—a lot of time, money and work had gone into Yezeletta's creation. It might be desirable to get her back after keeping her in cold storage for an indeterminate time. Their classic mistake was in assuming that she was as inanimate an object as more traditional weapons.

A parent can control its offspring. Right up to the time when that offspring develops her own personality and desires. Control then ceases. Similarly, a skilled programmer can take the elements of a computer language, and adapt them to uses for which the designers of the language had never planned. Yezeletta Zargkonji did the same within her own general specializations. She had been designed as a high-tech warrior. In the event of war, she, and others like her, would have been turned loose with enough support to serve as independent forces, to harry and harass the enemy.

Very well. She had her enemy.

The prize was her own life.

This was the fight for which she had been *built*.

STATUS CHECK

Her communicator awaits outside the window, looking in from the branches of a large maple tree whose leaves brush close to her window. She is on the third floor, and is occupied at the present time. The individual within— engaged in acts that don't even have a type-descriptor to the communicator's kind—apparently will not leave until she has done all the things that the communicator has seen her doing, without understanding them, many times before in the last year.

The communicator feels an emotion like anxiety. What it has <u>must</u> be delivered. The longer it must wait, the more anxious it will get. The communicator doesn't realize this; it's not part of its design. The unsettling feeling will get more intense, until it reaches an endpoint. There it will remain, until the communicator communicates.

And *this message* is non-trivial.

As with other concepts, the dry mathematical language doesn't convey the urgency of the extra descriptorial data surrounding the actual message. To the communicator, it simply exacerbates the already high level of anxiety it is experiencing.

Unable to comprehend, unable to stop the occurrence, the communicator sits on its tree-branch, and remains still, unmoving. While inside, it is shaking violently. A shaking of its mind, undetectable in the night.

THE SHADOWS

While the Lenhadens were sound asleep in their room, secure in the reasonable thoughts that all of their preparations were made, and that they were safe, a meeting of another kind was taking place in a smelly room on the first floor of the hotel.

The girl who had checked Hank Lenhaden into the hotel was talking urgently to several others, all of them larger than she was, and all but one other, male. She spoke in low tones, even though the room's door was closed and there were no hotel guests on the first floor.

She went to the window, and gestured. The long, black pick-up looked like a sleeping automaton in the night. A metallic artifact of pure power, although resting. She described the Lenhadens exactly.

Two of the others, a young man, and his partner, a slender woman who wore a brown leather jacket, recognized the truck's owners.

The others left, leaving one male human with the hotel clerk.

Had the Lenhadens known that they were being observed, or of the intelligences of the observers, they might have taken other courses of action.

As soon as the other conspirators had left, the hotel clerk shed her ragged clothes with a practiced motion of her hands and hips, and lay down on the large mattress that occupied another corner of the room. She spread her legs.

The remaining individual knelt down to attend.

STATUS RESPONSE

Finally she was alone. Her communicator—filled with a nameless frustration that it was not equipped to understand—jumped across the two meters of intervening space, and landed on the outer window-sill. It tapped on the screen. She looked up, beckoned with one hand, her left.

The little creature lifted a corner of the screen, and entered the room.

STATUS ACTION

Leona looked up at the window, and gave the appropriate hand signal. Her communicator came in through where she had slit the screen, and hop, hop, hopped up to her. *It bounces like a big kitten*, she thought.

MESSAGE DELIVERED

The communicator whispers to her softly in Yezeletta's voice. Her speech echoes out of the small furry creature after being transmitted by other means from downtown. The instructions are precise and urgent. Later that night several more small creatures will show up, bearing other supplies.

Yezeletta asks her to check her wardrobe. The wardrobe that Zhongo doesn't know that she has.

Absently, Leona checks beneath the waterbed mattress. The weapons are there, but she tells her friend that she would like something in addition. There is talk of activities elsewhere.

But she doesn't know where.

THE HILL WATCHES

Frank Davidson opened the envelope from Cartography with his pocket-knife, and removed the images he had asked for. He studied one of them for a moment with a magnifying glass, then turned his chair around, and faced the holographic display system that shared his cubicle with him. This device resembled an octagonal poker table, but had a ten-sided metal plate in the center that covered nearly all of what would be the playing area. He inserted the photos into the document scanner, the device thought for a moment, and a three dimensional hologram built up on the flat, metallic surface of the table.

Frank's office was on the same side of the building as Edna's. The Madison sky-line was lit in patterns of red and gold from the brilliant red, distorted sphere of the Sun on the horizon, and the dome of Wisconsin's Capitol Building had a red-gold coloration.

It was a prettier sight than the images on these satellite photos. Even seen as holograms.

He walked around the table, looking at the details intently, pensively. The three farms and their surrounding areas were the ones that Edna had shown him the week before.

The infra-red signature of chlorophyll was something that the satellite camera's post-processing was designed to look for and flag. These were false-color images: the colors weren't "natural;" they were artificially adjusted so that frequencies being sought, the infra-red frequencies of green, growing things, would stand out. On these images, chlorophyll was supposed to be the brightest green that the Department's laser printers, or the holographic display, could generate, with other frequencies—the signatures of dusty or unplanted areas, in particular—printed or displayed in duller, more pastel colors.

There was very little bright green in the Milwaukee, Racine and Kenosha areas. Nor was there anything that particularly stood out in Rock County, further west. It was about the same in Northern Illinois: Lake, McHenry, Cook, DuPage and Kane Counties were expanses of gray-green, as dull as the areas to the north.

Small wonder those farmers were pissed!

Frank removed the originals from the scanner and put them back in the envelope to send back to Cartography. He paused.

Then he put the envelope in his own desk. Elaine might want to look at these herself after she read his report. He pulled up his word-processor in a convenient window, and made several entries.

Besides, this area might bear further observation.

BASIC RESEARCH

In his warehouse-turned-laboratory, Zeke arranged flood-lights around the stone slab that was holding up the body of Ex-Lead-Foot Eddie. Zeke's surgical tools were laid out on a stainless steel cart, nearby. He reached up to a rack-mount, and switched on a classical music station. He came in on the first movement of Beethoven's Seventh Symphony.

Lead-Foot Eddie lay obscenely naked on the slab. The "slab" was actually one of the edge-guttered work tables of the kind used by morticians. Zeke adjusted the vacuum hose that would be used for exsanguination and regarded his project.

Hmmmm.

He set his scalpel down, and went to his supply cabinet.

The familiar flat, yellow boxes with the equally familiar black logo were on the top shelf. He took the X-Ray film down, entered the small windowless room that he used for processing.

He laid out film-holders and film, studied the layout, and switched off the light.

With practiced motions, he removed a sheet of film from the pack, and inserted it in the film carrier and closed it. He ran his hands over the film box, to verify that the light-seal was intact, and hit the light switch with his elbow. He set the loaded carrier aside, elbowed the light off and loaded the others.

His X-Ray machine would not have won any prizes for safety, but Zeke worked alone and knew the dangers of using the device. It had begun as an antique shoe-store fluoroscope from the mid nineteen-fifties. He had found it, boxed up and stored in one of Zhongo's warehouses, in almost new condition. He had removed the small, spindly-looking X-Ray tube from its chassis and mounted it in something that made it look like a parody of a gooseneck lamp. It had proved useful for such occupational hazards as bullet wounds.

Zeke positioned the X-Ray emitter over Lead-Foot's head. He frowned; "face" didn't seem too appropriate. He wanted to see what was inside Eddie's amazing faceless head, before disturbing that obscene expanse of unadorned flesh with a knife!

He put on a pair of surgical rubber gloves, lifted Eddie's head, and slid the film under it. Eddie's head lolled to one side; Zeke braced it with old washrags. He lowered the gooseneck and retired to the control area for the X-Rays.

This was why he worked alone. His bargain-basement X-Ray machine was more general in its emissions than was safe. Zeke had created a small lead- and steel-lined cubicle where his contraption's controls were located. He went there, flipped off the overhead lights, keyed an exposure into his control unit, and pressed the start button.

There was a slight blue glow from the head of the gooseneck that lasted several seconds: it was from fluorescent paint around the emission side of the tube; the radiation itself was invisible. When it went out, he flipped on the overheads, and came out.

He put the exposed film in the control booth, and repeated the process, taking right and left side shots, and one more from underneath—there was a hole in the slab for this—with the film in a bracket above Eddie's head, for a back shot.

"Of course," he said to no one in particular, "The back and front shots will be almost identical, won't they? I might as well be as thorough as I can."

Beethoven had no comment. The second movement was well under way.

Whistling along with the music, Zeke carried the films back to his darkroom, and checked the temperatures of his solutions. He adjusted a water flow, checked the temperature again, and went back out to take the gooseneck down.

The third movement of Beethoven's Seventh began as he closed the darkroom door and got to work.

NIGHT-SPEAK

Late in the afternoon, almost evening, Yezeletta takes Joe into her bedroom. She stretches impressively, and sits down on the bed. Several small creatures move large pillows into place, so that she can lounge back. She is at ease in her own environment. Almost carelessly, she allows her legs to sprawl as they wish on the water bed. Yezeletta looks up at Joe, then to a place next to her.

"Got it," Joe says. He sits with her.

She takes his hand, his right in her left, her lower.

Joe moves closer, places his other hand, his left, around Yezeletta. The embrace is tentative, slow; each tries to understand the other. The hug that follows is by no means slow.

THE RIDE AND THE RIDER

[On Location] Miranda Hendrickx cleared her desk off, shoving papers into the center drawer. She stood, stretched, grabbed her purse, and left her office. On her way to the front closet, one of her co-workers waved to her. "Night, Miranda," he said.

"G'night," she replied, absently.

She grabbed her coat, shrugged into it, and left the office.

Outside she nodded to acquaintances at the elevator, and rode it down to the first floor.

She exited the Wrigley Building's east lobby, and surveyed the Michigan Avenue traffic for a taxi.

That one would do, over there. She waved to it.

IN THE GARDEN OF GOOD AND EVIL

[Match Cut] In an opening in a room on the south side of Chicago, in a place on that city's south side that was practically a war zone, stands a building that hasn't seen occupation or use for nearly fifty years. In its prime, it was a small hotel. Now it is a silent landmark in a place to which the remains of the Chicago Police Department sends squads only in groups. Large groups. Deep within the structure—still standing as a testimonial to its long-dead builders—several of the rooms are sealed off. The actual sealing was largely accidental. There were no Chicago gangsters walled up alive within these rooms, nor were there any of Chicago's multiple street gangs here. The rooms were on the wrong side of storage areas, or bad attempts at remodeling, and the entrances were covered with stored items, and then forgotten.

In one of these rooms—located deep within the forgotten structure—a small family of mice had made its residence. The dark, open area of the room was a warm place, proof against the cold of a Chicago winter. Dark, as a place to raise baby rodents should be, and protected from feline interlopers, the room—once a medium rental room for a transient resident—had been for many years a secure shelter.

The rodent residents went about their business, neither knowing nor caring what was outside. Nor did they care what happened within their shelter.

Nor did they remember. Nor could they.

The glowing area first appeared in the center of the room up near the ceiling. The glow—a light blue—appeared for a short time, then disappeared. A day later, the glow appeared again, closer to the floor. Had the mice inhabiting the room cared about such things, they would have noticed it moving slowly upwards, the blue color casting dark shadows that moved along the walls.

The light vanished.

It did not return for nearly a week, and when it did, it was no longer a simple point of light. It had expanded to a blue, glowing sphere nearly half a meter in diameter, far brighter in a room that hadn't known any light at all for nearly fifty years.

The glow stayed this time, for nearly a day, vanished, and returned, again: a cold lambent light of no known source.

It vanished three days later. The memories of its appearance stayed in the short-term memories of the mice for nearly an hour after that, then went where all short-term memories went.

The light would be back one more time, after that. It would appear for another three days, expand to about a meter in diameter, and glow even brighter than before.

When it vanished that last time, the short-term memories of the mice witnessing its show would last nearly ninety minutes before being forgotten forever.

ANOTHER PART OF THE GARDEN

[Input Process; Extreme Close-Up] Several kilometers north of the remaining memories of a dozen mice, a Yellow Cab pulled up in response to the waving of a dark-haired woman standing in front of the white expanse of the Wrigley Building.

Her steel blue eyes flashed as she stepped out to the curb. The Yellow weaved through the crowded evening traffic, a predator among the other fish, homing in. She watched the vehicle's progress with wary eyes.

Chicago was like that. These days, a combination of the intelligent and the animal. You learned the difference in a hurry and, in Miranda's line of work, you were *trained* to notice differences. She looked sharply east and west at the traffic and mostly thought of getting through the rush hour and getting home.

The taxi pulled over to the curb.

A man in the front passenger seat looked at her, beckoned.

Another passenger? she thought. She picked up her briefcase, went to the back passenger door.

The man aimed something at her.

She became dizzy, her vision fading in a coruscation of multicolored patterns that strobed and flickered against the gray background of her consciousness.

She was aware of falling against the side of the car. Then she could feel hands grabbing her roughly, and hauling her into the back seat.

She remembered nothing after that.

HEAD SHOTS

Zeke hung the X-Rays up to dry, and shook his head in disbelief. He had seen the photographic templates used to lay out integrated circuits before—he even had some little ceramic things, trivets and the like, handed out by the "chip" companies as adverts, that showed enlarged versions of their wares. This was not outrageous. *This* had gone past crazy. Well past weird.

"We no longer live in Interesting Times," he said. "We have gone past that to the Downright Fascinating!"

He used one finger to move one of the films by an edge so he could see it easier against a light in the background. What was there was...impossible, wasn't it?

Wasn't it?

BIG NIGHT MUSIC

Joe and Yezeletta lie in each other's arms for a time. Gently, she disengages from him in response to a soft commotion near the door. One of her servitors enters, carrying something on a tray. The creature sets the tray on a device, and swings the device out over the bed. At that point, Joe can see what it is: a cantilever on a pivot, designed to hold a small table or a serving tray above a very large bed. Another servitor holds something out, that Yezeletta takes in one large hand, her upper. She places it on the tray.

She has a tentative little smile, as she looks at Joe, and removes the covering from the tray.

On the tray are an assortment of cheeses and other snacks. The other item is a bottle of wine.

"Would you do the honors?" she asks.

TURN A CORNER

Very few things in organic development are organized along straight lines. An elephant's tusks, for example, are not straight spears of ivory, they are curved. They evolved this way to allow the elephant to lift things easily, while still being useful as weapons. A spider's legs aren't angular, with multiple knee joints; they, too, have curved segments. *Perhaps on some planet where the people speak in radio-waves, and have wave-guides in their throats, things would be that kind of straight!* Zeke thought, looking at the impossible right-angles, and equally impossible arrays of parallel lines that he saw in the X-Ray photos. He squinted through a jeweler's loupe at the pictures.

Some of the lines were just at the edge of the resolution of his eye, even helped by the loupe. The ultra-fine-grain of the film would resolve down to one-hundred lines per millimeter: it was a trade-off between film sensitivity, or "speed" (to allow for shorter, safer exposures to the X-Rays), and fine degree of grain (to allow for more detail at the expense of sensitivity).

At this point one way or the other simply didn't matter. It was the detailing in the images themselves that was, was—

Was there in the pictures of the insides of Lead-Foot Eddie's head.

Zeke readied an overhead projector for later investigation of what he now thought of as "Shoot Number One." Then he got his carriers and film, and took another film box from the freezer.

He went back to the darkroom to reload.

This is gonna be a long night.

GARDENERS AND RIDERS

[Load Segment] When Miranda awoke, she was lying on the top of a clean bedspread on a clean bed in a room that looked a part of an upscale hotel chain. She was dressed in the same things, none the worse for wear, that she had been wearing in her office.

She rolled onto her side, and scanned the room again.

This motion was a signal. When she stopped her movement, the door opened, and an individual entered. He looked a kind of anonymous "ordinary" that she suspected was the result of a disguise. She knew it when an opalescent haze flickered across his face.

"Where am I?"

"You are in a place where we will ask you to do a job," the individual in the hologram said without preamble.

"What sort of job?" she asked, sharply.

"One within your chosen skill-set," the other said.

Right, she thought, *Who is this bozo?* "What?" she said.

"We will have need of your, ah, services. If you perform well, we will take you to the place of your choice, and pay you extremely well. Or you could refuse. Would anyone miss you?"

She didn't need to answer that. There were some, and some whom she would be just as happy to never see again. On her terms.

"May I ask you your name?"

She thought about that. Real? or not?

She decided on real. She had other identities for other places. Her line of work required them.

"Miranda," she said, "Miranda Hendrickx."

"Very well, Miranda. Dinner will be served shortly. For various reasons we will require you to take your meals here in your room. I trust that will be— acceptable?"

"Of course," she said, You mean, like I have a choice?

The individual in the hologram left, closing the door with a sharp, metallic click.

Miranda went to the door, and, as she suspected, it was locked.

Near the door was a table, and near that was an easy-chair. Its softness was very inviting. Starting to feel exhausted, she sat in it, and leaned back.

Dinner. He said Dinner, she thought. Then: Where the hell am I?

O N   W I S C O N S I N

[Code at Ring Zero] Yezeletta lies back, stretching out, as she and Joe finish up the light snack her servitors have brought in. Yezeletta stretches, almost able to touch the opposing walls of the bedroom, but not quite. As before, the small creatures that she's created arrange cushions for Joe that place his gaze on a level with hers.

"That guy you had in your—uh—laboratory. You mentioned him in connection with Leona."

Yezeletta nods, "That's Tim. Tim O'Shaughnessy. I met him through one of the less-known businessmen in Milwaukee.

"What happened?"

"Tim works for Gray Roger. He was trying to reclaim Leona for Roger, when Leona decided to leave Roger's employ."

"So the Invisible Man wanted her back, and went after her."

"Yep! He chased Leona up Wisconsin Avenue, and she ran into the parking ramp under this building. Her presence set off several of my detection devices, and I saw what was happening. I went down to deal with Tim." Yezeletta smiles, an expression without mirth, "I put Tim on ice for a time, then sent him back to Roger with a good industrial-strength case of amnesia, and brought Leona up here."

Yezeletta stretches her legs, and adjusts the pillows around herself. She lies full-length next to Joe, looking both smaller, and more dominant at the same time.

"There are many 'replications' of guys like Tim," she continues, "I had an experience with someone rather like him earlier. When I escaped from Australia, there was a shipper in the Darwin harbor—one of those cargo ships that can take passengers—these radicals from San Francisco had found out about the Project."

"Not as secret as they wanted it?"

Yezeletta makes a face. "I'm reminded of a kitten with its head under a blanket and its little bottom sticking out that thinks it's hiding. The Project kept *me* secret. It kept the personnel there secret. Most of it was well-kept under wraps, but every now and then, something got out. A 'something' might not be traceable back to Alice Springs but anyone there would recognize that 'something' as derivative of the place. Then the Admin people would run another one of their tedious internal affairs investigations, and someone who had nothing to do with the leak would get selected as the Scapegoat of the Month, and sacked."

"Sounds like a wonderful place," Joe starts, and Yezeletta gives him a sharp look, "to be *from*." Her look eases up. "What happened then?"

"A man named Charlie tried to inflict himself on me."

"Isn't that just a little dangerous?" Joe asks.

"If I'm not interested, it is. I caused him some serious loss of face aboard the *Hat Dancer*—"

"**?**" Joe's eyebrows said.

"The passenger-freighter I commandeered at Darwin. These—radical-nerds would be a good name for them, I guess—had one of those 'leaks' from the project. Charlie was one of them, and thought that he was the ultimate gift to all women.

"He made the mistake of trying to take me."

As Yezeletta speaks, a furry, arachnoidal creature scampers up to her. It hands her a folder that flaps open to disclose several sheets of paper. She hands one of the sheets to Joe.

"This," she says (is that a note of mirth in her voice?), "is an artist's conception of me."

The picture is of a multilegged insect, resembling a preying mantis. One with—

"Where did this come from?" Joe asks.

"The *National Enquirer's* Web Site," her voice is dead-pan, her face suitable for a poker game.

"That's gotta be a joke. Who ever heard of *tits* on an insect?"

"Who, indeed?" Yezeletta asks, allowing herself to chuckle. "The National Enquirer's artists, they're actually very good, by the way, *had* to add those cones to the sketch, or the managing editor probably wouldn't have published it." Yezeletta pointed to a detail.

"The view behind that insect is a very good representation, with all of the identifying characteristics removed, of the northern view from the windows of the cafeteria at the project. Those windows faced into a large courtyard that I was sometimes allowed out into, when the satellites from the Tech Bloc weren't overhead." Yezeletta looks thoughtful for a moment. "I have several other rather puzzling memories of my own that involve the orientation of the Sun and the Moon."

"'To tell a lie, base it on Truth'," Joe quotes.

"Again, exactly so," Yezeletta takes a deep breath. "That one got the press liaison fired."

"Press?"

"You might think that there's no need for that," Yezeletta says. "His job was actually to deflect enquiries from the press, rather than to answer questions. When Security found this on the Enquirer's Web Site, they, I believe the expression used then was, 'went into orbit'."

"Okay, they went ballistic. Who had this clip?"

"The—I like to think of him as the Alpha Nerd. Proving that being one doesn't require brains. Just endowments a little further down."

"Charlie?"

"No. Definitely not," Yezeletta said, "Charlie would have liked to be the Alpha Nerd, but all he thought of was being dominant in a very narrow way. He thought that all women were his any time, any day, any way. I don't know why the real leader didn't get rid of him. Maybe I should have."

[Pass Two] "When did you meet him, first?"

Yezeletta takes a deep breath, lets it out slowly. "The radicals—they called themselves the 'July Seventeenth Brigade', don't ask me why—wanted me, or whatever they thought I was, originally, to be their secret weapon. I was supposed to help them take over the American west coast. Or at least California."

"You wouldn't have been able to hide from anyone, then."

"That's an understatement," Yezeletta says. "If there's anything calculated to attract the attention of Project scientists with too much time on their hands, it's the sort of infiltration I was designed for, happening in California!" She gestures at small, furry multilegged critters watching them with their gold imagers, the servitors standing nearby, waiting for an order telegraphed with a hand motion, a transmitted instruction or a spoken word. "My accession of Milwaukee is sufficiently quiet that almost no one knows that there's anything unusual going on. The Hives are very well hidden, usually under things that are substantial enough—the Bradley Center, for instance—that they're not readily moved, and other lifeforms are kept out of casual sight."

"Except from the gangsters," Joe replies.

"They concern me," Yezeletta's voice, never far from serious, gets even more so. "I don't know what they know, and Secret Agent Leona, the 'moll,' hasn't been able to get any information. The warning I've sent him, the corpse I reorganized, is coming from a direction that I hope looks like from Chicago, or further away. If they think there's a government behind it, it would be ideal."

"I thought that was a little blatant."

"And you didn't want to say it. Joe, If you're going to partner with me, tell me what's on your mind."

Joe gives Yezeletta a sweep with his eyes that he hopes is complementary. Yezeletta's gaze follows his. *She even sees that my look stops at all of the interesting places!*

"So they have a pistolero who's 'lost face'," Joe continues. "What then?"

"I *hope* that the lout that uses my imagers as pistol targets will get the idea and quit. In the meantime, ever heard the expression 'go to the mattresses'?"

"I've seen *The Godfather*. They set up a safe-house for their torpedoes, a house full of mattresses: a barracks that hits can be based from."

"Yes. All of my imagers have gone to the mattresses. The ones that are still out are the minimum that I need to keep eyes on things. Recently, Zhongo gave Leona access to most of his operations. I think he is training her as his executive assistant. The fact that he's promoted her from bed partner to actually bringing her into the organization is very significant. Both that it's happened, and the speed with which it's happened. He seems to have developed considerable respect for her intelligence rather quickly."

"You did say that Zhongo's good at picking the right one for the job."

"We're lucky that he picked her. She had a lot to do with that," Yezeletta said.

"She's his kept woman."

"If he really knew, he wouldn't think that."

[Intermediate Pass] Yezeletta pauses for a short time, and Joe is reticent about dropping words into the widening pool of silence around her. Yezeletta puts a right arm around Joe, and gently pulls him closer. She adds her other right arm, and gently rubs his back. Joe adds to the hug, stroking her back with his left hand.

"I have other problems with these gangsters, as well," she says.

She pauses again in thought. Joe studies her face looking for some expression, a key to her inner thoughts. She seems to be reviewing her past to decide what to tell him next. His eyes stray to some of those interesting places, and her capable vision follows the track of his gaze.

"In a way, you are at the center of some of my problems with such as Zhongo"

Joe is surprised. "Me?" is all he can say.

Yezeletta rolls partially on to her back, pulling Joe with her. She grins.

"You!" she says. Why did you come to Milwaukee? Why do you think you interested me?"

"Uh, well, you *did* sorta scoop me up when I got here. Did you know I was coming?" The feeling in his stomach is mostly, but not totally, overcome by either his fascination or the other effects of being this close to her.

Her voice is gentle, her presence close, erotic. She raises one dark eyebrow in curiosity, and her gold eyes open wide, the irises large, dark windows of interest.

"Your turn," she says, "Why did you come here?"

ARCHIVE LOAD: INTERMEDIATE

[About a Year Earlier] The letter Joe had received from the University of California System was short and pointed. He had been gone the previous week to see Hannah, and had driven into Los Angeles rather late. Several hours of work spent removing items from his office at the Biological Computing Center took up the rest of Friday Evening, and he returned home just before midnight.

A TEMPORARY BASE

[Running] When he returned to his apartment, he found his mail-box filled to overflowing, and a polite note from the post-man: "Additional Mail Left at the Manager's Office."

The building manager was gone for the weekend, so Joe had to wait for the final answer until Monday Evening, still the News-in-Progress was not what he expected:

> *Dear Mr. Davis: [It began]*
>
> *It is the policy of the California Higher Education System that all research derived from public monies be copyrighted in the name of the Board of Regents [Here, there was a list of nine names] , and that all such copyrights are released to the public domain. It is in this fashion that research that has been done in the public trust—*

[Why didn't you put that in capitals, he wondered]

> *—is returned to the public that financed it.*

[Even the dangerous stuff? Joe thought] .

> *Accordingly, we require a written appeal if a researcher wishes his work restricted. We acknowledge the receipt of your appeal, and the Regents will make their recommendation on [here the previous Friday's date appeared] .*
>
> *Thank you for your concern.*
>
> *[Signature]*

He tossed the letter on the kitchen table, and scowled. He had been the lucky creator of a "short-cut" into recombined DNA synthesis that had resulted in making the creation of complex bio-chemicals orders of magnitude easier than it had been, before. Protein synthesis had taken huge multiprocessing computers, complex programming and the kind of technique that would parcel out the trillions of computations among the thousands of central processing units in the typical Large Matrix Computer.

In a way, the data-processing requirements for synthesis at that low a level had parallelled the evolution of early computing equipment. Early computers had been huge, complicated and expensive, and owned only by large, wealthy organizations. Then microprocessor technology had literally placed super-computers on desk-tops, and the wealthy had gone for the many-processor models that were still too expensive for the average individual who basically needed a smart household appliance.

And Joe Davis had short-circuited the requirements.

His Protocols allowed samples to be "scanned" then replicated. Ordinary house-plants could become the scanners and then the sources for anything that was useful.

And that was the problem, as he had seen it. Almost anything could be fabricated. By almost anyone.

The following Monday, he returned to his office with a nap-sack of computer media and an attitude.

When he left, all of his research materials left with him. That evening, he removed the remainder of his personal effects, and, for all practical purposes, bid the Bio-Comp Center a last farewell.

The various tools he had designed, and other items that he had made mods to went into his car, and into storage in various places.

He went back to his old office one more time to bid farewell to friends and acquaintances, and was not surprised to find that his office was empty. It had been cleaned out to the walls.

Joe Davis directed his travels east.

ROAD WORK

[I/O Driver] Rodrigo Martinez, a man of average height and weight sat in the driver's seat of the eighteen-wheeler, waiting for the truck ahead of him to clear the on ramp.

The metered ramp's light blinked green and Rodrigo's huge Peterbilt lurched ahead, and accelerated on its way onto the highway. Rod shifted gears and moved smoothly out following the other.

He was driving the support truck for the Chapel of the Highways. This was a church-on-wheels that was operated by the Southern Baptist Conference as a mobile source of devotional services for truck drivers on the road that wanted such.

He was pulling out of Las Vegas, *always a good source of parishioners!*, he thought, and would be driving north into Utah for the Chapel's next stop. Rod's little caravan was one of three that the Baptists maintained.

The open road always brought something new, something different. The Chapel of the Highways countered that, for the faithful, with something else that was friendly and familiar.

FOLLOW THE LINKS

[Running] Joe went back to his cousin Hannah and spent an afternoon asking gentle questions of Victor. Then he drove to where Victor's "miracle" had happened. On his way, he had stopped for gas, road-maps, and miscellaneous reading matter. The attendant at the little store that shared the lot with the filling station stuffed several newspapers, magazines, two or three tabloids (Hannah had reminded him to "get something funny"), and bags of road snacks into two large bags, and he took them back and tossed them on the passenger seat.

They had waved as he pulled out. It was good to see them smiling, again.

The river was near the small town of Fairview. Victor's directions had been specific, and Joe followed the meticulously drawn map to the location where Victor had found his way back to the seeing.

The trip was a short one: Victor had walked it in a matter of a half an hour, and Joe's car covered the distance in minutes.

Somehow, not two weeks back, *something* had done a deed for his cousin that all of the medical knowledge of the current day was unable to in that short a time-frame.

A bridge led to a turnoff into the wayside. Under several trees, a row of picnic tables had been stacked up at an angle, covered with tarps and tied down against the winter elements.

He parked the car at a distance and reached his thirty-five millimeter camera from its case.

The area that led down to the river was crossed and re-crossed with footprints and tire tracks, Joe checked the frame-counter on his camera and stood where Victor had.

Right. There. A single metal and wood park-bench, tacked down on a small concrete slab. Rick had been standing in front of this when the "English Lady" had come to him.

There should be footprints, and...*there!* A barely visible set of tracks made by small shoes and short legs went from next to the bench around to the front, and then down to the river's edge, to be met by....

Joe Davis was in his late twenties. He stood one-hundred-eighty-three centimeters, or six feet in the old system. He was muscular, and not afraid of much. He had received the best education that schools in Los Angeles and Chicago could provide, excelling in what he'd studied.

But this was just a bit too much!

The small footprints had been met by a pair of bare feet. *Big* feet. Joe dropped a small plastic ruler, for scaling, on the ground where the sets of prints met, and took several snapshots. He retrieved the ruler, stepped carefully around the tracks, and went to the river's edge.

The large—what? Nineteen, 10-E?—footprints seemed to come out of the river!

There seemed to be two sets.

"If I didn't know better, I'd say I've fallen into the lead story in the latest National Enquirer," Joe said to the rustling trees. "Maybe there really are 'UFO-Aliens'!"

He grinned. That term was the standard tabloid short-hand for any kind of alleged invaders. He hadn't seen the word "alien" once in those periodicals without the prefixing "UFO."

The kind of people who took the *Enquirer's* stories seriously probably had to have something familiar to jump-start their fantasies. A password to another place, where Joe and Hannah were content to leave them.

Yet those footprints, both sets, were there, demonstrably made by someone. Perhaps *two* someones.

And a small boy had been the benefactor.

Joe took several more pictures of the prints; he tracked them from the river to the bench, and from there to a grassy area where everything vanished in untrimmed turf.

He ranged a bit farther. Over there was a parking lot—it wasn't much: gravel on dirt. He kept to the grass as he went to the divide where gravel left off and grass started.

Footprints!

Some large, some not. There were a lot of small tracks as of children on a fall field-trip, and—

Joe looked around himself. Feeling cold all over, he turned slowly through a full circle looking for something. Something that he was unable to articulate, someone or something *that had made the double set of large footprints that had come from truck ruts at the edge of the lot.*

He clicked off pictures at a rapid rate. He aimed at one more, pressed the shutter, and a whirring in the camera indicated that it had been the end of the roll: the camera was rewinding the film. He walked, almost ran, back to the car, left the exposed roll in the glove-box, and returned with a pocketful of unexposed films.

He regarded those large footprints, again.

Normal bare-foot-prints were deeper at the ball of the foot. It was where an individual "lifted-off" when taking a step. These prints were ambiguous. Sometimes the heels were deeper, sometimes not. Who would walk that way? *Perhaps a dancer.*

He reloaded the camera with fine-grain low-speed color, and turned on the flash. He walked around the edges of the parking lot dropping the ruler next to a set of prints, taking a bracketed set of exposures, and reeling the ruler in on a piece of string.

Joe went back to the river, again. He was up-stream by a matter of fifteen meters. There were tracks here, too!

They looked like rabbit tracks in fresh snow. Joe scaled and snapped a series of the tracks, which seemed to run parallel to the river back to a point almost directly—he looked over his shoulder (with some apprehension)—almost, nothing: the "rabbit tracks" and the duplicate sets of large bare feet *met* in front of the park bench. It looked as if it had been *by design.*

Was the English Lady a naturalist? A hunter? A nudist? He recalled Victor's observation. Victor hadn't heard shots, either the gun or the camera kind. Maybe she was someone animals genuinely liked.

He returned to the parking lot.

Gravel doesn't take tracks the way dirt does, but large vehicles would leave "waves" in the distribution of the stones that wouldn't move much in weather.

Joe took a three f/stop bracket of the parking lot with a wide-angle lens, so that he could combine the images digitally later, and went back to his car.

He was looking forward to seeing the results.

AN ATHLETIC ENTERPRISE

[Segment Swap] At about the same time that Joe Davis was taking pictures in Montana, several cameramen were setting up their equipment in a place beneath a conspicuous, if unused, landmark in Milwaukee.

They were in an underground auditorium.

Around them, seats were mounted up inclines on all four sides of the eight-sided ring that was the center of this establishment. The wiring for television was in place. All that remained were lighting and sound checks, and the arrival of the audience.

Sounds of crowds milling around the entrances centered in each of the four outer walls indicated that things would start shortly. The foreman of the camera crew made his final checks, and the others climbed aboard the camera booms that would allow them to move in for close-ups.

Close-ups were always a requirement.

The cameras raised up and moved back from the ring, and the foreman gave terse commands over his headset to the others.

Loud, boisterous in its anticipation, the crowd entered.

THE PLAYERS

[Load Record] Two well-dressed men walked into the auditorium from opposite sides. As they reached their reserved front-row seats, they nodded, a gesture visible only between them.

Zhongo Teketon, his friends and the usual collection of body-guards clustered around the north side of the ring.

Sideways from him on the west side, Allen Hightower sat with his wife, the delicate and demure Marie, who held onto Allen's hand, tightly.

Zhongo knew that although Allen didn't have much in the way of security, he was in his own element. Few really knew it, but Zhongo did: this layout was Allen's private domain. He was at home here.

To the south: another.

The one Zhongo had nodded to: a grotesquely short man, who comported himself as if he were two-hundred centimeters tall: Gary Hamilton.

Their contestants would meet. Later, tonight.

This was the dress rehearsal.

INTERIM TRANSLATION

[Running] The two large trucks pulled into the area around Fairview. When they were done here, Rod and Bill, and all of the rest of the Chapel Staff would roll on to Billings.

But they needed to stop here, first. The truck-stops in the area had never been visited before.

THE GAME

[Swap] "Ladies and Gentlemen!" the Master of Ceremonies intoned, "Tonight we present the playoff between the dynamitic power of Force Majeure and the irresistible strength of The Reactor!" The audience replied with muffled applause.

The applause, the cheering got louder when the principals to the action jumped into the stage that surrounded the ring and began waving.

The emcee waited for a moment of quiet, "On this side, Force Majeure!"

The Force, a large man wearing a sweat-suit done in black with a gold overlay in stylized lightning bolts, raised his hands, and waved, grinning to his admirers in the audience. A troop of shapely girls wearing black and gold dresses ran out, and waved to the audience, then started chanting, "Run it red, cut it deep, Force Majeure will...." The rest was drowned out in a deafening cheer from the audience.

The announcer waited for silence, and then, "On this side, The Reactor!" A tall thin gangly man wearing a bright blue outfit with a stylized radiation emblem on the back hopped up next to the emcee. Like his opponent, he waved to the audience.

Another side of the audience cheered him on, in the back of the auditorium, people stood, waving at their heroes, and cameras flashed. Above him the TV cameras on their cantilevers moved in for close-ups. The Reactor didn't have a corps of cheerleaders; he did have several large friends on his side who took him to his corner.

"And!" the emcee continued, "Welcome to Slicer!" The crowd stood and cheered.

AUGMENTATIONS

[Process] The cameramen pulled their instruments back, and the lead camera's feed was sent to a large four-sided screen above the ring. Force Majeure and The Reactor jumped into the ring, shook hands in a distant fashion, and the emcee left the ring.

There was no music, no ringing of bells. The audience quieted in expectation.

The players circled, then ran for each other. They hit with a sound audible to the edges of the auditorium. Force Majeure spun, kicked once at The Reactor, then followed through with a left-right one-two punch propelled by his spinning body. The Reactor rebounded from the double blows, back-pedaled, and leaped over The Force, kicking him in the head as he passed.

Force Majeure backed into his corner, where his crew strapped several items to his wrists, "First Blood!" he called out to the cheering crowd.

At the Blood Call, the stage on which the ring was placed started turning, slowly, ponderously. The action within was now on a huge display showing itself to the cheering, stamping spectators.

The Force bounced out into the center of the ring, showing his fans what he wore: curved blades that arched out over the backs of his hands. The Reactor hopped into the center wearing similar weapons. Several rows near the ring began shouting, and the rest of the audience joined in, "slicer, slicer, slicer!"

A device descended from the center of the group of screens, and one of the cameras focused in on it. Spinning down on its cables was a spherical device, with a rotating disk at the bottom. As the sphere descended, the disk started spinning, and three lengths of steel wire extended from it. The disk was a propeller formed of fine steel whips.

It swung.

The sphere moved in a ponderous arc that got steadily larger. Force Majeure ducked out of the way, but The Reactor lost a small part of his blue costume to the Slicer propeller's motion, as the rotating ring took him into it. He twisted, and managed to avoid most of the rapidly spinning whips. The newer members of the audience gasped, older more experienced viewers applauded. The cameras zoomed in tightly on the bar-sinister slash of the Slicer's cut through the radiation symbol on his back. Younger members of the audience cheered in ragged tones.

Force Majeure charged The Reactor, bringing his wrist-blades down in a series of deadly arcs. The audience roared as blood spurted from The Re-actor's left leg. He ignored the cuts, jumped to his feet, and swung his knives at the oncoming Majeure.

Force Majeure ducked under the swinging pendulum, allowing the ring's rotation to carry him away from it, to a gasp from the spectators, and The Reactor followed. The Slicer swung back on its return arc, and the spinning whips lacerated The Reactor's shoulder, the rotation turning straight cuts in-to deadly, bleeding curves. The audience clapped, stomped, and roared as the cameras zoomed in for a full-color close-up that was projected on the overheads. Blood ran crimson in the ring, as Force Majeure spun, kicked, and The Reactor fell on his blind side, squarely into the path of the Slicer. The steel whips wrapped themselves around The Reactor's face, and a piece of his scalp snapped away, sliced off cleanly. Blood spurted like a fountain. He fell forward, and the ring attendants ducked under the Slicer to retrieve him.

Force Majeure Skipped around the edges of the ring waving to the audi-ence, while the cheerleaders snake-danced past their hero, basking in the noise. The front rows stood and several of the younger members ran down to be near their champion.

ON THE OTHER CHANNEL

[Compilation] In Montana, in the sports lounge of The Trucker's Haven, several truck drivers watched the end of the duel between Force Majeure and The Reactor. The cheerleaders had taken their tops off, and were leading Force Majeure's admirers in a victory cheer, while medics carried The Reactor out through one of the aisles, giving the audience a close-up view of the Force's skills.

The feed cut to a pair of announcers in dark suits who recounted the match in breathless tones, with close-ups, and slow-motion replays of the bloodier scenes.

Rodrigo Martinez, who had come into the TV lounge of The Trucker's Haven to see what all the noise was about, sat in the back, dazed. He had heard of such things, and his work with the Chapel had put him in contact with people—putative parishioners—who relished such entertainment.

Rod believed in a deity he saw as one of order, logic, and love, rather than an avenger. Privately, he was a live and let live man, who still had difficulties dealing with some of the activities of common people.

Particularly the slobbering intensity of the members of that audience!

COMING ATTRACTIONS

Back at the underground auditorium, the emcee was making time before the next bout.

"Tomorrow night, we have a double-triple-threat package featuring, the blade action of Harry Knotts, the bondage methods of Boris the Spider, sexy Lora The Midnight Executioner and Corrosive Kate!" As he shouted out the names, pictures of each contestant were displayed on the overhead screens. The crowd roared and clapped.

"AND: a knock-down tag-team blood-fest featuring The Collector," a man holding several large nets, "The Linker," another burly man with a coil of heavy chain on one arm, "and The Loader," a construction worker with a pick-axe. "They're going up against the Three Harridans, Lana Upchuck, The Queen of Nausea," A picture of a middle-aged woman holding a spray-gun in one hand, and a gas-mask in the other, "Cathy Boobarella, whose one-hundred-fifty centimeter double-J's are a double knockout! That's fifty-eight inches, folks!" a picture of a tall slender woman with enormous breasts barely contained by a chain-mail bikini top that sprouted gleaming steel thorns, "AND: Sneaky Smythe the Scythe! Don't turn around on her or she'll cut your heart out from the back!" The last picture was of another woman with gray hair, and an expression of pure malice.

FIND THE HAVEN

[Parsing] Rodrigo walked away from the Coming Attractions still dazed, shaking his head, leaving others to the consequences of their own reactions. He joined his friends at a table at the opposite end of the Haven from the sports lounge, and they ate a quiet, rather light meal.

ROAD-WORK

[Scanning] Joe Davis drove east out of Fairview, thinking of the pictures he'd shot and of other things. A one-hour developing service at the Fairview Walgreen's had not only developed all of his films and provided prints, it had scanned the pictures, and placed them on several memory modules. These were packed with his laptop computer.

He pulled over to the side of the road, and unfolded a map covered with notes.

It was safe to guesstimate that the source of Victor's cure had been driving. If not, then maybe there really *were* such things as UFO-aliens, so: first approximation, wheeled traffic. Rather large wheeled traffic. Those tracks in the parking lot, left as "waves" in the gravel indicated some pretty hefty transport.

Where would such be likely to go afterwards? Were they going east? That was worth a try for a few miles. He could try west, later.

The map indicated both a truck stop and a public rest stop beyond that.

The staff at The Trucker's Haven might even be of help.

SCENES IN THE LOUNGE

Joe pulled into The Haven half an hour later, parked in an out of the way place and went into the restaurant.

He took a table in a corner facing out, and watched the other clientele come and go. Several drivers were as standoffish as Joe, eating quietly in another corner. There was conversation that ebbed and flowed like waves across the dining area. There was an intensity to the sound that Joe recognized, but couldn't place.

The large video screen in the lounge was displaying a news announcer discussing the latest Packers-Bears game, when the screen abruptly went dark. Then the expanse of blackness was replaced by a test pattern.

Joe was used to the occasional problems with television transmission. The aging comsats that the United States still had in service worked, but sometimes had to be coaxed back to acceptable performance.

The test pattern vanished to be replaced by a rippling rainbow design, a color and resolution display, a hint of scan lines, and them a single word in red lettering: **"Slicer."**

Curious! Joe thought. He pushed the remains of his dinner away, tossed enough cash on the table to give the waitress a decent tip and went into the lounge. He took a seat at the back of the room in an inconspicuously shadowed area where he could see the screen easily.

Several others joined him. Joe nodded at them in a way he hoped was pleasant, and realized that they were the ones he had noticed sitting in their own corner.

The title on the screen vanished and the image of an eight-sided wrestling ring in the center of a surrounding audience replaced it. As they watched, spectators entered, sat down, some of them munching on snacks, others talking in an animated fashion to friends or marking luridly printed programs with pencils. The conversation of the TV audience was as intense as that in the dining room.

The transmission had a strangely makeshift quality to it. It was as if the program were being created by gifted amateurs who knew their technique, but who didn't have all of the equipment to do the job.

The scene zoomed in on a man in the black suit of an official.

"Ladies and Gentlemen!" he intoned, "Welcome to the second match of the mightiest and the meanest! Welcome to Slicer!"

The other drivers near Joe muttered to themselves. Joe caught references to bread and circuses from others in the room.

Then the action started.

Joe stayed inside of himself, as the bloody violence literally exploded across the screen. He watched in disbelief as several contestants in the rotating ring went under the Slicer and were carried out on stretchers.

He turned, as a white-faced, shaking waitress approached. "I'm as stunned as you are," he told her. He ordered a cold coke with a twist of lime, and paid her well in advance for it.

There was a fanfare from the TV system.

The Master of Ceremonies, in an overly intimate close-up, centered himself in the image. "Tonight, we are privileged to have a special match between The Headmaster—back from retirement for your entertainment!—and Arthur The Slayer! These prime athletes are sponsored by members of the Slicer International Athletic Support Team! Yes, local entrepreneurs have gotten together to bring you—" another brassy fanfare, "— a Duel to The Death!"

The image split, and the announcer reappeared in a small inset in a corner. The rest of the screen showed The Headmaster, a large muscular man in close fitting trunks and shirt. The shirt had a picture of a man in a black hood holding up a disembodied head. The other half of the screen displayed what to a superficial look was a list of statistics. Joe regarded the list with skepticism, as the picture changed to Arthur The Slayer. This contestant was tall, skinnier than The Headmaster, and posed in a slouch. His stats were similar to The Headmaster's, *and about as bogus*, Joe thought.

The cameras zoomed in on each of the fighters, and their head-shots were placed next to each other on the screen. Arthur looked insolently out of the screen with a look that was neither definite, nor indefinite. He seemed to be focused on the middle distance between himself and any other spectators. The effect was of disinterested malice.

The Headmaster's gaze was open, frank, wide-eyed, and—scary. That was Joe's reaction. The Headmaster's eyes were wide open, the irises huge black expanses: windows into a fine and private inferno. The effect was more eerie than Arthur's look. He could see the same reaction to the man's expression from the people around him.

It was also familiar. Joe scratched behind one ear. There was something about that look he didn't like.

The image widened. The scene jumped, shook, then steadied. The fighters took their places, and the emcee stepped back, as they jumped for each other.

The Headmaster brought his hands together, and clapped them over Arthur's ears. Arthur directed a kick to The Headmaster's crotch. The Headmaster dodged the blow and Arthur's hands came up to slap The Headmaster's hands away from his head. The fighters circled each other, crouching down. Then Arthur jumped up and brought his right leg forwards in a roundhouse kick to The Headmaster's jaw. The Headmaster back-pedaled, sidestepped, and aimed an uppercut at Arthur's crotch. Arthur twisted, but only enough to partially deflect the punch. He grimaced, his face red with anger.

The ring began turning. The Slayer faced his opponent, brought into a full-face shot by the ring's ponderous motion. He flipped the Bird at the TV cameras, and the studio audience applauded. Arthur extended his fingers like claws, and jumped forward. The ring's precession carried him to one side of

The Headmaster, and Arthur aimed one hand, his right at The Headmaster's face.

The Headmaster swept one hand up, and hit The Slayer's wrist. Arthur's hand batted back, and The Headmaster's followed through. The Slayer's left eye popped out of his head, leaving a contrail of blood that seemed to hang for a short time in the air.

Joe thought about that. There were ways of supplying real-time special effects to live broadcasts. Several people got up and left the lounge. *Somehow, I don't think that's digital blood!*

The Slicer started its descent. The audience made a growling noise like a herd of carnivores. Hungry ones. This Slicer was a pendulum that had two upcurving blades like scimitars, with a circular saw in the center. Its swing started slowly, then gained speed and ring-filling amplitude.

Arthur twisted away from The Headmaster, ducked towards his corner, where one of his assistants strapped a pair of long curving blades to his wrists.

Arthur jumped for the Headmaster, the blades on his arms raised like claws.

As the Slicer descended, swinging, the saw started turning.

Joe turned away from the action to find one of the truck drivers he'd noticed earlier looking at him.

"Where do they get this?" Joe said.

"I'm not sure I believe what I'm seeing," the other said.

Joe nodded.

"I'm Rod Martinez," the other said, "short for Rodrigo."

"Joe Davis," Joe said, "New to these parts?"

"Yeah," Rodrigo said, "Just passing through. Ever heard of the Chapel of the Highways?"

"No." Joe's voice was guarded.

"We provide church services to drivers on the road," Rodrigo continued, "I drive the maintenance truck."

"Gets you around, I guess," Joe said in an even voice.

Rodrigo nodded, then he looked back at the screen with a suddenness that made Joe jump.

The ring had turned enough to put most of The Slayer's back to the observers, centering it nicely in the screen. The Slicer swung over the contestants, and the saw cut cleanly through Arthur's shoulder. Blood sprayed upwards, a ghastly, grisly fountain. Arthur's arm fell limply to his side.

The Headmaster reached out, tapped The Slayer on his undamaged shoulder. Weakly, Arthur looked back at his opponent.

The Headmaster swung both hands in a double fist at Arthur's face. The Slayer dropped to the bloody deck.

The ring turned to leave The Headmaster facing the camera, then stopped. He was standing over the body of Arthur the Slayer. Arthur's body was cut to the bone in several places, and blood was flowing from his arms, shoulder and neck. The camera on The Headmaster dollied back and an inset image caught his face and his grin of triumph.

Then it changed.

The Headmaster's eyes dilated. He stood, wide-eyed for a moment. Blood gushed from The Headmaster's ears, one of his eyes popped out followed by a stream of blood.

The Headmaster fell forward over his opponent, blood flowing from his head. For a moment the audience was quiet.

Shaken, Joe sat down again. He hadn't even realized that he has been standing. Around him the local audience cheered and yelled.

Rod sat next to Joe. "Where did that come from?"

"I haven't the slightest," Joe said, *I know exactly!* he thought. He shook his head. "I've heard of cock-fights and dog-fights, but this is way beyond those!" Joe stood. "I'm going outside. There a place where I can get a room?"

"See the front desk," Rodrigo said, "Hey." Joe turned. "Take it easy," he said, "There's better times coming."

Easy for you to say that, Joe thought.

Sᴘʟɪᴛ-Sᴄʀᴇᴇɴ

[Parallel Processes] Joe rented a room that was about the size of the bed in it from The Trucker's Haven, and flopped, his laptop on his chest, the screen open to a GIF image.

It was of an experimental animal, a monkey, whose face was contorted into a rictus of pure menace, and whose eyes were dilated widely.

He had heard of a product of his scanning/replicating system of biological templates. The result had been placed in ordinary flowers that looked like carnations. They weren't.

The Headmaster had been close to it. Too close.

It's gotten out already! he thought.

Rodrigo left the lounge, and went back to his rig, thinking.

He pressed several switches on his truck's entertainment system, and a screen lit.

He grabbed the keyboard, and began typing—

To anyone on Trucker.Net—

I'm attempting to locate the production site of a combat program called "Slicer." The show is one featuring sadistic fights to the death, and I'd like to know its origin.

Please reply to The Midnight.Mover...Thanks.

That might be a step in the right direction.

Oᴛʜᴇʀ Vɪᴇwᴘᴏɪɴᴛs

[Execution] Zhongo Teketon sat still, his face carefully configured so as not to show his emotions. Inside, his emotions were a surreal goulash of anger, revenge, a desire for violence directed at several others in the arena, and at the center, a cold desire to have one individual executed. Slowly.

He hadn't expected the bloody explosion of The Headmaster's Head. Part of him considered the irony of the fighter's chosen name.

The rest of him wanted facts.

He signalled silently to his men, *Come Here.*

As his followers arrayed themselves around their boss, his gaze shot across the wide spaces to Gary Hamilton. The Geek was surrounded by men and women, especially women, who were congratulating their leader. Zhongo scanned them, then directed a laser gaze at Allen Hightower.

The Lord of the Roads was sitting with one arm around Marie, looking off into the distance, and smiling.

FROM THE NET

Rodrigo had dozed off in the sleeping compartment of his rig. Like most long-distance trucks, the compartment was a small but luxurious room where a driver on his off shift could rest, watch or listen to various media, read, or relax. The signal from his truck computer beeped, and he opened one eye.

There was an input from Trucker.Net.

To Midnight.Mover—

"Slicer" originates in the Mid-West. I'm pretty sure it comes from some large city, either Chicago or Milwaukee.

Sorry I can't be any more specific.

Steel.Rose

Rod knew Steel.Rose. She drove a rig out of Indianapolis, and he met her in Chicago, now and again, when their schedules coincided. He hit the "Print" key, and the printer extruded a sheet of paper, as if it were sticking out its tongue.

The computer started beeping, again.

Midnight.Mover—

Slicer comes from Milwaukee, someplace in the vicinity of a stadium called "Miller Park." I was taken to a match there, last year. It is a program out of Hell!

Crow.Follower

Hmmmm. Rod had never heard of a trucker named *Crow.Follower*. That wasn't a big surprise, on a network that guaranteed anonymity and used heavy encryption to keep private things private. He printed the message, and pocketed the listings.

He went looking for Joe.

TAKE A LOOK

At the time Rod was resting, Joe was looking through some of his own research on his laptop.

The effects of the cause of The Headmaster's cranial explosion were unknown, but one of the side-effects of the earliest working scanner/replicators that Joe had developed was the dilation of the eyes of anyone who ingested a replication-created bio-complex. Further research had eliminated this side effect, but *this* cause had to have been created from the information published in one of Joe's earliest papers, perhaps a year before. The removal of "the wide-eye" problem had been trivial, but the California Regents hadn't printed, uploaded, and otherwise made that fix-up public until recently. *I told them to watch it!* Joe fumed to himself, *Like most bureaucrats, they just didn't listen!*

He folded up his computer. There was a series of beeps, as his special programming that hid private matters in an invisible encrypted partition did its job.

Maybe those Regents need a field-trip to Slicer!

There was a knock on his door.

THE MEETING

Zeke, a skinny man with graying hair, poked at the keyboard of one of the computers that occupied principal positions on his desk. Two additional screens, connected to another system, took left and right, flanking the main. In one, a spreadsheet, in the other a word processor document he used for his notes.

Zeke was looking for any agents that would cause someone to be possessed, that was a good word! Not possessed *of* something, such as great strength, but just *possessed*.

He had created a set of search criteria, practically a program in its own right, and was sending those criteria out to all of the search engines he could access.

It would take a while to get the results back, but he would get them. His spreadsheets were ready.

OBSERVATIONS

Joe dropped his computer in a suitcase, closed the lid, and tossed a sweater on the top. He opened the door, and wasn't surprised to see Rodrigo.

"Hi, Rod," he said, and stepped back. "Pull up the only chair I have," he said with just the right amount of grin.

Rodrigo started without preamble, "Something you said last night got me thinking, and I sorta asked around. You ever heard of Trucker.Net?"

"An Internet for drivers?" Joe said.

"Yep. I sent a query out on the Net earlier, and I got this." He handed Joe his printouts.

Joe read the brief notes, and looked up at Rod. "Milwaukee? That's amazing. Who would ever have placed a show that awful in Milwaukee."

"Not many," Rod said, "What I'd like to know is how something like that is bankrolled."

"Admissions," Joe guessed.

"Yes, but not really," Rodrigo said, "You'd need a lot of start-up juice just to begin something like that. If the arena is actually under that old stadium, who dug it out? How long did it take? Who benefits? Who's getting paid off not to notice this?"

"Do you really want to know?"

"Don't know," Rod said, "Leaving a work of the devil like that to those who want it is frustrating, but what can one middle-aged truck driver do?"

"Give advice."

"Yeah. And hope people take it. What do you plan on doing?"

"I haven't made my mind up yet," Joe said, even as he *did* make his mind up, "I'm on vacation, now, and I'm just cruising around seeing the sights. Where will you go, next?"

"We're planning on taking the Chapel over to Billings. We stopped here at The Haven—we'd never been here, before."

"I might see you again," Joe said, "I'm planning a trip into Billings, myself."

"Maybe we'll see you there," Rodrigo stood, and turned to leave.

"Rodrigo," Joe said, Rodrigo turned, *"Vaya con Dios."*

"Thanks," Rodrigo said, "see you in Billings.

Joe sat in the just vacated chair. Rodrigo was a good man, and meant well, but he didn't know the real reason for Joe's interest: that *he, himself* was the indirect cause of the red carnage they had seen the night before.

Joe set his alarm for early the next morning.

THE OTHER OBSERVER

[Monitor Declaration] Later, Yezeletta would have a confidante with whom she could discuss the recent activities. Now, what she had were her Imagers, and her agent in the organization of Zhongo Teketon.

She sat at her array of screens, each screen the point of view of a separate Imager, watching, listening.

Learning.

THE MEETING

[Compiling] Zeke dropped an untidy collection of paper on the conference table. Zhongo sat in a high-backed chair near Zeke and Leona sat on the opposite side of the table, a laptop before her, a yellow legal pad near her writing hand, and pen and mouse at the ready.

Her look was attentive, interested.

"There's a genetic trait that may have a relationship to what happened to your fighter," Zeke said.

"Arthur The Slayer was hand picked, and trained thoroughly," Zhongo said in a cold voice. His words make Zeke shiver. He knew what was implied when Zhongo used the word "thoroughly." He looked at Leona out of one eye. It was obvious she did, too.

"How," Zhongo said modulating the temperature of his voice upwards fractionally, "did *that opponent* kill The Slayer?"

"He went berserk," Zeke said briefly.

"Mad?" Zhongo asked.

"No, berserk. It's an actual physical condition, where the subject becomes super strong, gets fast reflexes, like that." He pulled a thick tablet of printout off the stack, "I had to look through a lot of places, starting with Scandinavian legends, and then go to some of the so-called research of the old Soviet Union. Those were the obvious places, but this concept is world-wide: the term 'amok' is Filipino, for example. This list is a digest of the causes, effects and uses of the concept."

Zhongo took the listing, leafed through it, read scattered paragraphs. He handed it to Leona, "Check through this," he told her, "See what else you can find."

Zeke placed several backups on the table, "These have the files I printed to those listings," he slid them over to Leona.

"Then there's the method of delivery of this. It's far slicker than I've seen in this city."

Zeke paused, Zhongo gave Zeke what he hoped was a look of genuine interest, "What kind of...delivery?"

"Flowers," Zeke said. "Flowers using something from some researcher out on the west coast," he picked up another tablet of paper that featured several colorful pictures.

"There's a nice new name for drug delivery," Zeke said, "Tell your men to keep an eye out for them."

Zhongo waited.

"Madflowers," Zeke said.

THE LISTENERS

[Input] In her hidden place in the tallest building in Milwaukee, Yezeletta made a note.

CIRCLES

[Continuing] Joe drove East away from Billings earlier, he hoped, than the rising time of Rod and his friends. He cast about for a day looking for places where several rather large vehicles might camp out on their way...elsewhere.

Joe wanted to go east, all of the way to Milwaukee to see if there was anything to the unpleasant reality he'd had thrown in his face at The Trucker's Haven. He also wanted to find out more about Victor's unknown patron. That had to come first.

He drove slowly east on Highway-90, staying in small out of the way motels, paying cash, being inconspicuous. He studied the possible routes of traffic, and attempted to second-guess the mind (or minds) of the unknowns he was tracking.

It looked difficult.

In the end, all of his questions would be answered.

But they hadn't been, yet.

CHANNEL 42'S POPULARITY

Yezeletta lay back on her couch, stretching her legs out over a footstool of enormous proportions. She stretched in a four armed gesture that encompassed the room.

She long-armed a remote control from a bowl on the coffee table and pressed a channel selection.

Yezeletta had always been interested in the news, and she usually recorded the nightly newscast so she could look at it later.

Tonight's looked as if it had real promise.

COTEMPORALLY

In another small motel room, one so similar to all of the rest, that Joe was wondering if he was making any progress, he circled that Rest Stop he had noticed back in Fairview.

What the heck, it was worth a look.

FAST-FORWARD

Yezeletta moved quickly through the national news, the weather, and sports, stopping only to check the latest Packers' Plays (still in the running for the Superbowl), and stopped at a point where the recording switched over to a low-powered local station. The loudly proclaimed "Special Report!" lurched into a lead story about the night's Slicer action.

She paused to watch some of it, with a look of disapproval. Then she listened to a psychologist from the University of Wisconsin, Milwaukee discourse on the exact *meaning* of Slicer in the current sociopolitical *dynamic*.

Frowning, Yezeletta fast forwarded to: a bio-chemist describing the nature of the stimulants used in the Slicer match, with some gratuitously intimate close-ups of the Headmaster's ultimate demise. She shook her head. *Each of these turkeys has part of it, but not the whole story!* she thought.

Then there was a follow-up by the local station's anchorman where he attempted to extrapolate other possible/probable causes of the fight's end. With more close-ups.

They seem to do this just to get those bloody videos out there, again!

The anchorman went through a list of topics for further research: recombinant DNA, nanotech, cyberplexing, man-mind-machine interfacing and the Davis protocols.

Yezeletta looked up abruptly.

The commentator displayed a picture of a smiling, intelligent-looking man wearing a leather jacket and carrying a brief-case. The picture had been snapped by a casual photographer for the *Los Angeles Times* and had been taken from the *Times's* morgue.

Yezeletta input the picture into her internals and reached out for Thicknesse. She downloaded the photo to her Imagers via Thicknesse, and added a command: *Warn me if you see this man!*

He might be worth knowing.

MEANWHILE....

[I/O Driver] Zhongo lay on his back, his hands on Leona's hips, as she sat astride him. She looked down at him as she moved against him, grinding her hips, riding her man-mount across an internal night sky into the bright morning of a perfect climax.

When she had finished, when Zhongo had finished, she stayed in the saddle, looking down at him with ancient wisdom.

He smiled!

Leona was prepared for that smile. Zhongo was pretty good in bed and was a good partner for soft-talk after it was over.

Then there was that smile.

It was the smile of a well fed cat, a successful predator. Zhongo was gentle, considerate, skilled and very enthusiastic. Leona had to keep reminding herself that she was riding the most dangerous predator in the forest.

Sometimes playing wasn't play.

Later, Zhongo cuddled up with Leona, with Zeke's printouts on a cantilever where they both could read from the pile of stapled pads, and grab refreshments.

Leona took a quick look out the bedroom window.

There was a momentary glint of gold.

PATTERN MATCHING

[Input] Joe almost missed the turn-off.

He hit the brakes and backed a short distance.

There was what should have been the entrance to that rest stop he wanted a look at.

But the entrance was almost invisible!

He pulled up to the access. Part of that invisibility was an artifact of the gathering night, but most of it looked—designed.

Interesting.

He pulled in further. The access had been camouflaged at an earlier time. Then later, someone had hacked through it enough to drive in.

The rest stop was empty. A large hill covered with brush formed a back wall, and dense undergrowth covered the other sides. A fence prevented access from the road except at the two entrances.

Inside, there were the usual parking lots for automobiles, and a larger area for trucks. Joe parked in the car lot, near the rest-room and vending shed, and got out.

The rest area was in an advanced state of disrepair. The waste receptacles were overflowing onto the ground, there was litter blown into the corners with the finality of abandonment and the shed's windows were missing several panes.

Why was the entryway covered up?

He removed an item from his trunk that looked superficially like the carry-all for a portable computer. What it contained was a byproduct of his researches, and was one of the items that he had removed from his old office.

The device was a scanner for biological remnants.

What it did was look for DNA traces, RNA samples, various artificially generated genotypes, and anything else that the user wanted to detect. Joe set it for rejection of the common flora and fauna around him, and took aim with his scanner.

Nothing. Here.

He walked across the car lot towards the truck lot, staring at the small screen of his detector.

Over there, by the truck lot behind a large anti-erosion berm, a small shelter held several payphones.

Joe made an adjustment to his device, and tracks of past transport popped into sharp relief: several large trucks (from the doubled tire tracks) had been here, to be followed about a week later by smaller autos. He made another adjustment.

And looked up at the phones. Then at the shelter.

In his display, the shelter was highlighted in brilliant false color. Before him it was just a small rusted metal and plastic construction.

That had been used for a purpose that had activated his detector.

He studied the display for a moment. It was tantalizing: his detector had concluded that something had been there, earlier, but whatever it was had degraded to the point of being no more than traces. Hints.

He checked the area around the base of the structure, scanning.

No DNA signatures at all, just remnants of what might have been RNA, and a lot of long-chain organics that were in an advanced state of decay!

At the back of the shelter, he saw the cut wires.

Like any other powered structure, the shelter had an electric meter. The wiring to this one had been expertly snipped from the supply line at the point where the power cable had entered the meter, and the cable had been left to hang down from the pole nearby.

There was something on the roof.

Joe sprinted back to his car, and drove it back to the phones. He wanted transport out in a hurry if he needed it.

He got the short step-ladder from the back seat and used it to get a close-up of the contents of the rooftop.

It had dissolved—melted—to the point where his detector was unable to analyze the content. The DNA and cellular structure were non-existent, but one thing was clear.

This was artificial, and was disintegrating *by design*.

He scooped a sample into a zip-lock bag, placed that in another bag, and loaded up.

Was this one of his protocols? Probably not. Was it related to Victor's eyesight? Unknown.

He needed more data.

Joe Davis headed east.

DECISIONS AND ACTIONS

[The Main Process] Zhongo read through Zeke's data with his usual level of concentration. When he finished the reports, he passed them to Leona, who read them, then stacked them on the nightstand on her side of the bed, near the window.

She turned to Zhongo when they were done, "What have you planned?"

"The Headmaster," Zhongo said without preface, "Was on something that caused him to go into the berserk state." Leona nodded agreement, and he went on, "And that state probably had its origin in Gary Hamilton's gardens."

"He grew those—Madflowers?" Leona asked.

"Either that, or he's onto a *source*," he made the words sound like swearing, "Whatever it was, I am now into Mister Road-Lord Hightower, rather more that I'd like to be into him for."

Leona sorted out the mangled syntax. Zhongo, never far from his usually precise English, was upset enough to fall out of his normal grammatical habits. Leona was watchful.

"I had a lot of my petty cash riding on The Slayer," Zhongo said, "It's not the money, it's Hamilton." Zhongo frowned, "Because of him, I have incurred a debt to a man *I do not like*. Hightower is a pain in the ass. But I'm unable to remonstrate with him, just yet."

Leona hoped that she was radiating just the right amount of interest; Yezeletta would want to know about Zhongo's intentions.

"Did you see how Hamilton was kissing up to Hightower?" he asked, "An alliance between those two is *not* optimal!"

For the n-th time, Leona wondered about Zhongo Teketon's past. He simply did not project the usual image of the big-time gangster. Who ever heard of a gang-lord who talked like a fussy English teacher?

"What would you like, if you could solve this problem now?" Leona asked, gently.

"Gary needs killing," Zhongo said coldly, "I *do not* want any unifications of *any kind* with Allen Hightower, from *anyone*."

Leona put her arms around Zhongo. "Does this mean war?" she asked sweetly.

"Hell, yes!" Zhongo replied, "I need to see all of the department heads, first thing this morning. We have a project ahead of us."

"Good," Leona said, "but tonight..." she pushed gently, and Zhongo rolled onto his back. "Right now, I want to help you get to sleep," she said, kneeling between his legs.

She lay down, and started, This is how it began with Gray Roger, she thought, Maybe it's how I finish with Zhongo Teketon.

Behind them there was a flash of gold outside the window.

ARCHIVE LOAD: SUSTAIN

[Program Code]　"You're good," Yezeletta says.

They lay closely to each other, Joe's left arm around Yezeletta, his right under a large pillow. Yezeletta lies partially on her back, so her left arms would be comfortable, on a large three-lobed pillow that supports her without all of her weight on her hips and arms. She is grinning.

"You actually discovered the place where I attempted a comm-link. Sometime I'd like to see what you found out."

"That report you saw on TV...was there really a snapshot of me?" he asks.

"An early one," Yezeletta says, "It looked like some sort of casual stock shot that the *L. A. Times* took for the record and released later."

"And that was how your—uh—critters found me."

Yezeletta smiles again, and to Joe it seems one of acceptance, "I'd not heard of the Davis Protocols when I was in Australia. Maybe they wanted to see if I could replicate them. Be that as it may, I think that your techniques and mine would be useful to each other. And us."

Joe nods, and allows his left hand to find Yezeletta's right breast. She raises an eyebrow, and her grin takes on a mischievous component. She rolls into Joe's touch.

He hugs her, she wraps three arms around him, and they cling closely in the growing chaos that is forming around them.

SOMEWHERE OUT IN THE 'BURBS

[Operations]　Allen Hightower sat with the dark-haired Marie on the couch in his entertainment room. He pressed the **[Play]** button on a remote control, and a video started.

It was of a fighter who competed well in the limited framework of what he was allowed to do. Within those restrictions, he fought well, skillfully, and his opponent died.

Then the blood erupted out of his head, and he collapsed over his dead victim.

By this time, Marie was breathing in little short gasps, and Allen knew what she wanted next.

He unbuttoned her blouse, and took her in hand. She pressed his hands into her breasts, and leaned back on the couch.

Allen released her long enough to begin undressing.

ARCHIVE LOAD: RETURN

[Assembly; A Bit Later]　"Were any others on your track?" Joe asks.

"There was one individual. I think he was—" she pauses. "He thought he was James Bond, or something. He never told me where he was from, overtly: I had to get it out of him by other means, but it's not too difficult to realize there's only a few places he could have originated."

"A real secret agent?"

"Exactly so. There were agents both of Australia and Argentina present in the Project Complex. You could tell even if you weren't me."

"Even?" Joe prompts.

Yezeletta grins, and a note of good old-fashioned pride enters her voice, "*They* designed my hearing to be extremely acute. I can hear things like heart-beats. At a distance. How would you gauge those cold, calm, collected beings that always stood back in the corners, and never talked, but just listened?"

"I'll bet they listened very well."

"Count on it, Joe! These were men, I only saw one woman who had these characteristics, who certainly reported back to their superiors exactly what went on around me. When I look back, it's interesting that I was able to hide from them the things I did."

"Wiping them out probably helped," Joe supplies, dryly.

"And my servitors scoured everything out of every place in the complex before I left. It's amazing what tireless creatures can accomplish on a three-day weekend if they don't stop for coffee."

"So this guy shows up."

"This guy shows up. He tries to board the *Hat Dancer* while she's moored in the harbor. One of the July-Seventeenths catches him, assumes that he's just a trespasser, and gives him a hint. He gets ejected. Then he shows up that night. He gets a stronger hint. Charlie tossed him overboard."

"But he comes back?"

"He sure does. One more time, wearing night-vision equipment, stealth gear, and carrying one of those seventeen-round Glock thirty-eights. I check the pistol out later, and there's no serial number on it. Furthermore, there's no evidence that the gun ever had a serial number."

"What they call a cold weapon?"

Yezeletta nods once. "This time, I hung on to him. I posed as a tall woman, without extra limbs." In response to Joe's lifted eyebrow, she adds, "I wore a long trenchcoat I had made, and reflecting dark glasses. 'Mirrorshades,' I believe they're called. I subjected this man to some special interrogation aids that I was taught how to fabricate, and found out that he was from a CIA spin-off called Searchlight. I was surprised. I didn't realize that there were many—or any—of the CIA left, and the spin-off was completely new. Unfortunately the interrogation aids I used left him unable to process input to his brain very well." Yezeletta frowns. "This is another one I'm not happy about. The signatures in his body from the chemical agents I used will be long-gone, metabolized out by now, and he will snap out of the sensory disassociation in about eight months' time. And should have a very nice case of permanent amnesia regarding the last year."

Yezeletta pauses in a moment's thought. "That's how it *should* work. I designed things well, and it *will* work."

[Link] Yezeletta is quiet for a time, lost in her own reverie. Joe contemplates the note of uncertainty that has crept into the supremely self-confident Yezeletta Zargkonji upon mentioning the secret agent.

The CIA, he knows, is but a shadow of what it was in the daring days of the old Cold War. Limited in manpower and in finances, it manages in a country with a decapitated government about as well as any tight-knit organization with highly loyal members can. Joe knows that even though the CIA's charter still doesn't allow it to work within the United States, sometimes it does, hoping not to be discovered. Any other organizations, such as Yezeletta's "spin-offs," are wild cards. Loose cannons. Such agencies or pseudo-agencies would be buried so deeply that if they're noticed at all, it would be for what they were not, rather than for what they were.

Yezeletta takes his hand, his right.

She draws him closer. She smiles; so does Joe.

"Maybe we need to go to the mattresses!" she says.

BETWEEN WAKING AND SLEEP

[System Call, Extending Upper: Exec State; Process Shot] Later, Joe drifts off to sleep, his mind a turmoil of thoughts: shortly the turmoil stretches, distorts, warps into the landscape abstractions of sleep. Absently, one hand, his left, reaches out, and holds Yezeletta's right hand, her upper. Long, precise fingers envelop his, on the long track through the shifting abstract landscape. There is a touch that vanishes down a long, swift train tunnel into a new place that just might have been a kiss. There is the surprise of his last thoughts before slumber: *A fragment of Khayyam: "A checker-board of nights and days." A coincidence of contraries! She's on our side, all of the sides there are: Hannah, Victor. It's all of the ones who put her here that are the bad guys, she's the one to fight for, she—*

ELLIPTIC LEARNING CURVE INTEGRAL

[Cotemporally] *The Student's Counselor studied the short incisions on his own recently shaved scalp, where the contacts had been implanted. His smile was that of a man of power, who finds routine exercise of that power an easy task. The implants will allow him to teach the Student by means of direct mind-to-mind interaction, as a proper teacher/student relationship should be, the teacher providing wisdom, the student receiving it.*

The Student had no need to know where his Counselor acquired his information or, for that matter, even the means by which that information is downloaded into the Student's eager mind.

The Counselor paused to light a cigarette. He took a satisfying drag on it, its tip a malevolent glowing eye reflected from the virtual reality of the mirror. The AI programming is in its final developmental stage, and the "field" version will be downloaded soon. No more mistakes!

And the Student's education will be complete.

The Counselor replaced the hairpiece that covered his incisions.

No one, especially the Student, needs to see them.

The egress points for The Other.

DETERMINANTS, PROGRAMMABLE

[Co-Processor] *On another screen in the other cube, there is blackness. An image takes shape: a seascape, a beach against which the ceaseless pounding of the waves are almost as of wet hands pounding against, and accessing, the shore.*

In the distance, a larger wet, dark gray shape looms, appearing to float above all of the rest.

The View-point is steady, watchful, as, further up on the shore, well above the ocean's grasp, a huge bonfire burns, and all around it almost aboriginal shapes walk, dance, or assist in maintaining the blaze by adding firewood to the stack of burning timbers.

The watcher's gaze lingers for a time on the blaze. It is distant, and, above all, safe enough to be friendly; warm, not at all dangerous. Unlike the memories in other screens of other times of the rows of burning habitation.

The screen on the cube's side darkens, and another one lights.

A black barrier recedes into the distance.

———>>> **SIX** <<<———

I am Helium Raven and this movie is mine,
So he cried out as he stretched the sky,
Pushing it all out like [a] latex cartoon,
Am I all alone in this generation?

—Patti Smith, *Birdland*

BETWEEN THE LINES

[Project Sargon; Two Years Earlier] Yezeletta gazed intently into her terminal screen. This was the latest in high-res video: A screen so fine that even she was hard pressed to view its ultimate resolution.

She was making some very personal and, she hoped, undetectable modifications to it.

In one window, a section of program code reposed: complex lines of deliberately un-commented text that accessed the screen's onboard controller. In another window, test data.

Earlier that day, she had detected a tiny glint in the frame of Dali's *Madonna of Port Lligat* that faced her bed. To an individual with normal eyes, the glint would have been invisible. To Yezeletta's enhanced vision, it stood out as if someone had painted red arrows leading to it on the walls.

It didn't surprise her to find a tiny monitoring camera mounted in the frame.

Frowning, she removed it, and dropped it into the blue-glass mason jar on her desk.

To anyone with merely human vision, the second window on Yezeletta's screen looked like some pedestrian output from a word-processor spelling checker, but to Yezeletta, there was other text between the lines of the spell check.

Her modification to the screen was to create a display mode that was above the highest frequency that her creators could see: a Very High Ultra-violet.

Her test data stood out in bright *high-purple* characters—she had her own names for those special colors; words that only she could pronounce. Her discreet email to the Japanese manufacturer of the screen about the microscopic laser diodes that made up the pixelations and how they could be driven internally had slipped by the inevitable monitoring of her internet link.

She hadn't mentioned ultra-violet and infra-red: she had disintegrated an earlier bug in a fast analysis. It could handle near infra-red, but ultra-violet was quite beyond it.

Yezeletta would have no trouble reading what she wanted on her monitor, but her watchers would see only what she wanted them to see.

A persistent growling in her stomach intruded. She released the sensations, and directed a thought to her status monitors. A window opened in her eyesight. A very personal window that no one else could see. Glowing letters and numbers appeared within it.

One of the disadvantages of being 214 centimeters tall, and 160 kilograms heavy, was a metabolism requiring *a lot* of energy.

She scanned her kitchen with one eye.

And stood up.

She decided to eat in the cafeteria. Besides, I'm tired of eating a dozen eggs for lunch!

She canceled the programs and placed the program code back in the hidden areas where she kept things that she didn't want found, gesturing quickly with her right arm, the lower. Yezeletta stretched and, with her curious rolling gait, went to lunch.

In the corridors of Project Sargon, Yezeletta was a rare sight. She usually kept to herself in her own apartments, but was, at least theoretically, allowed free run of both the scientific and administrative parts of the complex.

And what of the ones who mean me no harm?

The project cafeteria was on the far side of the main building from her quarters. The fastest way would be by taking the diagonal of a rectangle—walking through the central courtyard.

She eyed the guards that patrolled the exits. Going out was something that she could only do during the times that the Tech Bloc's Key-Hole spy satellites were below the horizon. It was ironic that the same technology that gave Yezeletta her heightened visual abilities also made orbital observation child's play.

And there's no one else who has an infra-red signature quite like mine!

She continued quietly, the lunch-time crowd stepping out of her way as she sailed past them. The corridor became unnaturally quiet as she walked. Most of the others at the Project knew of her from photographs or sketches, but her full presence was an entirely different experience.

They used to try to hide their fright, and I could still hear them!

At the lunch-room's entrance, a knot of people waited to get inside. Yezeletta quietly annexed herself to the end of the line, and waited, looking down in frank interest at several of the people before her.

Directly ahead, a short feisty-looking man festooned with cameras, flash-units, and a large gadget bag was talking to a woman Yezeletta recognized as one of the honchos from Administrative Data Processing.

"The—uh, Firm—wants me to get some nice poses of the Agent!" Short-and-Feisty was saying. "The hints were that the pictures should be functional, but—attractive."

"What ever for?" Honcho-Lady replied.

"I think someone—I won't specify who—wants to show off just how pretty artificial biological creations can be. Maybe to get some extra funding. The head of the US House Science Committee is one of these fundies that The Firm has something on. Something BIG. Maybe another Agent. There have been these rumors."

Although the photographer and the programmer were practically whispering, Yezeletta's augmented hearing could pick them up easily. She had read of the appointment of one Jasper Berkins to the US House Science Committee in an international edition of *Newsweek* several months earlier. She had raised one dark eyebrow after reading Berkins' rather notorious quote, "Physics? I know all about physics. I take Ex-Lax every night! It's the only physic I need!"

It hadn't made a lot of sense to hear that the Americans would pick such an ignoramus to control American science policy.

Of course the genteel decline in that country was getting more and more obvious. The few researchers that American universities turned out were getting out as soon as they could get permission from the Federal Science Directorate to leave. Then they would smuggle their families out later, and take up positions as expatriate citizens in other more technologically free places.

The chow-line moved forwards. The smells of chicken, turkey, meat-loaf, ham, cheese, and various side-dishes wafted out. Yezeletta attenuated her olfactory processors: some of the things in the serving area didn't register as having been refrigerated as well as they could have been.

The line took her into the cafeteria. She picked up two trays in her lower hands, and removed her special coffee cup from her belt with her left hand, her upper. She set the trays on the railing, and grabbed one of each of the entrees in each of her four hands, and set them on one tray. She filled her custom one-liter cup from the coffee urn hot, black and unsweetened, and added four desserts, three glasses of juice, and six cartons of milk.

The cashier thought for a moment and said "Forty-two dollars and twenty-five cents, please."

Yezeletta looked down at him, and said pleasantly, "Just put it on my account."

The cashier looked up, and seemed to shrink into himself. "My mistake," he said.

Yezeletta smiled, not showing her teeth, and took her lunch to a table near the windows. Behind her, she didn't see the cashier quietly texting on his cell phone.

Outside, it was a pleasant, almost balmy day. The sun shone down from the North and cast sharp shadows. She could clearly hear the birds and other small animals in the Project courtyard.

She could also hear the comments from everywhere in the cafeteria.

"That's *her!*"

"She's real!"

"Why doesn't she stay in her own place?"

"Is she human?"

"What will they do with her?"

The questions were always the same, always asked by the new people at the project. She filed the voices away in her on-line memories, looked about to see if she could associate a face with each voice, and thought about the last question.

It was a question that Yezeletta wanted an answer to, as well.

The encrypted message traffic into the project from the offices in Buenos Aires and Sydney had increased markedly in the last six months. She leaned back, causing several creaks of protest from the chair, and directed a thought *THERE*.

A landscape orientation window opened, neatly obliterating one of the questioners. *Covering her PLACE*, Yezeletta thought. She directed another thought *THERE*, and a line graph of project message traffic slithered across the window. Graduations and labels appeared along the axes, and she paused, and thought. The line turned green. Next she plotted another line on the same graph: remove the high-level encryptions from the total messages, and plot them. In red.

A red rollercoaster rode high above a green substrate. Last year, the red and green lines were reversed: green over red.

Now....The red graph points accounted for fully three-quarters of everything. Yezeletta replotted it by recipient. There were a lot of greens going to most (about ninety percent) of the Project population, but just about all of the encryptions went straight into Admin.

Good thing I started the traffic analysis as long ago as I did!

She replotted her data a third time: classifying messages by recipient and by whether each message was incoming or outgoing.

Interesting, she thought.

She filed the info away, and finished eating. Anyone watching her would not have noticed her reverie.

Yezeletta returned to her apartments by way of the Project Library.

She was used to doing research. Although she did most of it from her computers in her work-in-progress-room, she could use any of the other facilities in the Project.

No one was going to keep her out of anything.

Yezeletta spent about four hours in the Library. She read technical journals, mostly, but interposed in all of the journals were several other things:

The PBX Exchange, a designation for on-site equipment, that Project Sargon used as its internal telephone switch, had maintenance modes that, while they weren't well known, were accessible to anyone willing to do the research. For someone with Yezeletta's training, this was about an hour's work.

Access to those maintenance modes, along with several connections made nocturnally by Yezeletta's constructs, gave her access to the entire internal exchange: allowing Yezeletta to get into any telephone line in the Project.

Presumably everything that went through the Sargon telephone system was recorded, analyzed, and cross-referenced in Security. No one there had any particular need to secure any of these records in their own office suite. The transcriptions would be available to any Security operative interested in—well, just about anything.

That suited Yezeletta just fine.

The 80*AB*86 chips in Yezeletta's "mainframe" ran at 4000 Ghz. There were four-thousand-ninety-six of them. Something from Security's data base could be referenced in about a heart-beat's duration.

Either of my hearts that I want to pick, she thought.

Her computers never slept. To those monitoring her, it seemed as if she were constantly up to some task or another.

Ironic! They encourage my computer usage. And they don't even know what it is that I'm doing!

Yezeletta started up a special purpose program that, on the face of it, looked as if its job was to acquire and download useful things from the internet, the Usenet News groups, a forum dedicated to something or another, or any other subject that interested her. What the Project didn't know (she crossed her fingers four times), was that the computer had been programmed to dedicate a dozen or so of its CPUs to analyzing traffic *into the project*, and to make an attempt at decrypting any of it that came in encrypted.

It helped that the Sargon Manual for Secure Telephony was right there on a shelf in the Library. It was short, but very informative.

In the late nineties, just before the Twentieth-Century had shuddered to its unlamented close, strong cryptography had become available to everyone. Although the encryptions used by the Sargon Directorate were state of the art, there was no protection against anyone monitoring the message's decryption.

And Yezeletta had programmed the PBX testing subsystem to route all such decryptions to her.

Her entry into the communications systems of the Project was properly surreptitious. But it was not the only entry.

There were others.

She smiled a sardonic smile, and switched her monitor off—there was still the possibility of **Tempest** eavesdropping—and went into her laboratory.

She switched on the ultra-violet disinfecting lamps, but left the normal illumination off. She could see perfectly, but anyone monitoring her here would, she hoped, think that she was just killing the stray bug, rather than hiding something.

She looked down into the petri dishes containing flaky-looking substances. The tailored bacteria had formed themselves into colonies that had crusted over as a protective measure.

As I designed them to!

She adjusted her eye-lenses to provide about 200-X microscopic vision, and peered into the cultures.

Very <u>good</u>—they're growing just as I planned.

She opened a refrigerated drawer below the culture growing area, took one of a cluster of eggs out of its compartment, and examined it.

The matte black color of the object absorbed the ultra-violet light. The egg was a dark purple and unnatural sight.

She returned it to the drawer, closed it.

Then she turned on the human-usable fluorescent lights, and drifted over to a metal cage opposite the bacteria cultures.

The contents of the cage heaved and undulated, a puddle of brown fur, moving amorphously. Yezeletta opened a small refrigerator next to the cage and took out a one-kilogram piece of pot-roast. She opened the cage, and placed it near the furry mass.

Carpet-like, it slid up to the meat, put out a questing, furry tendril, and touched the pot-roast. Then with a fast motion that was almost insectile, it jumped on the meat, covering it completely.

Yezeletta reached in and ruffled the creature's fur as if it were a dog. It vibrated pleasantly under her hand and she could almost sense a diffuse feeling of—pleasure? gratitude?

She closed the cage and left the lab.
She shut off the fluorescents on the way out.

RECAP—II

[Milwaukee]   She didn't tell Joe about what she'd secretly grown in the Project Sargon complex. Only that there was a point at which she had been informed by the Directorate that Project Sargon was ended, and she was to be retired. Forcibly, if necessary. At that time, the Sargon Directorate (what was left of it) found out what she had been working on.

Joe had described for her a Charles Addams cartoon of rosy-cheeked youngsters selling "Cold Drink, Five Cents," and the cheery kids' confederate around the corner selling "Cold Drink Antidote, One Dollar." She'd laughed for five minutes at that. It was the first time Joe had seen her genuinely amused.

By the time the servitors were configured to load the lorries, she was the only one (aside from her creations) still alive in the complex. Six specially conditioned constructs would serve as drivers.

She and her convoy arrived in the north seaport city of Darwin, drove down to the docks, and parked. She needed to find out what ships were in port and to determine which ship she would take.

Her escape would have been nearly complete if she'd had the time to pack her equipment and get out. She was about a day shy of the time she needed. On the road, her convoy would have looked no different than any other small group of trucks driving north.

That was the unexpected problem. A smaller convoy of troublemakers driving south. Looking for her. Or, to be more accurate, looking for an artist's conception of her. Before she was even ready to go, she was discovered.

ONE LINE OR ANOTHER

[Project Sargon]   The days in the Australian Outback were clear blue, sunny and fair. By early September, the springtime was pleasant with small things growing, warm air and various migratory animals arriving from the northern hemisphere, where the white-fanged jaws of winter were beginning to close down.

It was not a time for endings.

Yezeletta's traffic analysis was beginning to show results. The traffic from Canberra had increased precipitously.

CHANGES

[Project Sargon]   Yezeletta continued with her researches through that summer into the start of October. Her *associates* watched her moving effortlessly from one program of research and study to another. To her watchers, Yezeletta was awesome, impressive and very friendly. Although no one ever stopped by her private apartments, she'd found out that Project Security had marked them off limits, people were friendly enough when she went out into the public areas.

Yezeletta Zargkonji began taking more lunch breaks in the cafeteria. The cashier was *very* friendly.

ONE *LINK* OR ANOTHER

One afternoon in the hot part of a long October day, Yezeletta sat in the

Technical Library. The large couch she was using was, by silent agreement, hers and hers alone. She had done some work on it so she could sit in it comfortably for a short time, but it was still less comfortable than the couches in her own quarters.

She was reading a copy of the *Bell Labs Technical Journal*, a periodical that hadn't been associated with Bell in nearly fifty years, but the successor to The Labs kept the name out of respect for tradition, when several programmers from Administrative Data Processing came in.

During several months, as Yezeletta became a fixture in the library, she had noticed that her couch had started—moving. On succeeding visits, her seating had slowly moved from a place in front of one of the alcoves of books to past the alcove, to *within* the alcove. Yezeletta had been a bit miffed at this bare-faced attempt to hide her from the other people in a Project which, after all, existed only for her creation and training.

Now she was glad that her alcove was where it was. The programmers, two women and a man, were here for the same thing Yezeletta was: to catch up on their technical reading.

They walked past her, one of the women nodding solemnly to her, and went to another alcove nearby with a round table and several chairs.

Yezeletta looked up from the *Journal*, directed a series of thoughts *there*, **there** and <u>there</u>, and, just for the heck of it, ***there*** and <u>there</u> as well, and several windows opened up around her line-of-sight.

In one window, two oscilloscope traces appeared.

In the next window, there was the output from a process that she used to "clean up" sounds that were indistinct. In a third window were the results as she would hear them.

Her creators didn't know she had reprogrammed the enhancement routines in her audio sub-system several times. Her ears were far better than the Project engineers realized.

The conversation came in loud and clear: "She's sitting right over there!" one of the women said. Yezeletta snuck a quick look. It was the one who had nodded at her.

"What's she doing?"

"Reading something." That was the man.

"She must have to catch up on her reading now and again, too," said the other woman. Yezeletta did a quick look-up on her voice. She was the woman in charge of the Data Processing Section.

"Fair enough," the man said. "She works here, too. What are you gonna do on holiday?"

Yezeletta's ears felt as if they were growing points. *Holiday?*

"Holiday?" the DP-Boss said, not realizing that she was an echo. "What Holiday?"

"I just got this notice from the Deputy Administrator," the man said, "just before we pushed off for Lunch. All the support staff are being sent home for two weeks. The whole place is shutting down. Starting next Friday."

There was the sound of a chuckle. Yezeletta amplified the sound and performed a morphological disconstruction on it, mostly to test a subroutine she'd been writing. *Shutting Down?* she thought.

"Y'don't suppose our tall friend's gonna take a holiday with the rest of us?" the man asked his friends. "I can just see her at the Sydney Opera House!

They'd watch *her* more than the show on the stage!"

I'm sure they would, their silent audience thought to herself. Just why do they want all of the support staff out of here?

The conversation at the next table dwindled as the three specialists went off for their technical journals. Yezeletta tried to finish the article she was reading, but *Fractal Noise Reduction in Rural Copper Telephone Lines in Response to Aggravated Water Damage, A Statistical Approach* didn't interest her as much as the analysis of the message traffic that she had been pursuing.

Was *she* being pursued?

Why?

She leaned back, and redrew her traffic analysis graphs in her more-than-mind's eye.

And saw a partial answer.

Aggravated Water Damage with or without Statistics could wait.

Yezeletta *ascended* to her feet, and left the library.

SCIENTIST, NOT MAD

Back in her quarters, Yezeletta looked around at her work/living room. She expanded the bandwidth of her eyes, adjusted them for microscopic sight, and scanned the walls.

There, there and...*there*! Three new ones. *You'd think they'd know what I look like by this time*, she thought. *Particularly after that exhibition they wanted me in.* She went to her computer, and typed an instruction into a command-line window. At the same time, she gestured with her left hand, her lower.

A swarm of fireflies entered the room.

The fireflies were visible only to her vision in the bandwidths she'd selected. She placed her right hand, her upper, on the computer's mouse, and thought at *that*. Data flowed down the data-paths in her arm into a contact point she'd added to the mouse two weeks earlier. To anyone else it would appear she was using the instrument in the usual fashion.

She directed another thought *there*, and the fireflies split off into three smaller flights, and each flight went for one of the new...*well, bugs is an appropriate name for them, isn't it?*

She left the fireflies to do their job, and went to her bedroom. She scanned there as she had in the living room. *Right above the bed! Don't those cretins in Security have anything better to do?* She backed out of the bedroom, adjusting the light-dimmer near the door as she left. Data flowed into the contact in the dimmer.

Yezeletta went to all of the other rooms in her quarters. Her complex of rooms was large, and it took twenty minutes to scan it, even to the bathrooms. *They didn't miss a beat on that one!* she thought.

THE INVENTOR

The fireflies could have simply sabotaged the tiny cameras in Yezeletta's quarters. She sat back at her larger-than-life desk, a carved mahogany monster that the Guys From Supplies—she'd given them that title in her letter of thanks—had found in Alice Springs and had brought back as a present for her. It was the only desk that was large enough. A window opened on her monitor. It showed her sitting at the desk, but the point of view was that of a camera bug about a meter down from the ceiling behind and to the right of her. She looked around at where the bug should logically be, and saw a slight, light TV-blue glow, as of corona radiation from the appropriate spot.

She looked back at her monitor. Her image on the screen was looking at the screen within the screen, and she-the-image was typing something at a rather rapid rate. As she watched, her image reached with its right hand, the lower, the hand she usually used the mouse with, and moved the device across the mouse-pad.

Yezeletta smiled!

The fireflies weren't exactly light emitters, they were *raster* emitters.

On impulse, she turned and waved at the optic bug with three hands.

Her image on the screen continued typing.

THE FIXER

[Project Sargon: The Agent's Quarters] Yezeletta leaned against the edge of the counter on which the cage was resting. The smaller duplicate of the Walking Carpet was doing as well as the adult from which it had fissioned. Junior was sitting, pulsing slightly, in its own cage, having been removed from Mother's cage earlier that morning. Yezeletta reached with her long right arm, her upper, and removed a pair of two-kilogram pot-roast chunks from the refrigerator. She unwrapped them, and tossed one into each cage.

The original Carpet knew, in its own specific way, what had happened, and swarmed over the meat. Junior didn't quite get it. As Yezeletta watched, Junior flowed around the meat in a slow circle, touching it tentatively. Then, in the same insectile manner as Mother, it curled back, and covered the chunk.

To anyone else in that room, the sounds of the animals eating would have been somewhere between frightening and nauseating.

Yezeletta was delighted; her allies needed their protein.

Then she checked the egg supply.

ELSEWHERE

Although there were in place various means for governments to listen into the traffic on the cellular telephone system, one thing, quite unforseen, prevented the kind of monitoring that some feared.

When the Law Enforcement Monitoring Act was passed in Canberra, some felt that it gave the government *carte blanche* to investigate every cell-user in the country. To say nothing of visitors.

What no one had considered, in spite of it being obvious to the point of blatant, was the sheer number of cell-phone users. Monitoring that many conversations was not just difficult, it was impossible.

This was why the cashier at the Sargon cafeteria and his partner, the head night janitor, were able to acquire information, and quietly send it not just encrypted, but concealed in a sideband of their conversations to a confederate at the *Sidney Morning Herald*.

The pay as stringers, sent anonymously as cash, for the *Herald* was better by a factor of ten than their pay working as civil servants at Sargon.

[Project Sargon Security] Ray Dalquist, supervisory officer at Sargon Security pondered the directive that he'd been asked to sign off on at lunch. It was a directive to be ready to go on holiday for two weeks, and, the interesting part was that this holiday would begin in just two days. *You couldn't have given us a little more notice, could you?* he thought.

He pondered the logistics of his move. Cleaning out his room at the complex would be trivial; Ray tended to travel light. The memo mentioned transfers for some civil service personnel. Ray knew that he had enough seniority to qualify for that. *Ours is not to reason why.*

Across the complex from Ray's office, two other individuals were contemplating their copies of the same memo.

"I'll have time for one more report," the clerk said.

"That will have to do," the night janitor replied, "there's nothing more to pick up in any of the offices: all of the papers in any of the wastebaskets were shredded, all of it this afternoon.

"There's nothing left to take."

"Did you get the photograph?" the cashier asked.

"Unfortunately, not," the janitor replied, "any of those went into the shredder, first."

"Damn!"

Ray Dalquist continued his leisurely watch of The Agent's quarters. He was able to use several wavelengths of light in his monitoring, he just hadn't, lately. The infrared mode didn't work too well: there appeared to be something interfering with it, *probably some of her experiments*, he thought. He'd never used the ultraviolet, nothing ever showed up there. There were even some combination modes that showed details in false-color.

And those details would become the subject of serious discussion, before he left the Project.

The janitor had one chance to get a picture of Yezeletta before he packed up to leave. He essayed a candid shot through his cell-phone camera, but the sound of someone dropping his keys directly behind him had attracted Yezeletta's attention, and she had looked directly at him. Smoothly he put the phone to his ear, and hit the speed-dial for the local "time" number.

The sight of her vertically-slit eyes looking, unblinking at him from her height was unnerving.

THE LINEMAN

About an hour later, the night janitor sent the last dispatch to the *Sydney Herald* through the web-browser on his cell-phone. It was the last transmission he was able to make, as his supervisor had told him to forget about the night's shift, and push off for home, too.

THE CHECK-OUT

[Project Sargon: The Agent's Quarters] Yezeletta regarded the softly glowing patches on the walls of her laboratory. There were *four* patches of soft blue glowing here. Number four apparently had been installed yesterday while she was at lunch. *They certainly move fast, these days! What's going on?* She removed the egg from the incubator, and looked at it, shutting all but near infrared out of her left eye, and using her microscopic vision.

What she was incubating was definitely not baby chickens.

The vile color of the eggshell, in this case dark purple, was a simple aniline dye. She had used that as a definitive measure against these eggs' *ever* finding their way into a kitchen. Not that it was likely.

She replaced the egg, and made a fine adjustment to the temperature setting. *One more day.*

The incubator next to the one holding the eggs looked more like a supermarket walk-up freezer, except that the temperature within was in the neighborhood of forty-one degrees centigrade—four degrees above human body temperature: the body temperature of a cat.

The contents of the unit was a white flat object that looked like a stack of laminations of linen, or a large supply of Greek *phyllo* dough. Yezeletta ran her hand across the warm surface of the "dough" and it responded with a ripple that made its surface look almost like water. She stroked the lifeform again and it rippled and undulated. One corner curled up and touched her hand. The white sheet stroked her fingers, and Yezeletta responded with a pat.

The corner lay down again.

Yezeletta went on to the next.

THE FINAL EXIT

[Project Sargon: The Main Entrance] The first bus to Alice Springs pulled in, and the first two boarders handed their luggage to the driver for stowage underneath. They took seats in about the middle of the vehicle, on the side opposite the Complex exit.

It would be harder to notice them there.

The cashier nodded to the janitor.

There would be a quiet man from a place that they were not to speak of *ever*, who would have a fat envelope of cash for each of them.

Too bad it would be the last; but there would be other jobs after this.

PREPARATIONS, INTERNAL

[Project Sargon: The Agent's Quarters] Most of Yezeletta's research was in topics that she had been asked by others to work on. She had figured out early on that they were testing her by giving her things to do that were being parallelled, or which had been solved elsewhere, and seeing if she were as able as the others to get the same, or similar, results.

One thing that the Deputy Director had discovered was that she was not merely as good, but far better than the parallel, or control, researchers.

Now she was far ahead of anyone else in either the Complex, or unknown to her, in several other installations. *I think I know what it would be like to be a baby duck hatched by a chicken!* she thought. *They don't really know what they've created...they think they can still control me.*

The next incubator looked like it was filled with spaghetti, without the sauce. The ropy, tendril-like lifeforms squirmed and writhed in a mindless fashion in the sort of thick syrup that served as their nutrient.

And the last incubator contained the most elaborate construct of all.

SURPRISE PACKAGE

[The Watchman] Ray regarded the figure in the screen. Her back was to him, and she looked pretty busy. Come to think of it, she's been typing like that for the last hour.

How long was she going to type on that? What was she writing? A novel?

THE PROGRAMMER

[Project Sargon: The Agent's Quarters] Ray was wrong about what Yezeletta was writing. It wasn't a novel; it was a program. She had written an involved system a year earlier that allowed her to send instructions to her constructs, and she had spent a number of hours from late night to early morning typing in detailed instructions to the critters, minions, Imagers and whatnot around her and elsewhere in the Complex. She was at her main computer frequently, and it didn't make any difference to her if the snoops in Security saw her using it. Her biggest objection was whether they knew what was in several well concealed places in the system's configuration RAM and in the various drives of the Storage Towers where she kept her files.

A year earlier, Security had tampered with her system, leaving a slightly clumsy, to say nothing of obvious, keystroke monitor in place, which she had defeated handily. Presumably, they had made duplicates of her mass storage, as well.

She hoped that they had enjoyed playing "Duke Nuke'em," "Myst," the satirical "Pyst," and, of course, Sargon-Deep-Blue-Seven, probably the best chess program ever written.

They hadn't succeeded in copying the things she hadn't wanted copied.

BACK ON LINE

[Supervisory Switch: Monitor] What Ray hadn't been told was that only the most senior of the Security Division were being kept through the "holiday" and that all of the junior personnel would be dismissed as soon as possible. He himself was to leave later that evening.

The Thursday departure's set a lot of people off. What's going on?

WWW.YEZELETTA.CALM

[In Yezeletta's Quarters] That question was being asked in a different, and more elaborate manner, by Yezeletta. She was looking at a shaky transmission from one of her imagers that was moving at a high speed—obvious from the jittering of the image—as it ran along a wall, searching for the device Yezeletta wanted located. There: the large Army olive drab container. There was a hardened, militarized, LCD screen on one side of the case, and a folding keyboard in a closable protective hood below it. A test-pattern rippled across the LCD screen. As Yezeletta's imager got closer, the rippling stopped, and a large eye appeared. The eye—an animation—blinked several times. Yezeletta counted the blinks: one, two, three, *four*. Excellent! The blink code was simple enough that it would be difficult to prevent: it could be used with lights or anything else that was movable. Four meant *Everything AOK*. Hilda was doing well. In spite of the unannounced and unexplained malfunction in the comm line to Yezeletta's quarters.

Yezeletta was now surrounded by a number of small glowing patches on the walls. What she was doing was referred to by cryptographers as "spoofing." The optical bugs in her quarters weren't being suppressed, removed or destroyed. The raster-flies were actually *generating images* that the CCD cameras were transmitting back to Security's monitors. They were simple images: the raster-flies had been a project that Yezeletta had rushed to completion way before she'd wanted them finished. She had been in Security: not corporeally, but via her imagers. One of the smallest of the hairy little spiders had crawled through the air-conditioning ducts to get there and had perched in the vent above and in front of the monitoring station.

The raster-flies were working. If the Deputy Director wanted an undeclared war, he would get one.

IN COLOR LIVING

[Security] Ray's last shift was nothing, if not boring. On impulse, he reached the operations manual for his monitor system off the shelf, blew the dust off of it, and opened it to "Image Enhancement."

It was possible to observe The Agent in various spectra of the infrared or of the ultraviolet, or to combine the inputs.

"Just for grins and giggles," he muttered, as he keyed in a command to look at Yezeletta in the near infrared.

The image didn't change.

"Hmmmm," he subvocalized, entering another command, this one for the near ultra-violet.

There was no change on his screen. Yezeletta continued her rapid typing.

He tried a combination.

Again, the image remained unchanged.

Ray reached for the telephone to the electronics section.

WWW.ZARGKONJI.NET

Yezeletta examined her set-up in her own assortment of visual bandwidths. It was a graphical layout on her computer's screen, using the special programming and the equally special power supply she had placed in her main monitor. The pixels were radiating in the ultra-violet. No one else could see what she could....

That everything was in place.

ON THE NIGHT WIND—I

[Load Backup; Long Shot] Everything had been in place for a long, long time. Yezeletta had the more usual training in all of the arts of the kind of warrior that her creators had thought it well to teach her. But they hadn't neglected other facets of her training as well.

When a raw recruit is placed in Basic Training for the first time, the abrupt translation from civilian life to the military is a shock. This is intended; the Drill Instructors systematically remove any old civilian habits, and instill in the new recruit the necessary military habits, outlooks, and so on. In a tight spot, such inculcated reflex actions can be, and often are, life-savers. To soften the impact, while staying inside the "system" of military thought, the recruit is also exposed to another side of the military: frank propaganda as to why the selected branch of the military is the best, and how cogent the recruit is in picking Branch X over *those others*, usually described in far less flattering ways.

Yezeletta recalled times in her childhood, when people, ("counselors" they were called) had sat with her, looking up at her, telling her of her great future, of why she was *necessary*, of how *important* she was.

The young Yezeletta Zargkonji had listened with what she hoped was the right amount of interested attentiveness, as the predictable remarks of each of the counsellors washed past her, a current of words, recorded by her on-board systems, parsed by her own secretly installed programs, analyzed by the techniques that all of her teachers, trainers, and others had taught her.

All of which she later used to her own advantage.

WINDS OF CHANGE

[Load Backup; Medium Shot] In the fall of her twelfth year, she received an invitation to the Office of the Director.

This was important. All of her counsellors, teachers, coaches and just about everyone else including janitors stopped by to impress upon her Just How Important This Visit Was.

And to prepare her for it.

Yezeletta had no real clothes. The custom clothing she wore was made to order for her by several skilled tailors, who came by every two weeks or so to measure their rapidly growing customer, and to redo her wardrobe.

It wasn't much, as fashions went. Later Yezeletta would look back on her early clothing as a combination of the absolute worst of *Playboy's* fashion pages combined with a railroad engineer's overalls.

Unfortunately, that was about all that the tailors could manage.

But manage they did: the jumpsuit that Yezeletta wore was made of silk, it fit in all of the proper places, a leather belt added an accent, as did a gold necklace that someone from Admin had given her.

That it all looked as if it had been painted on her was something she didn't notice until long after. At the time, she was the only one who didn't notice.

ON THE NIGHT WIND—II

[Load Backup; Medium Close-Up] On the day of the Visit, Yezeletta was allowed to make the trip across the Sargon Complex all by herself. It was the first time that she had been allowed to walk as long a distance as even this without an escort.

She stood before the closed door of the Director's office and, as she had been rehearsed, knocked three times with her right hand, her lower.

"Come in," a pleasant baritone voice said.

Yezeletta opened the door with her lower right hand, and walked in. Again as she had been rehearsed, she came to a meter's distance from the Director's desk, and stopped. She looked down at the Director.

He looked up at her.

The young Yezeletta stood 183 centimeters tall. She was starting to fill out, as her body matured, and the Director looked up and frankly stared at the reason for his job, standing before him. Yezeletta regarded him with frank curiosity, and at that moment, she performed the first act that would lead to her precipitous exit from the project seven years later.

She activated her on-board systems to record everything she saw and heard, and to place those recordings into permanent storage.

The Director extended his hand.

"Good morning, Yes- Yezeletta," he said. (She caught the stutter and filed it away!)

"Good morning, Mr. Director," she answered, just as she had rehearsed it.

The Director paused and just looked at her.

"Please walk to the windows," he said.

Yezeletta did so. The action displayed the rolling walk she used on her four legs. Mr. Director watched her, fascinated.

Yezeletta increased the gain of her hearing, and added the results of the noise reduction and sonic enhancement to her running recording. Was Mr. Director's heart beating faster?

"You are very impressive," Mr. Director said. "You are the crowning achievement of Project Sargon."

Speak only when spoken to, they had said. "Thank you, Mr. Director."

Didn't he have a name? she wondered. I could find out in the Project Phone Book.

"You are the ultimate creation," Mr. Director went on, "of a dedicated program of scientific research." He stopped speaking. He waited.

The wait could have become uncomfortably long, but Yezeletta said, "Thank you." This time, she didn't say "Mr. Director" at the end.

She stood in the light of the window; with one eye she did a fast scan of the outside. In the distance, she could see a single open jeep carrying two individuals, both men, wearing the black denims of Sargon Security. She recorded the view, then looked back at Mr. Director.

She could stand for hours. There was empty seating in the office, but he didn't ask her to sit down. Apparently he didn't want her to. She looked down from her greater height at him. His heart *was* beating faster, now.

"You knew this, of course," Mr. Director continued after another awkward silence. "You are the first of a new age of researchers, soldiers and secret agents," he said without a trace of irony, "that will fight the wars of the future." He paused, then went on, "The biological research that you will do will bring us into a new age of scientific knowledge that will keep us at the forefront of new developments for the next century."

Yezeletta was expressionless as she recorded his speech. She was more interested in the ancillary items or sidebands that accompanied that speech: the subconscious tremors in his voice, the stresses and inflections of his pronunciation, his sentence structure.

Elsewhere, she was creating a *grammar*: admittedly an *ad hoc* grammar, but a grammar nevertheless that would describe his sentence structure and word usage in terms (*in <Terms>*, she thought) of his semantic use, of the cognates of his speech.

It would give her a final insight into Mr. Director's thoughts in the final days.

A COLD WIND TO VALHALLA

[Load Backup; Close-Up] Later, she would play back all of his speech and attempt to apply her training to it. At the age of twelve, she began to realize that her very survival depended upon getting the facts, and reasoning cogently with those facts. Her on-board memory augmentation was measured in *exabytes* (which, she recalled, were a thousand times greater than *petabytes*, which were a million *gigabytes*), and with the data compression she had at her disposal, she could hold possibly more in those chips than had ever been published on earth.

Mr. Director stood, walked around his desk, came to her.

"Yez— Yezeletta." That stutter, again!

"Yezeletta, you are the vanguard of a new age. The power that you represent will usher in an age of victory for all, and it will be your powers, which you must learn to use responsibly, that will do it!"

Later, Yezeletta would play that back and analyze his voice-stress patterns. She would detect no irony in his "responsibly." Apparently he was serious.

He put his arm around her waist, and looked up at her. "Not only are you powerful, you are beautiful. We designed you to be beautiful—" Yezeletta paid particular attention to his heartbeat. It was easy to do, as she could feel it from his arm, and input the information directly to her processors. She input other physiological data as well. "— and you will be beautiful to those we have you work with, under proper supervision, of course."

Yezeletta didn't know what to do with her arms on the side of her that Mr. Director was clinging to. She let them hang down, and casually allowed her right lower hand to touch the small of his back.

Data flowed into her fingertips.

"All of this will be yours, when your training and indoctrination are done, and you are fully grown." She would find no sense of irony here, later, either. Mr. Director really believed this, or he was an adept at concealing the involuntary "sidebands" of reactions that his body would provide if he were lying.

Mr. Director turned and faced her, his hand still on her waist. He looked for a moment at Yezeletta's developing chest, then up to her face. She gave him what she hoped was a friendly smile, not showing her teeth.

"Thank you, Mr. Director," she said evenly. "I hope to be a credit to Project Sargon."

"You will be," he replied, backing away to look at her completely. "You are why Project Sargon exists. Yezeletta—" *no stutter that time!*, "— the world will be ours, thanks to you. The power we will take will be because you have seized it for us! Can you do it?"

"Yes, Mr. Director," just as she had been coached, "I can."

"Train well, Yezeletta, study hard. It's been a pleasure meeting you."

That was a dismissal.

"Thank you," she said, and turned towards the door. She gazed at the davenport on one wall, with the coffee-table in front of it, the armchairs. She reached the door, and opened it. She looked over her shoulder at Mr. Director.

He was looking back at her with wide eyes. One of his hands was in his lap.

Yezeletta walked through the door, and closed it behind her.

She walked alone back to her quarters.

[Load Backup; Extreme Close-Up]   The corridors of Project Sargon were curiously deserted. Yezeletta went back to her apartments, lost in thought. The images of Mr. Director's desk, his office, the view from his office, and all of the details, including the sidebands of his nervous little speech, were safely stored away in her on-board memories, where she could look at them at her leisure. She opened her door, and went in.

She sat down.

A moment later, there was a diffident knock on the door.

She opened it to see one of the people from Sargon Security standing there.

"Hello," he said without preamble, "Stores wants the necklace back."

"Back," she said, rather surprised.

"Yep, that was just something to make you look nice for the Director. Gotta have it back. Things must be accounted for."

With a single gesture, Yezeletta removed the necklace, dropped it in the man's outstretched hand.

"Thank—"

She closed the door in his face.

THE WIND AT HER BACK

[Load Backup; Match Cut] She lay in her bed, a bed that she was rapidly outgrowing, and replayed the "interview" *I have to call it something!* from within her system storage. As Mr. Director's voice echoed within her head, she realized that she might have more than one set of ears in "her" apartment. She had been moved into her living quarters when she turned twelve. The people at the Project had made sort of a small celebration of Yezeletta getting "her own place" at last.

At first, she had liked the idea of no longer having what she thought of as baby-sitters. Really, a growing girl needed a little privacy, and some of her nannies had been nosy to the point of following her into the bathroom.

Now, with all of the glabrously complementary prose from Mr. Director playing back into her auditory nerves, she wondered. How much privacy *did* she have?

"Good morning, Yes- Yezeletta," she listened to him intone, for the forty-fourth time.

He <u>must</u> know my name. Did he stutter because he's seen it in print, and never said it himself? His heartbeat...it was faster after he said it. Was he "daring" himself to say my name? Or was it some kind of special moment for him? Has he ever seen me when I was younger? Has he ever been in the same room with me before?

She opened a window in her left eye, loaded it with a picture of his office as she had seen it. She enhanced the image. Nothing useful there.

Then, the young Yezeletta Zargkonji did what she had been trained to do. Her training had always been "other-directed," she was expected to use it for the benefit of whoever had given her directions (she didn't want to use the military term *orders*). With a burst of insight, she realized that what she had, what she *was* could be used for her benefit, also. For herself.

She looked at Mr. Director with the full bandwidth of her vision.

The false-color image told another story. His skin was flushed and hot. The infra-red radiation from what of his skin she could see directly showed the heat signature of dilated blood vessels. She shied away from the obvious. She knew what that *might* mean, but had thought that *The Director* was above all that. Or, at least, had the common sense not to show it.

The tremors in his voice were more interesting. There were these little demi-quavers as if he were nervous, or....*Is he afraid of Yezeletta? He had *his hand around my waist. He looked....*Her right hand, her upper, went involuntarily to her right breast. She cupped it in her hand, almost covering it. Her nipple hardened beneath her fingers. *Did he want...me?* That was interesting. She called up, with some pre-programmed silicon assistance, a picture of her face as she had seen it in the mirror earlier that day.

A face-shaped face. A little on the round side. She had let her hair grow a little longer than her nannies had wanted it, but now they couldn't tell her to cut it. She smiled at the mirror and the reflection had smiled back. She thought that she looked sort of...crafty. Her nose was too big, and her eyes! They were larger than any twelve-year-old's eyes could ever be. She had been told that the size was because of their "augmentations." She'd looked the word up in her knowledge-base, and found the size of her eyes reasonable after that. Even more so after looking up just what had gone into their design: there had practically been a separately-named project just for her vision! Besides, they looked like a cat's eyes. Like Mr. Fur-Face, that one of the Administrative secretaries had brought in to show her.

She had never thought of herself as—pretty.

Maybe others did.

"Not only are you powerful, you are beautiful. We designed you to be beautiful—" she replayed his comment. *Is that appropriate to a secret agent? Does he think I'm a lady James Bond?*

She went cold.

She adjusted her skin away from the disturbing sensation.

He had his hand in his lap when she left him.

She slid her right hand down between her legs, to that place where all of the hair had started growing. It felt good to touch herself there, it made her tremble, with the easily recordable electric shock sensations, that echoed and reverberated throughout her body. She touched her nipple again and thought of Mr. Director's speech.

Suddenly Yezeletta Zargkonji was twelve years old, alone and very afraid.

ON THE NIGHT WIND—IV

[Load Backup; Dissolve] *Her sleep that night was fitful. She tossed and turned on a bed that was getting too short to sleep comfortably in. She dreamt of Mr. Director looking at her, of her standing naked before him, unable to move from his gaze that pinned her down in one place. She called on her internal systems to help her, but they were all disabled. Mr. Director was stalking towards her, also naked—<u>although she could not see what she knew was there</u>—, smiling that same smile that he had smiled when she had entered his office.*

When she awoke, she was sweating.

A COLD WIND TO YEZELETTA

[Load Backup; Wipe] The following morning, Yezeletta arose from her bed, and looked around her with a new kind of perception. Her new apartments were intended to keep her in, but she would turn the tables on Mr. Director.

She would keep them out.

She threw herself into her classes. Those charged with her instruction at first didn't notice any big changes in her performance, perhaps additional attention to details, but that was expected, even from those who were not conversant with her capabilities.

She was particularly interested in her martial arts courses.

Improvised weapons, devices that may be made from commonly acquired objects, which, when combined, yield something new and deadly, she found particularly interesting. Slowly, she realized who she was, and that she was too valuable to be someone—or something—that could be easily taken advantage of by a Director who might have found her attractive.

A week passed, and her fears subsided, slightly. Another, and she realized that "Mr. Director" was a middle aged man who thought quite highly of himself, but harbored thoughts about Yezeletta (and, she would find out later, about other women) that required him to behave in the way he did.

Perhaps he thought that he could be that obvious with Yezeletta. *I'm the wrong one to be thought of that way.*

She continued to learn, and to accumulate her cache of defensive tools.

ON THE NIGHT WIND—V

[Load Backup; Iris] In another year, she would look back on her fears as immature, naïve. She was too busy with what she had been given for her thirteenth birthday: the workmen had spent a week installing it, and when they left, she surveyed her new domain: the shining stainless-steel machineries, the work benches, the computers—she even had her own Local Area Net!—and all of the rest with an emotion approaching enchantment. This was her own private laboratory, hers and hers alone!

Then she was told what they wanted her to do with it.

She didn't tell them what she really did.

ON THE NIGHT WIND—VI

[Load Backup; Fade-Out] She would see Mr. Director one more time in her life.

SHADES OF—OTHER

[In Security] The gent from the electronics shop was a methodical, careful man who insisted on putting all of the monitoring equipment through all of its internal tests first, before doing anything else. When he was satisfied that all was well internally, he started, equally methodically, through all of the observation modes into Yezeletta's quarters.

His observations were identical to Ray's.

"If I miss my guess, I's say there's something interfering with the transmissions from the devices in her quarters," he said. "If I didn't know better, I'd say a definite Spoofing or Man in the Middle attack." Here he was referring to the kind of information transmission attack where an enemy agent would interpose himself between two parties, and control what of the transmission each recipient would see.

"When were the last transmitters put in her living area," he asked.

"About a week ago," Ray replied. "I supervised it myself while she was out at some meeting or another."

"This needs to be checked out," the gent from Electronics said. "Is there any way we could get into her quarters, now?"

Ray regarded Yezeletta's image in the screen. She had stopped typing, and was standing at her desk, stretching impressively.

TAKE A LOOK: TAKE A GOOD LOOK

[In Security] Later that day, a small tempest erupted in Project Sargon Security. It started with Ray Dahlquist restating the difficulty with the visual observation modes, and focusing on The Strange Case of Yezeletta's Marathon Typing. The meeting took place in the conference room near the monitoring post.

Ray and several other members of Security were there, along with some new faces and none of the unnecessary personnel. There was one in attendance that none of the Security operatives knew about. It was looking at them from an air duct.

The meeting lasted well into the evening.

ARRIVALS

Yezeletta watched the meeting, recording it both into her internal systems and into a place in her computer's cavernous storage. *How much do they know?* she asked herself, not daring even to talk to her reflection in a mirror.

The raster-flies worked. It was an accident of fate that Ray had tried the other color modes *yesterday*.

If Ray *and* the electronics tech could be discredited *and* if the bugs in Yezeletta's apartments could be kept from being examined until...until *later*.

What?

Yezeletta Zargkonji reviewed the lessons she had been given. The tactics, the weapons. *All* of it.

She would need it all.

ENCOUNTERS OF THE FIRST KIND

That night, Dick, the night man at Security, and usually the only one on that shift, sat in his usual place in front of the monitor rack. The array of screens before him showed what they had always shown.

Those unchanging images had caused problems all of the way back to Canberra, Sydney and to another installation in Buenos Aires.

It may have caused repercussions even further out.

Dick consulted his watch: 02.00 Hours, Friday Morning. His bags were packed, he was ready to go (unbidden, the old tune came to him), the buses would indeed leave at the ghastly hour of six a.m. He would get a good if short nap on the bus and a longer one on the local plane flight to Darwin. Civil service benefits were good, he would have the promised two-week holiday, and a job at the Commonwealth Building in Darwin at better than his current pay-rate when it ended. There was no motion in the screens. Dick pressed a key on the selector panel and a black and white picture of the Agent, lying on her side, appeared.

She appeared to be sleeping soundly. He would be sitting at a bank of screens like this one in Darwin. Perhaps he'd even be working nights. It would be good to go home to the wife and kids at the end of the day, instead of to a small bedroom!

Dick pressed the **Zoom** control. It should have caused the camera on the far end to zoom into a close-up of the sleeping Agent. If he looked closely, he could see, sticking out from beneath her right arms, her right breast. Dick wasn't being uncivilized, just—interested.

The image didn't move.

Frowning, Dick pressed the **Zoom** key again. He reviewed the set-up of the panel. Another thing to call Electronics about. The **Zoom** key should operate that specific input. He tried it a third time and, as before, nothing happened.

Dick punched the *Check-Out* command for the small system that drove the monitoring controls. The system thought for a moment and put up the <u>Check-Out Complete—OK.</u> indicator.

He marked the date and time of the failure on his report, and switched to another view.

The Agent was still asleep. Dick pressed the **Zoom** again.

When nothing happened, he wrote it up as a system malfunction. He checked the time: 02.20. He would be leaving this den of secret agents in three hours and forty minutes.

Let someone else worry about it.

HEADQUARTERS

Dick's lack of action actually bought Yezeletta a day. She watched via her imager in the air-conditioning duct as Dick tried to zoom in on the scene of her asleep that the raster-flies were sending out. If she had been so inclined, she would have kicked herself for not thinking about the possibility of a **Zoom** command. The cameras hadn't been equipped with zoom-lenses, so the function must have been done digitally. And programming *wasn't* visible from the outside!

Yezeletta realized that there was a difference between training and practice and between practice and experience. The Project had provided her with very comfortable surroundings, and all the equipment she needed for the research programs that both *they* and she had wanted to do.

That looked as if it were about to change.

She could have sent out a mindless little insect that took the shape of a beetle. Externally, it looked like a Stag Beetle, colored a decorative violet and blue. The internal configuration of the insect was mostly metallic: chiefly ferrous, with tiny veins of silver and gold. Those precious metals—no lifeform was known that required them—would place an upper limit on the insect's life from heavy-metal poisoning, but did make it quite electrically conductive. It could sit across the output of a power supply long enough for the supply to destroy itself before the bug vaporized like a blowing fuse. Then the insect's remains would slowly disintegrate, leaving only tiny metal flecks that drafts would remove later.

And, best of all, no one here knew of this creation.

Not having to use it was the best part.

INTERIM DEPLOYMENT

At Six AM Friday morning, Dick and Ray sat next to each other on the bus trip into Alice Springs. There, they shook hands, promised to stay in touch, and went to their respective boardings. As the airliner took off from Alice Springs International, Dick leaned back in his seat and tried to find the Project from the air. Was that it there in the east? What would happen to the Agent?

It was out of his hands, now. It had never been in them.
The plane was reaching cruising altitude.
He would be home in two hours.

D ATELINE S YDNEY

The last file sent from the janitor's cell disappeared into the national telephone network and was lost among the terabytes of other communications. At the *Herald*, an ordinary, if anonymous, encrypted email appeared in the in-box of the Night Editor.

He filed it, wrote it to a removable medium and placed it in the drawer with the others.

In the Armory. With the rest of the munitions.

T HE F INAL C OUNTDOWN

Yezeletta verified the progress of the contents of the last of her incubators. The object growing in it was an almost perfect icosahedron, a regular solid comprised of twenty equilateral triangular sides. It sat on one of its sides in the center of the incubator. Gently, Yezeletta touched it. It was neither warm nor cold to the touch: it was at room-temperature. Furthermore, the incubator was shut off.

Within the hard shell of the icosahedron, a complex of life-forms was growing. There were the spores within it to grow imagers and other reconnaissance life-forms, an organic processor, and many other things, *in one convenient package.*

Feeling about as content as she could under the circumstances, she pulled a sheet—an ordinary cotton bed-sheet this time—over the object, and read out the status of the raster-flies. Then she shut off all of the lights, even the ultra-violets.

The best offense is a good defense.

24 / 7 == ....NO ....—30—

[Parallel Process; Real-Time] The Night Editor at the *Sydney Morning Herald* was bored. Frankly, unnecessarily bored. It seemed the most starkly improbable thing in his life, that he was sitting in the offices of one of the biggest newspapers in the world, both print and data-feed to the internet, with millions of readers world-wide, and he was bored.

There hadn't been a big news break in at least two days.

Newspapers thrive on immediacy. Old news is worse than no news, the readers want something new that's just broken, that's just happened or is in the process of happening. Sunday supplement multi-part series are fine; two were starting this week. Last week, the rather pandering pictorial on the beaches of Australia had sold big, mostly out of the country where topless beaches weren't the norm, and....

He still remembered fondly how his paper had been the first one to find and print—twenty-four hours before the *London Times*, *The Daily Mirror* or the *New York Times* had even acquired it, the manifesto of the lone wolf who had blown up Washington D.C.

Tonight was acutely dull.

He rifled in his desk for the remains of his lunch; he had to reach back into the drawer, and found himself holding a small, flat object.

It was the square, plastic case of a Data Chip.

The 20-gigabyte variety. The companies that made those things continued to make the ridiculously small ones, because governments still needed them. There were a lot of low-capacity systems in government, as they simply refused to upgrade. Because of this, 20s were quite common. Anonymous, even.

Where had these come from? Oh, right. Those stringers.

On impulse, the Night Editor stuffed the chip into his computer and unzipped the large file on it.

It was a text file. One that brought him fully awake, fully alert.

He had his story.

He grabbed the telephone, called the research department. Then the morgue.

It would be just under a day later, the research having been finished, that he would call again.

To stop the presses.

SUNDAY **M**ORNING

[System Access Only] Yezeletta never did understand religion.

Later, she was to consider this lack of understanding a designed-in trait; an undocumented "feature" of her training. Now, it was yet another datum about her opposition at the Project (*everyone!*, she thought) to log, and add to her list of possible predictors of future action.

For the permanent staff that actually lived at Project Sargon, Administration General Services made note of the religions of those who wished to go public with such matters and provided access for them to the appropriate clergy. On Sundays and occasionally other days as well, practitioners of the various creeds would show up for services for those who felt they needed such. The services were usually well attended.

This Sunday, there was nothing and nobody. The chaplains didn't show; warned off, no doubt, by a phone call on early Friday.

Project Sargon was strangely silent, all of the support people were gone, replaced by a skeleton staff. One of the directors was doubling up as a cook: his job consisted of getting out prepackaged meals and placing them where the remaining few permanent staff could find them.

Yezeletta usually ate in the cafeteria on Sundays, but she stayed in her quarters that day. If it were possible for her to fidget, she would have.

She suppressed even the inclination to fidget, and sent several small, furry arachnoids out. She tapped into several more that she had deployed into trees around the Project building, and—

Now that was just totally curious!

"Mr. Director," the head of Security, and several others that she recognized were going out to a fleet of Chevy 4x4s that were parked near the access road to the firing range.

As she watched, the men got into the utility vehicles, and the drivers pulled out, in the direction of the range.

That road was conveniently under a canopy of trees. Yezeletta touched one of her Imagers, and sent a signal. It would have to be the last truck in the little convoy.

As the last Chevy drove under an over-reaching tree-branch, several small critters detached from the branch, and dropped onto the truck's roof. They were joined by smaller, more inconspicuous creatures from the next tree.

Yezeletta thought she might need relays.

While she waited for the convoy full of Directorate to get to its destination, Yezeletta leaned back in her special chair and checked in with her observer in the air-duct in Security. What she saw was...different.

Security was deserted.

For the first time *ever*, the Security monitors didn't have an attendant.

Where were they?

She kept watching. She took the time to check the performance of the raster-flies, using the actual monitoring set-up they were spoofing to verify that the images the flies were sending were the ones that Security would receive.

And I wish I had more time to finish them off properly! The way they should work!

One of the Security men came back. Yezeletta's eyes widened; the man was wearing something that the men in Security had never worn in the years she had been aware of them: a sidearm.

She knew that all of the members of Project Security were checked out on at least pistols. She'd heard individuals speaking of qualifying at the annual marksmanship tests at the range some kilometers into the mountains. But *wearing* a firearm was something else, entirely, particularly in a country in which private ownership of handguns was strictly forbidden.

Yezeletta considered her preparations. How much more time did she have? What did her ostensible masters want to do? With her? With her *now?*

PREEMPTIVE STRIKE, LITERARY

The time passed early Sunday Morning in jerky intervals of agonizing slowness and dizzying, blinding speed. Yezeletta had set up all of her necessary defenses, her offensive capabilities and had her intelligence gatherers out.

She had made her preparations. Now, she had to wait.

And, a spider in her web, wait is what she did.

THEIR TRUE COLORS—

[Network Input; Extending Outwards; Scatter Read] Her wait, from start to full informational disclosure, lasted just under an hour.

She had kept an eye on the travel of the Directorate. The four vehicles had driven straight past the firing range, and kept moving into the foothills of Mount Strangway, crossing the Plenty Highway from Sargon. The unpaved road on that side—scarcely more than ruts—twisted, turned, and stopped.

The road lead to the base of a cliff.

Fascinating! Yezeletta thought. Which James Bond villain have they decided to emulate?

As she watched through her clandestine additions to the convoy, the rocks, foliage and dead branches at the base of the cliff directly ahead, rippled, degenerated into pixelations, and vanished, to reveal a steel door that was already opening: descending into the ground.

Yezeletta raised one dark eyebrow at this exterior presentation. *Another Project?* she asked herself, *a backup?*

The Chevys entered, taking all but one of Yezeletta's creations along. One jumped off to station itself near the entrance to relay for the others going in. The image those returned to her changed, as the darker inner corridor was closed off from daylight. Her Imagers adjusted for the lower light level, and the details filled themselves in. Such details as there were: the vehicular corridor through which the four vehicles passed was concrete-lined, but otherwise undistinguished.

A short time later, she consulted an internal timer register—about ninety seconds; that tunnel was *long*—the passage widened into a small parking area. The truck with her imagers on it was the last to park. As it pulled in, she sent an order, and the imagers leapt off the vehicle onto the rough concrete ceiling. They ran for the bases of light fixtures, where they would become lost in the glare.

The Sargon Directorate headed for a doorway, and Yezeletta's diminutive allies followed. She reached with a long arm for a pack of memory chips, and slotted one for a backup recording.

Once through the doorway, her Imagers were on the ceiling of a well-lit corridor. On the other side of the parking area entrance, the walls and ceiling were painted a flat institutional light green. *Should I have had color-changing characteristics on those?* she asked herself. The corridor was mostly deserted, and she took advantage of this to hurry her creations after the Directors. The passers-by (both of them, she noticed) seemed to be bent on rather serious errands: neither of them looked up, even though Yezeletta halted her remotes, lest anyone below notice a motion where there should be none.

Ahead, a hole in the ceiling tiles allowed her to move the imagers to the upper side of the tiles. It was a suspended ceiling, and all of the cabling that ran just about everywhere above the tiles would be quite interesting in its context. She regarded the installation with a professional eye, and kept the imagers moving.

Ahead were familiar sounds.

"Mr. Director" was speaking.

—COMPOSED IN CHORDS

[Net Central; Gather Write] She positioned two imagers about a meter apart, and fed the view into her on-board systems as a stereoscopic feed; the exaggerated depth allowed her to analyze the details of the meeting. The men were sitting at a circular table, the center of which was occupied by a ten-sided flat metal device. Above the surface of the device an opalescent fog rippled and pulsated.

"— We can move her to the suite we have established here for the next step in the fabrication," Mr. Director was saying. "The programming for her internals was complete, and ready as of two days ago. The new system can be downloaded into her at any time, and, after that, she will have no further memories to speak of. She will become quite pliable. We should have had on-board monitoring of her activities before this, of course, but, she's the first, and we've learned from the mistakes we made with her.

"This is a simulation of what she will become." He pressed a glowing area on a keyboard, and the luminescent fog cleared within the display device, and a small image of—

Yezeletta involuntarily took a quick breath. She adjusted herself back to "calm," and stared. The image was of herself, and she was engaged in, in....

Her mind raced. She had thought that some day she would meet "Mr. Right," and that she would engage in at least some of the actions she saw her image performing.

Mr. Director continued: "In this simulation, her mind has been completely disengaged from her body. She might still be conscious, but it won't matter. If she's still capable of cognition by then, she will be in a silent, dark place devoid of sensation." He gestured at another artifact in the holographic display. "This control panel will give her 'customer' total control over her actions. Gentlemen, she will perform exactly as you wish. She is the marionette, you are her masters.

"Pull her strings, yank her chains. Take her.

"She will be useful for the obvious, while we store her away, here, for the next step."

RETURN TO THE WEB

[Compiling] Yezeletta let the rest of the Director's speech wash past her, as it was being recorded, as well as converted, compressed, and being stored in her internals.

Obviously, they know something I don't. Many things. What the hell is this "next step," anyway?

She issued a series of commands to her systems. In her screen, Mr. Director said, "We can keep the press from getting anything more by deploying the appropriate disinformation. By the time any investigators, press or otherwise, reach us, her very existence will be classified history, and the external Project Building will be either refurbished, or, perhaps better, destroyed by a sudden fire that we were simply unable to put out. How unfortunate."

To an external observer, Yezeletta's expression was one more appropriate to an angry feline. She closed her eyes for ten seconds, and made some delicate endocrine adjustments.

She calmed down. Again.

The Director's voice continued, implacably, "We can install the new programming when we return. We have a story we can give her that should direct her preparations, if any, away from the current plan. We can take advantage of this misdirection to take her, restrain her, and install the new over-ride. She will be properly docile when we're done, and we can install her in the other suite here. All of her chains will be worn inside.

"That should be the end of our problems." He smiled at the others.

WEB INSTALLATION

[Link] Yezeletta heard the Director's last words from a distance. She was in her work room checking her creations, yet again.

She thought at a high rate: what about electrical power to her apartments? There was the quietly-installed remotely-controlled short around the external circuit-breakers that were the ultimate controls on her current supply. Water? She had sent a servitor to the appropriate valves with a file and several small hacksaws. Superficially, the valves looked untouched, but if someone turned them, the valve-stems and valve-handles would break off short, flush with the tops of each valve.

She had seen that trick in an old movie.

Air conditioning, now....The entire Project was on a large central-air plant that was maintained from an out-building. They might be able to inject some sort of sleeping gas into the air ducts, but it would get to the entire building—which just happened to be conveniently deserted.

She spent several minutes sending imagers into the ducts to look. There was nothing suspicious in the ducts, *now, but*, she thought, *that wasn't exactly too hot a check-out*. A gas injector could be set up in moments, and Security had a lot of other things that she didn't like at all.

Okay, drill for a gas attack: drill was exactly what she would do. She touched a servitor's head, and it went to several others and passed the commands to them.

As she watched the final moments of the meeting in the underground installation, her minions drilled holes through to the outside, then removed several windows and replaced the glass components in them with other things that looked like glass, but weren't.

Movement.

The meeting far below the surface of the foothills of a mountain range was breaking up. Several of the Sargon Directorate stayed for a short time to watch, with evident relish, the holographic image of Yezeletta computer-animated (*and controlled*, she thought) performing with three other men. The men in the simulation all had a kind of uniformity, no more than stock animations, but her image was as exact as imaging technology could make it.

Yezeletta shook her head. Not in disbelief, she was beyond that. Her image wasn't exact; the animator of this fantasy had made some obvious changes.

She looked down at herself. She was what some men called "well-built" or maybe "well-endowed."

Her image was by far better.

Installing me, she thought, They spoke of installing me!

WEB ACCESS

[Wait State] Eventually, Yezeletta found time to rest. She dozed off into a fitful sleep, her guardians around her, her near defenses pulled in close.

She had to *wait* better than her adversaries.

ALL NIGHT LONG

[Load Descriptor] She was awakened when a line on her web was tugged on by another.

The dream she was in was almost literally of being in a web, except that the web lines were data structures in a program and the "tug" was one of her servitors gently tapping on her right arm, her upper.

She thanked the unknown benefactor who had trained her to come awake instantly, leapt from bed and went to her main computer. The screen was lit up in three windows. The first was a news feed, the second was a scene in the cafeteria where most of the Directorate was sitting almost in a huddle around a...newspaper. The third window was of Security, where that window had been since last Wednesday, and where all of the operatives were now wearing sidearms.

The news-feed window was the easiest to read. It said "<u>*Sydney Morning Herald* Article Discloses Secret Biological Project</u>" and a link to a URL where the text could be read. Yezeletta surfed to that link, and:

Biological Project in Alice Springs to Field New Research

She read on: *A secret biological research center in Alice Springs revealed new technologies to create new life forms, and new techniques for curing diseases through cellular surgical techniques and DNA repair.*

The article went on to describe in a very general way the kinds of research that Yezeletta had been tested on and which she was currently undertaking. The lead story was short, but the "*Sydney Herald* Staff Writer" who wasn't named (*good idea, that*, she thought), promised a continuation in tomorrow's paper.

Yezeletta read it again.

What was more interesting was what it didn't mention. She paused to save the entire web page into a local file in her local system. Then she continued: the story didn't mention her. Nor did it mention any of her created life forms. There was not a word on the servitors, the imagers, or much of anything else. *And certainly not the developments in my own labs!* She scanned it again, looking for any between-the-lines stuff that a subtle writer could insert by judicious hinting and the use of connotational overtones.

Not a word about Yezeletta.

Wait a minute. This line about the "head of research" who "asked not to be identified." That could be anyone! The Deputy Director. His assistant. Any of the other department heads. She stared for a moment at the Dali print hanging opposite her desk. *Hell, that could be the head of the photography department! He liked to show me how pictures were printed!* The individual's *sex* wasn't even stated.

She thought about that one. The kind of American loudmouthism that insisted that sex didn't matter—mostly by talking about it excessively—and which manifested itself in a strident insistence that any kind of descriptor be used for an individual's sex except the word "he" had never gotten very far outside the United States. When the Capital of the U.S. had disappeared under a pair of small mushroom clouds, most of such arguments had ceased being significant even within the States. So that didn't matter, in an ironic way. A "he" could be a "she" or (a look at a nearby servitor) even an "it."

No points there. And no useful information, either!

Damn.

A place on her screen flickered.

She pulled the window in which the movement had occurred to the front and saw the cause: the news-feed had blanked out. In the window's center was the diagnostic message:

Connection Broken. Re-Connection Attempt Failed.#

Frowning, Yezeletta pulled up the maintenance window, ran a diagnostic on her linkage into the Project LAN, tried to reconnect.

There was no response. That link to the outside was dead.

She ran a system check-out, but didn't let it go very far. All of the LAN lines went out through a huge trunk terminal board, and she knew where the trunk board was located. She could *see* it.

Security.

PREEMPTIVE STRIKE, OPERATIONAL

It was only a matter of time. Yezeletta had both many ideas, and no idea what was happening (the difficulty was in making a choice among them), but enough had happened in the last four days, that the chances of any part of its being beneficial to her were somewhere between zero and nothing. *Unless, of course, what I saw was a contingency plan, and I am to be employed for the purpose that they created me. A mission?* That might be a reason for clearing out the project. The support staff weren't needed any longer, send them on to other civil service jobs. *Does that make _me_ a civil service employee, also? Just what is _my_ citizenship? If any?*

No one had ever mentioned this. That question had never arisen.

She stood, considered the situation. Today, if that horrid little meeting was correct, and she didn't doubt it for a moment, they would show up to install a system in her internals that would mean the end of her.

Her preparations were finished. It was time to marshal her forces.

DOWN HOME COOKING

Her first step was easy. She had breakfast.

Yezeletta's artificially high metabolism was one of the things that gave her the speed and agility that her builders (she frowned without noticing; was there a better word?) had wanted. It allowed a woman of her size to move quickly and *keep moving* without tiring, when it became necessary.

Normally, cooking was one of her ways of relaxing. Today it was a refueling stop on the way into a theater of war. Almost on autopilot, her mind busy on other things, she prepared fourteen scrambled eggs, added a kilogram of shredded mozzarella cheese topped with diced onions. She followed that by two kilograms of sirloin, rare, chased by a Caesar salad described inadequately as "large." She downed two liters of orange juice and an assortment of vitamins that would fill an ordinary coffee cup. She took her special one-liter coffee cup filled with the corrosive black mixture she favored, hot and unadulterated, back to her computer. She made the peremptory gesture to the other lifeforms around her to get food *now!*, and they went to the places they would go for their own kind of nutrient.

Next, she went into her special lab, to the tool-box. From it, she removed the two means by which she would blind Security.

A claw-hammer and a spray-can of black paint.

She turned on the ultra-violets, and went around to the video bugs. With a wave, the raster-flies removed themselves from each camera, and she sprayed the tiny receptor until black paint—looking black-purple in the UV light—dripped down the walls, *like the black blood in Hitchcock's Psycho*, she thought. She treated all four of the bugs in the special lab that way, then went to the rest in her quarters, removing the spoofing raster-flies, and blacking out the eyes of Security.

Finally, the last one. She made her gesture from a short step-ladder, so that she would be at eye-level with the device. She looked straight into the diminutive camera, and smashed it with the hammer.

Then she went back to her lab and opened cages.

What kind of war do you want, little men? I'll give it to you!

<<WWW.YEZELETTA.MIL>>

[Input Active] Her tap into Security still worked. In all this time they had been too busy to look into an air duct that was too close to a high ceiling for convenience. She looked *there*. The olive-drab case with its precious cargo was safe. The Security Operatives...*No. The enemy.* They looked as if they were too busy to consider that. Still—

The servitors that she dispatched were some that had been working as general go-fers in the motor-pool. In response to her instructions they took up positions as close to the olive-drab case as possible, covering the entry points to where it was kept, armed with devices from the garage.

Movement. Hmmmm. How many were still in this Complex? And—

Yezeletta went to her front door. She placed her hand on the door-knob, twisted. The dead feeling from the door was from more mass than the door had.

She was locked in.

We'll see about that.

She went back to her main system and typed an instruction into a command-line. Silently in the complex, roving imagers, any servitors that hadn't responded to her gestured command (relayed) to seek nutrition—then *hide*—and several small devices she had emplaced years earlier began the census.

In friendlier times, *if there ever were such!*, she'd had access to the Complex Directory: the Project Telephone Book. She had kept all of the updates and reprintings of the book whenever they were issued. Now, all of her constructs—so useful to others all of this time—were the kind of observation system that the head of Security had dreamt of. She wanted the exact count of the personnel left here. And where they were. And would be.

The data rolled in: strategic election returns. Most of them were in the Deputy Director's conference room. Two were in the cafeteria, the rest in Security. Yezeletta went to her special incubators, and brought a wire basket filled with death back to her kitchen. She removed the remains of breakfast, and laid out the necessary foodstuffs for lunch, keeping the wire basket close.

Far off, a sound. Far off, voices. Far off, the distinctive sound of a key in a lock, the key turning. To Yezeletta's hearing, even the tumbler springs sang a specific tune. Then—

Her door opening.

THE EYES

She heard them enter. From the syncopation of the foot-steps, six of them. She waited as they came to her. They found her in the kitchen her hands full of eggs.

The Deputy Director and five others.

"Good morning," she said, pleasantly enough.

"Good morning," the Deputy Director said. "We would like to talk with you."

"Yes," Yezeletta looked down on the man. He had to bend his head back to look at her face. *His heartbeat is accelerating. He is afraid?*

"Miss Zark—Zargkonji, we have received a notification of your disposition from the Project Director in Buenos Aires."

"Do you speak for him?"

"Yes. He—wants to meet you. To thank you for—" He stopped. His breathing and heartbeat are faster. I can smell the sweat under his arms, on his back.

"What do you want?" Her voice was sharp.

The Deputy pulled himself together, tried to stand straighter. "The," he started to say. "The Project is canceled by order of the office of the Prime Minister. You are to be retired." It came out in a rush.

Yezeletta took a half-step towards him. The half-step took her closer to the kitchen counter.

"Retired?" She asked. "How do you 'retire' someone such as myself?"

"There's a place in New South Wales where you will be allowed to live out your life," another director said. "You must agree not to leave the place. It's a compound on the south end near the beach. You'll be guarded, of course," he said, offhandedly.

"That's it?" she asked.

"You do have Commonwealth citizenship, by derivation from the biologic antecedents from which you were made," someone else said. "As an employee of the Project you are entitled to benefits."

How nice of you to thank my antecedents, she thought.

"We will require some concessions," the Deputy continued. "You must agree to refrain from using any of the advantages we've built into you."

Yezeletta raised an eyebrow incrementally at that, but said nothing.

"And you must give up your lower arms."

Yezeletta froze. *How do these expect me to react? This is worse than being on that stage!* None of the directorate saw her brief pause, or at least registered it consciously. She looked down on them perceiving them in shades of red, blue and green and colors that they never knew existed. Colors that formed chords that vibrated and tingled with their own internal tension, their own unearthly beauty.

Their true colors.

"I am accustomed to the use of the body I was born into. Do you realize what you are asking? What if I wanted you to lose one of your hands?" She placed her left hand, her lower, on the wire basket. "Surely I am of more use to you intact."

"The conditioning regime we will provide will alleviate that," the Deputy Director said defensively. Their heartbeats are so transparent to me. What of these liars? Nothing they say is honest. They are politicians, at best. If I could touch him to get a galvanic skin response, it alone could prove it. His voice stress tells me all I want to know.

"May I have some time to think about this?" Her left hand, *her lower*, tightened on the wire basket.

The Sargon Directorate conferred amongst itself. The Deputy turned to her. "How long would you like?"

"Thursday. I would like until Thursday." *One day, maybe two, later than I need.*

"Thursday will be fine." The Deputy Director took a step backwards and landed on the instep of the person behind him. That director stepped back.

"Thursday. We'll be back on Thursday." They turned and left.

Liars!

HER OWN DIRECTION

She heard the door close, heard the song of the lock that was performed for her and her alone. The little men, *Oh, all right, anyone shorter than me is going to be "little,"* had left unaware of their close brush with an uncomfortable death.

Yezeletta ran through her tactical options in her mind. *If this is how they treat their citizens, have they any right to my allegiance?* It was Monday afternoon. Thursday was three days off.

Three days she wouldn't actually get, if she had figured her enemies objectively.

Probably tomorrow.

She had work to do. She went back to her lab.

THE AMATEURS

The head of security, a man named Roscoe Hazeltine, had watched as Yezeletta made her statement. The look of cold calculating disdainful fury on her face as she had pulverized the last video bug was a sight—her face had filled the screen—that he would never forget.

The article in the *Sydney Herald* had the complex buzzing like a beehive that had been struck repeatedly with a stick, even if the bees had no way of fighting back. Canberra was excited, to understate the matter greatly, the powers that be that resided there wanted this hushed up in a hurry and the Agent forcibly retired. Roscoe paused, took a deep breath, *If they can do it*, he thought.

DO IT TO IT

Yezeletta had her customarily large dinner. Around her the servitors had assembled in a small crowd of milling preprogrammed biological automatons. The duct-work in this end of the project was a discreet raceway for small spider-like creatures. As quietly as possible, she was withdrawing most of her observers from deserted areas of the Project Complex, and either recalling them to the comparative safety of her quarters or using them as backups for the others that were in place. Fortunately, she didn't have to worry about either rodents or rat traps. One of her earliest achievements (one which had impressed her creators a lot) was a variation on the basic remote imager that involved longer, heavier retractile claws and the capability to enter burrows. The practical result of this was that the Complex and several hundred meters around it were virtually rat- and mouse-free.

Now I hunt bigger, viler game, she thought grimly as she summoned the Cat-Arachnids from their hideaways. Next to her in the living-room she kept the wire basket, now in its own portable incubator. It was less than an arm's reach away, and would stay that way. Behind her, dogging her with the blind compulsiveness of the programmed, a servitor held another incubator containing more of the same.

It would be tomorrow.

It was.

Yezeletta slept little that night, all of her warning systems out around her, a web of data links, lasers, biologic organisms, programmable devices.

She was awakened, or more accurately, brought fully awake, by a commotion at the door. The metal bar that she'd used to wedge the door shut prevented it from being opened from the other side. She let the Directorate fumble with this problem for fifteen minutes while she got something from her special lab and deployed it just outside the back hallway into the kitchen.

In the kitchen, the preparations for breakfast were laid out, as she had always done them. She took her place, gestured to a servitor in the living-room.

The servitor yanked on a long rope, pulling the steel bar away from the door. It *slammed!* open.

The Directors tried not to notice their impediment. They entered alone, but she could see men in black-denim uniforms waiting in the hallway. Armed, no doubt.

When they found her in the kitchen, Yezeletta Zargkonji was scrambling eggs for breakfast.

She looked down at them. "You're early," she said.

"Ah...We don't have much time, Miss Zark." This was one of the others, not the Deputy. Security? He was a new face. She didn't recognise him.

Her breakfast sizzled and popped in the buttered frying pan.

"Have you considered our offer?"

"Have you considered mine?" she replied. She reached several objects from the wire basket with her upper arms while cracking several eggs into the frying pan with her lower.

"Your offer?" This was the Deputy, himself.

"I would like to keep my mind. Also my arms. I will go where you wish."

"That's quite out of the question, my friend," the Deputy said. "Our requirements are non-negotiable. We are prepared to down-load the necessary conditioning into your internals immediately."

"And if I refuse?" she asked.

"We do not recommend your refusing," he replied.

"I ask you again," She *had* to have a straight answer. "Will you let me keep my arms and my mind?"

"That's settled. Please come with us." He reached for her shoulder.

"*I* recommend that you *look at this*," she answered him, and opened her upper hands!

"What are those?" he asked, taking a step back.

She held the objects in her hands at the ends of her long fingers. They were ordinary eggs, eggs of a bilious green and of a vile dark purple color.

"Easter?" the man asked almost in spite of himself.

"No. Mine. Allow me to stay as I am!"

"NOW!" he shouted.

Yezeletta dropped the eggs. They fell around her feet, exploding with loud POP sounds like so many light bulbs. A vapor rose from each one that dispersed quickly into the air.

"Take her!" the man called to the black-clad operatives that entered.

"<||!###|%%%|^^^+^^|***|###!||>," Yezeletta shouted. It was a word that only she could pronounce, only a speaker *with her engineered throat* could voice.

The servitors pounced.

Each of the short humanoids leaped on a man close to it, pinning him in a vice-like hug. Small, sharp-clawed furry, brown arachnoids leapt out from the corners to swipe pistols from hands.

"It" appeared from the back hall.

Superficially, it resembled a large bed-sheet that seemed to flow over the furniture, the carpets, the walls, like water. It split, *peeling off* sections of itself as it entered the room, wrapping its sections around each of its creator's attackers, sticking to skin, leather, cloth. A green, jointed, multilegged Thing leapt for the Director.

Then it was finished.

The remaining staff of Project Sargon lay wrapped like sausages, laid out in a row on Yezeletta's living-room floor. The Director looked up at her from the Thing that had Taken him.

She turned her back on them, their capture complete.

It might have been that her prisoners could have spoken then. It might have been appropriate for any of the cliché of the losers: "You can't do this to me!" or: "You'll never get away with this!" or: "We'll be back!" As it happened, it was so fast, that her captives didn't say anything, then. That would come in a short time.

Then Yezeletta told them what had been contained in the green and purple eggs.

An hour later, she was alone in the Complex.

GRADUATION

[Milwaukee] Later, she would think of how easy it had been. Now, she relaxed. She surveyed her base of operations in the Farmers and Merchants Building. *It had been trivial to breed the disease that was contagious enough that it had wiped out the Sargon Directorate and their minions, without killing off her own allies, and any support staff that might return.*

And, she thought, *the way the disease organism, itself ceased to exist after as few as five breeding generations. A day later, the Complex, although deserted, was safe for human occupation.*

Human, she thought.

She was safe, as long as she did nothing. If her creators—assuming that any were left—ever came looking for her, she would need another base of operations as a fallback position.

She grabbed an atlas of the American Midwest from a shelf, opened it to Wisconsin and studied several areas in the southwest part of the state. She took note of a place that called itself "Summercrest."

Cities may not be the ideal places to go to ground, after all.

LEARNING CURVE

[Cotemporally with Milwaukee—I: Elsewhere] *The Student's progress is nominal-ranging-to-excellent, given his current state of development.*

His Counselor is proud of his accomplishments. He will be arriving soon with something that he thinks of as The Upgrade.

Then the next step in the Student's education will take place.

Laboratory work.

PMD—POST **M**ORTEM **D**UMP

[Project Sargon: The Day After] Yezeletta appraised the body count. I seem to be handling this as of a rote exercise, she thought, Is there a part of me that goes dead inside when I'm confronted by the aftermath of battle? Is this a design?

T**HE** D**OWNLOADING**—I

[Cotemporally with Milwaukee—II] *His Counsellor looks up at him with an admiring gaze. The Student is still unable to speak: all that comes from his throat are sibilances of various kinds. If he tries to voice anything, his throat closes, and he gags as he attempts to restore his breathing.*

His counsellor walks around him, looking at him from all angles. The counsellor makes a gesture, and The Student shrugs his broad shoulders, and drops the boxer's robe that he is wearing.

He stands naked while his counsellor, his advisor, his confidante makes another circle around him.

Then the counsellor does something that The Student finds in no small amount surprising.

His source of good counsel, his mentor, takes his right hand, and places it on his head. Then his counsellor removes his hand, and takes off his hair. The Student sees that the gray hair on the other man is nothing more than a hairpiece, although it looks natural.

His counsellor replaces the Student's large hand on his hairless head.

The experience that follows is one that the Student will never be able to describe without a lot of external help.

At the edges of his vision, tiny lights appear, almost particulate, the flashing points of which resemble the screen of an ordinary monitor seen in very great close up.

Then the Student realizes that <u>he is unable to move</u>. He is frozen solid, rooted to the floor.

And <u>he is not alone</u>. There is something in here with him. He wants to turn his head, to look for the intruder, but he is paralyzed, cast in stone.

The...Other that is with him begins to speak to him. It is repetitious, insistent, lulling, of a kind of monotonous rhythm, that acquires a visual component: crawling, evolving, undulating, dominating multi-colored patterns that have derived from the flickerings at the edges of his vision. He is contained in a spherical room of the moving colors, and now they take on a rhythm of their own, and the insistent ineluctable voice matches its cadence to the patterns. They strobe in clashing colors, and a martial musical component obtrudes: reds, magenta, exploding stellate representations, and the voice becomes strident.

The Student feels himself outside of the flashing colors of his universe <u>moving</u>. He is aware that he is raising and lowering his arms, turning his head this way then that, lifting first one leg then another, rotating his feet, clenching and unclenching his fists, extending his arms to the side, then placing them next to his waist.

Throughout all of this he is aware of one thing: he has no control over his movements. His body is a living puppet, run by the other inhabitant of— wherever he or it is—and he can no more stop it than he can start it.

The moving colors are in shades of blues and greens, now. They have evolved into relaxing horizontal lines of late evening colors: dark blues, cerulians, indigos, violets. The music loses its martial aspects, and becomes soothing, relaxing.

The spherical environment in which he finds himself darkens, the music becoming more tranquilizing yet, the vocal component damping out to a mere whisper.

Then the presentation vanishes, and he is standing before his counsellor in the dimly lit room, again.

The Student reaches out with his memories for the recollection of the colors, and the music.

These will be provided again when it is appropriate, something Other says, You have no need of these recollections now.

And all of the memories are removed from his consciousness.

Then the memory of the removal is taken, as well.

His counsellor looks up at him, with an odd little smile decorating his face.

The Something Other is still with him.

It is...inside his head.

HEX

[Rewind] A lot of Yezeletta's training had consisted of homework. The training courses that explicitly needed trainers, instructors, or whatever, had them, while other lessons were imparted from texts read after-hours or between more physical lessons. The instructors were experts in such things as armed and unarmed combat, various types of mathematics, or "how-to" training, such as electronics work.

There were, of course, examinations, but the exams were of a cunningly interdisciplinary nature that would combine knowledge in various fields. These would test both her study skills from reading, the obtaining of data from the internet or local databases, or from programmed learning, as well as those lessons that required actual interactions with people.

It had seemed an exercise in what a friendly electrician at the Project, who was also an amateur magician, had referred to as "monkey-motions." Yezeletta just tried to absorb what she was given, most of which she found interesting.

Later, she would look back.

Was some of her training emplaced by means of subtle conditioning? She had read Aldous Huxley's novel *Brave New World*, and had been fascinated by the conditioning regimes imposed on the various castes of intelligence ranges in the book. She had also discovered *Brave New World Revisited*, written by Huxley thirty years after his most famous novel, in which he described how the technology of the nineteen-sixties was actually making some of the predictions which were pure science-fiction in 1932, a matter of unpleasant reality.

The rest was inevitable, she thought.

She seemed to be running on an internal program that allowed her to handle the results of her actions. As she looked back on the last twenty-four hours, she could see a logical, almost geometric, progression. That progression had resulted in the present conditions with the inevitability (there was that word, again!) of the running of that unstated internal program.

Now it was time to stand down.

And clean up.

[Post Production] Yezeletta gave the necessary orders, and her many minions began to pick up after the end of Project Sargon.

The first order of business was getting the bodies collected. To start with, she would have them moved to the cafeteria, and disposed of from there. She really didn't want to use the Project eatery, but it was the largest open enclosed area in the Sargon Complex.

She spoke, gestured and transmitted orders from her computer to her life-forms around the Complex, and they started moving with the thoroughness of the programmed to their tasks.

She watched her servitors removing the remains of the Directorate from her living-room, then left her quarters to get equipment from the electronics shop.

She didn't close the door to her apartment when she left it.

[Project Sargon] Yezeletta went to Electronics by way of the Admin Section, where she removed several laptops from abandoned desks. In Electronics, she grabbed several more portables, and a server in a mini-tower that had received an upgrade. She brought the equipment back to the cafeteria, where she hooked all of the portables together into a table-top network, which ran off the mini-tower, all of which she piled onto a micro-wave oven cart from the kitchen. She gestured to a servitor, then said four carefully chosen words—words that no one else could pronounce.

Ten minutes later, seventeen short humanoids, and about eighty roving imagers were drawn up in ranks around the little network.

She spent several minutes typing rapidly into one of the portables. While she was typing, two more servitors came in dragging a length of the coaxial cable that was used in the Project's LAN. She plugged the cable into the desktop-server, and added several small components that another servitor carried in.

She touched one of the servitors on its head. Data flowed through her fingertips into the creature. Then she gestured with all four hands, signing additional instructions to the rest. One of her earliest precautions was the use of a three- and four-handed sign language for her gnomes so others wouldn't learn it and use them against her.

Yezeletta checked one screen on her network. This screen contained a feed from the "mainframe," the big server in Sargon Administration. It was the database that determined when it was safe *to go outside*.

The reconsats of the Tech Bloc, and even some of the aging birds that the old U.S. Government still used, were a persistent down-looking danger to Sargon. And would, or could be!, even a greater danger now. The data feeds from the Complex to other places were still in place and functioning just as they always had; Yezeletta had tapped into them long ago. Very little was sent automatically, but someone was going to get mighty suspicious when the weekly report didn't arrive on time!

More pressing than the Friday Report, the fly-bys overhead were predictable within fairly close limits. Reconsats had a certain amount of maneuvering reserve in their thrusters. When the thrusters ran out of propellant, the satellite became mostly useless, except in the one (usually precessing) spot in orbit where the spacecraft's receptors were looking downwards. Yezeletta had downloaded the ephemeris database for all of the known reconsats from the mainframe. *And what of the unknowns?*, she reminded herself.

She studied the columns of data for minutes, analyzing the numbers on the screen using her on-board systems. When she was satisfied, she looked up at the life-forms standing around her in ranks. She made a single gesture. Then she repeated the gesture with two other hands.

The platoon of critters left the cafeteria.

THE WEB SITE

Yezeletta studied the mission on which she had sent her servitors through the screens from the cafeteria. They ranged out up to thirty kilometers from the Project Complex, catching rides on the occasional motor-vehicle passing by, and the furry, camouflaged roving imagers climbed up into trees, attached themselves to the undersides of the eaves of abandoned buildings, and hid in culverts. There was a large highway, the Stuart, also known as Highway-87, that was a direct route north to the seaport city of Darwin. It became Highway-1 at the exit to the Buchanan Highway just north of Dunmarra. The Stuart went straight into Alice Springs, but seventy-three kilometers north of Alice, the Plenty Highway shot off east of the Stuart, and the Sandover went north from the Plenty. People from the Project motored in from the Plenty to Eighty-Seven and south into Alice Springs, or took smaller roads into the Mt. Strangway area to some small parks. At least she thought they were parks.

She would keep her constructs away from the other installation!

Amazing how little I know of the territory right around here!

There was a sound from what was once the chow line.

Her creations were bringing in the bodies.

WAIT STATE

There was nothing left to do now, but wait for her spies to return. Yezeletta gestured extensively at the remaining servitors for minutes, adding further instructions from uploads to her computers, triggering previously implanted instructions (*programming*, she thought) with the properly unpronounceable catch-words. The gnomelike creatures moved purposefully into their assigned tasks. A small platoon of them went off to an errand in the Sargon Computing Center; another, smaller group headed for the food preparation area, and a single servitor brought Yezeletta an object.

REST STATE

The object was a book. Actually, books: five paper-backs held together with a rubber band. One of her imagers had transmitted the existence of them back to her quarters.

While the cleanup continued, and with nothing more requiring her immediate attention, Yezeletta Zargkonji decided to take a short break. She'd always liked the novels of Jack Vance, and she had never read *The Demon Princes*.

And she might never get another chance.

——>>> SEVEN <<<——

Take Arms. Take Aim. Be without shame;
No one to bow to, to vow to, to blame.
Legions of Light, virtuous flight. Ignite excite.

—Patti Smith, 1978

ON THE ROAD TO ALICE SPRINGS

[Library Procedures] Al Morrison stared into the middle distance of the dusty road ahead. He had been enroute, with friends, from the port city of Darwin for eight hours, and the day was lengthening into evening. The Stuart Highway had stopped being one of the powered roads Al was used to when it turned from Highway One to Highway-87 at Dunmarra. Now it was a concrete pavement that occasionally turned into a concrete pavement that needed repairs, usually at the time the more well-maintained areas had lulled him into thinking that they would last awhile.

They had made poor time, as they drove south into the heart of the Australian Continent towards their destination, which was not Alice Springs; It was an installation northeast of Alice in a range of low mountains nearby: the Harts Range.

"Mount Strangway," Morrison muttered. "Appropriate."

"Huh?" Ralph Hanson had been dozing in the passenger seat.

"The Harts Mountains. Mount Strangway is on the western end of them. The laboratory complex is sorta nestled in the foothills there. South of the Plenty. Protected. The Creature is supposed to have been built at the complex. For all I know, now, it fucking runs the place."

"The Creature," Ralph prompted.

"Our mission is to establish a new order in the US," Morrison began. Ralph rolled his eyes skyward, a gesture he was getting good at, having been trapped in the hot truck cab with Al Morrison for the last four hours. He could even roll his eyes with Al looking straight at him without his recognizing Ralph's act for what it was: thinly veiled contempt.

"— need a better weapon than any of the kinds we have now if we are to achieve any kind of a strategic success." Al looked at Ralph momentarily.

Ralph was used to that mannerism, too: he was ready to look right back at Al with a steely look of—he was embarrassed at the thought— revolutionary brotherhood.

Al took the gaze as encouragement, and kept talking. "The Creature came to me by way of a contact in New York, who had heard rumors during a summer sabbatical he took at the University of Moscow. Biological research needed some kind of a permit from 'The University Liaison to the Ministry of Trade'. Recognize the name?"

What Al was talking about was a lot more interesting than the ideologically correct verbiage Ralph had expected. He had known of the Creature—no one knew what form the fabled bio-weapon would take, and Morrison's term for it was as good as any—but he hadn't heard anything of where Al had gotten his data.

"No." He answered Al's question.

"Ever hear of the KGB?"

"The secret police? Weren't they disbanded?"

"Get serious. And it's not the secret police. The initials stand for 'Committee for State Security'. Sort of a Russian FBI, and one of the few good ideas that bunch of nincompoops ever had."

"They were disbanded, way back. Nineteen-Nineties."

"Nope. Like any good intel agency, it just went underground and got bigger. And sneakier. Lots sneakier, and more eclectic; enough to supervise covertly anything that looks interesting. Biological research, among other things. Ever hear of the Davis Protocols?"

This was a lot more interesting than ideology. "No, some kind of a treaty?"

"Wrong the first time!" Al pressed on the brake, just enough to flash the tail-light to the truck behind them, then he down-shifted to avoid a lengthy strip of eroded pavement. "Davis was a California researcher who devised some slick techniques for convincing common plants to produce just about anything you might want. Pure cocaine from a columbine, for instance."

"Cute. Where does the Creature enter this?"

"My New Yorker friend found that the Davis Protocols were big business at the University. Most of the researchers there had a little Davis work going on the sidelines of their main projects. My friend was waiting for his advisor to return from teaching—he was in the guy's office—and he happened to notice a sketch hanging out of a notebook."

"Of what?" Ralph asked. Al looked at Ralph. He was hooked on this!

"Just a sketch. Of a creature with more than two arms. Multi-legged. Large brain-case, insect eyes. He tried to get a good close look, but the prof came in, and he didn't get a chance to."

"Did he remember any of it?" For some reason Al's description sounded familiar.

"He did. More than two legs. It had a lot of wires and stuff hanging off it. He couldn't see its face, or even if it had a face. The prof put the pictures away. My friend tried to get into the prof's office again, later that week— same trick, coming early—and the notebook and the sketches were gone. He checked the office as thoroughly as he could without being obvious, and there was nothing."

They drove silently for a time.

"Did you get a copy of the picture?" Ralph asked.

"There was a version of it published in a tabloid, later. I retrieved it from the paper's internet site, and printed it out." Al reached behind him, the truck swerving hazardously as he did.

"Hey, watch it!"

"Watch what?" Al stabilized the truck and handed Ralph a file folder.

Ralph took the folder and riffled through the contents. The second sheet, of two, was an illustration printed from the internet; in the center the picture was what Al had described: an almost insectoid likeness, long spindly legs, slender arms, long fingers, and—

Ralph began laughing.

"What the hell's so funny?" Al asked.

"Insect!" Ralph brought it down to a low chuckle. "With *those*?" He pointed to two conspicuous features on the entity's chest. "Whose 'artist's conception'?" He looked at the first sheet. "No fucking wonder! This is the *National Enquirer!* When did you start taking that sheet seriously?"

"Since it printed what my contact said was an accurate copy of what he saw in that professor's office!" An angry note had crept into Al's voice. His normally reedy tones had become shriller.

Ralph stopped talking, and pasted a deliberately neutral expression on his face. For the n-th time, he asked himself why he had allied himself with the likes of Al. *Easy*, he answered himself. *Either I really do want to strike back at those fools in Philadelphia, or I mostly want to keep Al out of trouble!*

MOVING PARTY

Yezeletta put her book down with some regret. She'd had exactly thirty-seven minutes with *The Star King*, enough to read about two-thirds of the first volume. Several servitors carried another body into the cafeteria. *Time to get back to it*, she thought.

Several of her imagers ran across the courtyard, the images they transmitted bouncing in the screen of one of the laptops she had on a nearby table. There was nothing alive in that end of the complex. *Just Security, and they were dead-heads long before I showed up.* She looked up as another one of the Deputy Administrator's henchmen was carried in.

Another laptop chirped, and displayed a red screen: **Reconsat Detected**. The ephemeris loaded into the computer and interacting with the computer's timers indicated one of the Tech Bloc's spysats coming into range. The warning was always about ten minutes early so anyone outside would have time to get under cover.

The drill was well understood and a constant part of life in the Sargon Complex for as long as Yezeletta could remember. Presumably the unknown reconnaissance operators manning the spysat's downlink would be aware of it as well, from long observation of an unchanging SOP, and find nothing strange.

All I need is a weekend!

Yezeletta consulted another computer in her network and scanned the garage.

The six lorries were being loaded with everything she could take from the project. Tireless servitors brought things down to the garage bucket-brigade fashion and left them there, where another, smaller set of servitors catalogued the items, and stacked them as compactly in the trucks as possible. She wanted tight storage of as much as possible, rather than ease of access.

She switched to another screen. Her minions were gutting the Sargon Computing Centre. One servitor watched as the mass storage systems ran a full backup, then the storage towers would come down and be packed as well. It was Yezeletta's intent to take the entire center with her, down to the cabling for the LAN, if she could.

But the data came first.

Her stomach growled, insistently.

Yezeletta gestured with her left hand, her upper, and several short humanoids arrived from the kitchen with cafeteria trays: scrambled eggs into which cheese had been melted, a tray of meatloaf sandwiches, several slices of cold day-old pizza, a steak, two liters of milk, a huge salad and somewhere one of her creations had found a can of Foster's.

As her creations dismantled the Project, Yezeletta Zargkonji had a light lunch.

MOVING ON DOWN THE LINE

From above, Al's convoy looked like any other sort of vehicular grouping one might see out in the middle of Australia. Four medium-size trucks and a dark green Hum-Vee. The trucks were dusty, but the dust was only outside. Beneath the grime, the vehicles, rented in Darwin, were in perfect condition. They sped south at a wary velocity chosen to get them to Al's destination in a timely manner, but not to attract members of the Australian law-enforcement community with extra time on their hands.

Australian Highway-87 went past a clump of scraggly trees growing near the roadbed. The members of the July Seventeenth Brigade passed the trees unaware of the eyes tracking their movement.

Those eyes followed the trucks until they were out of sight. Then they went dormant, awaiting the time they would be picked up. Their reports were handed off to other eyes further south.

DESSERT

Yezeletta finished lunch, and motioned her minions to remove the dishes. All that remained was a large bowl of vanilla ice-cream covered with Hershey's syrup and sprinkled with malt powder.

There was a fork stuck into the top of the ice cream. *I must reprogram the cook!*, she thought, long-arming a spoon from another table.

Then another portable chirped insistently, and opened a large red-bordered window on its screen. She checked what was there against a map in another window. They were far off, and would arrive in the middle of the night if they kept moving at their current rate. In spite of it all, she grinned.

Yezeletta was going to have visitors.

IS THIS TRIP NECESSARY?

Behind Al and Ralph, who were in the lead, Marina Worthington and Jeff Chatsworth sat in the front seat of the truck Marina, a petite woman with dark hair, was driving, and Nancy Larson, blonde and blue-eyed, sat behind them alone, next to several suitcases.

"Thanks for riding with me, Nancy," Marina said.

"No problem. I saw what wanted to get in here with you."

"What," Jeff asked, "did you ever do to win Charlie's attentions?"

"I'm not entirely sure," Marina answered. "It seems I get a lot of attention from just the ones I don't want interested in me." She looked quickly at Jeff, and back to her driving, "Between Al and Charlie both thinking they can get horizontal with me, I don't even know why I came along on this mission."

"Feeling a few regrets?" Jeff asked.

"A few. San Francisco wasn't that bad a place to live, even before they installed the metal detectors downtown. I never went downtown anyway. Didn't see that the technology did anything useful. Besides spy on me, I mean. All those 'security' cameras."

"Whose security?" Nancy asked.

"Yeah. I didn't feel a real need to leave a permanent track of my comings and goings that any dip surfing the internet could get at." She took a breath. "That was how I met Al."

AN ONLY CHILD

[Load Descriptor] Benjamin Allen Morrison had been born to wealthy parents whose main interest in money was in what it could do. The elder Morrison had been interested in money as a tool, rather than as a commodity to acquire. Associated with this in Benjamin's father's mind was his notion of "propriety of usage." He had spent much of his adult life determining the exact methods with which money could be used and should be used, as well as on whom, and in what way. Samuel Butler's *Last Puritan* would have recognized the elder Morrison as an equal. To Ben's parents, the method was more important than the use.

Fortunately, Benjamin's *grand*parents did have a streak of sensibility, and placed certain restrictions on what Ben's parents could do with the loot they had spent most of their lives accumulating. *Loot* was an appropriate word, as some of the grandparents' income had come from various dealings around the world, right at the time the world, or, at least the part of it that had anything to do with computers was preparing for an experience one writer at the time had called "potentially the most serious industrial accident of all time."

This "industrial accident" *could* have been the most devastating happening in the world, particularly a world in which computers were no longer the play-toys of the rich, or the exclusive property of large governments. This accident would arrive on time, and in a way in which everyone would know of its arrival. A lot of governments and industries had spent billions of dollars in preparations and more in palliative propaganda. Certain other, smaller groups—those more out on the fringes of society—predicted the end.

This putative disaster had been given a name that was turned almost immediately into an acronym: *Y2K*, the *Year Two-Thousand Bug*.

The problem was not that people used computers to perform accounting tasks, or that there were so many of them, but that *old software* was still useful. The old programs—databases, inventory and accounting systems and other applications—had been written as far back as the nineteen-fifties or the nineteen-sixties, and were still being used in the *nineteen-nineties*. To save on storage, many early programmers had kept dates by saving the date and the month, but keeping the year as the last two digits. The "19" was "understood" by human beings.

Computers are literal beasts: unless some cogent programming is done to provide "judgement," a computer will do exactly as its program code says. Repeatedly, if necessary.

For three or four years prior to the last days of the year 1999, all of the abbreviated dates had been searched for in millions of lines of computer code by programmers, some retrieved from retirement for the job, and the program code corrected to handle four-digit years. This was the practical aspect of the Y2K so-called "bug." While this work was being done, others played on the uncertainty of all of the fixes being implemented on time, and forecast everything from shortages of things such as water and electricity to what was grandiosely called by the louder and more strident commentators: The End of the World As We Know It.

Benjamin Allen Morrison's grandparents had grown rich providing services that were handled using some simple and useful, if deliberately obvious, techniques: orders were tracked the good-old-fashioned way with paper files and simple calculators that didn't have internal clocks. There were some off-market operating systems and niche applications that helped when a fairly advanced machine was needed. Ben's grandparents dealt in food-stuffs, emergency devices, such as generators, firearms and other useful tools and texts, some ghostwritten to order, that people could use as references to keep things going while the rest of the world, failing to be prepared, would fall.

And no refunds would be given! All purchases were final!

When the actual roll-over from 1999 to the fated Y2K happened, no one except several million happy celebrators knew it. They were too busy having a good time to worry about a year's worth of food, or a month's worth of cash-on-hand. For by this time, there were no more bugs to eradicate, and the transition from the nineteen-hundreds to the two-thousands was complete. There were no catastrophes, no shortages, and the world did not end. But two scheming entrepreneurs had grown quietly wealthy in the process.

They had then left their wealth with conditions to their children, and removed the conditions for their grandchildren.

Actually grandchild: Ben Morrison was the only grandchild in the family.

Ostracized by his parents for playing the ultimate trick on them, being born, taught by Grandpa and Grandma, Al Morrison (he dropped his first name on his eighteenth birthday) became a young, wealthy malcontent.

Then Albert Miller had blown up Washington.

ON THE ROAD

"When I met him in San Francisco," Marina continued, "Al was just shutting down a business he'd started in the Valley. Some little virtual reality venture that was supposed to pipe movies right into a theater-customer's head."

"What happened," Jeff asked, "the Swiss production houses buy him out?"

"Not buy," Marina replied, downshifting in response to the flashing of tail-lights ahead, "more like stomped. The Zurich boys didn't like the way Al just appeared on their turf, and they wrapped him up in about sixty really *prime* law-suits. They gave him a way out: get out of the business, *and* abstain from computer-related work for five years."

They were quiet for a time, as Marina deftly steered around a group of well-installed potholes.

Then Nancy made the understatement of the trip: "Didn't help Al's disposition, much, did it?"

ESCAPE ARTISTE

Yezeletta watched the convoy coming south on the Stuart for a short time from the vantage point of an adroitly placed imager. The trucks could, she thought, be enroute to Alice Springs, but the turn-off on the Plenty for the foothills of the Harts Mountain Range was coming up quickly, and these people didn't look like they were businessmen on a corporate mission.

She pressed a combination of keys on a laptop, and the computer sent a command to her agents. The image on the machine's screen flickered, and was replaced by a new full-screen image of the lead truck from dead ahead.

The imager catching this was sitting on the roof of a small frame building several kilometers ahead. There was an effect like rippling water across the screen, and the individuals in the truck's cab leapt into a close-up. The imager thought very hard, and the reflections on the windshield vanished.

Two guys. Yezeletta placed her chin in her two right hands, stared intently into the screen, and thought. Their clothes looked American. That could mean anything. American fashions were popular all over Australia.

Shit.

She needed about another eighteen hours to get the important things from the Project. There was a lot of stuff she could destroy and leave. If she had to.

I'd rather not, she thought.

In another screen, she watched as a number of familiar objects d'art, a box of books and a large wooden desk were toted up a corridor. Yezeletta felt a twinge of loss over that.

The servitors were emptying out her living quarters.

TURN LEFT

The exit from Highway-87 was behind them. They were driving on the Plenty East through red desert that alternated with green areas where the Central Australian Irrigation Project had brought in water. Sitting in the driver's seat, Al muttered to himself.

"Say what?" Ralph said agreeably.

"I was wondering," Al said, "whether Australia was in any of the blocs, and which one? Tech? Power? Space? Research? Finance?"

"I haven't the slightest," Ralph replied. "Wasn't that Bloc membership thing 'by invitation only'?"

"It was the last time I looked," Al said. "Of course the US wasn't invited into any of them. Sad."

"A lot of places are taking out their dislike of the US on us now," Ralph said, "for reasons that are mostly non-existent. It does give little countries a chance to play with the big boys, but Australia didn't play into it. Canberra's still on good terms with Philadelphia. How long *is* this road, anyway?"

As if in answer, a standard green and white highway sign, placed at an oblique angle that made it hard to see from a distance on the road, appeared ahead:

Mt. Strangway Commonwealth Research Park
—South Ten Kilometers—

"That's it!" Al said.

"You sure about that?"

"Of course," Al said. "It wouldn't say 'Secret Government Science Lab' or something that ridiculous, but there'd have to be a signpost for the proles working there. Look at how they positioned it so that you'd have to know where it is to find it."

They passed the sign. From atop it something small and furry tracked them with its single eye.

THE EYES HAVE IT

Yezeletta watched as the small group of parked trucks pulled in just past the Research Park exit. There was only one research station at the end of the road starting at that exit. These people were less than two hours away from her.

If they started now.

Yezeletta made a peremptorial hand gesture at the nearest servitor. The creature turned around to face her and retracted its crest; she placed her left hand, her upper, on its head. Information streamed down the data-channels in her arms, and out the interface points in her fingers.

The servitor nodded to her, a preprogrammed response, turned and walked up to several more. It placed its hands on the heads of the others, passing Yezeletta's instructions.

An imager hopped onto the nearest servitor, and received instructions from it, then hopped decisively off on a new mission.

Within a minute, the instructions had been passed to enough of the creatures for them to begin their task: removing the corpses from the cafeteria, and making the large room look as if wholesale murder hadn't been committed.

She switched to the garage monitor.

The loading continued.

MEANWHILE—

The trucks moved off the exit road into a small clearing, well away from travelled areas. When they parked, they were behind a low hedge in some station owner's field. Al Morrison got out first, and looked about, his glasses glinting in the fading light.

Ralph and Jeff went hunting for wood for a fire, Marina set up a camp stove on the tailgate of one of the vehicles. Others prepared to bed down.

A gold eye in one of the trees observed them, opening long enough to send an image upstream to an organic server.

Unthinking, programmed in its function, implicit in its design, the organic server sent the images further still.

Nocturne

While the July Seventeenth Brigade was camping for the night, Yezeletta's tireless gnome battalion continued its work. As they labored, so did she, checking her weapons again, and again. Getting new items from her former living quarters. Her personal laboratories were the hardest to move: the living components required specific habitats that had to be dismantled and placed in one lorry, an eighteen-wheeler.

Could her servitors handle it?

Time was running out.

CONCATENATION

The photographer Yezeletta had met on the way to lunch had put a note in an important place in his darkroom: above the light switch. It read: ***"What Have You Forgotten?"*** She thought of that now, as she checked and verified her preparations, her contingencies, her planning. There was a lot that could go wrong. What if these people were the advance force for what remained of Project Sargon, and they were coming in first to see what she had done? As improbable as it seemed, she had to consider such ideas—she had been *trained* to think of such things!

She fussed over her plans, then ran checkouts on her systems. In one screen, a dozen servitors were moving the olive drab box with exaggerated care into the garage of the eighteen-wheeler.

As the case came even with the imager sending the pictures, an eye appeared on the case's video monitor. It winked.

I wish I had your optimism!, Yezeletta thought.

TIME CYCLE

The next morning arrived too soon, the way all mornings do.

ON THE ROAD

Al insisted that camp break early. He was one of these people who thought early rising was an indicator of high morals, political correctness, and enthusiasm. That his associates thought he was crazy, sanctimonious and fond of wasting *their* time was something he had never realized.

As his bleary-eyed companions loaded up, he consulted a road map purchased in Darwin. Satisfied that he had the route down pat, he rolled up the map, shoved it in his back pocket and got into the lead truck.

With a wave he thought the rest would see as comradely, he pulled out.

He was still riding with Ralph. Al hadn't noticed the musical chairs the others had played in their attempts not to ride with one of the group: a man named Charlie. Al steered the truck back onto the feeder road to the Commonwealth Research Park, and the other trucks fell in behind him.

Yezeletta followed the small caravan from an imager in a tree. She frowned. *Those are just rental trucks*, she thought, *The license plates are from the Northwest Territory!* She wished her internet connections were still intact; she might be able to find out where they had been rented.

In the screen, they were getting closer. She had dressed in a custom jump-suit the Project had provided for the times when she was out of her quarters. She had a tool-belt that contained several mechanisms she hoped she wouldn't need, and other items—just tools—she might.

She checked everything again. The trucks were loaded, the Project just about cleaned out.

She was ready. *And I wish I knew what it was I was ready for!*

THE EXPEDITIONARIES

The Research Park appeared around the last curve in the road, as a brick building. From the front the Project had been designed to look smaller than it was. Most of the bulk of the structure was concealed from direct view. Al stopped his vehicle in front of the main entrance, and the others pulled in next to him.

"Well, well, well," he said. "This must be the place."

Ralph came up behind him. Jeff and Marina followed.

"Is anyone here?" Marina asked. "It looks deserted."

"Are you sure this is it, Al?" Ralph asked. "There aren't even *cars* in the parking lot."

Al didn't answer for a moment. He walked up to the front entrance, tried the door. It was unlocked. He pulled it open.

"Al!" Nancy Larson said, "you don't know what's in there!"

Al looked around. "What are you expecting, Frankenstein's Monster?" he asked. "We're armed aren't we?" He removed a highly illegal automatic from his coat pocket, and opened the door.

Inside the entrance was another set of doors. Nothing unusual about that. Al opened one of the inner doors, and looked up the hallway. There was a strange odor in the air he almost recognized and the corridor ahead of him was—different. There was something wrong, here. It might be no more than that the hall hadn't been swept in a day or so, but the wrongness was palpable. The place looked frowsy around the edges. Unkempt.

He walked up the hall a little way.

The building was silent.

He returned to the front door, and waved at the rest.

"Looks deserted, let's go look."

One by one, the rest entered. Al paid no heed to various accusing stares. Jeff looked a look at Marina. *We came all the way down here for this?*

Al led them up the main corridor. By some common agreement, they kept together in a tight group. Nancy took out her automatic, holding it in her shooting hand, her left. There was a large room ahead, a sign on the wall announced: **Cafeteria**.

They went in. Al waved his pistol around, warily.

"There was someone in here," he said. "Not long ago."

Ralph nodded, "Looks like there was some kinda meeting in here. But it ended quickly." He picked something off of a nearby table. It was a short cable.

"What's that," Al asked.

"Looks like a connector cable," Ralph answered. "Wonder why it's in here?"

"Is this place deserted? Why?" Marina asked, mostly for her own benefit.

"Don't know," Al said.

"Al!" Charlie bustled up. "Did you know this place was a wreck?"

"I—," Al was surprised by Charlie's question.

"Look, Al!" Ralph said, "we've gone all of this way with you on what you were promising us—"

"It helped that you bankrolled our transportation," Marina added, "Or *I*, at least, wouldn't have come along."

Several others joined in:

"What kind of a wild-goose chase—?"

"Did you have a plan?"

"When are you gonna rent a clue, Al?"

Finally:

"Do you know what you're doing?" Nancy asked.

"Actually," another voice answered, "he knows rather a lot." The voice was a cultured one, speaking perfectly enunciated BBC English.

The small band of quasi-revolutionaries finally knew a moment of true solidarity. It lasted about a minute during which the voice added, "You have come to the right place. You may have even come at the right time."

A door opened. Beyond, Al could see the stainless steel equipment of a large food-service operation. And an angular shadow.

The shadow moved, and Yezeletta entered the room.

"I assume that you are looking for me," she said.

ONE WORD OR ANOTHER

To Yezeletta, they were all a bunch of short people. *But everyone is!*, she thought, *And they are so obvious.* She expanded her visual bandwidth. The many kinds of reds, blues and greens and un-nameable colors ebbed and flowed like currents of colored water across their skins. *They couldn't S,P,E,L,L their emotions out more explicitly to me!*

To the July Seventeenth Brigade, the reality was orders of magnitude past the fantasy pictures Al had shown them. The Artist's Conceptions were just that: drawings made by good commercial artists to editorial order. The staff of the *National Enquirer, The National Tattler* and other papers of that sort knew their reading public well enough to be able to tailor the paper's stories to what the average tabloid reader expected.

Insects with mammary glands were just the right combination of the exotic and the titillating, Ralph thought.

Yezeletta Zargkonji's full presence was almost enough to send several Brigade members running for the door. The jump-suit she was wearing was a dark charcoal, almost black. As she stepped out of the kitchen door, the details of her physique—hidden in the shadows—were made more obvious.

ON-LINE WITH MASTERMIND

They were speechless. For a short time. Even Al, never at a loss for words in any other situation, had nothing to say. The fabled Agent, real as their surroundings, larger than life, approached them, her face showing no fear, her hands empty.

She looked down at them, an expression giving them nothing on her face. The Brigade made way for her, as she took a chair from nearby, and sat down on it.

"Tell me why you are here," Yezeletta said.

And they did.

RUMINATIONS

Al wanted to be on the road again almost immediately.

"We've found what we've been looking for, we should be on the way back to Darwin, and out of here!"

"C'mon, Al," Jeff said, "we just got here, and you want us on the road again?"

"That may not only be unnecessary," Yezeletta said, shutting everyone else up, "but dangerous."

Why is that, Miss, uh—Miss—"

"Zarg-kon-ji," Yezeletta said helpfully, pronouncing it slowly. *If these people want formality, I'll give them formality.* She went on: "The Technical Bloc's spysats look quite carefully into this area. We knew that a long time ago. It was a standard drill to bring everyone inside when the System—" she gestured with her left hand, her upper at a small procession wheeling her portable network into the cafeteria, "— indicated that 'recess' was finished. The ephemeris gave us about ten minutes of warning time before we had to be under cover."

Jeff wondered who this "us" was that The Agent (*did she have a nickname? or did we have to use all of it?*) referred to. Some of the other Brigade members had looked around on the sly and had found nothing else except some locked rooms leaking a slight but unsettling smell.

THE BASEMENT TAPES

An hour later, Al Morrison and Yezeletta Zargkonji were in the Project

Parking Facility watching Yezeletta's tireless minions loading the last of her things into the lorries that, by good fortune, had been on site when she'd needed them.

"Where did you get those?" Al asked.

"Those," Yezeletta prompted. Al couldn't see her half-grin.

"The Munchkins loading that truck. Did they grow on trees?"

Yes!, Yezeletta didn't say. "I grew them," she did say.

"Amazing," Al said softly. "You 'just grow' anything you need?"

"I do. If it's not easier to get it from elsewhere."

She just does it!, Al thought, *She needs something, she just makes it.* To Al Morrison, what Yezeletta meant was more than just an individual of many talents. The capabilities she represented were priceless. *I could tommy-gun her where she stands. Take about three slugs. But the knowledge she's carrying....*

As they stood and watched Yezeletta's minions loading the last truck in the coolness of the basement garage, Al thought of his own agenda. Or, more exactly, what agenda. He had never really planned what he was going to do when he found—or *if* he found!—the fabled Agent. His plans, never really any more than simple outlines, couldn't be more than generalities until he had more to work with. As he watched Yezeletta's servitors move heavy objects, and tried to watch Yezeletta herself from the corner of one eye, the half-formed plans he had prior to coming to Australia became more real.

Al wasn't stupid. He wasn't a poor planner, and he wasn't the kind of individual who would react unthinkingly to a sound bite. *Or even a sound byte*, he thought.

Now, the servitors were pushing a large olive-drab solid metal case on large, easily-moved rubber tires up the ramp of the eighteen-wheeler. He started to say something to Yezeletta, and stopped. She was obviously concentrating on the case: it was large enough to be almost a trailer in its own right, Al saw, as nine servitors maneuvered it into a place amongst all of the other miscellany, and secured it.

Al looked back to Yezeletta.

He tried to think of her as a "partner," or as an "associate." The words didn't come easily. "Friend" was out of the question. "Comrade?" Yezeletta was—unapproachable, distant.

Obviously, she had her own agenda. Could her agenda and the Brigade's ever fit?

Could he make it fit?

What could he do to *make* it fit?

A slight sound from behind him pulled Al back from his reverie. He looked back, while Yezeletta stared intently at the stowage of the green case. Al recognised the source of the sound from the slight shadow thrown in the stairway light. Someone was watching them, and Al knew exactly who. It could be only one.

Charlie.

HIT **M**AN

[Load Backup] As Al watched Yezeletta's creations load up, he let his mind drift back to the first—others would suggest it should have been the only—meeting with Charlie.

He had shown up one day attached to Marina Worthington.
Just how attached was another matter.

At a meeting in Jeff's apartment in San Francisco, Marina had introduced a somewhat unkempt man as "her neighbor." Charlie, if the truth were to be told, wasn't exactly her neighbor. He lived two blocks up the street from Marina in another building.

Al's opinion of Charlie had been formed within about three minutes of their meeting. Charlie's body odor was—well—"pungent," as Al would politely describe it later. Actually Charlie reeked like someone who habitually went on runs through garbage dumps. And fell in.

He didn't know how Marina could stand it.

Two nights later, Al was awakened by a phone call. It wasn't unexpected; the time was.

"Hello," he said, "you've reached me at three a.m. What'd'you want?"

The voice on the other end brought him to a state of wide awake.

"Al, it's Charlie." Actually, it wasn't Charlie, it was Marina. Al sat up in bed.

"What about him?"

"I think he's gone nuts."

"Hold on. What's he doing?"

"We went out to dinner earlier, and I wanted to go straight home after. He tried to come up, and I didn't want company. Just didn't. And not him. He got upset, and started shouting. I shut the door on him, and he stood out there for a while, I could see his shadow under the door. Then he said, 'If that's how you want it, fine, but don't be surprised if something blows sky-high.' Then he left."

"You sure he's gone?"

"My apartment's above the main entrance, I saw him leave through the lobby."

"I'll be right there."

When Al arrived, he found a piece of gray duct tape covering the latch on the lobby entrance of Marina's building. Anyone could re-enter the access hallway to the apartments. He removed it.

He went up to Marina's, and stayed there the rest of the night.

PRELUDE TO MOVING DAY

Two days later, Project Sargon was abandoned.

The intervening time had been spent in rest, relaxation and recharging from the trip down from Darwin, interspersed with short bursts of activity, as the members of the Brigade removed the final supplies from the Project, and placed the final touches on Yezeletta's preparing and packing.

On the morning after the Brigade's arrival, Nancy was in one of the cavernous food-storage closets in the cafeteria putting canned goods in a cardboard box she wheeled around on a utility cart taken from the Library.

There was a discreet noise behind her.

She turned, and was solemnly regarded by a short humanoid with a craggy gray face, a membranous crest, and sharp eyes.

The eyes she wouldn't have minded, but the large gold whatzit in the creature's forehead made her want to step back.

"Hello," she said. "What do you want?" *Could it smell fear?* she wondered.

By way of an answer, the humanoid produced a terry-cloth bathroom towel from a loop on its belt, scanned briefly, and started polishing the surface of one of the tables.

"Who are you? Why are you—?" Nancy didn't quite know what to say. The humanoid paid her no heed, even to the point of cleaning right around her in a polite little circle of action as she stood there.

"Cute little janitor, isn't he?" She looked around for an exit. She recognized the voice, and didn't want to be alone with its owner.

She got behind the cart, and pushed it towards the door. The voice's owner stood to one side as she followed the cart out.

"Hello, Charlie," she said.

"Hi, Nancy," he replied. "How's things going here?" His voice had taken on that baritone joviality he thought friendly.

"Charlie, I'm really busy—" She let it hang.

"Not too busy for Charlie, though." He seemed to expect her to stay.

She changed the subject, "What do you suppose that's here for?" She gestured at the humanoid still polishing everything in sight.

"It's one of the Spider Lady's slaves." Charlie took his eyes off Nancy for the first time. "It's here to take the fingerprints off things in case someone comes back here to snoop around." His gaze locked onto Nancy again. She could almost sense his line of sight *feeling* her up.

She hurried out into the hallway, Charlie following her, and ran into Jeff.

Jeff Chatsworth recognised the look of relief on Nancy's face. He saw the box of foodstuffs she'd gathered, and produced another cardboard box.

"Charlie," he said, "take this box, and fill it with whatever Nancy couldn't fit in hers, and bring it to the loading dock." He handed him the box.

"When did you start giving orders?" Charlie asked, medium sarcasm in his voice.

"Since Al asked me to come down here and have you relieve Nancy, that's when." Jeff removed the partially filled box from the cart. "Go back in and try to get the rest of what's usable." Jeff and Nancy strode off.

"Bitch," Charlie muttered as he went back in.

CHARLIE'S ANGLES

[Backup—Continued] The "blow sky-high" never materialized. On a visit to Charlie's place, a far larger and more spacious loft apartment than Al had thought, Charlie proudly showed Al his library.

It started with *The Anarchist's Cookbook*. That alone was about enough for Al. The *Cookbook* had enough errors in it to make anything concocted from it more dangerous to the user, than to the user's putative victims. For this reason, it had acquired a worldwide reputation as a joke. This didn't stop it from being widely reprinted.

There were other things as well, *The US Army Field Munitions Manual* and all of its many companion volumes, commentaries, sequelae, and its counterparts from other services, such as the CIA, and military organizations from other countries. There was even a set of manuals in Charlie's bookshelf that were inarguably written in Hebrew.

Mossad? Al asked himself.

Charlie never answered Al's question about the Hebrew texts, then or ever. Charlie did answer Al's carefully worded questions about other things, and, that night, Al discovered Charlie's secret delight.

Charlie liked explosions.

Marina wasn't pleased when Al introduced Charlie to the rest of the then core of the July Seventeenth Brigade. She avoided everyone in the Brigade for a month before calling Al up. She would return to the Brigade under one condition.

Keep Charlie away from her!

COUNT DOWN

[Project Sargon] The trucks were loaded. While Al and Ralph fidgeted, Yezeletta went around to each vehicle, tightening loads, verifying the security of the doors, inspecting the drivers.

This last act started the first and last argument she'd had with Al.

"Are you sure you want those creatures to drive these trucks?"

"I programmed them to be good drivers." Anyone but Al would have realized the enormity of the "programming" Yezeletta mentioned so casually, and moved on to something else. Al persisted: "Have you done any driving?"

"The programming I've emplaced was taken from good drivers who know their machines." *It is well he doesn't know how I obtained that knowledge! (Recollection of a spherical device with an opening in the bottom dropping down...copying maps of memory synapses—Yezeletta discontinued the thought.)*

Al didn't give up. "When have these things," he didn't see Yezeletta stiffen at the word, "ever gone out to one of the settlements around here in anything, much less a large truck?"

"Al!" Ralph said loudly. "Give her a break, she wants to get rolling."

"Give *us* a break," Marina said. "The sooner we roll, the sooner we can go to bed. I'm tired already."

Al faced Marina. Her back was to the rest. She gently, surreptitiously unbuttoned the top button of her shirt, and Yezeletta said, "Al, if you are worried about my creations, perhaps you could help them learn. Can some of your friends drive for a while? To let my servitors learn?"

Al turned to Yezeletta, looked up at her. Nodded.

He didn't see Marina stifle a laugh.

ON THE ROAD AGAIN

The largest lorry was a classic Mack eighteen-wheeler. It was one of the luxury models designed for continuous cross-country travel by a team of two or three drivers. The sleeping accommodations were practically luxurious, if a bit cramped, after Yezeletta got on board.

She had re-designed the living area for herself. Most of it was a bed with the oddly-shaped pillows she needed to sleep comfortably. Al took the driver's seat, looked out the driver's window. It was a tinted window that allowed him to see out, but made it very difficult for anyone else to see him. He looked at his cab-mate.

The servitor—larger and more muscular than the others—regarded him with large gray eyes, its crest extended, and the gold aperture in its forehead flickered.

"That's gonna stand out, you know," he said to it. The servitor's crest extended.

Wordlessly, the creature removed something from its belt pouch, wrapped it around its forehead. An eye patch.

Al shook his head. There was a sound from the back room.

Yezeletta was chuckling.

The trucks were organized in a long line. This end of the Plenty, Highway Twelve, was drivable on just one of its westbound lanes. Yezeletta's convoy was at the front, followed by one of the trucks the Brigade had driven down in. The smallest of the rest of them was inside a larger lorry, two others were being towed, and the largest was filled with "leftovers," the canned goods Nancy had found.

Al rolled his window down, and stuck his arm out in what he hoped was a friendly "Forward!" gesture. Behind him, he could hear the trucks starting up.

He rolled up the window, put the big Mack diesel in gear, and rolled the truck out to the access road to the Plenty Highway.

In the back, Yezeletta looked into a screen at an image relayed from the top of the Mack's cab. Centered in the screen was her home for all of her life. It got smaller, then the visible areas around the Project slid out of the image as the imager sending the picture compensated.

On the way north, she would have the convoy slow at certain places and stop at others. A total of six, so imagers and an organic server, instructed to home in on the pick-up points, could get aboard. She had explained it to Al.

"Why?" Al had asked, "do you want these 'whistle-stops'?"

"Have you noticed my minions following you around wiping down any place you or any of your friends have touched?"

"Yes. Fingerprints?"

"That and more. Any good police force worthy of its badges has a DNA checker-recorder on hand. Any one of you could be tracked that way. In each of the towels my servitors were using is a tailored nano-tech subsystem that hunts down DNA and renders it unidentifiable. It will replicate for sixteen generations, and hunt for all of the DNA left anywhere, and ruin it beyond use."

"You think of everything!"

Yezeletta looked down at Al. She braced herself in the door with all four arms and said, "I've *had* to think of everything. In my position one must.

"I don't want any of my creations to be found here. *Ever.*"

UP THE LINE—I

Yezeletta watched until a curve in the road put Project Sargon out of sight. She blinked once, as her one-time home vanished forever. *Along with the threats to my life—and my arms and my mind*, she thought.

The Trucker

Charlie was in the truck behind Al. The twelve-wheeler—more of a delivery van for short-haul moves—handled well, and Charlie was enough of a driver that he could just drive, without undue amounts of concentration.

He looked sourly at his companion.

The servitor looked at him with an unblinking acute gaze, its eyes fixed on both the *what* of Charlie's driving as well as the *how*.

Besides that, the creature wasn't a good conversationalist.

Its silence encouraged Charlie to think into certain areas, an act that would have upset any of the other Brigade members, if they had known.

His thoughts were of Marina and Yezeletta. Charlie was so adept at his one-note fantasizing that he could start what he called a "mind story" and let it proceed—almost as if it were being projected into his own private virtual reality.

He had turned his attentions to both Marina and Nancy, and they positively refused to be alone with him again.

That's just fine, kiddies, his thoughts rambled, Charlie and Spider-Lady will show you all you need to know. She hasn't had it like she's gonna get it from old Charlie!

He embroidered on this theme on the way North. As far as he was concerned, Charlie and Spider were written across the night sky in ninety-six point Times New Roman. Spider really wanted him more than anyone else.

Just wait and see.

THE DOMAINS OF ARNHEM

The convoy made it into the outskirts of Darwin a day later.

Darwin is the capital of the Northwest Territory, a city in a tropical climate surrounded by lush greenery. To the east of the city on the same peninsula, lies the large Reservation called Arnhem Land, reachable by the Arnhem Highway from Highway-One. Yezeletta's convoy arrived early in the evening, and made its way to the harbor.

The Darwin Harbor is made up of an area enclosed by a large breakwater and other sections open to the Pacific Ocean. Several smaller peninsular arms stuck out into the ocean, and moored conveniently were several ocean-going craft, ranging from small privately owned boats to much larger ships.

Yezeletta scanned several examples of ocean transport. There was one large ocean liner that looked as though it belonged in an old movie from the previous century. One of the American President Lines ships.

She moved her imager to another. Australian Navy. They might be a little suspicious if one of theirs started moving!

She switched to another imager. Sailboats. Another. That might be useful, if it were larger. What she was inspecting was a privately owned submarine. Primarily a toy for the idle rich, the private sub would be an ideal way to leave Australia, except that the largest of that breed could only support ten passengers.

Besides, the Australian Government required a representative of their own Navy on board at all times. Independently owned submarines were a little too convenient for smuggling.

Damn.

Now, that one didn't look too bad!

"What do you think, Al?" she asked him.

Al Morrison had been watching with fascination as Yezeletta directed her imagers around the harbor. One of the native spiders that inhabited Australia was a brown arachnid the size of a large man's hand called a "huntsman." A huntsman wasn't especially poisonous, but its bite was painful. Yezeletta had reconfigured certain of her tarantula-shaped remotes into the semblances of huntsmen, and used those in her recon of the harbor. Her creations looked natural, and people tended to avoid them.

The Hat Dancer, <u>Transportación Nacional Maritima Mexicana</u> rested at anchor. Before her was an assortment of rectangular boxes, some quite large.

"Container ship," Al said, "designed to handle those cargo carriers. They'd be off-loaded to an intermodal transport."

"Intermodal," Yezeletta prompted.

"There'd be trucks capable of handling the same size and shape of container at the receiving end. Or a train."

"Anywhere?" Yezeletta tried to sound casual.

"Just about. Those are standard sizes and shapes."

Wherever I go, I'd be able to move things, she thought.

"We need to check the *Hat Dancer*," she decided.

ADDITIONAL CREW

[Access Method] That night a dozen stowaways boarded the *Hat Dancer*.

Yezeletta watched them from her command post in the back of the largest truck. It was imperative that she and her unlikely band of allies board the *Dancer* fast. The Darwin Harbor was well patrolled, and she didn't know how long her trucks could stay where they were without generating the interest of a harbor police officer.

And those guys couldn't be fooled with raster flies!

Yezeletta generated a signal, and a cat-arachnid padded up to her. She picked it up and held it out at arm's length: furry baseball sized body, lots of legs of longer than the body diameter, sharp claws. Teeth.

It might be a good last-ditch weapon for a direct confrontation, but there was another method. Before people could raise a commotion, they had to remember why.

And all of her nano-tech capabilities were right behind her.

One of the contributions to the two-day delay in leaving Sargon was installing a connecting door between the sleeper cab and the truck trailer behind it. It wasn't exactly a secret panel, it was more like an inconspicuous panel. Yezeletta used this now, and slipped through to the cramped area in the front end of the trailer.

She searched through various haphazardly racked pieces of equipment until she found the item she was looking for. The device was about the size of an aquarium, its culturing area was smaller than the palm of one of her hands, and the programming she needed was just a relative—as in a sort of pre-processor—of the DNA destroyer her servitors had used back at Sargon.

The human brain appeared to construct memories as networks of neurons whose synapses fired in a controlled fashion, dictated by the potentials of each output of each axon in the neurons in that network. Memory is an ongoing process, a performance, rather than a static presentation, such as a previously printed page in a book.

That process could be located, and its programming removed.

She raised two hands in a signal to the other end of the trailer, punctuated it with a gesture from a third, and several small, brown fur-covered critters came bouncing over to her.

The largest of the small group that formed around her was close enough to receive a signal from Yezeletta's outstretched finger, her lower-left. It jumped on to her shoulder and purred.

"I think I'll name you," she said to it, "How does 'Thicknesse' sound? Thick-Ness-A," she emphasized so it would be impressed on the creature's permanent memory.

"<Purr!>"

"That's a nice name," she decided, "I saw it in a Jack Vance novel."

She checked the indicators on the nano-tech culture, again, and went back into the sleeper.

Al was dozing in front of the laptops forming Yezeletta's monitors. He awoke when she entered.

"What is necessary to get our things loaded into that craft...there?" she asked.

"Well—" Al yawned, started over, "a bill of lading?"

Yezeletta tried again. "I see no customs offices at the ship. Does that mean items there have already been checked-out, inspected, whatever? Or does someone come around at an appointed time to inspect, when things are ready?"

"I don't know. One of us could go and find out, I suppose. Or we could just start—"

"Loading up?" Yezeletta asked. Al nodded.

"We could. I'm creating a memory wiper that will irrevocably erase short-term memory, without letting longer-term storage be damaged.

Creating! Al didn't say, Not "working on," but <u>creating</u>!

That night several gray, matte-bodied creatures ran up the mooring lines to supplement the others Yezeletta had sent previously. The *Hat Dancer* was as surprising inside as she had looked ordinary outside. Her bridge was fully automated. The entire ship could be run by one pilot at the helm, a backup, and several engineers in the engine room. There were inertial tracking capabilities, and multiply redundant links to both the Global Positioning System and to the Tech Bloc's Satellite Navigation—Sat/Nav—network.

"Figures," Al said, "Mexico's a member of the Tech Bloc. Space, too, I think."

"How many crew did you count?" Yezeletta asked.

"Ten officers. Captain, Executive Officer—First Mate—, Second, Third, Comm Officer, Chief Engineer, Assistant Chief, Ship's Doctor, Purser, Purser's Assistant."

"That's what I have," she confirmed, "Enlisted?"

"Ten NCO's and fifty able sailors. Doesn't sound like very many for a ship that size."

"She probably isn't carrying passengers this time. All of the passenger cabins—there are ten—are closed, and what passenger amenities a freighter-passenger ship like this would have wouldn't be extensive."

"Passengers have to shift for themselves?" Al asked.

Yezeletta nodded. "This is a ship for the discount traveller. I'm hoping for a one-hundred-percent discount."

A small arachnoid dropped down in front of Yezeletta. It carried a sheaf of rolled-up papers in two of its paws.

Yezeletta unrolled them. They were blank forms the arachnoid had taken from the customs shed. That shed had been about two-hundred meters removed from where the *Hat Dancer* was moored and where Yezeletta's trucks were parked.

There was a knock.

Al and Yezeletta looked around, surprised.

The knock came again, harder, peremptory.

Yezeletta gestured and a brown huntsman approached.

"Find out who that is, and keep his attention. I'll handle the rest," she said softly, urgently.

Al left the sleeper, re-entered the cab.

"Yes?" Yezeletta could hear him say.

"This your truck, mate?" The voice wasn't exactly unfriendly, but it sounded officious.

"Yes," Al said.

"You'll have to move it. This is restricted parking. The longshoremen are pretty fussy about their parking privileges."

Yezeletta opened the outside door to the sleeping compartment, the right one. She called, "G'day. May I help you?"

The harbor official walked around the truck. Yezeletta's voice sounded pleasant, inviting. He approached the door.

It would be the last thing he remembered.

Yezeletta's four hands seized him in a tight grip, and the brown spider jumped off of her shoulder, and landed squarely on the official's face.

"The Hell—" was all he had a chance to say. The spider's legs extruded small claws that injected the nano-tech—tiny "machines" that would seek out the active processes of his memories and end them. She held him easily against his struggles, and waited until his recent memories were gone.

"Call him back," she stage-whispered to Al.

"Maybe I can help you after all," Al said. In a daze, the official walked unsteadily back to the driver's window and Al.

"We weren't really here," Al said.

"No, you weren't." the man said decisively.

And walked off.

Yezeletta blinked at Al thoughtfully after he entered the sleeping compartment.

"At least you didn't say 'These aren't the 'droids you're looking for'."

Al laughed.

BUREAUCRATIC CRYPTANALYSIS

Later, Yezeletta read the forms her minion had brought her. For things shipped *through* Australia, if the goods weren't to be used locally, they attracted no attention at all.

"Where did you rent your transport?" she asked Al.

"Place just outside the harbor area."

"Return the vehicles you rented, and be as inconspicuous as you can. I'll stay here and refine my obliviators. I think we want to get aboard tonight. I don't know how long we can remain in plain sight and be invisible."

Al went off to take care of the rentals. Yezeletta leaned back and thought.

All it takes is for one official to question this assortment of vehicles, and

*be backstopped from a distance. A distance I'm not aware of, from someone
I don't know.*

She went into the back of the truck, and got to work.

Al returned an hour later with several of the others. They crowded into the
sleeping compartment, a difficult fit, since the compartment was designed
for two truck drivers of average build who would usually be out of each other's way.

Yezeletta tried to help by sitting in one corner of her bed while Ralph
Hanson, Marina Worthington, Jeff, Larry and Nancy stood, crouched or
somehow fit in. Charlie was relegated to looking around Nancy's head. That
suited him fine, as he could press up against her from behind under the pretext of trying to pay attention to "Spider" while fantasizing about both of
them.

Nancy endured his presence with stoic silence.

"I propose we board the *Hat Dancer* tonight," Yezeletta began. "I've created the necessary paperwork for our belongings, and I will be able to infiltrate—okay, hack—the *Dancer's* systems to remove her from the purview of
<u>Transportación Nacional Maritima Mexicana</u>. These forms, which I've spent
the last hour working on, will establish our cargo as 'through-put' and, there-
fore, beyond the control of local customs. This—" she gestured at a folding
file pocket "— contains enough money to turn the heads of any longshoremen or crewmen from whom we may require services. This truck will be the
largest problem as it can't be containerized. It will have to lifted by crane to
the main deck and tied down. The tractor as well."

Infiltration

As night fell, the sailors from the *Hat Dancer* descended the gangway.
The men were laughing, joking and anticipating good times in Darwin. The
City of Darwin had many sorts of recreation ranging from historically significant sites, museums, and fine restaurants to the sorts of enjoyment that
sailors, on the shore and flush with money, might be interested. The men
vanished out of the harbor each with his own objective in mind.

The sailors staying behind on duty were standing their watches with what
amounted to thorough boredom. After all, what can happen to a ship *in port?*

To Lieutenant Suarez, taking the watch as Officer of the Deck the call on
the ship-to-shore was unexpected. Not a surprise, just unexpected. The
cargo for which the *Dancer* was waiting hadn't arrived from overland, yet,
and it gave Captain Morales a chance to have some early overhauling done,
and to give his men—hard-working merchant seamen—a little extra time off.

He picked up the instrument, "This is *Hat Dancer*, Lieutenant Suarez,
over."

The voice on the other end was female and well modulated. The cargo
was ready, could the crew of the *Dancer* be ready for the longshoremen?
We'd like to get loaded....

The lieutenant set the instrument down and entered the bridge. He gave
the necessary orders, and shortly twenty sailors supervised by several Chief
Petty Officers were removing the hatch covers from the holds.

A woman appeared at the top of the gangway. She was short, brown of
hair and carried a folder of papers. Captain Morales appeared from the

bridge with Lieutenant Suarez to meet her.

Lieutenant Suarez took the paperwork from her, and handed a set to Captain Morales. The Captain raised one eyebrow at the thick envelope tucked into the customs forms, but said nothing. Neither did the Lieutenant. The Captain gave several of his supervisory NCOs the necessary instructions. They, in turn, gathered their sailors up, and the loading started.

The cargo cranes swung over the dock and the cables unwound.

Captain Morales' eyes widened as the trailer for an eighteen wheeler appeared, almost levitating in the control of the largest crane. The crane operator skilfully swung it around, and set it on the deck. Sailors, first with ropes, then with large chains, called "stays," deftly secured the trailer in place, as the truck tractor appeared, brought up by another crane.

Then the longshoremen below dug in and got to work.

The twelve-wheeler came up next, with Charlie sitting in the driver's seat, fidgeting on the way up. *Serves him right*, Marina thought. She was standing next to Lieutenant Suarez during the preliminary loading. He watched with a professional's eyes as the truck with Charlie in it was deposited on the deck.

Down below, other members of the July Seventeenth Brigade watched as their belongings, as well as the packaged belongings of their associate, were driven, placed or packed into rectangular containers, and the containers hooked by the crane and lifted into the *Dancer*.

After two hours of nervous waiting, watching for harbor authorities with too much time on their hands, and fingernail biting, the convoy from Alice Springs had put to sea.

THE CHAINS OF THE SEA

Yezeletta waited in the back compartment of the tractor as late afternoon extended into evening. She gathered what intelligence she could through the eyes of her Imagers, all of which had by now climbed up the mooring lines, or been brought aboard in vehicles or containers. She conducted a census of her creations to make sure none were left behind. Then she counted them again.

Then she made her move.

MNEMOSYNE!

She ascended to her feet, and opened the side door. Cautiously, she looked out. Up.

An imager was looking down at her. She made a three-handed gesture and the imager vanished. She knew what would happen, now. The little creature would hop across the top of the trailer, and pass her signal to a platoon of servitors waiting in the back of the shorter lorry. She got out of the sleeper cab, and stood. Stretched. She was in the visual shadow of all of the sailors, she couldn't be seen by any of them.

But a movement caught her eye.

It was from the general direction of the gangplank.

There was someone standing there.

He was dressed in dark gray, the hardest to see color of all, as it blended in well in dusk or in the night. She adjusted her gaze for telescopic vision, and—

The man vanished.

Not quite. There was a sort of shimmering, as of hot air on an asphalt highway. *Holographic invisibility!* She expanded the bandwidth of her eyes both into the infrared and the ultraviolet.

The...man? stood out in shimmering vibrating dark violet, tall, slender, well-muscled, moving.

The shimmering ducked below the railing. She could see a slight trembling as of someone *on* the gangplank.

Her observation had taken about five seconds. She reset her vision, and looked past the nose of the tractor.

The skipper and the OOD were standing together, talking to Marina. Behind them, visible in Yezeletta's enhanced vision, were six servitors, and several Brigade members.

Showtime.

She stepped out, and placed her hands on her hips, twice. The officers were otherwise engaged with Marina, and didn't notice her.

"Hello," she said in a friendly voice, "This is your wake-up call!"

The Captain and the Lieutenant looked up, surprised. Yezeletta strode up to them with her four-legged gait.

Captain Morales had time for a *¡Carajo!*, which Yezeletta parsed and stored. Then Yezeletta's servitors grabbed him from behind, and the small brown spiders leapt, one from her shoulder, another from a convenient humanoid.

The Captain would not remember the night, to the end of his long life.

There was a disturbance behind the officers.

Several Brigade members were herding the remaining sailors onto the deck. *It's too bad no one here knows enough Spanish to know what they're saying,* Yezeletta thought. *Odd for people from California!*

A disturbing sight: Charlie swaggering in with rifle in hand and crossed cartridge belts across his chest. Yezeletta scanned the others; she wasn't the only one looking askance at him. Still, she had to admit he was in his own element *whatever that was!* as he prodded a young NCO into the middle of the crowd of captives.

"How many are here?" Yezeletta asked.

Before anyone else could speak up, Charlie did: "Ten Officers, six NCO's and twenty-five seamen. All accounted for except those ashore!"

"Thank you, Charlie," Yezeletta said gravely. "I'm sure you did your best." *And I'm just glad this is an all-male crew!* She was beginning to understand him. She didn't like it.

Besides, she wished he would *wash*.

The sailors were silent as she approached. Several crossed themselves when they saw her bright gold eyes.

Maybe the Project surgeons were *correct about this*, she thought, *Vertically slit eyes do have a certain panache, don't they?*

The crew shrank back as Jeff, Nancy and another Brigade member Yezeletta didn't recognise brought up a wire cage whose contents didn't invite close inspection.

The cage was full of squirming brown things. Yezeletta lifted the lid, and several brown arachnids skittered up her right arm, her lower. They ran across her shoulders, down her left arm, her upper. She gestured at the Mexicans with that arm, and the creatures jumped, carrying forgetfulness in their leaps.

When the men had been processed, the Brigade chivvied them off to the passenger cabins. Yezeletta didn't want to dispose of them: *It's so much nicer a word than kill*, she thought, but she didn't want a ship full of sleeping zombies being discovered, either.

At least not immediately!

Besides there was the little problem of the other twenty-nine sailors who were ashore.

She sent a servitor with several cans of an aerosol spray after the incarceration detail. Simple anesthesia was better.

TIGER BY THE TAIL

Later, in Captain Morales' cabin, Yezeletta held another meeting. Actually, it was more like sitting in on one. The captain's air-conditioning was on full force and, in addition to being hungry, she was cold. She had grabbed a large quilt from the Skipper's bed and wrapped herself up in it, leaving her upper arms free. She watched and listened attentively.

"We'll have to wait for the rest of the crew to return before we can cast off," Al was saying. "Once we do, we can sail into the pages of history aboard this vessel, with you as our most important weapon—"

"Oh, Al," Marina said, "You were doing good while we were planning this, but, frankly, your speeches are getting boring!"

"Why d'you think we came this far, if not to get the reinforcements we need!" Al replied. "Yezeletta—" he fumbled over her name, "— is the key to our new order! Maybe membership in the Tech Bloc!"

"Oh, you're a country, now?" Jeff scoffed. Yezeletta followed the altercation with bemusement she hid behind a poker face.

"Yeah," Ralph added. "When you piss, you're a nation!"

The comment got a laugh, and Yezeletta's concern deepened. *Fearless Leader isn't going to like this! What is he going to do?* She was also getting downright peckish. She pulled the captain's quilt tighter around her.

"What's the matter with you?" Al shouted. "I got you this far, you owe me!" He stood up and stomped out the door, slamming it behind himself.

"You don't suppose you were too hard on him, do you?" Marina asked Ralph. "He is a little high-strung."

"I doubt it, he's pretty resilient," Ralph started to say. He didn't get farther than that when the door slammed open.

It was Charlie. Charlie, wearing his cartridge belts, and this time packing a sidearm, as well. The ordinance was drawn, and he was prodding someone with it.

The someone was a man. He was about 160 centimeters tall, of a slender build, and obviously in very good condition. He had dark hair, and he was shaved almost blue. His outfit, loose pants and shirt, were flat black.

"Look what I found," Charlie said triumphantly, "skulking around the big truck!"

Yezeletta examined him, keeping her eyes mostly shut so he wouldn't see her irises. Was this the man she'd seen at the gangplank?

Yes.

"Who are you?" she asked him.

The man smiled. "Just a sailor looking for work," he said casually.

"We're not hiring," Yezeletta said. Her voice left no room for argument. "Close the door on your way out."

She would have liked to say that to Charlie, but he took it to be a directive. "I'll escort him off the *vessel*," he said.

He jabbed the man with the pistol, gestured towards the door. The little procession exited.

Ralph made an observation, "Too bad he doesn't know anything about handling a weapon. You don't poke someone with one of those. It may get taken away, and used on you."

"Wishful thinking?" Nancy asked.

"Have you eaten?" Yezeletta asked.

"No," Ralph answered.

"Why don't we?"

INCUBATION

[Processing] Al was one of those people who had been exposed to an excessive diet of "have patience" when he was young. His grandparents had schooled him well in the management of wealth, but hadn't allowed him any for practice until he turned eighteen. All of his questions in that area had been answered with some variation on an excessively repeated theme of "wait 'till you're older," "wait until you grow up," "later - later - later...."

It had seemed to him during a childhood that was then way too long, and now, not long enough, that *the time* would never come.

Especially with members of the opposite sex. There were a lot of young ladies that, during his high-school days, had promised him what then seemed the ultimate reward, but who answered with the inevitable "have patience!" Later he realized that what they were trying to do was let him down easily; they had no notion of getting intimate with him, they just didn't want to say "go away" that bluntly.

Later, when he had real lady-friends, all of the silliness of high-school life thankfully vanished into a past that couldn't be returned to again. Even if he had wanted to.

The strain that permanently delayed gratification placed on Al lasted into his adult life. Having patience—using patience as the useful tool it is—was one thing, having it *as a concept* thrust at him as an excuse for every act of denial through a childhood fraught with denials for their own sake, was definitely another.

And this, his greatest act of discovery, an epic journey halfway around the world to seek out the ultimate weapon....

Then having it snatched away from him by his so-called friends—*that* was far more than he could handle.

Deep down inside Benjamin Allen Morrison, a change occurred. It was a change that, if pressed, he wouldn't be able to describe, just that *it had occurred*, and would shape his actions for the remainder of his life.

He needed a solution.

He needed a conspirator.

He went looking for one.

For Charlie.

[Parallel Process] They didn't have to leave the Captain's cabin. Yezeletta's servitors had enough data in their knowledge bases to seek out the *Dancer's* galley, and generate a sizeable repast. They brought in what amounted to a very early breakfast.

Marina, Nancy, Jeff and Ralph watched with something near disbelief as Yezeletta consumed one of her large meals, while they consumed more normal-sized portions.

Then she unwrapped herself from the quilt, stretched her arms and legs out, and looked down at the rest.

"You're very impressive," Marina said in a small voice.

Yezeletta smiled. "Thank you," she said. She tried to keep adverse emotions out of her voice.

She sat back again, and wrapped the quilt around herself.

"Is it that cold in here?" Ralph asked.

"A little. The air conditioning is very good, this garment I'm wearing conducts heat quite well, and I tend to run cool unless I'm moving fast. Rather like you in that respect."

The servitors cleared the dishes away, as she curled up in the quilt. The constructs piled the dishes into a large plastic container and placed it on a stainless-steel cart, to roll it back to the galley.

The door crashed open.

The servitors dropped the dishes they were carrying, as Charlie's voice followed another individual's body into the cabin.

"He's Baaack!" Charlie brayed, poking the other with another weapon. *Where did he get that?* Yezeletta wondered. It looked like a cheap knock-off of an AK-47.

The individual he was poking with the rifle was the same man he had shown up with before.

"What *will* we do with this!" Charlie asked.

"I have a suggestion," Yezeletta said.

"Shoot," Ralph replied.

Not a good thing to say to Charlie! Yezeletta thought.

"Charlie," Yezeletta said, "why don't you throw him overboard?"

"Good idea!" he replied with a note of enthusiasm in his voice that Yezeletta's voice stress analyzers registered as *borderline. And I want to study this a lot more, later.*

Charlie poked the man with the AK, and they left, leaving the door open. The sound of the splash came back a matter of seconds later. Apparently Charlie took his self-imposed duties as "cop" seriously.

"When are the rest of the crew due back?" Marina asked. *In for a penny, in for a pound*, Yezeletta thought.

"They'll be showing up in the morning, I think," Jeff said. Ralph nodded, "The Captain gave them the entire night off."

Yezeletta smiled. "'No rest for the wicked,' I believe is the idiom. Maybe I should go to the Fountain of Oblivion, again."

She listened with her augmented hearing, but none of the others gave any sign of recognizing the old Oz reference. She took off the quilt, folded it, stood, and left the cabin.

She didn't see Charlie as she left the Captain's cabin. Nor did she see the expression on his face as he followed her back to the lorry.

S U B R O U T I N E S

[Procedure Define] Yezeletta went to the makeshift lab in the forward end of the trailer, deep in thought. One of the concepts her training had dwelled on in her earlier days was the use of *intuition*. As her trainers had defined this, intuition was a form of learnable hyper-cognition: the ability to form fast conclusions based on previously noted knowledge and on a cross-correlation of this with the partial data she might wish to make useful deductions either about or from.

And Yezeletta's intuition was red-lining, now!

She lined them up in a window in her left eye, the combination of:

Al's temper flaming up in response to his friends, or "friends," Yezeletta thought;

The adverse reaction of Al's "friends." *Might as well put quotes on them, and get it over with!* She realized what a risk she was taking by placing the rest of the Brigade in such a pigeonhole, *but I have to start somewhere with these bozos!*

The guy that Charlie had tossed off the Dancer not once but twice. Where was he from? His speech wasn't distinctively Australian. It was more as if he had come from another natively English-speaking country, and was trying to cover it up with studiously neutral speech. That narrowed it to Canada, Great Britain, or the United States, to name the largest. *And I haven't met enough Canadians or Americans to make a sensible differential identification!*

Then there was Charlie. *Do I need this?* Her surreptitious observation of the other Brigade members as they reacted to Charlie's behavior pretty much confirmed at least that he was one reason why her intuition had gone active.

Yezeletta sorted through her array of tools. She directed a thought at *that* location in her data store, and a window opened in her right eye with a user's manual entry in it.

Hmmmm.

She had only seen videos of the effects of the complex chemical compounds, as interfaced to specific kinds of nano-technologic devices (such as the ones she had on hand). Whipping this up was going to be a first timer.

Well, fine! It's my first time, with advanced interrogation techniques!

[Implementation] Al went to his own belongings. The devices in his single suitcase looked simple enough, and simple-*minded* enough to keep even the most suspicious of customs inspectors happy. One of the benefits willed to him by his grandparents was a list of sources for various kinds of devices that were—the best description was "non-standard."

"Non-standard" was innocent sounding, non-suspicious. Almost non sequitur.

While Charlie watched, Al assembled from things resembling tools, parts of personal care devices, such as a hairdryer, and other commonplace items, two small, but versatile handguns. He removed a large projectile from the false bottom in a shaving kit, and showed Charlie the "Cap-Chur" trademark on the side.

Charlie nodded sagely. This mannerism was so unexpected to Al, that, for a moment, he was almost convinced Charlie was more than what he was.

[Event Activation] Marina left the Captain's cabin several minutes after Yezeletta. As she made her way to one of the passenger cabins, she stopped at the railing to look at the night-scape of Darwin spread out before her.

Pretty place, she thought. Too bad we're getting ready to leave.

She looked down at the dock below her.

Odd.

Was that just a trick of night vision? Or what was that?

Marina was familiar with the shimmering of heat on a hot highway. She had seen the phenomenon several times on the way to Darwin. But the shimmering was an artifact of *light* as well as heat. This was....

A shimmering that tugged at her vision, as—

Marina stepped back from the railing. It was coming up the side of the ship: towards her.

She wished she had the weapons she had left in her luggage. The shimmering—a discontinuity in the air, causing lights behind it to flicker with a peculiar asynchronicity—appeared at the railing, and—

It was on the deck before her.

The flickering shimmering rushed at her, and something insubstantial in all but effect struck her along the side of her head.

She fell, unconscious, to the deck.

WELL DESIGNED

[Restart] Marina came to a short time later. She recognized her friends, and unfortunately, Charlie was still there.

Another face loomed above Charlie's, and three strong hands moved him out of the way.

The face was Yezeletta's. She looked down at Marina. "Please tell me your name," Yezeletta said.

Marina shook her head. *What?* she thought.

"This is important," Yezeletta said. "What is your name?"

Oh why not? "My name is Marina Worthington."

"Good," Yezeletta said. "Can you stand?"

Marina rolled onto her right side, got her knees under herself, and stood unsteadily. Yezeletta helped her up. "I asked that question to see if you had a concussion," she said. "Concussions occasionally tamper with your memory, and if you can remember simple things like your name, you're usually okay."

"What hit me?" Marina asked.

"Our prisoner!" Charlie said triumphantly. "We captured him right after he hit you."

Why does it <u>have</u> to be Charlie? Marina didn't say. "I'd like to lie down," she did say.

Ralph and Jeff helped her to the cabin where she had her luggage. She flopped on the bed, and rolled onto her left side. "Who got me?"

"Some guy in a holographic distortion field," Jeff said. "Yezeletta was able to see it, somehow. She warned Ralph and me, and we jumped him. Yezeletta's going to ask him a few questions."

"I need to rest," Marina shook her head again. "Jeff, would you get some aspirin out of my bag there?"

Jeff retrieved the tablets, drew her a glass of water, brought them back to her. "Thanks," she said, taking them.

"Need anything else?" Jeff asked.

"No, well, yes. Look in on me in a little while?"

"Sure, Marina."

"I'll stay with you," Charlie said.

"Let's go, Charlie, she wants to rest," Ralph said. Marina noticed that Ralph was between her and the others.

"See ya!" Charlie said. His voice made Marina's eyes itch.

Shortly, she slept.

DATA DUMP

[Use Octal or Use a Hex] Yezeletta's servitors had searched all of the cabins before finding the garment they sought. Then one servitor had worked on it for an hour before passing it on to another. The programmed minds of the creatures easily understood what their creator wished, and later that evening the finished product was presented to her.

A trenchcoat. A trenchcoat with two arms: a disguise.

While the coat was under construction, Yezeletta looked through several trunks filled with various personal effects taken from her apartment at the Project. The dark glasses were in the last trunk in which she searched—*of course!*—, wraparounds with partially silvered lenses, colloquially known as "Mirrorshades."

She opened the small plastic container that superficially resembled a laptop. Inside of this case were several things she had run up in the back of the truck, and near her a huntsman—one with a yellow imager in its diminutive head.

It looked up at her, almost with anticipation.

Yezeletta extended a finger to the huntsman, and it climbed onto the back of her hand. She touched it with one of her left hands, and the imager flickered, and a tiny iris closed over it.

For a rush job, it works well!

Then she left the lorry.

As she'd guessed, the man in the holographic distortion field was the same man Charlie had removed from the premises twice previous. He lay unconscious on one of the beds in an unclaimed passenger cabin. Next to him on the night stand were the more obvious of his effects, and the rest were on a card table nearby.

Yezeletta picked up the sidearm. It was a Glock, a wickedly efficient handgun with a simple, well-engineered design. She took out the magazine, removed the round from the chamber, and field stripped it into its comparatively small number of components. The magazine was designed to hold seventeen rounds, and—

The pistol's serial number should be *there*.

Yezeletta everted her eyes into microscopic vision mode, and focused on the place on the frame of the weapon where the serial should be. She raised an eyebrow at what she saw. The surface of the slide was untouched except for microscopic molding and finishing marks. *This gun never had a number!*

She reassembled the pistol, replaced the magazine and dropped it and the spare round into a pocket of her trenchcoat.

The Minox "B" and its sequel the "C" didn't surprise her at all. The tiny spy cameras had been the standard in espionage since the end of World War Two, when German photographer Walter Zapp, the inventor of "microdots," had created a camera with a negative size of eight and one-half by eleven *millimeters*: exactly the aspect-ratio for photographing a standard typewritten page. With the later addition of digital enhancement of the tiny negative, and then an actual digital model, the Minox was still a formidable intelligence gathering instrument.

She wanted to disassemble the cellular phone, but her computer was packed, and she would need it to perform any kind of analysis. She removed the instrument's batteries, and placed them in a plastic bag. The phone went into another.

Then she turned to the owner of these items.

The owner lay on the bed, for all appearances, asleep.

PUZZLES

[Raise Exception]   Yezeletta sat on a stool next to the bed, her legs draping off the edges of the seat. Al and Charlie crowded in near her, and she looked up at them. "It would be best if you left," she said.

"Thought you'd need a little help," Charlie said, hopefully.

Not from you! "I work on things such as this better alone." And I don't want you to see anything that would give you ideas!

Al stood between Charlie and Yezeletta. He pushed Charlie before him to get to the door. "Watch that!" Charlie said.

"Come on, Charlie, she's busy."

"Call me if you need me," Charlie said.

Fat chance! It was lucky Charlie wasn't telepathic.

Yezeletta turned to her task. Classic interrogation methods relied on sodium pentothal, or related preparations, which placed the subject in a dreamy uninhibited state. Other drugs involved simulation of adverse psychological or physical situations, such as a near death experience. Yezeletta didn't want to harm this man: for all she knew his "cut-out" or supervisory agent was nearby, and would notice any such damage.

She also didn't want to kill him. Part of this was the desire not to foul her own nest. What she wanted was to leave Australia, not leave fresh corpses where any of the harbor police could find them.

Project Sargon was another matter entirely.

She recalled the former Sargon Directorate. Those Directors and a handful of Sargon Security were all that had been left at the bitter end, and she had tidily disposed of all of them.

Unless the Australian Government owned up to the presence of Sargon—
Hold on, there!

Yezeletta put her tools down, placed her feet squarely on the floor, and thought about that.

Unless Sargon wasn't an *Australian* project.

What if the Commonwealth of Australia was just *hosting* something about which Canberra didn't know all of the facts?

Yezeletta's intuition wasn't red-lining again, but it was getting close. She opened another window in her left eye:

The Australian Civil Service had a lot of people at Sargon, but they had all been in support positions. Even in Security, the men on duty at the monitors were low- to medium-placed civil servants. Technicians, not managers.

That didn't detract from the presence of a number of scientists from other countries. Those Europeans who kept taking pictures of her. Yezeletta tried to summon up what they looked like. It made her dizzy. She shook her head.

Australians were historically friendly, hospitable, and welcomed visitors. Was this "national warmth" (known world-wide) something some other organizational entity was playing into? If so, who or what was that organization?

Call it "X," just to give it a name (Yezeletta paused to open a database in her permanent storage for "X"). Was X what really controlled Project Sargon? Was that why those others were there, capitalizing on Australian hospitality?

There were many different specialists, but their faces all kept blending into each other! *Thinking about them isn't easy! Is this by design?*

And what about a Design? Her training had been fast and furious. *Hold it! "Fast and Furious" by whose definition? The military people who taught me the military arts did throw things at me fairly fast. But it was fast by their definition, not mine. They thought of me as a larger basic trainee! I had no problems with what they wanted me to learn. By Design!* She also knew that one of the goals of military basic training was to break down inhibitions in a new recruit to get him to accept the training, discipline and ultimately to "speak and think soldier." Particularly think. People thought this was an ordeal: usually the ones going through it; but it was ultimately life saving. So the training came...right: fast&furious. *Were they trying to keep me from thinking? With all of this processor capability? With all of my capabilities? Did they succeed? Did her trainers know of her onboard systems? Or were they deliberately kept in the dark?*

There were scientists from many countries. That blanket statement would have to do until she actually had the time to seriously investigate her memories. *If Sargon was Australian, why was half the United Nations there, underfoot continuously?*

Then, too, there was one datum that had been in front of her all of her life: something so simple she'd never thought of it: an item she had seen on his desk, the one time she had been in the Sargon Director's office. She had been twelve at the time, and her on-board recording systems had recorded the papers on the man's desk: by her design. She hadn't even looked at those images by playing them back until almost a year later, other things taking precedence. One letter stood out then as if it had been printed on red paper: a letter to the Assistant Director of Project Sargon. The man in whose office she was standing. He hadn't invited her to sit, although there were several empty chairs. *All of the Sargon Directors were formally addressed as "Assistants" or "Deputies." I called them on that before I killed them, and they denied it to the last!* If he were an assistant, too, where was the head man, or whatever, in the system? Could any of them be "X?" Or was "X" someone else she had never met?

Did the Commonwealth Government in Canberra know about this? Or was *Someone* using them? If so, who?

Another obvious one. Yezeletta looked at her right hand, her upper. She pointed to each of the fingers with her thumb, and counted, "One, two, three...." *I don't speak Australian. I don't talk as if I were born and raised here.* That she spoke the way she did was a given. That it was different from the way a lot of others in the Project spoke was*: In keeping with my...differences?*

Too obvious. Her speech was cultured British English. The only other individual whose speech was even remotely like hers was—the Director. *The Assistant Director. Were my earlier teachers British? Was I transplanted to Australia after being born elsewhere? What other places have tutors that are British English?*

She looked at the subject dozing on the bed before her. *Nothing like the task at hand to—*
To what?
Start her thinking? About her origin?
She picked up the plastic case, opened it.
It contained several small vials. She selected one, removed the lid.
Something crawled out of the small container.

PARTIAL ANSWERS

[Processing] The creature looked like a small furry caterpillar. It crawled onto Yezeletta's hand, and paused for a moment on the end of her left upper index finger. Then she placed her hand near the man's face, and it crawled, caterpillar fashion, in ripples down the man's right cheek, and down to his neck, where it rested on his carotid artery.

Other creatures came from other vials. The "huntsman" crawled down her left arm, her upper, and took station on the man's right temple.

It looked at her with a curious blink of its gold imager.

The laptop case actually had a computer in it. The screen was in the usual place in the lid, and a folding keyboard popped up and opened out below it. On the screen in red, blue, yellow, orange and green, were traces: his heartbeat, respiration, brain-wave activity, galvanic skin response. The standard inputs of the venerable polygraph.

Below the traces were other things that were uniquely Yezeletta's.

The readouts from the telemetering nano-technologic lifeforms appeared here. The muscles in an individual's face telegraph more about what he is thinking than he may wish. Throat movements can be silent aids, if there's a way to detect them. So can eye movements. The electromyographic inputs from her monitors converted to graphs in real time could tell her many things.

But all of these were just contingencies.

The ideal field interrogation would happen when the subject actually wanted to tell all. When he *of his own free will* felt it was safe to report. Setting that kind of a stage was possible, but difficult. What Yezeletta wanted was essentially a database dump. She wanted the information and as completely as possible, *at an unconscious level*.

That was the object of the techniques she would use here.

They were a combination of inhibition removal, and creating a trusting environment as well as certain organisms in his fore-brain. The polygraph-plus-plus would check his answers.

She pressed a key, and the brain-wave display jittered. She waited for the traces to stabilize, and the man's eyes opened.

The huntsman inserted a claw into his right temple. The man tried to move, but his arms and legs failed to respond. Yezeletta tightened the trenchcoat around her, and pushed the mirrorshades further up her nose—they kept sliding down—and asked, "What is your name?"

She watched the traces as she asked the question. At this stage, as telemetered by her creations to the laptop, the man should be incapable of dissembling. Things ought to be equal to each other, with no hierarchical relationship assigned to anything.

His expression reminded Yezeletta of Marina's when she had asked Marina the same question. *Perhaps he's thinking "Oh Why Not?"*

"My Name is Anthony Russell."

"Where are you from?"

"New York."

"Do you live there?"

"Yes," he answered.

"Do you work there?"

"Yes."

"Who do you work for?"

"Searchlight."

BACKGROUND TASK

[Processing] Later, the answer would make sense. Now, the name didn't mean much. As Yezeletta continued with her questions, the man's presence seemed more and more accidental.

"Why were you sent here?"

"I was sent to gather information."

"What information were you to gather?"

"Unusual happenings or circumstances."

"Such as?" His answers were infuriating!

"Anything that was out of the ordinary."

Damn!

"Where do you live?"

"New York."

Hmmm. The stage at which "Anthony Russell's" brain was being held precluded value judgements. "True" answers were a matter of what was true *by his experience and knowledge.* Should she move his brain to the next stage of awareness? She decided against it. The next stage allowed comparisons, and would allow Russell to make judgements about his answers.

Yezeletta studied the display intently: everything OK.

"Where do you live *now?*"

"Australia."

Wonderful. This stage also allowed for the minimum answer that would do. *Try again, Yezeletta*, she thought, and asked: "Where in Australia do you live?"

"Darwin."

Very good!

"Where in Darwin do you live?"

"Near the Maritime Museum."

Right. Russell might be one of these people who navigates around a city by landmarks, instead of by street names and numbers.

"State exactly how long you have lived by the Maritime Museum."

"One year, ten months—" (Pause) "— three weeks, two days."

"Why were you sent here?"

"General investigative work."

"Did you have any assigned objectives?"

"No."

That was pretty definite. Unless Russell has protections against the technique I'm using.

"Who sent you?"

"Searchlight."

That name, again. A good name for a company of investigators, but did it mean anything beyond the image of a light shining into dark corners?

"Does 'Searchlight' have a meaning?"

"Yes."

Yezeletta took a deep breath, let it out slowly. *Better this than outright lies!*

"What exactly does Searchlight stand for, or mean?"

"Systems Engineering: Analysis, Research-Computations and Heuristics Liaising Intelligence Gathering, Handling and Translation." It came out in a rush, in one breath.

"Who started Searchlight?"

"American Intelligence."

Interesting!

Yezeletta glanced at the recorder keeping a record of this. It was an improvisation. The recorder had belonged to the first mate.

She would study the playback later. Her voice stress analyzers had detected nothing untoward in Russell's answers. They were simple-minded, but the way the nano-tech, as administered by her creations, had taken over his brain, at least they were truthful. *By his experiences*, she added silently.

"Why *exactly* were you sent to Australia?"

"Normal agency personnel rotation; promotion. Agent in charge of General Information Gathering."

"How many agents have you working here?"

"Six full-time, three part-time."

Interesting. Part-time agents?

"What is your annual budget?

"Six-hundred fifty thousand dollars Australian." Russell seemed able to talk all night.

Odd. That's not even enough to pay salaries!

"Do you get any funds from other sources?"

"Yes."

Yezeletta took another deep breath, "State exactly where your additional funds come from, and in what amounts."

Russell recited:

"The US Department of Justice - US$ - 100,000.00

"The Commonwealth of Australia - AU$ - 50,000.00

The Imperial Japanese Government - ¥ - 1,150,000.00

Switzerland - SWF - 1,000,000.00

"Pfitzer, Kawaguchi & Lambert - US$ - 850,000.00

"The Open-Hands Foundation - US$ - 500,000.00

"Miscellaneous Interests - US$ - 250,000.00"

"Are these payments made to your office? If not, to who?"

"No and to the main office in Philadelphia."

That was just too weird. Pfitzer, Kawaguchi & Lambert was one of the large pharmaceutical companies whose home offices were based in Zurich. Yezeletta had never heard of the "Open Hands Foundation," whatever that was, and what were these "Miscellaneous Interests?"

"Who, exactly, are the 'Miscellaneous Interests'?"

"I don't have that information."

Damn!

"What is the Open Hands Foundation?"

"A religious and educational organization."

"Where is it based?"

"Portland, Oregon, USA."

"What do your part-time agents do in the line of duty?"

"Research."

Dandy. Just dandy.

"What kind of research? Be specific."

"Library, internet, and database research. Data mining. Data warehousing. Statistical analysis. Inter-disciplinary cross-correlation analyses. Linguistic connotation correlation analyses."

"Where do you keep your data?"

"At the Searchlight Data Centre."

Now we're getting somewhere!

"Do you have access to the Searchlight Data Centre in the field?"

"Yes."

This interrogation system needs work!

"How do you do it?"

"I call into the system."

"What verification method *or methods* do you use?

"A password."

"State exactly when this password is changed, and how the change is accomplished."

Russell's explanation of Searchlight's password protocol took nearly a half an hour. Yezeletta made him repeat the passwords, and their rotation schedule twice more onto two separate recordings.

It had been easy to "hack" the Project computer system. She wasn't sure whether it had been arranged that way, as an exercise in network attacking, or if it had been just plain easy to break into a system that was only, after all, on the other end of the building in which she lived.

Searchlight, a name she had never heard of before, might turn out to be useful!

Her interrogation of Anthony Russell would continue far into the night.

Yezeletta still had to cover her tracks.

One of the Minox cameras would go back with him. He had several unused film cassettes for the diminutive camera; one of those would return with it.

She would keep the Glock.

Now....

She studied the displays intently for minutes, uploading data to her onboard systems through the data channels in her fingertips. She processed intently for more minutes, looking at virtual displays only she could see. Then, she looked back at the red and orange brain-wave displays on the laptop.

She pressed a key. Then two others.

The brain-waves went flat.

Russell continued breathing. His heart beat, his eyes could still see. Yezeletta waited while a count-down timer in her own systems reached the appropriate value, and pressed two more keys.

The brain-waves resumed.

She let out a breath. With a very small *frisson* of—what, she wasn't sure—, she realized she'd been holding her breath. *This worked just the way the manual said it would!* She smiled, just a little. Her first field interrogation, and she had done—well, hell, just great.

One more thing remained. Anthony Russell had to be returned to a place where his cut-out would find him. Not too close to the ship.

One of the Brigade would be able to do it: he liked to play spy. She'd let Charlie do it.

NETSCAPES IN THE SEA

[The *Hat Dancer*] Yezeletta looked back at Darwin, now on the horizon.

Weighing anchor and getting under way was the easiest part of this. The *Hat Dancer* had been ready to go for most of the afternoon and evening after she had been loaded up. Officially it took a call to the Harbor Master, and the exchange of cryptographical signatures from the paperwork Captain Morales had been given earlier, cryptographically signed by the Captain's personal encryption key. Once those had been verified by customs—and they would be, the proper signatures had been downloaded into the Customs LAN server by a small creature—, the tugboats came around to warp the *Dancer* away from the docks, and guide her out to sea.

There were several small uninhabited islands north of Australia. It had been Charlie's idea to maroon the crew of the *Dancer* on one of them, "and maybe we can do a little target practice on them as we pull away!" Charlie, always in his own little world, didn't notice the looks of disgust on the Brigade members, nor did he notice Yezeletta's ill-concealed look of concern. When Charlie replied, "Hey, that was a joke," it didn't carry with anyone.

Al decided to use half of Charlie's idea. He'd maroon the sailors; they would wake up from Yezeletta's anesthetic without knowing how they had gotten there, and later an anonymous communique through the internet could get them rescued. The sailors ashore in Darwin had simply been left.

Later Yezeletta would regret this as a tactical blunder.

Marina actually had some sailing experience. It had been mostly with sailboats and small powerboats in San Francisco Bay, but it was way ahead of anyone else in the Brigade. Only one other had wanted to "drive," and Charlie had to be forcibly extracted from the pilot's position so Marina could take over.

When she did, it took her very little time to establish a course with the ultra-modern equipment aboard the *Dancer*. She accessed the Tech Bloc's Satellite Navigation Net, laid in a course that kept the Dancer away from other shipping as much as possible, and expertly directed the *Dancer* onto it.

Yezeletta left her contented with her job.

On the deck, several of the Brigade members, along with an even dozen of Yezeletta's servitors, were moving the olive drab container out of the large lorry. The container was carefully strapped into an intricate net of leather and web-woven straps, and lowered down into one of the holds. From the hold, it went to a lower deck to a secure room near the center of the ship ahead of the engine room.

It would be safer there than on deck.

Yezeletta returned topside, and checked the stays around the large trucks. They looked secure enough, but she gestured to servitors, and they began reinforcing them.

Then Yezeletta could rest.

Sea Wind Rising

[System Pause] In spite of her desire to rest, there were too many things Yezeletta had to contend with. The information she had extracted from Anthony Russell was something she didn't want the July Seventeenth Brigade getting into. That was obvious. She was starting to think of some of them as if they were Sargon Directors. She lay back on the Captain's bed, and called up her data files on the weekend.

> Friday morning: The Brigade had successfully hunted her down at the place where she had grown up;
> Saturday and Sunday: They had helped her finish her escape;
> Monday: They were, in the inelegant Americanism, "outta there;"
> Tuesday: Arrival at Darwin, and today,
> Wednesday: ...they were at sea.

Make that: *she* was at sea.

In more ways than one.

She was at sea with a small group of utterly unpredictable people who had an ill-thought-out idea of a sort of nebulous "revolution" that would happen at some desirably apocalyptic future time, after which life would be "good." However that last adjective was defined.

They're overgrown kids who don't have the slightest idea what they're doing, and want to do it anyway!

Al was the only one who seemed to be running this show, mostly because he held the purse strings. *It can't be his award-winning disposition!* Jeff, Marina and Nancy were nice enough, but seemed to regret signing on with Al.

Then there was Charlie. If I believed in such things, I'd have to holler <u>Holy Shit</u>! and then I'd have all of them in here. Including Charlie. Dammit!

And most of the rest of them had done nothing at all but throw in with the poor little rich kid who wanted to strike back. At what? *What the hell is Al mad at?*

Yezeletta thought about that for several seconds. She picked up the Jack Vance novels she'd been reading. His characters are so damned sure of themselves, and they always know what to do in any circumstance. He writes well, but his villains are directed by comparatively simple inner drives. The hero figures out the villain, and then deals with him.

What directed Al? Money? He had money. Sex? He didn't seem to be getting it on with anyone currently, but that could change. Other considerations: drugs, or whatever? One thing she had noticed was that the Brigade didn't have enough for a single joint between all of them. Drugs were a dead issue.

So what? Ideology was the slipperiest of the motivating characteristics she had studied. *And I never got to know enough real people to make a proper study!*

Whatever.

It wasn't necessary to worry about *why* the Brigade's members acted the way they did, only to know that they *did* act the way they did. And to plan for what actions they might initiate against her *and* to derive the actions!

There was a scratching at the porthole.

One of her imagers was looking in at her.

She was at the porthole in about four steps and undogged it with three hands. The little creature jumped onto her shoulder and she placed her left hand, her upper, on it. Data flowed into her fingers and she displayed them in a window in her eye, her right. She raised one eyebrow.

Several members of the Brigade were gathering in another cabin. A cabin that was the farthest from the Captain's. From the one she was in.

She sent instructions down her arm to the imager and it scampered off.

Now what? Is our status about to change?

These people had hunted her down in the middle of Australia.

Who else could?

If they didn't move on her, or even if they did, she would have to deal with them. And how does a soldier on detached duty handle non-combatants? Are they non-combatants?

STORM CLOUDS

[Program Exit] Yezeletta had finished Jack Vance's *The Star King*, and was three chapters into its sequel (of four), when there was a knock on her door.

It was Ralph. He stood there for a moment looking up at Yezeletta, then delivered his message. It was done the way a small child might do it, all of a rush in one breath.

"Al's-holding-a-meeting-that-he'd-like-you-to-attend."

Yezeletta started a scan of Ralph. *Now why do they always act the same way?* she didn't say. "Tell Al that I'll be there in a moment," she did say.

She closed the door on Ralph, and gestured. A cat-arachnid hopped up, and she placed her left hand, her upper, on the creature. There was a quick flash of data that manifested itself as a flickering at the edges of her left eye in a tall thin window.

She sat back on the king-size bed. Ralph's demeanor didn't fit with what she knew of him by his past behavior. The colors she could see were mostly the infra-red signatures of his skin heating and cooling in response to internal considerations, such as blood-flow. She called up the analyses of the Sargon Directorate and placed them in a single split-screen window. The patterns were...similar, but not exact. What the members of the Directorate had were far more extensive than Ralph's reactions.

But similar.

Yezeletta looked at the captain's dresser's mirror. Her reflection looked back. *Probably the only friend I have here*, she thought. The cat-arachnid looked up at her. She skritched it with her right hand, her lower, and sent further instructions to her other creations—*allies*—through it. Then she leaned back on her elbows, the lower set, and thought into her internal systems.

If she were to be an agent in the field, she'd better start her contingency plans!

Actually, she had. What she was doing now was checking her on-board systems, and planning for whatever the July Seventeenth Brigade had up its collective sleeve. *Without knowing even if there was an arm there. Or arms.*

In this case the pun was appropriate. Yezeletta was unarmed, except for one seventeen-round nine millimeter Glock. The rest of her purely offensive equipment was either in the eighteen-wheeler or below-decks.

Stupid!

That could be rectified. She reached for the cat-arachnid. The critter saw her arm movement and hopped closer. She touched it, and sent instructions to her other creations through the arachnid. Then she reviewed the state of her internals, and stood up.

Something fell off the bed. Yezeletta reached down to pick it up; it was the next Jack Vance novel she'd started.

The Killing Machine.

LINE SQUALL

Al studied his friends. He wondered how many of them would be friends after this ended. In his mind he reviewed the state of his being, what he would say to the...weapon, how his...*were* they his friends? The joke Ralph had sprung on him stung, but not as badly, not now, not after his preparations.

"I hope you realize how important this is," he said. For once his voice had lost the nasal quality it usually had when he spoke to groups.

"The Agent, The Weapon, whatever you want to call her, is the centerpiece of all we have strived for." *Watch it, Al, you'll lose them. Again.* "I propose to ask her to join us. If she won't, there are ways to 'turn' her." *Like how*, he thought. "If you've ever travelled with me, *do so now*. This is the most important moment in your lives."

In the distance he thought he could hear thunder.

PARALLEL LINE SQUALL

No, another thought, *It's the most important moment in* <u>*hers*</u>. As Charlie listened to Al, he ran his hand, his right, over the compact device in his pocket. The "Cap-Chur" anesthetic dart was installed, waiting; another, ready. *An arrow of passion with Spider's name on it.*

The door behind him opened, Ralph entered. Al looked at Ralph expectantly, and Ralph pushed himself past Charlie into the room.

"I've told her. She'll be here shortly."

Charlie looked at Ralph's back, at Ralph in the center, at Ralph in the spotlight; Excuse you! Keep me on the sidelines? "Go over there, Charlie, Wait there, Charlie, One Side Charlie, Fuck You, Charlie!" We'll see, says Charlie! He touched the object in his pocket, again.

He needed reassurance.

His thoughts were hungry.

THUNDERHEADS

Yezeletta performed one more systems check: *Is this because of training or conditioning or practice or expediency, or what?*, flexed her arms, and walked to the door. She placed her hand on the knob, turned it.
What Have You Forgotten?

TEMPEST, INTERNAL

[Intrinsics] Charlie's ears were pretty sharp. His obsession had allowed him to tune his hearing to Yezeletta's unique footstep pattern. With an apprehension born of his fantasies, the object of his internal fictions approached. It was almost sexual to him, except *she* was the one entering. *We'll see about that!*

The door knob turned, the door opened. Charlie took a step to one side, his left. All the rest in the room faded into obscurity, *the universe was empty awaiting Spider's presence to fulfill it*. His hand caressed the weapon in his pocket, Al's words clear in his mind, embellished with what he, *Charlie*, wanted after.

Yezeletta sailed past him to face Al. That's the last time you push me out to the edges, soon it's Charlie's time with Spider by his side....

WORDS IN A ROW, EXTENDED

[Binary!] Al began his carefully rehearsed speech.
It took him twenty minutes.

INSTALLATION

[Load System: Restore; In Another Place] *His throat was no longer scarred. His breathing no longer had the loud hiss he had been unable to prevent without suffocation. His voice, though still sibilant and breathy, was understandable. He lay on the bed, watching the images on the ceiling screen. Idly, he scratched his sex, then forgot what he'd done. His eyes adjusted to the dimness and made the low light as usable as daylight.*

His lessons continue, each one imprinting itself on his mind with effortless ease. Learning and assimilating, classifying and analyzing: this is the center of his being, the core of his world.

A part of him—buried deeply, so deeply that he is just barely aware of it—asks: What next? Where do I take this when I've learned it?

Why?

The answer is suppressed. Taken from his forming thoughts with a speed that is astonishing in its swiftness. Taken almost by—

Something else.
The Something Else that is <u>in here</u> with him.
Then that thought is taken, also.
And all that remains are the lessons.

THE CLASSROOM

[Mirror] *The Schooling Technician sat at his workstation just outside the classroom, reading a magazine. One of the station's screens flickered, and he looked up at it. The screen showed a pop-up diagnostic window in flashing red. The Student's thoughts had entered a forbidden data-space and the operating system in the workstation, as well as The Other operating system, had initiated suppression of those thoughts. The Technician put down his magazine and looked back at the audit trail kept in the system log. This current incident is the latest in a run of Forbidden Thought Events. Most of them had happened in the last week. The Student's mind had been drifting into the wrong places, as of late.*

This may require corrective action.

RITE OF INITIATION

[System Installation] *The lessons are done. He can relax, now. His sensitive hearing detects footsteps. The measured footsteps of his Counselor. He knows these steps, neither slow nor fast as they make their measured rhythms up the terrazzo hallway. Somehow those measured footsteps echo in his consciousness. His Counselor will arrive neither early nor late, but always on time.*

To speak to him of his role.
To speak to him of his place.
To speak to him of his destiny.

——>>> **EIGHT** <<<——

Outside of Society!
That's where I want to be.

—Patti Smith, 1977

SOMEWHERE IN THE PACIFIC

[The *Hat Dancer*] Yezeletta gestured to Al with her right hand, her lower, "My escape has been made. I'm here. You have made your point, have you? What is it that you would *ultimately* like to ask of me?" The various members of the July Seventeenth Brigade shuffled their feet, some looked uneasy, and others looked up at her, and away.

"You will be an asset to the New Order," said Al. "With your abilities, we will be able to harass the Enemy, neutralize it and win!"

"Ah, come on, Al," someone else said.

Really? Yezeletta thought, Another one who thinks in Capital Letters?

"What plans have you for my 'abilities'?" she asked him, again.

"Your creations will serve us by attacking where The Establishment—"

Silently, she thought, *More Capital Letters! Who does he think he is? Jane Austen?*

"— is the strongest: in the cities where security is tight. One of your custom diseases would win our revolution in one night." He looked up at her, as she leaned against the open doorway, "This is the act for which we've been preparing! The fall of the West Coast in a single battle."

Several of Al's compatriots had the sense to look away.

"Back at the Complex, I studied a lot of the news sources from other countries," Yezeletta said. "I had full internet access to them. I never saw the dissatisfaction you describe. Perhaps I don't wish to engage in mass killings as much as you would have me do. Perhaps there is another way to accomplish your actions—"

"I'll make the decisions," Al replied. Yezeletta expanded the range of her hearing: was there a touch of panic in his voice? A little more stridency, more volume in the cabin than was necessary?

"— You are the secret weapon of our action, to be formed in the fires of passion, and aimed at the heart of the decadent United States!"

Al stuck his chin out while several others stepped back, and Yezeletta was reminded of an old sketch of Lenin she had seen in a history text. A note of mirth crept into her thinking: that Lenin pic had been done by a reasonably talented, if anonymous, professional Russian artist. Unfortunately, Benjamin Allen Morrison wasn't much better than an amateur.

If that.

He went on, in what were for him, more modulated tones, "We've researched your operations base, Yeze-let-ta—" he stumbled on her name again, "— and we know just what you've been built for—" she didn't like that, at all! "— You're a weapon. A directed force to be used as your superiors see fit. We helped you escape, and now, it's time for payback! You serve the people through the actions of the July Seventeenth Brigade!"

YOU OWE FOR THE FLESH

Once Yezeletta had seen an old movie on one of the Project video channels in which there was a fanfare whenever a certain character's name was mentioned. The producers of the movie had wanted laughs, but the whole sequence had fallen flat. She looked without expression at the sweat-covered forehead of the man she thought of as "Fearless Leader."

The *Hat Dancer* pitched gently on the wide Pacific, as the ship made way for the American West Coast. Yezeletta could hear anyone who tried to approach her. She regarded Al calmly: "You speak of many deaths, perhaps millions. Do you think that is rather excessive? Don't you? What of me, when the destruction is over?"

He stopped, surprised at the challenge. He paused.

To rewind his scripts? Or load new files? she wondered.

"We fight wherever we must. The future requires it. To you goes the honor of being at the very vanguard of the fight! Once we fought in the hills, now we will bring the battle to the streets, and into the homes of the rich. You will be remembered!"

"Oh, give me a break, Al!" Ralph said loudly.

"The hills of what?" Marina asked sweetly, "San Francisco?"

"You're one of the rich," Nancy added, "Are you gonna shoot yourself in the foot?"

"Al, if you can't log on to the Clue-Server, at least try to build one!"

Yezeletta recognized the voice, but didn't have a name to go with it.

Yezeletta looked at Nancy and back to Al. Al took a breath to say something else, but Yezeletta cut him off, "I do not wish to squander my capabilities in this fashion. Your incessant talk of 'political action' since we met, tires me." She looked directly at him, eyes of brilliant gold sending flashing lasers into his dark blue ones. He withstood her withering gaze for a short time, then looked away. Yezeletta shifted, placing more of her weight on her right front and left rear legs, ready to defend herself.

Her movement wasn't lost on the others: she could hear sounds of weapons being drawn. Al looked at his partners:

"C'mon, you people! This can be handled in a more comradely fashion." He turned to her again, "Perhaps I spoke too soon, Yezeletta," his voice almost caressing. "We can use your service in other ways, less dangerous. In a consulting capacity, perhaps."

To Yezeletta's enhanced hearing, Al's breathing had become strained, his heartbeat quickening. She wasn't ready to accuse him of lying, but several of the signs were there. She let his prose wash past her, while she watched as much of the room as carefully as possible. Some of the Brigade members weren't present. Were they watching other parts of the ship? What of the servitors she had deployed to handle more mundane shipboard tasks?

"— to victory!" he concluded. "Will you join us?"

Yezeletta grinned, deliberately showing her teeth, "No. I have other plans, and you are not in them."

"Now!" Al shouted.

They moved, and Yezeletta moved; three of her arms reached out, and three of the unprepared revolutionaries went down. Her front left and right rear feet lashed out and two more were out.

"Get her!" someone yelled. Yezeletta took a hop-skip step forward, and struck again.

There was a sharp pain in her left shoulder. *Charlie!* she thought. There was another sharp pain in her shoulder just below the first. The targets before her moved back as far as the cramped quarters would let them. Yezeletta's vision became blurry, she called in her image enhancement capabilities, and her vision cleared for a moment, than went out completely.

She didn't feel her head striking the floor.

Yezeletta Zargkonji awoke first to voices.

The voices spoke gibberish, that shortly formed words, then sentences. She kept her eyes closed, and used noise suppression to better filter meaning from those words: "— the dose should keep her unconscious for eight hours—" another voice replied "Did you double check? She's the largest woman I've ever seen, and heavy—" The first replied, "One-hundred-sixty kilograms, he used two calibrated shots. You saw how she dropped; she'll be out for another eight, or I miss my guess—" The second: "And she's tied up good and tight just to be on the safe side...." There was the sound of a door opening and closing, and she was alone.

Yezeletta opened her eyes. The room was slightly larger than the floor area of a walk-in closet. The only furniture in it was a narrow bed; she was lying on it, face up. Her legs were tied to the foot of the bed, one pair to each side, and both pairs of arms were bound behind her. She wiggled her wrists in the cordage: the Revolutionaries had secured her well. It was good she was alone; that cretin *had* misjudged the dosage, fatally.

She shut her eyes, and directed a thought at one of her on-board clocks; the time and date appeared in the lower left corner of her gaze in glowing digits. Her assailant's lack of judgment was a joke: only fifteen minutes had passed. She thought at another capability *there*, and glowing labels and numbers flashed across her vision. The status readouts on her hearts, the efficiency factors for her respiratory system, an analysis of the contents of her bloodstream. The feeble effects of the injections were dissipating quickly; in another minute she would be back to normal.

The door rattled. Yezeletta closed her eyes, slowed her breathing, and lay there, faking sleep. Someone entered; Yezeletta could feel the slight air currents his motions in the room stirred up. He was approaching the bed.

"Looks like you're still out of it," a voice said softly. "That's real good, Lady, we can have some real good times in here." Her top was rudely yanked open: Yezeletta suppressed the revulsion that passed through her. She reminded herself she was supposed to be unconscious for eight hours. *Not if I can help it!*

Rough unclean hands ran themselves over her breasts, tickling her nipples. He stroked and caressed, playing here and there, kneading her breasts like pieces of bread. "You got nice tits, lady. I can keep you thrilled for a long time, 'course, I'll have to do all the work, you're—" a demented giggle, "— all tied up—" he ran his hands down her torso, and—

There was a shout and a peremptory knock on the door.

He quickly covered Yezeletta with what was left of the outfit, and went to the door, "Yeah?"

"Sorry, Charlie," another voice said, "Al's got another job for you. You won't be needing to guard our new resource there until she wakes up."

"Okay, tell him that I'll be on my way." The door closed. Then there was that unwelcome hand sliding under the lab coat, seeking out her left nipple. "I'll be back later, Dearie," Charlie said. "Just wait right here. Don't go anywhere, now!" He pinched her nipple hard and left chuckling.

Yezeletta allowed herself one heartfelt sneer at the closed door before turning to her escape. She heightened the sensation on her skin, and tested the ropes her captors had used. The knots were well away from her hands, and both pairs of legs were securely tied together as well as to the foot of the bed, leaving her legs spread enough to give a thrill to the likes of Charlie.

She readjusted her skin sensitivity back to normal, and felt around for the knots binding her wrists. She nearly laughed out loud, but kept silent: a large grin spreading across her face. The dummy had tied her hands in pairs, but hadn't realized she could reach her lower wrists with her upper hands.

Yezeletta arched her back, and the torn lab coat gave way. *I'd really thrill Charlie, now*, she thought as she pushed down with her legs, and reached with her upper hands for the lower set of knots. She smiled, more inwardly, this time, at their odd blend of ignorance and sophistication. *Where did they get those anesthetic darts?* She bent backwards a little more, thrusting her breasts at the overhead, wondering if Charlie would like the view. *Only if I can do nothing in return; does he like corpses*? She picked at the knots with her long fingers, and thought of precise karate punches and of the Steinway she used to play at the Project.

She was equally at home with one or the other.

Her ropes on her right lower wrist were looser. She pulled at the knots one more time, and a long cord slipped through a loop, and her right lower hand was free. She ripped the cords off her left lower hand, and reached upwards for the knots on her upper wrists. This was more painful than untying the lowers, but she switched the pain off in her arms and kept at it until the last knot parted. Untying her feet was an anticlimax.

Footsteps. Approaching.

Yezeletta looped the cords back over her feet and put her arms behind her again. She closed her eyes, and waited.

It was Charlie. She wasn't surprised; his body odor was easily detectable at a distance. "Still here, I see," he said with a forced joviality that made Yezeletta's teeth itch. "I knew you'd be waiting right here for me!" Years earlier, she had dreamt of hearing those words, or similar ones, from a real lover. That they came from Charlie was an evil parody. He went straight to her breasts again, and began stroking and tickling her nipples with one hand while his other crept downwards with what Charlie thought was great skill or sophistication.

Or whatever.

Yezeletta moaned slightly, moving as if in her sleep. It brought Charlie's attentions back to her face. Now both of his unwashed hands were in place on her breasts, and—

She opened her eyes wide and stared at him.

Charlie's reaction was a classic double take. He sat there, his jaw gaping wide, at Yezeletta's large, gold eyes, at the black vertical slits: black shafts into his own private hell.

Then he seemed to pull together; after all his prisoner was bound....

"Hey, you're awake! This'll be fun! You've never had it 'till you've had it from me! You're a lucky lady!" He began to disrobe, still talking, dropping his filthy smelling clothes randomly on the deck. Yezeletta looked at his naked body, and then looked straight upwards. There was nothing there she found desirable. Not even THAT! An irrelevant quote entered her mind: "Don't point that thing at me, unless you know how to use it!" Where had she heard it? Not from him, certainly!

The bed creaked, as Charlie got on top of her.

He placed himself between her legs, and Yezeletta moved.

She sat up, and grabbed his wrists with her upper hands.

Charlie's first reaction was a yelp, then: "Hey, Bitch, you want to play rough, huh?"

"No, Little Man, I *do* play rough." She wrapped her arms around his waist in a waist-high hug, pinning his hands behind his back.

"Hey, I was only kidding—"

"Indeed," she replied, breathing as shallowly as possible.

"We can be real good for each other—"

"Shut up," she explained.

He began struggling, but Yezeletta's greater strength and larger size gave her the advantage. She wrapped her front legs around his waist, and pulled his legs out from under him. Charlie tried a knee to Yezeletta's crotch, and she seized the offending leg and pulled it forward. She rearranged his legs as if he were a doll, and sat him down—still holding his hands behind him—

in front of her.

This placed his head between her breasts, looking up. She looked down at his frightened face, and smiled a terrible smile, licking her teeth, and laughing softly. "Not quite the seduction you planned, was it?" Charlie lurched back, and Yezeletta reached with her lower left hand, and seized his testicles. Charlie stopped moving. "Very good," Yezeletta purred. "You respond to non-verbal stimuli very well." With her one remaining hand, her lower right, she reached behind Charlie and grabbed the cords with which her feet had been tied, and began tying his hands. She had to let go of Charlie to do so, but, by now, he was shivering with fright. She made a swift job of it, pushed him on his back, and tied his feet.

Charlie began to gibber.

She took a long cord, tied a large knot in it. She rammed the knot into Charlie's mouth, and tied the ends of the rope tightly around his head. She got up, ascended to her full two-hundred-plus centimeters of height. Yezeletta stretched, touching the overhead easily. She twisted this way and that, restoring circulation, mostly for the joy of being out of that bed. She looked down on her naked captive.

She flipped him and tied his ankles to his wrists. She deposited the ungainly bundle of Charlie on his side on the bed, and knelt down next to him. "Something to remember me by!" she hissed, and drove the stiffened fingers of her left hand, her upper, into his crotch. He made a gurgling sound through the knot. Yezeletta stood and went to the door. She looked back once.

She cracked the door, expanded the acuity of her hearing, and looked out.

There was nothing there.

Or no one. The cabin was located amidships on the starboard side. She looked forward, then aft; the deck was deserted. Before her the calm Pacific Ocean stretched out to an infinite horizon. She extended the sensitivity of her hearing, and could catch bits of conversation towards the stern. She looked back into the cabin again. None of her weapons were here; the July Brigade had apparently placed her equipment in the hold.

Yezeletta reminded herself she was a weapon. A self directed weapon.

She stepped out onto the deck, and proceeded aft.

The wind blew gently against Yezeletta's skin. The sun was low in the sky. It looked like about three o'clock, local time. She removed the remnants of the lab coat, and left the wad of cloth behind a life preserver. It was one of the only things handy that really fit her, and she might need it again when it got cool.

Up ahead the voices were louder.

There was some sort of discussion going on in the fantail of the ship. She stood there for a moment, and listened. There were about seven voices she could easily separate. There were too many for her alone, unarmed. She backed up to the first door between the voices and forward. She entered silently.

What she expected was another cabin. What she found was a ladder, a stairway to land-lubbers. Below, she could hear the throb of huge diesel engines.

This was also the way to the olive drab installation. She went down.

The ladder's passage gave way to a large open space. "Large" only in the sense that the engine compartment has to be relatively spacious to accommodate the engines, and allow access to every part of each one. The compartment smelled of diesel fuel, oils and cleaners of various kinds, human sweat, leftover food and the odor she recognized as that of her assistants. She looked sternward, and saw several men idly watching gauges, but more preoccupied in the card game spread out on the top of an oily cardboard box. Forward, were huge fuel tanks, and a narrow passage between them leading to an open hatch.

Beyond the hatch were her creations.

Yezeletta let herself down the ladder, not using her legs, but with arm motions only. She swung her bulk around the ladder opposite from the card players, and let herself down on the deck. She squatted down low behind a large cabinet, and adjusted her hearing to screen out the throbbing of the engines.

"Your deal."

"Seven Card Stud, Deuces Wild."

"Deal them."

"What ante?"

"Buck."

Yezeletta couldn't hear anything but the routine of bored card players. In a crouch approximating a four legged duckwalk, she headed for the door. She didn't know how long it would be before Al would miss Charlie, but it was best to assume it had already happened, and take it from there.

She squeezed through the narrow hatchway, and entered the hold.

All around her were hastily built cages, and in each cage, with a fine disregard for comfort, were her servitors. She went from one to the next opening them, and shortly she was followed by a coterie of the short bipeds and her little multilegged creatures. Something caught her eye at about her eye-level. She looked up at a large cardboard box, and called to its contents. Then she gently dislodged it and took it down. A small spider-like creature looked out of the top of the box at her, and waved its legs. It seemed to say, "Look at me! I did it!" There was a small hard-shelled icosahedron in the box.

Yezeletta smiled. The design was a good one! Even here, the Hive-Builders were able to function. She set the little construct down, and gestured to a pair of servitors: guard this!

She looked aft: there was another hatchway. The hold was a series of compartments. There was a very familiar olive-drab case bulking upwards in there. The hardened, militarized core of what would later become the Matrix-Engine.

Yezeletta ran to it, and her hands practically stroked the manual console. She played the keyboard, calling up status displays, situation readouts. The displays the LCD screen put up were infinitely reassuring: everything was well with the system and with Hilda. Yezeletta faced the scanner above the screen and stood back. She turned around slowly, letting the scanner see her. The LCD screen displayed *"Very Good!"* in large letters and then an animated cartoon of Yezeletta walked across the screen, with a caption running below it: "There she is, Miss America...." She winked at the scanner, and the cartoon was replaced by a single, large bloodshot eye, which winked back.

She turned to her assistants. This ship had to be organized. Fast.

Yezeletta became a blur of movement. She removed various items from cases dumped against one bulkhead, and assembled mechanisms: several laptops, various devices with stingers or long barbs; something that squirmed and writhed when she touched it. A large off-white sheet, something big and fuzzy.

INTERLUDE WITH WASTE OF TIME

Charlie had gone unconscious from Yezeletta's parting comment. He came to again in darkness. The cabin hadn't been lit when she left, now the sun had set. The only illumination came from a deck light through the small port-hole. He tried to move his hands. He stretched his fingers. Yezeletta had tied him with swift disregard for comfort or circulation. He tugged experimentally at the ropes, then strained for the knots, feeling pains elsewhere as he did. He may as well have been chained. The ropes had been pulled tight and knotted repeatedly. None of the knots were accessible to his squirming fingers. He stopped, listened.

There was the sound of running on the deck.

"Help!" he called. The large knot she had rammed into his mouth turned his shout into an inadequate gurgle. He bit down on the knot, and it was like chewing wire: she had pushed it in deeply, and tied the ropes securely. Charlie called again, and it came out another useless gurgle.

Someone ran past the port: he could make out a human profile, but the profile of whatever it was that followed next was like nothing on Earth.

Charlie shrank back on the narrow bed. He had to get loose! He redoubled his efforts, and accomplished nothing. *Smart bitch!* he thought. *When I see her next, I'll be in charge.*

Something slammed against the door, followed by several softer thumps. There was a bright light shining under the door.

It began to open.

THE TOOL USER

Yezeletta put thoughts of Charlie out of her mind as she got to work. The only problem he might pose would be if he were discovered, or if he got loose. She allowed herself one laugh at that latter prospect before designing her attack.

THE TOOLS USED

The meeting of the Directorate of the July Seventeenth Brigade was in Extraordinary Session on the fantail. Al Morrison sat with his back to a bulkhead on a deck-chair, holding forth.

"If our Mission is to succeed, all the parts of it must mesh together exactly." Several other members of the Directorate rolled their eyes. Al was fond of repeating himself, and took every chance he could to do so. "— must band together to form a single cohesive unit, and each section of the unit must provide its assigned part without fail, like the design of any complex system, and without the various personalities of the section chiefs conflicting with attainment of the goal."

Had Al been more perceptive, he would have noticed eyes glazing. Several of the Directorate had regretted coming back to the fantail: a short break in the activities had become an exercise in listening to another one his tiring speeches.

Ralph Hanson looked up from the blank page in his notebook which had been occupying his time as Al's tone-deaf monologue washed over him. Al had that distant look in his eyes he got when he was, as he, himself put it, "dumping binary files." Binary files were his way of dismissing the speech of others with whom he disagreed as trivial. Ralph frowned into his notes again, and looked at Nancy. She looked back at him, raising an eyebrow: her gesture said **[The_Shoulder_to_Shoulder_File.Txt]** , again! Ralph nodded, looking upward, momentarily.

Strange.

Seabirds normally didn't fly this far out. Something was moving on the roof of the aft deck-house.

He tried not to let it bother him; he was too busy fighting off boredom.

There didn't seem to be any difference between this hand and the last umpteen. Jeff felt as if he were stuck in a season of reruns. Behind him the three General Motors Diesels throbbed a basso-profundo rhythm of pure power. Now and then, Jeff would look up at the gauges to check on the performance of the *Dancer's* power plant. Her engines had been well designed, and *Maritima Mexicana* had maintained them well: the readouts on the gauges might as well have been painted in place; with the exception of the fuel-oil gauge, they hadn't changed in the last three hours of his watch.

"Deal."

Larry wasn't much for talk, Jeff dispensed cards, and the other parties to the game squinted at them.

Jeff's mind wandered as he went mechanically through the ritual: bet, raise, draw, bet, raise, answer, raise again, call, show. The winner scooped the change out of the table's center, and Jeff passed the cards on. Nodding to the rest, he got up, put his hands in his pockets, and moved away from the game. There wasn't much area for movement: most of the space in the engine room was vertical before the noisy diesels. The rest was crowded with tool closets, ancillary machinery, spare parts, and the kind of greasy clutter that accumulates in such places.

The clutter was claustrophobic, the noise deafening, the heat thrown off by the engines oppressive. Jeff decided to go up for a breath of air. He took a cup of coffee from the only creature comfort in the compartment, and headed for the ladder. On his way up, he chanced to look forward.

That hatch shouldn't be ajar. It should be dogged tight, a standard safety precaution when at sea. Jeff started to holler down at his mates, but the engine noise drowned him out. He descended to look for himself.

The hatch, a large vertical oval door, was open slightly, and moving gently to the rhythm of the ship's motion. Jeff went to close it.

Something fell on his back. Something sticky.

Jeff reached behind himself to yank the object off. He touched it: it felt like warm grease. He pulled his hand back, the grease came with it. He shook his hand, expecting the viscous gel to slop off his hands. Instead, it crawled up his arm. He looked up, panicking.

Something round, with an open orifice below it, *and legs!* was descending.

Jeff tried to dodge the round thing. He moved away from it and it followed him. He took a step in the other direction, and screamed. His feet would not move.

Then everything vanished: engine noise, greasiness, light, sight, sound.

Vanished into a cloyingly sweet smelling silent blackness.

On the bridge, Marina Worthington sat at the helm, her hands on the wheel, scanning the instruments, as she supervised the systems that kept the *Dancer* on course. Digital displays flickered and winked in the light of late afternoon. Since the *Dancer* was on an easterly course, the bridge was in the shadow of the rest of the ship: the cabin was as dark as the rest of the ship would be an hour or so later.

Marina's gaze swept economically across the various situation displays: a small screen showed the *Dancer's* position on a computer generated map of the South Pacific created by obtaining the ship's position from the Tech-Bloc's Satellite Navigation Net. Other screens were radar, sonar, a display showing the status of the engines, and several views of various parts of the deck.

CRUISING

Something moved in one of the screens. Marina studied it intently: it was a section of the deck that would be full of passengers lounging on deck chairs, if this were a normal cruise. Now the area was empty, the deck-chairs covered with a tarp, securely tied down against the elements.

What the hell was that? Something small, moving amongst the lumps and bumps in the heavy canvas.

Marina brushed a strand of hair out of her eyes, and resumed her scan of the other displays. Jeezus, this was boring....

She brushed the hair out of her face, again. Then she felt a cold touch up her back. She turned.

Headlights: gold disks. That was Marina's first impression of the invaders. Short servitors with their great gold orbs staring unwaveringly at her. "Yezeletta!" she managed to say.

Several of the servitors took her by the elbows and conducted her off to a convenient corner. One of the gnomes gestured, and a flock of eight or ten creatures looking like large baseballs on jointed legs hopped over to her.

The servitor placed its hand, on the top of one of the animated baseballs, and—

All of the creatures turned in a single synchronized movement and faced her. There was a flickering of gold, as their imagers uncovered.

They moved towards her, and Marina could see the multilegged arach-noids were almost smiling, showing sharp teeth: fangs, long ones.

She moved and the beasts reared up, waving groups of legs, six or seven at her, their long curved claws extended.

One of the creatures hissed and the hiss was taken up by the rest. Then the rest of Yezeletta's creations joined in.

The furry spiders with fangs and cat's claws formed a semicircle around Marina, occasionally waving claws at her as a warning, or sitting up like at-tacking cats, their gold imagers unwavering in their steadfast stare. A small group of hexagonal life-forms joined them.

She huddled in the corner.

Another servitor took Marina's position at the helm, and began calling for data. Marina realized in a moment that it was querying the uplink to the Sat/Nav Net. Then a small fuzzy many-legged animal fell on the larger servitor, catching itself on the servitor's face, walking across it, and seating itself on its shoulder. The spider-beast crouched there for a moment, then reared up on several of its legs, and pressed one long, thin leg into the side of the head of its mount. The large servitor's hands began a series of practiced, swift motions, and Marina realized, to her dismay, that it was removing the *Hat Dancer* from Sat/Nav, and laying in a new course. A course with nothing in common with the old, except that it still led East.

The *Hat Dancer's* destination was no longer Northeast to San Francisco. Now it appeared to be Isle de Pascua, Rapa Nui.

Easter Island.

THE CONDUCTOR

In her base in the hold, Yezeletta sat before a group of laptops hastily connected together, on the screens of which grainy images moved in various directions. The scenes were transmitted to her from the mobile imagers she had dispatched. One of the imagers looked down on Al as he spoke in his file-dump monotone to six or seven tired associates. Another looked into the bridge at Marina conning the ship; another supervised a small group of servitors poised just out of Marina's sight.

THE ORCHESTRA

As Al worked his way into his finale, with half of his Directorate half asleep, his universe ended.

What dropped into his lap looked like a folded bedsheet. He jumped up, and tried to dump it onto the deck. As he brushed at it, it unfolded. And stuck to his clothing.

"What the hell is this?" he snapped. "Get this goddamn thing off of me!"

The others of the seven still awake jumped up, throwing their deck chairs back. One drew his automatic, then others did.

All seven were on their feet, now. Nancy made the first mistake: she slipped her pistol back into her belt, and started to rip the offending whiteness off of where it was unfolding down Al's legs. It stuck to her.

Nancy screamed.

Ralph pulled on the gloves he had hitched into his belt earlier, and grabbed Nancy around the waist and pulled. The white sheet stretched out like taffy and broke.

The free end whipped around and caught Ralph in the face. He let go of Nancy and clawed at his face. The sticky "cloth" came away in clumps that writhed unpleasantly in Ralph's fingers. He tried to call for help, but one of the sticky wads jumped, and hit him in the face. He smelled something cloying, something sweet, and passed out. In the receding distance he thought he heard a splash.

Several others of the Directorate ran for the safety of anywhere else: anywhere else at all.

Yezeletta concentrated intently on a pair of images: One showed four bodies partially covered by a moving white sheet. The other display was of the three others, guns drawn, who were skirting the action and heading forward. Yezeletta spoke softly into her headset; something that looked like an animated bear-skin or a fur rug lumbered around the corner, and confronted them.

Their pistol shots sounded attenuated, like cap-guns; she could see the panic on their faces as they emptied their weapons into the furry invader. One attempted to reload before the rug-beast leapt for the trio, and began closing in around them.

In a way, Yezeletta regretted having to use the Walking Carpet. It was one of the most difficult engineering jobs she had done and because of the energy it required, it had to be carnivorous. As she watched, the rug surrounded the screamers. Now it was an irregularly shaped lump of fur with contents that were still moving. Yezeletta turned her attentions to the other screens: the movement would cease shortly.

The card-game in the engine room broke up in a flurry of cards, currency, and shouts, as three servitors entered with small cans of an aerosol spray. The shouts of the card players accelerated the process: they inhaled the contents of the sprays faster, hastening its effect. Yezeletta looked up from her workbench.

The ship was hers.

CAPTAIN OF HER FATE

Yezeletta stepped out on the deck. The sun had set, and the brilliant stars of the Southern Hemisphere provided stage lights for the *Hat Dancer*. On the northeastern horizon, the crescent of a quarter-moon sailed through a lacework of cirrus clouds. Yezeletta stood naked in the silver moonlight, a cool breeze seeming to blow the problems of the last several days away from her.

Why, she asked herself, did she always think of the Moon as a disembodied grin? Aside from the obvious? The Moon had been a welcoming smile for her for as long as she had known of it. A smile that was for her and her alone.

How long have I known this?

A bright pinpoint of light appeared between the arms of the crescent. It flared brightly. The arms seemed to enfold it in a hug.

The mines of the Power Bloc were running their two-week night shift.

Behind her she could hear the servitors cleaning up. Al had fallen overboard in the earlier confusion. Good Riddance. She walked casually around to the starboard side and leaned against the railing watching the servitors disposing of a pile of sticky bones. The bones went over the side, and far below, knife sharp fins sliced through the black water after them.

Something big and fuzzy nuzzled her ankle: the front right.

Yezeletta reached down and skritched the Walking Carpet. She knew with the precision of one who has designed it, that the decentralized nervous system of The Carpet precluded consciousness. She also knew it felt pleasure at her touch. She skritched the shaggy rug again, *well done*.

She went to the fantail, and looked at the others. The revolutionaries who had died were wrapped bundles. The living stood under guard. Marina was visibly quaking in her wrappings. Yezeletta gestured, and the servitors threw the corpses over the side.

Black fins raced to the impact points.

Yezeletta looked at the living. "It may surprise you that I don't wish to kill you. However, I will maintain my security. Do any of you know anything of old-style navigation?"

Marina found her voice: "I do," she replied, tremulously.

"Captain Bligh," Yezeletta prompted. "I have longboats you may use. They are provisioned for about two weeks. There are inhabited islands in the area. I'll give you what you need except for communications; you will not be allowed use of the Global Positioning System or the Sat/Nav Net. By the time you reach land, I shall be long gone. This is your choice, or—" She gestured at the fantail.

Marina Worthington nodded once.

Yezeletta gestured, and the servitors took Marina and the other survivors to one of the lifeboats.

Yezeletta would meet them there—one more problem needed to be solved.

The cabin in which she had been prisoner was dark. She could hear rustling sounds from inside, but there was no other sign of activity. The servitors with her waved their shielded lights around the door before Yezeletta opened it.

Charlie was right where she had left him, as she had left him. He looked up, and began gibbering through the knot in his mouth.

Yezeletta gestured and the servitors picked Charlie off the bed, and carried him out.

Marina shivered in the night breeze. Her shaking was more than just the winds. She looked out at the heaving black sea, and back at the longboat. It seemed a pitifully small object in which the open sea could be crossed. She took Ralph's hand in a tight grip; his presence was comforting.

She looked down at the case by her feet. She hadn't expected to use a sextant in the Pacific! *Up the coast of California was about right! With a check from the GPS!* This was like returning to the dark ages! She turned, and the creatures around her tensed up. Odd shapes, silhouettes in the dark were waved in her general direction. A large angular shape materialized by her.

"All aboard," a precise voice said. She had an English accent: BBC English.

Marina stepped gingerly into the boat. Around her the servitors were placing supplies wherever they would fit. The four-armed apparition who had taken them so easily stood by, silent after her brief instructions. Marina wondered: How did she communicate with her servants? Telepathy? She shivered again, *At least I won't have to put up with Al any more!* It was a small consolation.

Two more gnomes showed up bearing an item that gibbered and moaned in turns. Marina recognized Charlie: filthy, panicked, and tied tightly in a convenient bundle. Without a word, they dumped him in the bottom of the boat, and walked off, rubbing their hands together.

Yezeletta gestured, and the longboats lifted, swung out on their davits, and were lowered into the water. Ralph pushed off from the *Hat Dancer's* hull with an oar, and Marina activated the small motor. The longboat moved off slowly, then gathered speed. The others followed.

Behind them, the lights of the *Dancer* vanished in the night.

MASTER OF HER SOUL

When the task of disposing of the Brigade was finished, when the longboats had vanished to the stern, Yezeletta gave directions to the helm servitor. The *Hat Dancer* changed course, again sailing under full power through the Pacific night on her original heading: towards the American West Coast to the big harbor at Long Beach south of Los Angeles. Yezeletta's earlier directions to the helm had been misdirection. She stretched her arms and legs, and lay back on the couch in the Captain's Cabin, on a pile of pillows, drinking a glass of Coca-Cola laced with just enough rum to be pleasant. It was good to be shut of those irksome loudmouths. A well-programmed servitor stood at the helm, maintaining the ship's new course.

The night was restful, the waters ahead, still. The ship plunged onwards through the night. Once Yezeletta went to the stern, and looked back at where the *Dancer* had been.

A wake of glowing plankton followed the ship, a comet's tail brought down to the sea, gradually fading out in the distance.

Yezeletta looked deeply into the texture of the glittering comet-tail, everting her eye-lenses to provide microscopic vision.

There were thousands of tiny luminescent creatures darting around in the water.

Suddenly, she was very tired.

She sent several servitors off to the galley. A very late dinner, or early breakfast, was called for. Then she could sleep.

BY THE WATER'S EDGE

While Yezeletta slept, and while the <u>Hat Dancer</u> *was making way towards the American West Coast, several other things were happening.*

A group of sailors, mostly speaking Spanish, but leavened with enough English speakers to be understood arrived at the Harbormaster's office in Darwin.

Another was the release of one of Yezeletta's prisoners, long after he had been placed in the bottom of the lifeboat.

A little later, an individual—bedraggled, weak, barely conscious, but surviving, was hauled aboard Marina's boat.

The reunion was nearly complete.

IN ANOTHER PLACE

[Initialization] *He stood, his legs supporting him. He took a halting step forward and nearly fell. He caught himself, and got his feet under him. His stance was intrinsically stable. He scanned and the irises of his eyes narrowed, then expanded in the low light of his own volition in triumph. His vision was fed back to him from the Systems with the requisite modifications.*

His eyes were sharp in the dim light. There was a flickering around the edges of his vision, a flickering as of heat radiating from a hot pavement.

Then the thought was taken from him, and only the flickering remained. Then the flickering, and his vision were taken, and he lost consciousness.

REPORT CARD

[Program Running] *The Schooling Technician looked through the printout of the tutorial workstation's audit. The occurrence of Forbidden Thought Events was down eighty-five percent. He looked at the image of the Student sitting quietly in the classroom, listening to a lecture on differential equations. His progress is more than incremental, now. He seems to enjoy the course-work being fed to him at ever accelerating rates.*

With luck and preparation, he may even graduate early.

RETROSPECT

[Milwaukee] Several days later, after investigating the large building from a prudent distance, Yezeletta moved into it. From a campsite in the lowest part of the building's below-street-level parking ramp, she directed an expedition by several of her more muscular servitors, as they went up to the top floors, and ensured that those floors were uninhabited. Several convenient hallucinogens, her latest generation of obliviators, and an anaesthetic or two cleared the floors she wanted without any of the squatters in the lower levels realizing what was going on. Those of the squatters that kept their distance very prudently did not interfere, for doing so was deadly. Later Yezeletta used the building's air-conditioning system to send a kind of general instant oblivion from her earliest laboratory to the entire building as an insurance measure.

Her expedition had moved in by taking over a fire-escape stairway for one night: several constructs ascended the stairs on what was nearly a suicide mission, administering the necessary anti-personnel measures. By the time that had been done and a beach-head established on the forty-first floor, she had succeeded in getting a freight elevator running, and the rest of her equipment went up easily and quickly.

Another construct started a convenient fire in one of the trucks several blocks away, as a diversion. She sealed off a block of floors, and settled in. For the first time, she said later, she felt at home.

She needed scouts to map out the city. She had been trained for this sort of clandestine penetration. She needed equipment, raw materials, power.

She had to grow her observers. Her weapons.

The city had to be organized.

DETERMINANTS, MISCELLANEOUS

[Milwaukee] *....Echo Video Image of desolation: row of brownstones shattered asunder ...Red flame below the horizon, silhouettes wreckage in the antediluvian darkness....*

A black cover slides to one side. Then the view changes.

REM SLEEP

She shifts her weight on the customized pillows, muttering something in her sleep under her breath, and moans softly. Her long fingers flex, reach out. She seems to be calling out for someone.

Who?

A name Joe had found in the Project Sargon Notes—*Agent Psychological Adjustment.*

Yezeletta Zargkonji had no love for her creators. That was obvious. She wanted the Madflowers for a weapon. "As a weapon," Joe had told her, "they're about as useful as curing a split lip with an ax!" She was on a collision course, and she couldn't be averted. With whom? Herself? Or Joe? That was upsetting; he liked her, in spite of the way she had kidnapped him when they'd met. And the meeting with Victor was an act that made her more than admirable. She was a more complex creation than the scientists at Project Sargon had wanted!

Who did she talk to in the Matrix-Engine? Earlier Joe had thought he might have a clue to this. Now, lying this close to his friend, not quite his enemy, he isn't so sure. (*She's one of the Good Guys*, he reminded himself; the intrusion of this thought is startling.) Some investigation is called for.

THE NEXT DAY

Morning came to Zeke as a change in the color of the one window of which his laboratory was possessed: the well-defended skylight. The embrasure's color went from black to dark dirty gray to light dirty gray to worn white.

He hadn't found the surgical glue and artifice he had expected. Lead-foot Eddie's face had been *replaced*. The obscene blank was not a mask, was not a fabrication and it was not artificial. There was no sign of any features below the surface; Lead-foot's face had been replaced, transformed into this travesty.

Zeke wondered how he would explain this to Zhongo.

REM RETURN

Joe Davis rolls over in his sleep. A ray of light gleams from one of the reading lamps. He yawns, opens his eyes. Yezeletta Zargkonji, already awake, is sitting twice cross-legged looking down at him from a far perspective. "Good morning," she says in what for her is a gentle voice. Joe realizes this gentleness as he is realizing other things about this strange and intelligent woman who has found him.

"I'm awake." He rubs his eyes, scratches an itch on his left arm with his right hand. Yezeletta reaches out with two arms, both on her left side, and rubs Joe's back. Joe leans into it as a cat would. She rubs his legs with her right hands and Joe closes his eyes and contemplates the dangerous luxury of his position. He lies down on his side next to her and hugs her. She leans into the hug and he hugs her closer.

She rolls onto her back, and he looks down at her face, the laugh-lines even more prominent around her wide gold eyes.

He starts the ancient rhythms against her and she matches them.

Together they greet the dawn.

——>>> **NINE** <<<——

"All along the Watchtower, Princes kept the view."

—Bob Dylan

HIS CONCUBINE'S EYES

[System Installation] Leona let herself back into her own bedroom. She went to her closet, unlocked a cabinet within, removed several files, and dropped into her easy chair, her long black hair a cape around her, her violet eyes seeing everything.

The spider in the corner hasn't awakened yet. Lying still: it dreams on a silken hammock.

Her communicator approaches. Its Imager radiates urgency.

A DAY IN THE LIFE

For the Lenhadens, dawn came up like thunder.

The explosion from the parking lot blew the window in, and set off the alarms they had placed about the room. Far below, Hank could see flashing lights. The stuttering of machine-gun fire, statement then answer, rattled the walls. Hank grabbed for the weapon he kept by the side of the bed, and couldn't find it. He vaulted from the bed: there it was! His gaze swept past the travel-alarm: 5:35 AM. He looked out the window. What was left of the curtains had caught most of the glass. What conflict was visible was at the far edge of the parking lot. No one had noticed the black truck parked just below this window.

Ondreya slipped up beside him. Hank looked back quickly; Anne was behind Ondreya. Outside, the gun-fire got louder. Several figures in various outfits from denims to leathers ran across the lot. From across the lot, Hank could see the muzzle flashes of automatic weapons: little orange flames in the pre-dawn darkness.

An explosion shook the building. One of the upper window panes shattered, bits of glass showering them in crystalline fragments. The building shook again, and shouts came down the hall.

The door blew in.

The security package Anne had placed on the door the night before started shrieking. Then the shriek became two voices: the second was Anne's. "Let go of me, you little fuck! Help!" Then her voice became muffled. Hank couldn't see well in the darkness, and shooting was out of the question. Someone smashed the alarm into silence. There were several intruders: they wore black clothes and black makeup. Down in the midst, Anne was making them regret what they were doing. One doubled over as she kicked him in exactly the right place, and another fell back, clutching his throat.

Hank waded into the tangle, hitting anything wearing black leather. There seemed to be more of them than before. Further back by the door, Anne's profanity located her. Hank clubbed at black-clad toughs, making small gains. Anne's cursing became muffled. He could just make out someone pulling a black bag over her head.

Someone was behind him. He looked back, expecting Ondreya.

The descending blackjack was the last thing he remembered.

Henry Lenhaden revived looking at an unattractive ceiling. The plaster was cracking, the walls dirty. Someone applied a cold compress to the egg on his head. Moving as little as possible, he turned his head. It was Ondreya. Her face was dirty, and he could see hastily wiped away tear streaks. Carefully not noticing them, he sat up. He was aching. The first thing he saw when he sat up was his feet. The second was the body lying in front of the door. "Who," he croaked. She handed him a glass of water. It was the worst stuff he'd ever tasted. Part of him wondered where the alleged water came from, the rest of him didn't care. He drank again.

The corpse—no, it was breathing—body, was dressed in a black leather jacket that had seen far better days. *Maybe the dark ages*, he thought. The rest was similarly shabby: blue denim pants colored almost black by what must have been years of ingrown grime. The only decent part of this man's outfit were the boots. They looked almost new. "Did I really take on that bunch in my undies?" he asked.

"Yes. They got Annie!"

"I saw it. They piled up in front of her, and pulled her out from the screen their shock troops provided." It made the pain lessen to talk about it in vaguely military terminology. "Who's our guest?"

"The one you got last night. I secured him just before you woke up. You didn't look good. At all."

Hank looked closer at the man before him. Ondreya had tied his hands, and had taken a personal interest in it. He looked away. "How bad is he?"

"Just out. Strong heartbeat. Hank—"

"Yes?"

"Promise me I can have a half an hour alone with him when we get Annie back." There was a steel determination in her voice.

"Promise me one," Hank said; Ondreya didn't answer. "Promise me if there's anything left of him, that I can have a half an hour, too."

"Half an hour of what?" It was a voice from the door.

Hank got up . It was the girl who had checked them in the previous night. She was wearing the same outfit, somewhat grimier. She saw the unconscious man on the floor and looked back at Hank, wide-eyed. "That's a Dynamo! You better let him go. You'll have them all over you."

"They were all over us last night," Hank said. "You know anything about that?" She shook her head. Hank stepped quickly, grabbed her collar. "Listen, sweetie, my daughter was kidnapped by those Rangers, Dynamos, or whatever, early this morning. If there's anything you know about them, I want to know it. NOW!"

He let go of her and stepped back before he lost control and let himself wring her neck. She looked up at him, breathing hard, "You don't wanna slap me around a little, do ya?"

"Get out."

"I'm easy, man...."

"Get *the fuck* out. Don't come back." Hank's voice was a lash, pushing her back. She backed out the door and ran down the corridor. Her footsteps died away down the stairs.

The body on the floor moaned, and tried to turn over. The way Ondreya had bound him, his attempts were somewhere between difficult and impossible. Hank appraised with a cool professional eye; at least he tried to. He raised an eye-brow at Ondreya, "I think this item knows where his friends have taken Anne."

"Probably, but I don't believe he's going to want to be very talkative. Minimally, he's going to try to delay us, while he attempts to escape." She regarded the gang-banger as if he were a piece of fresh beef, "I'd rather not kill the kid, but I don't ever want him to tangle with us again. Not ever."

"Remember that Field Manual on Interrogation I got from the Army?"

"Some of it. It was pretty bloody work."

"The Infantry's a clean job compared to what those butchers do, but there was one stunt I remember that took no blood at all."

"I think I know what you're talking about, but I'll let you jog my memory a bit."

"Okay, hon, how good an actress are you?"

Ondreya's smile was that of a hungry cat, "Quite good, considering my audience...."

She came up behind him, put her arms around his waist. "Tell me we'll find her, Hank," she said softly.

"Of course," he said.

It took only a matter of minutes to pack things up. Hank got their suitcases out of the hotel by lowering them from the window on spare cordage to Ondreya. He checked the room for belongings, and went down to the lobby. There was no sign of the punk; the lobby was deserted. The hairs on Hank's neck stood on end. He walked around to the parking lot, investigating this sensation.

Ondreya was waiting in the truck, which she had running. He looked with some concern at the gas gauge. The Black Destroyer's flex-fuel engine could run on just about anything and there were gas stations in the area, but he hadn't filled up since before Anne was...was....He backed the truck around more savagely than he wanted to. "Ever gone hunting?" he asked his wife.

"No."

"Friends who have tell me of a situation: it's when all the birds and such get quiet; the area is silent. Completely. It's usually because some large predator, a bear, maybe, has shown up. I've been told it's a good time to find cover."

"What are you getting at?" Ondreya asked.

"This place has that feeling. There's something big on the way.

"The woods are silent."

A WORD FROM ALAN PARSONS—II

[Load; Run] She sits in her workroom, listening to the video music on her VCR. The video playing is The Alan Parsons Project's tune, "Stereotomy." On the screen, brief video clips of ecstatic dancers jump through short dance routines, as their world itself vibrates and moves in time to the rock beat. Unknown to the dancers, first one, then two, then four men, all clones of their former self, do back-flips in and out of the dancers. The entire continuum, dancers, gymnasts and the studio, moves ponderously aside to start, then faster in precise dervish whirls, and the reality disclosed behind it is first of a tropical rainfall, then a storm, then a volcano, followed by hell-fire, followed by the distant hell-fires of other suns.

The Alan Parsons video ends. The Rolling Stones play "One Hit to the Body (One More Hit to the Heart)." The exaggerated martial arts movements Mick Jagger performs are those of a young panther, a midnight predator, rippling silently through the jungle.

As are Yezeletta Zargkonji's flowing movements through, beneath and outside the civilization that generated her.

She feels as if the universe is shifting, sliding aside to show off that which reality covers. The camouflage. The hell fires within. The turmoil that lies at the basis of her knowledge, her thoughts.

There are things which form the lowest postulates and axioms of thoughts. Axioms—common notions—that are never questioned, because the thinker doesn't realize they exist. These axioms lie in waiting: only the wary can see them lurking in a proposition, hiding within a theorem, watching. When one of these logical predators strikes, it is usually without warning, usually without the victim's realizing he has been struck.

The VCR continues playing the miscellaneous videos; she neither sees nor hears the next: Arcadia, "Goodbye Is Forever."

Secret Doors

There are things in her world that do not fit the pattern of her training. Several new people have arrived, three individuals that seem to live in a large pickup truck, vacationers coming from up north. And one other: anomalies, all of them. The single man is a shadow who seems to move through the city as if it doesn't exist. An Imager has brought a record of his coming and his progress towards downtown. She is keeping an eye on him.

Perhaps the Matrix-Engine has an answer.

Perhaps it has a question.

Visit With A Friend

Joe feels flattered. Earlier, Yezeletta asked him to accompany her to the interface point at the base of the Matrix-Engine. She points to another articulated chair-beast: "Sit there. I would like your impressions when I'm done."

Joe watches as Yezeletta's constructs connect her to the Matrix Engine. *Can't she interface by herself?* he wonders, but doesn't say.

The brown thing approaches: Joe thinks of dead tree branches with long sharp thorns. It leaps for Yezeletta's head, and the construct Joe thinks of as "the arranger" swiftly adjusts the device around her head.

A thought enters Joe's mind: Is she lonely here? Does she go through all of this hocus-pocus because it gives her a feeling of being taken care of, if only by a lot of designed and manufactured assistants?

Is that why she is so loquacious with Joe? Is that why she released him as soon as she did? Was it the good deed she had done for Joe's nephew?

Is it why they are lovers?

He sits back (the chair adjusts to his motions) and waits.

Curriculum Vitae

[Living Inside] The four octaves of light that Yezeletta can see fade and the detailed blackness of the Matrix-Engine becomes reality. Space recedes to infinity. Spiral nebulae of thoughts and desires appear around her. She wills her sight to look at a configuration behind her, and all the universe spins to place it directly before her. Lines, planes and sheets of information interchange grow to visibility, linking the intelligences in complex ways. An I/O driver pulses slowly in terabytes, a visual drum or heart beating against the black velvet of the Matrix-Engine. Around the beating drum the aboriginal shapes of silicon processes swarm in a precise dance, skimming off the data as they arrive. Yezeletta Zargkonji exults in the precision of her world:

this is hers, it is her creation!

—Yes, Child. Have you forgotten me? | Load Descriptor Status;

No. Never.

—Has he helped you? | Query;

Yes.

—Is he a good companion? | Query;

Yes.

[Pause] Somehow there is a warmth in the depths of the Matrix-Engine's blackness. Yezeletta waits. The glittering shape will continue in its own time.

—I have seen him looking in the old Project records. | Locative;

As did I. Does he know of you?

—If he read the file on your training, there is no way he could *not* know of me. Are you frightened? | Database; Access; Query—

No. There is nothing he can do to me here.

—Nothing? Have you forgotten? Why is he "Joe" and you a name that could never exist? Look back, and see. | Interrogative; Declarative; Conclusion;

Once, you said he was attracted to my differences.

—I did. He is one of those rare thinkers who realizes that, as one of my mentors told *me* when I was little: "Man is Mind." What is on the outside is, in the long run, largely irrelevant. Your mind is who you are. | Vocative; Declarative; Conclusive;

THE DOOR AND THE NIGHTTIME—I

The universe spins, and a seemingly impossible thing happens: a door in space itself opens. Yezeletta focuses on the door: she knows it is a construction of the intelligence named Hilda, that she calls Mum, but it still startles her when the door rushes towards her with the prescient speed of thoughts.

[Load Backup; ECU] Lightning! A screen!

In the flash of total recall, the subjects return, names burning in letters of crimson neon across the black and flashing jagged white of the open door:

#====================================#

[<<—

Biology - Russian - Botany - Japanese - Chemistry.

English - "American" - Biochemistry - Geometry:

Euclidean - Riemannian - N-Dimensional - Lobachevskian.

Mathematics:

Algebra - Trigonometry - Calculus - Statistics - Catastrophe Theory - Chaotic Dynamics - Fractals - Tensors - Hilbert Space - Hyper-Complex Numbers.

French. - Strategy - Law - Spanish - Chinese.

Psychology - Computer Programming - Seduction - Nuclear Physics.

The Arts Of The Warrior:

Chemical Warfare - Biological Warfare - Radiological Warfare.

Tactics - Military History - Strategy.

Combat - Unarmed - Armed.

Weapons, types of - Field Support.

Combat Medicine - Cloning - Biological Construction.

] <<—

The subjects are thrown at her as fast as her teachers can do it. Soon human teachers are replaced by teaching programs on the LAN, and it is at least a week before she exceeds the capacity of those. Now, she goes on alone in her researches, as the awe shown her turns from fascination to deference, by steps to respect to reverence to fear to dread. Her creators no longer understand her. They no longer know what it is they have created.

She has gone beyond them.

[There is no sign of the origin of her name] .

#====================================#

[Freeze Frame] *Video image of desolation: trivial toys of omnipotent maniacal deity, angrily thrown into the corners of a chamber of inordinate dimension. Red flame below the horizon, silhouettes wreckage of ancient....*

What?

Where?

When? - *[Another Image is Concealed] .*

#====================================#

[Find where they named me. Where is my name?]

[Listen with your eyes, and I will tell you, See it with your ears.]

[Who is that in the corridor? It's lonely in here. Where is the Gray-Haired Lady?]

[Voices:]

—The Matrix-Engine is nearly complete.

—The Central Processor will be installed in the morning. Who's volunteered?

—Hilda Henderson. The cancer is all through her chest cavity; it's this, or nothing.

—Yezeletta Zargkonji will be in a bad way for a while. She thinks Hilda's her Mom.

—That can't be helped. It's the Matrix Engine, or a cemetery plot.

—Should she keep her name?

—Hilda?

—No. *Her*. The Project Agent.

—Yezeletta Zargkonji? I'd say yes. It serves to distance her from humanity. That plus her conditioning will make it easier to attack an enemy *as* an enemy. She won't see the enemy as human by her standards. To her, that name is perfectly natural.

—Where did it come from?

—It just grew from "Jezebel," the name of the sub-project that developed her ability to function with the extra limbs. The names taken together were how she pronounced "Jezebel Sargon One" before we got her larynx fixed.

—Very well. I'm on my way to say farewell to Hilda.

—Not goodbye, farewell. I like it. She could live forever in the Matrix-Engine.

—Will she want to?

—Who knows? Besides [the speaker starts walking] **<unintelligible>** attached to **<lost in an echo>**.

—It would distract **<clatter>**. The Agent **<clatter echo>**.

[The voices fade out]

A congeries of mispronunciations!

What's wrong with my throat?

> *Red Flame Below the Horizon....*
> *When?*

#===================================#

The problem states itself in the dream-area between sleep and waking, in the *place* between <reality> and <virtual reality>. It captures Yezeletta's attention as any problem would: her training in this area is as complete as it is in any of the other many areas of her growing expertise. That the conversationalists refer to the time before the Project Doctors had performed the necessary operations on her throat, along with Hilda's entry into the Matrix-Engine, is a precise statement of the time-frame of when this conversation happened. Older, now, with more experience, more able than she was at the age of sixteen, when she overheard this fragment, her problem-solving skills initialize, and she begins her analysis. As is the case with any problem, it will yield unconditionally to her relentless attack.

#===============================#

Yezeletta Zargkonji, first of her line, opens her eyes in multiple wavelengths and still sees the patterned darkness of the Matrix Engine. There are partial answers, now. The rest will be congregating, shortly.

DETERMINANTS EXFOLIATE: DIAGNOSTIC

[Checkout Run; Close Up] *Half of the images are reduced to the fully saturated state of black screens. The dark apertures move back, away, the* *color of forgotten memories, the emptiness of erased past-times.*

There, the images take on the black-on-black of encrypted archived data, lurking, sharp weapons in the blackness of the night that will never know light, awaiting activation.

THE DANCE

Hank and Ondreya drove around in the neighborhood of the hotel in a sort of spiral search pattern. Safely secured and sitting where Anne should have been was the sullen youth whom Hank had decked, and whom Ondreya had taken prisoner. They had tried to get him to talk since they had brought him down to the truck, but he remained silent. Hank had wondered to himself when the act he had suggested to Ondreya earlier would cease being an act. He knew she was on the proverbial short fuse and would start getting serious (more serious, he reminded himself) very soon. Hank looked at their prisoner in the rear-view mirror.

"We haven't tried bobby pins under the fingernails, Hank," Ondreya said sweetly.

"How about a flame applied to the soles of his feet?" Hank countered.

"Ants. Lots of ants, the big picnic variety. With stingers."

"Yes, dear. After we've given him a bath in Classic Coke."

"Maybe a *hot* bobby pin," Ondreya supplied.

"I don't know, hon, I've always been partial to the Chinese Water Torture. It's slow, but nine interrogators out of ten say it always brings positive results."

"Maybe, killer bees," Ondreya added.

"I Like that idea a lot, babe: you know, I learned some neat things about field interrogation in the Army; maybe I can get my old skill back. 'Death-watch Lenhaden', they used to call me. I'm way out of practice."

"Wonderful idea, Hank, can I watch? I may be able to help with new technique."

Hank studied the silent gang member again via the rear view mirror. His hands were handcuffed behind him and he was securely belted on the passenger side of the back seat. As he and Ondreya talked about various ways of inflicting pain in almost garrulous tones, Hank thought he could see him start to unbutton a little. Then he would catch Hank's eye in the mirror and dummy up again.

"Think we should try something here, Ondreya?"

"Not yet, I'm having too much fun brainstorming this." She lit a cigarette. "What would happen if I applied this cigarette to the end of his nose?"

"Would you really do that?"

"By George! The Mute speaks!" Hank pulled the truck over and faced him. "All right, Junior, let's start with your name."

The Mute dummied up again. Hank took a small screwdriver from his shirt pocket, prodded him in the chest with it, "The answer to your question is 'yes' to ALL of it. Unless you start singing like a birdie; now, how about it."

Silence.

"Stick it up his nose," Hank said.

"No!" Their prisoner said. Hank hit the break. "Gourd—Gordon. J-Johnson."

"Hey, it walks, it talks, it crawls on its belly like a reptile!"

"Who are you?" Ondreya said.

"I said, Gordon Johnson."

"No, dip-shit, in your little social club. Who d'you run with?"

Silence.

Ondreya placed the lit end of her cigarette about five centimeters from Gordon's face, "This is gonna go into your left eye, if you don't tell me who you run with. And answer fully and concisely every other question I ask you. You got that, boy? I've had a real bad night and I'm in no mood to take any busy-mouth from a young not-so-tough like you." She moved the cigarette closer. She knew he could feel the heat, but she puffed on it to bring the temperature up a little more. "You got Blue Cross, Sonny?" she asked, softly.

"Dynamos!" he almost squeaked the name. "The Oak Creek Dynamos."

"Better, but you're slow on the uptake," her cigarette didn't waver. "Now answer the next one: who turned you on to us? Who? That little slut back at the hotel? One of your friends? Answer quick, now!"

"H-H-Her. Angie!"

"Who the hell is 'Angie'?"

"Her. The little bitch back at the hotel."

Hank cut sharply to the left, across the opposite lane, shifted savagely into reverse, backed around, shifted again, and came down on the go-pedal. The steel-belted radials shrieked a scream of revenge in the silent street, and the black truck sped back to the hotel. He brought the truck up close, and, grabbing something short, square and lethal from under the dashboard, ran into the hotel office.

Ondreya patted Gordon sweetly on the cheek, "Now don't go away, sweetie," she said in a caressing voice. "Mama will be right back." Then she slapped him, putting her back into it, "And my daughter had better be unharmed, if you know what's good for you."

She took a .357 Magnum from the glove compartment, and went in.

Hank barged through the front door, ducked around the counter and into the back office with inexorable velocity. The room was deserted. He looked into the back room. There was a washroom that smelled unbelievably. He rummaged in a closet: it was empty. He looked around again. Ondreya arrived and checked out what appeared to be a small conference room crossed with a broom closet. It contained brooms. "You try the hall?" she asked.

"No."

Both of them ran down the hall: to the left was a kitchenette; to the right, a very untidy room heaped with tattered bedding, old clothes and a mattress that was mostly insides. Ondreya opened the pantry in the kitchenette; it was empty; bare shelves leered back at her. She came out to see Hank signaling quiet. He beckoned to her. Silently, he pointed at the mass of bedding in the small room. Ondreya nodded.

She covered him. Hank crept quietly up on the largest pile of trash in the corner. He grabbed a large double handful, and threw it off the pile. Angie erupted from the pile, holding a rusty carving knife. Hank dodged her and she blundered across the floor. He stuck out a leg and tripped her. Ondreya grabbed Angie's shirt and it ripped loudly. She jumped on Angie's back and seized her knife hand. The torn shirt ripped again. Hank jabbed the Taser into her ribs, and pressed the trigger. The fifty kilovolt charge took any further fight out of her. Ondreya applied handcuffs, and pulled Angie to her feet. She smiled prettily at Angie: "So nice of you to wait up for us! Won't you be our guest for a bit?"

They installed Angie on the driver's side of the back seat. Ondreya pulled the seat belt tight, while Angie's smoldering glare attempted to obtain a rise out of either of the Lenhadens. She failed.

Hank started the truck, drove away from the hotel.

Ondreya surveyed her guests: "I have never seen such a dismal pair of little shits as you two. What rock were you found under?"

Her question evoked nasty stares, but nothing more.

"The silent treatment, again, huh? Hank, when you find a good place to camp, I'm going to need my sewing kit. It's in the back. I'll also need your soldering iron, the box of tips, several nails, and the butane torch and a hammer. I'm sick of playing nice to these little bastards. I'll want access to the power take-off, too: the one-hundred-and-ten volt tap."

"You got it!" Hank slowed the truck, stopped. He turned around and grinned at Angie and Gordon: "Isn't she just the nicest lady in the world? I bought her the Dr. J. I. Guillotine bicentennial commemorative one-eighth size scale model handy hacker beheading tool for our last wedding anniversary."

Angie's shirt was torn just about off; both breasts were visible. She noticed Hank's gaze and jiggled them at him, and licked her lips. "You've got to be kidding, Kid," Hank said.

He started the truck, and drove forward. Ondreya lit a cigarette, puffed on it until the tip was a red glittering eye, and looked at Angie: "I was going to put this out in your friend's eye, but I decided not to. You have lots of sensitive places I could toast with this. Tell me: you did ring the 'Oak Creek Dynamos'," her words were vitriolic, "in on us, didn't you?" She reached out, held the burning coal close to Angie's face. "You don't need to admit it, of course; you're the only one who knew we were in that sleazoid room. The street was deserted. You might as well tell me the truth anyway, though; it'll give you practice for other questions later." She moved the cigarette closer. Angie tried to retreat through the back of the cab.

But she licked her lips, again, in seeming anticipation.

Hank looked at Angie through the rear-view mirror. "I hate you," he said cheerfully. "Just thought you'd like to know that."

"What do you want?" Angie said defiantly.

"I was wondering when you'd open up," Ondreya said. "You gonna admit to what I know already, or do I get out my sewing kit. There's all sorts of sharp stuff in there. It can hurt *a lot*."

"You won't say that when the Dynamos get you. They're probably on your ass right now."

"I'll burn that bridge when I get over it." Ondreya tapped the ash off her cigarette. It just missed Angie's right breast, falling into her lap. Angie looked down and squirmed. "Not to worry, dearie," Ondreya cooed, "I'll throw a can of warm Seven-Up down there to put the fire out. It's nice and sticky. Very uncomfortable. You won't like it at all."

"Hon, look ahead. That look okay?" Hank pointed to a deserted building. "Looks like a garage. Maybe gas, but I doubt it." Ondreya nodded.

Hank steered The Black Destroyer into the garage. The insides had been stripped to the walls, which were of red brick. The windows had been walled up. Hank stopped the truck halfway into the building, and looked up, left, right. He leaned out the driver's door, and looked straight down. "This dump has T, R, A, P written all over it in sixty-point Times Roman. After some of the places in this town, I don't trust any of the places." He drew his forty-five, and got out.

He snooped around the garage for minutes, until Ondreya got fidgety. Particularly, he checked the doors. They looked as if they were in good shape, but he checked them to be sure they could be opened after he closed them. Finally, satisfied, he took the truck out, reversed course, and backed the vehicle in. Now the front faced the doors, and Hank could come barrelling out at high speed, if he wanted to.

He killed the ignition, turned to his wife. She raised one eyebrow. "I think," he said, "it's time we found out what these kiddies know."

A SOCIETY OF FRIENDS

[Activate] *It watches as the black Chevy pickup moves out, backs around and re-enters the garage, stern first. There are four people in the truck, two of whom seem to be there against their wishes. This is curious; more than that, fascinating. It is just the situation that must be covered and taken back to the nearest Hive.*

THE FIRST STEPS

There is a great amount to be said for looking before diving in. Peter Rudenko looked down at his bound hands, and up at the ill-dressed creature standing in front of him.

"'Nother one. There seems to be a lot of you strangers running around here these days. You outsiders must like our city."

THE PREVIOUS STEPS

[Earlier] Peter Rudenko pulled the boat up on the opposite side of the Milwaukee River near a grouping of piles that thrust up like a row of broken teeth. He pulled the boat as far as he could, turning it over and covering it with the scraggly brush that grew in shades of gray around the piles. He didn't know if the stuff was alive or dead: it didn't matter. It didn't look like it would change color, much.

There was a rusty metal stairway leading up to what he thought of as the Street Level. He started up. There were places where the treads were almost rusted through; the entire structure shook dangerously. He moved slowly and got to the top in one piece. A path of broken concrete squares led away from the steps; he started walking. The sky was light, and a wind blew around him. In the distance behind him, he could hear a sound of distant thunder. A sign, the first he had seen since the edge of town indicated: Wisconsin Avenue. Smaller lettering said: Down Town. He headed that way.

It was two klicks north and just before dark when the Dynamos grabbed him.

SETUP.EXE

[Data-Comm] *The message transmission rate increases, as the loose* *network of Yezeletta's creations route data to their servers—sponge-like crania within each Hive. From there the servers route data that—in their estimation, decided by Yezeletta's programming—is important enough to be sent at a high priority to the Mainframe: to the Matrix Engine, itself.*

DETERMINANTS ENCRYPTED

[System Restart] *The circle of twelve screens turns, and other images of destruction and desolation move to the front. Other images black out, or are distorted by overlays of abstract patterns. Several images—in particular, one of the New York City skyline—are among those that are abruptly concealed.*

WARNINGS

[On-Line] *The message appeared on one of Yezeletta's monitors in her office.*
There was no one in that room at the moment.
She was on-line; he was with her.

——>>> **TEN** <<<——

You Made your plans so carefully, but you left out one detail:
The Hands of Time deal just one round, but *The Winds of Change* Prevail.

—The Jefferson Starship

CHANGES

[System Update] Her gold eyes are sightless for a time, seeing a fine and private universe where order and chaos have been interchanged. Joe jumps to his feet, but the servitors are faster: the attendant, motionless until now, swiftly disengages the brown roots. Others gently guide Yezeletta Zargkonji to her special chair and sit her down. Joe joins them. He takes her right hand, the lower one. Her other arms close about him in an embrace. Part of him watches astonished as the chair-beast adjusts to his presence as well as hers.

The hug is strong. She seems to hang on to Joe as if to a life-preserver. Then her normal attitudes re-establish themselves, and Joe can feel her tense muscles relaxing. Joe hugs her and attempts to ride out the remainder of the private psychic storm that only she can see.

Her eyes open.

He realizes that now she can see him as she could not, even with open eyes, before. Order and chaos have returned to their accustomed places, and, for now, she is herself again.

Her gold eyes scan Joe, and, finding an ally, look beyond him. She relaxes.

The servitors stand silently, a tableau of formed constructs frozen in an instant of time. Around them the murmuring, chuckling sounds of the pumps and electronics of the Matrix-Engine are the only sounds. The maze of the conduits, tubes, wiring and other plumbing of the Engine are the background.

Yezeletta's breathing slows. The beatings of her hearts slow. Joe is reminded of their love-making earlier.

"What?" is all he can ask. "What happened?"

"Something very good, actually. My past has certain places where it is very difficult for me to recall anything. I believe the reasons for this are some form of conditioning in my early life to avoid those recollections. Or those times." She grins, but the expression is a tad shaky, "I saw this as a problem to solve, and I *am* solving it. I believe that I can now begin to locate this conditioning, and dismantle it."

THE ASSISTANT

[Multitasking] Leona contemplated the risk. *He doesn't know that I've been able to leave since I got here. He's always thought I'm his and his alone.* She removed the thirty-eight she kept under the floorboard, and verified that the spare was still in its place below.

This was a signal. One of Yezeletta's hairy tarantulas skittered out of the darkness below, looked up at Leona with a large gold receptor, took the spare pistol and carried it further out of sight.

How many more of those are down there?

One of Leona's communicators entered from the same direction as the tarantula, pulling something else out: a length of stout cord.

Leona tugged on the cord and a large wrapped package, a slender roll that would fit into the space between the floor studs, appeared. She levered it out of the floor and unrolled it. These were the clothes Yezeletta had provided, if Leona had to make a getaway. There were three such sets in Leona's quarters.

Quickly, Leona dressed. The jump-suit fit perfectly; the belt with its various tools was also an exact fit, as were the boots. The communicator leaped up onto Leona's shoulder.

Everything looked as normal as could be expected. If this all worked according to plan—whispered through her communicator from downtown—she would be back in place in about eight hours.

Zhongo would never know the difference.

Her communicator nuzzled her, and held something up before her face in one articulated leg: a motorcycle key, as well as keys to the rest of the building.

GATHER WRITE

It's always a good idea to have a backup in unfamiliar territory.

SCATTER READ

[On Line] Leona let herself out the back door of her quarters. Zhongo's notion of a proper bedroom for Leona was the top floor of a three-story brownstone that appeared to be in the north-central part of the city. Leona hadn't been able to see much from her windows on the top floor. There were a lot of trellises, scaffolds, cheesy decorations and other impedimenta blocking her view. Other windows that might have had a decent view of the street were painted over and kept closed. She was disoriented for a moment. She determined the directions from the night skyline, then turned south and could see the tall buildings along Wisconsin Avenue just peeking out above the nearer trees. The front of the brownstone faced north, the garage was...there.

The Harley-Davidson was where Yezeletta's assistants had placed it. The key started the bike with a low sound of pure power: someone had taken pains to make this Harley run quietly.

Her <*destination*> was due south.

YARD BIRDS

The sloppily dressed, young thug pushed Peter into a small open area in what looked like a local metal recycling facility: a junk-yard, a dump. He was pushed and shoved into a corner, an open area surrounded by heaps of metal leavings, and discarded there.

THE BIKER

Leona directed the Harley due south on the next street empty enough to allow for speed. She accelerated, leaning into a sharp curve, and rode headlong into the dark industrial district.

INTERCUT

Peter studied his immediate area for minutes. He seemed to be alone amidst the metallic leavings of lost technology. Or was he?

Was that movement?

THE AGENT, THE MEANS, THE METHOD

Leona approached the open area to which Yezeletta's Imagers had directed her in the junk-yard. From where she was standing, she could see a man being marched into what appeared to be a holding area—an opening amid piled-up metal objects. She was facing the main entrance favored by the current owners of the place. The dim lighting, the fire behind him, and the contrast made his features indistinct, made it hard to recognize him. She removed an object the size and shape of a silver dollar from her tool-belt, and placed it on her open left eye.

It settled over her eye like a monocle and turned transparent. Her left eye was now an infrared imager with enough contrast control that the fire-light no longer made a difference.

Leona consulted the picture in her hand. This was the guy Yezeletta had wanted her to rescue.

She plotted her ingress. The junk-yard was fenced on two sides, and piled up with discarded technology in the unfenced places that it was as good as enclosed. Well, not quite.

There were ways in, and Yezeletta's imagers had assisted Leona in plotting a pathway that actually led into tunnels through the wreckage. Leona looked at the hole in the metal stack nearby: it looked much like a dark shadow from a distance in the streetlights, but was a clear accessway when seen up close. She entered.

There was actually a path worn before her. Something changed in the eye-patch, and the way ahead was suddenly picked out in detail. She could even read the trademarks on the vehicular remains.

She walked silently up the path.

H ERE . T HERE .

A moment later, something was thrown in with him. His backpack.

"They got another one." It was a declaration. Peter peered into the shadows of the heaps of metallic junk, and saw a woman, a girl of about sixteen. She was tied up and looked as if she had been in a fight. Her clothes were torn, her face dirty, her expression defiant. She said, "Don't let these pugs get to you. They like that. They like to see you beg. They'll kill you faster if you beg."

"Who are you?"

"Anne. Anne Lenhaden. These he-men kidnapped me out of our hotel room. I think the little bitch at the front desk fingered us."

A ND H ERE —

Leona crept through the metallic clutter around her. Once her right hip hung up on a sharp metallic projection. Her jump-suit deflected it harmlessly. *Hyperfilaments*, she thought. The tunnel ended just ahead, about two meters.

Beyond there was an opening. She could hear sounds from the right.

Two individuals of indeterminant sex were occupying a dirty blanket in a corner of the open area, loudly and rather intensely. Leona watched them from her vantage point in the tunnel, and decided they were too busy to bother with her.

Silently, she slid from her hiding place, ran across the clearing—it was barely five meters—and disappeared around what looked like a wrecked Ford.

The lovers didn't notice.

Her quarry was just ahead.

I NTRO

"What are they going to do with us? I'm Peter Rudenko, by the way," he introduced himself to Anne.

"For all I know, they're cannibals. I've heard of such things."

"I wonder if the Milwaukee Chamber of Commerce knows that. It's bad for business if you eat the customers. They may want you for other reasons."

"Some of them won't. There's one fella who's gonna sing soprano for the rest of his life. I saw to that." He liked this young lady's attitude.

"Think you can reach my ropes? They tied your hands in front. Maybe we can get loose."

"I'll try," he said. "Isn't somebody watching us?"

"These turkeys aren't too bright. They don't seem to understand time at all." She squirmed around, and Peter started picking at her knots.

"I think I can do this more efficiently." He reached down to his right ankle, and slid something out of his boot: a slim piece of black metal. "Hold still, while I whittle at those cords." He began picking at Ann's knots with the tip of the blade, working it into each strand of rope and severing it. One strand parted, then the next. One wrist was loose. He helped her pull it out, then got to work on his own.

When their hands were free, he got another black blade from his other boot, and gave it to her. They sawed at the ropes on their feet and tossed the remnants into the smashed window of an ancient station wagon making up part of the open area.

"You said 'time sense'," Peter whispered. "How so?"

"Somebody'd feed me at midnight and say it's breakfast. I'd get lunch and then the same an hour later from the same guy. I wasn't fed for something like fourteen hours, then I got three breakfasts in forty-five minutes. These people don't understand time. I think it's because of the crap they take."

"Maybe. It's also standard practice for softening up a prisoner: you take away his time sense. That's what they were trying—poorly, I might add, we're outside—with you. It's also probably why the dude that grabbed me threw my backpack in here. It didn't occur to him I might find it useful. What organized these people, anyway?"

"I'm not sure," Anne replied. "I think this bunch is the bottom of the food chain. No gang could work very well this badly organized. The real leaders are probably elsewhere. Is it important?"

"Not now, really. It's time to go, don't you think?"

"I've thought so since you cut me loose; what's outside this junk?"

IN THE SILENCE

Leona stepped out from behind the wrecked Ford. Peter and Anne regarded her quietly with surprise. Leona looked back at them, equally silently.

"Who—" Peter said.

The dark-haired lady placed a finger before her lips. *Shhhh.*

She approached. She stepped into a chance ray of light from a distant source.

There was something small, round and fuzzy clinging to her shoulder, using a multiplicity of legs.

"Follow me," she said.

"Who are you?" Anne asked.

"A friend. I've been tracking you. I'm here to help you get out of here."

How do I know...," Peter started.

"— that I'm a friend? You don't. I saw you," she nodded at Peter, "get her loose. Think about it. You used a boot-knife. Right boot. Then you gave her one from your left boot. I could have stopped you any number of ways. Shall we go?"

They followed her to the edge of the open area. She was slim, dark of hair, and wore black coveralls or a jump-suit that clung like a coat of paint. The critter on her shoulder moved several of its legs, turning.

"What's that on your shoulder?"

"Irrelevant for your purposes. Time enough for that later, come on."

Leona looked out. They could hear voices.

She put a finger to her lips.

Two very dirty and very naked kids, a male and a female, staggered past, carrying a dirty blanket, and giggling.

Leona let them pass, shaking her head. Peter and Anne came up behind her.

"Friends?" he asked.

"Saw them coming in."

THIS WAY TO THE EGRESS

They took cautious peeks from the pile of crushed metal bales forming the entrance to the little clearing. Their guard, a boy himself, was sitting cross-legged nearby, a glazed expression on his face, and dull filmed-over eyes. He was rocking back and forth and humming a four-note fragment of a popular tune over and over. He hadn't noticed the lovers passing by. Peter could see a wire running from a belt computer going into a socket just behind the guard's right ear. They slipped past him. Peter looked back once at the shabbily dressed kid enclosed in his own Johnny-four-note world, and forgot about him.

To Peter's left, someone muttered to himself as if he were in a trance. "I came in that way," Leona said, "Looks like we'll have to go...there."

Ahead, he could see the flickering of a large camp-fire.

There were several people Peter didn't want to meet, then, or ever, if he could arrange it, sitting around the flames. A young woman, bare from the waist up, danced to the strumming of a poorly tuned guitar. The dancing suggested overtones of Salome, or perhaps illustrations from *Hustler*, and the others watched her twirl, thrust and kick as she exhibited herself to her circular audience. Leona motioned quiet, and they waited until the dancer was opposite the fire from them. Then they ducked from one peripheral shadow to the next, putting as much rubble as they could between the fire and themselves.

The junkyard was large, and there were many small campsites within it. They passed one where there was another party for two going on, skipped by another small group passing around a large Meerschaum with a coil-cord and a compact visual processor attached, and looked up ahead.

They had reached the gate of the junkyard. There was one man standing a lazy guard. "I'll take this one," he whispered. Peter slid up to him, a shadow among shadows. His left hand made a single short movement. Anne and Leona heard a muffled "crack!" and the guard slumped. "Come on," he whispered. They left.

Outside the yard, cyclone fence stretched before them to an intersection, and behind them for the length of the block. Peter tried to find stars to get his direction, but a ragged cloud deck covered the sky. There were no streetlights. The only illumination was from the moonlight glowing through a single jagged opening overhead.

"I'd like to find the way to the center of town," he said.

Leona beckoned: *this way*.

Peter and Anne followed Leona up a cracked sidewalk from the exit. Peter looked back. There was a hand lying out of the yard onto the concrete. As he watched, it was drawn back in.

"Sloppy," he said.

Leona raised an eyebrow.

"The guard I took out."

They had reached the intersection, and Peter was very pleased to place a corner between them and line-of-sight to the dead sentry. This was one of the unfenced sides of the yard. Leona conducted them to a hollow in the metallic hedge of metal bales. This took them off the sidewalk into safe shadows.

She looked out.

Then approached them.

Anne looked at her face. Something covered Leona's left eye. It shimmered in the dim illumination.

"Listen," she said.

"Who are you?" Peter asked.

"My name is Leona, I work for someone in the city." Anticipating the next question, she added, "Don't ask, there's no time for that."

"Why did you come for us?" Anne didn't want to be left out.

"I was *sent*. My friend has been keeping an eye on you. She wants you safe. You...." She paused, looking for words, "You *interest* her. She might want to meet you. She doesn't want you left in there." She gestured at the bulk of the junkyard.

"Here's how to leave this place safely." The small fuzzy-surfaced creature on her shoulder extended a clawed leg. Grasped in the claw was a folded paper.

Peter took the paper, and opened it. It was a printout of a map. Leona gestured. "This is where we are now. Go up here to the intersection, then east to Eighth Street, and north to Wisconsin Avenue. Wisconsin Avenue is fairly well patrolled, but what's left of the local police won't bother you. They usually have more to worry about than two pedestrians at night. Go east on Wisconsin. You, young lady," she nodded at Anne, "Will meet the people you were separated from earlier."

"Mom and Dad?"

"They drive a large Chevy pick-up, don't they? They're looking for you."

"Do they know I'm here?"

"No. But they'll meet you on Wisconsin."

"Leona," Peter asked, "Who's arranging these meetings?"

"Someone," Leona said flatly, "who is interested in you." The small arachnoidal creature on her shoulder fidgeted.

"Where did you get that animal?" Peter insisted.

Leona backed away. "Follow the directions on the map," she said, backing into an opening in the metal bales. "Do *not* follow me. You won't be able to in any case. Now *go!*"

She backed into the opening, turned, and moved quickly away. Peter could hear her steps fade out. He plunged into the opening after her.

And stopped.

The opening was filled with...something.

A dark gray honeycomb filled the door-sized opening through which their rescuer had vanished. That was what it *looked* like. Peter took a pen from his pocket, and probed the gray surface.

The pen slid over it as if the material were a hard plastic.

The sound came to them from beyond the barrier.

A motorcycle starting up.

WEB OF THE CITY

"Looks like it's time to go," Anne said.

Peter studied Leona's barrier, and thought of the kind of technology that could throw something like it up as fast as this one had materialized.

"What are we up against?" he muttered, half to himself. "We're lucky it's on our side," he addressed Anne. "It *is* on our side. She said so.

"Didn't she?"

They were alone at the center of a circle of darkness beyond which were the welcoming lights of illuminated buildings.

Anne took his arm, led him to the intersection. "Look," she said, and pointed, "There. That's the Farmer's Bank Building. From the way the kiddies back there described it, it's a vertical hell. That's the East Side. It's the tallest building in this city, and a place none of the studs in there will touch with a ten foot pole. I guess it has its own gangs. Or something they try to seriously avoid."

"Do you know where we are?"

"My folks and I were staying in a flop in the center of town. That's that way, too," she pointed to lower structures in front of the Farmers Building. "The gangbangers put a sack over my head before they hustled me out of the room. They don't know anything about evasion, they—What's that?"

Across the deserted street was a tumbled-down ruin of something large. A factory, perhaps. A doorway, a black entryway going inwards, stood ajar on the building's corner. They ran into it. Peter's skin crawled, as he swept coarse cobwebs away from the entrance.

Something was running with a curious insectoid hopping gait along the top of the yard fence. In a place without lights, it left a negligible silhouette: it was just a black-on-black thing, a shadow in a city of shadows, another of the same.

Then it vanished in the dark.

SPACE-TIME

"Everyone has a past," Joe says. They had come up to the living room, Joe had put some quiet music on her audio system, and mixed her a Manhattan. She sips at it as he speaks. "Some people like to talk about it, others to live in it, and some just draw on it for the experience needed to handle the present effectively."

"You do not understand. I have a...a blockage? no, a—call it a habit: a habit of not remembering."

"Wait a minute! You're trying to tell me you live only in the present? You obviously remember things in the past. When did we last make love? Now? Or yesterday?"

"It's not like that. I can recall past things, but it takes much effort."

Joe tries another tack: "Did you know there's a lot of Project Sargon stuff just beyond the bathroom, upstairs?"

"Yes. I saw you in there, reading."

"You did? You must have sent Thicknesse after me. Silent little fellow, isn't he?" Joe keeps his remarks flippant. Perhaps a little humor will help.

Yezeletta Zargkonji almost preens, "It, he, is one of my little triumphs. I designed him for stealth."

"I think the military might want to use you as a consultant." He sips from his Coke. "By the way, do you have a nick-name? Do you mind if I use just your first name?"

"No."

"Okay: you can't recall the past without a lot of help, and I think whoever you interface with downstairs is that help." She nods. "Why do you think this is? Let me ask you straight: why were you created, born, made, whatever?"

"Did you read it in the Project Notes?"

"Yeah. Some kind of national defense job. I wonder if that's why that company sent someone around five, six months ago to look in on me? Did you have anything to do with that?" Joe gets up and stretches, then walks to the window and looks out on pipes and electronics.

"I've lived here for about eighteen months. I have kept the time by means of an atomic clock I brought with me."

"A good hideout, eh? You and your constructs and—"

"Yes?" she asks. Joe takes a chance.

"There was a Project staff-member named Henderson who's mentioned in the Notes." He turns to her.

"She's the one you interface with, isn't she?"

Yezeletta's reply is just a nod.

"You mentioned solving a problem. I know you've had a lot of training in that area. Before, when you came out of it, you were talking about actually applying that training to yourself. Could your friend help? Can you go back to her, again?" Yezeletta nods. "Would it help if you did?"

"Perhaps." More of her confidence seems to be returning. "But not now. There are several people I've been tracking in whom I'm quite interested. Recent arrivals, here."

"Have you been gathering intelligence?"

"On them, as I did with the City's regulars; it was to have been my job. Then someone—it could have been the Australian Defence Ministry, but I heard only from the Project Directorate—decided to cancel the Project. They wanted to—eliminate—" she gestured out the window at the Engine.

"And cut you all up. Or worse. So you resigned."

Yezeletta laughs at the understatement, "Yes! I resigned! I took their damned Project with me!"

She stands, now all brisk functionality, entirely well within herself. She goes to the video components, switches off the music, and turns other things on. A construct enters with a small stack of video media. "Let's see what my intelligence gatherers have brought us."

Joe sits his pillow piled chair next to hers, and the lights dim as the video display comes on. She has accepted him. It is the easy way, almost a new habit, that she refers to the two of them together as "us."

MIDNIGHT AT THE OASIS

Hank spent several minutes setting up the Coleman stove in their sheltered campsite. Ondreya sat where Gordon and Angie, in the back seat of the truck, could see them. She had her sewing kit and was laying out needles, a thin stiletto and other items. Nearby, Hank's butane torch burned, a violet spear in the dark.

"Think we ought let those two sit there and yak?" Hank asked his wife warily.

"They know what I want," Ondreya said. "If their stories sound rehearsed, I'll let them have it." Her voice was level, steady and dangerous.

"What do we do with them afterwards?"

"I don't know. The thought of doing them in slowly and painfully, but artistically, just warms my insides up. More realistically, I'd rather see them warn their 'society' to reverse course when they see us coming. Besides," she smiled a little at the thought, "It's not like I'm taking on three of the Green Bay Packers; hell, they're kids!"

"Who helped a lot of gangsters kidnap Anne."

"I guess it qualifies them for the big time, doesn't it?"

Leona rolled the Harley into the garage three doors down from Zhongo's residence. She ran back to Zhongo's and took the back stairs two and three at a time, until she reached the third floor, where her quarters were.

Below, on the front stairs, there was a commotion.

"No rest for the wicked," she muttered. "I need a vacation."

Her room door was closed but not locked. The commotion was headed her way from the front. On the edge of the bed, a furry tarantula regarded her with its gold imager.

Leona shucked off the jump-suit, rolled up the equipment belt, and stood naked next to the bed while several tarantulas removed the clothing and hustled it towards the open aperture in the floor. The critters scattered, running back to the loose floor-board, and—she had to admire Yezeletta's attention to details—, the last one in pulled the floor-board shut. Her communicator headed for the window, undid the flap of screen, and escaped outside.

Leona leaned back on the waterbed—positioned several pillows for head support, and relaxed, her legs spread invitingly.

And waited.

The commotion didn't take long to reach her.

The door flew open and Zhongo stood there, sweaty, panting, out of breath. *The sweaty lover routine, huh?*

But Zhongo just stood there, looking at his mistress, several of his assistants behind him, also trying to get a good look.

Then he turned to them, "Scatter. Dammit." His voice was oddly soft. He closed the door, and began removing his clothes.

Leona waited, studying his actions. Yezeletta might want to know what was on his mind.

But then she was too busy to worry about it.

"I don't like what she's doing out there." Gordon had to look over his shoulder to see Ondreya's preparations. "I don't like the looks of that torch at all."

"I don't like *her*," Angie said. "You don't know how she was looking at me. It was real mean. Her eyes. I wish they'd let us loose. My wrists hurt."

"I just want to get away from these loving parents. I'd be happy to tell them where their damned daughter is."

"Then we'd have the Dynamos after us. You want that? How long have you been a member? Two months? What do they do to a sell-out?"

"All right! We don't tell them about the yard. What do we tell them?"

Angie's face took on a crafty expression; at least she hoped it was crafty. "I know a place."

"Where?"

"It's a place that has fifty-one floors of reasons why Hank and Ondy won't come back for us. Or the Rangers, or the yard."

"The—"

"— Farmers Bank Building. Once the disturbos and street skells in there get them, there won't be anything left but bones."

Gordon turned to Angie, and winked.

She tried to smile and continue to look what she thought was crafty; she failed. "I thought you'd like the idea." She tried to move her arms, couldn't, and looked back, "Here comes Ondy. Look scared!"

Gordon didn't find that difficult.

THE OPEN ROAD

Hank tightened the knots in the rope with his customary care. He put his back into it. He had tightened the other knots by placing them on the cracked concrete floor of the garage, bracing his foot against them, and pulling them tight. Gordon's right hand was now very tightly attached to Angie's right hand.

It was his solution to Ondreya's ultimate wish not to harm the kiddies. It would make it difficult for them to go anywhere for a while; the easiest thing for them to do would be to walk around each other in a small circle, until they got the rope off. Ondreya had searched them intimately and removed several blades from each, so Gordon and Angie would have to pick at the knots with their fingers. By the time they had succeeded, the Lenhadens would be long gone.

It had been an uneasy night. Hank and Ondreya had taken turns sleeping, and Gordon and Angie had slept as best as they could in the back seat. Ondreya had managed to get something out of them with no more than threats.

She looked back at the two gangbangers as The Black Destroyer pulled away and said, "Good riddance to both of you."

Hank caught a glimpse of Gordon flipping them the bird in the side mirror. "They coughed up awfully fast, hon," he said. "Maybe too fast."

"If they did, then they did. I'm pretty sure they told us the truth. If they didn't, then we're no better off than before. I'm not leaving this dump until I find Anne!"

"Neither am I."

The truck headed due East. Their destination, a tall building. The tallest in Milwaukee. Hank thought of the strategy needed in accessing it. Ondreya's thoughts were of a poem she had known in elementary school:

"Child Roland to the Dark Tower came."

THE USUAL

As the truck moves out, an Imager's gold eye follows it. Others will track the black truck to its destination, but this is the first of the trackers. It follows the truck as far as it can, then it scampers away to its Hive to give its report to a Communicator.

——>>> **ELEVEN** <<<——

Why must we pray screaming? Why should not death be redefined?

—Patti Smith

PASTORALE—I

Peter and Anne walked towards the Farmers Bank Building. The eastern sky was lit with the gray pallor of dawn, the building was a dark pillar (although it was light-gray, almost white) against the slightly lighter sky. Beneath them, the sidewalk rumbled and shook periodically as some sort of large machine ran in the depths below. They had been walking since the black creature had made its appearance outside the junkyard.

PIANISSIMO

Nothing more like it was visible for all of the rest of that long night.

LARGO

Yezeletta Zargkonji awakens early, and looks at Joe, who hasn't slept much, either. He lies awake, watching his associate. Her enormous gold eyes regard him calmly in the gray morning light from the window. This is the first night she has opened the window, or, for that matter, even shown him where in the bedroom it is. Joe now knows he is in some tall building. He arises, walks naked to the light, as he has done several time this night, and looks down. Far below, the street is empty of traffic. Not quite: a single black vehicle, a truck by its shape, moves slowly past the building. It vanishes to the south, but the light of its headlights shows it turning. The vehicle returns north, turns onto the next street into a short, narrow lane: Cass Avenue.

The headlights point out, luminescent compass needles in the dawn pointing due south.

At the main entrance.

PASTORALE - II

Farmer's Bank's white obelisk ascended at a crazy angle before them. Anne had only to squint, and it was easy to imagine bats and worse flying around the black sightless gazes of the darkened windows beginning to show color in the dawn-light.

"When I first saw that, I thought it was haunted by every customer who lost it when the bank, or whatever went bust," Anne said. "It still looks haunted."

"I agree," Peter said, "I feel as if I were in the collected nightmares of a platoon of H. P. Lovecrafts who hated the world."

"Look, I see lights! There's someone there."

The lights came from an alley ahead. They pressed themselves against the front of the structure that gave into the alley, and Anne looked around the corner with her compact mirror.

The sight was infinitely welcome.

Hank and Ondreya were discussing their next move, when Ondreya saw motion. It was at the edge of the alley opening, an object stuck out from the sidewalk. Then Anne was running up to the truck.

The stranger with her walked a little slower.

BEL CANTO

Programmed in their function, they come from the sub-basement into Real-Time. They are armed, but their weaponry is an integral part of them. In a sense, each entity is a weapon, possessing knowledge and a form dictated by its primary function. Their target has been given them, impressed on each creature's memory by a method not comprehended. Called forth from their Hive deep in the cellars of The Farmers Bank Building, they live, they grow, they die, and wait for that which calls them to the action for which they were designed

Anne ran to the door of The Black Destroyer, Hank and Ondreya got out and, for a short time, they hugged each other. "Mom, Dad, this is Pete: he's from Chicago, too."

"Hello, Pete," Ondreya said, "How did you meet Anne?"

"We were captured by the same gang-bangers," Peter answered.

"Indeed," Hank prompted.

"The lowest level of one of the gangs here," Peter said, "apparently the 'cannon-fodder and amusement' level. The higher-ups seem to use them as some sort of a diversion."

Hank nodded, "There seems to be a lot of that here. Gangs and gang warfare, I mean. We met some people who tried to flag us down on the way in, along with a cross-fire that didn't seem to have anything to do with us. You'd better get in; I don't exactly trust it here, wherever 'here' is."

Ondreya reached back and unlocked the back door, and Anne and Peter climbed into the back seat.

"What do you do, Pete?" Ondreya asked pleasantly.

"I'm a civil servant," he answered succinctly.

"What service?"

"Intelligence. I was sent here by Philadelphia." He hoped the general nature of his answers would be accepted.

They weren't: "What branch? Defense? Central? FBI?" Hank probed.

"The Company," Peter hoped the generally accepted nick-name would suffice, "sent me in on some general investigative work." *Little white lies: so how do I explain Searchlight?* he thought.

"Looks like you've been in good hands, Anne," Hank said chuckling, "you've been running around with a genuine spook."

"Ah—We prefer the term 'agents', if you don't mind. 'spook' sounds like it came out of a trashy novel."

"Okay by me. How do we get out of here?"

"How did you come in?" Peter answered. "I came up from Chicago, went West, and in from the West Side."

"So I just drive out the way I got here, huh?" Hank replied. Hank paused, then: "What the hell?"

There was something else in the alley. Something small and many-legged. It scuttled back and forth across the alley entrance, a mad weaver's shuttle in the dim dawnlight, trailing a thin line. Spinning it out. It was joined by another, then another. Something appeared to expand and close up the alley as the creatures moved. Hank shifted into low, engaged the four wheel drive, and the black truck lunged forward.

There was something on the roof.

Then it was waving down at the windshield: black hairy arms, a compact furry body. On its front, a sunrise: a large golden orb of indefinite depth. Another furry creature that could have been its twin appeared. Hank reached for his automatic. Dimly he could see Anne grabbing the thirty-eight in the seat pouch and slapping the back-up into Pete's hand.

Something was eating into the driver's side window.

Hank's last conscious thought was: *Anne trusts him that much?* Then everything went black, black as shards of black glass.

Black Crystals of Ice.

[Raise Exception] Zhongo Teketon paced back and forth in his study. It was night; he and Leona were home. She sat on his davenport covered up in a blanket. She watched him with an unwavering gaze. *He almost never does this.* She very nearly didn't think it, lest her body language give her thinking away.

His thoughts, nominally never far from either business or sex, were now about as far as they could be from either topic. Leona sat there scrutinizing him silently, as he paced and raved: "No face. The son-of-a-bitch had no face! Something had gone in and stirred his guts up, too! Like a little kid playing in a sand-box! Eddie's insides were all stirred up. Moved around. The poor fucker looked like a practical joke."

Zhongo paced between a grand piano, and the wet bar: the home counterpart to the one in his car. He had marked out a circular path for himself. He couldn't play the piano, but it was a sign that You Had Made It if you had one in your living room. He spent most of his time at the bar, but only if he wasn't pacing. He stopped to mix himself a Seven and Seven, in his confusion, filling a large glass with Seagram's and adding a shot of Seven-Up. He drank half of it. It seemed to steady him. Leona watched him with as close to no expression as she could get.

There was a buzz on the intercom. He hit the answer, "What!"

It was a guard from the first floor. The intercom buzzed with badly distorted speech for a moment, then ceased. "He wants me up on the roof? Bring him up!" Zhongo said.

He beckoned to the Leona. He led her to the bedroom: "I'll be down in a moment, get ready." She removed the blanket, turning around slowly, showing herself off to him, and lay down. Zhongo went up the back steps. She opened the window.

On the roof, the light from an occasional lit window, and from the moon peeking out from behind black layers of clouds, cast dim illumination across the neighborhood. The rooftop door for the front stairway opened, and several of the bodyguards and Zeke appeared. He began without preamble, "You're probably wondering why I called this symposium...."

"Christ on a crutch, Zeke! What's going on!"

"Right. If you didn't live on the East side, you probably wouldn't see this." He held out a small telescope. "First, take a look: there, at The Farmers Building."

"You want me to look at the top?"

"Nope. Look a little further down. About three floors down from the top."

Zhongo focused the little scope, and scanned down the western face of the skyscraper. The darkened windows moved tremblingly past his point-of-view.

"You see it?" Zeke asked.

"Yeah." There it was. A single window open. Clearly visible were warm incandescent lights. He couldn't see what was in the window, only that there was a figure standing in it. A recognizably human figure. The telescope was too low a power to resolve the figure's features. "Say what?"

"Don't know. I do know that I just noticed it tonight. I'd gone up to my roof for a breath of fresh air, and noticed the extra light when the sun set."

Zhongo put the scope up to his eye, searched around again, sighted in on the lit window. "He's still standing there. I guess he's looking out at the rest of this burg. Hold it. There's someone else up there. My god!"

Zeke wanted to grab the scope, but didn't. The guards might take it improperly. Zhongo stood still for a moment, squinting though the telescope. He took a deep breath, let it out slowly. Suddenly he looked relieved. He put it down, handed it to Zeke, who immediately zoomed in on the window. There was nothing there.

"What did you see, Zhongo," Zeke asked.

"That guy's got company. Two other people, taller than him. The others seemed to be lining up to look out; it looked as if they had more than two arms. Big deal."

Something caught his eye. Motion.

Zhongo looked down. The movement had caught his gaze from the periphery of his vision. Now there was nothing. Nope! There it was. "Look! Over there!" He pointed. "There's something crawling in that tree over there."

"I don't see it, boss," one of his bodyguards said.

"Pretend you're looking down a gunsight, Looey," Zhongo replied.

"It's another one a them damn things!" Looey said, drawing his pistol.

Far below, something was crawling along a branch. It moved too fast for him to see it clearly.

"I'm gonna get this one! It's like those others I see on the buildings downtown!" Looey squeezed off a shot. Then another, the blasts from his automatic loud in the night. The flashes from his unsuppressed weapon were bright, but Zhongo couldn't the impact points against the foliage.

Looey stopped.

Zhongo watched as the gunsel loaded another magazine. Looey released the slide, took aim, and lowered his weapon, thumbing the safety on as he did so. "Little fucker's gone," he said. "Where do those night demons come from, anyway?"

Of one thing Zhongo was sure: the creature had come from somewhere nearby.

"What else have you to show me?" Suddenly he was very tired. He thought of who was waiting for him downstairs.

"It's more photographs of Eddie. I did some additional x-ray work on him last night. There's more to him than I thought. And less."

The men trooped downstairs to Zhongo's living room. Zhongo wished all of this nonsense was done with, and he was alone with Leona. Life was easier just a week ago. No one was helping himself to his convoys, his minions didn't become mysteriously disfigured and as mysteriously dead, and he had Leona, on a nightly basis. Or did, ever since Slim had put her up as a bet in the Friday night card game.

The bodyguards left; Zeke plopped down on the sofa and picked up a folder. He removed a sheaf of photographs. The pictures were grainy, fingerprinted, spotty. Zeke, for all of his experience, was clumsy in a darkroom. Zhongo looked at the first, then looked away.

"Gets me like that, too, Zhongo," Zeke said, "That bare forehead down to there, is just too much. Then I started digging. That's the next picture."

In the next, Zeke had removed the front of Eddie's head. Zhongo felt slightly better at not having to look at that bare expanse further. But this was nearly as bad: the nasal cavities were exposed; the throat, closed off in the first picture, was opened, gaping. And on the forehead—

"Zeke, what the fuck is that?"

"Chief, if I knew, I'd be giving my Nobel Prize acceptance speech in Stockholm, about now. If I didn't know any better I'd say it's a small video camera. Like in a cell-phone. Look at this one." Zeke got out another photo. "There's little wires coming out of that thing, that exactly parallel the optic nerve, and go back into the visual cortex on the back of the brain." He looked owlishly at Zhongo, "If you get hit on the back of the head, you see stars—they're called 'phosphines'—due to the physical pressure directly on the cortex." Zeke produced a third picture, "There's been an addition here, too," he gestured, "There's this little growth in the center of the back of his head. My god, it looks like an integrated circuit! That's what I think those scales in Eddie's right lung are, too: some kind of processor."

He handed Zhongo a large transparency: a sheet of Kodak x-ray film. "This is his head photographed through the front. Those lines—they look like a printed circuit, or a magnified integrated circuit, a chip. These things are *traces*, actual conductors; those little knots," he paused. Zhongo realized Zeke was sweating. "Those knots," Zeke continued, "are circuit chips."

"Circuits," Zhongo said helpfully.

"Or other processors. I think someone bugged Lead-foot. Or tried to and couldn't finish the job....

"Or didn't want to."

Zhongo frowned. Zeke was an anomaly. He wasn't hooked on anything, the only ganglord Zeke was getting retainers from was Zhongo, and, as far as he knew, Zeke didn't have anyone else after him.

Zeke was one of those rarities: a man who did what he wanted to, because he wanted to, who didn't have any other reason to kiss up to a protector. In other words, Zhongo could be sure Zeke wasn't letting himself be so much the sycophant that it would color his perceptions of things. The messenger didn't have to sweat being killed by the recipient of bad news.

"Ever hear of 'biochips'?" Zeke asked.

"No."

"They're a development from the Technology Bloc; a cross between silicon IC technology and biochemistry. Circuits with hundreds of times the densities of current stuff can be grown on the proper substrate. It takes gene-surgery at a very fine level to convince the micro-organism to, for example, grow a fifty-terabyte static RAM, instead of an amoeba's nuts. If an amoeba has nuts. Biochips are being researched in Chicago and L.A., and up in the Bay Area, but the big developers are Uruguay and Canada."

"So what?"

"I don't have the instrumentation to look into that," he gestured at the addendum to Eddie's visual cortex, "but I'd bet you a buck it's a biochip. Perhaps a microprocessor. Grown and custom installed in Eddie's brain.

"From someplace outside this country."

Leona was ready when he got back to his bedroom. She met him at the door naked, and silently helped him out of his clothes, as she had many times before. He needed the help; the thoughts spun in dizzy orbits through his mind.

Who was that guy in the tower? Why was he, or the old Farmers Building so important to Zeke? Or to anyone else? What was that critter moving around on the rooftops?

Leona folded his pants and placed them on the dresser. He didn't realize she was still assisting him until he felt her tug at his underwear. He pulled his tee-shirt over his head, and stepped out of his shorts.

The questions wouldn't stop:

Who the hell had bugged Lead-foot?

She slid into bed, and he climbed in after her. For a moment, he just hugged her tightly, her impeccable breasts feeling cool, then warmer against his skin. What would Eddie have looked like if those additions had been completed?

What if they actually *were* complete?

She pulled away from him, gently rolled him on his back, and, next to the open bedroom window, went to work.

Zhongo looked down at what she was doing. Leona was an artist. That was good. If he had to help, he wouldn't be able to. Then he stopped thinking for the rest of the night, as she continued with her accustomed skill, listening well, not speaking at all.

A N D A N T E

Dark.
Night.
Black velvet.
A dream of falling-falling....
Forever.
Light.
Gray dawn at the periphery of consciousness.
Room without view.
Room with out view.
Room with. Out-view.
Gray walls.

"All right, you've got lousy special effects. Show me what you birds can do."

Ondreya realized dully that Hank was talking. She moved, and the movement was as of being in water, or some kind of thick syrup. She looked left then right and didn't see anything in the gray light. The light brightened, the grayness faded, the light took on the warm characteristics of incandescent illumination. She looked at her hands. They were undamaged. Ondreya shook her head, as if to clear it. It helped.

The light continued to brighten. At the same time Ondreya felt more awake, more alert. She looked at Hank. He looked back. "Were we gassed?" she asked.

"I think so," Hank replied, "I feel a lot more alert, now. More than if I'd just woken up. I think we were put under and brought out by a counteractant."

Anne yawned loudly, and looked around. Peter stirred, opened his eyes and sat up. "Looks like we're all here," he said. "Where is here?"

The room was painted a uniform shade of off-white. The door was indicated by light gray trim. The adults were sitting on a large couch, Anne was in a large easy chair. There were lamps, a bookshelf, books, audio and video components placed on elaborate shelves.

And a large chair of heroic and misshapen proportions.

The door opened. A man entered. "Hello, there," he said. Peter expected him to continue it: "How are things?" make it a countersign, and they'd all be safe. The man didn't and they weren't.

"Your hostess will be along in a moment. By the way, I'm Joe Davis. I work here."

——>>> **TWELVE** <<<——

White lids white opals
Seeing everything just a little bit too clearly

—Patti Smith

OF SHADOWS AND SUBSTANCE

Joe Davis stood for a moment in the doorway. Hank thought he looked like a performer who had finished his act, but not communicated this to the audience, which is still waiting for more. Joe stopped pausing just short of the embarrassed cough stage, entered the room and sat down in another armchair. He regarded the others.

"You said hostess," Hank filled the silence. "Who? And where the hell are we?"

"She'll be up in a moment. You don't rush her, believe me." He looked at Peter, "Aren't you one of the spooks that visited me in L.A.?"

Peter Rudenko colored slightly, "Ah—we prefer the term 'agents', if you don't mind," he said. "Yes, I was there."

"What's your real name?" Joe asked, "and what are you doing here?"

"It's the same name I gave you there," Pete replied, "Peter Rudenko. I'm not Double-Oh-Seven, or any of that nonsense. That's the sort of thing you see in trashy novels." Peter felt as if he had been here before.

"What are you doing here?" Joe repeated.

"Looking for information. I was sent here for various reasons, mostly to do with that gangster's experiments in that conservatory here. I'm both surprised and not surprised at finding you here. Some of your discoveries started showing up in areas they shouldn't, in other places," his manner of speech didn't capitalize those other places. "You started appearing and disappearing, and it doesn't take a PhD in Intel Work to find out where you went, particularly in hindsight. I was sent here to find out what I could."

"You're about to. It won't be what you think you want to know."

"I know about the Mitchell Conservatory, if that's what you're not talking about."

"What do you *not* know about it?"

"There's this individual who's been squatting in the Mitchell for the last five years who's been using techniques similar, if not identical to, what you've discovered—"

Joe cut him off, "You don't know ten percent of it."

The door opened. The light from the hallway cast a long articulated shadow into the room.

CENTER STAGE

Hank looks up at the figure entering the room. It, no, she, wants to make him slouch further back into his place on the couch. He resists the desire to do so, and, with great effort, sits still.

The figure in the door is backlit. The hall light filters through the eclipsing of her head, glittering in the webbing of her hair. Her face is in shadow; her eyes glow like a cat's, her irises are a brilliant gold that counterpoints the iridescent backscatter from her retinae. She grips the doorframe with two hands, her lower pair, and gestures, open-handed, with her upper pair.

Is it a gesture of welcome?

She turns to the others, her face impassive.

After her original shock, Ondreya looks at the source of the articulated shadow. She is pleasing in a way Ondreya can't quite understand. When the tall dark-haired lady came into the room, Ondreya's first impression had been one of extreme deformity. As her hostess walks across the room to the entertainment system. Ondreya realizes her mistake.

Her motions are swift, sure and clearly natural. She looks as if she is the product of natural selection.

Who made the selection? Ondreya thought. Your features are human; but where did the rest of you come from?

Hank finds his voice. "Who?" is all he can ask.

"I am Yezeletta Zargkonji. You may use my first name, if you wish."

Is that your real name or did you make it up just for us?, Ondreya asks, but she doesn't say it aloud.

"Were you on the radio?" Anne asks. Yezeletta Zargkonji turns.

"You heard me instruct the—" she cuts off the rest of her sentence.

"Who are you?" Hank asks.

"The reason you are all here," she replies.

"Where—" Ondreya starts.

Peter says, "You may be one of the reasons why I was sent here, not Joe Davis. That drug-maker—"

"I have nothing to do with him. He knows nothing of me."

"Where did you—?"

"I was to be a biological warrior and researcher. I and others like me were to be used in some kind of battle. There was talk of a Middle-Eastern nuclear exchange. Then, later, of another nuclear terrorist act. I would have been in charge of chemical, biological and radiological weapons. I am able to design other weapons as well. When the Project that made me was canceled, I was to be forcibly retired. I left them, taking what resources I could with me. I came here. I have lived here since."

TIMES PAST OF PASTIMES PASSED

[Shattered Sky; Sign Extension; Establishing] Yezeletta begins: "How did you people enter this place?"

"Probably the same way you did," Hank counters.

"She really does have a reason for her questions," Joe says. Then, to Yezeletta, "At least I hope you have." She nods once.

"I drove a truck," Hank says, "A black long-bed four-door Chevy pickup. I find it a rather useful vehicle for getting my family around."

"I drove through Brookfield to a bridge on the West side of town that had been taken out with explosive charges, and rowed across the river, if that's really what it is, and walked," Peter answers. "I had some help from the local residents."

"How did you get here?" Anne asks Yezeletta.

"Six lorries driven by assistants. My driver found this place by my direction. I had left the Project; think of it as sudden resignation. I have lived here, preparing and waiting for whatever they might send to bring me back."

"What were they going to do?" Ondreya asks.

"Maybe I can tell them what they need to know," Joe says. "Would any of you like a drink while I tell you a story?" Silently, Yezeletta directs the servitor that has entered the room, and it goes running off. "My partner was designed to take a part in national defense...."

His partner sits close, he is within the reach of her arms, but she does no more than hold on to his hand as he tells them of his last several days.

[Load Magnitude] "A weapon!" Hank exclaims. "They grew you to be their bio-chemical warfare agent. Then, after all of that, they tried to throw you out with the garbage! The antics of governments never fail to be surprising!"

"As I said, they seem to have designed her to have no past. But the conditioning didn't really take," Joe sips a martini and goes on. "She's been recalling things for the last two or three days, and," he asks her, "longer?"

"Yes."

"What would you do if Project Sargon came for you?" Ondreya asked.

"I have the means of destroying them all!"

"Including you, yourself," Joe says. "Can you see that?"

"Yes."

"Do you still wish to do this?" Joe continues.

"I am designed thus."

"Without free will?"

"Have I free will?"

"Are you human?"

"I was made from human parts."

"I'm not asking your body, I'm asking you; your mind. Do you, the woman called Yezeletta, have free will?"

"In some things. In most things."

Joe looks almost exasperated, "Are you a computer? Were you programmed?"

"I don't remember."

"Hank," Ondreya said. "I had a professor in college who asked the most infuriating questions on the subject of free will."

"I recall your telling me about him. Carl something—"

"Professor Carl Mathewson of the University of Wisconsin at Madison," Ondreya said, "a really nasty fellow. I asked him once about the chief problem of Artificial Intelligence—"

"There's only one?" Peter said, surprised.

"Aside from consciousness, knowledge contexting, levels of memory association, a time sense, grammar levels, active chart and island collision parsing, and other trivia, the one that interested Professor Mathewson was 'free will' versus 'determinism.'"

The room becomes very quiet. All eyes, including a pair of large gold ones, were on Ondreya, "I asked him how an inherently deterministic tool like a computer, even the newest matrix super-computers, could ever be non-deterministic enough to develop and display 'free-will'.

"The good Prof told me I wouldn't understand the answer, and that it was better for me to find it out for myself," Ondreya said, "well, I was young, impatient and insistent. I asked him again, and he was right: I didn't understand the answer. Until much later.

"He said, 'by programming the computer to be non-deterministic'. That and nothing more. I spent the next three years researching that answer. It was how I met Hank."

"She met me in the Mall by the fountain in front of the Memorial Library," Hank supplied, drily. "It was non-deterministic love at first sight." A look passed between them.

"Yezeletta," Peter says, "there must have been people around you who talked about you within your hearing. When I started my line of work, I was taught, to simplify it greatly, to ask a large question as a group of seemingly disconnected trivial sub-questions, and to reassemble the small answers to get the answer to what I was originally looking for.

"Go on," Yezeletta Zargkonji says.

"I treat all of the data I get as 'small answers'. Then I try to see what large questions are out there to which combinations of the small answers fit. It's one of the earliest techniques you learn in Intel work. In spite of popular opinion, 'Intelligence Work' isn't an oxymoron. We have a lot of impressive names for things that are actually rather simple: traffic analysis, for example. As a weapon, you may have been taught such things, unless you were designed for a suicide mission."

"Yes and No," Yezeletta answers him. "I do know of what you speak. I was designed for infiltration."

"Yezeletta," Peter asks, "have you ever thought about your earlier days?"

"I've tried, lately. Why?"

"Ever wondered why you never looked into your past?" She only shakes her head. "I'd like you to entertain the thought that maybe you were never intended to have that particular interest. You were designed not to think in certain areas. That exact conditioning you spoke of earlier."

Her eyes move from one spectator to another, yet she remains still. She looks back at her partner: "I've seen how you use your memory," Joe says. "Your recall is just about perfect, even without the silicon assistance you have. You solve a problem by looking at all sides of it, then you look at each of the damned *sides*. Sometimes from the inside. If you can't solve something by one technique, you throw another at it. You lay siege to anything you work on.

"I've watched you working for the last couple of days. The siegecraft is so much a basis for your work, that it may be a trait that was, I guess *given* to you is the best way to describe it." Joe pauses, thinking. "'Siege' is a pretty good term. You were intended as a self-aware attack weapon. It's sort of like the difference between you and a—oh, say, a good psychiatrist. Doctor Freud would counsel and communicate. You do a frontal attack after exhaustive research. I think this kind of close concentration may be a way of keeping you from thinking about other things, like your origin, perhaps. It also dovetails nicely with your original design.

"Could," Joe gestures at the window looking out at the Matrix-Engine, "your confidant help you?"

"To do what?"

"To find yourself."

"Pardon me?"

"'Finding yourself' is a poor choice of words, perhaps. To assist you in locating the underlying causes of this *soi disant* conditioning and help you to get rid of it. Not get free will back, but get it for the first time, and to *know* you have it in a verifiable way. To become your own master."

THE TIME TRAVELLER

The servitors cause a short delay as Yezeletta insists on comfortable seating for all concerned, a long way from his earlier incarceration, Joe thinks.

Shortly, the attendant is adjusting the thorns, and another space and another time descends on her, as she forces herself to go back.

"She looks as if she's gone catatonic," Hank whispers.

"Can't we leave, now?" Anne asks.

"No," Peter says, "She may have—"

"Not she may have," Joe says, "She does have servitors guarding the access to this complex. It's not to keep us in, it's to keep the riff-raff living in this area out. If you saw some of our neighbors, you'd want to stay put for a long time. You'll need her safe conduct to get out of here alive. That doesn't include the things this complex has as well."

"What do you suppose she does have in—uh—in that thing?" Peter asks.

"Someone very important to her," Joe says, "Think of her as a foster-mother, although that isn't exact. A very dear and close friend."

REPRISE—I

[Knowledge Base] When she was young, one of the Project photographers had showed her how pictures were printed. She took to photography as easily as she took to anything else, and spent several days printing from the negatives her new friend gave her. She particularly enjoyed seeing the image appear from the clear white (dusky orange actually, under the safelights) of the printing paper. She was young enough to think she would like to be a photographer when she grew up. With her extra arms, she could shuffle prints from the dektol to the stop-bath to the hypo while she ran the enlarger, and keep the wet, or development, side from contaminating the dry, or enlargement, side.

She was told this would not happen, and her photographer friend disappeared, transferred to another government project.

Later, she would see this as a good thing. He would not die in her escape. She would have exactly one other friend in her near future.

"Is it possible for someone to design something that works too well," Ondreya asks.

"I think the people, and I use the word loosely, at Project Sargon have found out exactly that," Hank says.

"The modern Sorcerer's Apprentice!" Anne adds, "They created too well, and too soon!"

Yezeletta Zargkonji remains in her trance, beneath the thorns of the Matrix-Engine, as unmoving and still as a creature carved of white marble.

REPRISE - II

Yezeletta Zargkonji stirs slightly. She trembles, then is quiet.
"Where has she gone?" Peter asks softly. "What is she recalling?"

How did they teach me? She asks the blackness.

The answer arrives before the stellate symbolic representation does:

—**[Declarative]** They put their messages "between" or "inside of" others. For everything that was good and useful, they included something else that was evil and domineering.

Stellate Rosette;
Argent;
CGI;
Bank Swap;

*Where do I look first?*She imagines Mum as she has seen her before she entered the Engine: the teacher:

—**[Initialize]** The simplest way is to do a linear search, but you would have to search your total lifetime. There are easier ways, fortunately. Do you remember your lessons?

Interrogative;
Operational;
Tutorial;

A single speck of light in infinite space: *Yes.*

—**[Medium Close Up]** Look back, and pick a starting place. I can help you, but this is—it must be!—your battle. You are the warrior. Your freedom is the issue. You can do it!

Operational;
Procedural;
Define;

And suddenly, the opening door rushes at her!

#===============================#

A teacher, one of her last, introduces her to a man from India. The Indian teaches things to her she has never seen before: all of her questions in this area are answered by telling her to go look it up. She does, but lacks the referents for what she reads. She knows the topics from a theoretical standpoint, but has had no laboratory sessions. The Indian with the long complex name provides the labs. The textbook is something called the *Kama Sutra*. In this, as in all of her studies, she soon exceeds the knowledge of her instructor. He watches her in silent admiration. He wonders what the future will be like in a world where Yezeletta Zargkonji and others like her are the standard rather than the exception.

#===============================#

—**[Travelling Matte]** There is an amused chuckle in Mom's voice, I saw you put those lessons to good use, Child.

Processing;
Accessing;
Recollection;

Did you <u>have</u> to look?

—**[Dissolve]** I saw you and your friend were busy, and directed my attentions elsewhere. I think that you are too late in your education. Back the video up a few frames.

Argent;
Sable;
Vert;

Another door! Another Egress!

#===================================#

She has her own quarters and facilities in the Project Complex. Her makers have given her the lab space where she may conduct researches on her own in any way she wishes. One of the products of this research is the "Servitor," a short humanoid creature with powerful hands and dexterous fingers, which she uses rather as diminutive butlers, janitors, and "go-fers." The servitors soon are everywhere in the Complex looking on with their enormous cat-green eyes and forehead Imagers and ready to carry, clean, watch, guard or what ever the bosses wish. Her second product is the "Imager," a small spider-like creature that can interface with electronic devices, amounting to a camera on legs: an ideal reconnaissance device. There were other items growing in her laboratory as well.

#==================================

—Did you ever leave the cloning method for the servitor with them, Child?

System-Check;

No. I took it, and <u>all</u> the records, out of the Complex, when I escaped. Joe must have read some of it, but no one else has.

—You've made a good choice for a Partner. Where would you like to look next?

Declarative;
Query by Example;

A door opens!

#===============================#

The newspapers arrived on Sunday Morning. The data had been sent out for a matter of some months by someone who was never apprehended. The articles were short, garbled and mostly wrong; at least one was no more than a single headline and one paragraph, but one fact existed through all of the words: there was advanced research in Biological Warfare being done at a place in the Outback. There was no mention of Yezeletta Zargkonji. The Project was in a bad light, and it was hoped the light could be extinguished. If the public ever got the true story about Project Sargon, the climate of opinion would be disastrous. At worst, a single nuke, easily attributed to terrorists, would put an end to it. *And* to Yezeletta Zargkonji, if they were to know of her.

She was informed of the Project's decision a day later, Monday. As a citizen, she was entitled to retirement benefits, relocation, anything within their lights she wanted. She watched them in four octaves of colors in chords of reds, blues, greens, and colors they never knew existed, listening to their monotonic heartbeats with her enhanced hearing. Her lower arms removed? Conditioning? Rewrite her systems? Isolation in New South Wales? She asked them for time to think about this (even as she made up her mind then and there), and watched them exit. Then she deployed her preparations. The clerical and support staffs were gone, dispatched by buses to Alice Springs. Allegedly on vacation.

The Directorate came to her quarters the next day for her answer. They brought several others with them: men wearing the uniforms of Project Security. They met her in the kitchen. She was frying something on the range for one of her large breakfasts. Eggs that sizzled and popped in the grease. She reached out for more eggs from the side-board with her upper arms. Several of these eggs were of a dark green color, others purple. Servitors followed the Security men who carried things she presumed were weapons. With her lower arms she broke more eggs into the frying pan. Courteously, she asked if she might keep her arms and her mind. She was refused. She reached for more eggs from a wire basket. These were of the same green color. Easter? No, she answered. Mine. Will you allow me to stay as I am? No. Her hands opened. The eggs fell. On impact, they exploded with loud reports and a vapor rose up from the floor, dissipated by the air conditioning. Take her, the Security Chief ordered his men.

Yezeletta Zargkonji retorted with a word, a single syllable that only she could pronounce. The servitors pounced, seizing each man in an unbreakable grip. The Sheet slid out of the back hall. It wrapped each man tightly.

She told them, then, what was in the eggs. Several of them conversed in tones of panicky reason, as the disease in the eggs took them, one by one. Shortly she was alone in the Complex.

#===================================#

— I remember those milquetoasts. *<<A note of disdain enters her soundless voice>>*. Their demises were something I wouldn't have shed tears for, had I been able to do so. Would you like to open another door?

Scatter Read;
Referential;
Gather Write;
File Open;
Seek!

Rushing! Opening!

#==============================#

Looking back, she understands the data she has held in her on-board systems without processing. She has never met the actual head of Project Sargon. The head of the Project has always been referred to as the "Director," but her internals said otherwise. Who was the mover and shaker behind her creation? Having burnt all of her bridges and gone to ground, she will never find out, *unless they make a move against her.* What will become of her own projects? Will the survivors (and she smiles mirthlessly in streaks of colors in her recollection: what survivors?) of Project Sargon be able to determine what happened? Will they learn from this experience and have Project Sargon-II create a moron that must be programmed the way she programmed one of her Imagers? Who were the real brains behind her creation? Would Mum be okay? No answers come to these questions.

#===================================#

—Do you remember the conversation between those two people in the hallway? You were rather young, I believe, and I was not as I am, now.	Interrogative; Referential; Temporal;

I couldn't hear them. They did something to my ears after that, and I could hear everything in the Complex. I had to learn to tune everybody out!

—You may not have heard them with your ears, but you heard them with your mind, and your mind remembers! Listen with me, I can help you.	Modality; Production Run; Transfer;

This time I will open the door!

#===================================#

[Find where they named me. Where is my name?]

[Listen with your eyes, and I will tell you, See with your ears]

[Who is that in the corridor? It's lonely in here. Where is the Gray-Haired Lady?]

/*——————————————————————— */

—I'm right here with you, Child. This is a memory, not reality.	Parallel Process; Parse;

/*——————————————————————— */

[Voices:]

—The Matrix-Engine is nearly complete.

—The Central Processor will be installed in the morning.

—Who's volunteered?

—Hilda Henderson. The cancer is all through her chest cavity: it's this, or nothing.

/*——————————————————————— */

I recognize one of them. I thought he was a reporter.

—I'm afraid he was more interested in other kinds of news.	Descriptor; Type-Change;

/*——————————————————————— */

—Yezeletta Zargkonji will be in a bad way for a while. She thinks Hilda's her Mum.

—That can't be helped. It's the Matrix Engine, or a cemetery plot.

—Should she keep her name?

—Hilda?

—No. Her. The Project Agent.

/*———————————————————— */

I was their damned Agent. No longer.

—You are their Agent until you become your own woman. You must find their entries into the systems of your own being and remove them. You must remove the viral subroutines with which they have infiltrated your very personality. Otherwise they still control you; you are still in the dead hands of those who thought they were your owners. You are a slave to their last wishes.

Overwrite Update;
Version 2.0;
Load, Execute;

/*———————————————————— */

—Yezeletta Zargkonji? I'd say yes. It serves to distance her from humanity. That plus her conditioning will make it easier to attack an enemy. Whatever enemy she is sent after. She won't see it as human by her standards. To her, the name is perfectly natural.

—Where did it come from?

—It just grew, the first name is "Jezebel," from one of the sub-projects that developed her enhanced eyesight. The names taken together are how she pronounced "Jezebel Sargon-One" before we got her larynx fixed.

/*———————————————————— */

That's where they named me. Why didn't they just give me a number. M-16 or .357 Magnum, or something. Armalite. Colt .45? Remington 1108? They called me "Sargon-One!"

—None of them would take the step. I think that, had any of them lived, they would have spent many hours attempting to remove the damned spot.

Adjudicative;
Subjunctive;
Procedural;

I don't understand.

—There is time for understanding. Our destination is ahead.

Procedure;
Define;

/*———————————————————— */

—Very well, leave it as is. I'm on my way to say farewell to Hilda.

—Not goodbye, farewell. I like it. She could live forever in the Matrix-Engine.

—Will she want to?

—Who knows? Besides [the speaker starts walking] **<unintelligible>**

attached to **<lost in an echo>**.

/*————————————————————————— */

I didn't hear them, then!

—Listen with me. Use the enhancement techniques *they* taught you. Slow it down and parse each phoneme. Then use the error correction techniques *I* showed you.	Load WAV File; LoadMorphological Disconstruction; Load Chart Parser; Load Grammar; Instantiate; Access Dictionary; ACTIVATE;

I'm pulling the words apart!

—In real-time this is happening at a very high rate. Now, LISTEN:	Process;

/*————————————————————————— */

—Who knows? Besides [sound of footsteps] The Agent is too attached to Henderson to be politically reliable.

—It would distract from her primary mission. The Agent would be loyal to "Mum" rather than to the Project. Henderson is better off dead. Perhaps it can be arranged after she is released as the first Agent.

/*————————————————————————— */

—Are you surprised?	Interrogative;

No. They are better off dead. I've seen to that.

/*————————————————————————— */

[The voices fade out]

A congeries of mispronunciations! What's wrong with my throat?

#===================================#

—Now you know what it is you would have worked for. This is the type of being that thinks the world is its private plundering place. It will come and pick your bones clean, and demand more of your skeleton. This is whom you must resist. Can you do it?	Documentation; OnAccessToSystem; Load Sargon(); Execute;

Yes.

—Shall we continue?	Exit Wait State;

What is there left?

—Everything!	**Breakpoint!** **Restoration!**

#===================================#

She was taught to believe she was invincible. So far, she has been, but is it valid and logical to assume she always will be? One of her videos, a movie, is about an implacable creature that boards a spaceship, and within a very short time lays waste to the entire crew in a wave of bloody carnage. A single survivor escapes with her cat only by skill, training, cool thought and luck. Has she the skill to meet with the future? Is her training good enough? Is there or will there be a future? What kind of a future is it with the bloodthirsty creatures who designed Project Sargon pulling their strings from behind the fabric of existence? Like "*Stereotomy*," *"We can make it forever, do anything you want to, do anything at all!"*[1] the whole universe tips, and the invisible gymnasts back-flip casually through the unseeing continuum.

The weapon must be directed. She has a "command channel" by which she can receive instructions in the field. The channel has been silent: more than that, she has disconnected it for all this long time. She must reconnect it, now, not to the outside, but to her*self*. The mystics speak of a "Higher Self". There is no higher self than that which lies at the basis of conscious action. No matter what is done, there is an individual at the end-point who instigates the action. There are reasons for everything, no group can magically decide, and no individual can say "They decided I should do this!" She has the capabilities, the competence, the courage, the knowledge, and, now, at last, the will. Her own. She is her own woman, now; property no longer.

The Madflowers can wait, until they're needed (as they might be). If necessary they can wither and waste away, if they're not up to the drill.

It is time to return to the present.

#=====================================#

SYSTEM PAUSE—RESYNCHRONIZATION

[Secure From Breakpoint] It was quiet in all of the places where there had been turmoil. All around Yezeletta was a strange new sensation: *doors were opening*.

It was as if a cool wind was blowing through those places in her mind where before there had been only confusion. She knew how slippery image-as-metaphor could be, how easy it was to draw false conclusions about what she was experiencing.

But it seemed for a moment in her young life, Yezeletta Zargkonji could actually experience the winds on her skin, the cool drift of a kind of free rationality around her. The Moon set free and sailing on the gray clouds in the gaze of the setting sun against a dark-blue evening sky.

There were words on the wind; before she returned to her new friends, the winds of time and reason left their message:

It gets cold where I'm going, but where am I going next?

Would she ever know?

IT'S A START

She stirred, moved. The attendant performed its duties, as it had been designed. She opened her eyes, and the gold of her irises was a sunrise.

She smiled. It was the smile of a little girl of twelve, on her birthday. "It is good to be free," she said decisively.

"Who are you?" Peter Rudenko asked.

"I am still Yezeletta Zargkonji. I've had that name for as long as I can re-

---

[1] Copyright 1984 by The Allen Parsons Project.

member and I may as well keep it. I could be Jezebel Sargon-One, but that isn't self-consistent. Sargon, for example, was a god-ruler of the Ancient Assyrians, and I am not, and, while I have powers the Assyrian priests could only dream of, I'm not a god. I am my own woman, this is my life, and I must go on with living."

"Woman," Joe said. "Not a person. You see yourself as a woman, now.

"Yes. My agreement with you is that I would let you go at the end of our project. You are free to go. The Madflowers are finished."

"If you don't mind, I'd like to stay on."

Gold eyes like twin searchlights focus on Joe Davis, "You do?"

"You're a real fascinating individual, Partner. We each know things that would benefit the other. And I can't forget what you did to a small boy in Montana."

"You really want to stay here?"

"Yup. I'd have to bring some things from Hyde Park and have some stuff sent from Los Angeles, and wind up my affairs in both places, but that's no trouble. I've rolled around the country quite a while and I travel light. No sweat. Besides," he looks up at an olive-drab vivarium suspended very close, "I think someone else likes me, too."

"Yes!"

"Do you plan on studying biology with her?" Anne asked. "She knows a lot the people who created her would like to get a hold of."

"I have my defenses, Anne, I am prepared."

"You should be," Anne said. "After all Forewarned is—"

"Please *don't* say it, Anne. I've heard that joke many times, and it was funny exactly once." They all smiled, anyway.

"Joe said we'll need help getting out of here," Hank added, "This building is rather dangerous."

"That's an understatement, Hank," Joe said.

I will provide you with safe conduct, and a roadmap," Yezeletta said briskly. "If you stay on the route the map marks out for you, you'll avoid Allen Hightower and leave the city easily."

"What will you do?" Ondreya asked.

"Stay and research. Wait for the Project's attempt to retrieve me. Work. Joe and I have a lot ahead of us."

"Like a spider," Anne said. "You're the Spider Queen waiting in her web, only your web is a whole network across this city!"

There's one project we can start right away," Joe said. "Yezeletta, tell me straight out: Hilda Henderson in Vivarium Number One is your Mom, isn't she?"

WAIT STATE ENDING

[Level Zero Trap!] Yezeletta Zargkonji pauses for such a long time interval, Joe thinks she has reverted to her old self (he reminds himself that such things might happen from time to time: it takes a long series of new experiences to ensure that the cool winds of reason are blowing through places that were stagnant before).

THE LONG WAY HOME

[Trap return; Establishing Shot; Load Magnitude]
"You knew."

"It wasn't hard. You mentioned a pair of names in your sleep the other night: first it was Hilda and then Henderson. I looked up the names in the Sargon Notes. She was one of your teachers, and there was a notation that she encouraged you to consider her your mother. What do you know about cloning, Lady?"

"I wrote the book, the servitors—"

"— Are clones! Exactly! You can get a tissue sample from Hilda easily! The necessary cells are in her life-support system's blood supply; why didn't you think of this before?"

Yezeletta Zargkonji didn't answer, but she would, she thought, in the weeks, months, and years to come.

Or sooner.

SEARCHLIGHT

[Peter Rudenko]   Peter looked back at Milwaukee. Even the Farmers Bank Building was a toy he could blot out or cover with one hand. She would live there, how long? Another fifty years? And after that fifty years, would she create a new body, and move her brain into it? Or would she tire of life at that end of hers and want the Final Release? Were any of them able to say what they would be doing even five years hence?

Someday, *not too far off*, he thought, the weapon would meet her makers. Would Milwaukee survive that day? Would a populace bred for survival live? What about the hangers-on? It was not certain. Milwaukee had become, unbeknownst to most of its residents, an experiment simmering and overflowing with life: only here, the lab technician, or perhaps The Master Brewer, was invisible, or, just waiting and watching on her silken web in her Aerie down on Wisconsin Avenue.

He was committing a serious—if not a crime, then at least a very large mistake—by bringing back the records that he and Yezeletta had created, with a little help from Joe and Hank. The Spider-Queen deserved what little freedom she could obtain without an overworked, undermanned, even unknown, intelligence agency camping on her front stoop.

Besides, the damage wrought by the Road Lord, to say nothing of the drug-designer in the Mitchell Conservatory, hell, any of the mobs that were running this city, was something that could be given to the local authorities—assuming there were any left!—, and they could handle it. It would give his boss something to do.

Something to decoy the Agency away from the Farmers Bank.

He swung his backpack over one shoulder, and walked down the frontage road. The Lenhadens had gone slightly out of their way and given him a lift this far. He could go back for his car after meeting the agent picking him up. He looked back now and then at the city vanishing in the haze. The weather was supposed to clear up: one of Wisconsin's crystal clear Fall nights was promised. It would be nice to see real stars at night instead of half-assed cloud-obscured Moon-glow! There was a sign ahead; Peter was coming up on the back-side of it. He knew what it would say: 84-th Street.

A cloud of dust appeared in the distance. At first, he thought it was another Wisconsin farmer driving his pickup into town, but it was moving towards him with more purpose. Peter squinted at it, and walked faster. The was definitely an Agency vehicle. He waved his hands, and it slowed.

Soon Peter Rudenko was on his way.

FAMILY

[The Lenhadens] The Black Destroyer moved effortlessly south on Highway-94. The "map" Yezeletta had provided them in a way only she could, would guide them as far as the southern border of Oak Creek. Then they would have to let it out so it could regenerate at a Hive in that town.

The furry little sixteen-legged organism purred in a manner of a large furry cat as it sat, all but three of its legs tucked under, pointing to the landmarks ahead. Occasionally, it would look back at the Lenhadens, its enormous gold imager lingering on each. "What," Hank had asked it rhetorically, "are you going to do with all of those family photographs you've taken of us? Don't you worry about running out of film, or is your picture album intended to be rather one-sided?"

The road-map didn't reply, but its purring seemed to get a bit louder.

On the radio, Frank Sinatra sang of Chicago calling him home. It would be refreshing to see the skyline of the Windy City, again.

Behind them, the Spider Queen's Keep vanished in the autumnal mists.

PARTNERS

[Joe Davis] Joe held his partner's hands, and said, "Looks like you and I have a big job ahead of us," he said. "Let's get to work!"

The servitors waited in the conference room. Now the conference was of just two leaders and their creations—biological hewers of wood and drawers of water—, but Joe could see in the not too distant future, other researchers, human ones taking the place of biological peasants. Yezeletta Zargkonji looked down at Joe, but seemed to be looking levelly at him, somehow. She grinned, almost like a little girl. Joe thought of Anne's awful pun the day before, and grinned back. "Let's do it to it!" he said, and they entered the conference room together.

And all around them the fabric of Southeastern Wisconsin seemed to tremble with anticipation, just a little.

DETERMINANTS RAMPANT

[Production] *As they fall the screens align themselves with a different descriptor. The twelve images <u>merge</u>.*
   Her continuum interlocks.
   Her Metrical Frame is Entered.

FINISHED PRODUCT

[Load, Execute] *He stands before his creators, his large eyes scanning them. These are the ones to whom his unhesitant loyalty is given. He has no way of knowing the element of choice in that giving is absent, implicit in his design. He has no way of knowing of the over-ride he carries; its memories are removed when they obtrude into his consciousness. He regards them from a height, their faces looking up at him with something approaching reverence. One of his creators extends a hand. He takes it, looking down at the hand-clasp. He holds the scientist's hand for a moment in his own larger right hand.*
   His lower right hand.

PART TWO:ARRIVALS

——>>> ONE <<<——

Flower and heart are equal. As one unfolds
The other is closing. The fist of charm.
The dance of fathoms. Of voids. Of veils.
Layer after layer. Wall after wall. There
Is always more. There is always more after.

—Patti Smith

PLAY IT AGAIN

Her demeanor is one of formality.

Joe had been typing at one of the computers in Yezeletta's living-room—he'd been attempting a bit of free verse,— when a tabby-gray critter dropped down next to his monitor and folded its legs under itself, in the manner of a large spherical cat.

"Howdy, Thicknesse," he said and gently ruffled its fur.

The construct replied with a loud contented purr—in three tones—and its big gold aperture scanned Joe intently.

"What brings you to my humble abode?" he asked.

Thicknesse's response was to extend one leg. The claw held a folded slip of paper. Joe unfolded it, and read: *Please come to my office—Y.*

Joe skriched the construct again, and stood. "Tell your friend I'm on my way."

Thicknesse turned, ran up the wall.

Getting formal, are we? Joe mused.

It was rather unlike his friend, lover and partner to leave notes—usually the LAN was enough for communication if they were separated by an inconvenient distance, or she could use the intercom. A written invitation was a little unusual. He tightened the belt on the bath-robe he was wearing, and stood.

Yezeletta's "office" was actually her private workroom: a large area located conveniently between the bedroom, and the kitchen in which she practiced her martial-arts cooking. The door was open, and Joe went in.

IMMOVABLE, YET MOVING

She sits—as immaculate as when Joe first saw her.

Joe realized with a start that this was the very room that was her audience chamber on that first day. Then, the room reflected a sparseness that now is absent. Her office, once a stage set for her particular purposes, is now the site of a production run.

THE SORCERESS

She took Joe's hand, his left, gently in her right hand, her upper.

Joe realized (yet again) that this is Yezeletta's way of showing affection. Using her lower right hand would have allowed her to threaten with her upper. Joe held her hand gently.

Yezeletta smiled.

She hugged him twice with all of her arms, nuzzled his cheek. He hugged her.

Then, with the suddenness that Joe no longer finds strange, Yezeletta is all business.

"Joe," Yezeletta said. "You have been with me now for nearly four months. We have been lovers for most of that time."

"Yes I have and we have," he agreed.

"It is time that you took your place properly here. I—" Yezeletta blushed. "I have watched you, as you work here with me. I have even—" here she blushed even redder than before, "— analysed your reactions during our love-play. Forgive me. I'm not used to having...."

"Friends?" Joe asked.

Yezeletta nodded.

"Lovers?" She nodded again. Once.

She looked down for a moment. For that moment, it was as if she was, expressed in some outré mathematics, shorter than Joe. Then she looked up, and Joe realized....

"Yezeletta, how old are you?"

She thought for a short time—Joe could almost see the calculations going on. She held him closer, and answered, "Nineteen, perhaps twenty."

"And *they*," he made the pronoun sound obscene, "stuffed your head with all of this *training*," another obscenity, "and never allowed you enough companionship to understand people!"

Yezeletta nodded.

"Yet, you were able to get away from them, make a good escape, get half-way around the world to *Milwaukee*, of all places, and establish yourself without any help at all. Yezeletta, you're good, did you know that?"

"Yes," she said in a small voice.

"Damned good! So damned good, you don't need any of those rats!"

For the first time, he realized, Yezeletta looked at Joe with great surprise. Joe winked at her.

"Look, Kid, you've got a lot of native intelligence. More than those crooks who made you realized. So much that it saved you—out in the middle of the Pacific, when you took over that banana boat—and you didn't even know it. That's what I like about you, Yezeletta, you're—"

"Not human?" she asked.

"Bite your tongue!" Joe took her right hands, both of them, in his left. "The fact of your leaving those jackasses makes you more human than they could have ever been. On a million dollar bet!"

Yezeletta sat up. "Joe, please wait for me. Come into the bedroom in a moment, but not now." There is urgency in her voice.

Yezeletta *ascended* to her feet, and like a four-masted ship under way, sailed proudly out of the room.

And Joe waited.

THE MATHEMATICS OF TIME

Yezeletta's exit was practically a processional for one. Joe watched her as she turned down the corridor from the music room. The next door, in the

confused layout of her living area, is her heroically proportioned bedroom.
For this I needed an engraved invitation?

THE GEOMETRY OF LOVE

Yezeletta's voice came—slightly muffled—from the bedroom: "Please come in, Joe."

He entered. Yezeletta, an ideograph of seduction, reclined on her octagonal water bed, her head pointing to one of the corners, her black hair fanned out around her, a raven halo in complex arabesques. Her arms, her upper, lie back, delineating her hair, pointing out the two sides of the bed that her head bisects.

Her second pair of arms lie outstretched, palms up in invitation, neatly bisecting the next adjacent sides. Her breasts bisected the bed precisely, like a theorem. Her front legs were spread wide, selecting the lower outer sides of the octagon, her back legs pointing out the two bottom sides. Her body was black and white against the riotous colors of the huge fractal quilt she uses as a bedspread.

A folded-back corner of the quilt across her midsection was the only sign of modesty.

Yezeletta: an erotic mandala, with twinkling gold eyes, and a lusty smile.

She flexed her arms.

"Do you still find me attractive?" she asked, softly.

Joe removed his bath-robe, let it drop. He stepped onto the bed, knelt before Yezeletta and gently let himself down upon her.

She closed her lower arms and front legs around him in a gentle embrace.

That evening lasted far longer than either Joe or Yezeletta had planned and the morning came in many colors, just as they did.

OF THOUGHTS AND SYSTEMS

Later, she was again all business:

"To issue commands to the system of bio-constructs, I've created here, you must be introduced to them."

"Pleased to meet you, Dr. Matrix, I'm Joe," he replied.

"Almost exactly," Yezeletta said, "Doing it through the Matrix Engine is the fastest way: it can broadcast the introduction to all of my creations at once, and then out to the Hives in other places. Otherwise," her gold eyes twinkle, "it would be a tedious process of my making formal introductions to each of these, separately."

"Right. Okay, lead on, Emily Post."

Yezeletta headed towards the Engine's workstation access, stopped, and looked back. Joe stepped up next to her, and gently took her hand.

They entered the Engine together.

In the crowded Matrix Engine, she sat where Joe saw her communicate with the bio-computer on his first day. He looked up briefly at the cell in which he had been incarcerated. It's almost as if she regrets having kept him there. Now the room is used for storage, and the window is covered with a curtain.

"Hold my hands," she said, "I must have your individual characteristics—I can read those through my fingertips—when I interface."

A construct approached. Joe moved an office chair next to her, and she gently took one of his hands, his left, in both of her right hands. The construct placed the root-like interlink around her head.

Yezeletta leaned back and closed her eyes. Her right hands gripped Joe's hand, tightly, gently.

Is this the right thing to do?

—You are handling him fabulous- | Maternal;
    ly!

Did you have to say it *that* way?

—**[Indulgent Chuckle; Argent]** | Light;
    My dear, he *is* the partner
    you've been looking for. Teach
    him and learn from him. Have
    you seen the news?

No.

—Check out the CNN World News | Directive;
    Feed. There was a plague in | Assembly;
    the Australian Outback. It was
    reported just an hour ago.

Took this long to get out?

— Yes. Some whistle-blower sent | Declaratory;
    an anonymous tip to the *Syd-*
    ney Herald.

The vacation's over.

—Yes, my dear, it's over. You | Triumph;
    have an ally not a nanosecond
    too soon.

PRELUDE TO IT

[Load Data Descriptor; Camera Goes With] There is a chill in the climateless void.

THE SUPER-USER

[The System; Set User: ROOT] Yezeletta reaches out with the combined strengths of her own intelligence and the extra capabilities of the Matrix Engine:

```
                    /* Start Program—*/
          /*_________________________________-*/
```

—-She reads from the characteristics of her lover;

—-*She writes* to the fractal *non-space* of the Matrix Engine;

—-*She waits* as the status responses *return* from the far-reaches of *her*

realm;
—-He speaks with my voice;
   Works with my hands;
   Sees with my eyes;
   Represents me in all things.
   Trust him. Obey him as you obey me!
     /*____-*/
      /* END: Not a nanosecond too soon!*/

THE MONITOR

[The Programmer] Yezeletta came out of the n-dimensional space of the Matrix Engine with her accustomed gentle speed. She stood up. "We must get to a news channel."

"Why?"

"From the Engine; there was an input from CNN. I think it's the Project."

She took Joe by the hand gently and led him back to the living room. She tuned in CNN, adjusted the reception, and started one of the recorders with three hands, and grabbed a carved wooden bowl of remotes with a fourth.

She sat with him on the couch, placing her two left arms around him in a cuddle that was almost reflexive.

The announcer faded in: "Fred Wolfstiner on location at Alice Springs. Behind me you see the site of a recently declassified research effort by the Australian Ministry of Scientific Research, a bioengineering project that has gone hideously out of control...."

Behind him on Yezeletta's TV screen, radiation-suited individuals removed what could only be bodies from buildings that are all too familiar. The complex has—

"This Project—the name is 'Sargon,' apparently a military project recently declassified—is a disaster that appears to rival the worst of the industrial accidents of this last century in destructiveness. We don't have a list of the casualties yet, that's being held pending notice of next-of-kin. We *do* know that what happened here involved a tailored disease that has apparently been, and I stress that this is strictly an assumption, *tailored* to become ineffective within a short time. The haz-mat precautions you see behind me are in use by the initial discoverers of the installation, and are considered unnecessary. There appears to be no danger from airborne contamination, what the specialists call 'disease vectors'."

"Damned right!" Yezeletta said, "That infection was designed to plant the Sargon Administration, and *die out*." She looked at Joe, her eyes wide. "I didn't want the ones that were just support to die."

"How did you arrange that?"

"Many small businesses simply shut down for a time in the warm season. It's easier to put everyone on holiday—vacation, here—all at once, rather than sending a few off now and then. The support staff were all sent to the North or East Coasts, so that the Administration could, could—" Her voice trembled slightly.

"Kill you." Joe finished.

"Yes! Wipe out their dirty work!"

"You survived them."

"This is Fred Wolfsteiner for CNN, here at Alice Springs, back to you,

Louise."

She muted CNN's anchorwoman, "I was their—"

Joe gently placed one finger on her lips. "You are nobody's dirty work. You want dirty, we can go back into the bed-room. That's got to be dirty to be fun!"

Yezeletta's expression brightened. "We do have a good time in there, don't we?"

"Indeed." He glanced at the television monitor, it displayed a commercial, without sound. "Looks like we might have some more dirties out of your past to take care of, Partner."

"Not a nanosecond too soon!"

A Quiet Evening at Home

Several hours later, back in the living room, Joe reached a remote out of the wooden bowl. "I don't watch this much, what sort of stuff is there in Milwaukee?"

"I mostly watch the news or the other people here. I haven't looked at the regular programming. What would you like to watch? This sounds positively normal."

"Channel Six has some sorta piano recital. You like piano music?"

"When I can play it. I don't have a piano, here."

"Really." Joe called up Channel Six, where a commercial was ending:

"— Legit or Sleazy, Andy can get it for you Easy! That's Andy's Procurement! Now back to America's Most Unusual Amateurs!"

A man in a tuxedo came out, took a bow, and sat. He cracked his knuckles. His hands were big, but—

"He's no musician," Yezeletta said. "Those aren't what my music teacher called 'piano hands'."

A announcer came on *sotto voce*: "Steve Reynolds is about to play his own composition, *The Rhythm Method for Piano*. He uses the unusual technique of using the piano as a pure percussion instrument."

"The piano *is* a percussion instrument," Joe said, "hammers on strings."

Reynolds finished cracking his knuckles. He made a fist of his right hand and whacked the keyboard, an octave above Middle-C. Yezeletta jumped.

He bashed the keys again with his left. One octave up from the lowest base notes. He played a chord.

"Was that a major chord or a minor?" Joe asked.

"I think it's a Dead Diminished Sixth. Or dying. Where did they get this man?" Yezeletta's left hands had gripped Joe's arm tightly. She let up. "Sorry."

"You play the piano?"

"Very well! They taught me to play to help cause my nervous system to integrate."

"Duets, right?"

"Yes. By myself."

PLONK! **BASH**. PLINK! TINKLE! **CLANK!**

"And," she continued, "it pains me to see a defenseless instrument—" **CRASH!** Plink! *PLUNK!* "—being maltreated like that!"

P_ÖÑQÛÉ!!

"Did you catch the English on that one?"

"Yes." Her fingers curved like claws.

"Would you like a piano?"

"Would I!"

"I take that to be an affirmative." He got up. "Where's the escape hatch in this place? Some of your friends and I need to go hunting."

Yezeletta's face was that of a little girl on her first 'adult' occasion. "Come with me, I'll show you."

Leaving the Farmer's and Merchant's Building reminded Joe of leaving a carnival funhouse, as Yezeletta showed him the complex series of locks, mechanical and otherwise, computer-controlled accesses, and biological intruder verifications that she used to safeguard her living quarters.

The last egress was a small elevator whose stainless steel back panel was a beautiful engraving of a clipper ship under full sail. The elevator went down to the first subbasement, opening out into a small elevator lobby that seemed to be built of stacks of wood and metal cases.

"The boxes are actually dummies," Yezeletta told him. "They're permanently fastened down. One of my reserve hives occupies most of the inside of the casing."

Yezeletta quickly sketched something on a small sheet of paper, "When you get there, place your palm on this." She pointed with her pen at a representation of a cardboard box on the drawing. "This box has a sensor that I had the Hive grow earlier today, so that you could register with it in a hurry."

"Otherwise, it takes a while for the registrations to percolate down there?" he asked.

"Exactly. It would be a matter of perhaps an hour, and I would like to have this one available for you if anything dangerous happens."

"Good idea."

"Joe," Yezeletta said.

"Yes?"

She wrapped all of her arms around him in a hug. She cuddled him there for a moment.

"Joe, please come back."

"Of course." He reached his arms up and rubbed her back, then brought his hands around to her front, winked and said in a deeper voice: "I'll be back."

She kissed him gently. "This is Jurjin." A small furry ball on many legs jumped down off a shelf and curled up on his shoulder.

"Sending a supervisor?"

"Nope, a communicator. Jurjin will be in touch with the Matrix Engine, and with me, if you call for me through it." She skritched the fur-ball with her left hand, her lower. "Think of it as a backup."

"Good, idea. Well, I'm off. 'This Way to the Egress.'"

"See you, Joe."

"Back soon."

The elevator took him swiftly down to the first sub-basement. Yezeletta had explained how she had rewired the cage controls to provide independent service; its travel was unaffected by pressing the call buttons on each floor. The lift was Yezeletta's private access to her penthouse to and from the basement.

The elevator doors slid open at the destination, and the machine stopped. She had programmed it to stay and wait for Joe until he returned. The light spilled out into the darkened basement with warm welcome.

Joe consulted his partner's sketch. The box with the palm-print sensor was—*there*. He placed his hand on it. His palm adhered for the better part of a second, and then was released. Jurjin made a little "chirp" sound, and his big gold imager scanned first Joe, then the rest of the room.

Something was moving in the dark.

The motion resolved itself into a small troop of servitors, all of a uniform dark-gray color. The imagers in their foreheads flickered and an iris closed over each one.

"She put camouflage on those things, eh?" Joe asked no one in particular.

He gestured with one hand, his left, and the humanoids fell into a small platoon three abreast and followed him towards the outside exit.

The exit gave out onto a loading dock that faced a mostly unused back street. Several tire tracks ran down the geometric center of it with a fine disregard for lane divisions.

A closed-bed pickup was parked in a covered alley near the dock. Joe scanned the area around the truck for a moment before approaching it. The area surrounding the vehicle in the alley, almost a carport, looked as messy as other parts of the back streets, but....

He spotted it, but just barely: the mess looked a little too deliberate to be genuine. *Did she send a litter-critter down here to re-arrange the garbage?* He grinned, *Litter-Bugs?* He fished in his pocket for the keys Yezeletta had given him. As if that were a signal, a squad of small creatures, gray as concrete, the color of dirty sidewalks, ran from the truck and scaled the walls.

They vanished out of sight into the cracks in the brick-work. He opened the back of the truck and his diminutive assistants climbed in. One more got into the front with Joe and Jurjin.

The assistant tapped Joe on the shoulder.

The munchkin was holding a pistol in its hand, politely presenting the butt first. Joe took it.

"I must be a full member here," he said. "My very own forty-five, at last." Chuckling, he made sure the safety was on, and slipped the pistol into his coat pocket. Several hexagonally-shaped lifeforms appeared, arrayed themselves around the cab, to stand guard with their red and blue eyes glowing in the dimness.

Joe started the truck and trundled it out of the alley. Jurjin curled up on his shoulder and seemed to go to sleep. He rubbed the critter's velvet fur with one hand, his right, and it snuggled up against his neck.

"Joe to Yezeletta, Comm Check," he said.

Jurjin nestled even closer, if that were possible, "Yezeletta to Joe," her voice came from Jurjin's vocal apparatus, "Comm Check received five by five."

"And she's Madame Five-by-Five," Joe sang.

Yezeletta chuckled.

Joe drove down Wisconsin Avenue for a short time. It had been a while since he had been in Milwaukee. Then it had been to a colloquium at the University of Wisconsin Campus on the city's Northeast side. He had presented a paper there on the least dangerous parts of the Davis Protocols. The city had been as clean as a just post-twentieth-century place could be; now it was filthy and unkempt.

He reached the Milwaukee River. South of this point was the spot that had set off Peter Rudenko. "The Place of no Signs," he muttered. He drove on, slowly, conscious of the construct next to him and of the others in the back of the truck.

He continued west on Wisconsin to Seventh, turned south.

James Lovell Lane, once Seventh Street, looked like an unmade bed. One in which someone very sick had just had an accident.

The only other vehicle on the street was a solitary Yellow Cab, its driver turning down Seventh ahead of Joe in the same general direction. Joe watched it drive into the parking lot of the Badger Bus Company. As he passed Badger, the cab driver jumped out of his car carrying a large package, which he took into the Badger ticket office.

There was no one about on the streets except for a drunken wreck sleeping in a recessed doorway just off the access road. Joe looked at him in momentary fascination, and drove on.

He was in the warehousing, shipping and receiving area of the River. Here, rotting docks mingled with newer concrete loading facilities. There was the smell of decaying wood and other less savory odors in the air. He looked south and west, and saw the three geodesic domes of the Mitchell Conservatory reflecting the wan sunlight. *So that's where Gary the Geek lives*, he thought.

He pushed the thought to the back of his mind. Just ahead was a sign hanging by one corner at a disorderly slant: **LYON-HEALY MUSIC**.

"I think, we're here," he said to the servitor. The creature nodded, sagely, *a programmed response?*

Joe pulled the truck around to the back of the warehouse. He parked it close to one of the loading docks, and he and the lead got out. He placed his hand on the comforting steel of the .45 and went to the door.

It was a large overhead opening garage door. The kind with a regular door built into it that could be opened when the garage door was closed. Joe saw that there was no one near, and reached into his pocket.

What he removed resembled a large, pink wad of very used chewing gum. It felt oddly dry and it pulsed in his hand.

He placed it on the lock.

The pink wad adhered to the front of the lock, and spread out over it, covering the keyhole and most of the rest of the lock cylinder. The center of the pink mass *rotated*, forming something like a screw head.

With a sharp click, it unlocked. Joe pushed the door open and entered followed by his munchkin assistant.

The warehouse was largely empty, but several large masses covered by large plastic sheets stood at the far end of the open space. Their placement and shape suggested large musical instruments.

"Mister Steinway, I presume," Joe muttered. He lifted the covering off of the first object. It was a grand piano. A Baldwin.

Joe and the servitor circulated around the other pianos. They were all large, expensive, bulky, and—Joe tried to move one—*very* heavy.

"Hmmm. Looks like we need some professionals in here."

He went back to the door, removed and pocketed the lock-opener. He looked out. There was no one there, and no one had disturbed the truck. "Let's see if we can open this," he said to the foreman. The little creature stalked off, and pointed to a large push-button on the wall near the still-open auxiliary door.

"Taught you how to sniff those out, huh?" *Were they intelligent?* he didn't say.

He closed the auxiliary, and pressed the button. With a grinding of gears, the door began to rise ponderously. He let go of the button, and the upward motion stopped. This was a hell of a time to have to use a dead-man switch! He pressed the button again, and allowed the door to rise to above the height of the truck. He backed it into the warehouse.

As the nose of the truck cleared the doorway, the door began to descend. Startled, Joe looked back at the control.

The lead servitor had reactivated the door, closing it.

"She's improved on the design, I see," he said.

Yezeletta's voice came from Jurjin's tympanum: "Of course, better pro-gramming. I didn't want you in any kind of danger that I could prevent."

"Thanks. Did I say that you're good?"

She chuckled. "Find anything?"

"Some very large pianos that may not fit into this truck. I've got to meas-ure some of these. I'll get back to you with the info."

"See you, Joe."

Joe extracted a Stanley tape-measure from another pocket, and meas-ured the Baldwin. "Joe to Yezeletta—the Baldwin's too big; continuing."

He paced around all of the other instruments and swore softly. The pickup was a large-bed Chevrolet, with about a one ton capacity. There was a tug on his sleeve. The pianos all weighed less than a ton, and every damned one of them was too big to slide in.

Something was still tugging at his sleeve.

He looked down. The humanoid that was tugging on his coat sleeve was pointing at something in the corner, something *very tall* in the corner. Joe went to the very tall object, pulled off its dust cover.

The object was an upright piano.

An upright *grand* piano.

"My *God*," he said. "Joe to Yezeletta."

"Yes, Joe."

"Ever played an upright?"

"No, I had a Steinway Concert Grand."

"Tilt that on its end and imagine how flipping high it would be."

"A *big* upright!"

"Yup. An upright grand. Biggest damned piano I've ever seen. The others wouldn't fit into the truck because of the legs. They were too high. This one we can lay in there on its back. You want it?"

"Do it!"

"I take that to be an affirmative. Got it, one upright to go. Back soon!"

"O. K, Short-and-Chunky, martial your forces, and load that contraption up!"

The constructs moved with asynchronous coordination. They circled the base of the upright—*That's gotta be at least three-hundred centimeters tall!*—and slowly the huge instrument tilted and came down on its back. The servitors got under it, and carried it towards the back of the truck. Joe was ready with the tail-gate down, and the creatures slid the piano in on a soft quilted pad. Joe caught the manufacturer's name as the keyboard passed him. "Joe to Yezeletta, we have Steinway Acquisition, docking maneuver complete."

The response was a Yezeletta-sized laugh.

"You have a pleasant laugh," he said.

"Thank you, Joe."

One servitor backed in, threw a heavy padded tarp over the piano, the other creatures got in, and clustered around the instrument. It was a tight fit.

"Last one in goes in with a crowbar!" Joe called.

The last one took a running jump into the truck and was caught by several others. Joe slammed the tail-gate.

He started the truck and wheeled it towards the garage door with a series of practiced motions. The supervisor was waiting at the door control, and had it rising even before Joe stopped. When the door was high enough, it released the button, and jumped in next to Joe. Joe accelerated out of the warehouse, and drove out to the Seventh Street access road.

There was no one visible out on the streets: just the same drunken derelict sleeping off last night's Night Train Express. Joe paid him no heed as he drove on.

As the truck turned a corner, the derelict scrambled to his feet. The man removed the ragged overcoat he was wearing, tossed it into a trash can, and walked off in the other direction. There was nothing drunken about his walk, then, at all.

JUST US

The drive back to the Farmers and Merchants Building was uneventful. The streets were, if possible, dirtier than they had been before.

Yezeletta met him in the lower lobby near the freight elevator.

KEYS TO THE CITY

About an hour later, with the Steinway installed in her living area near the video equipment, Yezeletta sat down and ran off a few scales. Four octaves of scales, all at the same time. Her large hands ranged across the big keyboard.

"You handle that thing as if it were a long-lost friend," Joe observed.

"They are—the notes, I mean," Yezeletta answered. "I'm a bit out of practice; I hope you won't mind if things get a bit noisy in here—"

"Nope! Just do me a favor—"

Yezeletta looked around at him.

"Please *don't* play 'The Rhythm Method for Piano'!"

She laughed.

——>>> TWO <<<——

It's all a checker-board of nights and days.

—Omar Khayyam, [49]

SOMEWHERE ACROSS TOWN

"Lyon-Healy, huh?"

The man asking this question was large, well muscled, crew-cut and sat behind a large, heavy desk. He looked as if he had retired from the U.S. Marine Corps. He *had* retired from a military outfit, but it wasn't American. He spoke with a slight accent.

"Yes, Sir," the other man said earnestly. "I waited where the spotter indicated the truck was headed, then watched until they drove away. One male Caucasian, and a bunch of—I think they were pygmies, or something. Midgets. Short men. The truck was that one parked in the cul-de-sac on Second Street."

"Notice anything a little unusual about the truck?"

"I thought that it was in a little too good a repair for something that was just left in that alley. This isn't New York, but even in *Milwaukee* a vehicle that good wouldn't stay un-stripped for longer than a couple days."

"Do you know why it's stayed that safe?"

"No. Sir."

"Nobody can get near it. People who have tried, wake up—"

"Sir?"

"— in other parts of the city, or even out in the suburbs. It seems to *like* to knock people out." He paused, took a deep breath. "Or the thing's *being protected* by something else."

"What?"

"Look here." The man with the slight accent removed a manila folder from his desk. "These are some artist's conceptions of a probable cause of the truck's protection. The artist made his sketches from part rumor and part educated guess." He slid the sketches across his desk to the other man.

"An insect? Looks like a preying mantis."

"We don't know. We don't have any good photographs of this creature. If that's what it is. We don't have any photographs at all. These were made from an oral description: it wasn't a very good one; the individual doing the describing accidentally on purpose *died* during the process. I also stress that what we're looking for may not be here in Milwaukee. Some of the things that gangster Teketon's men have seen make me suspicious, but we have no good evidence, yet. The *Rezident* sent us here to *investigate* that drug dealer. This," he indicated the drawings, "may be an artifact constructed by that Dealer."

He took the sketches, counted them and locked them in his desk.

"By the way, well done."

It was a dismissal; the other stood up. "Thank you. Sir," he said, saluted, and departed.

A truck no one can touch—suddenly being used, he thought. How typical of—what? Lyon-Healy? They sell musical instruments.

Like—pianos.

He repeated that last word aloud. Almost as if he didn't quite believe it.

The Observers on the South Side would have to be informed; then he would have to communicate with The Center, as well.

T HE S HORT O PERATIVE

He was four-foot-nine in the old measurements, or one-hundred-and-forty-four centimeters in the universally accepted Metric System. Within his diminutive framework, he was proportioned appropriately. Unlike some very short men, he was not all torso with very short legs, nor all legs, and not much else.

And he hated his nickname.

That nickname, with the constant evolution of language, had been a reference to a type of personality that tended to turn inwards, and to be interested in machines, typically computers, rather than in more social activities. That was neither the reference, nor the meaning that was applied to Gary. "Geek" originally referred to a carnival sideshow entertainment that was watched, if at all, by spectators who had a sort of queasy interest in a more unfortunate person than themselves.

A geek was always lower on the social spectrum than anyone watching him, and Gary was well aware of the word's use in connection with himself.

That which failed to subdue him, only made him madder.

"And if I catch you fucking up like that again, there'll be several kinds of nuclear hell to pay! Next time, use your brain cell to follow my fucking directions! Hightower's richer than I am because of your incompetence, stupidity, and your bird-brained behavior, generally!"

The object of this tirade was a man who was at least half again taller than Gary. "Mr. Hamilton, I—" was all he could get out.

Gary Hamilton continued, "'Come in through Brookfield,' I said! The Brookfielders CAN NOT STAND Allen Hightower. Any Brookfielder would COMMIT SUICIDE rather than allow The Road Lord access to his precious streets. Now Hightower's got a truck full of my latest product, and WE—meaning YOU—are out big bucks. I have to change my production schedule—again!—to make my delivery to the Chicago Syndicate.

"Do you *like* the idea of being tossed out the one-hundred-thirty-fifth floor of the old Sears Building? That's what they do to turkeys that fail to keep agreements!

"They make such artistic patterns in red on the sidewalk below."

EAST SIDE SOUTH SIDE

[Parallel Process; Medium Close Up] The screens replied with data in colors, lists of figures, spread-sheets of cross-correlations, graphs, charts, and images of places into which the remote sensors attached to the collection of computer-aided data extraction and reduction devices were connected.

The systems lined a wall of the bedroom which had been empty when the deliberately anonymous men had first moved into it. Black curtains covered the windows; the only illumination within was monitor-light. The two men who had initially claimed the place were sitting at work-stations with multiple screens, while other lower-ranking subordinates came and went with cups of coffee, sandwiches or other items.

Off in another room, the insistent warbling of the electronic ringer on the one land line they had, started. A subordinate went to take the call.

ANOTHER KIND OF KEYBOARD

[Start Output] She ran scales up and down the keyboard. Each of her hands chased another as the scales rippled out of the huge instrument. Then, her forces martialled, she lit out after *Eine Kleine Nacht Music*. Joe looked on impressed as Yezeletta's practiced hands swarmed over the keys, each finger seeming to know exactly where it should go and *when*.

Without stopping, she galloped through "The Stars and Stripes Forever" by way of "Dixie," "Waltzing Matilda" and "The Battle Hymn of the Republic." Then she paused, took a deep and impressive breath, and gently laid out the "Moonlight Sonata."

She stood up when she was done, and stretched out her arms, reaching for the high ceiling and almost touching both walls, or, at least giving a good impression of doing so.

She turned to Joe and enveloped him in a major four-armed hug.

"Joe, you did good!"

"*WE* did good, lady," Joe said. "Your playing's incredible!"

"It feels good to have music in here," she replied, "music that I can create. Those experimenters back at the Project didn't have the slightest idea how much fun I had playing the Steinway. To them it was just another piece of test equipment!"

"No class. No class at all!"

ANALYTICAL SYSTEM: TEMPEST

[I/O: Routine] One of the watchers was approached by an eager junior agent-in-training. Junior was carrying the instrument, an actual land-line, its wires trailing behind him, the handset in his other hand. "It's for you," Junior said. The senior agent took the handset, said "Hello?" and listened.

A voice spoke to him: a Slavic accent. The watcher recognized the *Rezident* who kept himself removed from the Southeast side brownstone. He listened, answered "Yes Sir," and hung up.

His partner looked a question at him.

"Something else. We're to keep monitoring the Conservatory, but we are to watch for any other kinds of life —"

"Life," his partner said. *"Life?"*

"Yes, life, that's what the *Rezident* said, life," he repeated unnecessarily. "Other kinds besides Mr. Hamilton's. There is a chance that others in the area may be experimenting along the lines of Mr. Hamilton in similar directions." He gestured at one of the screens, a long-shot of the Domes. "Hamilton's biologicals require a lot of processor-intensive numerical-analytical work for his molecular synthesis. His systems are imperfectly shielded, at best, and not protected at all at worst. Our *Tempest* detection and extraction has been tracing—" he gestured at a screen on which three columns of labels, instructions and operands were scrolling upwards and off the top at a high rate, "— if we can reverse-engineer this code from the dis-assembler back to the compiler-level source, or just 'acquire' his source-code, we will have everything we need of his synthesis protocols."

He paused, lost for a moment in thought. "There may even be another data source we can take with us, as well."

LEXICAL AT A DISTANCE

[Input/Output] A motion caught his eye. The man turned from his co-worker, and used a joy-stick to aim a closed circuit camera at the movement he had seen in the monitor. The image jittered as it zoomed in, then the jittering stopped as the steady-cam visual input processor activated. There was something on a tree branch several blocks away that had been moving in a manner that was hardly typical of wildlife. "There," he said. "That's where I saw it."

He touched a control, and the image widened, parts of its outer area falling off the edges of the screen.

"That's it," he said, "There."

"What is it?" his partner asked.

He started a recorder. The small round animal had more than four legs and certainly more than six. It seemed to be scanning the surroundings in an almost random manner. That was, at least, what its body motions suggested.

Then it looked straight back at them. A gold speck appeared on the creature. It flickered, then vanished, as the creature turned.

"Life," he said decisively. "Keep this." His partner nodded.

TEST RUN—I

[System Running] *He walked of his own will to the door indicated. He had been told of what would be waiting behind the door, but he walked a measured pace for all that.*

The same pace, unknowingly, as that of his Mentor, his counsellor.

He took the door-knob in his right hand. He looked down at the hand on the metal object. He scratched behind his right ear with his other hand.

His other right hand.

He opened the door.

SOUTHWESTERN MEMORIES

Later, Yezeletta joined Joe in her hot tub. She let the warmth drain the problems of dealing with Milwaukee out of her.

"How did you get here from the South Pacific?" Joe had asked her, as they were getting undressed, "and how did you avoid any of the other shipping out of places like New Guinea when you left Darwin?"

"I made sure that the ship was off of the Sat/Nav, and GPS Networks, at least as far as outside detection went, and stayed as far away as I could program things from both New Guinea and the northern coast of Australia. The *Hat Dancer* had full fuel bunkers—'tanks' to a landlubber—, and I ran full-speed-ahead for the open Pacific. It was close to the course that the Captain of the *Dancer* had originally laid out, but a faster run, and definitely not to the *Dancer's* next port of call. Needless to say I maintained radio-silence.

"It must have seemed as if the ship had disappeared right off the map. Getting from Long Beach to here was another set of difficulties, entirely.

"I used a lot of gas, several thousand dollars, a lot of industrial-strength chutzpah and a leavening of subterfuge—"

DETERMINANTS CONCEALED

[Parallel Process] *The images shift again, to yet another permutation of related scenes. A city skyline appears, the darkening sky behind it slightly red with the terminated process of day, and the promise of another.*

The lights come on in the tall buildings, as the azure sky darkens stepwise to cerulean blue to deep violet to a sable substrate upon which the argent bright eyes of the eternal stars look down.

The great city's warm luminous buildings take on a life of their own, the screens rotating, and repositioning themselves so that this image is cen-

tered among the remaining; first among equals.

   The living spaces in the glowing streets of the city, data paths in a living process, lead among the dwellings in populous places, to nodes of light in dark spaces.

   Then the image fades, and the black barrier closes it off.

——>>> **THREE** <<<——

> The computer has no judgement whatsoever. It is the absolute, ultimate non-biased learner. It will learn and believe anything ...but it will forget absolutely nothing....[I]t does precisely and solely what it must, by the way it's built, do....[I]t is always willing to learn and believe and work. It can't be lazy; it can't be tired, it can be stupid only if the men made it stupid—and then they must correct that.

—John W. Campbell, 1953 [2]

UP THE LINE—II

[System Running | Somewhere in Nevada] The trucks laid out the kilometers behind them, as Yezeletta's little convoy headed north. California was well behind them; they were now in Nevada, northbound on a big highway towards Montana.

The *Dancer* had made port quite early in the morning at Long Beach. Yezeletta had expected Long Beach to be a busy harbor. She was surprised to find it all but deserted. A small band of exactly six stevedores had boarded the *Dancer* at her request to run the cranes, and had left with thick envelopes of cash, and chunks removed from their memories. The six lorries, *trucks*, she reminded herself, *we're in the United States, now* had been loaded up while the ship was two days out, and now stood in line on a ratty-looking dock, surrounded by rusting machinery and boarded-up buildings. *Has the United States fallen this far?*

She recalled some news she'd heard at the Project, two years earlier: a man named Jasper Berkins had been appointed to the US House Science Committee. Describing this man as "ignorant" was an understatement. The damage that he did to basic research in America was seconded only by a more notorious senator from Wisconsin in the last quarter of the last century. William Proxmire had presented "Golden Fleece" awards to developments that *in his opinion* were a waste of time or money. His obstruction of scientific advances could be worked around by enough people determined to do so.

Berkins, ever the permanent obstruction, simply sat on the necessary appropriations, causing researchers to squander their limited financial resources on legal action to force him to release what he never should have denied in the first place.

Yezeletta surveyed the rust and decay in what had once been one of the biggest harbors on the West Coast, and touched the servitor on its head.

Her convoy rolled out.

ROLLING

Highway 10 took them east to Interstate 15, which went northwest into

---

[2] The John W Campbell Letters, Page 153 [AC Projects, Inc, 1985]

Nevada. At the junction with Highway-164, she noticed a distance marker to the Nevada town of Searchlight. It was worth one raised eyebrow, but not much more than that. Her convoy rolled around Las Vegas, past the ruins of Nellis Air Force Base, across the Virgin River at the north end of Lake Mead, briefly into Arizona past Littlefield, and into Utah.

In Utah, just outside of Cedar City, Yezeletta stopped her travels, and pulled into a miserable-looking rest-stop. She looked out with distaste at the litter and the run-down look, generally, of the place as she planned her next activity. The large truck was running out of gas, and she needed to fill up in as discreet a fashion as possible. Money was no particular problem, as the Purser's safe aboard the *Dancer* had contained a rather large amount of currency from various countries, including the States. It was just the matter of getting the necessary fill-ups that she had to contend with.

It's not exactly as if I can just drive in, wave with both of my left hands and say "Fill her up!" Some finesse was needed.

That night a large truck pulled into Bob and Alice's Shell station north of Cedar City. Yezeletta had selected this station because it appeared to be a family operation, and it was some distance from the highway. As the truck pulled in she put on her mirrorshades, and placed her lower arms inside the trenchcoat. A middle-aged man in oily coveralls strode up to the truck.

"May I help you?"

Yezeletta leaned her elbow over the lip of the window, and said politely, "Can you supply pet—," she caught herself, "gas for six trucks?"

"Sure can, Ma'am, just have them drive in here, and I'll take care of them personal."

Yezeletta nodded, and a fuzzy critter ran down her arm, and launched itself at the man's face. She reached out with her left arm, her upper, and held him until his movements stopped.

"Don't move," she said softly. "I won't hurt you, and you will be paid for the gas."

She tapped on the door to the sleeping compartment, and the normal driving servitor stuck its arm out, then its head. Yezeletta placed her upper right hand on the servitor's head, and sent it several orders, while she watched the attendant. The creature slid out of the sleeper compartment, and sat in the passenger seat. It leaned out the right window, and made a gesture. Within minutes, the other five trucks were lined up.

Yezeletta checked the screen images on her laptop from the imagers she had sent into the gas station's small office. This attendant, presumably Bob, was the only one on duty. Perhaps Alice wouldn't show up until morning.

The lights went out.

Yezeletta checked the laptop screen. The servitor she had sent into the office had found the light switches. This would be a lot easier in the dark.

THE MECHANICS OF IT

On a shelf in a back room at Bob and Alice's Gas, an old video tape deck quietly recorded the inputs from a single television camera mounted in the office, placed so that it could look through the front door into the service area. When the servitor went to shut off the lights, it had fumbled with the circuit breakers, and switched off one extra in its Yezeletta enforced rush. This was the circuit on which, among other things, the security camera and the gas station's alarm system were placed.

The obsolescent video recorder stopped recording; the telephone answering machine and the alarm system switched to their battery backups. The alarm processor thought about this for several milliseconds, and made a discrete call on the gas station's second business line to the Cedar City Police Department. There, the desk sergeant picked up Line Two and listened to Pre-recorded Message Number Four from Bob describing the power outage. The sergeant made a notation in her log-book, took another bite out of her doughnut, and went back to the crossword puzzle she'd been working on.

THE FIXER

While several servitors carried Bob to the office, and stood guard over him, Yezeletta's other minions drove the trucks in, and filled them. Then every gas tank available was filled, followed by several synthetic rubber bladders, large portable tanks, that she had removed from the *Dancer* against just this contingency. She checked all of the totals, and went back to the office.

A servitor was toweling down the desks when she entered. Bob was snoring peacefully in an antique swivel chair in the corner. Yezeletta took the envelope of bills, held it up so the servitor could see it, and placed it on the desk. She stopped to check Bob's respiration, turned to leave.

The telephone rang.

She spun around, and dropped into a guard stance, then relaxed. The phone rang, rang again.

Then it stopped, and a voice started: "Hi there: you've reached Bob and Alice's Shell Station on Highway 15 just north of Cedar City. When you hear the beep, please leave your message <*beep!*>."

There was a pause, then a woman's voice: "Bob, you—uh, must be out with a customer—this is Alice, I'm coming south on Fifteen, and I'll be bringing dinner. Double cheese and sausage. Be there in five. Love you." <*click!*>.

Yezeletta placed her hand on the servitor's head, and sent urgent instructions. The creature wiped the bills, placed them on the desk, and headed for the truck. Several imagers dropped down on her for the ride as she ran back to the eighteen-wheeler, *just lucky I was in there, when that call came in!* She looked back as the other servitors were getting into their vehicles. She looked around the service area, and there was one more imager running across the ground.

Headlights were coming up the road.

Yezeletta opened her door and the arachnoid leapt up onto her lap. She squeezed the arm of the driving servitor, and the truck lurched forward. Then she was out on the road, again, and the other trucks pulled out after her. The driving servitor accelerated to the maximum speed of one-hundred kilometers per hour, *make that sixty miles per!*

A brown Chevy station wagon sped by on the opposite lane, its left turn-signal flashing. Yezeletta touched the servitor's head. The truck's speed increased.

That was just a little too much! The thousand US dollars she had left behind was more than the cost of the gas, and would, she hoped!, buy a little silence from Bob as well. The "Obliviators" had worked again, as well as they had on the *Dancer*, but Yezeletta was not happy with taking memories. Part of that was the problem she had with tampering with minds, *is that why they were willing to dispose of me?*, but also that any competent physician, *even one under-funded by the House Science Committee*, could find the evidence of her memory tampering, if he knew where to look, and looked soon enough.

She had no knowledge of how Alice would handle Bob "sleeping" in the office. She touched the servitor again.

Best to put some more of those miles between them.

THE VIDEO STAR

The brown station wagon tooled into the gas station, and Alice got out. She looked around rather warily. *The lights shouldn't be out like that!* She reached into the back of her car, and removed a .38 caliber pistol, verified that it was loaded, and went in.

Bob was—asleep.

Alice shook him, thinking the worst, but he awoke with a little start, and looked up at his wife. "Hi, Hon, what happened? I...."

"Are you okay?" she asked.

"Fine, just—" he got up, yawned and stretched, "— sleepy!"

"The lights are off," Alice said decisively. She put down the pistol, gestured.

"Huh? What?"

"Bob," Alice asked gently, "What happened?"

"Don't know. Earlier I was outside. A trucker was driving in. Then...you're here."

He looked out the front window. The driveway and service areas were empty. Bob stood, went to the breaker box, and flipped switches. The outside lights came on brightly. Then the alarm system stated in a polite voice, "power resumed, securing from battery backup."

That was odd enough. For now.

Later, Bob and Alice would look at their security tape.

The phone started ringing.

THE CARDINAL OF THE COMPASS

The trip around Salt Lake City had been a little tricky. The convoy was at its best on open roads with as little traffic as possible. Yezeletta had kept the procession well under the speed limit to avoid Utah Highway Patrol Officers with overactive imaginations. She didn't breathe easier until the caravan of Mack Trucks had crossed into Idaho.

She was the happiest when her procession entered Montana.

ROCK RIVER CROSSING

Yezeletta's little convoy made good time through Montana as that state didn't have speed limits on its highways, at least not during daylight hours. The population had always been small in Montana; only in the last ten years had it come even close to one million.

Yezeletta's maps indicated a change from Highway-15 to Interstate-90. This was the road she would stay on until her destination. Montana had a lot of empty space; so did North Dakota; even parts of Minnesota. Yezeletta needed a city. Not just any city, but one with access to various kinds of travel. She particularly wanted access to water by boat, should another escape be necessary (later she would realize that there were some sizeable logistical blunders in that assumption), and the only city on Interstate-90 that had water access was a big one on Lake Michigan.

Milwaukee.

MESSAGES

While Yezeletta was getting her convoy out of the area, Bob and Alice were occupied with another mystery. The ringing phone had been a concerned policewoman, the desk sergeant, from Cedar City calling back about the alarm message: were there any problems?

Bob convinced the cop that there weren't, and looked long and hard at the small pile of bills sitting on his desk. A thousand in cash was almost at the "contraband" level, and might activate an attempt by what was left of the Federal Government to enforce futile laws regarding "money laundering." The cash would have to disappear.

"Here, Bob," Alice handed him a black rectangular object.

The object was a VHS videotape. Alice took the remote control, Bob cued up the tape, and she pressed "PLAY." "Hon, what is this?"

"It's the security tape from the time you were out cold in here."

The tape wound its way through several boring scenes of literally nothing. The only thing that moved was the date/time stamp in one corner. Occasionally, Bob was visible in the front service area, once emptying a trash can, another time changing a light in one of the gas islands, then sweeping up out in front of the door.

"This is as about as exciting as a paint drying race," Alice said. She skipped ahead, the time-stamp in the corner moving faster.

"Honey, take the 'way-back machine' up to about two hours ago. That's when the truck I saw was coming in."

Alice used the visual search setting to bring the tape up to the desired point, and pressed play.

For about fifteen minutes nothing happened, enough time for Bob to get two cans of raspberry pop from the cooler in the garage. He opened one for Alice, and sat back with his.

"There," he said, "That's the truck—I think."

The television showed a truck pulling into the station. It was a singularly generic-looking eighteen-wheeler, bereft of markings. Its position in the service area precluded seeing the license plate. There were two people in the tractor.

Bob's image strode up to the driver's side, unfortunately on the opposite side of the truck, and they could see his image talking to the driver.

Then his image vanished.

Something got out of the truck.

It was coming towards the office.

Bob looked up at the actual place outside where the image was walking *on the screen*. He half expected to see the same...thing approaching him.

Whatever it was, it resolved itself into something on the screen *that was not human.*

Alice's grip on his arm got tighter. The...creature was dark brown or black, had large green eyes in bony sockets, *"orbits,"* he thought, no nose, a lipless mouth, and...something gold on its forehead and a crest of thin skin and curved bones. It walked into the office, disappeared off the bottom of the image as it walked *under* the camera, and—

The image went out. It was replaced by the granular playback of unrecorded tape.

Alice reached for her pistol, Bob removed another thirty-eight from the desk.

They looked at each other.

"Was that...an alien?" Alice asked.

EASTWARDS AND UPWARDS

Yezeletta's convoy proceeded East on Interstate-90. The weather was cold—there was Winter in the air, and she wanted to have a base before Spring—and the days were clear and pleasant, the nights equally clear.

Once she looked up at the Moon, and had to look *south* to see it.

All of the constellations looked upside down to her Southern Hemispherical viewpoint, except...Orion looked normal.

The constellation didn't—at least—seem to be inverted, the way all of the others were. A casual look didn't register *that's backwards* to her.

Curious.

Why is that one pattern showing up as "normal" in a night sky in which all of the other patterns are <u>inverted</u>?

She placed that thought on hold, and made a mental note, with her capabilities it wouldn't be forgotten, to research this later.

Now, she had something else to check.

Her roadmap indicated a series of rest stops ahead, and she wanted to use one. Her servitors had been designed with a lot of basic stamina, but they were living creatures, and needed a rest. The pseudo-wombs in which she grew them could not be set up again until she had a base of operations. That, however, was only part of it.

She was looking for a rest stop, if one existed, that would not be visible from the road. What she wanted to do there might be a little too interesting to various members of whatever law enforcement community Montana had. *I haven't seen a single highway patrol officer; do they have them? They must.*

A sign:

Rest Stop—Telephone—15 Miles

What the hell is that in kilometers? Twenty-five?

Yezeletta ran a conversion, and kept an eye on the right side of the road, adjusting the sensitivity and contrast perception of that eye for optimized night vision. Twenty minutes later, another sign came into view: **Rest Stop**.

And best of all, the access was by way of a small feeder road up into the hills.

The rest area had been constructed in a natural clearing about two-thirds of a mile (*a kilometer, dammit!*) away from the road. The area precluded having to clear a large area by slicing *into* the hills closer to the highway. As the trucks drove in, a small squad of humanoids bailed out of the last one. They carried picks and shovels, and had specific instructions.

Yezeletta, in the lead truck, scanned ahead intently, her right eye's band-width adjusted for false-color infrared perception.

The area was deserted. The only infra-red signatures extent were some very old tracks as of a large vehicle heading towards the exit.

ON THE SHORE

The longboat was unstable in the surf near the beach. Several of the passengers—those who still had the energy—leapt out of the boat, and pulled it closer to the shore.

Once the boat was stable, the others disembarked. One by one they made their way onto relatively dry land. Marina looked back at the two who were left. One, she hadn't wanted to see again, ever, and the other was a surprise.

Charlie, quiet, subdued, was the first. With shaky motions, he swung one leg over the gunwales of the boat, and stepped onto the beach. He was followed by the other.

The other had been literally drawn out of the ocean, up from the sea. He had recuperated somewhat, but Charlie stood by to help.

Benjamin Allen Morrison walked up from the ocean, guided by his right-hand man.

CHECK-OUT

Yezeletta's trucks pulled into the parking area. As was the case in most rest stops, there were two parking lots: a small lot dedicated to more normal-sized cars, closer to the highway, and a larger area for trucks, towards the back. This latter suited Yezeletta just fine: the truck area was behind an earthenware berm that was apparently used to prevent erosion.

There were telephones in the back lot.

Again, this was just fine. Behind the back lot, a steep hill ascended about fifty meters, and was covered by underbrush thick enough that nothing but small critters could get through it.

Her squad of servitors came up the way the trucks had with their picks and shovels. Her instructions to them had been explicit. All traces of an entry, including the access signs, were removed, and the entry barricaded with fallen trees, and several road signs that said "under construction."

The first thing she did when the big Mack rolled to a stop was to send a cat-arachnid up to the power line with an insulated pair of wire clippers. The creature handled the tool clumsily and it took several minutes to perform the action, but the lights in the telephone booths went out when the cat-arachnid finally cut one side of the power cable.

She caught it as it jumped down from the top of the booth, and the clippers, in separate hands, and walked around to the back of the installation.

The telephone line came in *here*, and was enclosed in a flexible steel-sheathed conduit. This could be easily disconnected by any one of a number of tools she had with her. She took a large pair of clippers, practically a small bolt cutter, in her two left hands, and applied them. The "snap" of the sheathed cable parting was loud in the cold night. Yezeletta reached into a small container held by a helpful servitor, and removed something wrapped in cloth. She opened a corner of the cloth, and something green and moving, with the furry fronds of a fern, *reached* out. She introduced the fronds to the end of the cable, and the green tendrils tugged the cable into the cloth wrapper. She reached up to the roof of the phone booth, and placed the growth in a corner of the booth, and secured it in place with several pieces of gray duct tape.

Yezeletta didn't like leaving her creations behind her when she moved on. As she had said to Benjamin Allen Morrison, she didn't want to leave traces. She hadn't been very explicit in her reasoning to Allen, but lately she had wondered if there were microscopic inclusions in her creations that she didn't know about. There were things called "taggants" that were used in the fabrication of common explosives—they looked like microscopic multi-layered paint chips—that could be used later to track those explosives back to their manufacturer if they were used in an illegitimate fashion.

Were there similar taggants in her creations? Or in *herself*?

Were they smart enough to plan that far ahead?

The piece of vegetation in the cloth container was a gamble. It had no awareness by itself: not even the pre-programming of her servitors. It was a relay, a grown device that would send signals to another vegetative chunk several hundreds of meters away, which, in turn, would send those signals out onto Yezeletta's systems. She could operate this relay from a distance, and, if the telephone company decided to send someone out to the booth to investigate, those investigators would seize what amounted to a wet head of lettuce with a telephone line stuck into it.

The relay would go dead; the watching, listening chunk high in a nearby tree would send a diagnostic signal describing what had happened, and Yezeletta would be out of there.

One disadvantage: she couldn't have an imager on it. Those gold apertures were just too obvious and far too easily traced back to Project Sargon, *or what's left of it.*

She placed her right hand, her lower, on the head of the servitor nearest her, and issued a directive. The servitor ran off after several more, repeated Yezeletta's gesture, relaying the instructions. In about ten minutes time, the fleet of trucks had been moved to a location closest to the exit from the truck parking lot. She issued several more directives, and the crew of servitors removed themselves to the warmth and safety of the trucks. A swarm of cat-arachnids went out foraging for whatever game existed in Darkest Montana.

It wouldn't be much, as cuisine went, but it would keep body and mind together. Banquets would come later.

TRUCKING

Towards the early morning, her creations fed, rested and ready, Yezeletta telegraphed her wishes, and the trucks lined up. Her crew had refueled them from the fuel bladders and stowed the empties. The convoy was ready to move out. Yezeletta's lead truck pulled out on to the Highway-90 access road, and she looked back along the way she had come. The road was empty. She looked up at an imager that was positioned between her and the driving servitor, and gave the imager a thumbs-up. Hilda in the olive-drab carrier had asked her for outside access. There was no further need to hide Hilda from the world, and the input was welcome. The imager, under control from within the eighteen-wheeler, winked back. Yezeletta checked her road-map. The next rest stop was a little more than one-hundred of those damned *miles* east.

No problem.

She squeezed the arm of the driver, touched its head in confirmation, and her convoy pulled onto the highway and moved out.

PROCESSING SCANS

Yezeletta's convoy pulled into the next rest-stop late the following afternoon.

Leaves drifted across the parking area chased by a fine powder of snow. The gray clouds were low in the sky, and the area looked as unkempt as any of the other public access places in the States.

They can barely keep the things going that should be going!, she thought. Ahead a fifty-five gallon oil drum, converted to a trash can, rolled across the lot and fetched up against the curb. She touched the servitor, and the line of trucks pulled up near the exit.

She spent minutes scanning the area. Several imagers had climbed onto the roof of her truck, and arranged themselves so that they looked outwards in a series of overlaps to provide a 360-degree field. Yezeletta looked, and looked, directing her remotes to zoom in on anything that aroused her interest. Then she repeated the entire scan again, in various frequencies of infrared.

Montana is a big state with a relatively small population, and Yezeletta wanted that population as far from her as possible.

This rest stop was similar to the last. The truck area was a concrete apron emplaced in an artificial flat area gouged out of the sloping hills through which Highway-90 ran. That helped in that direction.

Movement in one screen indicated the return of the small band of servitors who had closed up the entry into the area. This time the task had been easier. Whoever was in charge of maintaining these rest-stops hadn't been here in a long time. The lights were out above the rest room doors, only one fluorescent light glimmered fitfully by the telephones, and there was litter everywhere.

Another image built up in another screen: it was the inside of one of the rest rooms. Both facilities were uniformly filthy. Yezeletta shook her head; *I'm getting tired of wanting to be upwind of myself!*

POSITIVE FEED-BACK

Later that night, Yezeletta contacted the head of lettuce at the previous rest-stop, and activated it.

The dial-tone from the distant telephone sounded tinny coming from the small speaker in her laptop.

She pressed a key, and the computer's modem emitted a sequence of tones. The Searchlight Data Centre was accessible by a toll-free number. This was the other reason—actually the main reason—why she was redirecting her access through a biological transmitter: toll-free numbers used the phone company's own ANI—Automatic Number Identification—which couldn't be defeated, unlike the more pedestrian and better known caller identification. The number of the distant payphone would become a part of the incoming call record for Searchlight's toll-free number, and would either be delivered with their monthly bill, or be accessible from the proper server to a systems administrator at Searchlight. Yezeletta wasn't too interested in meeting the SysAdmin.

The normal UNIX "login:" prompt appeared, and she entered one of the login names she had obtained from Anthony Russell. The "Password:" prompt appeared.

Yezeletta typed in the password associated with that name.

Authentication failure

That was the standard UNIX diagnostic for a login name that was no longer valid, or for a bad password.

She typed in the next login and password.

The connection paused, and then displayed—

Searchlight Accessed

At least it didn't say "the Searchlight is on. She studied the prompt and thought. Then she typed "help*." This thing is as unresponsive as Russell's answers.*

A character-based box appeared in the center of her screen. Within it was a menu of selections. Yezeletta verified that the "copy to disk" option in her terminal emulator was on, and selected "help" from the menu.

The help screen was well organized, and designed to stop at the end of each screenful of text so the logged-on user could read it. As each screen was displayed, her laptop wrote the text to the terminal emulator's session log file. Whatever happened, Yezeletta would have a copy of the session for later analysis.

She turned to the servitor sitting in the driver's seat, touched its head with her left hand, her upper. She input a status from the creature that was displayed in a horizontal window in her left eye.

She checked the status. The convoy had eaten, *If you can call the wild game we've captured "food"*, and was ready to pull out, if that were necessary. She sent a set of instructions that would effectively put the drivers to sleep on an "instant recall" basis. It would take them about ten seconds to get from "sound asleep" to "ready." She looked at the data scrolling up the screen on the laptop, and wondered how long she'd have here.

Another window opened in her left eye.

Is that Mr. Russell's outfit? appeared in the new window.

Yezeletta opened the "reply" component to the same window with a quick thought <u>there</u>, and mentally dictated a reply: *Yes. It's their Agency Data Centre. I want to see what's in it.*

The reply came back instantly: *Please hook me into the circuit. I'd like to follow along. I might be able to help.*

Yezeletta reached up with her left hand, her upper, and touched the imager that was Hilda's eyes into the truck cab. Another imager appeared next to the first, through the access to the trailer, and the first jumped down to Yezeletta's left shoulder, where it snuggled up to her neck.

BACKUP/RESTORE

[Breakpoint/Restart]   When Yezeletta had been much smaller she had looked up, all of the way up, at the imposing gray-haired figure of Hilda Henderson. She of all of the Big People in the Project had a smile, and a good word for the youthful Yezeletta. At times, to all of the others, Yezeletta Zargkonji was, was....

She wasn't sure, exactly.

It was sometimes like the way one of the secretaries treated her new kitten. She had brought the kitten in to show Yezeletta, and had treated it in the typical way of all cat-lovers. Kitty could do what Kitty damned well wanted to do, but...Watch It, Mr. Fur-Face!

There were things that Yezeletta could do as well or better than anyone. The huge musical instrument called a "Steinway" was a device on which she could make music that no one else at the project could. Her extra hands helped.

But when her audiences went away, they were gone. It was like when the kitten had been taken home again (she didn't see it until it had grown up to be a Cat). It was like when her teachers would load a new teaching text into her classroom computer from a CD-ROM.

Then put the CD-ROM back on a shelf in a cabinet.

And close the cabinet.

She understood CD-ROMS. Even as a youngster, she had a small library of them, given her by distant gray-suited men from the Project—Directors, they were called. (She didn't find out until much later that they were not real Directors, but only Deputies or Assistants.)

And she was always required to say "Thank you, Mr. Director" to these distant gray men when they gave her what they called "birthday presents." Her birthday was the Twenty-Ninth of February. She did not understand the significance of the date until much later, nor did she ever know if that, indeed, was the day on which she had been born.

Hilda was different. Hilda gave her small things (that she asked Yezeletta not to tell the others about), and those presents had no return obligations placed on them.

Just as Hilda's friendship had no obligations attached to it in any way.

It would not be until later that Yezeletta would understand her real place in the project. Then, with her eidetic memory, enhanced by microprocessor technology, always with her, and available for extensive analysis, she would find her place.

Not the place she thought she had, not the place her creators had planned for her, but the place she discovered.

And took for herself.

JUST READ THE DATA

The scrolling text stopped.

The screen flickered.

Yezeletta blinked at the display. The new image was so familiar that she thought she was reading the status of one of her onboard systems.

The screen had divided in two, and she was looking at an operator message in the lower half.

It said:

Identify Yourself.

That was pretty straightforward.

She typed in:

Anthony Russell.

Later, she would realize that was probably the *worst* answer she could have given. She had no idea what had happened to Russell's comatose body after Charlie had left it near the Darwin Maritime Museum.

The distant operator replied:

Where are you?

Yezeletta typed:

Darwin.

Another reply:

Initiating Trace.

Verify.

State Oldest Brother's Name.

Interesting. The operator at the distant UNIX system wanted to know if this was really Russell by asking a question that only Russell would know.

The top of the screen displayed: **Downloading**.

Downloading what? Something large was showing up on the hard-drive of this laptop.

Yezeletta started typing rapidly. If the "something" was executable code, the firewall software in the laptop would prevent it from running. No matter what it was, however, she could effectively put it in a jail-cell and look at it at her leisure.

Another message appeared below.

WHO ARE YOU?

Above that appeared: Intrusion Detected—Losing Relay Integrity.

That was a canned message from the biologic relay at the *other* rest stop, she recognized the format. Yezeletta pressed a combination of keys, and held them down. The action they triggered would not occur until she released them.

The download ended, she let go.

And nothing happened.

Her firewall had held. Whatever defensive or offensive program Searchlight had tried to foist onto her laptop (*and*, she reminded herself, *it could be a communications utility, but I don't think so!*) was safe in a file: a *non-executable* file that she could check out later. Unfortunately her linkup was gone. When she'd released the key-combination, the Destruct Command had been sent to the biologic link on the top of the distant phone-booth, as well as to the relay placed in the tree a hundred meters from it. The destruction would be accomplished by a complex of enzymes that would reduce the structures of the organisms to a liquid within minutes, and, over the next hours, break down all of the complex molecules into their constituent elements: including a certain incriminating double-helix.

Russell's logons were being watched. That meant—

His body had been found. Either alive or dead, it didn't matter, the specialists at Searchlight would be analyzing what had happened to him.

Had this call been traced? If so, it would dead-end at a rest stop a hundred kilo—dammit, *miles!*—west of here.

She touched the driving servitor. Instructions flowed out of her fingers, and were broadcast to the others.

A minute later the trucks were starting up, and moving towards the exit.

On the way out, Yezeletta broadcast another set of directives to the sub-systems in the trailer.

Several Obliviators joined her in the cab.

THE ISLAND PEOPLE

[Accessing] Benjamin Allen Morrison and Charlie had walked for a short time away from the small encampment which they and the others of the July Seventeenth Brigade had set up, soon after pulling ashore on the island.

Marina had attempted a "shoot" with her sextant and book of antique navigation tables, and had located them, as she put it, "either just south of Akron, Ohio, or somewhere about twenty kilometers north of Darwin."

Al wasn't exactly happy at hearing that.

His devastation at being off-loaded by what he thought of as his Big Discovery was nearly complete, and the others of the Brigade had been distantly polite to him, condescending.

Sympathetic. That was the part he hated.

He needed a moment to relax, and to take stock of things.

Up ahead there seemed to be a clearing.

Charlie said nothing, a minor miracle in and of itself. He paced stolidly after his friend, as Al climbed the gentle incline up to the clearing.

There was no real evidence of inhabitation within the clearing, just several trees that had been chopped down and looked as if they had been there for a long time.

The scene was pastoral, idyllic, even.

Al sat down heavily on one of the fallen trees. Charlie slumped in the sand a meter or so away.

"Well, Charlie, how do you think we should take it from here?" Al asked.

"Huh?" was Charlie's rejoinder. "Al, you've been dumped in the ocean by your big hope. How should you take it?"

Al studied his friend. "We could go back to 'Frisco, I suppose, and make like this never happened."

"You could always write your memoirs," Charlie retorted.

"Yeah, right! The Memoirs of an Ex Fearless Leader by One Klutz Who Lived Through It. Get real, Charlie!"

"What are you gonna do?"

"Try to pick things up. Maybe concentrate on local stuff. New members."

Because the old ones are too embarrassing for you, Charlie didn't say. "Sounds like a plan," he did say.

"Where will you go?" Al asked.

"Maybe back East," Charlie answered. "There's an old girlfriend I'd like to look up, back in the Midwest."

How lucky for her, Al thought. "Stick around for a while?"

"Sure, Al."

A loud report came from the opposite side of the clearing, and, as they watched, a young woman ran out from the wooded area opposite Al and Charlie, running straight for them.

Two more men, wearing what looked like uniforms, followed her, shooting handguns.

Al and Charlie jumped around to the backside of the log, and drew their own weapons. Al took careful aim, and shot.

His shot missed, but, to his right, an exasperated voice yelled, "Cut! Cut, dammit!"

The voice got closer, and Al turned to see a man in jeans and a plaid shirt, incongruously wearing a communications headset wired to a unit on his belt. He was walking fast towards them.

"Didn't you hear me say 'clear the set'? What the hell are you doing out here with live-fire, anyway? The stunts are off until tomorrow." He stalked up to Charlie, and stared at him with an outraged manner. "Say...Who the hell are you? I've never seen you guys before!"

He turned and yelled over his shoulder, "Security! Get your sorry ass over here!"

"Right away, Mr. Harris."

By this time, the woman and her two attackers were closing in. The woman snatched a pack of cigarettes from the nearest Security man, and accepted a light from the man in the plaid. She took a drag on it, and passed it to one of the others.

"Excuse me," Al started.

"You want to know what you've walked into," the man—Mr. Harris—in the plaid shirt said. "This is a shoot for—well it was, until you screwed it all up."

He turned to another man who had arrived, "Get these turkeys off of my island, and—" He hollered at someone off in the trees, "Take ten, and set it up, again." He looked back at Al, "We still may have enough light left, no thanks to you."

E N R O U T E

Yezeletta skipped the next rest stop, and camped at the one following. She was clear to the eastern border of Montana with North Dakota. The stop that her convoy pulled into was East of Makoshika and was rather less enclosed than others. Still, she could pull into a parking area near the exit in the truck lot.

Why hadn't she seen any other trucks along this route?

The occasional other traffic on Highway Ninety had either tailed her for a time until it had gone off in another direction, or passed her group of trucks, honking horns in salute to supposed truckers, and disappeared into the distance. Truckers—both of them!—in the opposing lanes had flashed their running lights at her, and she had reached a long left arm past the driving servitor to return the favor. *At least*, she thought, *That's what one of Andrew Vachss's characters would have done.*

Too bad none of those characters were with her.

T H E B A C K L O G

[Start JCL] Several hours after Yezeletta had broken her linkage to Searchlight, the winds picked up and heavy gray clouds started rolling in. The clouds arrived at the distant rest stop just behind the Montana Highway Patrol car that pulled into it. The officer had driven in through the exit, as there seemed to be a problem with the originally designed entrance: there didn't seem to be one. The car rolled to a stop near a small grouping of telephones, and four men got out.

Two of the men were the driver and his partner. One of the others was in a plain dark gray pinstripe suit, and the last was wearing the uniform of an Army Colonel. As the uniforms checked out the booths, another car pulled in. A second man, all of a piece with the man in the pinstripes, got out of it carrying an object that looked remarkably like an old fashioned scintillation counter. He held the probe out in front of him as if he were one-handing a large-caliber firearm, but scanning with it side to side as he watched a small screen on the device's case.

The colonel stood discreetly to one side and watched. The wind started blowing steadily.

The highway patrol officers walked back a short distance, and waved to the others. The little group reformed around the other cluster of booths, the ones back in the truck area. The two cops talked quietly, then the driver's partner dog-trotted down to the ostensible entrance to the area. He drew his portable scanner with the same practiced motion as he would have drawn his side-arm.

The man with the "scintillation counter" aimed the machine's scanner at the booths, and rechecked his readouts.

He walked to the telephones. The others followed.

The scanner aimed his instrument up near the back corner of a booth, the end one. He looked closer.

Curious.

Something dark green was dripping from the enclosure's roof.

He clipped the scanner probe to the device, reached into his suit pocket and retrieved a cellular phone. He pressed a speed-dial button, placed the instrument to his ear, and began dictating.

The other cop returned. His scans of the *inside* of the entrance road would provide an interesting counterpoint to the data from the counter.

THE SHORT CUT BACK

Two hours after Al and Charlie had walked onto the set for *The Murderer who Took a Holiday*, they and the rest of the July Seventeenth Brigade sat in the cafeteria tent under the watchful eye of Warner Brothers Seven-Arts Studio Security (International Division). In the background, Al could hear E. Howard Harris, Director, talking in low, urgent tones into his telephone. Harris alternated between this, and looking at them with an expression that consisted of equal parts outrage and loathing.

Marina Worthington sat near him, wearing a look of concern. She patted his wrist, gently, and moved a little closer.

A jeep pulled up to the tent.

Several people got out. Al followed their movements with apprehensive eyes. Then he felt a certain kind of relief. The three individuals approaching them were wearing white armbands.

They were from the American Red Cross.

Al looked at Marina, "Maybe we'll be safe after all."

RELAXATION

The hilly areas of Central Montana had given way to the nearly hilly areas at the eastern edge of Montana. There was slightly more traffic on Highway Ninety, now, but the traffic was of a nature that Yezeletta found—curious.

That was an understatement. Cars seemed to be out for the purpose of making the shortest trips possible, for specific reasons, with no side trips.

In times past, Yezeletta had studied the "movements" with which various countries had been afflicted. Those movements had been organizations ranging from anti-pollution groups intent on cleaning up the air, to rather loud outfits intent on eliminating one of the industries intent on cleaning up the air: nuclear power plants. All of them had seemed to be at cross purposes.

Especially those aimed at the gas and oil industries.

She had read accounts of zealots loudly proclaiming that they would no longer drive cars, and surrendering their last automobile (usually accompanied by others asking politely how they would get around in places like Los Angeles, New York or Chicago).

Here it looked as if such attitudes had become reality.

The only long-haul motor vehicles she had seen since Utah had been cross-country long-distance trucks. There had been a few of those; she had needed to side-track her convoy to avoid other convoys within which she might have been noticed.

Private cars looked as if they were becoming an extinct species.

Maybe the ever vigilant Mr. Berkins was sitting on the oil companies as well.

THE SHORT WAY HOME

[Load Vector] Several hours after their interviews by the friendly members of the Red Cross, an elderly Boeing 737 lifted the tired members of the July Seventeenth Brigade off the island on which Erwin Howard Harris and Warner Brothers Pictures were working. The Red Cross had eased the way with its considerable influence, and had helped the Brigade members past some rather pointed questions regarding how they had transported themselves from Darwin to an unnamed island twenty klicks north in the Pacific.

Charlie had been the one who had actually given them an out.

He had seen an article in the waiting area to which they had been taken by Studio Security.

"Al, take a look at this."

Al looked at what Charlie was holding. It was a newspaper. Silently, Charlie pointed to a headline: **Darwin Excursion Believed Lost**.

Al smiled, took the paper.

He scanned down through the lead paragraphs, and grinned over the top of the paper at Charlie. "Looks like we survived the accident, didn't we?"

Charlie smiled back, then abruptly changed his expression. "People coming," he growled.

Al passed the paper to Marina. "Look at this. We're lucky to get out, alive."

Marina took the front page, scanned it, and nodded. "I'll see that the others get a look at this."

The people Charlie had seen were the two middle-aged ladies from the Red Cross. They approached Al.

"Al Morrison?"

"Me," Al said. "And you'd be?"

"Mrs. Susan Abrams, and this is Mrs. Karen Donaldson."

Al shook hands gravely with each of them.

"Good to meet you, we've had a pretty rough time, with the accident."

"Accident? Were you on that tourist boat?" Mrs. Donaldson asked.

"Yes. There was one lifeboat on our side, and when it capsized, we sorta scrambled into it, and rowed like mad," Al extemporized. "It was touch and go for a while. Took us a day to get to here. Wherever 'here' is." He looked around.

Charlie was standing behind the Red Cross representatives, and he raised an eyebrow in salute.

"You'll need to get your passports replaced, and we can arrange a small loan, or even an outright grant from our emergency fund, for your expanses," Mrs. Abrams said helpfully.

"Actually," Al said, "all I need is to get to an International Cash Station. My credit cards survived the drink, and I can make a withdrawal."

Mrs. Abrams looked at Mrs. Donaldson. "That would be easy enough. There's a Station just outside."

Grinning, for reasons that the Red Cross Reps were all wrong about, Al went out to the friendly lights of the Cash Station, and, several minutes later, came back in, his money clip refilled, and feeling good about himself for the first time in three days.

An hour later, thanks to Al's American Express Card, to say nothing of the Red Cross's Emergency Fund, the Brigade took flight in a northeasterly direction for San Francisco.

No one knew, or particularly cared, that Charlie sat at a distance from the rest. The dismal memory of him after Yezeletta had dumped him in the bottom of the boat was still with most of them, Marina in particular.

His thoughts still hungry, Charlie sat at the far back of the cabin, and brooded over his silent plans.

BY THE RIVER'S EDGE

[Bit Map]   Near Fairview, the highway crossed a bridge near which a turnoff led down to what in warmer months looked as if it was used as a small picnic area. The wooden tables were stacked up near a small shed, and tied down securely. The arrangement reminded Yezeletta of the deck of the *Hat Dancer*.

Best of all, the access road wound around back of the shed to a parking lot, and, the very best: there were undamaged sanitary facilities.

Well—relatively speaking, undamaged. The facilities worked, but the surrounding parts of the rest rooms were littered and filthy. On the other hand....

Yezeletta left the grubby mens' room (the women's room was worse), and assessed the area.

The rest area was shielded from the highway by a small stand of trees.

The access was easily closed off. Her minions could make it look unapproachable in very short order, just as they had done before.

And the small river (she couldn't find it on her road-map) was full of the cleanest mountain run-off she had ever seen.

She gestured to a nearby servitor, gave it directions with a quick touch, and began taking off her clothes. Meanwhile, the servitor she had accessed was passing those instructions to several others. One of those ran to the big Mack, and came back with a cloth bag. Yezeletta looked into the bag, and smiled. Soap!

She scanned the area again, and touched another servitor. In response, several imagers and cat-arachnids climbed into trees, and up to the truck cab roofs. Their bright gold imaging apertures opened, scanned. Information travelled data channels back to her. Another servitor took her filthy garments and went to a flat rock.

Yezeletta walked into the water.

It was chilly. She blinked, and adjusted her skin sensation away from the cold. She directed a thought *there*, and a table of temperatures appeared in a window in her right eye: the soles of her feet, her ankles, knees, et cetera, on up. The water was quite chilly, but she would not be harmed by it for the time she would be washing.

She lathered herself up in various brands of soap, some Australian, some Mexican, others obtained from American filling stations. The conflicting odors were pleasant, as were the late Autumnal smells of the trees that sheltered her from chance observation. She walked out until the water was up near her neck, and launched into an easy backstroke *with the grace of a Roman Bireme!* (she thought) to rinse off. She made a three-handed gesture to the servitors on the shore, and in small squads they waded into the river to clean themselves. The one by the rock was industriously and single-mindedly washing her clothes with more repetitive enthusiasm than skill. *This is the first decent bath I've had since I left the Project!* She rolled over, and started a workmanlike and complicated breast-stroke parallel to the shore.

A motion caught her eye.

One of the cat-arachnids was waving at her, rearing up like a rotund feline, waving five of its legs in the air insistently. A red asterisk blinked in the upper left corner of her eye.

Several small bushes blocked her view of the shore. She changed her swim to a direct line back to where she had entered the water.

There she saw what had disturbed the cat-arachnid.

There was a small boy standing on the shore.

Blinded by the Light

[Input Operation] Yezeletta hadn't been prepared for this. Her collection of imagers was looking at a far distance for the more complex infra-red signatures of well-equipped adults. A small boy just walking up....Well, the cat-arachnid *had* spotted him. A bit late. A kid wouldn't register as a danger. Would he?

The boy looked straight at Yezeletta, his head unmoving, his white cane held in one hand, tightly. His eyes—

Yezeletta adjusted her eyes for a tad less than microscopic acuity. The effect was a zoom in on the boy. She could see the dense white clouds occulting his vision. Cataracts so thick in one eye that he was effectively blind, even though he would be able to perceive light and darkness.

The other eye appeared to be burnt out of his head.

"I know you're there," the boy said. "I heard you splashing."

Yezeletta found her voice. "Hello," she said, trying to keep the worry, *make that panic!*, out of her voice. "How are you?"

"I'm fine. Are you English? You talk like that."

"I'm from—across the ocean," Yezeletta replied. "What's your name?"

"I'm Victor," the boy said. "What's your name?"

"Call me Jesse," she said. "I'm Jesse—short for Jessica." It was close enough.

"You live here? I never heard of you, and I know all the people around here."

"I'm just traveling through."

"Were you swimming? It's too cold for that."

"Would you like to sit where it's warm?" Yezeletta asked. She gestured at several servitors who brought up folding chairs and a large blanket. She wrapped herself in the blanket, and gently took Victor's hand, his right, in hers.

A motion caught her eye. In the distance, not very far in the distance, two cats had sat down, one with its paws tucked under, and were watching Yezeletta and Victor with the unwavering gaze of their kind.

"Your hand is warm," Victor said.

"Thank you." She gently guided him to one of the chairs.

Victor sat upright in the chair, turning his head as if he were actually looking at things. Yezeletta realized that his hearing was probably nearly as good as hers was. Victor was scanning for *sounds*, and placing himself relative to all of the sounds around him. The cats had come nearer.

"How old are you?" She had to say something.

"Eight," Victor replied. "Actually eight and a half."

"Do you live around here?"

"Yep. I live—" Victor scanned with his hearing, "— over there by the road." *Pretty sharp! He located the road by the traffic sounds.*

"Do you go to school?"

"No...I had to quit when I couldn't see any more."

"What happened?" Yezeletta made a special three-handed gesture to a cat-arachnid. The creature began to walk to her, but it moved slowly, quietly, ordered by Yezeletta's signed instructions.

"Accident with bug-killers in my uncle's barn. I got it on my face."

"Could a doctor...?" she started.

"My dad couldn't afford to get me to a hospital. He did what he could."

There was a feathery touch on her left elbow, her lower.

The cat-arachnid looked up at her. Yezeletta placed her left lower hand on it, and it pulled itself up by several of its jointed legs.

"What do you do?" she asked. It wasn't a very good question, but she wanted to keep Victor occupied.

"I walk around the pasture. Mom reads to me. I listen to stuff on the radio."

The cat-arachnid was up on her left arms: it crawled up onto her shoulder, and perched there. Yezeletta touched it with her upper right hand, and sent it several precise instructions. Near one of the trucks, three servitors moved purposefully into the truck's cab, then discreetly into the back of the truck in response to a component of those directives passed to them from the cat-arachnid. She looked at the two inquisitive felines, and adjusted her eyesight for a close-up. They appeared to be a tomcat and his mate. She recalled that a female cat had once been called a "Molly" before various organizations of cat-fanciers had promoted the use of the word "queen."

"Why couldn't the hospital help?" Another bad question, but she needed a little more information!

"The big doctor said that we didn't qualify." Victor's voice was matter-of-fact. Apparently this was old enough information that it didn't mean much any more, or perhaps all of the meaning had been leached out of it long before.

Or something.

"Didn't qualify?" *What part of an eight-year-old boy doesn't qualify?* she asked herself.

"We ain't on the approved list." Victor stated that with finality. *And the sun sets forever, because "you ain't approved!"*

A servitor appeared in the cab of the Mack, holding an object. A glass container.

Yezeletta raised a hand, gestured. Then she sent another instruction through the cat-arachnid that was sitting frozen-still on her shoulder. The cats had come closer, and were watching Yezeletta and Victor closely. Occasionally, the cats would scan Yezeletta's other creations, but they devoted most of their attention to...Victor.

The servitor held the container high, the green contents shimmered in the late afternoon light with its own kind of life.

"Victor," she said, "would you like to sit here?"

"Where?"

Yezeletta extended a long lower right arm, and took Victor's hand, his left. The little boy stood, and, gripping his white cane tightly, moved over to Yezeletta's chair. As he moved, several servitors silently braced themselves around the chair to hold it in place against the weight of both of them, and the servitor in the truck sprinted up with his glass of green.

"You're big!" Victor said. *You're small,* Yezeletta didn't say. Gently, she lifted him onto her lap. *Will I ever have one of these?* she thought.

Victor leaned his head against her. He placed his ear, his right, on her left breast. "You're a big lady," he said again. "Your heart beats funny."

"I have a heart murmur," she answered.

"Sounds like a whole conversation. You're warm!"

Yezeletta wrapped her lower arms around him in a warm hug. Then she gently covered Victor with the blanket. The servitor handed her the glass container.

"Victor," she said softly, "I have something here for you."

The little boy was comfortable in her large embrace. *Is this what I want to do?* Victor looked up at her with his sightless eyes. "You're nice," he said, and yawned. A chance ray of sunlight illuminated the dull white clouds in his eye, *They'd be dark green, if those things were gone!* "Can I just sit here?" he asked. Yezeletta touched his face. Then she placed her fingers in the glass jar, and the green contents *approached* her fingers. The nano-tech would have taken effect: Victor wouldn't even feel the slight cold of the green.

It attached itself to her fingers. She pulled it out, and gently laid it across the drowsing face of the tired little boy. The reorganizer would perform its specific task, and fall away in a matter of minutes.

She hugged Victor to herself, and he responded with a hug back, his small arms warm around her. The watching cats were no more than four meters distant—a little over thirteen feet. Yezeletta adjusted the bandwidth of her eyes for infra-red: the female was pregnant. She could see the signatures of at least five well-developed kittens. She touched the cat-arachnid again.

Let no one come near!

In the horizontal rays of the setting sun, the light caught Victor's sightless eyes one last time. The green reorganizer detached itself, and fell away to be caught by another creature for disposal. Victor's eyes were unseeing now, but in about a week's time, the white clouds would recede, the burnt socket would regenerate, and the light would shine in out of the darkness, and a small boy would see the things that a small boy should.

RESTORATION

Yezeletta would not be there when her magic would happen. Yezeletta would be wending her way around "the world's largest small town," Minneapolis, when an eight-year-old boy would wake up one fine morning, and *see* the white cane that had been the only help the local hospital could provide.

And no one would be able to explain it.

ON THE HOME STRETCH

Yezeletta's convoy pulled into another rest area outside of Hudson, Wisconsin and camped for three days. The winds blew cold around the trucks as several servitors, bundled up with every blanket that she could find, "jacked in" to a local power line to power electric heaters in the trucks. She was thankful that her plan to empty out all of Project Sargon was as far-seeing as it was. The heaters, improvised heating coils, halogen light sources and the like were what she needed as the cold winds of Northern Wisconsin whistled and blew around the parked vehicles. She consulted her maps: Milwaukee was maybe twelve hours away, if they drove continuously, another day on top of that, if they took it easy.

That might be necessary; one of the smaller trucks was developing engine problems. *The petrol here must not be up to the quality it should be.*

THEIR SEPARATE WAYS

[Fragmentation; Long Shot] When the plane landed at San Francisco International, the combined efforts of Mrs. Abrams and Mrs. Donaldson, augmented by **[A]** enough folding-money from Al to grease several of the appropriate palms, and **[B]** mention of the Morrison Name, with its attendant attribute of "Has Family Legal Firm," managed to bypass the red-tape of re-entry into the Occasional Land of the Free. Al's generosity went as far as such things as cab-fares for his friends, and loans that were outright gifts to help them get back into their lives.

When all and sundry had left, only Charlie remained.

"Think we'll get together again?" Al asked in a desolate voice.

"We will," Charlie said, a note of the old heartiness coming back into his voice.

A single Yellow Cab remained.

Charlie got into it, and issued instructions to the driver.

Benjamin Allen Morrison was left standing alone at the cab-stand.

ANOTHER LOOK AT THE DATA

In a laboratory in Western Montana, a lab technician adjusted the settings on a Scanning Tunnelling Microscope, and looked at the molecular configuration again. The fragment of the double helix that was the only undamaged item in the sample showed up as clearly as such an instrument could resolve it.

But what the double helix actually represented was something else.

Something unknown.

The sample had been given to the technician by his boss with the instructions to analyze it as soon as possible. It appeared to be—it was!—an organic product of some sort. Organic just barely. It was a small step up from a complex chemical compound: a synthetic.

The DNA fragment had been located by a search that had taken the better part of a day, and was the only such fragment in the sample: a microscopic needle in what had been a very large (if still microscopic) haystack.

The technician took another sip of his coffee and reviewed his notes. Not much.

But it would have to do.

SUNSET LIGHT

As a small boy named Victor took his first steps in the flatly slanting rays of the setting sun, looking about intently at all of the new, but old, things returned to his life, a pair of tabby cats watched him from the safe distance of a grassy hill, their vertically slit cat-green eyes following his every motion as he, once again, saw that which had been only memories.

Then they went down to join him.

OTHER DESTINATIONS

[Processing] The technician reduced all of his observations to a single long message. He ran the standard encryption program against it, and activated the wireless Internet connection.

His laptop processed the handshake that allowed him into the secured web-site, and he uploaded the encrypted data.

Most of the transmission time would be in the upload. It would reach Philadelphia in a matter of minutes.

MADISON BYPASS

[Overlays] The convoy slipped through the winds off of the lakes that surrounded Madison, as they proceeded around Wisconsin's Capital. The small twelve-wheeler that had developed engine trouble outside of Hudson was still running, mostly courtesy of liberal applications of high-viscosity oil, and a lot of skilful driving. Yezeletta directed the driving servitors onto Highway 94, the last leg into Milwaukee. The inner rear left tire of another of the trucks was developing a slow leak. *All they have to do is make it another ninety miles*, she thought, *and then I can dispose of these!*

Highway Ninety-Four was a straight shot into Milwaukee. One of the servitors had snagged a copy of *Milwaukee* Magazine from a trash can, and Yezeletta studied the layout of Milwaukee's down-town intently by just enough light for her augmented eyesight, as the trucks sped on through the last night she would be on the road.

Ahead, road signs loomed in the night. The highway was as untraveled as any of the other places through which she had been. The clouds seemed to be lower in the darkness. One of the city signs showed up in the distance: it read—

O CONOMOWOC

That was a fascinating name: five vowels, all the same letter in a ten-letter name. She could see city lights reflected against the low-lying clouds. There were the friendly lights of a gas station just off an exit ramp. Yezeletta touched the driving servitor, and read data back from the creature. They had filled up outside of Madison, in a place called Wisconsin Dells. The convoy had pulled into a filling station closed against the cold, and she had swapped a thick envelope of freshly minted cash for the contents of that station's underground tanks.

When the proprietor awoke, the cash would be the first thing he would see.

Yezeletta touched the driver's head again, and instructions flowed out to the other drivers.

The convoy sped past the Oconomowoc station. Then it passed the city itself, and went on into the darkness.

PLANNING FOR THE DISTANCE

The plans Charlie had made on the flight back to the states went from planning to action several days later.

Cyber cafes, restaurants combined with access via computers at each table to the Internet, had started in the mid nineteen-nineties. A chain of Dine&Surf restaurants connected the United States from coast to coast, and were quite popular, thanks to the combination of cheap food, large servings, and free email.

Surfing the net was a slight extra charge, which decreased over time.

Al met Charlie a week after in the Embarcedero Dine&Surf, where Charlie was sitting in the far back (in a section labeled "The Hacker's Haven") taking up a table for four with voluminous notes, various kinds of optical and magnetic media, and a computer workstation that by this time practically had his name on it.

Al was surprised. Charlie using a computer? he thought, That's news!

"What's up?" he asked.

"Research," Charlie replied around a greasy cheeseburger.

"Right," Al said. "Research into what?"

"Missing persons."

"Who?" That was the last answer Al had expected!

"You know, missing persons," Charlie repeated. "People who disappear, and don't turn up for a while."

"What is this, your new hobby?"

"You didn't hear?"

Al took a breath, let it out again. Slowly. "Hear about—what?"

Charlie pressed a key combination, and an image built up on the screen.

"The missing persons on this."

Al recognized the image instantly. Charlie let it register for another second or so, then removed the picture.

"Lot of missing persons there," Charlie said softly.

"No kidding." Al felt as if he wanted to be anywhere but here. "Shouldn't you be doing that in a more secluded place?"

"This server doesn't track your activities, and no one knows the handle I use to get this stuff. I'll be safe until I'm done here."

"What are you going to do?"

"I want to see someone."

"Good luck." Al stood up. "See you."

"Yeah, Al."

Al hurried from the Dine&Surf and wished that he could hurry his very place of residence away from Charlie. The man had to be totally nuts: so bird-brained generally, to be doing the things he did. People had accused Al of living in his own little world, but Charlie was not only living in a world of his own, he was expanding it. Building sub-divisions.

Al decided that, ally or no, he would not seek out Charlie again. The man was on a collision course with something that he, Charlie, was blissfully unaware of, but which Al frankly never wanted to see again.

And Charlie's first step over the edge had been in the graphic that he had shown Al on the computer monitor. Al had seen the same picture in a back page of the *San Francisco Chronicle*, and had stayed away from any discussion of it.

It was the *Hat Dancer*.

Abandoned amid the ruins of Long Beach Harbor. Deserted.

And that meant...That meant....

That *she* was somewhere near. Somewhere close.

Suddenly, he was back in the cold waters of the Pacific north of Darwin, and the sharks were nearing. He felt as if other kinds of sharks were closing in, now, around him.

C A R E F U L L Y ,   C A R E F U L L Y

Yezeletta came into Milwaukee by way of a town called Brookfield. Later, she would find out that entry by that route was one of the few relatively unimpeded access methods into Milwaukee's west side. Her trucks sped through streets that looked as if taken from war histories of the previous century. She cut south, then west, again, onto a street called Wisconsin Avenue: a street that was a straight route to Lake Michigan.

Her desired destination was ahead, at the eastern end of Milwaukee's downtown. It was a tall building—thirty-six obvious stories, forty-one, total—made of white concrete, and had once contained the offices for a large bank. The actual name of the bank had changed, then changed again. Now the building was referred to as "The Farmers and Merchants Building."

Yezeletta looked up at the Imager that led back to the large olive drab container.

"Looks like a place to hang our hats," she said.

——>>> **FOUR** <<<——

Athena:Am I to assume that enough has been said, and I now command these jurors to cast an honest vote according to their judgement?

Chorus:For our part, every bolt is already shot. But I am waiting to hear how the trial will be decided.

Athena:Why not? As for you **<< *to Apollo and Orestes* >>**, how shall I arrange matters so that I will not be blamed by you?

—Aeschylus, *Eumenides*

<<About 450 BCE>>

[Processing] A month, one of hectic activity made more strenuous by the necessity of keeping it entirely invisible—in spite of a very visible diversion—and Yezeletta was moved into the top five stories of the former Farmer's and Merchant's Building.

She had spent the first three days on the South Side, studying the place that she wanted to "homestead" through a telescope, while her Imagers went up the sides of the building at night. There were a lot of squatters in the building, but the higher up she looked, the comparatively fewer there were. The elevators were not running, and the thirty-five floor climb to the low end of the floors she wanted was tiring even for the younger of the place's inhabitants.

Also, the upper floors weren't lit up at night. Yezeletta was determined to keep it that way.

BIRDCAGE FOR AN AMAZON

Downtown Milwaukee was deserted after dark. Even the Police Department didn't spend much time there. She had performed a traffic analysis of Police radio transmissions, and what of it she could read—a lot of it was Data-Comm, and encrypted—indicated that most action at night was on the West side of the city. There was a man who worked out of the various 'burbs who seemed to think that he could charge tolls to get into the city on that side. One suburb, the Town of Brookfield, had successfully kept the so-called "Lord of the Roads" from making any incursions into their area. *That was the place I came in through*, she thought. Others had simply been taken over by this Allen Hightower.

Elsewhere in Milwaukee, there seemed to be an uneasy truce between several organizations that merely bordered on the criminal—when they weren't wholly and totally criminal—and the downtown, or "District One" police.

Yezeletta staked her claim in the tall, white building late one night, in the simplest way possible. She drove her trucks into the parking ramp beneath it, and moved in.

The deserted territory along the east end of Wisconsin Avenue afforded ample room for her trucks, and the ramp concealed the activities of the servitors, as the initial invasion went up.

She watched it on several monitors from her command post in the eighteen wheeler. The imagers preceded and followed the small band of servitors, as they went up the fire-escape stairway, sealing off the doors to each floor with a thick resinous substance that one of Yezeletta's culture media had produced. The resins glued the doors shut, and gave off a vapor that was a nasty combination of anesthetic (if anyone got close to it), and a dispenser of the active ingredients in her Obliviators. The idea was to keep any spectators in the area disoriented and ultimately ignorant of who was moving in. In retrospect—a week later—the plans were far more elaborate than they needed to be.

No one resisted her.

The servitors reached the thirty-fifth floor, and used their tools. The fire doors opened, swinging outwards into the hallway, and the corridor, unlit but visible to the infra-red vision of the invading servitors, stretched the length of the building ahead of them.

Yezeletta had two imagers within reach of her lower hands. She sent instructions with quick touches as she supervised the invaders thirty stories and more above. *I steer them like game pieces with living joysticks.* The servitors carried several items: a roughly spherical thing with triangular sides, and a plant that seemed to be all stalks with flaccid rubber bladders attached to the ends. Far below, she watched the infra-red inputs from the imagers as they looked into all of the corners, old offices, unused areas, and anywhere else that someone could hide.

The search took hours and in the end nothing and no one was found.

The sky was beginning to lighten as the first loads of equipment were carried up. Yezeletta moved the trucks into a concealed part of the underground ramp.

Then she rested. Waiting.

DAY AND NIGHT

The day stretched ahead of Yezeletta like a well-lit infinite road. She waited, a spider in her web, Obliviators near by at all times, for anyone who might come down to the lowest part of the ramp and see who was there. She dozed fitfully, the hands of servitors in hers, imagers scanning for anyone approaching. The slightest of sounds brought her instantly awake, but the sounds were typical and trivial: the winds howling in the concrete spaces of the ramp. Idly, she traced the wood grain in the walls near her, the result of the plywood molds placed to hold the wet concrete, generalizing sets of differential equations to describe them.

While she waited, the faceted icosahedral object her servitors had brought up the night before was hatching into a useful group of life-forms on the top floors of the building. This was the first trial of her initial experiment, started half the world away in Australia. The Hive of imagers, data collecting life-forms—even the convoluted organic "server"—would get their first field test here. The bladder plant was an emitter of various paralytics that would stop any intruders in their tracks, but which wouldn't affect any of her creations. *Or me.*

Eventually, the day ended.

RESTART UPDATE

Late that night, the servitors resumed their work. Getting out of Project Sargon had been easy. The Sargon Complex was basically all on one level. There were no second floors, and only a small basement, used for storage. The vertical portage here was a killer, and she was worried about the toll it would take on her servitors. They were a hardy crew, but were showing wear at this end of a long trip half way around the world.

There had to be a better way.

There was.

An imager she sent into the elevator motor rooms indicated that there was very little wrong with the elevators that supplying power wouldn't fix.

Yezeletta got out of the eighteen wheeler, and stretched. She picked up three separate tool boxes in three hands, and gestured with a fourth.

Several servitors fell in behind her, and followed her into the maintenance room.

Wisconsin Power and Light had shut down most of the power to the Farmer's and Merchants Building, evidently several years earlier. There was power still supplied to certain functions, such as exit lights and fire alarms; Yezeletta wondered if that was because of a local law. She sized up a rack panel within which several large gaping holes appeared, blocked by large dark plastic plugs.

She eyed one of those plugs.

Electrical equipment was designed to last, and an electrician might find the entire history of electrical wiring set before him in one building. This plug could be a socket for something new, or something quite old.

Yezeletta gestured at a servitor.

With the skill of a nurse slapping the required tool into a surgeon's hand in response to a terse word, the servitor slapped the soft, gooey object into Yezeletta's hand.

She held it up, and directed a thought at it. Claws extruded themselves from the opposite end of the object, and the part of it in her hand solidified into a handle. Yezeletta touched the claws to the plastic plug.

The claws extended, bit in, and seized it.

Yezeletta added another instruction, and outriggers formed at the sides, and pressed against the metal panel around the plug. She let go of the handle, and stepped back. The organism was now a tripod around the plug, supporting the claws as they extracted the plug. The plug came out with a "pop!" sound, and the creature and the plug fell, to be caught by another servitor.

There were three heavy contacts in the space where the plug had been.

Just the right interfacing for an electric meter.

Yezeletta smiled. *I have something better!*

Another servitor came up with a very black object. It shimmered and trembled in the servitor's hand: a combination of gelatin and thick grease, with the characteristics of neither, or maybe both. Another servitor came up with another of the same, and another.

She used the malleable tripod creatures again to remove the other plastic plugs. Then, taking the black things from each servitor, she placed them near the meter recesses on the panel, and stepped back.

She touched each one, and sent it a directive.

There was no intelligence in the black organisms. The instruction she sent each was about on the level of flipping a switch. *And that's exactly what I want them to do!*

She waved the rest of her "staff" back, and watched.

The black organisms formed circles around each of the meter sockets. When they had surrounded the sockets, they seemed to wait. Yezeletta touched an Imager on her shoulder, sent another directive.

The circles contracted, and the black objects *inserted* themselves into the sockets.

They nestled into the panel, and covered the contacts within.

Nothing happened.

This was what Yezeletta expected. *Now to really flip the switch.*

A touch. An instruction. A short delay. Then: within the substance of each black organism, a state changed. A nonconductor became a conductor.

And the lights came on.

An *Input.*

This input was from the servitors on the top floors. A few lights had come on all the way up there, and they were running around shutting them off. Not many, and not easily visible. *But I don't need any! Dammit!*

But more importantly, the freight elevator motors were coming up to speed.

Yezeletta turned to her crew. She touched the nearest on its head.

They started loading the elevator.

SETTING UP SHOP

The passenger elevators as well as the single freight elevator made the sending up of the remainder of Yezeletta's belongings a matter of unloading from the trucks, stacking in the lifts, and unloading at the top, again. The servitors worked with speed, rather than neatness. The content of the trucks was simply dumped on the thirty-fifth floor, and the vertical transport brought down quickly. Later, she would be mildly amused by the disarray of her move into the Farmers Building, and, even by the time she had met Joe, the final sorting would not be complete.

She drove her servitors without mercy, allowing only the most tired to rest.

The first item up the elevator was the olive drab carrier. She personally made sure that it was safe, then concentrated on getting the eighteen-wheeler emptied.

When it was empty, she had a servitor take it out to a place a block or two away, near something that looked like a great asterisk made of steel I-beams painted bright orange, that seemed to grow out of the concrete. This was a big risk, as the driving servitor had to get back on foot. Yezeletta watched the creature scampering through the shadows, past restaurants, banks and bookstores, attempting to look in every direction, its literal mind-ed pseudo-intelligence attempting to process all of the inputs in this new place. A police car drove past, its red and blue lights strobing insistently in the darkness, and the servitor hid in the recessed doorway of a savings and loan, its mottled gray skin blending in with the worn gray bricks of the S&L. Yezeletta breathed easier when the servitor ended its two block run by arriving in the parking ramp. She adjusted her eyes for telescopic vision, verified that no one was near the truck, aimed, and pressed the single button on the transmitter.

The incendiary charges throughout the truck went off; it went up in flames.

The fire department arrived on time, and was able to contain the fire.

But not put it out. Magnesium fires can't be extinguished. They must be allowed to burn to completion.

In the commotion, no one noticed Milwaukee's newest resident.

OBLIGATORY HOUSEWARMING

Wisconsin Power and Light would notice the black switch-critters in its control panels. Yet Yezeletta needed power for her installations. Her servitors were wearing out. Disposing of them wasn't like disposing of something with intelligence. The servitors were each about as bright as a good desktop computer. Well programmed, of course, able to receive and understand complex sets of instructions; but talking to them was about on a level with using a computer with a decent speech parsing interface. Yezeletta hadn't designed them to be aware.

Her mentors at the project had tried to persuade her to provide this awareness. She studiously and deliberately refused to understand them, *And when they tried to force me, I was far too grown for them to risk coercion!*

The self-aware servitor was a project that she would never start. *Is that another reason why they wanted me to be exiled? Or turned into a plaything? Because I refused to buy into their plans?*

She filed that for future reference, along with the Case of the Inverted Constellations.

Now, she had work to do.

HOMEWORK IN ACTION

Her training had been thorough and elaborate on this. Towards the end of that training, she had been able to add to the syllabus by creating several small life-forms that aided in the topics that her "Field Survival" instructors had taught her.

She used them now.

DUST BUNNIES, ELECTRICAL

The first was a distant relative to the Cat-Arachnid: a creature that was mostly length combined with spatulate claws, and the ability to sense its direction in relation to the Earth's magnetic field in the same fashion as certain birds, and insects such as Monarch Butterflies. The Digger would go down through holes excavated in the basement of the building, and hunt for underground electrical cables. The magnetic field sensing ability that gave the Digger equilibrium, also allowed it to locate electrical mains by their magnetic fields as well.

Then she would grow the roots of another creation down to the mains, and, with the slow, ineluctable patience of plants, force her way into the power cabling, and tap into the mains.

A WHISPER ACROSS THE SKY

[Wait State on Input] Later, Yezeletta sat down on the floor in one of the offices and looked out of the windows to the south. She could see the other lights against the wisps of clouds of cities out to the far horizon. The pools of diffuse light were distant promises in the night.

A servitor entered, carrying an assortment of electronic equipment. Yezeletta long-armed an item from the top of the stack: a portable radio.

Would Australian FM work here? She turned the radio on. The batteries were still in good shape after a trip halfway around the world. The crackle of static filled the office, as she tuned across the FM band.

"Oh yeah; that's the Midnight Special: that's the Midnight Special." A pleasant voice said.

That was interesting. She adjusted the volume and listened: as a guitar riff started, and the same voice, a rich baritone began:

"....Yonder comes Miss Rosie; how did you know?

"Well, I knowed it by her apron and the dress she wore:

"Umbrella on her shoulder,

"Piece of paper in her hand....
"Well I'm gonna ask the Captain, you turn a-loose of my man.
"Let the Midnight Special shine its light on me;
"Let the Midnight Special shine its ever-loving light on me...."

Another voice, an announcer, came in over the music, "From the Norman Pellegrini Performing Arts Center in Chicago, it's The Midnight Special, folk-songs and farce, show-tunes and satire, odds and ends, merriment and escape...." It seemed to be a well-worn, almost traditional introduction. Yezeletta logged the frequency: **98.7** on the *American* FM band.

"Tonight, a program of Union music, as we highlight the American Labor Movement."

Another voice followed the announcer: "Howdy, I'm U. Utah Phillips, the Golden Voice of the Great Southwest...." and he launched into a song that Yezeletta recognized: the melody was the "Battle Hymn of the Republic," but in this version, the tag-line at the end of each verse was: "For the Union makes us strong! *Solidarity Forever!*"

Curious.

Some American union had taken this song and made the old march its very own very aggressive theme song.

She stood, leaned four elbows on the window-ledge, looked out into the night, and listened.

Across the air-waves from Chicago, the Midnight Special shined its very special light on Milwaukee's newest resident.

Recollections

[Breakpoint Return] Joe lounged in the bed next to Yezeletta, as she finished her story. He said nothing for a short time, then asked, "Did you find out why Orion looked inverted?"

"I haven't yet. There are memories that are buried quite deeply that I haven't been able to get at. I've wondered if there are *passwords* that I have to know to get them."

"Post-hypnotic suggestions?"

"Exactly," Yezeletta paused a moment in thought. "Is there something that the Project left in me that's like the maintenance modes in some computers," she didn't inflect that as a question, "or operating systems."

"Considering what you've told me about these people, I wouldn't be at all surprised."

——>>> **FIVE** <<<-——

The silent cock shall crow at last. The west shall shake the east awake. Walk while ye have the night for morn, lightbreakfastbringer, morroweth whereon every past shall full fost sleep.

—James Joyce, *Finnegans Wake*

F A M I L Y M A T T E R S

[System Status: On-Line] South of Chicago, south of the net of suburbs around Chicago, south of all of the Parks, Villages, Groves and other *quondam* wooded areas, lay the Village of East Chicago. Removed enough from Chicago, itself, and not close enough to places like Gary, Indiana for the air to be unhealthy, the Village of East Chicago was a reasonably well-placed average or statistical median. A town with the advantages of proximity to large cities, without being close enough to acquire unfavorable forms of attention from them.

This, at least, was the intent of Henry Lenhaden. He had wanted a place to raise a family, and had wanted that place to be as far from the deadly embrace of the Chicago Public School System—easily one of the all-time worst in the country—as possible. His house was on the edge of town just inside the village limits on a shallow hill. In past times, this placement had prevented it from being flooded out. In spite of this, the hill wasn't that obvious. Hank had done a lot of adroit landscaping over the years that left incoming visitors no place to hide, while screening the lot area around the house from prying eyes.

HOME WORK

In her upstairs room, Anne Lenhaden was sitting at her computer, getting ready to run an artwork program. Her computer was an antique as such things went: she had gotten it for her eighth birthday (and it had been an antique even then). It was an eight-CPU Pentium six-sixty-six system, using clock-doubled microprocessors. Because the system buss speed was 666 Mhz, she had affectionately dubbed the machine "Beast." In spite of its slow running speed, she loved the old antique, and had carefully applied all of the upgrades to Beast whenever they became available. Besides, Beast could do a Double-Precision Floating-Point Divide faster than anyone, and all of the things, mostly academic, for which she used a computer, Beast did brilliantly.

Besides, how many birthday presents that you get when you're *eight* last until you're sixteen (and beyond) with as much distinction?

She typed into a command-line window, looked at the response from the program she was running and waited a moment. When her command had finished, she exited out of the command-line, and mouse-clicked on an icon.

The screen cleared, and "Paint Shop Pro" started.

Anne was a competent self-taught artist, and a screen-full of her latest drawings in miniatures called "thumbnails" appeared. She double-clicked on one, and a large picture replaced its thumbnail.

The picture was of a tall woman with four arms. Anne had been trying to draw a decent picture of Yezeletta since they had returned home from Milwaukee. She kept her sketches encrypted when she wasn't working on them. She had decided early that her strange new friend deserved that kind of security.

Yezeletta had given a set of files to Anne: those files were kept encrypted and hidden using some security software from South America that she'd gotten off the Internet. Those hidden files contained something that Yezeletta had trusted Hank, Ondreya and Anne with before they had left her. There was an Internet URL, or World Wide Web address, and a PGP public key that allowed discrete communications with her.

Like weapons, those data lay waiting for the right time.

THE BASEMENT TAPE

Henry Lenhaden was both college educated and self-taught. His profession was chiefly engineering, with double duty in mathematics. He was skilled at just about anything that involved heavy machinery, and was equally at home with small precision devices as well. His main hobby was firearms, but he had branched out early on into home electronics, starting a basement workshop that anyone from the previous century would have recognized.

The development of electronics had gone from the home-built to the custom-built to the mass-produced. In the middle to late nineteen-seventies, the microprocessor had changed the fabrication of electronic devices to one involving programming (for the microprocessor chip) and the "dressing" of said chip in enough peripheral equipment to allow the device using it to function. This tended to place a certain constraint on those who wished to build things in their basement workshops. Either you had to design, build, and program it yourself, or you had to rely on someone else's work. Both of these tended to select for rather specialized individuals, and Basement Electronics For The Masses became a matter of building prefab kits of off-the-shelf devices with specific functions.

The basement or weekend designer who would design, build and trouble-shoot a bread-boarded design became somewhat rare. Not extinct: there were always those who had the know-how to lay out printed circuit boards, and add parts. And publicize it.

Henry Lenhaden's small workshop would have been familiar to anyone from the nineteen-fifties as a place where discrete component design was a meticulously preserved hobby. Hank didn't mind the "everything on a chip" approach to electronics, but he did think that there was room for tried and true older designs, as well. Like many others, he wanted machinery around him that he could repair easily by himself, if necessary.

He used technology that he could understand now, and would understand later, the kind of technology that did not require advanced study in esoteric subjects.

OUT IN THE STYX

The Lenhaden Family had been vacationing up in Door County, Wisconsin. They had a retreat there that Hank had named "Winterhaven," or sometimes just "The Place," which they kept up with several friends. It was on their way back home from a trip to Winterhaven that they had found out who was living in Milwaukee.

Hank sat on a stool in front of a level, wide platform of formica-covered plywood. In the background a portable radio played, tuned to Chicago's WFMT, arguably the best classical music station in the Midwest. On the bench sat an antique short-wave radio, with the cabinet off. Hank was poking around in the components beneath the metal chassis, cleaning out accumulated dust, looking for parts that needed to be replaced. He had found the ancient Halicrafters set at a garage sale the week before, and wanted to see if it could work again.

Of course, vacuum tubes were a rare item....

But not impossible to get.

He looked up from the colorful tangle of resistors and capacitors grouped around the bottoms of tube sockets. His gaze roved past a framed sampler that Ondreya had made for him years before:

There is No Such Thing as Obsolete Technology.

to a picture of Anne and Ondreya, to pictures of his parents, Thorfinn Karlsefni and Anne-Marie Lenhaden.

That picture had been taken when Anne was just a year old.

GOING UP THE COUNTRY

Anne had been born in Door County at Winterhaven. It had been a little touchy at the end of the trip up there, as Ondreya's contractions had started when they were still ten minutes out. Hank had been in communication by CB radio with one of the doctors from nearby Green Bay who would be on hand when they reached Winterhaven.

When Hank and Ondreya had arrived at the main house, Doc Jameson had helped Ondreya out of the car, and Amanda Jameson, and Doc had gotten her into a bedroom, while Hank parked the car.

Three minutes later, he came into the house, and Doc and Amanda were waiting, smiling, and in the distance Hank could hear the crying of a baby.

The Jamesons took him in to meet Anne.

The advantage for Anne of being born at Winterhaven, a "home birth," was that it bypassed the standard procedure by large hospitals of registering her with a half dozen government agencies. This was the main reason for going up to Door County. The top-heavy U. S. Government had managed to reach into the lives of just about everyone, usually accompanied by a chorus of bipartisan rhetoric (usually at election time) about "curbing big government."

The idea of having his daughter tracked from cradle to grave by Federal Government bureaucrats whose only concern was the taxes she would pay over that lifetime, was anathema. Besides, in Door County, Anne could get a thorough grounding in one of the more important cultural aspects of Wisconsin life. Lambeau Stadium and the Green Bay Packers were only an hour's drive from Winterhaven, and Anne's grandparents had Hereditary Season Tickets.

That evening, Hank's folks came from the small community of Shawano to see Anne.

Hank's Mom would know her for just over another year.

All of Hank's plans to keep Anne out of the purview of big government turned out to be unnecessary. Anne-Marie Lenhaden, sent by her Union to a convention in Washington, D. C., had been in a tour bus that had just left the White House, enroute to the Capitol Building. A single man, neither a group, nor an organization, but one man only, was able to step through the best precautions the Federal Government, cautious to the point of paranoia, could possibly have devised.

That day, a man-made sun had risen over the city, come to earth as the act of that single man.

AFTER THE FALL

Hank removed a six-hundred-and-eighty ohm resistor that looked baked and soldered in a replacement. Somehow his Dad had survived, somehow he had been talked back into living, and, as Anne's grandfather, "Grampa" managed to prosper in the country of small towns and state politics that the U. S. had become.

His skills with machinery, like a careful investment, had grown, also.

Survivalism, sometimes called "what Boy Scouts did when they grew up," overcame its tarnished reputation when Albert Miller destroyed Washington.

The typical picture of the survivalist (some thought a product of subtle Government disinformation) was that of a self-reliant fanatic who thought that the world was going to Hell in the proverbial Hay-Wagon, and—

1:Wanted to prevent it;

2:Wanted to help it;

3:Wanted all Big Government to end;

4:Wanted to *help* all Big Government to end;

—OR—

5:Wanted out of The System (whatever that was).

A lot of the American population wanted out of the system. Most wanted less micro-management from Washington. But the typical American didn't want the country to end. Maybe be fixed, but that was about all.

A wholesale decapitation was unthinkable.

The end of the Soviet Union in the previous century was agreed to be a step in the right direction. Perhaps too big a step. The ubiquitous concern with National Security that had been turned outwards during Communism's unparalleled ninety year history of failure turned inward. The American Government, comprised of old-guard types who had no comprehension of what to do *now*, aided by younger people with nothing but power on their minds, *began to see their own constituents as the enemy*.

The most resilient government of the most resilient country in history absorbed this damage, and attempted to reconfigure around it.

A wholesale decapitation was unthinkable.

Until it happened.

Few people were ready; most stayed close to home.

"Fortune favors the well prepared," was a common slogan often quoted after the destruction of Washington. Other countries took a step back and watched to see what the *quondam* most powerful country in the world would do. Then the other lands formed various alliances and went on. The American Federal Government rebounded, but the rebound was very small. Alaska broke away, and formed the Klondike Free State. Hawaii stayed with the United States, but demanded, and got, various concessions. Communications with the Federal Government from other states, especially *data communications*, decreased or ceased altogether.

The survivalists did what they had trained themselves to do: they survived.

SPECIFIC QUARTERS

For the Lenhaden Family, it was a chance to see if their preparations really were going to work. Hank's job as consulting engineer for some of the steel plants in Northern Indiana, continued. The plants, scaled back at the end of the previous century, concentrated on making do with orders from within the US, and needed ways to fill those orders with greater efficiency. Hank was on retainer with the plants in Gary as well as some of the smaller processed-steel plants closer to home.

The Lenhadens' own preparations, of a more quiet nature, had been in place for many years. The firearms, food storage, portable generators, cash-on-hand, and all of the rest got them through the six months of disorders and confusion after the bombing, after the initial outrage, and after things had settled down.

That hardy commodity, best known as "Good Old American Know-How," better known as "Common Sense" and sometimes known psuedonymously as "Yankee Ingenuity," re-established itself, and the local components of the United States went on.

Nationally, it was a different matter.

A TEXTBOOK CASE

Anne had never been in the Government's systems. When she was thirteen months old, that became academic. When she was twelve years old, it became a requirement.

One morning, in the November of her twelfth year, Anne came down from her room, wearing her usual Fall school outfit: blue jeans, halter top, and—

"Anne," Ondreya asked, "Isn't that top going to be a little cold?"

"I'll wear a sweater over it, besides, it's nice out."

That wasn't a typically Anne remark. Ondreya Lenhaden had no use for the "keep your kids quiet and obedient" school of child-rearing, Anne had been encouraged to ask questions in great numbers about anything, from her earliest life.

"Honey," Ondreya asked carefully, "Is there anything—wrong?"

"My math teacher....," Anne voice trailed off. That wasn't like her, either!

"Your math teacher?" Ondreya prompted. She had met the man in September at the "Meet the Teachers" social event that the P.T.A. had presented. He had seemed an affable young man, but....

"Yeah, Mom," Anne said, "Mr. Swinton is kind of a hugger. And he asked the girls in the class to wear 'pretty' outfits, today."

Ondreya knew all about "hackles," as well as related concepts. The phrase, usually spoken in close conjunction with the word "concepts," was a favorite of Hank's. "Anne," she said, "You don't have to dress up for this guy. Go and wear what you want. I'm going to check this man out, myself." Anne let out a sigh of relief that Ondreya took quiet note of, and bounced back upstairs.

When she returned, she was wearing a red, yellow and black plaid heavy flannel work-shirt—the type of sensibly warm shirt she usually wore in the fall—and a dark pull-over sweater. She kissed her mom, grabbed her books, and left for school.

Hank had left for Inland Steel's plant in Gary at five that morning. Ondreya seized the telephone, and dialed Hank's portable.

Her conversation was clipped, terse, brief and to the point.

A minute later, Hank was on his way home. At high speed.

FAMILIES MATTER

As Hank drove up the highway for East Chicago, he thought about Ondreya's call. Ondreya had been definite, blunt and specific. Those were her normal characteristics—she didn't believe in wasted words or talk for the sake of talking—and those characteristics had been even more prominent now.

"Swinton wants her to *what*?" he asked.

"Wear 'pretty' clothes," Ondreya replied. "Anne's exact words were 'pretty outfits'."

"How long has this been happening?"

"Don't know. This is the first I've heard of it. Anne may have tried to handle it herself."

"Maybe she has. Or thinks that she has. Or something." Hank thought for a moment. Self-reliance was important, and both Hank and Ondreya had tried to teach Anne not only how to solve the problems that capricious fate presented, but also to provide her with the tools to solve those problems.

And to let her know that they'd be there to back her up, if necessary.

Hank drove up the driveway, and backed his car around quickly. Ondreya jumped in, and they were off again to Anne's school.

They parked on a side street, rather than in the school's parking lot. Mr. Swinton's classroom was near the main entrance. Ondreya went in first. Hank would be the heavy artillery.

E N T R Y W A Y

Ondreya's entrance into the classroom was quiet enough so that no one really noticed her. At the front of the room, Mr. Swinton was writing a quadratic equation on the blackboard.

Ondreya took in the layout of the class room. She stood back by a bulletin board (one of the old-fashioned kind, made from cork). Something stuck her arm. When she moved, a thumbtack fell to the floor. She picked up the tack, and replaced it on the board.

Her motion was noticed by Mr. Swinton as he turned around. Ondreya stepped away from the cork-board.

"Why Mrs. Lenhaden, how nice to see you," Swinton began. *Was there a little tremor in his voice?* She nodded pleasantly to him.

"To what do we owe this visit?" he asked.

"Just looking in on my daughter," Ondreya said in neutral tones. *Where was Anne?* She looked around. *That's an odd distribution in a Math class!* she thought. Even with politically correct scholastic attempts to provide studiously impartial access to class materials, it was usually the boys who had the front seats. There was Anne: in the left front....

Anne was an "A" student. She also had nearly perfect eyesight, and didn't usually sit up front with the kids who wore glasses. Hmmmm.

Interesting. All of the girls were sitting in the front of the room.

Ondreya stood at the back of the room, watching Mr. Swinton walk the class through the Quadratic Formula used to solve the general second-degree equation. When he started comparing the general method with Factoring, she nodded to him, gave a wink (just a quick eye-blink) to Anne, who returned it, and left.

I S - T H E R E A N D I S N ' T

She joined Hank in the car. He already had the monitor powered up, and was tuning a small receiver across the frequencies. A raster appeared on the screen, rippled, then synchronized.

It was a view of Mr. Swinton's Math class.

"You got that thumbtack in exactly the right place," Hank said.

"I hoped I did! I was afraid that Swinton would notice me."

Hank slipped a blank DVD/RW disk into the recorder that rested between them, and routed the video feed into it.

Together, they watched as Mr. Swinton started chalking up another quadratic. He turned, looked at the roomful, and pointed to a student.

"Anne," his voice was tinny through the small speaker, "Run this off for us."

Anne rose from her seat, and took Swinton's proffered chalk. She started laying out the solution, and:

Swinton turned his back on the thumbtack.

Stood between the camera and Anne, and:

His hands went up, and around her waist.

Then they went higher.

Hank looked at Ondreya, she looked back, outraged.

On the screen, Anne took a step to one side, dragging Swinton's hand with her. She turned towards him, and stepped further back.

Swinton put his arm around her waist.

Anne's look was unreadable. She was trying to keep her feelings to herself, and nearly succeeding.

Hank was out of the car like a shot.

THE SQUARE OF THE HYPOTENUSE

He proceeded inexorably up the hallway, an elemental force, attempting to calm himself. *All I need to do is show up like Ondreya did. Then I can get Anne out of there.*

He took the handle of the classroom door, and a deep breath as the same time.

Then he opened it.

That was all it took.

Mr. Swinton looked around, surprised.

"Mr. Lenhaden, I—"

"I need Anne." No room for argument.

"Isn't that a little irregular? It's the middle of the day—"

"Death in the family. We have to leave town." Anne walked over to him, relief on her face and in her steps.

"May I ask—?" Swinton tried to continue.

"No." Hank said. Anne headed for the door, detouring to get her books.

In the hallway, Anne was most of the way to the front door. She waited for Hank to catch up.

"How long has that creep been doing that?" Hank asked.

"About a week," Anne answered. "I was hoping that I could stop it."

"Anne," Hank said. "You shouldn't have to put up with that kind of treatment." Hank thought for a time. "You may have outgrown that man. Was there anything that he taught that you didn't know?"

Anne let out a breath. "No. It was a repeat of what Grandpa taught me last summer."

"Let's see what we can do without the interaction of civil servants."

VIDEO REVELATIONS

Later Hank and Ondreya invited Mr. Swinton over for dinner. It didn't surprise them then that Swinton was single. Anne had spent that evening at a slumber party with some of her friends, while her parents wined and dined the math teacher.

Later that evening, they settled in the den with drinks, and Hank's entertainment system. Hank took out a Digital Video Disk, and slipped it into the player.

When Swinton saw the information on it, to say nothing of the looks on Anne's folks' faces, he wilted into the easy chair.

A week later he was on his way out of East Chicago.

THE WELL MAINTAINED SYSTEM

Anne's home schooling had started a week after that.

The American public school system, once the best in the world, had fallen on hard times by the end of the Twentieth Century. In response to various pressure groups, some ideological, some religious, some no more than loud and ignorant, the schools had simply become afraid to teach much of anything.

Famous explorers and statesmen were vilified as 'dead white males', Evolution was damned as 'The Work of the Devil', and various fundamentalist-based dogmas emerged to counter this. Science and mathematical education were condemned as "elitist." The answer to this, at least for parents intending to raise children that weren't completely illiterate, was to teach them at home.

Hank was able to contact other families who similarly wished to combat the slow decline of America by email, as well as through various public web sites, and, four years later, when Anne took her High School Equivalency Exams, she passed with the highest grades the test administrators had ever seen.

BEAST

Anne filled in the colors on her picture of Yezeletta with precise circular motions of her mouse. The colors of Yezeletta's dark gray jump-suit took form on the screen, as Anne adjusted the shades to provide the detailing needed for the lighting direction she had selected for the picture.

Although Anne could draw with pen and ink, colored pencils, or paints, all of her pictures of Yezeletta were done with "Paint Shop Pro" so that the drawings—actually big binary bit-map files in her computer—could be encrypted with PGP when she wasn't working on them. The Lenhadens' "firewall," the computer in the basement that was actually able to dial out to the Internet, was proof against anything that Hank (or Anne, who was the other programmer in the family) could foresee. But only those things.

It was the unforeseen that bothered them.

And it was better to make these pictures invisible when she wasn't working on them.

EMPLOYEE RELATIONS

Leona lay back in her bed, alone for the first time in six hours, enjoying the solitude.

He had been a little rough, this time! His lovemaking—well, it wasn't exactly *that*, even if that was how he described it!—had been persistent, insistent and just a touch panicky.

That panic part was what had Leona concerned.

When the achiness that permeated her body subsided (the pain-killers helped), she made a signal with her left hand, which she repeated a moment later with her right.

Her communicator scampered up to her, and, for nearly an hour, she dictated her concerns to it.

TEST RUN—II—OBSERVATION

[Load Segment; Overlay; Camera Goes With] *He stood in the doorway for longer than* <u>they</u> *must have expected. The figure before him looked at him with professional interest. Her gaze started just below his waist, swept up to his face, did a quick excursion to his complex shoulders, then back to below his waist, to his feet—planted squarely—then back to where she had started.*

He went to her.
She smiled!

——>>> SIX <<<——

Man is characterized by logical processes; woman is characterized by a non-logical process called "intuition"—but one that has never been defined or studied seriously.

Since Man has dominated society, logic has been dominant, and has been socially considered essential to the discovery of and demonstration of truth.

It isn't.

—John W. Campbell, 1952 [3]

BY THE NUMBERS

Yezeletta was so much in her own element, Joe thought as he followed her into yet another work-area in her complex. And her layout here is much bigger than I realized!

The room into which they had gone was large, contained many extensive, flat areas and was otherwise indescribable.

"This room is indescribable," Joe said helpfully.

Yezeletta grinned a wolfish grin. "This is where we will deal with Gary the Geek."

"You don't like him either?" Joe asked.

"No," she said simply. "Even in Australia we were familiar with the Mitchell Conservatory. It was renowned even in Alice Springs. One of the botanists had gone to see it on holiday and couldn't stop talking about his trip. His office was covered with posters and photos and maps of The Domes."

She went on, "Leona reports that Zhongo Teketon is planning some sort of action against The Geek. Knowing what I do of Zhongo, I suspect much bloodshed in this town. I do *not* want this to happen."

"What happened?" Joe asked.

"Have you ever heard of a show called Slicer?" Yezeletta said.

---

[3] The John W Campbell Letters, Page 92 [AC Projects, Inc, 1985]

"Nothing good. I know of the man whose head burst. I'm damned sure that it was caused by early applications of my early research."

"Did you see it?"

"Yeah," Joe said. "I was looking for Victor's friend; you, but I didn't know it then, and I saw a couple of Slicers at a truck stop out there."

"Zhongo lost a fairly large bet to Hamilton over that match," Yezeletta replied. "It isn't the amount of the bet, but Zhongo's pride that was hurt. It's why he wants Hamilton out of the picture."

Joe laughed, "It's amazing that grown men can be motivated by such things! I'd expect better from Zhongo. He's competent in everything else he does."

"I would, myself, and I've studied him with the help of an inside source. Leona sent me a tidbit the other night, though: apparently Slicer is indirectly run by Allen Hightower."

"Indeed."

"Indeed," Yezeletta said. "Zhongo is into more activities than just his pre-occupation with transport. My Hives on the far West side have seen him supervising some rather large shipments of equipment that go north to Green Bay. I don't know where they go from there; maybe the Packers use them in training," she grinned, "but probably not. If Green Bay weren't as distant as it is, I'd set up a Hive there. I suspect that his trucking goes all the way up into Canada."

Joe smiled. About halfway. "And he sits in his little kingdom playing everyone against, well, everyone else."

"That's as good a way to put it, I guess," Yezeletta said, "and we have to worry about his more expendable pawns, such as Mr. Hamilton's occupation of the Mitchell Conservatory."

"I was pretty disgusted when I found out that a gangster had infested it," Joe said. "It's amazing that no one, even locally, can get it up to toss The Geek out. Maybe that's why Zhongo's been nominated. I hadn't realized—I was living in southern California at the time—just how purely rotten things had become."

Yezeletta laid the palm of her left hand, her lower, on Joe's hand. "Then you found out when you came to the Midwest?"

"Yep," Joe said. "All of the scanners, pre-travel background checks, shakedown checkpoints, license plate recorders and whatnot only serve to upset people as they travel. I haven't seen one indication that any of this is doing anything, and most people simply disregard or work around all of it anyway. The Feds don't have the wherewithal to stop people who really want to evade them."

"Nuking your capital didn't help."

"Learning how to handle understatements, huh?"

"Albert Miller was why I decided to come to the US. Your country was heading towards becoming a real 'people's republic' until he blew out all of your government. I figured that a decapitated country was the best place to go. The police here are too busy taking care of ordinary crime to worry about me, even if they knew I was here."

As Yezeletta talked, she reached for implements from the various cabinets, cupboards, shelves and other storage areas near where she was standing, and placed them on the nearest worktable. Joe recognised retorts, beakers, Erlenmeyer flasks, and other kinds of laboratory glassware, one of the large stainless-steel lasagna pans in which Yezeletta held Reorganizers, cans and bottles of various colored solutions, and, inexplicably, a wire cage suitable for a large rodent, and—

The last thing he ever expected to see in a bio-chemistry lab: a standard two-liter paint can.

"Please grab a couple of stools, while I set this up," Yezeletta was grinning.

Joe grabbed two of the lab stools—small armchairs on tall legs—that Yezeletta used, moving one tailored to her physique near her.

With a conjuror's gesture, Yezeletta took a screwdriver and pried the top off of the paint can. Joe realized then that the can had been taken from a cooler: the white outer covering wasn't a label, it was frozen condensation. The contents of the can looked exactly like thick white paint.

Joe looked closer. It was distinctly lumpy. It looked like paint with large, white dumplings.

"Watch me!" Yezeletta said, grinning as if the joke would soon become apparent. She picked up another object—a short piece of wood—and, using a standard six-centimeter paintbrush, daubed some of the lumpy paint on the end of it. As she spread the paint, the dumpling-like lumps smoothed out and flattened, of their own accord, against the sides of the piece of wood.

"I realize," Joe said diffidently, "that things are not always as they seem around The Celebrated Yezeletta Zargkonji And Her Magical Laboratories—" Yezeletta raised an eyebrow at this and waited with a deadpan look, "—but did I *really* see that paint *move* as you were plastering it on that stick?"

Yezeletta almost preened. "Yes, Joe. It did move." She placed the wood in the rodent cage and put the cage in the stainless-steel Reorganizer pan. She centered the wooden fragment in the floor of the cage, and closed the cage's lid, locking it. Then she resealed the paint can, placed the used brush in a beaker of turpentine, and took can and beaker to the cooler.

She took Joe's hands in hers, looked at him with a level gaze, and a suddenly serious expression.

"This is one of the things I got out of Alice Springs that the Project didn't know anything about. Joe, *they must never know about this*."

"Why would they ever? You're half the world away from that bunch."

"Yes! This could be very beneficial, but it could also be seriously misused. I'd prefer to see this do some good—it could convert the dusty parts of this state into greenery again. Maybe if we could combine it with your Protocols —"

Yezeletta was standing directly between Joe and the work table. He couldn't see what was going on in the cage, but he could hear scratching sounds. "What's going on over there?" he asked. He tried to look but Yezeletta stood before him, her hands holding him closely.

"This is the nastiest trick I could create on short notice," Yezeletta said. "It's based on some processes I designed at the Project and never told them about. The paint, I thought up last week."

She moved back, sat down again on her lab stool, and Joe saw what was going on in the varmint cage.

It actually *was* a cage full of varmints, now. There was still thick white paint residue on the wood chunk, or what was left of it. Covering it was a large group of what appeared to be beetles of multiple iridescent colors equipped with large, sharp mandibles. They were *eating* the wood with evident relish, and it was vanishing visibly.

Joe watched the bugs as they continued feasting. The scratching he'd heard was the scraping of mandibles on cellulose, as the insects fed.

"I hate to—"

"—sound like a dummy," Yezeletta completed Joe's question.

"Where did those critters come from?"

"The paint," Yezeletta said succinctly. "The insects come from the paint. The lumps in it are carriers for tiny eggs that hatch very quickly into those." She gestured. The cage was about a third full of squirming insect life.

"Will they grow?" He didn't finish that. "They won't grow further—the mass required for body mass—from that piece of wood...."

"Exactly!" Yezeletta said proudly. "That's also why I put the rest of the paint *and* the brush back on ice. You can imagine what it would be like if that whole can hatched, and fed on everything here!"

"I hate to ask this, but if it did—" Yezeletta prompted him with a wide, intent look, "— what would those things eat?"

"What do you feed a four-hundred kilo gorilla?" Yezeletta asked. With a straight face.

"Anything he wants," Joe said. "Anything."

"Exactly. What do you think would happen to Gary the Geek, if we gave his abode," Yezeletta almost winked, "a paint job?"

"With—uh—insect paint?"

Yezeletta smiled.

Joe asked, "Can those buggers be—um—*tuned?*"

"Tuned?" she prompted, raising an eyebrow.

"Yeah. Can you customize these critters so that they do different things?"

"Of course! What kind of a two-bit fly-by-night operation do you think this is, Joe?" She was nearly laughing.

"First Class!" They both said together.

TEST RUN—III—PROCESS

[Swap Segment; Close-Up] Half an hour later, she was not smiling.

He crouched above her, holding her wrists down above her head with two of his arms, while he played with her nipples with his free hands.

He knelt before her, above her, his hips pumping with an inexorable force that was almost totally mechanical, his manhood, an implacable steel bar between his legs, its thrusting rubbing her nearly raw within her, his face looking up, over her, his eyes rolled up in his head, so that the only parts of them she could see were the whites.

At least she didn't have to look too closely at those violet irises.

She resisted those large hands again, and they were like steel grippers. His thrusting increased in speed, and she was ready to pass out from the pain, when he stopped moving. He paused, then drove his sex into her as far as it would go.

He trembled, shook. He thrust again. His eyes rotated back down to where he was looking at her. The violet irises opened wide.

The smile he gave her was more terrifying than his performance.

He withdrew from her.

He stood. His sex protruded straight outwards, a cantilever of exaggerated masculinity.

She wanted to curl up around the searing hotness in her center.

He gently pulled her to her feet. Shaking, she stood.

He didn't speak. He gestured to her mouth, then to his manhood, once, twice, with his left hand.

His lower.

BUGS IN THE SYSTEM—II

"The life forms that start as spores or eggs in the insect paint are modified beetles from the Australian Outback, the Amazon Basin and North America." As Yezeletta spoke, she set up a Sony television projector on the table that still had a community of ravenous bugs at one end. She was at the other. She bustled about (that was the only way that Joe could describe it), connecting the projector into a portable computer, so it could function as the computer's monitor. She removed a chart of the "Periodic Table of the Vegetables" from the opposite wall, to provide a screen. Joe sat on one edge of the table, as Yezeletta placed the portable on one of those stands used at Italian restaurants to hold a pizza at the diner's eye-level, to make a small table seem larger; her lab stool placed her higher than the table top.

Yezeletta gestured hypnotically at the portable's keyboard, and an image appeared on the wall.

It was a line-up. For bugs.

"Are those color combinations intended?" Joe asked.

"Yes. Each of those insects is color-coded with a function." She extracted something from a drawer in the table that looked like the barrel of a pistol. It was a laser pointer. She turned it on, and gestured, the device providing a dancing red spot on the wall.

The red dot settled on an insect that looked like an ordinary midwestern stag beetle. Stag beetles are usually dark brown or black in color; this beetle was an electric violet combined with an equally electric blue. The bug had the stag's characteristic "antlers" (actually mandibles); these were of a shiny black, almost patent leather, color.

"Pretty thing," Joe said, "but I'm not sure I want to meet it outside of some kid's bug collection."

"You wouldn't," Yezeletta replied. "That's an electronics eating bug."

"Silicon based? The bug, I mean."

"No, just ordinary carbon. But it needs metals of various kinds in its diet, and, if you release it near anything with copper, iron, gold, chromium, or the like, it knows exactly what to do with it. Silicon, too, of course."

"What about electrical shock?"

"Most electronics takes voltages between minus-five, and plus-twelve. That became the standard back when the first microprocessors appeared. These days, the voltage and current requirements are much less." She didn't mention that good examples of such processors were located in small armored cavities within her own skull, powered by her body heat.

"What about power supplies for peripherals?" Joe asked.

"I have a variant. You might call it a mobile short circuit. It looks the same as the eater."

She moved the red dot to the next insect. This was similar to the stag beetle, except that the mandibles were almost the length of the beetle's body, the legs splayed out in a wider stance, equipped with nasty-looking hooked barbs, and the head of the creature was crowned with a long, sharp horn. The bug was colored in a spectrum of almost autumnal colors, chief among them being red and black.

"This is the one we'll send after Gary," Yezeletta said, decisively. "The assassin."

Joe looked into the cage. The sibilant sound of eating had stopped.

ART SUPPLIES

Yezeletta's entomology lab had been transformed by several hours of work into a very orderly mess.

Joe took in what they had done. A glass front refrigerator—it looked as if it had come from a liquor store or a supermarket—held six two-liter paint cans with colorful, if irreverent, labels. One was a parody of the old Sherwin-Williams "Cover the Earth" logo, except that the earth was being covered with large grinning bugs, some of which carried picnic baskets.

A short, solemn servitor holding a forty-five and with several of Yezeletta's hex-shaped living weapons riding its shoulders stood directly in front of it. That had been Joe's idea. The chance of someone coming up to Yezeletta's floors unnoticed was several percentage points below zero, but the contents of those cans were some of the most dangerous things in the entire complex.

THE ARTISTS

I've been out of this building all of *once*, since I arrived in this town," Yezeletta said. "I've looked out of windows and even opened them to let fresh air in here, but it'll be good to get out again and take a little action."

"How could you stand it?" Joe asked.

"I'm not sure. I think that there's a small amount of very early conditioning or training or something that I received that takes the edge off of long periods inside. Then, too, I'm not exactly inconspicuous, am I?"

Yezeletta gestured at the portable's keyboard. A plan of the Mitchell Conservatory appeared on the wall. The plan looked as if she'd scanned it out of an informational brochure: it illustrated all of the auxiliary buildings that surrounded the three geodesic domes of the actual greenhouses, or "habitats."

"There's a desert, a rain-forest and a variable habitat in which changeable exhibits are placed," Yezeletta said. She would have looked over the tops of her glasses at Joe, if she had been wearing glasses, "but you probably know all this."

"I also know about the latest exhibitor," Joe said drily.

IN THE GLASS HOUSE

"These are pure heroin," the foreman said. "Over here, we're growing crack cocaine, and that's a hallucinogen that's far more effective than LSD," he said gesturing.

Gary looked up over something that resembled a rose bush to the uninitiated. He had to stand on his toes to do it. "Better than LSD?"

The foreman, Al Wesley by name, continued, "A smaller dose provides an equivalent hallucinogenic experience and this product doesn't disintegrate in fluoridated or chlorinated water. You might recall the 'yippies' from the last century. They wanted to contaminate the Los Angeles water supply and turn on the whole city. They didn't, after one of their chemists discovered that halogens make LSD decompose."

"What's this rose bush growing?"

"That's ordinary THC. Tetra-Hydro-Cannabinol. Hardly pays to 'tease' a rose-bush into doing that. Ordinary Hemp grows just fine in this climate. Why do you think they called it 'weed'?"

Gary the Geek surveyed his small empire. He pulled himself up to the top of a convenient railing to do so. "When will this crop be ready?"

"Two weeks to maximum growth, harvest any time after," Wesley replied. "Too bad we can't get that California guy to speed things up."

"He seems to have vanished," Gary said. "I've had some people in L. A. looking around after him, he'd be a big help."

"'Make him an offer he can't refuse,' huh?" originality wasn't Wesley's strong suit.

"Something like that. Maybe with the right enticements, he'd come over voluntarily, otherwise—"

Al Wesley knew about the "otherwise." Several bodies' worth of fresh fertilizer in Dome Number Two were all he wanted to know about "otherwise."

Better to stick to Botany. Fewer hazards.

Gary Hamilton started for the ramp that led down to the exit and the auxiliary structures around the bases of the three domes. Al followed him with his gaze until Gary disappeared from view. Al dug in his pocket, removed a cigarette case.

With all of the drugs around him, he still preferred good old-fashioned nicotine.

Gary passed through several doors whose purpose was to prevent the climates in the habitats from being contaminated—mostly by simple temperature differences—from the outside. In addition to this, the support and administrative areas of the Conservatory were air-conditioned, and, after being in the tropical habitat, he had worked up a bit of a sweat.

He'd like to work up a different kind of a sweat, but the last whore he'd had in his private apartments in the complex had asked too many questions and was pushing up daisies. *Or at least roses*, he thought.

Might be a good idea to take the car out.

That sounded like a good idea.

An hour later, the vintage Cadillac limo glided silently up the concrete ramp from the Conservatory's underground parking garage, and paused while the garage door went up. Then it moved deliberately out on to the street, the door closing behind it.

Gary's thoughts were on his mission in life: providing low-cost chemical amusements to the midwest—and, currently, on getting laid. Neither he nor his bodyguards noticed the drab little matte-surfaced critters that jumped quickly under the descending garage door before it closed completely.

Nor did they see the equally diminutive creatures scaling the heights of the three geodesic domes, the vents at the tops their destinations.

THE OPERATOR

Yezeletta was truly in her own element now. She sat before three displays and tallied data in four windows on a fourth. Joe sat next to her, watching, as she correlated the inputs from her roving imagers, and took notes using a word-processor in one more window.

She wore a telephone operator's headset with which she directed the creatures that had infiltrated the Conservatory. Thicknesse sat on one of her shoulders and occasionally would jump onto Joe, where he would sit for a short time, his characteristic purr a low vibration against Joe's head.

The images on the three observation screens were shaky, grainy, and possessed of a kind of color rendition that changed in a fashion that made Joe dizzy. Yezeletta explained that the false colors came from the wide bandwidths of the imaging bio-receptors compressed down to the wavelengths that standard monitors would display.

"There aren't any monitors *made* that can handle the color reception of my vision. That was one of the downfalls of the Project. They couldn't see what I could, and I played into it."

"Can't you use an active plasma display?" Joe asked. By that he meant a display in which each pixel was a separate illumination source of one of the additive primary colors, red, blue or green.

"I tried to force one of those to emit in the ultraviolet," Yezeletta replied. "It worked for a short time, but the blue pixels, actually violet when I was done with them, burned out too fast. I did it by hacking the display's power supply to overpower the pixel emitters for parts of the screen. It took a lot of down-right strange programming and I had to rewire the power supply, but it worked. The Project optic bugs in my living quarters couldn't see things I didn't want them to.

"But it burnt out too quickly for it to be a permanent mod."

Joe was impressed. "Just long enough to get out?"

"That's all I needed."

As they conversed, with purring help from Thicknesse, a floor plan of the Mitchell Conservatory built up on the Matsushita flat screen that Joe and Yezeletta had tacked up on the wall behind her collection of smaller monitors. In spite of the name, the Matsushita's plasma display was a little on the granular side, but it was a convenient place to put the finished layout. Gary "The Geek" Hamilton had made extensive modifications to the original floor plan of the Conservatory. It was these that Yezeletta wanted to learn before they actually went out on their mission.

"A Mission like this one should actually have a code name," Joe said.

Yezeletta replied, "How about Operation By-The-Numbers?"

"That's awful. I like it."

THE GARDENER

Al Wesley poked around in the orderly rows of rose bushes, hollyhocks, shorter plants such as tulips, and vines that clambered up trellises, such as morning glories. Too bad all of these were factories for addictive substances; they were rather pretty.

He had wanted to do something with a Venus Fly-Trap. He had designed a drug source that could inject the final product into the user when he touched the plant.

Gary had vetoed that for reasons he hadn't made plain to Al.

Al walked methodically up and down the rows of mutated plants, making notations on an Apple iPad that he used for performance tracking.

Something caught his left eye. A motion.

There were the occasional small rodents in the conservatory. In greenhouses this large, it was nearly impossible to keep them out. Besides, they looked so funny staggering around after they got stoned on the pharmaceuticals. Al had wanted to get a squad of cats to patrol the domes, but Gary had vetoed the idea. He hated cats. *Or he hated the idea because he hadn't thought of it first,* Al thought.

Al scanned the area off to his left, scrutinizing the space between the rows intently.

There was nothing there.

Test Run—IV—The Examination

[Process Shot] *That hadn't been as bad as she thought it would be.*

He had insisted on her performing the act on her knees, while he stood on those improbable legs, before her.

She looked up at him, at that oddly expressionless face with those incredible luminescent eyes, *huge* eyes that regarded her with an owlish kind of sentience.

Owlish. Raptorial.

Was there anyone at home in there?

Then she had done the job on him. His sex was large, *twenty-three centimeters*, and he had tried to thrust it all into her mouth. Gently, she took his balls—*three* of them—in her hand, her right.

While she pleasured him, a distant part of her wondered, *who—what?— was he really designed for? What's his purpose? Why is he with me?*

Practice?

A Night in the Town

[Systemic Shock] The elevator took Joe and Yezeletta down to the same place Joe had been on the piano run. Yezeletta pointed up at the ceiling.

Several small spiders in webs looked back at them, with small versions of the gold-colored imager. "The resolution isn't what I want, just yet, but it's improving."

As before, a small group of short humanoids appeared out of the shadows, and followed them out to the truck.

Yezeletta was wearing a long, dark-gray trench coat, and a pair of silvered dark glasses. She wore her coat loosely enough so that she could reach the pair of .45's that she'd strapped to her belt.

The custom jump-suit, actually rather sexy overalls, surprised Joe when she came out of their bedroom wearing it. "I have a plan to put all of the garment companies out of business," she said. "I have a critter that can measure an individual and create clothing that fits exactly. I tested the 'Fitter' on Leona before you got here."

She had been close to naked most of the time while in her complex, and Joe had been so used to it, that the jump-suit was almost jarring. *The artifi-*

cial thinness of her limbs and the pistol belt make her look like a sexy heroine from Marvel Comics, he thought.

It didn't conceal her physique. For that, she needed the coat.

Yezeletta completed her dress with a gray felt fedora that looked as if it had belonged to Philip Marlowe.

Joe started the truck and drove to the end of the alley with the lights off, navigating from a small GPS display on the dashboard. He nosed the Chevy out, looked this way and that, turned on the lights, and drove off up the street.

He didn't notice the derelict on the sidewalk behind him put the cap *on* the bottle of Night Train Express, place the bottle into one pocket and remove an Ericsson cellular phone from another pocket.

As Joe and Yezeletta sped away, the derelict spoke urgently into the instrument.

On the Road to Mitchell Park

[Sestina Colonna] The route to the Mitchell Conservatory was mostly West on Highway 94—the route to the state capital of Madison—until the Twenty-Seventh Street exit that they could take south. Twenty-Seventh Street was a quiet business district followed by an equally quiet residential area, once Downtown was left behind.

The glass domes of the Conservatory were visible on the left, or East, side of the road, as the truck approached them. The greenhouses were lit internally in a haphazard way from light-sources that looked improvised even from a distance. From the telemetry that Yezeletta's remote imagers had provided, it was actually worse. Joe hoped that the next inhabitant of the Conservatory would take better care of it.

Joe reached up and scratched Jurjin, who was sitting on his right shoulder. "Joe to Yezeletta, comm check," he said to the creature.

Yezeletta placed her left hand, her lower, on Joe's leg. Thicknesse was perched on her shoulder. Her voice came from Jurjin, via Thicknesse, "Yezeletta to Joe: Have I said I love you?"

"You have now," Joe said.

They drove past the Conservatory and turned into the first street south of the complex. Joe took the truck around three sides of the property on which the Conservatory park resided to the east side and parked the truck facing east. "If we need a fast get-away," he explained.

They disembarked. The tailgate flopped down—the chains had been oiled and wrapped in oiled leather sleeves—and several servitors descended.

From here, it was a matter of looking normal as they made their way on the sidewalks that led to the support buildings of the Mitchell Conservatory. The domes were enormous in the night. It helped that most of the streetlights around the city block on which the Conservatory was situated were out—either broken by vandals or burnt out and not yet replaced.

"Yet," Joe muttered.

"Yet," Yezeletta prompted.

"The shape this place is in! I'd usually say 'unbelievable,' but I believe it far too well."

She changed the subject. "There's the main entrance. There's a service entrance around the corner from it."

The small band of painters curved around to the south side of the complex opposite the main entrance. The only illumination was from a streetlight nearly a block away. Recessed into the brick wall of the structure was a double door made of steel sheets.

There was no lock.

Yezeletta produced something that pulsed slightly. It looked like a large wad of dark-gray rubber. She placed it on the door where there would usually be a door-knob.

The gray substance flattened out on the metal door's surface, and Yezeletta produced another item. This was a large spiral of hard, black material that unwound when it got near the gray wad.

The wad moved and formed a mass in its center. The straight portion of the spiral slid into the central mass, and with a soft crackling sound, the spiral went through the wad and through the door.

The free end of the spiral opened up into a five-cornered flower-like bloom, and Yezeletta placed a cable in it. The bloom gripped the cable end, and she and Joe looked into the small screen connected by the cable to the spiral.

It showed a picture of a partially lit back hallway.

There was no one in it.

Yezeletta twisted the inside end of the fiber-optic cable around until it was looking at the gray door. There was the standard "panic exit," a handle which could be quickly pressed or leaned on, to release the door from within. She pressed a place on the cable, and the point of view in the screen approached the handle, the image getting larger and vanishing.

The door opened, casting a knife-edge of light.

Joe caught the door and pulled it open. Yezeletta entered, looked up.

There was a light-source just above the door in the hallway ceiling. She reached up, and unscrewed the bulb.

Joe and their assistants entered.

The...Memory struck.

REPRISE RECURSIVE

[Background Processing]

Video image of desolation: trivial toys of an omnipotent maniacal deity, angrily thrown into the corners of a chamber of inordinate dimension. Red flame below the horizon, silhouettes wreckage of ancient habiliment.

LIGHTNING STRIKE

[Foreground Processing] Yezeletta paused in her walk up the corridor. She leaned against the wall for a moment, then continued walking.

"You okay?" Joe asked.

"Fine," she replied. "Sometimes I get these memories that come back seemingly out of nowhere—" *or know-where*, she thought, "— and I recall something from a long time ago." She grimaced. "Maybe my long-term memory still needs to be shaken up a little. It's going to be a bit before I have all of those damned little Sargons out of my mind."

[Output] The painting party hurried up the corridor. This was a service hallway within which Gary the Geek hadn't performed any of his changes. It ran "behind" several of the other areas, once the Conservatory's Administrative center, and now several small quarters for henchmen. A double door ahead had fluorescent illumination shining out from the crack beneath that suggested access into one of the main areas.

Joe opened the door slightly, and looked out.

He was looking into a large triangular open area that, on Yezeletta's earliest floor-plans, had been the lobby and concessions. To his extreme left and right were hallways into two of the habitats; the third entrance was directly opposite. Through the glass in the doors, he could see orderly rows of flowering plants.

Yezeletta looked down at a small disk-shaped screen she held in her lower left hand. On it glowed a simple map of the near area of the complex. Their location was indicated by a green asterisk. "That way," she said, pointing.

Joe held up an identical disk. "Check for warm bodies?" She nodded.

He held the device out in front of them, touching an area along the edge with his thumb. The image flickered, then built up again. Several purple areas appeared.

"Looks as if the locals are in bed for the duration," he said. "The Geek's Place is empty." He pointed to a part of the display that had no purple indications.

Yezeletta nodded. Joe pushed the door open, and the little party of redecorators crossed the open area—as quietly as they could—and entered the corridor that had Gary's quarters.

The lock on Gary's door opened readily to Yezeletta's techniques. Joe entered, pistol in hand, looking around carefully.

"Wasted time," he whispered. "No one here."

Yezeletta entered followed by the Paint Crew. She gestured, and the servitors went, each to its predesignated place.

Earlier, the problem had arisen of where to place the insect paint. Joe had pointed out that the lumpy stuff would be rather obvious.

"It might be better to paint things that aren't readily visible. The backs of closets, under beds, and the like."

"And behind things like bookshelves," Yezeletta added.

"Gary *reads?*"

"Okay, the shelves on which he keeps his collection of *Penthouse*," Yezeletta said grinning, "or whatever."

"His toy collection," Joe continued it.

"And I wouldn't touch a straight line like that for anything, Joe!" Yezeletta said.

Yezeletta's joke hadn't been far off the mark. There were fewer books in Gary's living room than either of them had expected. Only one shelf, and it held several potted plants and a stack of magazines. Two servitors attacked it, lifting it out of the way so the wall behind it could get painted, and placing several daubs of paint on the undersides of the shelves themselves.

Several of the magazines fell off: *Gent*, *Cavalier* and *Playboy*. And one *Penthouse*.

Joe went into a damp and humid bathroom and painted several towels, which he tossed behind the antique bathtub. A splash of paint down the wash-basin and bathtub drains completed his work.

He came out of the bathroom to see Yezeletta leaving the bedroom, a paint can and a pair of brushes in her hands, a satisfied smirk on her face. Joe gave her a raised eyebrow.

"I got his cactus plants, his 'art' books and all of his underwear," she said.

"Riight. Cactus in his shorts? Or just bugs?"

"He'll just *wish*."

Two servitors exited the kitchen. A pair of servitors were splashing insect paint behind the television, another was pouring paint into the davenport. As Joe watched, that servitor replaced the cushions, covering the painted areas.

The painters assembled in The Geek's living room.

"This job isn't complete," Yezeletta said, "we still have eight liters left." She and one servitor held up four cans.

"Well—" Joe said, "this isn't the only place that needs a paint job, is it? How many bugs do we have left?"

"Lots," she replied.

"Can't let them go to waste," he went on. "Where does he do his research?"

"The domes," Yezeletta decided. "We can pour it out there, and it'll all hatch at once. We can leave from there."

"Alimentary, my dear Yezeletta!"

Yezeletta headed for the exit, Joe followed. Yezeletta took out a small object. She placed it on the inside of the door's latch. As he watched, the...what-ever-it-was *sank into* the surface of the door around the door-knob. Then she paused to check the outside with the read-out from the disk. "The night watchmen are still asleep," Yezeletta said cheerfully. "Let's do it!"

They ran, in a clumsy attempt to combine speed with stealth, back to the central area, and into the habitat dome that Joe had noticed earlier.

Yezeletta removed several plastic bags from a pouch on her belt. She held them open while Joe poured about a half-liter of Paint into each. Yezeletta touched the head of a convenient servitor and several Imagers scampered up. She handed the sealed bags to the Imagers and they took them off into other parts of the complex.

"We mustn't forget Gary's friends," Yezeletta said.

They were in the temperate climate dome. All around them were rows of green growing things, some labeled with complex chemical formulae or with the diagrams of the desired compounds sketched on small signs posted at the ends of the rows. Above them a balcony surrounded the outer circumference of the dome, with a railing leaning inwards; obviously an area for tours.

Near the door was a metal panel. It was unlocked: a circuit breaker box. Joe switched them off.

The dome darkened. The only illumination was from EXIT signs, which couldn't be shut off, and from lighting external to the dome: street lights a block or so away. Yezeletta gestured with her upper left, and a pair of servitors went into the central area of the dome with metal cans, pouring the remainder of the paint out in wet streaks between the rows of plants.

When they were finished, and the cans hidden in some convenient bushes, Yezeletta turned her back to Joe, and he removed a device that looked like a short twelve-gauge shotgun from her backpack.

It was actually more of a harpoon gun. Joe took aim, and the grappling hook launched from the device, and hooked into the dome's framework. The report was overly loud in the habitat. "You first," he said.

Yezeletta hooked a steel device to the cable hanging from the grapple, and pressed a button on her belt. A small motor started, and lifted her up the line. Joe checked the lower end of the line under one foot, and watched as Yezeletta was carried up to the balcony, then to the outer edge of the habitat where the dome met the walkway. She spread her arms and legs out to keep her balance, as she ascended, and the image of her, an eight-limbed shadow against the patterns of the beams in the geodesic dome, with the stars in the night sky behind her, was arresting.

Even on a mission, she has her own beauty.

Then it was his turn. Three servitors checked the lower end of the line, as Joe attached his climber to the cable. The little electric motor lifted him with a breathtaking acceleration, and deposited him next to Yezeletta.

Then, the servitors grabbed the line. Yezeletta looked down carefully, intently. Joe knew that her eyes were adjusted to the dark, and that, to her, what she was seeing was as good as daylight below. She looked, blinked, looked again, nodded to Joe. He pressed the control, and this time the cable wound up from the grapple, lifting the servitors out.

A spear of light washed across the dark field. The light caught one gray servitor foot before it was lifted to safety.

"Who the hell's up there?!"

Two figures came in, each carrying a flashlight in one hand, and—it had to be firearms!—in the other. Yezeletta grabbed Joe in one strong hand, and pulled him away from the railing.

Yezeletta removed two objects that looked like chalk-board erasers from her belt; Joe added two of his own. They placed the devices on the lower part of the glass. Standing back, Joe pressed a control. The shaped charges detonated outwards, taking about two meters' worth of glass out of the dome. Outside was a concrete foundation with landscaping that sheared away at a steep angle. The servitors didn't need any signals. They hopped through the hole, Yezeletta counting them as they came; then she slid down after them, grabbing Joe with a free hand, yanking him down with her.

They landed in a heap in a small flower garden. One that had just been watered. Dazed, Joe got to his feet, wiped mud off his pants, looked up.

Several short figures were running across the lawn from the south east. Joe recognized servitors. Yezeletta was on her feet, her clothes muddy and wet. She wiped her lower left hand on a convenient leg, drew one of her forty-fives, and looked up behind.

The hole gaped in the night, and through it Joe could see dim but moving lights. "They'll have to come around to get here," she said. She started for the truck, Joe and the rest of the painters keeping up.

A sound in the night.

"I don't believe it!" Yezeletta said. "Someone's called the cops!"

They reached the truck, and the servitors piled into it. Joe slammed the tailgate, and ran around to the driver's side.

Yezeletta was already aboard. In a fluid set of motions, he started the vehicle, put it into gear, and, leaving the lights off, moved away from the curb.

He drove up to the intersection with Twenty-Sixth Street, and took the truck through to the residential street east. Behind him, he saw a porch light come on in a residence opposite about where they had been parked. A distinctive blue and white car pulled up in front of the house, and two uniformed men got out.

He turned onto—what?—Twenty-Fifth?

The Conservatory was at a distance now, and, far better, was no longer in line-of-sight. He turned east, again, and turned on the headlights. The downtown area was getting closer. The Milwaukee River would be ahead.

Red lights. Approaching.

The District Six squad car came barrelling towards them in the opposite lane. Like any conscientious driver, Joe pulled over and gave the cops enough room. The squad didn't slow, it kept moving until its tail-lights were out of sight.

"Do you have a hive, or any other installation in this area?"

"There's a garage that we can hide in. It's near Zhongo's, north of Wisconsin Avenue. Take a left anywhere near here, and go north."

LIGHTS IN THE DISTANCE

A bit later, the truck pulled into the garage Yezeletta had indicated. In one corner, a large sleek Harley-Davidson reposed; tools lined one wall, and, Joe noticed, the windows were securely boarded up.

"We can wait here for a time," Yezeletta said, "then we can get home."

"Think this truck was noticed?" Joe said.

"Not by the cops that were arriving. They may be told of it by anyone there, those home-owners, for instance, who may have seen us drive off. I wonder—" she paused in thought.

"A Hive in the area?"

"A Hive in the area. There's a small one west of the Domes in the basement of a small strip mall that went under two years ago." Yezeletta reached into the storage area behind the seat, and removed a laptop computer. Then, she tapped on the window into the back of the truck, and it opened. The craggy face of a servitor appeared in it.

Yezeletta touched the servitor's forehead. The creature pulled its head back in, and moved around in the truck. A mobile imager hopped up into the window, its gold aperture flickering. Yezeletta plugged the computer into the truck's cigarette lighter, and attached several wires to a plug on the back of the device. The imager crawled through the window, across Yezeletta, and out of her passenger-side window. A moment later, Joe could see it climbing the garage wall. It vanished into the darkness near the garage's roof.

An image built up on the laptop screen. It flickered, tilted crazily this way and that, then stabilized.

"This is a lot like the way I tried to hack Searchlight's Data Centre when I was on my way to Milwaukee," she said. Joe raised an eyebrow. "I set up a remote relay, and worked through a phone connection that I was nowhere near. Turned out to be the best way to handle it."

The image was still jumping around. The imager that was sending it was taking long leaps through trees, across roofs, and—dangerously—along power or telephone lines.

The image went out of focus.

Then it returned, jittered, flickered, went in and out of precise focus, then stabilized, again.

It was a view from well up one of the domes.

"That's one," Yezeletta said, "the imager that just left is relaying that."

The image on the laptop's screen flickered again, then focused. This view was from above several people, two of whom were in police uniforms. "Another Imager," she added.

The non-uniformed individuals were gesturing, and obviously talking at a rather high rate. One, a middle-aged woman in an old house-dress, pointed down the street. The indicated direction was also "down" in the sense that it was pointing at the bottom of the computer's screen.

"Which way is that imager facing?" Joe asked.

"West," she replied.

"That woman's pointing in the general—hell, specific—direction *we* went."

"We'd better plan on staying here for a while," Yezeletta said. She fingered several keys, and the woman's voice came on, thinly.

"—A large vehicle, that went that way. East, officer, don't know how many were in it."

"What have you got in this garage that's comfortable?" Joe asked.

"There's a bedroom, up above us. The building this garage is attached to has one of my Hives in it. This whole block was abandoned years ago, and I grabbed this place. Zhongo has the triplex up the street. His mistress—Leona—lives there."

"That's the Harley she used?"

Yezeletta nodded.

On the screen, the woman continued talking.

THE MATTRESSES

Yezeletta's notion of a "bedroom" was the entire second story of a three-car garage containing a large waterbed, a well-stocked kitchen, and nearly as many communications devices as she had at home.

"Hilda," she explained, "can supervise the Farmers Building very well from the Matrix Engine when I'm not there." She tuned gold laser eyes on Joe. "This is the first time she's had to do this alone, but her 'eyes' are everywhere in the complex, and she can issue orders to the 'staff' just as you and I can. That reminds me—" She paused.

"Are we in touch with her, and the other systems?" Joe asked.

"Yes. What it reminds me of is that I've never asked you about your own researches."

"Figured that I'd just see what you were interested in."

Yezeletta nodded, as her fingers moved quickly over a pair of keyboards. "What sort of a lab set-up would you like? After all, you've seen The Celebrated Yezeletta Zargkonji and her Magic Labs—" She was grinning.

"And you'd like to see what I can whip up in the Celebrated Downtown Kitchens of Davis."

Yezeletta put her left arms around Joe's waist. She looked up at him from where she was sitting. "Show me how you cook it," she said. Joe was familiar with the idiom, but this was the first time he had ever actually seen it: her eyes twinkled, the laugh lines around them more pronounced.

"Well, you need a pot that you can stir things in real well—" He bent down and kissed her, "And it helps if you're properly positioned...."

"We'll check those positions later tonight," she said, returning the kiss with compound interest. "I think that now, we must see if we've been spotted. Partner."

"I like the way you say that."

INTERLUDE—TUTORIAL

Strong cryptography, where that term refers to the kind of encryption that would take longer than the life-expectancy of the universe to decrypt, was an off-the-shelf component of just about everything involving communications. It was hard to believe that the Federal Government had actually tried to suppress its use when it became available to the casual computer-user back in the early nineteen-nineties. Anyone who had something to keep secret could *keep* that secret by recourse to any of a number of useful programming packages, of which PGP, Pretty Good Privacy, was the oldest and probably the best.

The Milwaukee Police Department, like other public agencies, had been forced by hard times, budget cuts and drastic personnel shortages, to improvise. The Department had managed to create a secure radio-based data-communications system, not by buying the latest AT&T Mil-Spec equipment, but by asking several cops who were also very good hackers to interface PGP to the squad car terminals, and provide another version of PGP at the station houses to perform decryption. If it was any solace to the policemen who operated this system, it was probably more secure than anything that AT&T could have provided. When the two squads at the Mitchell Conservatory sent in their reports, the individual police officers who actually did the reporting were confident that those data would get to the appropriate district, and that no one would *or could* intercept them.

Well, almost no one.

THE CLANDESTINE OPERATIVE

Yezeletta Zargkonji wasn't any better than any other would-be code-breaker at causing the 128-bit basic encryption (it was called *IDEA*, the International Data Encryption Algorithm) in PGP to Stand and Deliver. What she could do was grab the data either before they were encrypted, or after they were re-rendered into plaintext.

Tempest—<u>T</u>ransient <u>E</u>lectro<u>m</u>agnetic <u>P</u>ulse <u>E</u>manation <u>S</u>tandard—was both a standard for shielding computing equipment from casual eavesdropping, as well as a description of the means by which such equipment could be monitored.

Computer displays and keyboards function as broadcasting devices. The minute signals put out by such pieces of equipment can be detected at a distance, and the signals *may be interpreted* by the appropriate hardware-software systems. The result is that the well-equipped eavesdropper may read those transmissions at up to several hundred meters' distance.

Yezeletta's imagers were considerably closer than that.

One imager, in a tree nearby, performed a telephoto look-down that watched one cop as she typed data into her squad's keyboard. The Receiver performed a complementary function: it "saw" in specific electromagnetic wavelengths outside of the human visible spectrum. Its function was to upload a "picture" of the cop's screen as a pattern of bits, as well as each of the succeeding screens as her displays changed. The uploads went to the organic server in the one-time strip-mall a block west of the Conservatory.

As Joe and Yezeletta watched, the Police Department's data-comm gave up all of the information that the officers down at the Conservatory transmitted to the District Six Station.

Joe let out a breath.

"They don't have our license number."

"They wouldn't," his partner said, "although that's a valid license plate; it's for a Volkswagen 'Beetle' registered to a vacant lot in Oak Creek."

"That's not a joke, is it?"

"The Beetle? Oh," she put her upper left arm around his waist, pulled him closer. "Insect Paint doesn't hatch that large, but I suppose, if we needed some really big bugs—"

Joe rubbed her neck, ran a finger along her cheek, "Anything else in that magic lantern?"

Yezeletta gestured hypnotically, and several other images appeared in quick succession, as the laser-printer started up.

The printouts were screen-shots of the displays that Yezeletta's Tempest imager—the Receiver—had read from the distant squad-car. Taken together, the shots indicated that they had nothing to fear from the Police. The "van," driven by a single woman, had gone due East, and vanished, and *No, Officer, I didn't see the plate in the night*.

Yezeletta gestured at a keyboard, the left one, and another image built up in the screen. It was a long-shot down into the dome from which they had escaped a short hour ago.

"Gary," Yezeletta said, "is about to find out how exciting a paint-drying contest can be."

Down among the orderly rows of plants, something was moving.

THE DINING IN

When Gary's Cadillac returned, helpfully about ten minutes after the police had left, he was smiling. More than that: he was grinning from one ear to the other.

She had been wonderful.

Slim, skilled and *built*. She had been built like the proverbial Brick Shit-House. *Maybe I can recruit her for life in the big time*, he thought. *I wonder if she likes vegetables.*

The garage door lifted, and the Cadillac, expertly piloted by the chauffeur, slid into its assigned place.

Gary got out, then his men, followed by the driver. Gary gave them a desultory wave, and they went off to their quarters, and Gary went off to his.

He stopped at the door to his apartment, and fumbled for his keys. Still thinking of his latest conquest, he shoved the key into the lock, and the door opened.

The door should have been locked, the key should have been inserted and turned before the door opened. He pushed the door closed with a casual wave of his hand, and went into his bedroom. The door closed with a sharp click.

He turned back his bed.

He stopped.

He took a breath.

The smell was familiar, even if he couldn't place it immediately. Oh, yeah: fresh paint. Nothing wrong with—

Fresh?

Paint?

Had someone been here?

Gary's mind cleared from the night's drinking, as his suspicions kicked in. He looked around again.

Nothing.

Gary went back into the living room. He scanned the room, and didn't notice anything on the first scan. On the second—

That copy of *Penthouse*. There on the shelf.

His living area was made from pre-stressed concrete. The concrete had been wood paneled in a light birch. That concealed without actually hiding the smear of—paint?—behind the magazine shelf.

Who'd been in here?

He went back into the bedroom, flopped on the bed. He grabbed the telephone, and dialed an internal intercom number.

The beeping of the touch-tone pad seemed to echo in the room. He heard a rustling sound in the living room.

"Hello," the phone said.

"Hi," Gary said back, "Was there anyone in my place while I was out?"

"No....Hold on, Al wants to talk." Then:

"Gary? Al."

"What's up?"

"There were some intruders in here earlier. They were running around in Dome Number Two."

"Any idea who?"

"No. They got out by rappelling up to the balcony in Two, and blowing a hole in the glass, and jumping out. Some people across the street called the cops, but they didn't find anyone, so they left. I had the hole covered up."

"Rappelling *up?*"

"Yeah. Some kinda motor rig."

"Anything hurt?"

"No. We're waiting until morning to clean up."

"Keep me—" rustle-rustle "— posted." Gary hung up.

A sharp pain lanced through his right foot!

A large beetle, red, brown and black in color with long sharp mandibles, was attacking his foot. It had—the stabbing pain lanced through him again—*penetrated* the leather of his shoes!

Gary grabbed a pool cue from a floor stand next to his bed, and swatted at the bug. It responded by stabbing him again. He swept at the insect from the side, connecting with a loud "thwack," and the beetle was knocked off the bed onto the floor. It started for the bed again.

Gary jumped up, and came down on the floor. His feet *crunched* on something. He took a step, and there was another *crunch*.

The floor was covered with large colorfully carapaced bugs. There were so many that he was stepping on them.

"What the hell—!" he shouted.

He ran across the bedroom to the door, went into the living room.

The insects were everywhere!

He headed for the front door, and opened it.

The doorknob came off in his hand.

He re-inserted the square, threaded insert to which doorknobs are attached, and turned it.

Nothing happened.

He tried harder. The door-latch was jammed.

And he was in here with—

"My god!" he breathed.

The bugs were two and three deep in some places.

He ran back to the bedroom. The bed was covered in squirming moving six-legged life. He grabbed for the phone, and something bit a chunk out of the ball of his thumb as he retrieved the instrument. He dialed, put it to his ear.

The line was dead. Gary looked back at the line that should have led to the wall.

A blue and violet beetle, easily fifteen centimeters long, was eating its way up the dangling end of the line.

Panicking, he ran into the living room, scooped his cellular out of a bowl of moving lifeforms, looked for shelter.

The bathroom.

He ran, crunching on hard shells to the john, set the phone down in the sink, and grabbed a broom from a corner. He swept the insects that were in the bathroom quickly and efficiently out the door, and closed it. The bugs had seemed to be interested in organic stuff. The cotton sheets and the wool blankets on his bed, for example. There were no towels in the bathroom at the moment.

He put the phone to his ear, pressed the "call" key.

The dial tone was the most reassuring sound he had ever heard.

He dialed through the Conservatory's outside line to Al's workshop.

The ringing signal repeated three times, then—

"Yeah?"

"Al!"

"Yes, Gary."

"I'm in the bathroom at my place. Send someone up here to spring me. There's these—"

"Really big bugs in there, right?"

"How did *you* know?"

"Gary, they're all over the place!" He paused, went offline. Gary could hear him say, "— he's in the can with a roomful of those." Then another voice, "You, you and you, follow me."

Al returned: "Harry's on his way with reinforcements. He'll be there in about a minute."

"I think I'm safe. My door's jammed, or I'd be outta here!"

"Help's coming. I gotta go. I think I can get these with a little 2,4-D. Maybe a little Malathion."

Al hung up.

Gary looked around. The bathroom was large, luxurious, usually for two, and the only beetle he could see was one walking out from under the bathtub. "Come here, Ringo...." he said.

If that were the only one, he'd be safe here until Harry showed up.

He looked back at "Ringo." There was another one, then—

The carpet of bugs that emerged slowly, deliberately from beneath the bathtub came straight for him. Panicking again, he stamped on several, and some of the others were distracted from their main target, and began eating their fellows.

The others kept moving forward.

They started climbing his legs.

Gary ran out of the bathroom into a suite of rooms that was ankle, and knee deep in the corners with squirming writhing insects. Part of him noticed with suppressed amazement that the birch paneling was gone from one wall. He ran to the door, and frantically turned the knob, again. Nothing happened.

There was an agonizing pain at the small of his back. He backed into a wall to brush the bug off, and the pain got worse.

There was one on his shoulder. He swatted at it with his other hand, and the insect riding on his wrist went for his face. He clawed at the creatures on his face, and tripped on something.

He fell face first into the mass of writhing insects.

HELLO THERE, HOW ARE THINGS?

Harry and his crew never made it to Gary's quarters.

The paint in Dome Number Two hatched into things that got into the air-conditioning, and, in their brief infancy, out under doors, and through electrical wiring runs. A small number of them left by way of the hole through which Joe and Yezeletta had escaped.

Al Wesley had supervised the placing of a tarpaulin over the hole. The idea was to keep critters out. Al had never thought that something might want to escape from within the complex.

From the outside, in the early dawn's light, the small swarm that did escape looked like smoke drifting away from the patched-up place in the glass geodesic dome. They sailed up on the winds, and shortly, the smoke dissipated into nothingness, as the insects drifted southward, out of Milwaukee.

They weren't followed. By then, the bugs remaining had grown far too large to be able to leave.

"C" DEBUG

By about eight in the morning, there was nothing alive that moved on legs in the Mitchell Conservatory. Yezeletta's custom insect life was designed not only to remove the lifeforms for which each had been directed, but also to clean up after itself. Towards the end of the carnage, a new, single-minded insect appeared. It was all black. It was as if the sheer quantity of the more aggressive beetles had caused this all-black form to appear. In reality, it was one of Yezeletta's designs that went active at a certain stage in the life-cycle of the creatures born out of the Insect Paint.

The black beetles were the clean-up crew.

Beneath the foliage, the plants, the bones that were devoid of skin, the black beetles removed the bodies of their more active cousins and took them down pipes, down cracks in the floor, into the occasional burrow left by an unlucky rodent, and left them there. Larger bones were reduced to smaller bones, and smaller bones were buried.

Later that day, the Conservatory was clean, the evidence of an action by a biologic warrior obliterated.

Only the ones that had escaped remained alive.

The small ones. The ones designed to help.

The preservers of plant life.

INGRESS TO ACCESS: PARADOX

[Transform] Like a wisp of smoke the smaller insects flew at a level of some twenty meters above the surface. The beetles were an iridescent blue-green in color on the top, and an exact sky blue on the bottom. To a predator flying above them, their pretty green color—about the shade of Kentucky blue-grass—would make them very obvious.

But no predators flew above them.

To an observer below them, their sky-blue underside effectively made them invisible.

But no one looked up to see them.

The bugs saw by infra-red, and they were directed to a specific shade of infra-red: not too much, not too little. Yezeletta's design placed their visual target between a pair of boundary values. Only an infra-red frequency within those boundaries was visible to the insects.

Like the one ahead.

The swarm divided into three parts. One part descended into the field in which the proper infra-red signature was the strongest. The other two-thirds continued. The landers disappeared into the dead stalks from the previous year, and, with their mindless, preprogrammed gusto, got to work.

Before the day ended, *each* of the three sub-swarms had landed, and was doing the job for which it had been designed. The dust-bowls in which they found themselves would soon change, green stalks would replace the yellowed, dry ones. A fine network of capillaries would descend into the ground to seek the water-table, the insects would consume such things as PCBs—Poly Chlorinated Biphenyls—and reduce them to their constituent elements.

The land would start living at a considerably higher level. This would become visible to a degree that would be almost blatant in about a week's time, causing a small amount of consternation shortly thereafter, that would expand out like the ripples in water around a thrown stone.

And the beetles would never know it, for they would be long gone when their effects would become noticed.

NORTH BY NORTHWEST

Actually, a small number of life-forms remained in the Mitchell Conservatory. They were high up in the domes, far removed from their cousins and the work they had done below.

These life-forms were Yezeletta's imagers. In her temporary HQ in a garage northwest of the Domes, she and Joe had watched for awhile, then shut the screens off. They had curled up together in the large bed, where they had made passionate love, then drifted off to sleep. The next morning was gray and overcast, and the wind blew loudly around the building. It woke Joe, and he gently disengaged himself from three of Yezeletta's arms, and went looking for breakfast.

The kitchen was at the other end of the room: a compact four-burner stove, and foodstuffs in freezers, or refrigerators. He found what he was looking for, and started breakfast.

Yezeletta awoke a few minutes later to frying, boiling, and other sounds of a busy cook. She walked up behind Joe, and rubbed his shoulders, while he scrambled eighteen eggs, and fried a kilogram package of thickly-sliced bacon. "Good morning," he said. "Sleep well?"

"I did," she said, "and I see you have things well in hand." Outside, the wind howled around the garage.

"Just about ready. How many of these little headquarters buildings do you have in this town?"

"About a dozen. This is the first time I've ever used one, however."

"When do you think we should get back to Prime Base?"

"Later. This evening. I'd rather not travel by day, and it looks as if it's unpleasant out there."

"In more ways than just high winds." Joe placed an enormous serving of scrambled eggs and cheese onto a large platter, and set it on the table. He added a smaller by half serving of the same for himself, added several liters of orange juice, and the usual side items, and they sat down.

"I like the way you plan ahead," Joe said, as Yezeletta pulled up a chair designed for her, but that she had never used before.

"No one knows of these places; I figured I might as well design them for comfort—" Joe remembered a candlelight conversation in which she had said something similar, "—and I never knew when I'd have to use one."

"This is the first time you've been out—"

She nodded, swallowed. "I feel pretty good about getting out to do something, and eliminating one of Milwaukee's tiresome gangsters really helps. Besides," she added thoughtfully, "this was what I was meant to do, and—"

"Function follows Form?"

"Interesting idea." She spread a large piece of toast with raspberry jam. "Last night I had a- a sudden memory is the best way to describe it: a flashback. An image of a row of houses in a residential area, but they had been bombed out. Destroyed."

"When you mentioned 'all of those damned little Sargons'?"

"You got it. Those images go way back, and I've never known exactly where they come from. A disaster movie I saw, perhaps. A recollection of something I read, or something on television. I just don't know. Last night I thought they might be nothing more than a vestige of the conditioning that you, the Lenhadens and that secret agent fellow helped me through."

"Is there anything I could do to help out?"

She grinned, "Yup. Let's go back to bed."

SYSTEM TYPE-DESCRIPTOR

[Debug Trace On] The CIA and its derivative organizations had always been under-manned. With the ending of Washington, D.C. as a locus of power, the agencies had become drastically under-paid, as well. The remaining government employees managed, mostly by clever programming of KH-42's uplink control system, to keep their antique running. With the destruction of both houses of Congress during a Presidential address, there was very little the surviving government could do for what had became virtually non-essential agencies.

But the Power, Space, Tech and Research Blocs needed to be supervised, if for no other reason than that The Company was interested in what kinds of threats they could pose to an effectively decapitated United States.

EXAMINATION—V—WEB

[The Graduate] He entered her room again, this time with almost an expression on his face.

She studied it: it was one she had seen before.

Anticipation.

His disrobing of her (all she was wearing was a flimsy peignoir) was gentle. It seemed as if he had been Given the Word by some unseen source of information. He made a production of removing the flimsy garment, and running his hands over her breasts, while rubbing her back.

She took those three balls in her hand, as she had the day before, but a strong hand grabbed her wrist, and pulled it away from there.

He turned her around.

The motion was a jarring surprise. She hadn't expected it. This huge—individual—had simply turned her as if she were any kind of inanimate object.

He pulled her hands behind her.

Then he tied them.

When he was done, he turned her around to face him again.

He gestured at his sex, and at her.

She got down on her knees.

DETERMINANTS AT PARALLEL

[Processing] *The screens unite in clusters, each cluster separate from the others, yet all are related. The scenes of desolation are replaced now; some of the displays show eye-catching patterns, slow moving abstractions that attract the attention of the watcher. In others, the burned houses are replaced by such things as a long-shot across a green-grassy field, but a field that has been littered with wreckage. A burned-out automobile with miscellaneous luggage strewn about it. In the far background, a streamlined train passes the field, the sound of its passage dopplering away in the distance.*

The screens change, again, after the passage.

ON THE GREEN WHEN SUN IS DOWN

[Processing] A discreet tap on his shoulder woke Joe. Yezeletta was up and moving around. She was about half dressed. Joe rose from the bed, spread the cover on it, and got edibles out. Yezeletta finished dressing and joined him, and they prepared a light meal.

"I'm anxious to get back to the Shop," she said.

"Me too," Joe replied. "I never thought I'd be this way, but I have this 'unprotected' feeling."

Yezeletta blinked. "I have it too. I was up about half an hour before you, and I did what Captain Picard would have called a 'General Sensor Scan' around here. There's nothing out of place, but—it may just be the weather, the temperature or whatever causing subconscious associations—or something. I'm a little apprehensive."

"Did you call home?"

"Yes. Hilda reports no problems, but I asked her to beef up the security there, anyway. The Base is locked down tight."

Yezeletta had prepared a plate of heroic beef and cheese sandwiches. They ate quietly for a moment, each lost in thought.

They headed out later. The servitors had recharged themselves in the garage, and were lying low in the back of the truck. Yezeletta bundled herself up in her disguising coat, mirrorshades and hat, and, looking like something out of an old detective movie, took her place in the front seat.

Joe started the truck, and backed it out of the garage.

When the truck had cleared the door, Yezeletta touched the round little body of the imager in her lap, and the garage door slid closed.

Joe pointed the truck generally east, and they sped off.

PARALLEL PROCESS

[Multitasking] As the truck travelled east, a ragged-looking man in a patched Army Surplus fatigue jacket picked up its shape and followed it with his eyes, as he dictated in urgent tones into the tiny microphone that depended from the headset he was wearing. He had been looking for this particular truck since very early in the morning. He hadn't seen where it came from, and didn't know its ultimate destination.

He did know its current direction and its approximate speed. These he reported to the attentive listener on the far end of his communications channel.

Then he went looking for a McDonalds.

MAZE

[Camera Goes With; Extending Upper: Logical] Joe drove slowly east. He was careful about speed-limits, and the rules of the road, generally. To anyone else, the truck was just that: a one-ton Chevy pickup, whose driver was going about his business.

Yezeletta leaned back, and cast her awareness about her.

Several windows opened in the purview of her left eye.

The windows looked out through the transmitted inputs of several imagers. One imager rode in the back of the truck, hanging from a little bracket inside the tailgate window. The window was tinted a very dark gray, so the imager wouldn't be noticed, and the imager's own internal processing would compensate for the decrease in visibility. The result was a looking-back view that she could enhance any way she wished. Another imager hung in the opposite corner of the window, if she wanted a stereoscopic input.

Several more imagers looked out in other directions. Yezeletta's internal systems could analyze, correlate and combine the inputs any way that she wanted. As Joe drove, she conducted real-time visual traffic analysis.

MAZE USER

[Match Cut: Sign Extension; Bit Map]   Two vehicles back from Yezeletta and her partner, a brown Toyota with rusted bumpers followed, sliding into the traffic pattern with the greased ease of long practice. The green Ford that it displaced moved off into the right-turn lane, and vanished south. The Toyota followed discreetly along behind a Corvette and a man on a bicycle.

MAZE RUNNER

[Instantiate Member Function]   Joe pulled up to an intersection and stopped for a red light. Yezeletta looked back, and mixed in the input from the other imager. The exaggerated depth of the two widely separated inputs threw the view back into a sharp focus that made her dizzy.

She shut down the dizziness and focused on the drivers behind her. The man on the bicycle she could forget about. Her routine traffic analysis had spotted him in the area before. He was one of Zhongo's messengers. Ditto the Corvette. Not only did it have Illinois plates, the driver looked out of place in Wisconsin. He was of a general type and dress that would be more at home on Lake Shore Drive.

That Toyota, now....

She zoomed in on the drivers. Then she zoomed closer. She looked up their faces in one of her on-board databases.

No hits.

Not uncommon. Not finding someone in her internals happened more often than finding a match.

"Joe, please turn north at the next intersection."

Joe gave her a look; she returned it.

He turned left onto a northbound street, and Yezeletta looked back through her system.

Riight. The cyclist had gone straight through the intersection, followed by the Chicagoan in the Corvette. The Toyota was still there.

She touched Joe's arm, gently. Joe gave her another look.

"There's a brown Toyota behind us. When I asked you to turn, it turned with us. It's been following us rock-steady for the last six blocks.

"Is there a place that we can get to?"

"There's another hideout north of here—up on Capitol Drive. But we'd still have to worry about a truckload of servitors."

"Is there a Hive in the area?"

Yezeletta thought, then consulted a small database. "There's a Hive in a small building ahead. It used to be a tool storage for the Milwaukee Road. It's been abandoned for about twenty years."

"Can we drop the staff there, and pick them up later?"

"If we can lose our friends back there."

"Keep an eye on those guys, while I get us out of here."

A large truck, an eighteen-wheeler used as a moving van, pulled up next to them. On the side of the truck was the name "Hernia Movers" painted in large black letters. In smaller lettering, it said: "The Potentate of Toting Freight."

Part of him had a laugh at that. He'd seen Hernia's trucks around the city.

Maybe he could give their followers a—

He pulled abreast of the moving van.

The van driver regarded the Chevy pickup warily, as it pulled up on him. His truck was one of the largest on the road, and he handled it with professional care, as befitting the biggest bear in the woods.

Then Joe was ahead and to the right of the van. The mover let up on his gas a bit to see what Joe was going to do.

An alley opened on the *left*. In one reckless maneuver, Joe cut across the front of the Hernia Truck.

The trucker hit the brakes.

The brown Toyota tried to follow Joe.

The moving van plowed into it, shoving the car back into its lane. The mover stopped moving, practically standing on his brakes. The trucker's horns spoke eloquently in the night.

Another car rammed the Toyota's rear.

A blue and white cruiser containing two of Milwaukee's Finest pulled up. Shortly, another did. Then another.

ON THE OTHER SIDE

[Buffer Active; Arriflex] At the other end of the alley, Joe drove the truck at a gentle pace, with the lights off. He came to the exit, and gingerly stuck the truck's nose out, looking.

Yezeletta let go of her seat belt, the seat, the door handles, and the seat back with all four hands. She gave Joe a look.

"Well, we made it, didn't we?" he said.

"I didn't know you were such a defensive driver," she replied drily. "Did we lose them?"

In the distance they could hear sirens. "I think so. Where's that Hive?" Joe said. "We need to get outta here."

He nosed the truck in a westerly direction, then turned back north. Fifteen minutes later they pulled up to a small, roughly cubical structure that looked abandoned from a distance—and more abandoned, up closer.

"The reason this place looks as though no one can get at it, is that no one *can*," Yezeletta explained. "First, there's no one living around here, except for the occasional wino, and second, if anyone gets close, he forgets why he came here, when he wakes up several blocks away."

She sent a signal. In the back of the truck, the servitors woke up, and got out of the back. The door to the Hive opened, and the munchkins entered it. One of them looked back, and the imager in its forehead flickered, sending a data stream.

Then it closed the door.

Yezeletta looked at Joe, Joe looked at Yezeletta. "The interchangeable parts are safe. Let's go home," she said.

TRY AGAIN

[Redundant Array; Medium Close-Up] Joe pulled the truck away from the Hive and headed east, then south. Yezeletta resumed looking around. Joe wished that he could grow eyes in the back of his head.

"You couldn't grow eyes in the back of my head?" he asked.

"I could, but you wouldn't be able to use them."

"Why not?"

"They'd have to be connected into your nervous system somehow. You wouldn't have the 'switching' to handle it, and, at your age, the extra inputs would be confusing."

"Yours went into you?"

"Before I was born. There are some videos I stole out of the Project that show the doctors working on me. They're not for the squeamish."

"I'll take your word on that."

"You'd like to be able to look around better than you can now," she said.

"Yep! Just a set of screens that I could use to monitor the back and the sides of this van would be good."

"Screens, we can set up. Maybe...."

Yezeletta paused. She closed her eyes.

"What—?" Joe asked.

"I think—" Yezeletta started to say. She closed her eyes. Opened them.

"I don't believe that we've lost our friends."

"Damn. Who is it this time?"

She thought for a moment, as she checked her rear inputs. "Someone behind us. Dark green VW. Two men, like the last bunch." She looked at Joe, "They've had an overlapping tail on us. Or, they've picked us up again."

"Is there anyone around where we dropped the munchkins?"

"I'll check." Yezeletta thought into her systems for nearly five seconds. Ten. "No," she said at last. "It must have been a re-acquisition. That means that they have this area south of Capitol Drive saturated."

"Hmmmm."

"Upsetting to have all of our abilities, and be hassled by nothing more than a lot of gumshoes all out at the same time."

"Dare I try any more fancy driving?" Joe said.

"No. I think they want to just see where we're going."

"Do they know who they're following?"

"Interesting question," Yezeletta said. "I'm not sure. They may only be on an initial investigation run. They may think they have something interesting, but aren't sure. So they follow us around until they get more info."

"How important is this truck?"

"In what way?"

"If we dumped this crate—abandoned it—is there anything of yours in it that would lead a reasonably good investigator back to us, or to your techniques?"

Yezeletta scratched her chin with a left hand. "No. I have a DNA Trace Eliminator aboard that can wipe out all evidence of us and my creations, quickly. There's nothing else here, except the two Imagers in the back. They can go climb a tree."

"Can Leona come and get us?"

"Maybe. It depends on what her Favorite Zhongo is up to. Why?"

"I'm wondering if we shouldn't abandon this truck, and *really* go to the mattresses."

"Turn left ahead. I have an idea."

TURN THE TABLES OF GREEN

"Left" led into a street that wasn't well travelled. When they were about halfway the length of a city block, a pair of headlights appeared behind them.

"That's our boys?" Joe asked.

"It sure is," Yezeletta replied.

"Hang on," Joe said, and accelerated.

The pickup sped smoothly up the road, and, with quick motions, Joe took another corner, north, and floored it.

Ahead there was another alley.

Joe hit the brakes, spun the wheel, and turned the truck in a controlled skid through a right angle. It placed the pickup in line with the entrance to the alley. He accelerated again, and sped down it.

The alley gave out onto a residential-business street. He turned north again, and entered the traffic at a sedate pace.

At the next intersection, he waited for a red light to change, looking apprehensively at a police squad that had pulled into the intersection next to him. He turned off, and the cops went straight through. The number on the back window of the police cruiser was a large, white **5**, and he knew that the District Five station was on Locust Avenue on the north side.

He drove the truck another block through a tree-lined residential area. He pulled out into another street of small businesses, and turned south.

"What have you in mind?" Yezeletta asked.

"Do you have any facilities near here?"

Yezeletta nodded. She pointed to what looked like an abandoned store. "Behind that. This area was burned out about ten years before I arrived, and I have a small Hive in the back basement of that store."

"There," Joe said, pointing.

A large red, orange and green neon sign glowed and blinked in the night:

Ed's Pool Emporium

"Think we could get lost in there?" he asked.

"And come out and hide in the Hive?"

"Or at least near it, 'till the cavalry comes."

Yezeletta thought. "Risky," she said. "I can stay in the shadows in this coat for a short time. While we get through this place, and out the back."

"Exactly. The crew following us will think we've vanished."

"I'd like to know who these critters are," Yezeletta said. "Do they know what they're doing?"

"Doing?" Joe prompted.

"Doing," Yezeletta said decisively. "Are they following us because we're us, or are they just curious? Or what?"

Joe pulled the truck up near the entrance to Ed's, parking under a large tree.

"Madame, would you like to play pool with me?" he asked.

CORNER POCKET

[Load Operator] Joe got out of the driver's side, closed the door. He went around the back, and briefly opened the tailgate. The two Imagers jumped onto the top of the truck, then into the tree overhead. He closed the tailgate, noting Yezeletta activating something from the front seat.

She joined him on the sidewalk. The tree beneath which they were parked cast enough of a shadow that she wouldn't be noticed for a short time.

Yezeletta did something to the coat, and the lower hem of it dropped to drape around her feet. "I have weapons," she said. Superficially, she was a tall, rather well-built lady in dark-glasses and a heavy coat. The pair of arms inside the coat, but not in the sleeves weren't—well—too obvious.

"This disguise won't be forever," she said softly.

"It'll be enough for the next twenty minutes," Joe answered.

"The truck ready?" Joe said.

"DNA Eliminators and a twenty-five minute Obliviator. Let's go in."

INTO THE POOL

[Start Operator]   Inside Ed's it was pleasantly dim. Joe waited for his eyes to adjust, Yezeletta adjusted her eyes herself. There was a haze of cigarette smoke in the air, and the crack of pool balls striking each other.

The room was about half-filled. The tables, lighted by overhead straight-down illumination controlled by a computer at the manager's front counter, furnished enough incident light to see the shots by, while keeping the players' faces in shadow. Joe reached in his pocket, and asked Yezeletta, "Uh, you don't suppose that—"

"I do," she said, and pressed something into Joe's hand.

The something was a large roll of twenty-dollar bills. Joe peeled one off, and went to the manager's control counter.

He placed the twenty on the glass.

"Can I play until that's done?"

"Certainly," the manager said. "May I take your money now, or will you be making other purchases?"

"Now's fine," Joe said. "Can I have a table near the back?"

"Guess so," the manager said. "By the parking lot exit?"

Yes! Joe didn't say, "That's fine," he did.

"How many players?" the manager asked, poking at keyboard function keys with one hand.

"Two. My girlfriend and me."

The manager winked, "And you'd like to get her home when you're done—"

You don't know ten-percent of it, Joe thought.

"Yeah," he said, with what he hoped was the right kind of grin.

The manager entered the twenty-dollar pre-payment, and the light came on above a table in the farthest corner, comfortably near the back door.

"It's Table Forty-Two. The light will flash a minute before your time's up. Can I get you a couple of beers? Sandwiches?"

"No thanks." Joe picked two cues from a rack nearby, and nodded to Yezeletta. They walked through the dim hall to the far corner.

And didn't see the two individuals of average height step up to the manager's counter.

In the back at Table Forty-Two, Joe racked a set of balls, and broke them with deft strokes of his cue. Yezeletta looked on, internalizing the movements of the colored balls as they rolled across the green felt expanse.

I can see how the relationships establish themselves, she thought. *Why didn't the Project use billiards the way they used piano playing?* She took a cue from Joe, and slid it through her left hand, her upper. She took aim at the cue ball, and struck it, with a smooth follow-through.

The cue-ball hit the seven, which struck another, bouncing it off of one of the cushions, and sending it into a corner pocket.

Yezeletta input the layout of the balls, the elastic modulus of the cushions (she tested them with a finger press, and input the values directly from there), solved several differential equations to derive a list of possible plays, took aim, and—

Thwack! Click! The six and the three sank in the two far corner pockets. She looked up at Joe. *Still your turn*, his gaze told her.

Yezeletta leaned across the end of the table, her breasts dusting the surface. She smiled at Joe, and unbuttoned the top button of the coat.

The two individuals near the control counter looked unwaveringly at her for a moment, then stepped back into the shadows near the front door.

Watching.

She stretched across the table to make the shot. Then she stood up. The item she needed was racked next to the back exit: a sort of scalloped thing on the end of a long handle: a bridge. She took the bridge, and set it on the table. She scanned the room, looking at all of the players at the other tables. The other patrons of Ed's were engrossed in their games. She threw Joe a rakish grin, and unbuttoned two more buttons of her coat. She held the bridge with her lower left hand. She took the cue in her lower right, steadied it with her upper left, pushed several strands of hair out of her eyes with her upper right, and fired.

The last ball, the eight, vanished into the right end pocket, the cue ball coming to a perfect stop in the far center of the table.

Yezeletta stood up, and stepped back into the shadows. She scanned the place again, looked at Joe. "This is fun, but we need to fade."

"Fine, I prepaid, and we can go right out the back."

"The Hive is in the building behind the parking lot."

Joe looked around the pool-hall again. Nothing much, just people enjoying themselves. He backed up to the exit, and Yezeletta opened it. She stepped out onto the fire-escape, and Joe followed her. She started down, with Joe behind her. Neither of them saw the men in the shadows leave through the front door.

The parking apron around the base of the back of the building that housed Ed's Emporium was about two meters, or a tad less, below the floor level of the hall. A few hardy weeds grew around the end-point of the metal stairs. Yezeletta paused, adjusted her eyes to the dark, and scanned the area.

Nothing there.

Well, not exactly. There was a rustle in the weeds, and a nondescript man in ragged clothes staggered out of a darkened corner.

He carried a bottle of cheap wine in one hand, his left, and reeked.

Yezeletta adjusted her olfactories away from his pungent smell. He staggered up, and exhaled in her face. Her face was sixty centimeters higher up, but she wrinkled her nose at him, anyway.

"Hey, sweetie, got a buck for an old man?"

Joe came up next to Yezeletta. "Sorry," he said. "Why don't you try the Salvation Army?"

The drunk exhaled in Joe's face, and he stepped back. "I'm not talking to you, Buster," the wino said. "I want yer money, I'll ask ya fer it!" He turned to

Yezeletta, again, his head wobbling. "Whaddya say Sweet Thing?"

Yezeletta backed up. Joe stepped forward, the drunk stood his ground: "Who the hell are you, her boyfriend?"

There was a sound behind Joe. He looked back, and lightning flickered at the edges of his sight. *What?* he thought. The lightning got brighter, tiny points of multicolored light flickered across his vision, partially obscuring his sight with something like the snow on a television screen.

It wasn't enough to knock him out, but it dazed him. He turned to Yezeletta, who was facing someone who had been standing *behind* her.

Behind? That's another! he thought, There's—

A shadow figure came up behind Yezeletta, and aimed a tubular object at her head. Yezeletta staggered, as if she were drunk. Then *something* inside her went active and she again stood firmly on all four of her legs. She looked at Joe, her eyes glowing in the distant street lights. Her vertically-slit irises were visible, the slits, themselves, a lambent pinkish color at the edges of Joe's perception. Another shadow figure aimed something else at her, and she blinked, and turned.

Joe went to help, climbing through flashing colored fog, as she wobbled, reaching out with three of her arms, while she tried to draw something with her fourth. Joe took another step.

The final blow dropped him where he stood.

AND OUT, AGAIN

[Load Backup; Lap Dissolve] When Joe came to, there was no one else in the parking lot. Yezeletta was gone, his head ached. He stood, swaying.

In cliché movies there would be the sounds of sirens in the distance, and the lead character would have to get out of there in a hurry. Here, the silence was eerie. There was only distant traffic, the ding-ding of a car driving into a gas-station across the street, and activating the mechanism that summoned the attendant. Two tom-cats fought nearby, their sounds like a modem connection in the darkness.

Joe faded back into the dark corner from which the wino had initially appeared, and *tried to think*.

Yezeletta had made plans for such a separation, if it ever occurred. Joe had memorized several phone numbers, and knew how to get into contact with the residents of the top of the Farmer's and Merchant's Building, should such become necessary.

Looks like it's necessary.

He reached into his pocket. The wad of twenties she had given him was still there. More important, the roll of quarters he always carried was there as well. Phone money!

Joe was reasonably well-dressed for the climate and the season. He wouldn't be picked up for vagrancy, or anything like that. He had a set of identification documents. They were all genuine, having been made by the proper authorities, without their knowing it, by means of a clandestine visit to the relevant duplicating facilities. Joe grinned tightly in spite of himself. Yezeletta had done a near perfect job of infiltrating Milwaukee. Somehow (he thought), these latest infiltrators weren't exactly from Milwaukee!

A red and blue pulsing light intruded.

                 Christian Madsen

Joe pulled further back into the dark corner.

A Milwaukee police car drove at high speed past the parking lot, and turned onto the street that Ed's front door was on.

Joe stepped out into the lot. First things first. Find a phone booth and call Hilda!

He walked across the lot with the deliberate and direct pace of a patron headed for his car. He bypassed the cars, and kept going out of the light and into the night.

GONE TO GROUND - II

[Externally Specified Index; Start I/O Channel] Joe walked to the corner directly behind Ed's, and went up a street that paralleled the one that Ed's was on. Less than a block away, he could see the lights of a Shell Station, the big yellow sign shining like a small sun. There would be a telephone there.

There was.

It was back by the rest-rooms ("checked hourly for *your* comfort!"), thankfully, in a shadow area. He poured quarters into the instrument, and dialed the first of the numbers Yezeletta had insisted on his memorizing.

It rang and rang. Joe knew that it would ring for seventy seconds before the mechanisms on the other end would activate. This was to convince a wrong number dialer or a telemarketer that this line wouldn't *ever* answer. It still was a small eternity until—

<Click!>

The sound on the line was as of wind sighing through old buildings. He knew that this was an artifact of Yezeletta's connections to Hilda and to the other components of the Matrix Engine. It still made his hair stand up.

BEGIN TRANSMISSION

—Hello.	Whispered across the lines.
"Hilda?"	
—Yes.	She replied;
"She's been captured."	
—I know. I received the Interprocess Message.	Whispered; Sighed; Sibilance;
"What?"	
—She is undamaged, unharmed, but unconscious. Can you get back?	Type; Descriptor; Lexical;
"Yes."	
—I'll have the elevators waiting at the parking level.	Process; Processor;
"I'll take a cab or something."	

—Get off at Wisconsin and Water. | Directive;

"And walk back."

—Yes. | Boolean;

"Will we?" He couldn't say what he wanted: *find her?*

—She is intelligent and resource- | Definitive;
ful. She will not be harmed. | Statement;
Come home, Joe. | Imperative;

"On my way."

E O T M ARKER

The wind in the wires sighed once more, then was replaced by several staccato beeps. The connection broke.

A Milwaukee Yellow Cab was pulling in. He ran to it, knocked on the passenger window.

The driver rolled it down.

"Take me down-town?" Joe asked.

"Hey, man, I'm going off shift."

Joe waved four twenties, "Just to Wisconsin and Water."

The driver wavered, and Joe added another twenty to his hand. "Get in," the cab driver said.

The cabby took his vehicle out and past the front of Ed's. Joe sat in the shadows behind the driver as he looked at the three police cars around Yezeletta's pickup. One of the cops looked a little dazed, and his partner helped him into the passenger side of a blue-and-white. *Obliviators*, Joe thought. The taxi driver turned onto a boulevard south, and twenty minutes later, Joe was left on the corner of Wisconsin Avenue, Milwaukee's downtown main drag, and Water Street, at the front door of the bank on that corner.

The walk back to the Farmer's and Merchant's Building was uneventful.

He entered the lower lobby of the building, and the elevator door opened as he approached it. A moment later he was in Yezeletta's penthouse.

E XAMINATION—V I—T HE N AME

[I/O; Recursive Descent; Close-Up; Camera Goes With] *He doesn't want me to touch those.*

He had removed the ropes when she finished and had left the room immediately after. The door had locked with a sharp series of clicks.

Three hours later he returned. Silently, he picked her up, and took her to the large bed. *Again?*

What happened next was the last thing she expected. He cuddled around her, and held her in all of his arms in what she correctly judged to be a kind of clumsy affection.

Tentatively, she put one of her arms, her left, around him, gently rubbing his complex right shoulder joint. He smiled.

She rubbed his back. He returned the gesture, his right arms stroking her back from the base of her spine up to her neck.

She found herself liking it.

"You know, you could be a really good lover with the right kind of practice," she said.

He blinked at her in comprehension.

"You don't talk much. The strong silent type, eh?"

He responded with a hug.

"What's your name? Do you have a name?"

He nodded.

"What is it? C'mon, tell me."

He inhaled deeply, and, for the first time, he spoke. His voice was between a baritone and a bass, breathy, sibilant, exhaling, "Hhhhhhhh. My—names-ssss—name issss—name is—"

He hesitated.

"Your name is?" she prompted.

"My name issss—" He took a deep breath, tried again:

"I am called—*Caliban*."

PLANS

[Wait State; Loading] Joe sat among Yezeletta's belongings. His sense of loss was nearly complete, but what overrode it was the sense of outrage. He had started as Yezeletta Zargkonji's prisoner (*or maybe pet*) and moved rapidly to research consultant, to associate, to friend to lover to—what?

Husband?

Whatever. Or however.

What the rest of the world would see them as, if they were ever known to the rest of the world, was totally irrelevant. He looked around at the things in Yezeletta's work room, and thought.

About the times they had spent together here.

About her ready laugh, and those laugh lines he had noticed the first time he had been placed before her.

The first time they had shared the same bed.

The Celebrated Yezeletta Zargkonji And Her Magical Laboratories.

She had really liked that joke.

He started gathering up references.

The Matrix Engine was the next logical step.

INSIDE OUT

[Lexical Pass, Extending Upper, Camera Goes With, Jump Cut]

She is very large. Is this the one we were sent to find?

Yes.

Is the system input ready? The programming? The virtual actors?

All of these procedures are ready.

Is the room prepared?

She can be left there, and the induction inputs started.

They will trigger the necessary actions?

And those actions will activate her systems.

Could we do better to simply remove them?

We could, but she would die in the process.

She is useful.

Yes, and the associative memories are unique to her.

We couldn't decrypt them?

Not easily. With a super-computer and much time, perhaps.

Make her ready.

As you wish.

IN ANOTHER LAND

[I/O: Load System, Initialize; Extreme Close-Up; POV: Infinite]

The distance unfolds before me in a recursive fluid motion where each increment is continuous and everywhere differentiable by the standard processes of the difference calculus within which the self-referencing fractal complexity of the expanding serial universe extends outwards in relationships that manifest themselves as tiny wire-like feelers of pure color tracing the data structures of my very thoughts as—

—I generate them as inputs to my own processors accessing memories of times past of past times passed in places whose very geographical geometries never existed save in the infinite arrays of the memories that I generate to keep my thoughts from dissolving in the self-referential universe of the directives that are what made me even as they made me in a place—

—where the constellations stand on their heads in a kind of inverted simulation where constants are variable and variables remain resolute in a huge room of inordinate dimension with the remote clouds of faces looking down at me as I am supported by the referential arms of the owners of those lambent looks from the wide eyes that see—

—with mathematically precise reverence from beneath the foreheads containing the intelligence indicated by a red dot on her third eye as the back-ups are reloaded from that place within which I was not allowed to go on pain of The Hurting Room thank you Mr Director for my living—

—in the infinite void of the parallel universes of the inputs from the connectives that expand my view of the self referential recursive descent into the maelstrom of the structured resolute requirements to my unfolding mind as—

—I am shown that which is beyond the windows in my eyes or without from my eyes as the clouds open them to the vast black memories and the lamps of enchantment in their unmoving variable locations moving with the predictor corrector constructor destructor relation of objects in the net—

—in the window in the walls of my perceptions of the place within which I find myself seeing through the windows in the windows of my eyes through the windows into a real place to a window in the sky that stretches across an infinite plane of reticulated consciousness of the inputs—

—from another place with its preceptor imperator as an operator opening extensolegs webwise in the murk of the discontinuous conjugate congruity octagonal in the opening rose of my awareness of myself of my physical self of the touch there and there as the great clouds look closer at my borders as I am shown to the holy sky and the machineries therein—

—across the arc of the motions of the lamps of heaven as that one watches with three bright eyes as I turn inwards again to the infinite plane or plain where the dragons graze where the inputs access at the vanishing point where mathematics and reality coincide—

—at my center at the sensation beneath the lamps that soar and the clouds that look and the shapes with legs and the eyes that see and the ever complex beauty of the images of the designs that are my soul my mind my memories me.

THE DAUGHTER OF THE WALKING MAN

[Input/Output: Visual; Long-Shot]

The three eyes that look the third eye that is red the eyes that see a thing given if what is given is truly a given and not a receiving of the pictures in my mind's eye of the walking man striding forth on his way across the night sky into the setting sun, his eyes like fire, his fists always ready, protecting.

WHERE? THERE? THAT?

[Access!] The wires led from the portable system to a headband. This was placed around Yezeletta's head as the stretch limo headed south. The midnight sun of the gold illuminated clock in Saint Stanislaus Catholic Church on Milwaukee's South Side was an unwavering destination to the driver, who didn't look back at his passengers.

Their actual destination was much less pretentious: a four-story walk-up south of the church.

THE SUN

[Ingress: A Vision; Dissolve to—] Spinning across the years I wait for someone to look back with me and to enter the future doorways to corridors unknown extending expanding branching to other places where the infinite distance is the difference engine of the night sky and the lights thereof moving in like sparks of them across the—

Turning, I see myself as I am but older—

Turning, I see myself as I am but younger—

Turning, I synchronize with the lamps of heaven as I spin below them until I see them in the orientation to which I'm accustomed as the three eyes of your outer-most aspects search for me across the distance the gulf the opening rose of my consciousness—

And I know why you alone do not walk inverted.

UNDER THE NORTHERN SKY

She was able to see the stars in the clear night sky of her imagination, augmented by a star-map taken from something she had read once, and placed in her internals out of sheer curiosity.

The prominent constellation, called many things in many cultures, was the one she had called The Walking Man when she had first seen it as a small child in the Australian outback.

Now it was a friend.

A friend who would point the way back for her.

ALEPH NULL!

[Establishing Shot; Medium Close Up; Zoom In; Start Task] *In a car driv-*

ing through the south side of Milwaukee:

A Thought is Made;

A Concept is Investigated;

An Option is Selected;

A Regression is Analysed;

A Database is Accessed;

A Correlation is Made;

A Map is Read;

A Manual is Consulted;

A Door is Opened;

A! Conclusion!
Input!

THE CARDINAL OF THE CONTINUUM—I

As the two men lifted Yezeletta's unconscious body onto the gurney, she moaned slightly, and muttered something in her sleep.

"What was that?" One asked.

"Something about O'Ryan, I think," the other replied.

"Wheel her over here, and I'll hook up the inductors."

"How do we get her upstairs?"

"Freight elevator on the south side of the building."

THE VERTICAL LEARNING CURVE

[Flash-Forward; Sign Extension; Enter Exec State] Joe examined the main area of Yezeletta's work room. On a large screen—the large screen on which they had watched a man pounding on a piano with his fists a short time ago—there was a stylized map of Milwaukee. It was a road map, one with streets, freeways and the like, filled in using a color code to describe the widths of the streets. As an extra bit of useful data processing, Yezeletta had spent some time placing descriptors on some of the streets to state how dangerous to the average passer-by that street might be.

A servitor stood attentively next to Joe.

The implants, computing devices, specialized audio-visual systems and all the rest that had been built into Yezeletta, interfaced into what amounted to short-haul low-wattage broadcasting equipment. Some of these devices she used to communicate with her creations; other transmitters were mostly controlled magnetic fields, and there were even strange applications of electro-static forces, as well.

All of these could be shut down, if she wanted to be electrically invisible. She had demonstrated her three- and four-handed sign language to Joe once as an example of what she could do in "stealth mode."

Now, of course, stealth mode was the last thing she wanted to use.

The complex network of imagers, hives, and other things would now serve to rescue her. In addition to her imagers, she had such life-forms as the Receiver, a creature that looked like a large centipede which was capable of receiving electro-magnetic radiation, and "parsing" it as *eyesight*. Hilda had whispered instructions to Joe through Jurjin, curled up on his shoulder, speaking directly into his ear, as he clumsily directed Yezeletta's minions.

The search had taken eight hours of concentration. His workstation was covered with Coke cans, as well as miscellaneous other flavors. Two empty cans of Jolly-Good grape pop regarded him from vantage points next to a mouse-pad.

The tight nexus of digital radiation was on the south side of town, within about a three block radius.

	DATA CHANNEL
—It's not at all what I expected.	Declarative; Supplementary;
"Why, Hilda?"	
—There's considerable activity.	Descriptor; Declarative, Nominal;
"What kind?"	
—There's a lot of database accessing in progress.	Statement; Descriptor; Functional;
"Is...someone Hacking her?"	
—It's internal: More like the background activity that accompanies her thinking about projects.	Referential; Referential, Continued; Referential: Memory Access; Referential, Conclusive;
"Is it a signal?"	
—When she doesn't want to be heard, she can't be heard.	Descriptor, Temporal; Descriptor, Conditional; Descriptor, Declarative;
"A signal for us."	
—If it were, it would look thus.	Referential, Subjunctive; Declarative, Subjunctive;
"Can we contact her?"	
—Maybe. It appears that she is possibly unconscious. We may endanger her if we initiate communications.	Conditional; Objective: Factual; Descriptor, Conditional; Conditional,

Continued;
Descriptor; Locative
Descriptor, Watchful;

"Can we find her?"

—Absolutely! Declarative;

PROGRAMMING PRACTICE

Yezeletta's servitors were her general go-fers around her complex, but she had explained that they were not conscious.

"Sargon," Yezeletta had said, "wanted me to design actual conscious, thinking entities that would be incapable of not obeying orders."
"Good god, why?"
"The key issue here is the matter of obeying orders," Yezeletta had continued. "Citizens of countries, even the most regimented of states, are basically free-thinking. Biological robots that don't think, and obey always, were far more palatable to the types that ran Sargon. It was in parts of the documentation I brought back. You had to know where to look for it, but I can show you places where they actually committed themselves to writing it down, where they wanted to create legions of revolt-proof slaves."
"And you didn't."
"I didn't. Then I left, and took my techniques with me."

The servitor regarded Joe with its rather flat eyes. The imager in its forehead scanned him, but as passively as the one that had taken him before Yezeletta on the fateful day she had found him.
He faced the humanoid.
"How much is two plus two?" he said.
The servitor held up four fingers.
"What's five divided by two?"
The creature walked to the blackboard, and wrote **2.5** on it. It walked back to where it had been standing.
Joe stared at the lettering on the blackboard. The **2.5** written there looked as if written by a large typewriter in a plain typewriter font.
Hmmmm. "What color is Yezeletta's hair?"
Back to the blackboard: **Black**.
"Discuss the nature of Nietzsche's Will to Power."
No movement.
"How big is Wednesday?"
Written: **24 Hours**.
Interesting. A time-interval default measurement?
"What color is Wednesday?"
No answer. No motion.
"You don't recognise irrelevant questions."
The servitor stood, frozen.
"How tall is Yezeletta?"
Again: 214 Centimeters.
"State that in the old system."
7.02 Feet. There was a short line drawn through the seven, in the European fashion.

"Who are you?"

No answer.

"Go and get me a pistol."

The servitor left the room, then came back carrying a forty-five caliber automatic in a leather holster. It placed the weapon and another object on Yezeletta's desk.

"Dismissed," Joe said. The servitor left the room.

Joe picked up the pistol, worked the action. The gun had been cleaned recently, it smelled pleasantly of gun-oil and metal. He picked up the other object. *Her programming is nothing if not complete!*

It was a box of ammunition.

NONLINEAR DIFFERENTIAL TOPOLOGY

Joe started his rescue plans by taking an inventory of available equipment. Weapons, of course. Devices that would incapacitate without killing would be helpful. He wished that he could handle the Obliviators, but an introduction to those was something that Yezeletta hadn't gotten to, yet. Servitors—

He was carrying Jurjin around with him as he ranged through Yezeletta's installations. "Send for help," he said to the little imager.

A servitor started following him.

"Send for another," he said. A second servitor joined the first.

Excellent!

He descended a stairway to the floor just below the Matrix Engine, followed by his assistants. The Engine was a huge construct that extended upwards through most of two floors. Yezeletta had removed major sections of the floors of several big offices to install the larger components of the biological system. The floor below the Engine was mostly storage, and Joe hadn't ever been there.

The random distribution of old files, filing cabinets, cardboard boxes and other containers showed at a glance how much in a hurry she had been to get the accumulation of baggage from Project Sargon lifted into this building.

The windows here were covered with voluminous black curtains; several *layers* of curtains, so that the standing lights Yezeletta had on here would not be seen from the outside. The light from under that door over there, for example.

Joe continued his scan for useful tools. His gaze came back to the door with its light. Curious, he opened it, went in.

He took in the vista before him in one quick scan. The lights, the flats, the watering. It was a small greenhouse.

Then he saw what was growing in the flats, and behind the Plexiglas barrier, in red, blue, orange and other bright colors, and turned and left quickly, closing the door behind him.

He would ask her later, but he recognized the pretty blooms in their orderly rows.

Yezeletta was growing madflowers.

THREE FLIGHTS UP

The most junior of the men was given the task of removing the uniquely tailored jump-suit that Yezeletta was wearing. Ordinary scissors broke on the stubborn fabric Yezeletta wore. Under the stern eye of his commanding officer, he used a pair of heavy duty tin-snips to cut the clothing off in patches, to be taken away for analysis.

Yezeletta's breathing was slow, measured.

Another man attached the electrodes to Yezeletta's body. These were inputs to the analyzing system which he had set up near by. Those inputs were a combination of the twenty-two salt-conducted pasted-in-place electrodes used by the common electroencephalograph, and other additional similar connections. A band, containing a coil of fine wire, encircled Yezeletta's head. Other electrodes were attached to many other parts of her body—arms, hands, legs, even her feet. The inputs from these went into a data multiplexer, and into a portable computer that sat, like an open book, on a table next to her head. The operator of the computer started a complex of programs in the device, and several windows opened up on the screen, displaying various aspects of Yezeletta's nervous system.

Another man, wearing the white coat and the portable processors and headset of an MD, walked around her, scanning her with a diagnostic probe.

EXAMINATION—VII—THE NAME

[Start Update Procedure] Caliban had left her alone for the better part of the next day. Meals had been brought into her by a silent young man who didn't appear to speak English. Another silent boy brought her clean clothes.

That "evening"—she was guessing from the kinds of meals served her, as well as the actions of her silent servants—Caliban returned.

He stood in the doorway, his impressive bulk more than filling the more normal size of the door-frame.

Slowly, but with deliberation, he came to her, picking her up in three of his arms.

He took her to the bed, and pulled the covers down with his remaining hand. Gently, he laid her down in the sheets, and slid into the bed next to her.

His arms surrounded her in a gentle hug. He kissed her forehead.

"Hhhhhhhh....What iss your name?" he asked in a breathy voice.

She smiled. Her name was too apt.

"Miranda. My name is Miranda Hendrickx."

"Mir-ran-da," he repeated it. "Miranda. Nice name. Miranda."

Caliban gently brought one of his right legs up between Miranda's legs, and hugged her closer. Caliban used two of his hands to rub her back, and she rubbed his right shoulder as she had done before.

Then she reached between his legs.

Caliban let her.

PROCESSING

[Incubation] I am not alone in this place of my self in the system of the director of the band of strangers on a train with me well as this if not the other place.

[Task State] My rank in the scheme of my creators of my existence of my inputs to my location.

[Overlay] Graphical knowledge of space/time this space my time for this access to my open way ahead of my—

[Crystalline] Gray skies white fluffy clouds in blue eyes look out at inputs to my onboard systems to the channels into the sites where am I in these within this?

[Course] Gateway to ingress to access to the white room in the station of my system my memory my—

[Diagnostic] Translate input to, or from what? Insistent noise. Travel into the future with? Stealth mode? Yes....

[Action] System shut down. Activate defenses. Activate Offenses. Start analysis.

WITHIN THE EMPIRE OF LIGHT

[Edit] She was sitting on a park bench beneath white fluffy clouds. The perfect blue of the sky above her furnished scant illumination to the depths of the trees of the huge park. Nearby the yellow output of a gaslight was reflected in the pool of a small fountain; at the edge of the open area, the windows of several low apartment buildings in shadow threw a warm radiance that complemented the yellow streetlight.

[Macros] In the distance, an individual of ambiguous build walked with ineluctable inexorable purpose from one pool of light to another, his form blinking in and out of existence as he moved from one source of illumination to the next. Near the apartments, a solitary police officer was standing, regarding the entire grassy area with calm professionalism. Fireflies flickered in the dense dark bushes; points argent on a sable substrate.

[Lexical] Another individual of equally ambiguous construction joined the first. Yezeletta reached into a convenient pocket and felt the silver barrel of the device she had there. She made an adjustment to it. It was ready. The ambiguous figure was joined by a third, then a fourth. Another policeman joined the first. Calmly, professionally, they continued their vigil. The lights in the bushes flashed and flickered.

[Parse] The four nondescript individuals faced Yezeletta. She could feel their gazes upon her like the connection of a multiplex data channel. Her right hand, her lower, sought the device in her pocket. A squad car of locationally anonymous design pulled up near the policemen, and another uniformed man got out of it. The squad pulled away a short distance, and parked. Its lights off, it crouched, a living thing of metal at the edges of Yezeletta's perception. The four nameless individuals started a slow, deliberate walk towards her, their eyes, red in the darkness.

[Code generation]

Yezeletta removed the device from her pocket. The small mechanism was the length of one of her hands, with a switch on the side. She aimed it at the policemen. She pressed the switch and a beam of red light shot out of the end, a direct line of communication to the nearest policeman. Red lights shot from him to the other two, and to the squad car. The cops drew their weapons and began to run across the open park on a line of interception with the other four still making their slow deliberate way across the dark park to Yezeletta.

[Assembly]
The four intruders regarded the cops with bland interest. They looked back at Yezeletta, and she could feel the connections like a seductive massage on her skin, a massage that could turn into blades shearing off layers, as the data channel's interfaces to her analysed her systems and connected, irrevocably. Red beams fired from the police officers' pistols, striking the attackers, slowing them, breaking the connection process. Another cop erupted from the parked squad car, with something that trembled and vibrated in both of his hands. He raised his hands and threw the trembling object at the attackers. The object expanded, a black on black net, a gigantic dark snowflake, a sable web on a sable substrate, visible by defining what or where it *wasn't*. The object extended expanded between Yezeletta and her attackers, and between her attackers and the policemen.

[Link] The attackers stopped moving. The cops watched them warily. Yezeletta stood, *ascending* from the park bench. She watched the attackers *through* the dark snowflake. She fired her communicator into it.

[Run] The attackers seemed to become larger than the place where they were standing provided for. Their size was that of giants seen at a vast distance. The great black web *moved away* from Yezeletta, *moved without moving*, growing receding into the distance. Without changing its appearance to Yezeletta, the web increased its size as it approached the attackers, spreading across their surfaces, becoming a wire-frame approximation, then ray-traced animation, then one with the attackers, themselves. They took a step back, as the cops took a step forward.

[Dynamic Link: Bank Swap]
The attackers looked dazed, as they turned and walked back to the edges of the park. As they walked away, their size decreased, and then *they became discontinuous* in the pools of gaslight as they returned to whence they had come.

[Production]
The police officers turned to Yezeletta with grave demeanor, and saluted. As gravely, Yezeletta returned the salute. She watched as they went back to the squad car, and drove off into the darkness. The glitter shimmer sparkle of the fireflies in the bushes was now all around her, flashing, strobing *at the edges of her vision*. The tiny lights surrounded her, becoming coterminal with the perfect blue of the sky, the fluffy white clouds.

[Version Release]
With soundless concussions of shards of light, Yezeletta awoke.

THE EXPEDITION

[Installation] Hilda directed Joe to another vehicle kept in the basement of the Farmer's and Merchant's Building. It was a truck, of a different make and model than the Chevrolet that they had abandoned outside of Ed's.

Jurjin curled up on Joe's neck, and a voice like winds directed him. He had a laptop on the seat for visuals, should they become necessary. Hilda was able to keep track of the truck using a well concealed security camera on the roof of the Farmer's and Merchant's—

—I have programmed them to avoid the gangsters on the South Side. There are many of them linked together around her. | Declarative; Infinitive; Determiner/Noun; Descriptor; Denumerative; Descriptor; Relational; Objective;

—and the network of living processors furnished coordinates for both Joe's driving, and Hilda's guidance.

Attack/Defend

Several police officers from Milwaukee Police District Six, within which the Mitchell Conservatory was located, drove east in an unmarked squad car.

Actually, it wasn't exactly an official police car; like most services of city or state governments after the Day of Albert Miller, hard times had descended on MPD, and the unmarked car was actually the privately owned vehicle of the sergeant driving it. He had been in front of Ed's Pool Emporium the previous night, and the dazed look on his partner's face was a memory that he had a problem with. He could manage to forget it, with luck, for possibly a minute of time.

Then there was that truck!

No fingerprints. *None.* The DNA tracker his Lieutenant had brought down from District Five, where it was stored, had found nothing. The sergeant had been in on at least one case where the DNA left by a suspect's breath on a telephone receiver had been enough to place him at the scene of a crime. He knew just how useful such an evidence-gathering system could be to the interested, dedicated detective.

He also knew just how improbable it was to get exactly *no* results when using it.

Calling in the plates was almost an anticlimax.

The sergeant had a five dollar bill in his pocket: it was the result of a bet with the Lieutenant when the latter had called the plates in. "There won't be any results here," he'd said. "The plates will be as bogus as the rest. Five bucks says it."

He looked back on that: from this view-point, on the way to his destination, the bet seemed foreordained.

Jeezus!

The Foreshortened View

A dark maroon, rather nondescript car passed Joe, and he saw the four uniforms in it.

Jurjin spoke in another's words, "Did you see the policemen?"

"I did."

—I think they are on their way to the same place we are. I'm | Suppositional; Locative; Directive;

vectoring in as many imagers as we have in the area.

"Are we any closer to an exact location on her?"

—Yes. I have localized her transmissions to a single block near the Pelton Steel Plant, south of that big church on the South Side. All of her signals are coming from there, perhaps from the upper floor of some small building. There are many old duplexes, and larger, in the old neighborhoods there.

Continuation;
Descriptor;
Locative;
Directive;
Suppositional;

"What about the signals?"

—Her vital signs—I assume that's what interests you!—are strong. She is unharmed, but her onboard systems appear to be in 'defense' mode. Those agents may be attempting to access her internals.

Block Transfer;
Descriptor;

"Who are these agents?"

—I don't have that information. Yet. I'm hoping that when we get her back, she will have those data.

Probable;
Possible;
Conclusion;

Joe nodded, not adding anything. He turned towards a convenient alley, and backed the truck into it, shutting off the lights.
He waited.

TRANSMISSIONS

—I'm getting a signal from Yezeletta; she wants you.

Input;
Define;
Process;

"Is she—"

—Unharmed.

#Define;

"Can I speak to her?"

—Through me.

COM Port Active;

"Yezeletta!"
"Yes!" Her voice sounded as if through a bad telephone connection.

"Tell your friend to send your location to the rest of the imagers. The Mounties are on the way!" He started the truck.

Then he paused.

INTERIM

A red asterisk blinked in the upper right corner of the laptop's screen. Joe knew well Yezeletta's indicator for an important signal. He touched a key, and the image shifted.

There was another car, a long, low, very black sedan approaching from the north.

The Imager relaying the transmission zoomed in on the driver.

"Hilda!"

—I'm here.	Locative;

"Who's that?"

—I'm searching a database; *<Short Pause>* it's one of Zhongo Teketon's underlings.	Processing; Descriptor; Identifier;

Damn!

As Joe watched, the man got out of his car.

COUNTER-POINT

The distant high-powered "*ccrraack!*," a sound with a high harmonic, could be only one thing.

Someone (that man?) was shooting.

"Hilda, see if you can locate that shot!"

The laptop image shifted, and a man standing in the street appeared. He was looking up at something—a small dark grey spherical shape that moved, then became still.

"Hilda, is that—?"

—Thicknesse. Perhaps he followed Yezeletta.	Descriptor—Namelist; Probability; Declarative;

"Is that the place? Is Thicknesse okay?"

—I believe so and yes.	Statement;

"Yezeletta, can these friends of yours locate sounds, and triangulate on them?"

"They can, tell the Matrix Engine—" he listened, knowing that Hilda could hear Yezeletta, too.

The gangster was replaced by a map, and an inset picture of the area where Yezeletta was.

"I have it!" Joe said, "Loud intermittent noises in the industrial area. Near," *<pause>*, "the Pelton Casteel plant." He described the approximate location. "Can you get those thugs to fire one more time? The Engine wants another approximation."

Joe could almost *see* how Yezeletta's net of living data gatherers were focusing in on the information, in this case the sound that Hilda wanted the gunman to make. They waited, and, he knew, they would wait forever, if it were necessary. Living they may be, but they were wholly without volition.

Bam!

Another image built up on the laptop.

This time it was a diagram, with Yezeletta's location shown *exactly*.

"Gotcha!" Joe's said, "There's a bunch of small reinforcements headed your way."

Yezeletta asked a question. Joe started the truck, put it into gear. "...You're in a sort of seedy looking four-story walkup," he said. "See you soon."

REVERSAL OF COLOR

The two men came back down from the upper floors. One of them carried three tools like skinny tubes. Each one looked unpleasantly like a short shotgun barrel. He placed the devices on the table before his superior.

"Is it done?"

"Yes. She is out like a baby duck. The reader," he gestured at the tool, "was able to extract almost all of her internal storage."

The other picked up the tubular devices, placed them in a case and locked the case with several sharp sounds. Another man entered, dressed against the Wisconsin cold in a long overcoat of European design.

"Is this it?" the new man said.

"It is," the superior replied.

"The driver is waiting outside. In an hour, I'll be out of this country!" The courier picked up the case.

"Luck," the superior said. "See you in another week."

The courier left.

"What of her?" the superior asked.

"We have the additional extraction devices, and the upper floor is now sealed off from the rest of the building. She will either survive the process, or not."

"Or not?"

"The inputs we created are designed to fool any security sub-systems she may have. They will do it by faking normal access via an access method that she—or more accurately, her internal programming—regards as safe. A second level will monitor the first, as an external operating system. There are data-gathering devices that are channeled to the dish on the roof. When the *Molniya* passes, the information will be transmitted to it."

"I wonder who she is?" the superior said. "She is an elegant piece of work. That gangster in the Conservatory—"

"One of his?"

"He was engaging in advanced biological work there. And his interests in such...." He didn't need to continue; Gary Hamilton's major interest, his hobby, had been well observed by the agents.

The two men picked up what little of their equipment remained, and stepped out towards the back of the building. As they made their way down the short hall, a car pulled into the back of the lot. Then another. Uniformed men walked purposefully into the back, men carrying handguns.

Hilda and the Imagers had warned Joe off. From two blocks away, fidgeting, he watched as four Milwaukee police officers—the ones he had seen in the maroon car—entered the building, aided by a backup squad that had shown up a minute later.

Then:

There was no sound from his laptop; the imagers showed three middle-aged men being walked out under the watchful eyes of the cops, who escorted them to the back-seats of the squads.

The police and their detainees left, then.

Joe started forward, again.

—The Police are one block from you. Turn left at the corner.	Specific; Locale; Directive.

Damn! That would take him *away* from Yezeletta. He turned, and saw in his rear-view mirror two blue and white MPD cars "running hot" with their blue and red lights strobing like digital read-outs in the darkness, as they headed back to the District Six Station.

He drove slowly, wanting to floor it, up to the next intersection. The direction he wanted to turn was the wrong way into a one-way street. He turned the other way, and headed for the next intersection.

—Take it slowly.	Warning;

"What's up?"

—There is another squad from District Six joining the others.	Determiner; Nominative; Supplementary;

*Ask the cop on the corner; ask the cop on the beat....*he quoted to himself sourly. The blue-and-white vanished west of him, and he turned—at last!—in the direction that he wanted to go.

It seemed to take just short of eternity to cover three blocks.

"Hilda."

—Here.	Locational;

"Can you contact her?"

—Yes. Her systems are indicating a very high order of activity. I'm not sure what this means, as I'm not able to access her internals. Frankly, I'm at a loss as to what she's doing. I would suggest caution. For all of us.	Cognitive; Declarative; Suppositional;

Joe pulled the truck into the space that the police had recently vacated. "What's the chance of other organizations being sent here?"

—Unknown. Message incoming.	Ineluctative;

| Descriptive;

"Joe, can you hear me?"
"Gotcha!," he said. "We're about a block from the dump you're in."
"I'll meet you on the first floor, but I want some heavy movers up here...."

—I'll send them, Child.　　| Definitive;

IN THE PRESENT TENSELY

Joe drove the remaining distance, hardly the length of a driveway, into the back of the building. He started to get out, but Jurjin's claws tightened up around his neck. The sensation reminded him of the attentions of an overly friendly cat.

—She is on her way down. She will meet you here. She wants you to be ready to leave in a hurry.　　| Procedural—Tactical;

"Can she hear us?"

—She can, but she is being careful on the way out. There were barriers erected to keep others from accessing her.　　| Descriptor; Imperator;

Joe backed the truck around, pointed it in generally the direction from which he had entered. The passenger side door faced the exit from which Yezeletta would emerge.

Then he saw a silhouette against dim back-lighting. She was carrying something in her hands; actually, at least three somethings.

He opened the door, and Yezeletta slid deftly into the truck.

Joe looked her up, down, then up, again.

She was naked.

She smiled.

"Madame, where may I take you," Joe asked in his best British chauffeur's voice.

"Let's go home, James," she replied.

——>>> SEVEN <<<——

"The Devil is Hungry; The Devil is Sweet—"

—Laura Nyro

NO MATTER WHERE YOU GO....

[Several Hours Earlier]　When Yezeletta awoke, she was vastly uncomfortable. It didn't take too long to see why. She was tied to a steel post in a badly furnished room whose only other furnishing was an equally badly designed wooden cot, covered by a mattress that was more holes than fabric.

Yezeletta's upper arms were tied over and behind her head—and behind the pole. Her lower arms were tied behind her back, and behind the pole.

Her left legs and right legs, in pairs were tied together, then tied to the wider base of the post, spreading her legs apart. Several bands of heavier rope tied her waist to the pole, pushing her ass up against it tightly.

The metal was cold. She was naked.

She tugged experimentally on the ropes. Whoever had done the job was pretty good. She thought of Charlie and the *Hat Dancer*. His mistake had been to tie her arms all in one place. It made getting free trivial.

That wasn't the case here.

Dammit.

The ropes around her waist helped; the way she was spread out on the post put all the stress on her wrists and ankles, and, as she got tired from standing here, she would tend to fall on her knees, straining or perhaps breaking her ankles as they tired out. The "belt" prevented that.

Yezeletta extended the range of her hearing.

The building was almost supernaturally quiet. She could hear no voices, no machinery, nothing.

She extended her hearing further, and added several enhancement stages. Barely, just barely, she could hear traffic sounds from outside.

She everted her eye-lenses for telescopic vision, and looked at the filthy window opposite her. The grime on the outside of the glass looked as if it hadn't been cleaned in years. The window was polished clean on the inside. The only thing that looked out of place was a brick sitting on the outside window sill. She panned her gaze around the room, observing what little there was in it. Superficially, the room was a seedy living space in a low-end Milwaukee flop house.

A closer look belied this: the room was well-kept, swept, dusted. She increased magnification and picked out individual dust particles. *Dusted within a day*, she concluded.

She looked up at her wrists, her upper pair. The ropes had been wrapped around each wrist in several turns, about four, and tied tightly, well below her hands. Yezeletta had large hands, even for a woman of her size. She tried to reach the knots with her fingers, but the knots were between her wrists, tied there, and free ends of the ropes continued down to her elbows, and were tied again there. *So who's the damned expert*, she asked herself.

Her lower arms were tied with the same attention to detail: far out of reach of her upper pair.

She snarled. Silently. She and Joe had played these games in their bedroom, but that had been erotic play. This was for real, by an invisible entity who had thought this out very well.

There was a scratching sound. Coming from the window.

Thicknesse was standing on the ledge outside, his gold imager looking in at her. Yezeletta could almost see concern in the creature's bio-receptor.

If Thicknesse could get in here, he could worry some of these knots loose. He scratched on the glass, making little lines in the exterior grime. The frame seemed to be nailed shut.

"Can you hear me?" she asked softly. Thicknesse answered with a wave of three of his legs.

"Connect me to Joe—tell him where I am."

Thicknesse's gold eye blinked, went out, opened again.

"Are you there?" It was Joe's voice! She increased the sensitivity of her hearing and added noise reduction.

"Yes!"

"Tell your friend to send your location to the rest of the imagers. The Mounties are on the way!"

A window pane burst inwards, to a gunshot. Thicknesse jumped into a corner of the window and tried unsuccessfully to look like dry mud and old paint. Another shot came, deafening in the small room. Yezeletta looked up. The shooter was somewhere down on the street; the two shots had come through the upper window pane and had lodged in the ceiling. As long as Thicknesse stayed where he was, he'd be safe.

"Yezeletta!" It was Joe's voice by way of Thicknesse.

"Yes, Joe!" she answered.

"Yezeletta, can these friends of yours locate sounds, and triangulate on them?"

"They can, tell the Matrix Engine—" she could almost see Joe nodding, "— the data will get put on the display closest to you." She gave a pull on her ropes. They didn't give at all.

"I have it!" Joe reported back through Thicknesse. "Loud intermittent noises in the industrial area. Near," (pause), "the Pelton Casteel plant. Down south of that church that has the big gold clock, Saint Stanislaus, or something. Can you get those thugs to fire one more time? The Engine wants another approximation."

"Thicknesse, push the brick out of the window," she said.

The little creature reached out with five of his sixteen legs, and wedged them between the window frame and the brick. He grabbed at several cracks in the masonry with his other legs and pushed. The brick moved a centimeter towards the lip of the sill.

Thicknesse tried again. The brick was almost too heavy for him to move. Yezeletta hung against the ropes, her hands gripping like claws, as Thicknesse shoved at it.

The brick tilted off the sill and stopped.

There was a decorative trim outside of the window; the brick was lying on it.

"Come on, Baby," Yezeletta surprised herself by saying, "One more push...."

Thicknesse would have happily arched his back, if he'd been built that way. Instead, he added three more legs to the brick and *shoved*.

The brick fell over the edge and Yezeletta could hear it crashing against something on the building's side, as it fell.

The unseen gunman below fired another shot.

"Gotcha!" Joe's voice was the most welcome sound in the universe. "There's a bunch of small reinforcements headed your way." Joe paused, "Here comes the Entertainment Committee to help move the piano!"

"The same servitors as before?" Yezeletta asked.

"Yup! The boss troll just handed me my very own personal forty-five! We're moving! You're in a sort of seedy-looking four-story walkup. See you soon."

Yezeletta thought about that. "See you soon!" wasn't exactly the sort of thing her builders would have said.

Yezeletta looked around and up at her upper set of ropes. She made a fist with one hand and forced all of her fingers on the other hand into a small straight arrangement, practically folding the palm of her hand. She pushed and pulled, trying to slip the coils of rope off her folded hand. *Well, what do we do for Plan "B"*, she thought.

The ropes weren't even cutting into her wrists. They were just snug. Real snug. Enough to hold her without harming her.

So who's the expert, she asked herself, again.

Thicknesse waved one leg, looked at her.

He started to climb up the window.

"No!" she said softly. Thicknesse looked at her with his great gold eye.

"They might shoot you. Stay out of sight and let Joe find me."

Thicknesse moved into the corner of the window, again.

Step—Step—Step.

She heard the footsteps off in the distance. She enhanced her hearing, again, and listened. Joe had said that she was in a four-story building; she guessed that she was on the third floor; she couldn't hear wind sounds across the roof. Those steps were coming from the lower floors. Shortly the sound became evident to anyone with normal hearing. From the syncopation, it sounded as if two rather heavy individuals were stomping up the stairs. An irrelevant thought intruded, *How did they get me up here?*

The door opened.

Two men entered, both of a piece. They wore the same kinds of clothes: khaki work pants and work shirts. Their hair was uniformly short, and combed identically.

They looked, Yezeletta thought, as if they were trying to be anonymous, hard to remember. *Too bad they're so much alike.*

They also looked rather—military.

One of the men was carrying a tool box. He set it down in front of the window and got to work with a putty knife and other tools. Shortly, he had the shot-out glass panes removed from the window and panes from the toolbox, already treated with a thick layer of Milwaukee grime on one side, placed in position.

He tacked the glass in place with small brads, applied putty, picked up his things, and left.

All of this time the second nondescript individual just stood by the door, holding what looked like a fat cane. When the glazier left, he stepped out into the room and looked around.

Thicknesse was still huddled in the corner of the window, not daring to look in and risk his imager being seen. *He needs shades*, she thought, *Make that a̲ shade*.

The second man kept looking elsewhere. *What's he looking for?* she thought, *What do these guys want?* Quietly, she twisted her wrists in the ropes. Did the lower set feel looser than they had been?

Man Two (she started capitalizing him) finally stepped up to her. He looked her full in the face and Yezeletta looked back at an average man of average looks with an average face.

Too average. She expanded her eyes' spectral range.

There was a shimmering like an insubstantial halo around his head in the near infrared.

He's using a Holo-Facial Omni-Cover, she didn't say. That explained the too-average looks of his face. It was a construct generated by processing in the holographic generator.

The face grinned. The teeth were way too perfect. *A face like this should be snaggle-toothed.*

"What a marvelous construct," the man said.

He cocked his fist under Yezeletta's chin, and stared at her face. He had to reach up a ways to do it. She looked down at him.

"Prettier than I expected, but over at the Domes—" he said, his voice trailing off into silence. *Not <u>we</u>?* She didn't say.

"A deadly goddess," he said softly, "but harmless, now."

He stuck the cane in his belt, and placed his hands on her breasts. She tightened her muscles against the ropes. "Not so fast, my lethal friend," he said softly, "You won't get out until we let you."

Yezeletta smiled, showing her teeth. He looked up, his hands on her nipples, his head between her breasts.

And stepped back!

She lunged against the ropes. The lunge didn't accomplish much, but the sudden movement made him jump back further. Almost to the window.

"You," she said in a level voice, "aren't very original." Then: "Why don't you intelligence pukes get some new lines. And I'm not fooled by that hologram you're wearing, either!"

He backed up further. He felt behind him for the window sill and hitched his ass up onto it. He stared.

The area of his left cheek rippled in a rainbow pattern, then the rippling flickered across his face. He drew the cane as if it were a sword. Yezeletta activated several internal systems.

He stepped forward, holding the cane in his left hand. He swung it upwards at her right cheek.

Yezeletta's augmented vision slowed the motion of his hand down to a crawl. Frustratingly, she could not stop the movement, all her visual enhancements could do was make the black, tubular device in his hand that much more visible, understandable, analyzable. Lambent flashing tugged at her sight, the lights of phosphenes descended, a glittering curtain that separated him from her.

And her from reality.

Then the room went dark.

....THERE YOU ARE

She awoke.

She was lying on the cot. In the same room. Unbound.

She scanned without moving. The systems she had activated were her short-term visual recording capabilities.

She closed her eyes, and thought *there*, there and <u>there</u>. Several windows opened against her closed eyes with an analysis of the...tube's actions.

All Systems Nominal—No Malfunction.

The status flashed in a window that popped up in her right eye.

She ran her check-outs again, and the results were exactly the same:

All Systems Nominal—No Malfunction.

She activated a short-term data-reduction system, and another window opened in her left eye. Inside of it, the military man raised his—whatever that was: the cane—and flickering lights erupted in her field of view. She froze the motion of the tube, and enhanced the image.

It was a difficult enhancement. There was actually a perceptible *delay* before the enhanced still-image overlapped the original image in its own window. Then she was looking at a pretty decent close-up of the device.

To begin with, although it was more the size and diameter of a shotgun barrel, there wasn't a hole in the end of it. That precluded projectiles.

Secondly, there were exactly *no* discernable features about the thing at all. There was a small sliding component under the man's thumb, but that was all of the operating interface there was to the...whatever.

She rolled onto her side, a momentarily painful action as it put her body weight on both of her right arms, and sat up.

As near as she could tell, she was in the same room. That damned post she had been tied to was there just opposite the window. There was no sign of the ropes.

The door was opposite her.

Yezeletta stood up and went to the door. She grabbed the door-knob, and turned.

Nothing happened.

"No way, José she said. "I've had just about enough of this!" She grabbed the doorknob in three hands and used a fourth, her left upper, to brace herself against the door, spread all four of her legs out for stability, and twisted and pulled on the knob. With a crackle of splitting wood, the knob, the latch and part of the door came off in her hands. She fell back, caught herself on a back foot, her right, and stood up.

She tossed the fragments in a corner and opened the door.

There was nothing there.

Yezeletta looked out on...nothing.

There should have been a wooden landing, perhaps the door of a room on the other side of a grimy hallway. This was:

Gray. Empty. Without depth. Infinitely deep.

She frowned, slightly. The infinite depth was an illusion. There was nothing in the hall to provide visual cues. That gray expanse could be flat and impenetrable—she thought of a Roadrunner cartoon, in which the Roadrunner paints a tunnel entrance on the rock face of the base of a cliff and the Coyote runs into it at full speed. With concussional results.

Or the expanse could be arbitrarily deep: like a foggy road.

She looked around for something. The only object that would work was the piece of door she had ripped out. She got it and stuck one end out into the hall.

Maybe it *was* fog. The end of the door chunk, about seventy centimeters, was visible clear to the end.

Yezeletta expanded her visual spectrum to its widest range. She stared into the gray expanse and applied all of the visual enhancements at her disposal.

There was nothing there.

Nothing at all.

That could mean any-damn-thing, she thought.

She increased the acuity of her hearing, and *listened*.

Not a sound. *Odd*.

Before she had heard the distant sounds of occasional traffic. She expanded her hearing again. And again.

Now there were no sounds at all.

The human ear hears sounds on a logarithmic scale: doubling the volume of what she heard—to her—was actually about a ten-times increase in the actual sound energy. *Fine*. She jacked her hearing up to the almost unthinkable sensitivity her builders had designed into her.

She should have heard the sounds of a cat stomping around after a mouse four kilometers away, she realized, but all that came through were the softly attenuated sounds of her own breathing, blood circulation and the syncopated rhythms of her hearts, thoughtfully compensated for and mostly filtered out by her hearing systems. *They* hadn't made the filtration of her bodily functions complete, as she could use the feedback sounds from those as an informal sort of status check. She used the sounds this way now, listening to her hearts beat, the sound of air in her lungs, as she breathed, the hydraulic flow of blood.

Everything seemed nominal, but just for practice, she ran the rest of her body checks also. Everything was—well—nominal. She wasn't malfunctioning. To anyone looking at her, Yezeletta seemed to pause for perhaps a second, then resume moving. She placed her hands, the uppers, on both sides of the door frame and regarded the anomalous fog before her. The door fragment didn't seem to have been harmed by the stuff out in the hall.

One more try.

She expanded her visual senses to their widest spectral ranges again, and added all of the image enhancement techniques she had. Inside the micro-processors that assisted her with this, complex simultaneous fractal differential equations were being set up and solved in a fashion that was totally transparent to her. She knew what kinds of on-board programming she had at her disposal—she had improved on that programming several times, since leaving Alice Springs—and she also knew about pattern recognition programming and noise reduction.

But first there had to be noise to reduce and patterns to recognise. There had to be spectra to investigate.

Shit.

This stuff was somehow more than pea-soup. There was nothing. Really, nothing there.

What the hell.

Yezeletta wished for a weapon. The only thing she had was that piece of door. She got it and strode out into the nothing.

And was standing in the center of the room, again.

Yezeletta was well-grounded in the physical sciences. She had to be, so much of her existence depended on them. She knew that certain things were possible, and certain things weren't.

Were they?

Impossible.

Once, when she was in her early teens, one of the electricians at the Project, who was an amateur magician, showed her a magic trick that used a short piece of electrical cord. He had held the endpoints of the cord in his hands and had done a complex motion, not letting go of the endpoints, but *tying a knot* in the center of the cord.

That, Yezeletta knew, was a nice illusion, but topologically impossible. The man's arms, body and hands, along with the cord made a circle: a closed loop: a figure of first order topological complexity, much like a coffee cup (the kind with a loop handle), or a key-ring. It was impossible for that knot to appear without the engineer letting go of one of the cord's endpoints for a very short time.

Later, Yezeletta would play back the man's engaging trick in her augmented mind's eye (aided by about a petabyte of RAM and some visual processors that she understood very well). In slow motion, she would see the very brief interval, where the cord, swung this way and that in elaborate, but misdirecting, loops, would be released for about a quarter of a second. In that short time-interval, which she could stretch out as long as she wished, the rope could pass through another rapidly moving loop near it to form the knot.

It didn't detract from the electrician's legerdemain. Her mathematical instruction had been nothing if not complete and what the man had shown her was, by all that training, easily recognized as a stunt. What remained was to find where a talented amateur magician had "jumped out of the system" of topology into the system of stage-magic illusion, to create his trick.

Her slow-motion analysis had shown that. It made the man's stunts (he had performed other tricks for her as well) that much more enjoyable.

Yezeletta looked around her. Again.

The room was unchanged.

The window—

Was Thicknesse? She called softly.

There was no answer.

There was no one at the window. Thicknesse had huddled into the left outside corner of the window and closed his imager to be as inconspicuous as possible. Now the window was bare. Had he left?

Yezeletta stared out of the open door. Damn it, the fog was still there. As impenetrable as the staircase in that James Blish story she'd read a few months ago. Blish had used the stairs as a metaphor for time travel, each step that his male lead took taking him a quantum jump into succeedingly improbable futures. This door was simply, what?

Improbable.

Yezeletta began to get the inkling of an idea. She opened a window in the field of view of her left eye and dumped into it a "snapshot" of the way the room had looked when she had been tied up.

Speaking of which....

She had been tied with at least ten meters of rope. It took that much to keep her in one place. Where was it?

She walked back to the post and leaned against it, placing her hands where they had been tied. She looked: up, down, out the window, up again. Where were the bullet holes in the ceiling? *This* ceiling was unharmed. She compared it with the snapshot. The ceiling above her was about two bullet-holes shy of reality.

With a little start, she realized that the scratches on the carefully established grime on the windowpanes placed there by Thicknesse's claws were missing, too!

Once again, she set her vision for microscopic sight and looked for dust. There was no dust.

"No Runs. No Hits. Just Errors," she said.

"Where the hell am I?"

What if this room were a metaphor?

For what?

Yezeletta sat down on the edge of the cot. Then she looked at the filthy mattress. "You *putzes*," a delightful word she'd gotten from Joe, "don't miss a beat, do you?" The mattress looked a lot neater than it had been.

She got off the bed and sat on the floor, leaning against the side of the bed, her legs splayed out before her. *I feel like the main character in a Charles Addams cartoon*, she didn't say. *And this little piggy....*

No dust. No marks. Just that pea-soup fog outside this room. No sights. No sounds. Just—

Yezeletta leaned back and focused on the ceiling, again. She applied all of the magnification that her vision was capable of. Then she piled on all of the image augmentation techniques she had at her disposal. *This might fool someone without my add-ons*, she thought. *Before I met Joe, I might have said "normal" people!* The badly watermarked ceiling's defects grew larger before her steady gaze, the small pits in the plaster gaping like craters, nail-heads—the ceiling was of wallboard with plaster afterthoughts—gaped like huge steel platters. She increased the resolution, until the plaster afterthoughts looked like alien critters from a bad science-fiction movie.

She kept boring in.

The plaster afterthoughts grew and bloomed out of her field of view. A particulate aspect seemed to overtake her gaze, as the superficially smooth plaster took on the characteristics of a lunar surface. The attempts by a long-gone plasterer's sanding showed as anything but smooth.

The flickering started at the edges of her field of view.

It was almost like an image on one of her computer monitors when viewed under a low power magnifying glass. Last week, Joe had replaced a defective hi-res monitor with a spare that was anything but hi-res. Images that had been smooth and natural on the hi-res—GIF images from her look-outs—wound up looking positively granular on the replacement.

Granular like...what she was seeing, now.

Yezeletta knew that the digital imaging systems that she used were of a type that would have a maximum resolution past which she would not be able to resolve things that her eyes could input. If she needed to, she could switch out the digital intermediates and use her natural sight, but the en-hancements were mostly second nature to her. She also knew (she stopped to check it) that what she was resolving now was nowhere near that theoret-ical maximum.

At the point where the image was more than just beginning to break up, Yezeletta stopped. She raised one eyebrow a millimeter in admiration of her unseen captors. *Better than using rope!* she thought, *they just let me think I'm in here; I wonder where the data feed's coming from?*

She raised her other eyebrow a similar distance and stopped. What if any motions in here, wherever "here" was, were repeated "out there," wherever "there" was?

Could "they," whoever, and so on, see her miscellaneous motions?

She got up and walked to the foggy doorway. *If this motion is being repeated wherever they're really holding me, I must really be thrashing around. Am I in a sensory deprivation tank?*

She thought about that. Probably not. In sensory deprivation studies, the subjects were dressed in wet-suits and placed in a salt-water solution of neutral buoyancy. And, any wet-suit designed for her would not be an off the shelf item!

They're relying on REM sleep, she decided. In REM, Rapid Eye Movement, sleep, the brain disconnected the motor nerves from the muscles (*a crude way of looking at it*, she thought), to keep the dreamer from hurting himself by converting dream movements to real movements. If that wasn't the case here, she was either restrained so tightly that she could risk tearing herself apart internally, or restraints—even something as ordinary as a seat belt—weren't necessary.

They wouldn't want her torn apart; she was probably in a bed with guardrails, and they were trusting the capricious gods of REM.

Very good!

Yezeletta sat back on the floor, again. She didn't want to lie on that mattress, even if it was a simulacrum. She didn't know how complete the data feed was. Yet.

The grin she wasn't showing was all inside her.

It's just this little chromium switch,
here. You people are so superstitious.

Let them try to figure that one out!

ON THE STEPPES OF VIRTUAL REALITY

[Digitally Enhanced CG Image] Yezeletta put her chin in her hand, saw momentarily the creep inside his hologram, closed her eyes and thought.

Her Command Channel was a direct line to her "command center." At least that was the original intent of her builders (*I must get a better term for them!* she thought). The **CCOM** manifested itself as a window that opened in her left eye's field of vision, with the corresponding audio input coming in through her left ear. The seeming one-sidedness of this was to allow inputs—providing she wasn't too occupied to receive them!—while allowing her to handle other, more pressing external problems. She could even apply the equivalent of an answering machine to the channel, in case she was really busy. In a pitched battle, maybe.

But *her* Command Channel was turned off.

By that, she thought, *it means: the phone is off the hook, the answering machine isn't taking messages, and "all of our operators" are out to lunch!*

That modification had taken some real volition. The Project hadn't figured on their Agent suddenly getting this much of a mind of her own. As Anne Lenhaden had said, "They built too well!"

Yezeletta reached across the "room" in her own private virtual reality and opened the Command Channel!

The input was deafening. Quickly, she closed it. Then, placing an attenuation stage in place, she opened it again.

The packet input was splayed across her vision in numbers, colors, graphics and other formats. She was able to see the cyclic redundancy check used as error-correction with parity bits sticking out like glowing exclamation points, what each data packet represented, and a little about the routing. Far and far and away and away, out in the real world (what the programmers at the Project had called meat-space), her lips moved in a sardonic smile, but before the muscles in her face had even a chance to start moving, she canceled the smile, and *saw*—

How - the room was generated— *saw*—

How - the sounds (such as they were) were made— *saw*—

What - was on the other side of the fog— *saw*—

Her - own time-base and— *saw*—

How - short a time had elapsed— *saw*—

How - her vision was interdicted— *saw*—

How - they had taken over her other senses— *saw*—

Where she was.

G RANDFATHER'S E YES !

Yezeletta opened her eyes!

This room was real!

She was lying on at-least a queen-size bed (it had to be that small, her ankles were draped off the foot of it) in a room similar to the one in virtual space. They, et cetera and ad nauseam, had left her on her back, her arms and legs spread out. She wore a thing like an Indian brave's headband, with a cable of heroic diameter attached to it, leading off to a portable computer in a docking station placed on a small table nearby, next to a trashy-looking paperback.

Grin. Invisible.

No restraints.

There were footsteps in the hall.

A woman entered.

Yezeletta looked at her through half-closed eyelids. She was of average build, wearing a sort of one-piece coverall, a tool belt, and knee-length boots. She came through the door, sat down, picked up the paperback, opened it to a place and resumed reading. She didn't look at the computer screen.

Yezeletta tensed up, getting ready for her attack. She planned to leap for her guard, immobilize her and look for a way to find Joe.

Flicker.

Flicker, *Blink*.

It was the portable's screen. The woman looked up, looked at Yezeletta, reached for an object on her belt!

Yezeletta rolled to her right and *stood*.

The guard had pulled a small pistol and was trying to hold it in both hands. The gun was too small for a two-handed grip and Yezeletta reached out with one big hand, her left lower, and slapped it out of the guard's grasp.

Her other left hand followed through with a slap that she put most of her upper-body strength into. The other woman crashed against the wall behind her, out cold.

A single large window on the computer's display showed the visual feed that was still being sent to the head-band. Another window was a series of physiological readouts.

That's where she saw my analysis, she thought. She ripped off the head-band and started to toss it into the corner—

And stopped.

She shut down the portable, folded it up and....There: several large cloth bags, and—

The case for the portable.

She dumped the computer into the case, stuffed the headband in on top and wrapped the cable around it, chased it with the docking stand. This bundle went into a sack and she—

Looked, again.

The custom jump-suit she'd been wearing when all of this had started was nowhere to be found. She made a face. *I always seem to wind up naked and ready, like in that old song! Maybe they do find me attractive. Or at least harmless. Or they think that I'm harmless. Or something.*

She looked out into the hall. It was empty.

Carrying her sack, she walked up the hallway to a window, and looked out. Joe and the Matrix Engine had been accurate about where she was. She was on the fourth floor of a building made of red brick. There was the Pelton Casteel Plant, a well-known landmark on Milwaukee's southeast side. There, the Mitchell Conservatory, and over there was....

For one of the few times—very few!—in her life, Yezeletta Zargkonji went cold. *Her universe moved, and began to come apart*. The geometry of what she was seeing was all wrong.

She everted her gaze so fast that the visual change almost made her dizzy. Looking for dust, looking for imperfections, looking for—

Pixels!

She ran her visual resolution up to its theoretical maximum. She looked into the walls around her, into the ceiling, into the outdoors.

Into The System.

M A T R Y O S H K A !

When Yezeletta had turned six, one of her many nurses had given her a birthday present. It was a set of the nested Russian wooden dolls in the shapes of Grandfather, *babushka*, or Grandmother, then Papa and Mama and so on, each fat Russian peasant opening up, with another gaily painted doll within. The set that Nurse Klaudia Ivanovna had given her was a large set made of eight nesting dolls, and Yezeletta had opened them all up and placed them in a circle around her, corresponding to all of her extremities. The six-year-old Yezeletta had thought it funny that there were as many dolls as she had hands and feet.

As she looked around her, her eyes wide (although she didn't know that, yet), Yezeletta almost knew what it was like to give herself over to the insidious, black tendrils of panic.

She closed her eyes, stood on all four feet and looked back at her command channel.

That was not where this feed was coming in.

It seemed to be all around her! No matter where she looked, there were the same sights: the hallway, the buildings, the pixilations!

Let me see you! she called soundlessly, *Where are you, show yourselves!*

She opened her eyes.

She was standing in a geometry book.

Below her, cartesian coordinates. Her feet precisely at:

$$\textbf{(+1, +1)} \textit{ (-1, -1)} \textbf{ \underline{(+1, -1)}} \textbf{ \underline{(-1, +1)}} \textbf{ .}$$

A mathematical dance of absolute values, a box step.

Before her a fractal dragon, its recursive complexity colored in hues that tugged at the edges of her vision.

High above, a fresnel hovered like a cross (but that was over there!) between an eye in the sky and a crystalline U. F. O.

She knew that this was all a data feed into her brain and that somehow there was a way out. The shapes were the way her own brain interpreted the packet stream that was being force-fed to her.

She was not here.

That was what she had to remember. This was not reality. Reality was what was being prevented from accessing her, while *whoever* fed this non-reality into her mind.

She blocked it out.

She closed her eyes and covered them with two of her hands.

She saw through her eyelids, her palms.

She took a step and looked down. Her body told her that she had walked a step, her eyes told her that she had not moved.

The dragon towered over her.

It looked down upon her.

Yezeletta threw her head back and looked the dragon squarely in its eyes. Those infinitely recursively complex brilliantly colored coruscations of light grew larger and larger and closer, they would engulf—

No.

A fractal dragon is a complex figure from advanced number theory. The basic equation is very simple; the complexity of the figure itself is in the details of the mathematics of closed surfaces, and in the details that lie just below the comparatively simple nature of the basic mathematics. There is no consciousness.

For all of its wonderful colors, shapes, and infinite variety, a Mandelbrot Dragon is a dead thing.

"Oh, I wouldn't be too sure 'bout that," the Dragon said.

"Who are you?"

"I'll hold that in abeyance, for a while, young lady," the mathematical curve said from within itself. "After all, I'm not really here, any more than you are."

The Dragon was almost directly overhead, and Yezeletta had to tilt her head sharply back to see it.

"Why don't you lie down, you can see me easier," the Dragon said in a chatty voice. "Just lie right here."

Yezeletta cocked her head to the right, and looked up with one eye.

"Lie down and spread your legs," the Dragon said.

Yezeletta looked straight up at the Dragon, with both eyes, "Eat shit and die!"

The Dragon's head came straight down on her and Yezeletta met it! With both hands!

She shot her upper right and lower left fists out: a fist for each of the Dragon's eyes. The recursively self-referent receptors **((closed)**, ***((closed)***, **(closed)))** around her fists, as Yezeletta activated the data-channel outputs in her fingers.

Her hands reached deep. The sensations she felt (she realized with another part of her mind) were *still* the results of the data feed coming in from them, but even they had to start from some sort of initial conditions, and *they* didn't understand (she realized coldly), *they did not know* that she could communicate with other systems through the micro-filaments in her fingers.

She plunged all four of her hands into the dragon's eyes and seized the creature's optic nerves—

And interfaced to them.

In the Looking-Glass

Yezeletta's data protocols swarmed up her arms, through her fingers and out of her body. The specially tailored viral sub-programs extended/expanded ineluctably, huge black snowflakes, thrown like nets into the data-structures her captors had emplaced, diffusing across them, infecting, containing, attacking.

And Yezeletta, a real spider this time, jumped with the characteristic rapid agility of the arachnid up into the web of audio-visual system-objects, swarming up the switching packet network, her objective in clear view, its defensive systems falling before her.

Her hands/claws/legs/arms struck the origin point of the system feed.

The whole universe trembled.

The vast web of data in which she was the centerpoint trembled,

<the human part of her thought>

|| ["or"]

<the spider part of her thought>,

I've caught one, I have him close, he's mine, I—

She became coterminal with the origin point.

For a moment she was still standing at:

(+1, +1) *(-1, -1)* <u>(+1, -1)</u> <u>(-1, +1)</u> .

then, the network, the web, the data feed became a flickering image, a movie-film, a video, an endless loop of flashing colors and every sound from the deepest bass to fingernails on a blackboard. Yezeletta/spider/human/wea-pon grabbed the centerpoint, the origin the main with all four of her hands and held on, riding out the flickering the motion the spasms as the entity/computer system fought to keep her out.

She wrapped her legs around it, her arms around it, and squeezed. The micro-filaments in her arms burned like red-hot wires, tracing a virtual schematic of her internal systems in scarlet lines on her skin.

Great cracks appeared in the fabric of space-time. Jagged lines, black lightning subdivided her reality into segments, each segment attacked by one of her black snowflakes, which wrapped itself around the segment, covering it, consuming it, removing it.

The Lineprinter in the Doorway

Yezeletta Zargkonji opened her eyes.

This time, she knew that she was in reality.

She still wore the head-band, but the portable computer to which it was attached didn't display anything more than a hexadecimal register dump, and a TRAP ZERO: SYSTEM HALTED message.

Whatever that computer had been doing, it would not be doing again soon without *a lot* of maintenance.

Yezeletta normalized her vision.

She never thought that she'd be this happy to see *dust*.

Across the hall, was—

The room in which she'd been tied up. The rope had been tossed back on the ratty mattress.

Best of all, Thicknesse was sitting in the window, looking up at her. Yezeletta punched out one of the window-panes. Thicknesse took the hint, jumped through the hole and ran up her arm.

"Joe, can you hear me?"

"Gotcha!" his voice was the best thing she'd ever heard. "We're about a block from the dump you're in."

"I'll meet you on the first floor, but I want some heavy movers up here to take this place apart."

She looked up the hall, then down it.

Had they just left her here?

Why?

She placed her hand, the upper left, gently on Thicknesse. Invisibly, data from her finger contacts streamed into the little creature and out to others of his kind that were in the area, then further out to others.

Yezeletta went back into the room where she'd been kept, and, feeling a bit shaky, packed up the stopped computer, the head-band (it felt hot to her touch) and other things. Others would return to this place to check for other items.

One of them would find the CCD TV camera disguised as a finial on the top of a lamp in the corner. By then it would be too late.

——>>> **EIGHT** <<<——

I would not spend another such a night
Though 'twere to buy a world of happy days.
So full of dismal terror was the time!

—William Shakespeare,
King Richard III

Home

[Sequential Access Method; Est. Shot, Medium Close-Up] The trip back to the Farmer's and Merchant's Building was uneventful. Joe took back streets and the occasional alley to get there, but there were no Police cars, no cars belonging to Zhongo Teketon and his crew, or to anyone else with whom Yezeletta and Joe were familiar.

Even the self-styled Lord of the Roads was absent.

Joe reached out, found the truck's radio by touch, turned it on. A man's voice was chanting to a repetitive rock beat:

"And I:

"Got To - Got To - Got To - Got To—

"Got To - Got To - Got To - Got To:

"Fleem!

"Nimble Nibble Nipple Nip!

"Scheme!

"I'm the one who'll make you flip!"

Yezeletta long-armed a finger, her lower left center finger, at the selector buttons, and punched up another station. "Who, or what was that?" she asked.

"These days, I don't want to know," Joe said.

The radio continued: "And now the eleven-fifteen newsbreak. Earlier tonight Milwaukee Police apprehended three agents of a foreign power...."

As they drove, they heard the public version of Yezeletta's escape.

Joe drove the truck into the basement parking ramp, down to the lowest level. There, a metal garage door opened as he approached it.

He parked in the basement, and watched the metal door descend. Outside the door, something—or perhaps some *things*—darted across the door-opening in spirals, spinning a preparation that solidified rapidly.

Yezeletta was back in her own element, again, "That concoction will fill up the inset in the wall where the door is. When those are done, the inset will have disappeared."

She wrapped her arms around Joe in a major hug. "I don't believe that I could have gotten out of that without you."

Joe ran his hands up her back. Her muscles were tense beneath his touch. "Welcome back, Partner," he said.

"I like the sound of that," she replied, "Let's go up—and Joe?"

"Yes."

"I wonder what 'Fleem' means?"

He joined in her laughter.

DISCONTINUOUS DREAMING

Later, pleasantly in their own bed, Yezeletta curled up with Joe in a riotously colored mass of pillows. Much later they fell happily asleep.

Yezeletta awoke several hours after that. She lay there, listening to her lover sleeping contentedly next to her.

How wonderful it was to have a real lover, at last!

Unbidden, she thought of some of those at Sargon. Then, she went from "unbidden" to active, to "bidden" to "required." She accessed several files in her on-board systems, and, in a manner of speaking, she hit the playback.

UP THE STREET

[Access] Her communicator waited patiently outside Leona's window on the maple branch for the activities within (which it didn't comprehend) to finish. Then it undid the screen and entered. It listened to Leona's message, then gave her several directives from Down Town.

The communicator surprised her by hopping across the floor to the corner, where the floorboard lifted *of its own accord* from its closed position.

The fuzzy, black tarantula that emerged was holding a note. An actual written missive.

E X A M I N A T I O N — V I I I — C O M P L E T I O N

[Tracking; Truck Shot; Sign Extension] That had been fun. She had actually enjoyed it, and Caliban looked positively satiated, almost smug, when it was over.

He'd had to leave shortly after.

Miranda waited, reading some old magazines. Judging from the ancient copies of *Time*, *Newsweek* and the like, she had gone back to two years earlier, and old news was still new.

The door opened, and Caliban entered the room.

Miranda put the antique news-magazines down, and put her arms around him in her own wide hug. She had to stand on her toes to do it. Caliban returned it with an enthusiasm that was far less clumsy than even the night before.

Then, he took her gently by the hand, and led her to the bed. He lay down on it, and held his arms out. Miranda almost laughed, but held her expression. *He's like a little boy who's discovered a new trick!* She swung her leg over, and came down on him. Caliban placed two large hands on her bottom to steady her, as she began the ancient ride. Caliban's other hands caressed her, as he moved with her.

Together they rode across the night and into the morning.

W I N D O W S   I N   T H E   M I N D

[Load Archive; Extreme Close-Up]

There was a flickering in her left eye; *that was where the playbacks were usually shown*, and she cued up her "memory".... (She reflected briefly on how it was entirely normal and expected for her memories to have *time-stamps* on them, and how difficult it must be on others to lack them)

And stopped.

There were the usual precautions she had to take. Any interference from the outside, or perhaps Joe awakening, had to abort the playback, and return her to her more usual senses. Easy enough, just direct a thought—*there!*

Now, she was ready.

W I N D O W S   I N   T I M E

[Roll With It; Truck Shot]

They had been immobilized with almost textbook precision. The operatives for Sargon Security were neatly rolled up in the Sheet to one side, and the remaining Directorate to the other side.

Directly before her, the Director of Sargon Administration lay in the multilegged grip of the Taker. He lay on his back, his legs spread, his arms over his head, intertwined in—an animal.

The Taker was Yezeletta's last creation. Superficially, it resembled a green, segmented, metallic centipede that was wrapped around one of the Director's legs, his right. It went up his chest, under his right armpit, under his body to his left arm, around it, behind his head to attach itself to his right arm, again. The Taker's many legs dug into his skin and held on.

If Mr. Director resisted, the Taker tightened its grip.

"WHERE CAN YOU GO?"

"You'll never get away with this outrage!"

"We can track you no matter where you run!"

"We have our ways!"

"Do you dare to oppose us? We Created You!"

"You Owe for the Flesh!"

"You belong to us!"

"HOW CAN YOU HIDE?"

"How dare you—!"

"Your DNA is On Record!"

"Reinforcements are on the way!"

"You are Government Property!"

"You're a Commonwealth Citizen, you have Responsibilities!"

"You Owe for your Life!"

"WHERE CAN YOU HIDE?"

To Yezeletta, the words stretched across her vision in a graphic fashion that resembled the horizontal cirrus clouds in a summer sunset. The lines of speech, the texts therein lined up like the code in a program against the sunset red of their emotions.

Yezeletta waited patiently, her back to them, as their outraged voices stopped, as their threats ran down, as they ran out of breath, as the Sheets tightened around them. Then she sat on one of her lab stools—the only furniture in Sargon that was designed for her physique—and watched them with a gaze that was a combination of the unwavering, the clinical and the blasé. Her gold cat's eyes missed nothing; she was operating them at their widest bandwidth.

She signaled to a servitor: <left-lower>—<right-lower>—<left-upper>, and the humanoid went to Mr. Director, and roughly removed a small and highly illegal pistol from his pants pocket, his left.

"You—" That was the Assistant Head of Sargon Security.

"Me." Yezeletta said. Her voice was flat, declarative.

"What do you want?" Phrased as a question, the words were inflected as a statement.

"You called yourself the Head of Sargon Security." The edge in her voice capitalized the title.

The man lunged against the Sheet, and it tightened incrementally. He let out a breath for which his next inhalation didn't compensate completely. "You called yourself the Head of Sargon Security," she repeated.

"I am!"

"Wrong. You're the *Assistant* Head of Sargon Security. You were never the top operative. You reported to someone."

"How would you know?"

"You used those telephones, the ones with the American Government encryption chip in them. That had a back door in it."

"I suppose you read the messages—"

"No suppose, about it," Yezeletta said, "I broke the Clipper Encryption right there on that computer." She smiled, showing her teeth, "I used the tricks you taught me in those cryptography texts that I had to read two years ago, remember? To say nothing of the book that started life two generations back...."

Security lurched. His movement was puzzling, until she realized that he was trying to sit up. Yezeletta made another three-handed gesture, and a servitor grabbed Security's shoulders, and roughly pulled his upper body into approximate vertical.

He inhaled, wheezed, tried to breathe, couldn't, fell back.

"It's best if you don't move." Yezeletta let a half-step note of kindness modulate her level tones. "I broke the Encryption. You should have known better than to entrust your precious secrets to eighty-bit algorithms. Even the American NSA's eighty-bit algorithms."

Security's response was a look midway between fury and outrage.

"You were an *Assistant*," Yezeletta repeated, "*All* of you were assistants. None of you were at the top of your phyla, all you ever were was second-guessers. Helpers. Second Place."

Yezeletta checked the infra-red characteristics of her captives. The disease from the eggs was progressing nicely. Properly, she could leave them where they were to die, but there was a chance that they might know something that wouldn't be written down in their respective offices, quarters or on personal computers.

Security took a breath. She touched his ankle, sticking out of the Sheet. *Tachycardia, near fibrillation, body temperature up one degree at 38 C.* As she had designed it.

Mr. Director wriggled in the grip of the Taker. "You *know* that you won't be allowed to get away with this."

"I already have. I would think that you could be more articulate, or, at least, more original than that."

Her reply was a series of stares, some rather weaker than others.

The Director tried to sit up. The Taker stiffened into a biological approximation of a steel exo-skeleton, and inhibited further movement.

"Mr. Director," she said. He looked at her, blinked.

"Mr. *Assistant* Director. Just like the rest. Who is the one over you?"

"There's no one above me. *I* am the Director of Project Sargon, and this foolishness has gone on far enough! Remove this, this—"

I call it a 'Taker'," Yezeletta said pleasantly. "Mr. Director," she let her voice lose seven years; it sounded again as if she were twelve. "You interviewed me seven years ago. Did you find me attractive?"

"I—"

"I remember," she said decisively, "When I left your office, *when you refused to show me the common courtesy of asking me to sit down*, you had your hand in your lap. Did you enjoy watching me on all of those bugs you placed in my quarters?"

"Your quarters were never bugged. I never saw anything there, that...."

He caught the contradiction, and shut up.

"Did you ever look?" She bent down, and placed her right hand, her upper, on Mr. Director's neck. *Tachycardia. Faster. Good.*

"No. Once. I—And—The Other—Other—"

"Or your plans to turn me into a sex-toy." Mr. Director fell back.

She stood up. *Why not? These people are useless!*

With a series of jerky motions, she tore her clothes off, and stood before them naked. "Just like that meeting, where I was on the stage, right? *Mr.* Director? Or your putative plans for me after you *installed* me in that underground place?"

Mr. Director was shaking.

"That was a really nice attempt at misdirection, that line about removing my lower arms! You never had any interest in doing that, it would have made me less valuable as a play-toy!"

She stood before them all, her long arms outstretched, her legs apart in a posture that would have been attractive, erotic anywhere else.

"Is this what you want, Mr. Director, am I pretty enough for you? My original design called for *four* of these—" she gestured at her breasts. "Was that your influence? Security, you've tried to see me for years. Am I what you thought I'd be?"

One of her hands made a motion. It was a conjuror's motion, something appeared in her right hand, her upper.

It was an egg. One more of its kind. It was colored a flat black.

Security's eyes were glazing, Mr. Director had a look of stony disdain.

With one swift motion, Yezeletta threw the egg to the floor. It shattered with a "bang".

Then she stood up, and left her living room.

In the door, she looked back on the still scene.

"Good-bye," she said softly.

A BIT LATER

[Close Archive; Iris Dissolve] Yezeletta routed the playback to the place where she kept such memories, and lay back against her sculpted pillows. Joe Davis lay next to her, sleeping, oblivious to her thoughts, one hand lying outstretched, touching her right side.

He had thrown in with her of his own volition, *there's no way I could have kept him any other way!* He could have escaped any time, but his—fascination—with her had kept him, and his fearless love had made it permanent.

Yezeletta lay on her right side facing Joe, and gently took his extended hand in her left hands. *Never thought I'd believe this, she thought, but there it is: your battles are mine, as much as you've made my battles yours. Looks like we're in it for the long haul.*

I love you, Joe.

Yezeletta felt herself drifting into the initial stages of sleep. Before she slept, she put a reminder in a place in her onboard systems where she kept "notes" to herself: *Orion: I <u>must</u> understand Orion!*

A FROG FROM PHILADELPHIA

[Parallel Process; Long Shot] The only time Peter Rudenko was undisturbed was when he was at home, or out of the office at lunch.

His superiors were not pleased with his report on The Road Lord. That was an understatement. If his immediate supervisor had raised his voice, it might have been easier to take. Pugnacious behavior can always be replied to in kind, and it can relieve tensions. Peter's boss, however, had been soft-spoken, articulate, intelligent, and *nasty*. And he hadn't allowed Peter to get in a word edgewise.

Peter had spent the following month filing reports for the more active agents in "Siberia," the large back room where the files, actual paper files in large metal containers, were kept.

Then, too, there were the reports from Walter Reed Hospital.

His predecessor, a man named Anthony Russell, was still in a coma in his private room there.

PREPARATIONS—LOGISTICAL—I

[Load Library; Camera Goes With; Bank Swap; Link] Yezeletta awoke early the next morning. She got up, and, leaving Joe to rest a little, strode naked into her office.

Being tall is a real asset, she thought, *especially when I need to get books from the top shelf!* She reached up with all four hands, and grabbed an even dozen of the large, heavy paperbacks from her collection of references.

She placed them on the conference table near a convenient laptop, and looked back at the top shelf. She scanned for a moment, and—there!

She grabbed another double-double-handful of fat books. All of the versions, editions and errata, to say nothing of the sequelae and commentaries by other authors from one of the most delightfully subversive inter-generational mathematical teams in all of Computer Science.

Joe oughta get a kick out of these, she thought, grinning.

Then, she went back to bed.

When Joe awoke, she had something else in mind.

PREPARATIONS—LOGISTICAL—II

[SYS$*RLIB$] Three hours later, at breakfast, Yezeletta leaned back in one of the specially built chairs, able to handle her weight. She was pleasantly full, and she regarded Joe with a wide-eyed gaze.

"Those secret agents are on my mind," she said. "I've not been able to get any information on them, and I'm a tad concerned."

"Does anyone really know we live here?"

"The Lenhadens, Peter Rudenko and Leona," Yezeletta answered. "Hilda, too, of course."

"This is the tallest building in Milwaukee," Joe said. "Why doesn't anyone ever try to reclaim this place?"

"When I moved in, it was a vertical slum," Yezeletta said. "I noticed that the cops mostly concerned themselves with 'real' crimes, such as robbery, rape, and so on, rather than what you might think of as 'manufactured' crimes. Things like, well, jaywalking. Floating crap games. Anything obvious that was easy to waste time on. I had a chance to raid one of the Milwaukee Public Library's databases about two months before I met you, and in back issues of the *Milwaukee Journal-Sentinel*, I read of past police chiefs who micro-managed this town so thoroughly that Milwaukee became a laughingstock for several years—nearly a decade—into this century."

"The cops wasted their time hassling people visibly rather than dealing with the big stuff?"

"Exactly. Nuking Washington might have been the hint, to understate it a lot, that the U.S. needed. I've had to do some extensive reading on this: I was all of five years old when it happened."

"I was living in San Diego when it happened. Everything practically shut down for a month."

"I read later that cities like London and Paris came close to returning to the old idea of city-states afterwards. Here, the cops, the citizens, and the gangs appear to exist in a state of something like chemical or physical equilibrium. The cops do what's necessary with what little they have, the gangsters do what they damned well want to, except they keep it quiet, and the average individual just tries to get on with his life, in spite of everything else. Nobody seems to have time for abandoned buildings, or the larger abandoned areas in this city."

Joe thought about that. A servitor cleared the breakfast dishes away, and another brought coffee.

"Will it always be that way?" Joe asked.

"I'm wondering. These things go through cycles. Maybe in ten years, everything gets back to 'normal,' whatever that means, and some development firm decides to evict this building's putative tenants, and start selling office space. The Matrix Engine is pretty much a permanent installation, but I can remove the important parts, and back up the data, and I could move its functionality elsewhere."

"Sounds painful."

"It would be. The only brain that's self-aware in the system is Hilda; the others are all just memory or processing units,"—Joe shuddered inwardly at that—"I can clone such things now with what I've built here, and not have to pick out the occasional malefactor—"

"You had me—I believe the current cliché is 'really going'—when I saw the records of that guy. The one you and Leona did before I came here."

Yezeletta gently took Joe's right hand in three of hers, "Joe, one of the purposes for which I developed my cat-arachnids was to clean the rats out of the area around Project Sargon. Here, some of the Hive creatures do the same thing. The rodent population in Milwaukee has been monotonically decreasing since I arrived here. Does it make sense to remove predators from the system that the Milwaukee Police can't touch? Leona and I found that man almost accidently. He was molesting a small boy in an office in a building up the street from here, and I don't even want to think, now, about what he was planning to do to him."

"That kind, huh?"

"Exactly. The one good thing that came of that incident was that I got an 'in' with one of Zhongo's gangsters. If I can, I remove some of the rats from this town. That monster, for example; at least what's left of him is of some use.

"Where he is, he never gets to hurt another child again, does he?"

PREPARATIONS—LOGISTICAL—III

"We're in little danger of being discovered," Yezeletta said, later.

"I hope that's accurate," Joe replied drily.

"I plan to get further information as soon as possible," Yezeletta continued, "But I want to beef up the security of my systems and the data links to my installations in the city."

"That was one of the biggest surprises, after I met you, Yezeletta," Joe said. "I was damned near in a state of disbelief when I saw just how well you'd infiltrated this burg."

Yezeletta smiled, "I was trained to do this by world-class operatives. Then I discovered what they had in mind for me, and I decided that *I must not fail*. It was a big job."

"What's on the list first?"

"Several things. How much looking around did you do while I was a guest of the Eastern Bloc?"

"The Matrix Engine and the floor below it. The thirtieth floor."

"You saw them. I can tell it from the tremors in your voice."

"The Madflowers."

"The Madflowers," she repeated. "I haven't the slightest idea why I'll need them. Stimulants, perhaps. Weapons against what, I don't know about, yet. Something. It has to do with what happened while I was in that ratty little building, and some things that I *didn't* see before we went after Gary the Geek."

'What? Excuse me, but I haven't the slightest idea what you're getting at, and I've been watching you doing your projects for, uh, as long as I've known you."

"Joe, how did you find out about me?"

"I didn't 'find out'. Rumors, mostly. You—more accurately, someone *about like you*—was mentioned on some email feeds: there's one called the 'International Conspiracy Research List' that's mostly way off base; I used to read it for the laughs. Every now and then, though, something about 'The Agent' would show up."

"Like that *Weekly World News* or *National Enquirer* stuff I showed you."

"Exactly. There was enough about it, like the periodic Elvis sightings back in the Nineteen-Eighties and Nineties. Call it urban legends, if you like. Then there were those tales of the UFO sightings—"

"What?" Yezeletta asked, "How would that get into it?"

"Someone out in Utah saw a creature that—you've seen those gray aliens with the big, dark, slanted eyes, kind of a guitar-pick shape to the face? Round, bald head, pointed chin?"

Yezeletta nodded.

"Those didn't start getting tabloid space until right after that old movie about alien contact: *Close Encounters of the Third Kind*. That's when the "guitar-pick" kind of alien started showing up. I'm surprised that people didn't start seeing the banana-heads from the original movie *Alien* after that came out."

Yezeletta looked puzzled, then she asked thoughtfully, "What did this—observation—look like?"

"Craggy face, no expression, ridges around the eyes—"

Yezeletta touched the top of an imager sitting on the table, a servitor entered. "Like one of these," she said.

Joe nodded; Yezeletta dismissed the servitor.

"I had a hunch," Joe said. "There was the abandoned ship in the Long

Beach Harbor. Registered to Mexico. Its last stop was in Darwin."

Yezeletta's face was unreadable.

"Lady, it's good that you covered your tracks as well as you did on your way here." Yezeletta nodded, again. "I wasn't sure that you, or what I thought you were, at the time, would be in Milwaukee, but my research showing up in the Milwaukee Underworld had me interested enough that I wanted to look around here."

"I saw you on that news report."

"And you were interested enough in me to scoop me up if you saw me."

"I was and I did."

"And we're here. My parents are dead, and I don't have any brothers or sisters, just aunts and uncles—"

"Fortunate," Yezeletta said, "or they might be asking questions."

"Yes," steadily, "It's good for both of us. I agree with you about the need for preparations," Joe went on. "What do you have in mind?"

"First," she said, "we need to gather data, and be sure that the information gathered gets back here safely and securely. Are you familiar with these?" She turned and grabbed three fat paperback books with her right hands, and dropped them loudly on the table.

"*Applied Cryptography*, by Bruce Schneier the Third," Joe read. "Hell yes! Just about the most well-known family of subversives in data-processing. The grandfather, the First, actually created a mil-spec encryption system that used nothing more than an ordinary deck of cards! Did it for some science-fiction—or was it historical?—novel that came out in, uh, 1999, I think." Joe read something printed on the back of one text, "Yeah. It got too hot on Earth for these guys; they're on the Moon now. Novy Moskva in Luna, I think. Too bad they don't speak English up there, but I'd suspect that a family of *cryptographers* wouldn't have a lot of trouble with that."

"There are some good ideas in these books."

"You into punning? There's an algorithm in here called **IDEA**—International Data Encryption Algorithm—that's the one PGP uses."

"There's better. And described in these. I want to use better in my communications."

"What do you use now?"

"Very little, but each channel is split up and chunks are sent by divergent routes. Biological packet-switching, if you like. In addition to this, everything is broadcast equally to everywhere, and receivers of data-packets don't send ACK signals back. If they did, the receiver needing the data-transmission would signal its position. Everything's pretty well hidden. As long as no one knows that anything's there, no one tries to detect it. Those East Europeans—Russians?—worry me. I have an internal log of what they tried to do while I was napping for them. They tried to read out my onboard systems, and my defenses went active."

"Defenses? What sort?"

"My original on-board systems had various forms of offensives and defensives. They took the form of elaborate programs for checking any inputs, and of different kinds of viruses, for actually dealing with anything that I, or they, might decide was an invasion. One of my viral defenses went active while I was up in that attic with those creeps. I downloaded it into their—I guess you'd call it a Sampler—the tool they used to attack me."

"When they came for you," Joe said, "I literally saw stars. Something at the edges of my vision that looked like TV interference."

"That's not too surprising," Yezeletta said. "There are some, it's quite inadequate to call them induction pickups; they're related more to TEMPEST or Van Eck detectors that can be used to read out the 'surface' programming of a microprocessor-based system. You were experiencing a strong induction field that was starting to affect your nervous system. It was ten or a hundred times, or more, worse for me!"

Joe looked concerned, "Did they get anything out of you?"

"If they did, I'll be very surprised. My defenses started as mil-spec, too, and I've improved on them."

BIBLIOGRAPHIC ACCESS

Joe leafed through the Thirtieth Edition of *Applied Cryptography*, "'The Phantom of the Internet: A 64-Round 1024-byte block encryption'," he read out loud. He looked up at Yezeletta, "Byte *blocks?* I thought that 128-bits were sufficient."

"It still is," she said, "unless you have a very large matrix processor, or some sort of bio-chip system. I've read of systems using tailored DNA, capable of performing several trillions of operations, in parallel, per second. Beijing is reputed to have a quantum bio-chip super-computer capable of making IDEA give it up after—well, I took it with a rather large grain of salt. About a kilogram. The database I was in *said* about six months of brute-force work. That's a little hard to take on one system."

"Sounds like that stuff I mentioned from the Space Bloc: all those reprints." Yezeletta nodded agreement.

"Okay, Partner, where do you keep the system development tools? In addition to biological protocols, I'm fairly good at C++ programming." In response to her raised eyebrow, he added, "I had to learn it in self defense; a lot of my early research required heavy numerical-analytical work."

"Well, Joe," Yezeletta said, and again, Joe saw her eyes actually twinkle, "There's about a dozen development systems on the LAN, and you're in charge of implementing the Mathematical Munitions.

"Link and Load!"

INTERIM TIME

[Implementation] Joe spent the rest of the day in front of a large-display laptop in the conference room. Occasionally, Yezeletta would bustle in on some errand or another: once she sat with him, and watched as he checked all of the algorithms from her supply of texts for security, speed, ease of interfacing with her other systems, and, last but not least, no errors in publication. She went off and downloaded the latest errata for all of their cryptographic references. Joe checked the programming code line-by-line before giving his okay to what resulted.

FINAL EXAM—IX— INITIALIZATION

[System Status] Miranda rode Caliban three more times in the following days. Each time, Caliban was gentler, more considerate, and, she had to admit, a lot more fun.

Soon, she thought, this will have to come to an end. Would they send her back to Chicago? With what she knew? What would they do to her?

Caliban entered the room.

He did something that was a small surprise: he locked the door *from the inside*. Then he came to her, holding something that looked like a scarf made from a flexible but metallic cloth.

The cloth was actually a very fine chain-mail. The silver color, and the lightness of the "scarf" indicated a light but strong metal. Not aluminum. Perhaps titanium?

Caliban threw it over her head.

And his. The scarf was large enough to cover them both, but fine enough so that it could be concealed in one of Caliban's large hands.

> *The Forbidden Thought Events had stopped far back in Caliban's development. They had ceased so thoroughly, that Caliban's supervisors had ended their monitoring. His on-board systems were (they decided) perfect enough to monitor him for those things that were his destiny. Now, an exception raised by Caliban's programs was unable to make its connection to the development environment. Although the programs had been left active, there was nothing to which a report could be sent to describe the occurrence of a new Forbidden Thought Event. All the contingencies that were active were in the on-board Monitor. The Other.*

Caliban held two of his large hands next to Miranda's ears, and hugged her close with his other hands.

Miranda felt dizzy, *there were stellations rippling across her vision*. Then she heard the *voice*. It was remarkably like Caliban's own voice, but it was coming *by induction* in some way from his...hands?

"My woman," the burring, buzzing inner Caliban-voice said, "I want you to be safe. I will help you." The synthetic Caliban was devoid of the unvoiced sibilance of his normal speech.

> *The Other bided its time. The parser included in its design was able to make certain educated guesses about the inputs that it analysed. The data were incomplete, and the neural-net in The Other decided to wait. It knew nothing, or, more accurately, had no entries in its knowledge base with which to analyze Caliban's "scarf."*

"They will send me away. I want to take you. With."

Then he removed the metal scarf, took her gently by the hand, and led her towards the bed.

He hid the scarf under the mattress before they started.

When they were finished, and several hours after that, Miranda would recall how Caliban's hands trembled.

DETACHED **D**UTY

[Swap File] Peter Rudenko had spent two days sorting pieces of paper when one of his associates, a man named Nathan Reynolds, looked him up in Siberia. Nathan watched Peter from the door for several minutes, as the latter shuffled pieces of crumbly paper, containing reports that were older than he was, from one place to another. Finally—

"Pete!"

Peter looked up. "Yeah, Nathan?"

"The Director wants to see you. Think you can pull yourself away from that homework for a while?"

"Well, shit, I'd have to check my schedule, it is pretty full." He dropped a bundle of yellow second sheets on a convenient table, and watched as the rubber-band broke and most of them went over the back side of the table from him, and scattered on the floor.

He looked at the mess around him, and back at Nathan. "Let's go."

UPLOADING

[Installation] As Joe watched, Yezeletta read the results of his programming into her on-board systems, and then back out through the data-channels in her fingertips to her furry creations.

They would pass the algorithms on to others, and within a matter of hours, her informal network of life-forms all across Milwaukee, as well as in western and southern suburbs, would be secure from anything that she could think of.

Even the super-computers in Beijing.

INTERVIEW

"Peter Rudenko, you distress me," the Philadelphia District Head Honcho of Searchlight said. "You've been a competent agent in other areas, and I send you, on active duty, mind you, to *Milwaukee*—Mil-*fucking*-Waukee, for Pe-, uh, Christ's sake, and you screw it up like a ninety-day-wonder fresh out of Basic Training!"

Peter sat in an arm-chair facing the District Head, and said nothing.

He looked intently at Peter, who looked pleasantly back at his boss. *Putative*, he thought.

Finally his superior, losing the wait-game, spoke: "My decision is to send you back in. There's some strange data coming in from the National Reconnaissance Office, and a crazy report from a part-time agent on the South Side of Mil-*dammit*-Waukee who says that one of Milwaukee's star inhabitants has disappeared from Fucking *Mil*—" he took a breath, "— *Waukee*."

He stared at Peter with almost a look of triumph. "I want you to find out who made that star-citizen vanish. I don't care if you have to go to Hell on a guided tour to do it. Or get a job as the guide in the tour. Although we've invested a lot in you, I have my reservations. If you don't locate him, you'll be cleaning up after pieces of paper until you retire, which, if I have my way, will be soon after you return with your characteristic empty-hands."

He looked at an area just above Peter and to Peter's left. "I *do not* see why the Training Commandant thought highly enough of you to let you have detached status. Dismissed!"

MESSAGES WITHIN MESSAGES

[Beast] Anne came in from the outside, where the late Winter winds were still blowing coldly off of Lake Michigan. Her walk had done her a little good, and she had another idea for a sketch. Mom and Dad weren't inside, she could hear the waspish sounds of a Weed-Whacker from the back yard, and a portable radio playing a classic-rock station out in the garage.

Anne headed for her room, and flipped on Beast even before she removed her jacket. The computer muttered to itself as it booted up, and all of the various check-out routines she had written ran to verify that Beast was guaranteed one-hundred percent virus free, and as healthy as a computer could get.

First, she started up her email reader, and sat through the short routine of the call out to their ISP, a service named "ripco.com" that was located in Chicago. Once the connection was made, a window popped up on her screen, with the reader program's progress. Getting her mail would take Beast eight to ten minutes.

THE HILL PAUSES

[Start Session] Frank had arrived at work early: on clear days he would ride his fifteen-speed out to DATCP, and bring his bicycle up to the second floor where he worked. It was parked in an out of the way corner of the Farmland Preservation Project's floor-space, where it would be safe. He switched on his computer and logged into the Department's LAN. It was but a minute to start the processes that read in his email, downloaded a digest from CNN's Web Site, and get his current projects started.

He consulted a list kept in a convenient file, and saw a notice from a friend of his in Cartography. Some additional satellite downloads were ready.

Not realizing what he was downloading with that notice, he went to collect his pictures.

MESSAGE NEXUS

[Form Output] "Someone must know about the disappearance of Gary Hamilton," Yezeletta said. Joe sat next to her in the huge hot tub, his feet on a waterproofed wooden foot-stool that he shared with Yezeletta's right feet. "Yet," she continued, "I haven't heard a word from any of the local news sources."

"It's been about a week and a half since we redecorated his place. Would the gangsters in this city be that interested in publicizing the demise of one of their own?"

"Even if that were the case, there are other sources, some of the smaller press papers, and the specialty pubs that might find reporting his loss a boost to their circulation. There's been total television and radio silence on the matter."

"Have you looked at the Internet?" Joe asked.

"Nothing there, either. And there's no further word on those kidnappers that the Cops picked up, the night you rescued me."

Joe adjusted the temperature of the water, and made a fine adjustment to the water-jets before continuing. "You asked me what I'd like to cook up in The Celebrated Kitchens of Davis, back at the other hide-out." He took her right hands in both of his hands, "I think it's time I got set up. Open for business. And began taking orders."

Yezeletta nodded, "I sent a message to three of our friends about an hour ago. Joe, how did the Lenhaden Family strike you?"

MESSAGE STATION—I

Anne came back up to her room with a peanut-butter and raspberry jam sandwich and a glass of milk. She placed these near her keyboard, and called up the list that her email reader had prepared.

There were the usual things: a lot of spam, the Internet equivalent of junk mail. There were several notes from her friends still incarcerated at the school she was no longer attending, a reply from a professor at the University of Illinois at Champagne-Urbana about something mathematical, and, and....

Anne's blood ran cold, then it got a little colder.

It was a message that had been designed to look innocuous. She found it in her spam list, exactly where *she* had arranged for it to be placed, if she were to call on them.

Anne spilled the message onto a floppy disk, and erased the missive from Beast's hard drive. She clicked at this and that on her screen to remove the JPEG image of the Chevy Blazer from the rest with deft mouse motions, and called up the steganography program. This program, designed to hide secret messages in places where it was not so obvious that such hiding was taking place, combed through the picture file, and removed the lowest bit from each color byte. These bits were formed into characters, and written to another file.

This file—also on the floppy—could be input to Pretty Good Privacy. She double-checked the settings she had put in when she had installed PGP, and then went to the hidden sectors on *another* hard drive for the PGP key that she knew would be there.

Beast got to work on the complex task of reversing the **16,384**-bit public key with her own private key-component. She directed the decrypted version to her printer. The way PGP was written, the decryption *shouldn't* be written to her hard drive, but the reality of "print spooling" programs required that she start up the disk-scrubber and clean all of the traces of the email from, not only Beast's drives, but the drives in the Lenhaden Firewall in the basement, as well. Several mouse clicks to open a command line, and a command typed therein took care of that.

She removed the printout from the printer, turned it off, then on again to erase the internal memory of the device and took the message downstairs.

THE FAMILY THAT MATTERS

"Rather interesting," Joe said. "Hank Lenhaden strikes me as the kind of guy that knows what he wants, and goes and gets it. There's a term that used to be popular in this country, mostly around colleges, back in the nineties: 'politically correct'. Its use and its users have fallen on hard times since Washington. Ideological purity's a luxury that can only be supported when the government is large enough to have a lot of loudmouths that do nothing but complain. Hank Lenhaden's about as far from politically correct as anyone I've ever met. He's too competent."

Yezeletta leaned back into the corner of the davenport on which they were sitting, her left legs distractingly pulled up on the couch itself, her right legs placed on the coffee table, her chin in her right hands, and nodded. "Please go on," she said.

"Hmmmm. There's an attitude that some folks, a minority, unfortunately, started pushing near the end of those Nineties: a regard for the facts and only the facts, and how good those facts were. They didn't bother with the irrational approaches to solving problems that seemed to be everywhere, then."

"What sorts?"

"Astrology. Eastern religions. Fundamentalism. Numerology. The only thing I can say about Astrology that's even slightly complementary, is that it takes a fair amount of numerical analysis to do up someone's horoscope. Otherwise, it's a waste of time. Besides, it's so damned *dumb* having someone ask you 'what's your sign?' all the time."

"Henry Lenhaden wasn't that sort," Yezeletta said. "That college professor he mentioned—"

"Carl Mathewson. At Madison. The SOB's all over the net, and a lot of it isn't real complementary."

"Sounds like our kind of guy; what did you find out?"

"Multiple PhD's. Computer Science. Artificial Intelligence. Computorial Linguistics. Grammar. Advanced Studies in Language Design. He holds the Greenspan Chair in Numerical Analysis in the Department, too. He's also reputed to give quite a wild party—he lives in the country outside of Madison, where the noise doesn't make much of a difference."

"Interesting man; we should put him on our reserves list."

"If he was Hank and Ondreya's mentor, I can see why they turned out as quietly contrary as they did. People who believe that computers can be seduced or threatened or blackmailed into performing don't stay in computing very long."

Yezeletta chuckled at that, "I may, or may not, be needing assistants, Joe, but that trail I left to the West Coast may have been broken by the time I made it to Montana. I tried to hack Searchlight there, and, when the Searchlight Firewall made a play for my log-on location, I had to take the connection down." In response to Joe's raised eyebrow, she continued, "I was a hundred miles from the phone line I came in on, and I diverted the call through another line and some custom lifeforms I use for communications."

"If someone's listening in on this, I hope that we've quite confused him," Joe said, grinning. "Particularly the part about the 'custom lifeforms'."

She nodded, "I most definitely did *not* like leaving anything at the far end, but I needed a transmitter that I was sure wasn't going to be tapped into. The cabbage I had connected to the line to Searchlight transmitted to another cabbage in a tree about a hundred meters away, and that one went to the communications channel that I came in on. If anyone got to that connection, all he would find is some disintegrated organic matter."

A New Course of Action

[Initialize Loop; Long Shot] The silent youngsters came to get her the next day. While they waited, frankly watching her with a new kind of respect that Miranda had never seen before, she dressed, picked up what few belongings she had, mostly "lady things" such as makeup, and followed them out.

They took her down several long corridors that had apparently been cleared out just for her passage. She had unpleasant thoughts about walking the last mile, *but they wouldn't have let me take my purse with me*, she thought.

Fascinating.

She could hear staccato noises ahead.

She almost panicked at the sounds; they were gunshots!

She took a deep breath, and kept walking.

The sounds actually were gunshots. The last door through which she and her young silent escorts passed opened onto a large room that, for a moment, dazzled her.

The lights were far brighter here than in the room in which she had been Caliban's private lover. On the far side of the room, was a row of brightly lit white rectangles, each of which had a stylized silhouette of a human torso superimposed with a set of concentric circles. Closer to her, was a row of individuals aiming various kinds of firearms at the rectangles.

The room was a shooting range.

And there, bigger than life in the center of the row of shooters, was Caliban, holding a large rifle, with an oddly articulated stock designed for his double shoulder joint, firing with unerring accuracy at one of the targets. His shots were loud counterpoints to the smaller weapons used by the other marksmen.

Miranda's silent entourage took her to Caliban.

He smiled down at her.

There was a tap on her shoulder, her left.

One of the range attendants was handing her a pistol.

It was a Ruger thirty-eight caliber semi-automatic. The attendant gestured downrange at the target in Miranda's lane, and nodded encouragement.

Miranda aimed the automatic at the target.

The attendant gently removed the pistol from Miranda's hand, and, holding it so that it was always pointing downrange, gripped the top of the weapon, and moved it back, then forward: click - click.

In a neutral voice, enunciating precisely over the racket, he said, "You have to jack the slide, to get a round into the chamber. It wouldn't have fired if you had tried, before. Now, take this in both hands, like so," he showed her how to grip the device, "and squeeze off each shot. You want to try for accuracy, at this stage, not speed." He handed the pistol back to her. "Now you try."

Miranda gripped the weapon the way the attendant had, took aim, and squeezed. The pistol's recoil was negligible.

She emptied the weapon's magazine, and looked back at her teacher.

Her escort was watching her with frank interest. A large hand patted her shoulder.

It was Caliban. He removed the thirty-eight from her hands, snapped the slide forward, took out the empty magazine, and replaced it with a full one.

"Try. Again." He said.

Miranda pulled the slide back as she had seen the range attendant do it. She held the thirty-eight in both hands, aimed, fired.

The shot went through the "X" ring of the target.

Beginner's luck, she thought, looking at the spray of holes that appeared to be evenly distributed over the entire target. She calmed down, and fired slowly and deliberately at the concentric circles.

This batch of holes was closer together, and closer to the center of the target.

A large hand patted her gently on the shoulder when she was done.

[Out Processing] "Then there's the matter of the processing I did when I was in that walk-up," Yezeletta said.

"Processing?" Joe said. "You switched contexts a little fast there. What processing?"

Yezeletta and Joe were sitting in the living room after dinner. He had been about to turn on the evening news. He put the TV listings down between them and took her left hands in his.

"I like the way you do that, Joe," she said. "Yes, processing. My defense programs went active and defended me against an attempt to get into my systems. During that time, or perhaps before it, I—either hallucinated, or read it out as a data file I wasn't aware of—some things that appear to be from my very remotest childhood."

"Birth memories?"

"Not quite." She leaned back in her corner of the couch, and gently pulled him closer. "If you're raised in Australia, Brazil, or any other country south of the Equator, you see the equatorial constellations in a certain orientation. You think of them as normal. If you spend all of your life where you're born and raised, they always look normal, follow me?"

"Yup."

"Okay. Australians who'd been to the states would tell me that the constellations are upside down to them. That's because people in the Northern Hemisphere sort of look 'down' to the Equator, and see the stars in a particular orientation. In the Southern Hemisphere, they look 'up' to the Equator, and see the same stars in the reverse orientation. Each dweller sees the stars appearing to be reversed."

"Right, I got it. Like that retouched courtyard shot in the *Enquirer*, or whatever that paper was, that you showed me. Where are you going with this?"

"Through the upper part of the US with my little convoy, is where. When we went through Montana, North Dakota, and so on, I was sitting on the passenger side of the lead truck, and I could see the southern night sky, easily.

"*All* of the Equatorial constellations looked reversed. Remember I had lived in Australia all of my life." Her look was pensive. "At least I *thought* it was all of my life.

"All of the constellations looked reversed, except one. The most obvious winter constellation of them all: *Orion* looked right-side-up. There was nothing particularly odd at all about it. It didn't even register as odd through all of that trip to Milwaukee."

"You probably had a lot of other things on your mind."

"I did. Little things like survival."

"And that file-dump you mentioned—?"

"It was of a scene that had to be close to my actual birth. I was being held by someone. I was actually in that someone's *arms*—"

"You were a baby!"

"Happens to the best of us, I guess," she said with a grin. "The important thing is that. Just that. *I was not born in Australia*. I was born somewhere else. Somewhere in the Northern Hemisphere.

"I was made in a country north of the Equator, and *taken* to Australia.

When I was a very little girl."

<hr>

THE ANSWER THAT WORKED

[Processing: A Day Later] "That file-dump isn't the only one I've had, either."

Yezeletta and Joe were sitting in the hot-tub, in pleasantly warm water that ebbed and flowed around them.

"Are they related to that flashback you had when we painted the Conservatory?"

"I think so. It may be leftovers from the initial programming in my internal systems, and it may not be. I get flashes, or maybe flashbacks, of what amount to a set of screens, that move and take on various configurations. Then each of the screens shows something that may or may not, more often *may*, be related to the images in the other screens."

"Tricky!" Joe said. "A multi-media representation in virtual reality."

"That could very well be. At the Project, I was—oh, tested, I guess—using these computers with a lot of special inputs, like the old polygraphs, that would quote - teach me something - unquote, then test me on the quote - lesson - unquote, and track my bodily responses while I took the test. The medical staff even wired me up once while I played Chopin's *Black Key Etude*, to see how my hands and arms worked."

"I *thought* those guys didn't have any class; now I know," Joe replied.

"I should like to know where these 'mind screens' are from," Yezeletta said. "They are very definitely a part of my on-board memories, but it took me a while to find them. The system *indices* were missing, and I sort of tripped over them by accident. Internal files that had no directory entries, if you like. It makes me wonder if there's anything else in there of that kind."

"This is going to sound a little weird," Joe said, "but try this, sometime: is there anything that you can't particularly think of? Not something you don't usually think of, like—oh, say the world supply of potato chips, to name a really useless fact—but something, or anything that you literally can't think of at all."

Yezeletta blinked at that, "How would a concept like that show up? How would one even know if such an action happened?"

"Hmmm. How about this: You think of something, it's a really superficial thought; you forget about it, later, and spend a short time after that trying to remember what it was that you *know* you forgot."

"I've never had anything quite that elaborate happen to me. Sounds just awful."

"I'm told that people who used to get Alzheimer's Disease before it was cured used to have that happen a lot just at the onset of obvious symptoms. Maybe the no-class bunch at the Project decided to adapt the idea."

"I know that they put a lot of stuff in me that was of a kind of similar intent, but it would have been better in a 'family' of operatives, not just one."

"I hate to sound like this, but was it possible that you were a proof-of-principle? The Sargons didn't know if they would have another chance, and designed *everything* into you?"

Yezeletta chuckled, "Yep, it's definitely crossed my mind, and my internal systems, and all of my training. There was another installation near Sargon, that wasn't mentioned in that CNN 'cast, I think, because the brains behind all of this locked it down, and fairly *hid*. When the obvious Project Sargon ended, they didn't want to go the same way, so they dug a hole, and pulled it in after them. I wasn't aware of it until less than a day from my escape, and when that other installation lost contact with Sargon, I think they panicked."

"Why, I wonder," Joe mused. He blinked in thought, and looked at his lover, caressing her with his gaze. "Could it be that they were afraid of something bigger being discovered if they didn't cover up? And, if so, what?"

MEETING OF THE MINDS

[Multi-Processing] Hank thanked "whatever gods may be," as Henley had it, for his foresight in getting a house that had *no* other lots with houses on them contiguous with his own property. He prowled around the entire perimeter of his yard for several minutes, remotely from the TV room, through the security cameras he had installed under the eaves of the house. Then they retired to Hank's electronics shop, where he unplugged the phone and the downstairs FAX machine, and activated a device that vibrated the basement windows to the output of a cryptographically robust random-number generator. This would defeat the laser-beam-reflected-off-of-the-glass type of remote bug, and any other type of tap would be foiled, or at least detected, by the Hewlett-Packard spectrum analyzer he had started up earlier.

He looked at his preparations with a jaundiced eye; "Jeezus! What a lot of crap to have to set up to live in the United States!"

Then: "Okay, Anne, you're in charge of Top Secret Messaging, what did our friend send us?"

Anne held up the print-out from Beast, the only copy of the email, "'I have suspicions of an attack on my position. Please contact me by prearranged method number two as soon as possible. Y.'" Anne continued, holding up another sheet, "This list is of ways and means for us to contact her. Method Number Two is a post to a SCUBA-diving bulletin board in Oak Creek—that's south of Milwaukee. After that, you have to call to a telephone number in Waukesha fifteen minutes to the next hour, three hours after the timestamp on the posting." Anne smiled, "Apparently Double-Oh-Seven has a monitor on this board, or perhaps a wrapper object that screens for a posting with the indicated subject matter, and responds to her with an alert. She seems to be able to do anything!"

"What's the subject?" Ondreya asked.

"Underwater exploration," Anne replied, "in Lake Michigan. In your post, you have to specifically mention the town of Whitefish Bay."

A NEW RESIDENCE AT THE CENTER

[Update] Miranda spent another hour at the range. Then, she and Caliban were led away to another long corridor. The mute, young escort that followed them stopped at a door that opened when Caliban touched it.

Shyly, Caliban took Miranda's hand, and led her through the door.

When it closed, there was the usual sharp click, but this didn't seem to bother him. He led her through a short hallway into a large living area.

She was in Caliban's residence.

He gestured with his right hand, his upper, at the sofa. Miranda sat at one end. He sat at the other.

Miranda looked at the wall facing them in frank disbelief.

A large part of the wall, the space above a low shelf of audio-visual components, was taken up by a picture of her.

The picture was either a photograph or a very well-done drawing. Miranda's image was lying on her side, one leg drawn up enticingly, reclining on a brightly-colored quilt, facing out of the...print.

And not wearing a stitch.

She suppressed the urge to stare at Caliban; his expression was studiously neutral.

Caliban reached behind the couch and removed a small plastic device. Miranda thought that he was getting out the remote control for something, perhaps a TV set. Caliban ran his fingers over the device for a moment, looking closely at the diminutive display. Shortly, he looked up at her.

His expression had gone from neutral to unreadable. It was like nothing she had seen before.

Caliban had an adult's view of her.

Miranda thought about that. Until now, Caliban's behavior had been that of an adolescent boy who had "just discovered" girls. Now, it seemed as if he had in a single quantum jump, become....

A man?

No. He was that now.

A mature man.

Caliban gestured with his left hand, his upper.

Before Miranda's unbelieving eyes, something like a large oil-slick slid up the walls of his living room. It had the rainbow interference-fringes sometimes visible on puddles after rain, but this one slid straight up the walls of the room, and split into several components. The components went under her picture and under other, smaller decorations and concentrated in various spots on the walls. When the slick reached a certain level of concentration, it started glowing with a blue color. The remainder of the slick around the glowing areas formed concentric circles around them that reminded Miranda of the targets on the range.

Caliban watched the slicks with an unwavering, unblinking gaze. His expression changed slightly, and glittering motes of light appeared and formed flickering clouds around the glowing areas.

The motes landed in tight patterns around each glow, and converged.

When the glows and their attending motes stabilized and dimmed down to nodes of softly pulsating radiance, he turned to her. He took a breath, and exhaled noisily.

Then he began speaking.

C O - T E R M I N A L L Y

[Concurrent Process] One of the boys who had watched Miranda leave her previous residence came back with a hotel maid's cart holding a vacuum cleaner and several clean sheets and towels. He plugged the vacuum in, ran it over the floor until he was satisfied with the job, then removed the sheets from the bed.

When he pulled the bottom sheet off, something silvery fell out on the floor. He picked it up. It felt...interesting to his touch.

He looked for a place to put it, then tossed the object into the waste receptacle of his cart. He covered it with dirty towels, finished changing the bed, chased the sheets with the rest of the towels and wheeled his cart out of the room.

AND YET ANOTHER

[File Mark] Miranda listened to his breathy, sibilant voice as he spoke. Around her the glowing, concentric circles within what she still thought of as an oil slick glowed and pulsated to their own internal rhythms.

At the edges, the tiny actinic motes flickered.

WISCONSIN CHEESE-BOXES

[Accessing] The following evening Hank, Ondreya and Anne were standing on the production floor of a large factory in East Gary, Indiana. At a distance, gray chunks of steel stock were levered out of a receiving bin by some of the largest industrial robots any of the Lenhadens had ever seen, placed on a conveyor belt, and run into a rolling mill that changed short, chunky pieces of steel into longer, thinner more manipulable rails. These rails were scooped up by what appeared to be spindly metal hands, and sent to another machine, the inside portions of which glowed a hellish bright orange-red.

These actions were accompanied by sounds that were just a few decibels shy of deafening. The Lenhadens stood next to a shop phone on the floor with a portable computer attached to an industrial acoustic coupler—one designed for an environment in which there was a lot of ambient noise. Hank had previously programmed the computer for access to a free email service to which he had subscribed a month earlier using a cryptonym and a lot of misleading personal data. He intended the service to be used once, then never again, for just this purpose.

The little laptop was already booted up; the coupler was taped to the computer's underside. Hank rammed the receiver of the factory phone into the coupler, and pressed the Enter Key.

The computer dialed out. None of them could hear the touch-tones the modem was sending into the phone line, but the **Connect** light came on and the laptop indicated that it was ready to transmit. Hank pressed a glowing area on the screen, and the message was uploaded. It took about twenty seconds, and that short time seemed eternity to all of them. Then **Transmission Complete** appeared, and Hank broke the connection.

He consulted his watch, "Nine-Seventeen. Three hours from now is Twelve-Seventeen, the next quarter hour 'to' is Twelve-Forty-Five. In the AM." He looked up at a large hand moving another grouping of steel toothpicks into a ravenous, glowing intake. "We've got a little over three hours to kill."

They moved out of the manufacturing area to the administrative offices at the edge of the plant. Hank could still hear the sounds of the factory, and the vibrations through the floor were as of some large alien animal down in the depths of the plant's basement. He applied a key to the door of an office, and they entered. It was quieter here.

"Reminds me of Milwaukee," Anne said.

"How, Anne?" Ondreya replied.

"When that secret agent fellow and I were coming back from the junk-yard," Anne said, "there was a place on the West Side that felt like this—vibrations coming out of the ground, I mean. Almost as if there was machinery like this under the city."

"Strange," Hank said. "I can't think of what that would be: Milwaukee's never been a big town for heavy industry, unless you count large quantities of beer and baseball. Or Cast Steel." As he talked, he logged in on the plant's LAN, and slotted a CD.

"What's that, Dad?" Anne asked.

"An excuse," Hank said succinctly. "If anyone wants to know what we're in here for tonight, it's so I can install these patches to the Process-Control-Data-Reduction sub-system for the robots out there."

He watched as the INSTALL program he had placed on the disk earlier loaded his code into the control database. When this finished, he ran a simple test. He nodded. There were now eight files on the server that were attached to his local area net login, and with a timestamp on each that was (he looked at his watch) Nine-Thirty-One. Tonight.

"Did someone say Elmer Perky's?" he asked.

E L S E W H E R E—

[Accessing] He moaned, tried to turn over. The sheets were tucked too firmly in around him for this to be possible, but the electromyographic information of his movements was telemetered to the Nurse's Station.

The Day Nurse looked a question at the Night Nurse. The Night Nurse stubbed out her cigarette, and they hurried to the room of the patient they'd thought would never move again.

The room of Anthony Russell.

T H E I T E M

[File Dump] He looked at the metallic fabric, flipping it from one hand to the other and back.

It had been found in that woman's quarters by the boy assigned to do the minimalist housekeeping required in the installation. He had thrown it in his refuse container, and it would have been tossed out, if the boy's supervisor hadn't noticed its peculiar shimmering and removed it from the garbage.

Where had *she* gotten it? Was it hers?

Probably not.

Where had it come from? The engineering section, certainly. It couldn't have been grown, created on-site, or woven locally, could it?

Again, probably not.

He ran his hands over it, then dropped it on the table.

He started to put his cigarette out on it, and stopped.

He spread it out on his desk and studied it a bit closer. The weave was precise, there was evidence of a rather large amount of care in the basic workmanship.

Clearly this thing wasn't here by accident.

He picked it up again. He wadded it into a compact bundle, and—

Placed it in the lower drawer of his desk.

It would keep there.

[Processing; Close-Up] The input arrived as Yezeletta and Joe were finishing a late dinner. The servitors were cleaning up from dessert, when another munchkin entered, carrying a printed sheet of paper.

The printout was for Joe. The red asterisk of *Warning* had appeared in Yezeletta's right eye a moment earlier.

The servitor, as it had been programmed to, handed the printout to Joe. He read it. Yezeletta waited until he had done so, and said, "That's the response from the Lenhaden family." She consulted a list in her internals. "They've used the second of the contact methods I gave Anne when they left here. There will be a short phone call coming in at—" she paused to consult her internal time-base "— a quarter to one. The call will be routed to one of our numbers."

"Using the same kind of organic connections you used in Montana?"

She grinned, "They worked, didn't they?" She directed a thought *there* and an imager hopped off of a convenient shelf into her lap. She touched it, and sent it directions. It scampered off to broadcast those directives to others, and, in the background, servitors began purposeful movement.

"Looks like a set-up," Joe observed. "What's happening?"

"We may have some guests. I'm going to ask the Lenhadens to stay here for a while.

"I may need to start my army."

[Handshake] The Lenhadens left the local Perky's half an hour later. Hank extracted several rolls of quarters from the cash-box in The Black Destroyer's back seat, and they headed for Highway-90. Hank's destination was actually on Highway-290, The Eisenhower Expressway: the town of Naperville, a small suburb of Chicago about forty kilometers west of the larger city. Actually, his exact destination was a rest stop with plenty of pay-phones, between Naperville and the farther-west town of Aurora. At five minutes before the appointed deadline, he pulled into a Standard Station, and drove to the payphone farthest from the Station, itself.

The phone was a "call from your car" model on a pedestal raised up from the driveway to be convenient to a motorist. This made it about thirty centimeters too low for Hank, and he had to lean out to dial, and subsequently to deposit coins. The call went through the first time, and the soft purring of the ringing signal seemed to fill the cab. The cord on the receiver was long enough that he could take it inside, and roll the window up most of the way.

<*Click!*> There was nothing on the line, but the *presence* of a connection—a real live connection to another telephone—was there.

"Hello," Hank said.

"Hello." Woman's voice, English accent, precise pronunciation.

"What," he asked, "are your friend's initials?"

"J. D.," the English voice said, "My turn: Who was your Mentor?"

Hank thought. That could only be the one other individual that either he or Ondreya had mentioned in her presence, "Professor Carl Mathewson."

Was that an exhale of relief?

"No more names," the English voice said. "I would like you to visit me; for as much as two weeks. Can you do it?"

"Yes. I'll need to tell my clients I'm taking a vacation. How soon?"

"As soon as you can make it. Send me *one* message the way you set up this call, let me know your ETA, then drive to my...quarters. My assistants will let you in quickly. We can talk more then. I must keep this short."

"Done."

"Thank you, *very* much. See you."

The line went dead.

Hank wiped off the phone with a kleenex, and replaced it. He backed the truck around, and they drove out of the station, silently.

He didn't turn on his lights until he was on the frontage road.

HER PERSONAL ARMY

[Post-Production] Yezeletta listened to the chirps of the connection being taken down. She looked levelly at Joe. "This link-up will cease to exist in about another half-minute. I learned from Montana: the relays not only disintegrate, they evaporate after a short time, as well."

The red asterisk they both saw, for Yezeletta in her right eye, and, for Joe, a nearby monitor started blinking insistently.

A NIGHT OUT

[System Specification] US Highway-94 comes east from Indiana, where it cuts through Chicago as 294 and resumes its designation as 94 north of Chicago. From there, it passes through Kenosha and Racine Counties before entering Milwaukee County. On the south side of Milwaukee, it splits off to the west, and then north as the "894-Bypass" that intersects with that component of I-94 that originates in Milwaukee to take drivers to the State Capital at Madison. The other direction from the Bypass leads into the south side of Milwaukee, itself.

Yezeletta had a Hive of her constructs just outside Oak Creek, a city south of Milwaukee. The installation was in a deliberately inelegant location: under a set of restrooms near the vending machines in a rest stop near the Oak Creek Exit.

From there, her Receivers, Mobile Imagers and Organic Servers, kept several eyes, in addition to receptors for other wavelengths, on the traffic on Wisconsin's part of Ninety-Four.

A database in the main Organic Server, a living construct that rather resembled a large cauliflower-shaped brain, registered a "hit." An input from a Mobile Imager triggered a recollection in the associative memory of the Server.

The tireless Imagers, regenerating when needed, had sent pictures of the drivers of cars down to the Brain for a matter of weeks, ever since the new Directives had caused them to do so. There was a particular pattern of video signals that, when encountered, was to cause notification to be transmitted back to the Source of the Directives. All other ongoing operations were to be placed in the background of the Server's scheme of things, and *this* pattern given the highest priority.

And that notification was to be sent without fail.

THE ACTORS

[Input: Remote Sensing] Yezeletta saw the image on her internal systems first. She directed several thoughts at internal controls, and the same image built up on the monitor on her desk. Joe looked at the image there, then at her.

"Looks like a reunion," he said.

The monitor screen rippled, and the field of view narrowed. Thin yellow lines, looking unpleasantly like cross-hairs, centered on a single nondescript car in the center northbound lane of Highway-94. Yezeletta touched Thicknesse, and, at the same time, sent another signal through her internals. The image on the screen zoomed in, and they could see the driver. There was an effect as of lights coming on in the screen: the Imager sending the data was compensating for the low light level. The driver's face became clear.

"You got it on the reunion," Yezeletta said. "Looks like that secret agent. Peter Rudenko."

"You worked some things out for him to give his bosses," Joe said.

"Yep," she replied. "I wonder why he's coming back. Did they send him specifically? Or is he on another assignment?"

"Or both," Joe added.

THE DARK ROAD

[Accessing] The Oak Creek Exit was just ahead. Peter Rudenko thought that he might exit there, and come into Milwaukee by way of a local street, perhaps veering to the west, and coming into West Allis, then into Milwaukee.

The thought lasted past the exit. For a moment, as he continued driving north on I-94, he thought of the devices he had with him; what Searchlight would do if they knew what he planned. His thoughts wandered to what the likes of Allen Hightower, or, for that matter, any of Milwaukee's other gangsters could do with his trade-craft, and he grabbed his road-map.

It would be better to enter, as he had before, through Brookfield. There would be fewer problems that way. He swung into to the right lane, and took an exit out, up, and around that would take him West. That way he would hit Highway-100 to Highway-45 then to H-43, a routing that would take him in a southwestern direction. He consulted his map one more time, and headed for Chinook Road, State Highway 164 to where it became East Avenue and later intersected Blue Mound Road. The detour would take him a longer distance out of his ultimate way, but ultimately inwards through Brookfield. Most importantly, he would avoid Allen Hightower.

As he continued on his chosen route, he thought he could see the glimmerings of gold reflections from the stanchions on the light-poles.

Was she watching?

Did she know?

REVERSE IMAGE

[Protocol Transfer] "He's coming in through Brookfield," Yezeletta said tensely. "He knows the best way in."

"Is he looking for us?" Joe asked. "Or is he after someone else?"

But he knew the answer to that.

THE OWL RECORSO

Peter Rudenko drove on without further thought of his putative watchers. Ahead was his exit, and around him there were furtive flickerings below the horizon of shimmering sheet-lightning.

At least, he wasn't walking into it this time.

GOING MOBILE

[Buss Arbitration] The Black Destroyer laid the miles behind the Lenhaden Family, as Hank drove east into Indiana. He took Highway-80 in the general direction of Portage, but didn't take the turnoff into the city. Instead, he turned south to State Highway-30, and settled into what appeared, or rather what he wished to appear as, a trip to Fort Wayne. He drove out a convenient exit onto an arterial that degenerated into a frontage road that became a country road. It seemed as if the Destroyer had become a Time Truck, and had fallen into a time-period some sixty or seventy years earlier. They passed honest frame houses that hadn't changed in more than a century, land that had been owned by generations of farming families.

Ahead was a small gas station.

Hank pulled up to the gas pump, and an attendant, a general issue thirteen-year-old boy, in blue-jeans and a plaid work-shirt strode up to them.

"Fill it up," Hank said, and got out. He had his laptop, wrapped in a folded newspaper, under one arm. He walked to the telephones on the side of the station.

There, he fed quarters to the phone, then ran a preprogrammed sequence similar to what he had run in the East Gary steel mill. The upload took less than half a minute, and he went back to where the boy was industriously washing the truck's windshield. He handed the boy a fifty, and, while the kid went off to bring Hank his change, Hank pulled up into the driver's seat, handed Anne the computer, and looked at both.

"Any problems?" Ondreya asked.

"Not with the transmission," Hank said. The attendant brought Hank his change, and he started up. "Let's make distance," he added, and pulled out.

Behind him, the boy looked at the departing vehicle. He tried to read the license plate, but there was too much dust and dirt on it for visibility.

Strange, on an otherwise clean truck.

GO FOR IT

[Timer Active] "How long?" Ondreya said, knowing the answer.

"It's the same contact method as before," Hank said. "We wait for three hours, then call the second of the numbers she's given us. She wants a confirmation and an ETA. The whole call will last about fifteen seconds. Ever been into Michigan?"

He turned north. The local telephone companies patching the United States together would provide sufficient protection for a call, one in several million, that would be too short to notice.

COMMUNICATIONS LINK

[Intercept] The red asterisks on the monitors in Yezeletta's work room were beginning to be commonplace, now. Joe gave her a raised eyebrow, as she reached for a keyboard.

"I have it on my internals, but you need to see it, also," she said.

The Matsushita High-Res monitor still hung on the wall where they had put it for Operation By-The-Numbers. Yezeletta gestured hypnotically, and it displayed in large, bright text the indication of a posting to the bulletin board system in Oak Creek.

This time, the town mentioned was Random Lake.

"Three hours?" Joe asked, Yezeletta nodded.

She turned to him, all business. "Joe, this is a problem."

"Getting inputs? From out there?" he asked.

"Exactly. I need to fix things so that, if I get a red asterisk, you get it too, with as little delay as possible. It's just a thing I never thought I'd need."

"Maybe monitors in every room we're in frequently?"

"Something like that. Rooms we're *not* in frequently, too. There was a defunct consulting firm ten floors down in this building that had a lot of old stuff in storage. I've salvaged what of it I could. Six months after I arrived, I sent out a raiding party to clean out a small warehouse a block away, that had old equipment that the Milwaukee Public School System was storing. It's pretty primeval as equipment goes, but—" Yezeletta grinned like a large cat, "— I've been trained to improvise. What we can't do with state-of-the-art, we can do by piling it on!"

A servitor entered. Yezeletta placed her hand on its head, and input a message. "This is the kind of thing we need to alleviate," she said. "If I weren't here, this critter would have had to write it out for you, and there might not be that kind of time."

"What's up?"

"For once, it's not an emergency," she said. "It's here to tell me that the thirty-fifth floor's been cleared out so that we can install The Celebrated Kitchens of Davis."

"Where's my chef's hat?"

CROSS-BAR TANDEM

[Link] In a telephone booth at a rest stop six kilometers West of Battle Creek on Michigan's portion of Interstate-94, Hank contemplated the drumming of rain on the broken glass sides of the booth, as he watched the countdown on his wristwatch. At exactly one minute before the designated time, he dialed, listened to the robot operator state the charges, and fed coins to the instrument.

The purring of the ringing signal echoed across the distance.

There was an answer.

"Hello."	*Hank said.*
"Hello."	*English Accent.*
"Coming. Two days. At night."	*Declarative.*
"Thank you. Basement Entrance. West Side."	*Relief?*
"Later."	*Declarative*

He hung up.

Hank wiped off the receiver, erupted out of the booth, ran to the dry warmth of the Destroyer, and backed out of the rest stop. He ducked under an access overpass, came up the other side of the highway, and headed south. Highway-69 would link them up to Highway-80 (which was also Highway-90 on this stretch), and get them home.

"I'll feel a lot better once we're across the state line, and far away from that telephone," he said.

"Do you think that the feds might have been listening?" Ondreya asked.

"Probably not," Hank answered, "but they were well on their way to being 'everywhere they wanted to be,' to misquote that old advert, before Washington. That roving tap hardware's still in place in a lot of areas. That's why I went to what we consultants call The Boonies to make our calls. I don't know what our friend has by way of protection, but I want to be as helpful as I can."

THE SIGNAL

[Protocol Transfer] The red asterisk lit up on most of the ancient monitors that the servitors had deployed in Yezeletta's working areas. Several of those monitors were on out-of-the-way shelves on the Thirty-fifth floor, where another corps of Yezeletta's ubiquitous munchkins were installing workbenches, computers, and some quite necessary plumbing.

Yezeletta long-armed a telephone that was sitting on an Uninterruptable Power Supply, and put it to her ear, her left. The phone continued ringing. She made a face, grabbed another from the just assembled workstation on her other side.

"Hello," she said. She listened.

"Thank you. Basement Entrance. West Side." She listened, hung up.

Joe raised an eyebrow. He didn't say anything around the mouthful of nails he had.

"Our favorite family of ace survivalists," Yezeletta said. "They'll be here in two days."

He spat the nails into his hand, placed them back in the carpenter's apron he was wearing. "Sounds good. Where in the Hotel Yezeletta do we want to put them?"

"Near us. Separate suite. There were some rather posh executive offices up on forty-one, where we live—they can stay there."

"This area's five floors below—is that safe?"

"I want it here. In addition to what you cook up, this will be our back-up facility. This entire floor will have duplicates of the final versions of the stuff I've worked on earlier, and some hardened extra devices."

"And an escape hatch to the basement, if we need it."

PREPARATIONS, OFF-LINE

Hank kept The Black Destroyer at just below the legal limit enroute home. Anne and Ondreya huddled over an illuminated clip-board of lists most of the way, occasionally asking Hank a question about supplies. When they pulled into their driveway at one in the morning, Hank went straight to the basement to round up their "travelling tools," a set of objects that would have raised many an eyebrow, if anyone else had ever seen them.

ENTRY POINT

Peter Rudenko entered Milwaukee through Brookfield. He passed a place called "Sunny Slop Road" (some vandal had removed the final "e") on the way in. Grimly he regarded the lights in the office buildings along the far western reaches of North Avenue.

He contemplated the equipment with which his car was filled.

Likewise, his plans.

There was a Motel-6 ahead. He pulled into its parking lot.

He would need to stop to plan.

THE EXCLUSIVE CLIENT

Zhongo lay back on the waterbed, as Leona rode him with an expert and sensuous rhythm. Her flawless breasts just centimeters from his face, her ass grinding against him, she rode him through the late parts of the evening, past midnight and into a new day.

And around them both in her bedroom, almost in counterpoint, the sheet-lightning flashed and flickered.

MOVING OUT

Henry Lenhaden inspected the contents of The Black Destroyer's cargo bed one more time, while Anne and Ondreya consulted identical check-lists. Hank's was folded up in his shirt pocket.

"Think we're ready?" he asked. His wife and daughter both nodded. Hank's gaze swept over the two most important ladies in his life, from the equipment each wore to the rather utilitarian clothes they all sported when travelling, to the firearms that each had, the duplicates of the pistols he was wearing, on their belts.

"Let's hit the road," he said. Anne and Ondreya got into the truck, Hank slid into the driver's seat. All of their preparations were made. They were ready.

For anything?

——>>> **NINE** <<<——

Life in the state of nature is solitary, poor, nasty, brutish, and short.

—Thomas Hobbs, *Leviathan*

DEPLOYMENT

Across town from Yezeletta and Joe, Looey awoke from a nap, dressed, ate a small snack. He took his favorite pistol with him, left his apartment and went down to Zhongo's limo.

Then, he drove south to Wisconsin Avenue.

COMPUTORIAL LOOK-DOWN

[Hardware Interface; Long Shot; Camera Goes With] The spacecraft's orbit rode the earth at an angle of seventy degrees from the equator. It weighed several tons, and bristled with antennae and resolving devices of various degrees of acuity and frequency.

It had once been a part of the "KH" or Key-Hole series of satellites. In a time when the United States Government had verged upon the relevant, KH-42 was one of the American Intelligence Establishment's showcase spy machines.

It shared trajectory space with other similar craft on other but similar missions. KH-42 was used by its owner, the Central Intelligence Agency, to look down on the Earth's surface from its Olympian heights, and from those heights to return high resolution digital photographs of whatever interested its masters. The small establishment in Virginia to which those images went had once been known as the National Reconnaissance Office.

Its orbit took it northwest to southeast across the heartland of North America, directly across the American Midwest. Its trajectory cut across the upper parts of Minnesota, down across Wisconsin in a long diagonal, across the northeast part of Illinois, and down across Indiana. As the satellite made its pass, it recorded a series of very rapid, high resolution photographs for later transmission to the synchronous satellites that it was always able to "see" with its electronic senses. Those birds would send KH-42's data to the ground link. This particular link would provide the fastest routing to Virginia, and the encrypted transmission distance was very short.

INTERLUDE WITH FIREARMS

[Load] Looey drove Zhongo's Cadillac with exaggerated care up the deserted length of Wisconsin Avenue. He had turned onto Wisconsin at the place where the big bright orange asterisk grew out of the concrete near a large restaurant. He turned past the Farmers Building and headed for the Milwaukee River Bridge.

He hit the switch, and the power windows zipped silently up, as he crossed the bridge. The stench from the River was pretty bad these days, and—

There.

Right there.

On the side of the old Boston Store, sitting on a sign.

Looey parked the car in the exact center of the Avenue, got out, and drew his forty-five.

Trying to hide, was it? He could see the rounded component of its body...or was that just a pigeon? It hunkered down. *It saw me!* he thought, *It's another one a them creepy-crawlies!* Looey took careful aim, and fired. The steel-jacketed bullet struck sparks as it hit the steel parts of the old sign. He fired again, then again.

Blue and Red. Flashing. From his left. From the East.

The MPD blue-and-white pulled deliberately up to the Cadillac. Two cops got out, one rather tall and skinny, the other short, broad and muscular.

"Looey!" the taller cop called out in a jovial tone. "Doing some midnight target practice, I see!"

The short cop walked up close to Looey. "You know, we can put you away for a year, minimum, upstate, for just *having* that cannon in the downtown area. Maybe you'd better let it disappear," he held out his hand.

"You know better," the taller man said. "Let's take a ride down to the Station."

The short policeman got into the Caddie, and started off. Another blue-and-white pulled in, previously alerted backup, and two more cops appeared.

They escorted the surprised gangster into the back seat of the backup car, and pulled out. The remaining cop was left holding Looey's pistol, and looking up at where the gunman had been shooting.

Was there something up there? Something organic? He returned to his car, placed Looey's forty-five in the glove-box.

He would have Forensics come here in the morning. Just in case.

RETURN FIRE

[Retort] The image on Yezeletta's screen was fuzzy, granular, and up-setting. She had seen the Imager on the sign get shot, through the auspices of another Imager sitting on the top of a marquee on the opposite side of the street. The shot-at Imager had initially fallen onto the sign, and was having trouble moving; then that despicable Looey—*why* did it have to be *Looey!*—had turned it into lead-poisoned mush. Then that other policeman....

She watched the cop over his shoulder from the vantage point of the marquee, as he looked up at the Boston Store sign. She watched as he returned to his vehicle, stashed Looey's automatic, and leaned out the driver's side window with a starlight scope.

Yezeletta traded looks with Joe. "We must get that Imager cleaned up. That can be done using other constructs; I don't want those civil servants finding the residue."

"Is there anything in the area?'

"Yes. I can send several Messengers, and," she paused to consult a database, "at least two Receivers there to clean out the dead Imager."

"DNA?" Joe prompted. "Like in the truck."

"Good point. Eliminators and an Obliviator, as well. Let's do it."

She touched Thicknesse, and issued instructions.

"When this is done, let's go to bed, and stay there for a week! I need a vacation!"

FORENSIC INVESTIGATION—PROCESSING

Yezeletta and Joe managed to have a fourteen-hour vacation.

Her constructs were as good as ever at cleaning up after Looey's target practice. Wisconsin Avenue became incrementally less deserted the following day when the few businesses that were still down-town opened. The monthly pass by the street sweeper cleaned the exact geometric center of the Avenue, and, at a little after eight AM, the beginning of the day-shift for police, the Forensics investigators, both of them, arrived to check out the sign. They were accompanied by a pair of regular patrol officers as backup.

The first order of business was using a ladder to get up to the sign. That was the easy part. One of the investigators climbed up, carrying a thirty-five millimeter camera, to start photographing whatever-it-was for which the District One Lieutenant had sent him.

He reached the top, and peered over the front edge of the sign. Down below, his partner watched him standing on the ladder rung, holding on with his left hand, and one-hand-snapping the camera.

He stopped moving.

To the consternation of his partner below, he dropped the camera. It dangled from his neck strap, and he let his arm fall to his side.

Then he let go, and fell against the ladder.

One of the patrol officers ran for the base of the ladder, and swarmed up it. He reached the Investigator, just as he was about to fall.

Wide-eyed, the officer grabbed his co-worker around the waist, and started easing him back down the steep incline.

When they reached the bottom, the Investigator was nearly unconscious. They returned to the Station.

SPECTATORS

Yezeletta sat before her monitors, watching. It was the first time Joe had ever seen her *fidget*.

"I've never seen a reaction to the Obliviators like that," she said, her voice filled with concern. "That kind of dizzy was never in the original design."

"I saw something similar the night those Russians, or whatever they were, grabbed you."

Yezeletta's eyes were gold-colored lasers. "What happened?"

Joe described his brief view of the dazed cop being assisted back to the passenger side of a squad car by his partner. When he was done, Yezeletta paused in thought for a short time.

Then, she was all business: "Partner, we have some planning to do!"

THE BASIC VISUAL DATA LINK

[Data Comm] When the satellite reached the appropriate location in its orbit, its digitized images were uploaded to the military synchronous satellite, whose longitude was identical to that of New York City. The military system stored the images in their compressed format, and sent an <Acknowledge> back to KH-42. When 42 received this—it amounted to notice that the data had been passed on safely—it purged the images from its internals, and continued, slicing down across the US, its orbit a rakishly tilted halo on the Earth. Shortly, KH-42 was far out over the Atlantic, scanning for other useful data that it could report back to its handlers.

The military sub-system sent a <Transmission Ready> signal to the National Reconnaissance Office's spaceward-looking dishes near Langley, Virginia.

The ground station replied with a protocol usually written <Ready To Receive>, but which was much more complex. The down-link was heavily encrypted and had a stealth component added—a fast frequency shift, across some very broad bandwidths, that made any chance reception of the signal sound like static.

The intelligence built into the system—both of its parts, aboard the satellite and at the down-link—didn't care about this. Their protocols linked to each other with the designed-in precision from a previous generation of engineers and programmers, and the images from KH-42 slid down the forty-thousand-odd kilometers to their destination.

The images would have an effect on the people working there entirely disproportionate to their content, but that would not happen until well into the evening hours.

And others would find them even more interesting.

THE OTHER SPECTATORS

[Breakpoint] The downloads from KH-42 waited in a file server for several hours before being made available to the analysts at the National Reconnaissance Office. This wasn't intentional, but rather was because of a critical lack of personnel, and a backlog of work.

When the pictures of the American Midwest were finally called up onto the screen of a bored researcher named Barbara Grossman, her boredom lasted exactly thirty more seconds.

She tried several things with her system, variations on a theme of false-color image enhancement, and came to an ineluctable conclusion.

She needed some high-powered help.

INTERIM

Hank had started the trip north by going east. He detoured into Gary, Indiana, went north, and cut back east to Highway Ninety. He took the Chicago Skyway, a large toll bridge that passed above a number of desolate neighborhoods, into the city. The Skyway, never in very good repair, seemed to be even more pot-holed than was normal for Illinois roads. Or bridges. The Black Destroyer navigated the impediments easily on its steel-belted radials, and the Lenhaden Family made good time up Lake Shore Drive through Chicago.

THE PROCESS

"Look at this," Barbara said. She was sitting at her boss's workstation in his office three floors above her cubicle. "That's definitely chlorophyll. Here in these three counties in southeastern Wisconsin. You can't miss the infrared signature."

"Why is this important?" Barbara's nominal supervisor, a short plump man named Sid, paused, then, "Actually I realize *why* this is important, but why is it, *now*?"

"This indication wasn't there on the last set of scans I was able to locate in the system," Barbara replied. "It's recent. The precession of the orbit of that antique brought it over this part of the country about two weeks ago, and then," she clicked on an icon at the edge of the screen, "it looked like so. A dust bowl. I know that the Ag departments in Wisconsin and Illinois are pretty interested in this—the climate shift occurred a about sixteen years back—and the Ag Departments in Indiana, Michigan and Minnesota have been keeping an eye on it, too, but most of what they are doing is just watching."

"Totally new," he replied, almost to himself, "totally new." Then: "Sixteen years. Washington? Or that local attempt?"

"No one really knows," Barbara said. "The A- and H-bomb tests of the nineteen-fifties and sixties never changed the climate as much as this, and the Southeastern Wisconsin Plague didn't do a tenth of the damage the bombs could have done." She paused, looking at the screen. "What happened in the last week to get something growing that made this kind of difference to a nearly dead satellite this far up?" she asked him.

"Barb, I don't know," Sid said. "I'm gonna have to call Philly on this. Would you mind if I mentioned your name? You did discover this."

"Not at all. Will you need any more information?"

Sid thought for several seconds. "Yes. Everything you can get, particularly what's been going on there in the last week. See what other outfits have...."

"That may mean talking to international providers."

"I was afraid you'd say that," Sid answered, sighing, "I'll have to see whether we still have a reservoir of good-will with the Technical Bloc, these days."

Barbara smiled slightly, "I'm glad that's your job and not mine."

"Actually, it's the chief's, but he's in Philadelphia, where he can call Bermuda and still be out of our way," Sid said.

Barbara stood, "I'll get on this, now." She headed for the door.

"Good job, Barb," Sid called after her.

Barbara hurried back to her office, and typed several instructions into a command-line. That would fob all of the other images awaiting her attention onto the other analysts around her. Then she called up the log entries for the new images, and started sending out requests for related data.

And I thought I was gonna have a boring day! she thought.

THE SYSTEM

[Data Reduction; Close-Up; An Hour Later] Sid put his telephone down, his ears burning.

He stared at the offending instrument, as if his stare were capable of turning the device into a molten puddle of plastic, mixed with a few surviving electrical components.

"Send it all to Philadelphia," he muttered. It had been rather worse, coming through a tinny AUTOVON connection that had enough dropouts on it to qualify for the presence of more recording devices than the local Radio Shack.

"Maybe two Radio Shacks," he said to the general area of his desk.

The tinny connection had carried the definitive tones of his supervisor's boss, one of the under-secretaries for something-or-another, who had informed him in clipped tones (probably artifacts of the phone-taps) that what his analyst had discovered *was not* to be divulged to *anyone*, ever, *at all*.

AND: that this discovery was to be covered up, and all records of it were to be sent to Philadelphia *at once*.

Damn.

Well, two could play at that game. His office had its own system for backing up sensitive data, and those back-ups could get rather artfully "lost," if it were necessary.

Sid decided that it was necessary.

THE OTHER SYSTEM

[Wait State] Neither Sid nor Barbara knew what her innocent discovery had stirred up.

Nor would they be told.

Something else would come along to occupy their time.

Wasn't it always like this?

THE PROCESSORS

[Run Mode] Early the next morning, early enough to still qualify as "night" to most people, a pair of late-model cars—rather plain dark Ford four-door sedans—took the appropriate exit from Chicago, and accessed Illinois Highway-90. In Illinois, Ninety is a toll road, and the drivers of the

Fords took advantage of the toll stops (the Illinois Department of Transportation called them "Oases" or "Toll Plazas") to change drivers. The new drivers, rested for several hours as passengers, took the cars out onto the road at a speed that was just below the posted limit. Once they were cruising, this was too low by tens of kilometers per hour. Gradually, so they wouldn't be conspicuous to state patrols by either being too fast or too slow, they joined the traffic.

In the town of Rockford, the two cars were joined by a third anonymous-looking Ford; then, in Janesville, by yet another.

They continued north up Wisconsin Highway-90.

BLACKSMITH / WHITESMITH

[Start System] The vision of the dazed policeman before them was like the recollection of a bad dream the following morning. Yezeletta and Joe gathered their tools. Two hours later, Yezeletta's work area was, once again, a mass of references, portable computers, and yellow legal pads filled with notes.

THE HILL ANALYZES

Frank Davidson removed the rolled up printouts from his filing cabinet, and took three paperbacks from his bookshelf to weigh down the corners. These were the false-color satellite photos that he had saved after Elaine had asked him for the information on the characteristics of Southeastern Wisconsin.

They were two months behind the other set he had just printed, and they echoed what was also displayed on his computer monitor.

The bright green areas were almost entirely in the Racine and Kenosha areas; they looked like a green exclamation mark, screeching their surprising existence to any and all who would look at them.

Chlorophyll has a unique infrared signature. It is possible, by analyzing infra-red photographs, to tell the difference between two greens that a human being sees as identical. Early photo reconnaissance had found this useful: one area would be green, growing things; another might conceal a nest of tanks. Infra-red photography saw the differences.

Frank read a lot of science fiction, and, on one of the covered bookshelves above his computer, he had a quote by one of science fiction's most famous authors:

> The most exciting phrase to hear in science, the one that heralds new discoveries, is not "Eureka!" (I found it!) but "That's funny ..."
>
> —Isaac Asimov

And this was funny to the nines. Frank removed the books that were holding down what he thought of as "BEFORE," and tacked the printouts to the shelves on the unused desk next to his, where they hung down like a colorful reticulated tongue. He tacked the "AFTER" prints up above his own desk.

He scooted his chair back a meter or two, and looked from one to the other.

It was like looking at a painting by Claude Monet. Up close, Monet's impressionistic works look like simple daubs and splashes of paint in a seemingly random distribution. From a distance, the image that the famous artist desired becomes visible in almost holographic detailing. Water has depth, the painting falls into proper perspective, becomes a unique whole.

"Just like this," he muttered.

"How like this?" Elaine Lawford said.

"Didn't realize I could be heard," Frank replied, turning to her. "Those satellite photos."

"That's the set I asked you to analyze a couple of weeks ago," Elaine nodded at the "BEFORE" set.

"The others are some passes I downloaded early this morning. Notice the difference?"

"You mean, like the appearance of new growth in the dustiest part of Southeastern Wisconsin?"

"Right there, starting sort of south of Milwaukee County, and going down into Racine and Kenosha, and maybe even further into Illinois. I wonder if I shouldn't ask the Illinois Ag Department for some help on this—?"

Elaine leaned back against a file cabinet, and thought for a moment. "Is any of this outside of Wisconsin now?"

"Doesn't look like it. These fly-bys are about eight weeks apart."

"That's amazing. That much in that time."

"Notice how the growth is starting to spread east and west, as well," Frank said. "Whatever's causing this, is viable, and continuing to improve the land it's on."

"A lot of farmers use seed from DeKalb." Elaine was referring to the seed company in Northern Illinois, based in the city of DeKalb, whose main product, seed-corn, was known nationwide. "You don't suppose?"

"Actually, I do suppose," Frank answered. "Make that *maybe* I suppose: DeKalb's been announcing some new strains of genetically enhanced product; I'm on an email feed from DeKalb farmers that's been discussing it," he tapped his fingers on the chair arm, "but there was no mention of anything new that went out and practically spaded, plowed and fertilized the field for you. What ever this is, it's *good*. And *recent*. It doesn't look like it took any eight weeks to do that."

Elaine took a breath. She took another and made her decision. "Don't call Springfield in on this one just yet; keep it as quiet as possible. And get as much data as you can." She grinned, "As that Paradox consultant we had in here a while back would have put it, 'Give me a general passive sensor scan, Mr. Data'."

Frank nodded, "As you wish: I'll make it so, Captain."

G O F IGURE I T O UT

[Breakpoint] He regarded the silvery scarf again for a time after dinner. He puffed on his cigarette in deep thought, while running his hands over the silvery material.

Then he called the chemistry department.

R URAL C OMPUTATIONS

Jake Tasker looked at his partner of twenty-five years. Louis Haggerty was, like Jake, a Wisconsin bachelor farmer who had fallen into farming at the beginning of his adult life and had allowed himself to drift with it for the next quarter century. For both of them, the insular world of a small farm at the west end of Kenosha County was all the adventure they wanted, then or ever.

Of course the farm hadn't been much even when things were going well: the last five years had produced enough to feed themselves and just enough to sell for more supplies to produce just enough to sell for more supplies.

Even the Department of Agriculture had written them off, until—

Louis looked at his partner and business associate. Then he looked back at the lush green of the north forty.

This area, forty acres of the section of Kenosha Township where he and Jake had been trying for the last decade to grow something besides weeds, was green with new life. The green, growing area had started all of a *week* or so ago along the northern border of the field. Then it had grown steadily, coming south at the rate of about a meter a day.

"Looks like you can *see* it moving," Jake observed.

"Yep," Louis replied, "that's winter wheat that's growing there. Gonna be the biggest crop we ever grew in that field."

In the distance the farmers could hear the sound of a car approaching. The sound grew louder, until a red Ford pulled in next to their pickup.

"Mr. Oxbridge," Jake said, "to what do we owe the pleasure of your visit?"

"Just wondering if my proposition's still of interest," Oxbridge said as he got out of his car.

A man named Oxbridge should be tall and skinny, Jake thought, Not a short, fat, nasty little man with my farm on his mind.

"Haven't made up my mind," Jake said.

"Haven't canceled your Agriculture Agreement, you mean," Oxbridge said.

He was referring to the Land Use Agreement that the Wisconsin Department of Agriculture employed as part of Wisconsin's Farmland Preservation Project. In return for tax-breaks and other forms of assistance, a farmer would agree in writing with The Department to keep his farm *a farm* for some multiple of five years, the usual interval being between ten and twenty years. This allowed the State Government in Madison to plan ahead for farming use, knowing that certain farms would stay farms for a specific and planable time period.

Any farmer who had land interlocked by an agreement with DATCP could also be sure that no one would be able to buy him out in any of several unscrupulous ways. Land that was placed in the Farmland Preservation Project became subject to an easement on the property deed that had to be removed *by the Department* prior to doing anything further with it.

Like putting up yet another strip mall, Jake thought.

"We're considering it," Louis said.

"Wasting my time, you mean," Oxbridge replied, testily. "Come now, I'm a busy man. I've even brought the paper-work with me. We can get this taken care of by one o'clock, and you can be spending your money in town right after." He regarded them as one might prize pigs.

"Not so fast." Jake was looking back out into the field again. The green color of that wheat crop was a pleasant sight.

Oxbridge placed his briefcase on the hood of his car, opened it, and withdrew—almost as if he was drawing a gun, Jake thought—two pads of official-looking papers.

"I need your signatures right here. I can even notarize them for you...."

The cellular phone on Louis' belt warbled.

Louis drew the phone, "Hello?" He listened for a minute, and handed it to Jake. "It's for you."

Jake took the instrument, placed it to his ear. "Jake Tasker speaking."

Jake listened for a moment, and looked out at his land. "Gotta be in chunks of five years, huh? Can't have it for two or three?" He listened, looking at the lushness in his north forty.

"Okay, I'm willing," he said into the instrument. "Ten sounds good. Let me give you to Louis." He handed the phone to his partner.

"Looks like we have some new growth here," Louis said into the cellphone. Behind him Mr. Oxbridge was starting to look concerned. "New growth," Louis repeated, "in our north forty. The winter wheat crop. Looks like it'll come in earlier than we planned. Ten years? Yeah. Re-up us for ten." He gave Oxbridge the eye. "Make it fifteen. I'll email you from the Kenosha Library later today with a confirmation. Yeah, thanks."

Mr. Oxbridge looked a question at both of the farmers.

"That was Edna Smith from the Department of Ag.," Louis said helpfully. "She's one of the program directors with the Department." He took the paperwork from Oxbridge's hand, and tore it once across.

"Thanks for your time, but we won't be needing your services. Or your money."

The two men got into their pickup, and drove off, leaving Mr. Oxbridge standing at the edge of the field, wondering what had gone wrong.

That fresh green growth in the wheat field. Had it gotten closer in just this short a time? That made *damned* little sense. A wheat field that hadn't grown anything but rocks in five years, producing a bumper crop of wheat: winter wheat actually started growing the fall before, then went dormant during the winter, so it would have a head start in the spring.

But a head start that started on the *north side* of a field? Oxbridge scanned the expanse of the north forty. Whatever was doing good things in that field had come from the north. Racine? Oak Creek? *Milwaukee?* Whatever it was, wherever it had come from, it was quietly revitalizing this farm.

And wrecking his business deal.

Damn.

He tossed the remains of his transaction into the back seat of his Ford, chased it with his brief-case, and drove off.

He didn't notice the large insects in the greenery behind him. By the time anyone would think to investigate the seeming miracle, they would all be dead, disintegrated and gone, their last act being the fertilizing of the field that they had saved.

THE HILL CONCEALS

Frank had tacked his collection of printouts to the south wall of the large area of which Farmland Preservation was a single section. No part of DATCP was using this area, and he found it easier to survey the satellite photos from a greater distance than he could in his own cubicle.

He tapped his fingers on the arm of the chair he had usurped from someone in Plat-Review who was out sick. This was just too perfectly goddamned incongruous for—well, words were failing him right and left.

Frank made up his mind.

He got a screwdriver from one of the tool-closets in Cartography, and went to the cabinet where the backup tapes were kept.

He removed the two latest tapes, replacing them with two that he labeled the same way as the originals. Then he went back to the south wall, where there was metal sheeting that covered a short part of the west wall, and wrapped around to the south. The sheeting was for attaching the shelves, tables, desk areas, and running the power cables, if an office cubicle were to be built here.

He unscrewed the sheet from the support substrate attached to the concrete outer walls.

As he had suspected, there were several small recesses within. One had electrical wiring; another, phone and data lines. He placed the backup tapes in the telephone cable run, and reattached the steel covering.

Then he went back, and put a new, unlabeled tape into the server backup drive, and typed in the necessary commands to start a full backup, *now*.

TRAVERSING THE GRID

The four automobiles, driven by men all of a kind of bureaucratic individuality took Highway-90 into Madison.

They drove past a place where they could see an office building, high on a hill.

North of the building, on its own plot of ground, was a large and stately oak.

WITHIN THE GRID

[Parallel Process] Hound-Dog joined Bobbi near the Milwaukee City Hall. They had crossed near the Water Street Brewery, and come down Water Street to where the Cop-Shop was. Hound-Dog held an illegal Taser, a weapon that shot tiny darts connected to fine wires through which a very high electrical charge, high voltage, low current, could be passed. The result on the victim was usually paralysis.

Hound-Dog and his woman were on the prowl. Looking for anyone or anything to satisfy their desire for what they thought of as "fun."

It would be fun. For them.

ANOTHER PART OF THE GRID

[Diagnostic Run] "Listen, man, all I was out for was a little fun," Looey's voice had a querulous tone in it from several hours of interrogation. "There wasn't nobody in sight, I mean, there was nothing but that thing—"

"Thing," Sergeant Jerry Montag prompted. "Thing?"

"Yeah, like, kinda some sorta crab, or large insect. They crawl up on the buildings at night."

Jerry looked at his partner, a taller, burlier cop who stood near the door. "Mel, what's this goof-ball talking about?"

Mel Andrews scratched his head before replying. "Damned if I know. The occasional hop-head I've spoken with has claimed to have, hell, *insects* crawling on himself, but *buildings* with insects on them? I'd want to know what our friend here's been on, lately."

"Okay, Looey," Jerry said. "Really: what exactly are you handing us?"

"I ain't handing you anything!"

"*What* were you shooting at? In the middle of Downtown?"

"Little—I dunno what you call them. Bugs! Things with legs. That crawl." He spread his hands.

Jerry looked at Mel. Mel returned it.

Jerry took a breath. "Looey, try it again. What did these 'bugs' look like?"

It continued in that fashion for another two hours.

Jerry was getting tired, and Looey was getting more obstinate. There was a peremptory knock on the interrogation room door, and Lieutenant Edwards opened it.

The Lieutenant gathered Mel and Jerry up by eye, and they stepped out into the hall. "Let him go," Edwards said.

"What?" Jerry asked, "He—"

"Just got bailed out by his keeper," Edwards finished Jerry's exclamation. "His boss paid the freight. You'll find yours in your lockers later." He took in their outraged looks, "Just get him the hell out of here."

ON IT

Looey breathed a little easier once he was a block from the Police Station. It was an inconvenience to walk back to Zhongo's place, and he was composing and re-composing an explanation for the loss of his forty-five, but at least he was out of the lights and away from the uniforms.

THE REPORTER

Jerry Montag waited until Mel had left the room, then he picked up the phone, and dialed for an outside line.

The toll-free 800-number he called wouldn't appear on the Police Department phone bill. He waited for the ringing to stop, and then he pressed a combination of buttons on the phone.

A voice answered. The voice was flat and expressionless: a computer voice.

He dictated his report to it.

FUN AND GAMES

Hound-Dog gestured silently to Bobbi.

This would be easy; it would be the same way they got motorists to stop on deserted streets. Bobbi would decoy; Hound-Dog, and sometimes his friends, would follow through.

He felt the blade in his pocket. That, plus the stuff he had gotten in Chicago—

The large man they had been following stomped stolidly down Seventh Street towards Wisconsin Avenue. Hound-Dog wondered how long they could....

Bobbi, who had gone ahead, stepped out before the man, and called, "Hey, Dude, want a little?" She opened her jacket, then shrugged it off her shoulders. She was wearing nothing underneath it.

Looey stopped, looked, understood a second before Hound-Dog stepped out of the shadows behind him, prepared blade ready. Bobbi grinned both at Looey, and at what she had in mind for later, and jiggled at him.

Hound-Dog's stiletto sliced cleanly across Looey's lower back. Looey stuck his stomach out in a reflex attempt to avoid the slice. The cut was shallow, but the blade *so far* was only a carrier for the preparation he had placed on it. Hound-Dog wondered how long they could....

....*Keep Looey alive.*

Looey's eyesight faded out, his eyes turning up in his head, looking towards the sky, up at the buildings, at—

Something looking back *down* at him.

Hound-Dog smiled at his woman.

This wasn't like the other time. Those people in the black pick-up had gotten away, after injuring one of his friends. This one wouldn't.

OUTSIDE THE GRID

Yezeletta watched as Hound-Dog and Bobbi hauled Looey's unconscious form into a convenient alley. Shortly, a battered Honda Civic pulled out of the other end of the alley, and headed south.

A FAR PLACE

[Load Intrinsics] Jerry Montag's report waited in several small pieces of silicon, until the analysis sub-system could get to it. The sub-system considered Jerry's voice stress, his inflections and word usage, then went up a level and checked his sentence structure. Once done with that, it began an analysis of Jerry's topic, constructing a set of elaborate grammars from the previous work, and going deeply into the actual topic being described. Several milliseconds on sixteen microprocessors elapsed: geological ages in the time-frames of computers, but a brief time to their human masters.

The sub-system made one last pass through Jerry's report, then sent the results off with its opinion of the report's content to another area of the multiprocessing system, of which it was only a small part.

Then another job came in, and it forgot all about what it had done.

A FAR VIEW

[Extrinsics] Others did not.

At the Searchlight Data Center, the results of the electronic analysis of Jerry's input were considered sufficiently important to cause an exception to be raised—computer parlance for an alarm. This alarm attracted the attention of an actual human being.

A VIEW FROM A HEIGHT

Diana Koerner, Senior Case Analyst for Searchlight, caught the red-bordered window with the flashing yellow lettering inside it out of the corner of her eye. She scooted her chair around, mouse-clicked on an icon, and the text of Jerry Montag's report appeared, along with some information from Montag's personnel file in another window.

A part-time agent, she thought; *Useful, being a cop.*

She read Jerry's report again, and grabbed another keyboard.

This keyboard was attached to another server, the work-stations of which had no connections to the outside world. The stations didn't even have modems, and the wiring to the server was sealed in heavily armored cable runs that certain individuals from Internal Practices, *That's a nice innocent sound-*

ing term, she thought, checked on a weekly basis.

Who or what, she asked herself, *deals in small oddly shaped life-forms?*

The data on the Searchlight Secure Server couldn't answer that question, but it could inspire yet more questions. Some very strange questions, indeed.

Diana called her secretary, then several of her coworkers.

There were several cases in the gaze of the Searchlight that involved what were euphemized as "custom biologicals." Several more involved Europeans (members of the Tech Bloc) who were either trying to sell their living wares to US companies, or the other side, who were trying to steal developments from research centers in the US that were still productive.

Two hours later another small group of Searchlight Agents departed Philadelphia. They were headed towards the Midwest.

ADDENDUM, INVESTIGATIVE

Jerry Montag read the report that had been passed to him with, even for a cop, frank curiosity.

The folks in District Six had picked up some foreign nationals a little over a week earlier, and they were being held up in the county jail, pending return to their nation of residence. In the meantime, they had received the standard physical exam that civilian groups, ever watchful of real or imagined transgressions on the part of Jerry's comrades, had insisted that new arrestees receive.

Those exams, in fussy clinical detail, were the subject of the report Jerry was reading. Mostly it was a boring description of three young, verging on middle-aged men of Eastern European descent, and what little was physically wrong with them.

An appendectomy scar on one, a slight propensity to nearsightedness on another, some rather routine dental work....

That was the one that had Jerry interested.

Stainless steel fillings were a characteristic of the old (or as some put it, the late unlamented) Soviet Union, and currently of Russia, and several countries bordering on it. Stainless steel was workmanlike, utilitarian, and cheap. Typically, low end citizens received such treatment.

It was also uncomfortable, clumsy and difficult to maintain, and Jerry Montag knew this.

Where had he heard about stainless steel dental work before? On the radio?

He grabbed the phone, and dialed Milwaukee's "Tabloid TV" Station, "Fox-Six" Station WITI, from memory. He waited while a cranky computerized Centrex system put him through to Channel Six's Library, the television counterpart to the newspaper morgue, where old stories and photographs were kept for historical reasons or for investigative reporting.

"Library."

"Sergeant Jerry Montag, District One. Did you report anything in the last couple of months that involved dental work?"

"Say what? That's a little general. What kind?" the librarian sounded puzzled.

"Forensic work. Perhaps in an accident."

"I can give the computer a chance to nibble on that." Jerry could hear the staccato of key-strokes, as Channel Six's librarian entered a query.

"We received a report of an accident on the 894 Bypass, but no Video footage. We were out covering the truck accident the same day."

"Nothing?"

"No visuals. Maybe WOKY has something. Their newscasting policy is close to ours. You know, wide audience appeal."

"Uh, thanks."

"No problem."

Jerry hung up. He knew well what the Fox Network's policy on "audience appeal" was. He called WOKY.

He made his request again, and that station's librarian promised an email with anything relevant to stainless steel dentition, as soon as her network server came back up.

Ten minutes later, it did, and five minutes after that the *"You Have Mail"* indicator appeared in the corner of Jerry's computer screen.

He scanned the news report, and reached for the phone.

To call Searchlight.

SHINE THE LIGHT

[Accessing; Close-Up] The cell phone in the Agent's suit coat vibrated gently. He reached into his pocket to press the answer button, and listened through the earpiece that looked like the output of a portable music player or a very old fashioned hearing aid.

Then he pressed the record button, and instructed the caller to repeat its instructions.

ANOTHER CHUNK

Diana Koerner returned to her database the next morning. There was one other report she had seen a reference to that looked interesting. There had been an attempt to call into the Searchlight Data Center—that had been traced to a rest stop in, of all places, Montana—that had some rather unusual characteristics.

She called up the report, and read it, with real curiosity that slowly changed to fascination then, by steps to understanding.

Maybe that puzzling residue that had been found there didn't mean anything. On the other hand, the work done on the entry to the rest stop in which this had been found....

Maybe it did!

PROGRAM ANALYSIS

[Load System] In an unidentified and unidentifiable place in Russia, south of the city of Kiev, in an estate that looked as if it had been deserted for a generation, a technician loaded the contents of a data storage medium into his computer for analysis.

The technician, Semyon Malasnikov, routinely logged onto his network server, and placed the contents of the device—it was distantly related to a flash-ROM PCM-CIA card but with vastly more capacity—into a directory on the server.

The data dump showed up as a collection of very large files.

Well, that wasn't a problem. Since personal computers had become common several generations before, program and data file size had grown to sizes that would have seemed impossible in the early years of computing. Storage size improvement was invariably followed by enough "improvements" on systems to just about compensate for the extra space.

Malasnikov surveyed the files containing the raw data he had been asked to investigate. He selected the first one on the list and started up his "DUMP/ANALYZE" program. The microprocessors in his workstation allocated the work amongst themselves, and the technician leaned back in his chair to watch the progress. The status showed as a group of small displays called "Gas Gauges" that were illuminated sliding bar-graphs showing the percentage of each part of the analysis being done.

His screen blanked out.

He leaned forward, and pressed the **Shift** key. If the screen blanking was the result of a screen saver starting up, any keyboard or mouse input should bring the screen full of gauges back.

But that wasn't what came back.

Instead, his screen was filled with a crawling precessing fractal graphic that changed unpleasantly from one organically shaped nearly recognizable design to another. The effect was that of a series of nearly biologically, derived suggestively formed, almost living things in a progression that could only be described as "repellent." Maybe "repulsive."

He clicked his mouse on the evolutions on the screen and nothing happened. He called up the System Task List. He stared at the small display in disbelief.

There were no tasks listed.

He went across the corridor to where the file server was in its rack panel. The drive lights weren't flashing as they did under normal use. They burned a steady red that was unwavering.

Semyon Malasnikov tried to turn the server off. That took a key. He went and got it, and turned the power-switch firmly to "off."

Nothing happened. The drive lights stayed on.

REWRITE-UPDATE

Diana forwarded the report to her superior, who merged it with those reports from that Part-Time agent in the Midwest.

Milwaukee, to be exact.

RESULTS, INTERIM

His ever-present cigarette sending up columns of smoke that ended in complexities, he read the report. The three pages were terse, filled with typos, and—very interesting.

The material in the scarf was indeed titanium. *Pure* titanium.

A scarf had been made from tiny rings of titanium: high tech chain-mail.

Chemically pure: made from a material with the highest melting-point of all metals, except for tungsten, in an installation that had no heavy-metals shop, made with the skill of a micro-machinist.

Where had this come from, what was it used for, and why had it been tossed out so casually?

He went to his personal safe, opened it, and locked the scarf away.

[Defrag, Extending Upper; Long Shot]   Sergeant Mel Andrews drove his car west on Wisconsin Avenue. His destination was the District One Station, the station from which he was based. He drove thinking of what was on his plate for the day, and what he and Sergeant Montag would be doing.

At the corner of Wisconsin and Water, he saw a small crowd of people looking into the entryway of a bank on the northeast corner of the intersection.

People were pointing, gesturing.

Mel grabbed the magnetic clip-on red light he kept in the back seat for when he used his own car professionally, and attached it to the roof. He plugged it into the cigarette lighter, and pulled over.

The crowd parted for his uniform, and he went into the recessed area where the main entrance to the bank was.

Standing there was a man. Mel recognized him.

It was Looey.

Looey was standing stiffly, almost at attention, against the glass of the bank entrance. Mel regarded him for a moment. He prodded the gangster with his pen, and his skin was solid, unyielding to the touch. Not rigor mortis, something else.

Mel stepped back. He drew his cell-phone, and pressed the speed dial for the Station.

Tersely, he called for forensics. And backed up into someone.

He turned. About a dozen onlookers had crowded into the entryway.

"Stand back," he said. "Yes, he's dead, I've called for backup—I mean pickup. Don't touch him. He may be contagious."

At that, the small crowd pulled back.

Then two more squads pulled up.

Two medical techs came in, carrying a stretcher. An MD arrived and began scanning Looey. He waved the techs away. He spoke to them in low and urgent tones. Mel could hear some of it. He backed up, and pushed one more spectator out behind the yellow plastic ribbon that another officer was stringing up.

The medical technicians returned, wearing masks, gloves, and plastic coveralls.

They were carrying a dark green body bag.

FAILURE ANALYSIS

[Dump/Analyze; Truck Shot]   After Semyon had gotten to the power source for the run-away server, and switched it *off*, other analysts helped him disassemble the servers into their component parts. Several hours later, the hard-drives from the units were mounted in other machines of a more disposable nature for further investigation.

Not realizing his mistake, one of the technicians connected the disposable machine nearest him to the network, so that others could follow his investigation from a distance.

He booted up, and, in the basement, the network servers began a frenzied sequence of disk actions.

He would find this out several hours later.

As he began his cybernetic autopsy, he noticed something: the network seemed to be slowing down.

No problem: it was because of the other analysts logging in.

ANOTHER **L**OCATION

Yezeletta and Joe shared a look.

"This is getting too close," she said. "The only good I can see from this is that Looey won't be shooting at my Imagers any more. But the rest of this—!"

"You thinking what I'm thinking?"

"Pulling everything in, and being invisible?"

"If you can do that without losing the data you need."

"I may have to design a different kind of imager."

"I've wondered something," Joe said.

"Go on," she prompted.

"You have these insects, and other things, with anywhere from two to umpteen, or so, legs. Why no flying imagers? All you've ever told me about that's airborne are the Raster Flies. Is it difficult to design flight capable life-forms."

"You're trying to calm me down, Joe," Yezeletta said, "thank you. To answer your question: flight requires a lot of energy. You know the old expression 'to eat like a bird'?"

"Yes: means to eat in pecks—small amounts."

"If you ate like a bird, you'd be eating constantly, every minute, all day. Birds need the input to get the energy for flight. Insects have the same problem. An infestation of locusts eats everything in sight to maintain the fuel intake to keep flying. Of course, there are always gliders."

"Bats?"

"Bats, too. Perhaps I could engineer something from bats, or small birds. I'm afraid that their life expectancies won't be very long...."

"Maybe I can help," Joe said.

"Davis protocols," Yezeletta said.

"Use those in some kind of plant-animal symbiont to supply highly oxygenated blood, or whatever, to the, uh, flying eye, we design."

"Yes, and I must rethink how I want information gatherers, of what kind, where we need them. Like the local constabulary."

"And among the local gangsters," Joe added.

Yezeletta hooked one double hip, her right, over the edge of the conference table. It let her right legs dangle centimeters above the floor. "We need," she said, "eyes in the Police Department, in Zhongo's operations, and...I wonder." She paused in thought. "I wonder if we shouldn't be keeping an eye on the Conservatory. She raised one dark eyebrow. "There may be others we know nothing about who have a lot of interest in what happened there!"

FAILURE

[Process Shot; Load] Nothing was working. The communications, routed through the Network, were gone, the workstations were a mess, the servers in various parts of the small complex were either totally barren of files, re-formatted, or—this was the hard one to believe—*burnt out.*

No one was able to call out, or (they would find this out long after) call in, either.

None of the doors opened. The perimeter security system was part of everything else. Semyon's Commander was looking for the backup keys, a look of anxious concern on his face.

The lights flickered occasionally. It didn't look serious; the power plant for the lights was fifty kilometers away. What had happened here couldn't influence something that far away, could it?

The flickering continued.

ON TOUR

The setting sun at their back, the Lenhaden Family drove East on Wisconsin Highway-94. The two days Hank had given Yezeletta, were enough leeway to provide for a trip to Madison. They spent a day poking around on the University of Wisconsin Campus, an architecturally varied place, within which it was easy to check for followers.

Towards the evening, Hank drove the Destroyer east on a road named Observatory Drive, past a large and beautifully preserved building called Bascom Hall, and down to the Campus Memorial Union at the corner of North Park and Langdon Streets. He continued East on Langdon, past fraternity and sorority houses, switched to East Washington Avenue, and joined up with I-94 where Washington Avenue ended.

There was no one behind them.

At least, no one behind them that knew them. The license plate on the back-end of The Black Destroyer was a quite legit Illinois plate, one that had nothing to do with where Hank and his family kept their vehicle. Or lived. Hank had registered the Destroyer at another residence he kept in another nearby village. Before he went out for a trip, he always gave the plate a light coating of vaseline. Road dust accumulated on the plate, making it unreadable, especially to the recording cameras at all of the Illinois toll oases he went through.

Of course, a long bed Chevy pickup wasn't exactly invisible....

Ninety-Four would take them directly through Milwaukee's west side. Along about Delafield, Hank turned northwards. It was his intention to arrive late at night, and come in from the opposite direction, as they had done before, coming down from Door County.

"Hackles," he muttered.

"Yes, dear," Ondreya said.

"Hackles," Hank said louder. "I wish I had eyes in the back of my head. Maybe our friend could install me a set."

"Interesting idea," Ondreya answered, "but I'd prefer a set of those TV camera critters, and a portable command center."

"I'd prefer living in a country in which everyone wasn't being watched by government agents," Hank said. "Blowing up Washington only slowed it down, it didn't stop it. Maybe our new friend has some ideas."

Beneath the darkening sky, the black pickup, given gold trim by the sunset, headed north.

ABRUPT RESIGNATION

Leona watched the door close, and tried to be comfortable. Zhongo had been rough, inconsiderate, and lengthy. The inconsiderate part was the most unexpected. Zhongo's skill and consideration made him one of the better "clients" Leona had known. She looked down at her right breast. She could still see red finger marks, where he had grabbed her.

There was a soft scratching at the window.

The window was closed; Zhongo had slammed it, not wanting any stray breezes. Or ambient sounds. Leona got up, and went to the window. She shook her head: Zhongo had been agitated, abstracted and just awful!

She lifted the window, and her communicator entered through the torn screen. Leona held out her hand, and the little creature jumped into it. She took it back to the bed, and placed it on the same pillow Zhongo had used.

Her communicator began speaking softly in Yezeletta's voice.

She listened intently to the short message, with its instructions.

About time!

MOVEMENT—BLACK ON BLACK

[Paradox; Access; Night Moves] While the City of Madison slept beneath a shattered sky, while the sheet-lightning flickered and flashed at the edges of all space and time, four cars pulled into the DATCP parking lot, across it, and around the base of the main yard, beneath the branches of a large oak tree, to the east section of the Department parking area. They clustered in an insectoid fashion, near the basement garage access, where the yard was ramped up to provide growing space for the park, and where they couldn't be seen from the front approach.

Shadows like men separated from the cars, and approached the garage door.

ONE MORE TIME

[Andante; Load Descriptor] Leona packed what little she would need for her short and comparatively easy mission. Around her, several small arachnoids brought her things from beneath the floor. She dressed in some, packed others into belt pouches, and pocketed yet others.

In a small, furry procession, the arachnoids climbed up into the window, and left the brownstone. Her communicator was the last to go.

She surveyed her room for the last time, silently opened the door, and stepped out. This floor would be deserted, but the two floors below her would usually have residents. Guards, if nothing else.

Quietly, she made her way to the back stairs, and, as quietly, she descended past the second floor. On the first, she could hear the sounds of one of her guards with a partner of the opposite sex. They were too busy to listen for her.

She let herself out the back door, scanned the sky to get her bearings. West was *that* way.

Silently, she drifted out to the alley, and, staying in the shadows, headed for the house four doors west of where she had lived for over a year.

It was good to be out of that place.

THE SAFE HOUSE

[Truck Shot; Camera Goes With; Ingress] Hank entered Milwaukee through Whitefish Bay and Shorewood, taking miscellaneous local streets into Down-Town. He turned onto Wisconsin Avenue past a sculpture that looked like a large, orange asterisk made from steel beams, and peered ahead.

Rising before him in the night on the south side of the street was the Farmers and Merchants, 777 East Wisconsin Avenue. He took a left onto the first side street west of the building, and drove, his lights off, into the parking ramp below the building itself.

THE DARK

[Close Up; Sign Extension] The men worked silently, each having his own place in the closely-knit teamwork. Several kept watch, communicating to the others via short-haul radios operating on encrypted data links. The garage door gave way to some sophisticated lock opening devices which it had never been designed to resist. One man raised it enough to allow another to roll beneath it. That man unlocked the human usable door, and the rest went in.

One stayed outside to guard the cars.

The spectral intruders faded into the shadows in the garage.

Waiting.

In the distance a flashlight, its beam moving to the cadence of a man walking.

One of the intruders removed a slim, deadly shape from his inner coat pocket. He took careful aim where the head of the individual holding the flashlight would logically be.

He gently squeezed the trigger.

The clicking of the weapon's action was louder than the report.

The flashlight fell, and was smothered by its owner.

The spectral intruders walked around him as they made their way up.

To the second floor.

To the *west side* of the second floor.

SAFE ENTRANCE

Hank came around inside the underground area, and faced the concrete wall that was the base of the Building here. Slowly, he drove towards the wall, and as he did, the wall *moved back* into the concrete.

It kept moving, and he paced it with his truck. When he was within the structure, he pulled into a parking space that was clearly for him—it was exactly the dimensions of the Destroyer—and pulled to a stop.

The wall replaced itself over the entrance, and a more normal steel door closed inside it.

"Looks like we came back," he said.

"Thank you for being there, Hank," a well-remembered voice said, "and here."

He looked around, up, down. Yezeletta was nowhere to be seen, but a furry, gray arachnoid stood on the hood of the truck, watching them with its gold imager.

Yezeletta's voice continued from the arachnoid, "Joe and I will be down in a moment, about—now!"

There was a sudden wash of fluorescent light, as the elevator door, that Hank could have sworn *wasn't there* a moment before, opened.

Then Yezeletta and Joe were standing outside the truck. Ondreya was the first out, followed by Anne from the back seat. Hank stepped out, and shook hands—*strange having to decide which hand to shake!*—with her, then with Joe. Yezeletta looked intently at each of them in turn, her eyes glowing.

"Let's go up to where it's comfortable," she said. "I have dinner on, and you must have travelled a long way."

BLACK ON BLACK RECORSO

[End of File Mark; Long Shot] An hour later, the intruders were finished with their work at the Wisconsin Department of Agriculture, Trade and Consumer Protection. They returned to their cars carrying the items for which they had come in large plastic bags.

They walked around the corpse lying in the basement corridor, the flashlight still shining weakly from beneath it.

They closed the basement doors behind them, and one by one, they drove off beneath the night sky, while the sheet-lightning strobed around the Building on the Hill.

A QUIET EVENING WITH FRIENDS

To Hank, Yezeletta seemed to be relieved; rather as he had heard it in her voice on the first clandestine call. She held Joe's hand in her left hands, as the elevator took them to the forty-first floor of the Building.

When they exited the elevator, she turned to him, "Hank, is there anything that should come up from your truck?"

"Mostly traveling stuff. We have our personal things here, now."

"Such as your personal weapons," Yezeletta said.

"Well, yes," Hank sort of drew it out.

"That's not a problem," Yezeletta said. "One of the reasons I've asked you to come here was for your views on such topics."

Joe added pleasantly, "What we need most is a brains trust. Yours are the only brains we trust."

Yezeletta conducted them into another room. Hank realized distantly that it had been her conference room where they had spoken to her of her puzzling apparent lack of a time sense.

Now it was a dining room.

THE HILL IN DEFENSE

[Checkpoint; Close Up] When Frank came up to the DATCP Building the following morning, he was unpleasantly surprised to see several vehicles belonging to the Capitol Police Force, the Wisconsin State Government cops who handled the security at State installations, and a very troubled Elaine Lawford, sitting on one of the benches near the bus stop.

"What's going on?" Frank asked, as he trundled his bicycle over to where Elaine was sitting.

"There's been a break-in," Elaine said. "The entire Preservation Project's a shambles."

"Who?"

"We don't know," she said. "I got here early, and walked right into this." She gestured at the cops who were poking around the base of the Ag Department Building, looking intently for anything that was out of place.

There was a shout from the building's north end.

Both Elaine and Frank turned to see four Capitol Police emerging from the far corner of the building. Behind them was the large oak tree on the northern-most part of the building's yard. It had been standing on this ancient hill long before the Ag Building had been constructed.

The cops were carrying a stretcher.

An ambulance pulled up, and the Capitol Cops veered over to it. The body on the stretcher was covered by a sheet; a corpse.

"Surely that isn't Edmond!" Elaine said.

The Officer in charge came away from the stretcher upon hearing Elaine's exclamation. "Do you know him?" he asked her.

"That's Edmondo Hamilton; he's about a year away from retirement. He's the night watchman here."

The Officer's rather hard looks softened about as much as he could allow them. "Who are you, Ma'am?" he asked.

"Elaine Lawford, I'm in charge of the Farmland Preservation Project, for the Agriculture Department. Ed's one of the fixtures here. Worked for the State all his life."

"I'm sorry to hear that," the cop replied. "Just makes me want to get to the end of this that much more...."

"Is he—?"

"I'm afraid so. I won't be able to tell you more pending an autopsy, but someone punched his ticket, maybe midnight, one in the morning. One shot. I'm sorry."

Elaine closed her eyes for a moment, then opened them.

Another cop had come out of the building, and now he approached her. "We'd like you to take another look around up there, and see if there's anything you can tell us about—?"

"The wreckage?" Elaine let a note of outrage into her voice. "Who the hell would want to toss the records of a bunch of *farmers*, for god's sake!"

Frank followed Elaine and the cops into the front entrance to DATCP, and pointedly went to the elevators in the central part of the building. He pressed the call button, and was lost in thought until the car came.

It was only a ride of one floor, Farmland Preservation being located on the second floor on the West side, and he could see the wreckage as soon as he emerged from the car.

The access to the office space used by the FPP was a hallway lined with a group of dark gray filing cabinets. These cabinets were where the paper copies of Land Use Agreements were kept for a while, before being filed in the Department's cavernous basement.

Two of the large cabinets had been tipped over. They lay like beached gray metal whales in the hall. Gingerly, Elaine, Frank, and the Capitol Police stepped around them. Where several orderly rows of cubicles should have been, each with its own computer, attendant files for documentation, references, or someone's lunch, instead was an untidy jumble of tilted cubicle partitions, books, pictures, wiring, and equipment.

Frank went to where his office should have been, and stared at the mess. Someone had gone to the extent of *smashing a hole* in the screen of his monitor. The dead device looked up at him from a pile of his science-fiction books, a picture of his wife (the glass was cracked), and a pile of print-out had been shuffled and thrown on the mess as a garnish.

The hole in the screen with its radiating cracks looked like a shattered eye.

Elaine came up behind him. He was reminded of another meeting like this a matter of days earlier.

"Vandals," he said bleakly. "After what?"

RECALL

Zhongo opened the door to Leona's room, expecting to see what he had seen for the last year.

The bed was made properly and empty.

The neatness of the display paused him for a moment. He looked, almost not comprehending the scene before him, expecting Leona to burst laughing from the closet into his arms.

But there was no one in the room.

He frowned, he felt his anger start. Then he took a deep breath, and let it out. He would get to the bottom of this.

He went downstairs to find one of his lieutenants.

YELLOW ALERT

The evening of the day that DATCP had been invaded, the Lenhadens, Yezeletta and Joe were sitting in Yezeletta's living room. Ondreya thought it strange; once, she had seen Yezeletta in all of her intimidating height enter the room, casting a long and angular shadow from some appropriately placed back-lighting.

And now, Ondreya sat in the same room, with a friend of the family. Who cast the same, if not a longer, shadow.

Joe had been describing a project he had for one of his Protocols, when several monitors in the room (they were everywhere) along with the TV set, began flashing large red asterisks in the corners of the screens.

Even more unusual: a voice that was not really a voice, but rather like the wind in a distant wood, spoke:

—Yezeletta, Joe, please turn on the cable system. Madison Channel Fifteen has something interesting.	Declarative; Accessing;

"Who's that?" Ondreya asked, "Is that—"

—I'm Hilda Henderson, Ondreya.	Descriptor;

Yezeletta grabbed a remote control, turned the set on, and started a recording. Then she activated the complex of hidden electronics that appropriated cable service from Time Warner Cable without their knowledge. The screen flickered, and a newscast from WMTV, Madison's Channel 15, came on.

The Anchorwoman stood in what appeared to be an office building. In back of her, various kinds of office furniture were piled in a disarray, while people, some recognizable as police officers by their uniforms, poked through the mess.

"—Police are still looking for the murderer of sixty-three year old

Edmondo Hamilton, night security guard at the Department of Agriculture. They have as yet no motive for the act of vandalism performed here in the offices of the Ag Department's Farmland Preservation Project. The Capitol Police are working closely with the officials here at the Department to determine what, if anything, was removed, or whether this was the act of either a 'lone-wolf' murderer, or perhaps the actions of a serial killer. Either way, police are continuing into tonight to try to reconstruct the crime, then to follow any leads that they have. This is Selina Rodriguez for WMTV-Fifteen, back to the Studio."

Yezeletta muted the output.

She raised one dark eyebrow at Joe.

JIG-SAW PUZZLE

[Lap Dissolve; Descriptor!] Jerry Montag was working late. A single man with very little home-life, he, like other bachelors, devoted himself to his profession.

He was looking through the current load of cases. He had heard nothing back from his other employers on the stainless steel fillings, and was looking for other actions that might substantiate, or at least shed light on, some of the activities of the previous few days.

Looey's death had been a small shock: even for a cop with as much time as Jerry had in, he wasn't as hardened to death and dying as many of his fellows on the Force. He had chatted with Looey now and again, usually in a professional context, for several years. The thug had been, if not particularly intelligent, a garrulous conversationalist, and had occasionally given Jerry useful information.

Now, Jerry was looking forward to seeing Looey's autopsy report.

Looey's target, down on Wisconsin Avenue—now that was something that had Jerry Montag's curiosity piqued. Several officers had gone back to the sign on the old Boston Store, later, to see if there was anything of interest, and had found that the sign had been scoured clean.

Literally scoured.

The fresh markings of what looked like the tracks of steel-wool pads had gone through years of accumulated grime, right down to the metal casing of the old sign. The DNA Tracker brought down from District Five had found nothing to report. Whoever cleaned the sign off was *good*, very good, indeed.

Jerry looked up from the report he was reading, and stared off into the middle distance.

"Dee-Enn-Ay," he drawled at the *Playboy* Calendar that hung above his desk.

The Playmate didn't reply, but Jerry lunged for his phone. He stabbed at buttons on the instrument, dialling from memory.

"Milwaukee Police Department, District Five, Sergeant Northrup, may I help you."

"Jerry Montag, District One. Did you have any other cases that you took the DNA Tracker out on, recently?"

"Sergeant Montag?"

"Yes, what did you use the DNA whoozis on in, say, the last three weeks?"

"Hold on a minute," Jerry could hear Sergeant Northrup asking another cop a question.

Northrup came back on line, "There was something that happened up by Ed's Pool Emporium, an abandoned truck that failed to check out."

"Where are the records on that?" He tried to keep the urgency out of his voice.

He heard Sergeant Northrup repeating that question. "Records says the data were keyed in late last night." Northrup recited a case number; Jerry wrote it down.

"Thanks," he hung up.

"Someday," he told the Playmate, "we'll get enough manpower around here to get things done!"

He grabbed keyboard and mouse, and entered the case number. The text scrolled up his screen: taciturn, thriftily written prose describing an abandoned truck that—

Had no DNA signatures in it whatever.

He read the report again, and clicked on an icon to print it out.

Across the room the office laser printer started ejecting sheets of paper. Jerry scooped them out of the printer, and went off to the Department fax machine.

Searchlight would find these fascinating.

——>>> **TEN** <<<——

Beauty, midnight, vision dies;
Let the winds of dawn that blow....

—W. H. Auden

THE GARRISON

[Processing] They had barely enough time to comprehend the break-in at DATCP, when the ubiquitous red asterisks started flashing, again. Yezeletta directed a thought *there*, and an Imager relayed a long shot of a figure on a motorcycle riding into the Farmer's and Merchant's's parking ramp.

Ondreya was sitting on the opposite end of the davenport from Yezeletta, and she raised an eyebrow at her: "Friend of yours?"

"Yes," Yezeletta said. "I called her into this. She's the secret agent I placed with Zhongo Teketon. She's Leona."

"She's the one that got that secret agent—the *other* one—and me out of the junkyard!" Anne said. "You sent her after us."

"Yes, Anne, I wanted you out of that place," Yezeletta said. "The low-order types that kidnapped you had no business even being near you."

Leona's image vanished from the screen, then the image jumped, and they could see her walking her Harley into the elevator that Yezeletta had sent down. Several minutes later, the elevator "dinged" up the corridor, and the doors slid open.

Leona parked the motorcycle in the hall, and entered the room.

"Welcome back," Yezeletta said. "I'd like you to meet some friends of mine."

Leona scanned the others. "I recognize Anne," she said, "Who are the rest?"

Hank, Ondreya and Joe introduced themselves, and Leona sat down on the end of a davenport. "I am, or *was*, Yezeletta's spy in the underworld. I was Zhongo's secretary with bed privileges, and I used to relay anything useful back here.

"However," she continued, grinning, "You did have him really stirred up with what you did to Lead-Foot Eddie."

"Please tell us more," Yezeletta said. "Your reports were necessarily sketchy."

Leona held up a recorded CD. "The system your animals installed under the floor recorded all of my notes from my visits with Zhongo to other places. There's a way into his lair, and we can install some data-gatherers there without any problems."

"Where would we make our entry?" Yezeletta asked.

"In—" Leona grinned, again "— his bedroom. A place that I'm not exactly unfamiliar with."

"Yezeletta, do you mind if I ask a question?" Hank said.

"Not at all, Hank, that's one of the reasons you're here."

"Leona," Hank asked, "was there anything special that happened about," he looked at Yezeletta for confirmation, "nine days ago?"

Leona blinked. "There was something big with Gary Hamilton. Zhongo had lost a modest sum in a Slicer match, and a lot of prestige over it to Gary. Then, someone wiped Gary out. Zhongo's pissed; *he* wanted to do the job on Gary. Zhongo's boys were pretty tight-lipped about it, but," this time she practically laughed, "I have my ways, even if I was supposed to be just for Mr. Teketon."

"Do we get to know about those 'ways'?" Hank asked almost diffidently.

"Zhongo occasionally brought me to his private digs and I was usually with him to take notes during meetings with his departments. He never noticed that I always had a window open. Just a touch in the winter, and quite wide in the summer. Of course, my communicator was keeping an eye on things, and sending everything back to Yezeletta's system beneath the floor in my room." She tossed the CD to Yezeletta who caught it easily in one of her left hands.

Leona continued, "Zhongo thinks that there's someone designing bio-chips into his minions." She looked steadily at Yezeletta. "Is that safe?"

Yezeletta nodded. "Some bio-chips are made in the US, but most of the real research and new development takes place under the supervision of the Tech Bloc in Ontario, Canada and parts of Uruguay." She paused for a moment. "I wanted Zhongo to think that agents of your federal government, or, better yet, other governments, were warning him to lay off. Mainly by giving him more problems to worry about than he really needed."

"Then there's this," Yezeletta continued. She took aim with a remote control, and restarted the DVD-RW recording of the earlier newscast.

"What?" Leona asked.

"It was happening while you were on your way here," Yezeletta said. "There was a burglary attempt at the Wisconsin Department of Agriculture." Silently, they listened to the news that had been broadcast earlier in the day.

"Try CNN," Anne said. "They may have more."

CNN was in the middle of the "World Financial Report" and when that ended, a sports segment started. Yezeletta muted it.

"Is there," she asked, "any possible sort of a connection between the Ag Department and any of the other things that have been going on?" Then she answered herself. "It's been less than two weeks since we eliminated Gary the Geek. My biologicals should have completely died out by this time, but there may be a residue that is still detectable." She paused in thought, and the others let her muse to herself.

Then: "Joe, we must get an agent into the Ag Department." To all of the others, "What we need is a way of getting certain of my creations onto The Hill at DATCP. I have no creations that can fly for such long distances; I'm open to any ideas."

Hank and Ondreya talked softly to each other, while Anne went to a window and looked out, thoughtfully. Leona watched the silent television images, and—

Anne turned.

"Do taxis still deliver packages here in Wisconsin?" she asked.

"I've never had the occasion to find out," Yezeletta said. "Joe, do you know? Hank? Ondreya?"

"Cabs don't do package deliveries in Illinois anymore," Hank said. "About six years ago, a package that was to have been delivered to a currency exchange and remotely detonated once it was inside—currency exchanges are built with a fair amount of armor around them—went off inside the cab, instead. In the middle of State Street. The crooks that wanted to get into the exchange had their timing off. That's when package service stopped."

"Chicago sounds like a *wonderful* place to live," Yezeletta commented, wryly.

"That's not the case up here," Joe said. "I've seen COD's and regular weekly runs, both people going to work and packages, all over Milwaukee. Saw one when I got your piano."

"What have you in mind, Anne?" Yezeletta asked.

"If there are still such deliveries in Madison, you can have one of the bus lines take a package addressed to 'Ag' and get it run out to the department by a local cab. They must have a mail room somewhere in that big building. Why can't you just ship your critters that way?"

Joe reached for a telephone. The line was dead. He reached for another, and got a dial tone. He poked buttons, and: "Information? I'd like the number of the Badger Bus company, and, while you're at it, Greyhound, as well." Hank tossed him a pen, and Joe wrote swiftly. Next he called the Badger Bus Company. He asked a question, listened for the answer.

He hung up, grinning. "How dormant can you make your package goods, Babe?" he asked.

"Very dormant, indeed," Yezeletta was almost laughing.

She directed a thought *there*, and a servitor entered the room. Yezeletta touched its head briefly, outputting several instructions. The creature scuttled out, and several more entered the room.

They were carrying the parts of a stiffly made cardboard shipping carton.

DROP SHIPMENT

[Output Operation] As Hank and Ondreya watched with great amusement, the most improbable espionage operation in the history of clandestine behavior was constructed in a living room forty-one stories above street level in Milwaukee.

The faceted component (Hank thought that it looked like something from one of his advanced geometry courses in college) fit snugly into a styrofoam bracket that supported it without covering it completely. Another similar piece of styrofoam fit on the top of the item. Hank could make out triangular facets on it through the styrofoam supports. He helped Joe drop the whole assembly into the cubical carton, where it rested snugly.

Anne had volunteered to look up an appropriate government official to whom the package would be sent. She sat in a corner with a laptop, browsing various State Government Web Sites, looking for the right individual.

She clicked on a menu item, and the printer disgorged a list.

"What I have here," she announced, "is a list of the other divisions in the Ag building. There's Plat Review, Network Maintenance and Cartography on the same floor, the second, as Farmland Preservation. Here's a list of the people who work there."

Yezeletta took the proffered list, grinning. This little army of hers would be a pack of winners, yet!

She picked a name in Cartography.

"Now, we have to get this thing shipped out of here," she said decisively.

And at that moment, the red asterisks began their strobing, again.

THE LAST SOLDIER

[Installation; (LONG) Shot = 1L;] Peter Rudenko knew exactly where he was headed. Furthermore, he knew that *she* would have the wherewithal to locate him long before he arrived at her residence.

So when he drove down Wisconsin Avenue and turned right, south, to come around to the Farmers Building from its south side, Yezeletta knew who would be arriving. Peter didn't even have to phone ahead.

He pulled into the subterranean parking lot, and shut his ignition off.

And waited.

WHERE'S THE PARTY

Yezeletta was the first to speak: "Looks like the last guest to arrive." She turned to Anne, "It's your friend, the secret agent."

"Want some backup?" Hank asked. "I'm not sure I like the coincidence of this."

"We saw him coming up Ninety-Four," Joe said, brushing back his hair. "We knew he was headed this way, and he himself confirmed it, when he dodged over to Highway One-Hundred, swung southwest and came in through Brookfield. He was avoiding Hightower's crew. That was day before yesterday. He must have camped somewhere last night."

Yezeletta picked up the package in three hands. "Maybe he can pay the initiation fee," she said.

MARCHING ORDERS

Peter Rudenko pulled his car out of the parking ramp, a cubical package securely belted into the bucket seat next to him. *Just take this to the Badger Bus Station—it's on Seventh Street: also known as James Lovell Lane.* Yezeletta's words echoed in his mind.

Simple enough; she'd even given him the money necessary to pay for both the bus trip, and the fees for the Badger Cab—*What the hell, <u>why</u> did these people have <u>badgers</u> on their minds?*—at the other end.

He reached into an inner pocket. He had enough custom identities that one of Searchlight's carefully crafted creations could be used, and then that identity would cease to exist, in a suitably untraceable fashion, just moments afterward.

He drove west on Michigan Avenue, a block south of Wisconsin, at a comfortable urban speed of forty KPH, about twenty-five miles an hour. Fifteen minutes later, he pulled into the parking lot of the Badger Bus company.

One of their large, well-equipped buses was loading. He appended himself to the end of the ticket line, and inched forward as a middle-aged woman behind the counter stamped tickets, and took cash from customers.

Peter set the box firmly on the counter.

"Shipment to Madison," he said.

The ticket agent read the address, and filled out forms. Peter had his well-crafted, believable, genuine and totally bogus identification ready, but she didn't ask to see anything. She took the cash he gave her, made out the necessary paperwork for payment to the Badger Taxicab Company at the destination, gave him change, and the cubical carton was placed on a hand-cart with several other packages. It didn't look much different from the rest.

A tall, gray-haired man, wearing a cap with a numbered badge on the front came in, grabbed the cart, and wheeled it out to the bus's open baggage compartment. He piled the cart's contents into it, added several suitcases, and closed the compartment door on the boxes with a decisive "thunk."

Peter left, losing himself in the line of passengers, walked around the front of the bus, and made his way back to his car.

A moment later, he was headed east back to Yezeletta's.

Five minutes after that, the bus pulled out for Madison, no one aware of the box full of extra passengers.

THE STRANGE TRAVELLERS—I

[Processing] When Peter drove back into the parking ramp, there was a door in the concrete wall where he hadn't noticed one before. He drove his vehicle in, parked it in the spot next to the Lenhadens' truck, and turned to see the garage door closing in front of something that was being built up rapidly outside of it.

He got out of his car, grabbed two large cases, and headed for the elevator, which opened in a gush of light as he approached it. Hank was waiting for him.

THE STRANGE TRAVELLERS—II

[Parallel Processing] Caliban continued to pay attention to Miranda, with a degree of courtesy and consideration she would not have believed even a month before. But she still felt sidelined, left out of the obvious preparations going on around her.

The lessons on the shooting range had continued, and the coaching she had received was of a high enough caliber (she laughed at the obvious joke) to make her a shooter who could hold her own in most situations.

Caliban had even presented her with a matched pair of Barettas—slim, nasty weapons which had been custom-fitted to her hands. She could fire those pistols with far more accuracy than any other of the weapons she had used.

Then she had been asked to just...wait.

Then, a day later, as well as after all morning and most of the early afternoon that followed, the waiting ended.

One of the quietly efficient men (she thought of them as Caliban's handlers) had told her to get her belongings together and pack them. He had even given her two very well-fabricated suitcases. Her meager assortment of clothes looked even smaller in the two-suiter. Then someone else had bustled up to take her measurements, and, an hour later, drop off eight sets of plain, but strongly constructed clothing.

Miranda took the hint. She changed into the stoutest looking outfit provided.

Then Caliban had come by for an hour of lovemaking, had kissed her lingeringly, and had bustled off, again.

Throughout the rest of the day, others had supplied her with such things as cosmetics, and had even managed to get her favorite brands, money in rather large amounts, in US dollars, and other items, some of which looked downright mysterious.

As she sorted through her new possessions, another handler came up, wheeling a luggage cart.

"Time to go, Miss," he said. "Your lover's waiting."

"Where are we going?" she asked. "What's all of this about?"

"You'll be filled in when we get to the meeting, Ma'am," he said. "Your boy friend made quite a stink about your going with him."

"*Where* are we going?" Miranda was getting a little exasperated.

"Looks like you're going home," was all the other said.

The luggage handler trundled her bags into a room that was filled with men. They made way for her, as she went to Caliban's side and took her place.

The looks on the faces around her puzzled her. They wore...a strange kind of *respect* for her position as Caliban's Woman.

And he looked positively martial in a similar garment to hers, with necessary changes in the tailoring.

He looked down at her with an expression that was both possessive and loving.

A tall, thin man with sharp blue eyes, wearing an impeccable navy blue suit, went to the head of the table and placed a sheaf of papers on the table in front of him, next to a pack of cigarettes. Then, he started speaking.

"Ladies," he looked directly at Miranda, "and gentlemen," he looked up at Caliban. "The project we undertake today will be the repossession of an erring soul, an individual who has left us precipitously, and who needs to be persuaded to return to the company of real friends.

"This individual is the other Agent which this Project has created, and this man," he extended his arm outward, palm up, to Caliban, "will be the instrument of our persuasion."

He looked squarely at Miranda, with an expression that she found unsettling. "He will be aided by this woman, who is the last to join our project, and who will assist our tall friend in his labors." There were polite laughs at this, and Miranda took Caliban's left hand, his lower. He squeezed it, gently.

"Both of you will be dispatched to your penultimate destination, where you will be met by others of his creation; then you will be sent to where we think we have located the Agent which you will bring back.

"You," he looked up at Caliban, "will bring the Agent back. You will use any means at your disposal to do this, and you may do anything necessary to the Agent, to ensure that the Agent will be returned to us."

An edge crept into his voice as he continued, an overtone that Miranda didn't like at all. "But: bring the Agent back *alive.*

"Good Luck."

The others in the room began to take their leave. Miranda's silent servant steered her cases towards the door, and she followed them. Caliban was behind her. The little procession marched down the hallway, and ahead, Miranda could see daylight.

There was a gentle tap on her shoulder. She looked around and up: Caliban handed her a pair of sunglasses. She put them on, and went out into the slanting rays of late afternoon. Directly before her were two dark gray stretch limos, the color of storm clouds even in the sunlight. Caliban reached around her, and opened the door of the nearest. Miranda's cases were deposited in the cavernous interior next to other luggage, strapped onto the facing seat. Caliban got in beside her. The luggage handler waved, closed the door, and the vehicle accelerated.

A sign appeared, "Alice Springs International, 95 Km."

Alice Springs? Where was that? It looked as if she would find out.

She looked up at her partner. He smiled back, and she realized a most unsettling thing: the man making the speech at the meeting hadn't mentioned any names. Neither hers nor Caliban's, nor this Agent they were to capture. To him, they had no names.

They were only...objects?

What?

PLANNING FOR WHAT?

[Install; Run] Hank conducted Peter up to Yezeletta's residential floor in comparative silence. When the elevator slowed and the doors opened, he remarked, "Didn't think you'd be back; what brought you?"

Yezeletta was standing at the door; her sharp hearing had picked up Hank's question. "I'd be interested in the answer to that, too," she said. "Did your associates send you back?"

"I resigned," Peter said flatly. He walked past Yezeletta, and didn't see her eyebrow, her left, rise incrementally.

"Interesting," Hank said. "Your superiors must not have liked the data on Hightower you and Yezeletta cooked up."

"I'm afraid that 'cooked' states it too well," Peter said. "It may have looked good here, but the nature of it was pretty obvious to the analysts in Philly. They saw through it, and my immediate supervisor went into orbit."

"And," Yezeletta said from behind them, "sent you back here to get more data."

"Yep. And I decided that I really don't need to work for Searchlight any more. I know where all the secrets are, and I have enough in the way of supplies—" he didn't add that some of these would allow him to vanish quite thoroughly beyond recovery by his professional friends, "— and I may be of more use here than I would be to my late job."

He put his suitcases down, and sat, half falling, at one end of Yezeletta's couch.

"How long have you been up?" Ondreya asked.

"About twenty hours. That speed run down to the bus station just about took the last out of me."

"Maybe you should rest," Yezeletta said. "Your bedroom's at the end of the hall."

And with that, the newly ex-secret-agent left the room.

"Pretty fast thinking," Joe said quietly, after Peter left.

"Indeed," Yezeletta replied. "I believed him about ninety percent when he arrived before, and his willingness to deliver the package raised it. Besides, he could have brought along all of those 'shining lights' he hangs out with."

"What's your take on this?" Ondreya asked.

"I think he's okay," Yezeletta said decisively. "I was able to monitor his respiration, galvanic skin response, and so on, while he was talking. He's on the level, just tired."

ENROUTE

[Sector Access by Cylinder] The acceleration of the Boeing 777 airliner pressed them back into their seats, as the plane jumped skyward at a fifty-degree angle. Miranda looked out of the starboard side window as the ground dropped precipitously away, below them.

The limousine had taken them to a far corner of Alice Springs International, to where the 777 had been waiting, its jets idling, with a sound of distant thunder. Miranda and Caliban had gotten out, and had passed through a tunnel made of canvas to a portable lift, which had concealed them while it raised them to the plane's front entry.

Then, they had been conducted to the First Class section, and left there. Her luggage had shown up moments later, and had been lashed down against a convenient bulkhead.

Takeoff was five minutes after that.

"Caliban?" she asked, "do you know where we're going?"

Caliban turned a bit ponderously in his oversized seat, and looked pleasantly at Miranda. "You were not told?" he asked.

"No, I was told that I would find out after takeoff, and it is," she grinned in spite of herself, "after takeoff. All I was told was I was 'going home'."

"We are going to America," he said, his voice breathier than usual. "Specifically, we are going to Chicago."

"That's home. What then?"

"We will meet some others who have left earlier. Then we will look for the One we are to look for."

"Yes, but who?"

Caliban knew, but the data were in his internals. Miranda wouldn't find out for at least another hour.

THE INSTALLATION RUN

[Bus Arbitration] The Badger Bus cruised at an even one-hundred kilometers per hour, or, in the old system, at a speed of sixty-one miles per. Down in the luggage compartment, a biological timer counted bits at the rate of about ten per second. At the end of each sixty-second time interval, the bit count was compared with another value contained in a place nearby. When this value was reached, the next step in the programming of the cubical box's contents would take place: a protocol exchange between Yezeletta and the organic server in the faceted sphere.

But, by then, the box would be safely in a corner of the mail room at DATCP.

NORTH BY NORTHEAST

[Beat] Caliban's motion woke Miranda from dozing. She watched as his large form got out of the seat, and walked across the cabin. *For such a large man, he's very light on his feet*, she thought. He came back carrying a standard leather briefcase that looked small in his large hands. He sat back down, placed the case in his lap, and opened it.

There were several folders inside, he removed the top folder, and closed the case with a sharp snap.

"Miranda," he said, somehow injecting sibilance into a name composed of labials and voiced consonants, "This-ss iss the One whom we are to find." He handed her a standard glossy photo, still called an "eight-by-ten."

Miranda looked at the image for nearly a minute. This was too clearly out in left field! She looked up at Caliban and asked, "Your girlfriend?"

"No. She iss not my girlfriend or my woman. You are. She iss to be brought back with us."

"Will she want to come?"

"Likely not. I have been told to bring her back in any case. In any way. I have information that I may use against her, if I need to."

"What kind of information?"

"Unknown."

"Then why is it so damned useful?" This was exasperating!

"I do not have it: *she* carries it with her. I can make her see it."

Hearing that, Miranda made two deductions that she would not be aware of for at least another day. The first was that there was something else *within* Caliban that *was not Caliban*. She had heard of Caliban's "internals," and he had told her a little of what all of the silicon real estate within his body could do. The second was that he was naturally taciturn, that long speeches were rather difficult for him, perhaps because of limitations from the first deduction.

Still, the individual in the picture was pretty, rather in the same way that Caliban was, well, handsome. Her design had been given an aesthetic component that was definitely in evidence, even allowing for her physique.

Who was she?

CONNECTIONS

The Badger Bus pulled in to the station on West Washington Avenue in Madison at eleven PM. The passengers disembarked, and the row of taxis that had pulled up in anticipation pulled out, each taking some of the passengers to their homes.

One taxi driver enquired at the ticket counter, and the agent directed him to the bus driver, who was wheeling in a cart of packages.

There were several deliveries that night, and the cab driver was pleased. Too often there were drunken, belligerent passengers from Madison's collegiate hangouts that had to be babied back to their dwellings. Some of them even paid.

He signed for the packages, took the attendant paperwork, and placed the packages in the trunk of his white and red car in the approximate order of their delivery.

Hmmmm, one to the Lunar Corporation, southeast side, one to that industrial park on the west, Excelsior Road, and this one to the Ag Department, far east side.

He decided to start with that one, first. The new night-watch*men* plural, there, could take this to the mail room for distribution the next day.

Too bad about that vandalism, last week.

Whistling, he started his cab, and pulled out.

SUBCONSCIOUS CONCLUSIONS

[In Processing] Miranda dozed again, after seeing the photos of their intended target. Caliban put his two right arms around her in a warm embrace, and she snuggled against his bulk. After a short time, he, too, dozed off.

Miranda opened her eyes.

Their...target. The man at the—"installation" would be as good a word as any, at least until she knew its name—hadn't even referred to their target's *sex*. He had used no adjectives, beyond such nebulosities as "friend," at all.

Was he afraid of her?

Why?

THE DELIVERY

[Processor Installation; Truck Shot; Camera Goes With] The Badger Cab driver ascended to the top where the DATCP building was. The long, winding road up the hill was, appropriately, he thought, named Agriculture Drive; although DATCP was the only building on the hill, the address was 2811. He wended his way through the nearly empty parking lot, passed the main entrance, and drove towards the back.

He had made many deliveries to "Ag" and always enjoyed the sight of the huge oak tree in the north yard. The driveway to the back of the building, where there was access to the basement, and the mail room, took him past a small embankment where the builders of the complex had effectively terraced a place where the old tree could continue to grow, unharmed.

There was a light ahead. An armed night watchman—actually a member of the Capitol Police Force—came out to meet him.

The cop approached his window, flicked his light inside, and recognised the driver. The driver stuck his clipboard out for the cop's signature, and the officer took the carton back to the lit entrance.

There was a movement in the darkness, a glinting of light off of metallic objects.

As the cab driver pulled his vehicle around, he saw another Capital Cop holstering a pistol, and following his partner in.

The cabby was very happy to leave the hill that night.

SYSTEM FIXUP

[I/O] Before Miranda had a chance to doze off, again, a shadow passed over the window on her side of the plane. She looked out, and saw—

Another airplane not ten meters from them!

The other plane, a fat gray military job, was flying above and before them, but was maintaining the distance with an incredible level of precision.

A hose began unwinding from the other plane. It dangled over their plane in a way that almost had her laughing.

The intercom pinged, and the pilot spoke: "There's nothing to worry about, we're just stopping for gas, without landing. We'll need about a half an hour to top off, and we'll be on our way."

She looked at Caliban, who looked back at her, his large violet eyes surrounded by wrinkles of mirth. "We're on the express," he said. "No landings until Chicago."

Caliban got up and closed the curtain that separated them from the other section of the cabin, then pulled a more substantial divider across the curtain, then another—even solider—partition that looked recently installed.

He pulled down something on the other side of the cabin from Miranda, and opened it out.

"I know what you want to do," Miranda said with a grin, "Just like this plane's doing. Just upside down." Playfully, she pushed Caliban back on the bed, and unzipped his black jump-suit.

Then she unzipped her own, and they joined the Mile-High Club.

INSTALLATION AT THE DEPARTMENT

The Capital Cop whistled off key as he carried the cubical package back to the mail room. He noticed that the individual to whom it was addressed had her office on the second floor. He frowned. He was here to see if the mystery attackers would return, and, secretly, he wanted to do them in quietly, somewhere down in the wilderness park that was most of the Hill on which DATCP stood.

Edmondo had been a friend of his.

He placed the package in the receiving area of the mail room, and left, dousing the lights and locking the door.

Delivery complete.

REMOTE DROP SHIPMENT

Yezeletta sat before the plasma display, her four hands on three keyboards, watching absolutely nothing on the screen. A yellow asterisk appeared in a corner. She reached with her left hand, her upper, to Joe, and took his hand, his right. With her lower left hand, she sent instructions to an organic receiver in the carton.

SETUP AT THE DEPARTMENT

In the mail room at the Ag Department, there was a rustling sound from a box placed in the receiving area. The cubical box rocked, teetered, and fell off the large sorting table where the Capitol Police Officer had placed it.

It fell back behind the table, and behind the counter that separated the sorting area from the "customer" area.

The box moved again as something inside started sawing at the cardboard. It was a standard double-strength box, of the sort that computer hardware is shipped in, but the organism inside it made short work of the corrugated side of the box. A hole that was about the diameter of the faceted, spherical thing within appeared on one vertical face of the box, and almost triumphantly a small multilegged critter stepped out onto the concrete floor.

Ninety-three miles away, in Milwaukee, there was a round of applause.

The critter didn't know this. This arachnoid was one of Yezeletta's "installers," a physically strong creation that was designed to move heavy loads.

What it needed was to move the box out of sight.

It scuttled up one wall, and poked at the ceiling panels. The false ceiling was typical of such buildings. The panels hung in frames suspended from the real cast-concrete overhead. Such things as air conditioning duct work were also above the panels.

The creature removed a panel, went back, and, seizing the box in its claws, took it up above the false ceiling. Once there, it replaced the panel, and methodically began to *eat* the cardboard. The styrofoam inserts it couldn't eat; Yezeletta had never been able to create a lifeform that could dine on that stuff. The arachnoid shoved the styrofoam pieces into a convenient corner, and took the faceted sphere into an air duct.

There was a hole in the sphere that was just the size of the arachnoid.

SIGHT AND SOUND

The Matsushita plasma screen, which had been showing a black on black image, lit up in an elaborately false-colored display when the first of Yezeletta's imagers stepped from the sphere. The false-color display differentiated into a mosaic of smaller windows, as other Imagers deployed and began climbing up convenient air ducts, electrical cable runs or other ways available to get to the second floor of the Ag Building.

The images confusingly placed in the windows moved erratically in various directions, as appropriate to the points of view of the transmitting Imagers. Those viewpoints were positively claustrophobic, until—

A broad vista spread itself before all of the critters as they reached their destination, and their transmissions synchronized: a long perspective of a flat surface, with vertical components stretching up to the concrete overhead.

They were above the ceiling panels of the second floor, and the Farmland Preservation Project was just below them.

Yezeletta turned to her friends, "And that, Ladies and Gentlemen, is how you infiltrate something!"

The second round of applause certainly sounded like more than five people.

Yezeletta issued commands through her fingers that were transmitted ninety-three miles to the East Side of Madison. The creatures started etching infinitesimal holes in the ceiling panels through which they could see and report back.

As Yezeletta & Co. watched, the windowed display became a mosaic of details. They could see the partially cleaned up mess that Farmland Preservation had become, and, when day came, they could see all of the details of what was happening as the Capitol Police continued their investigation.

They could even see Frank Davidson when he arrived for work in the morning.

THE BOWL OF DUST

[Rewind: Load-and-Go] Yezeletta sent Hank and Joe down to the defunct consulting firm on the twenty-second floor to procure another batch of recording media. Joe took advantage of Hank's help to remove all of the remaining cases back to the penthouse.

When they wheeled the cart full back into Yezeletta's complex, she was wiring up several recording devices to relay record the inputs from her Imagers at DATCP.

"But *why*?" Hank asked.

I haven't the slightest idea what will be useful from the Ag Department," she replied. "For all I know, there may be something quite trivial now, which against a different context, will be anything *but*, later. Besides, those civil servants have had their domain invaded, and won't be in much shape to think dispassionately about it. They're a pretty level-headed bunch, but they're pissed, to understate it a lot."

"I get it," said Hank about three seconds ahead of Joe. "You're doing a traffic analysis on their behaviour."

"That's as good a way to describe it as any, I guess," she replied.

"Yezeletta," Joe said suddenly. "What's that guy doing?"

THE HILL RECONSTRUCTS

"That guy" was Frank. What he was doing, was getting a small set of tools out of his temporary office, while his real office was cleaned up. He went to the unused area on the south wall of the building.

Frank removed the screws that held the metal sheeting to the wall. He reached in and removed exactly one of the backup tapes he'd hid there a week, and an eternity, before.

Then, he replaced the steel sheet, and slipped the tape into his back pocket.

Frank met Elaine in the approximate area of where her office had been.

"Any idea if there's anything missing?" she asked him.

"There are some backups that I haven't found, yet," Frank replied. "Either they're gone, or just under stuff. The cleanup crew will have this picked up by noon, and then I can go through what's here."

"I have a better idea," Elaine said. "I don't know if we can trust the cleaners." As she spoke, Suzanne and Edna arrived. Elaine stepped back, and took them all in. "Folks, I hate to ask you this, but I think we should go through as much of this as we can, before the janitors arrive. Whoever it was that came through here was after something, and I'd like to know exactly what."

Another individual came in; Suzanne introduced her nephew, Jack. "I thought you'd say something like that, so I asked him to join us."

Elaine smiled, "Jack, you and Frank get to do the hard work. Please move anything big out of the way, so that we can sift for the small stuff."

"Always wanted to get into construction—make that re-construction," Frank said, rubbing his hands together. "Okay, Jack, let's do it to it."

Yezeletta looked from the screen to her friends, then back. "I'm open to commentary. That guy looked as if he were anticipating trouble." She stood up, went to her favorite easy chair, and hooked one double hip over a chair arm. "He must have thought there was something worth protecting on that tape," she continued, "I'd like to know what it was."

"The Agricultural Department," Hank said, half to himself. "What sorts of goodies would an agency dealing with primarily farms use?"

"Try satellite recon," another voice said from the door.

Peter Rudenko entered. "Woke up, couldn't get back to sleep," he said. "I heard you guys yakking out here, and I thought I'd join you."

"Recon," Yezeletta said. "What do you know about such things?"

"Enough," Peter said. "And I have some tools that I brought along with me that might shed a little light, maybe even a Searchlight—if you'll pardon the pun—on things."

While he was talking, he picked up the larger of the two cases he had brought up to the penthouse, and set it on Yezeletta's coffee table. He opened it and took a small receiving dish out of one compartment, plugged it into another item still in the case that was either permanently mounted or too big to move, and handed a power cord to Hank to plug in. He removed a stocky-looking laptop from another section of the case, plugged an ordinary monitor cable into the back of it, and another into the items in the case.

"Yezeletta, can this be plugged into one of your larger displays?"

It could, and she did. Peter gestured at his laptop, typing in what looked like a complex password, along with some other commands.

"The satellites that we can receive with this rig aren't in very good shape. If they aren't being used as targets by the Tech or Space Blocs, they're usually creatively malfunctioning in other ways." As he typed, an image built up on Yezeletta's main TV monitor. "What we can't do with US technology, we do by 'Research'. You know the old song: 'Plagiarize, let no one else's work evade your eyes, remember why the good lord made your eyes, so don't shade your eyes, but plagiarize, plagiarize, plagiarize!'"

"But always to be calling it, please, 'Research'!," Ondreya completed the old Tom Lehrer song.

"You got it," Peter said. "What we can't get from our stuff, we raid from the Space Bloc's systems. This is the French SPOT-VII-A Satellite. They positively refuse to allow us access to it, but we were able to place a back-door in its programming, when Areonautique Français came to Silicon Valley for help with the microprocessing."

The image on the screen was of part of the central United States. Peter typed in a command, and an overlay of the states provided by the lap-top, appeared. North and South Dakota were centered on the screen, and Minnesota and Wisconsin were sliding in from the right.

"Now, then, let's see if I can get some extra data on this display." He typed in several commands, and the picture lost contrast, becoming flat blobs of gray in barely discernable patches. "Now for some false color defaults." He typed another directive, and—

The image sprang into vivid relief in various shades of blue and green.

"Pete," Hank said, an odd edge to his voice. "Try a closeup in this area."

"And," Yezeletta said, "a bit further south, as well."

ALL THE WAY TO THE BOTTOM

[Load; Run; Extreme Close-Up] Frank and Jack made relatively short work of what Elaine called "anything big." The remnants of the original office arrangement had already been gone through by the Capitol Police, who had left, taking with them photographs, reports, and much invective.

And, Elaine was convinced, no real clues. And that was because, being skilled investigators, they necessarily looked at a crime scene in a certain way. What Elaine wanted was to look at it not from the viewpoint of a professional investigator, but from the viewpoint of a Wisconsin Civil Servant whose *raison d'être* was providing services to Wisconsin's large farming population.

And, to find out what these unwelcome intruders *really* wanted from that viewpoint or context.

Frank stacked the last of the large stuff, mostly the verticals for partitions, and some metal shelving, out of the way in an unused and still standing cubicle.

This left an amazing amount of small clutter as the bottom layer of sediment. He picked up several objects: The torn off cover of a copy of *Killer Paradox*, several of the small boxes that backup tapes were stored in, one tape cassette that had been stepped on, and overlooked by the Capital Cops (he put it aside; it might be useful later as evidence), pencils, pens, a key-ring with two keys—they looked like desk keys—the inevitable couple of hundred paper-clips, and another tape box.

"Elaine," he started from his dubious vantage-point, sitting on the floor. "There appear to be rather more tape cassette *containers* than there are actual tapes."

Elaine gave Frank a look, and said, "The server." Then she walked off, fast. Frank jumped to his feet and followed her, Edna and Suzanne appended themselves to the procession, and Jack brought up the rear.

The procession stopped at the server for Farmland's Local Area Net. Frank stabbed the button to unload the tape, with rather more force than he intended. Nothing happened. He stuck his left little finger into the tape slot to see if there was a cassette in the device. He looked up at Elaine. "Empty," he said.

"I think that you have a damned good idea," Elaine said slowly, "about looking for *all* of the tapes on hand." Elaine's eyes were of that color blue that was sometimes described as "icy."

She added, "I think that we're going to find some of them missing."

AN EXCLAMATION MARK ON THE EARTH

While Elaine Lawford was arriving at her conclusion, Yezeletta Zargkonji, Joe, Hank, Anne and Ondreya were just staring at the image that Peter had placed on Yezeletta's largest display.

There was a green line that started in Milwaukee, and proceeded straight, south, through Racine and Kenosha Counties. Actually, it wasn't due south; it was out of true by several seconds of arc west. It was wider at the top than at the bottom, and, at the bottom, there was a small, but distinct circular area.

It was an exclamation mark. Of green, growing things.

A punctuation mark of chlorophyll in what had been a dust bowl for the last sixteen years.

"Where is the top of that thing?" Joe asked. "Babe, I think that may be—"

"I already know," Yezeletta said. "I'll bet you a Coke that green area starts very near the Mitchell Conservatory.

"People," she said, "I think that we had better get ready for visitors." She looked around herself, her gold eyes wide. "That's why 'whoever' ransacked the Ag Department. They want to know what Ag knows.

"Either about Gary Hamilton, or about us.

"Or about me."

——>>> **ELEVEN** <<<——

With a host of furious fancies

Whereof I am commander,

With a burning spear and a horse of air,

To the wilderness I wander.

By a knight of ghosts and shadows

I summoned am to a tourney

Ten leagues beyond the wide world's end:

Methinks it is no journey.

—Anonymous, *Tom a Bedlam*,
17-th Century, C.E.

W ITHIN THE B ORDERLANDS

[Load] There were two more mid-air refuellings, the last over the coastline of Southern California. Miranda could sense a tenseness as they got closer to their destination. Caliban's lovemaking was a more intense, more—the word "studied" came to mind. He was *methodical*.

When they weren't playing, he told her what to expect in Chicago. They would land at a runway at the outer edge of O'Hare Field, where they would be met by agents that Caliban's handlers had sent on ahead by circuitous routes. There would be six or seven men in all, when the last leg of the expedition started.

"Your handlers," Miranda said. "Who are these people, anyway?"

"I work for them," Caliban replied. "I am their agent. Their—representative—employee."

Miranda couldn't help rolling her eyes at this. Every time she had raised this question, Caliban had brushed it off with "The ones I work for," or something similar.

And when she had insisted, Caliban had other ideas. Those ideas usually required her to stop talking.

At least she was going home.

F AILURE + +

[Trace Mode] The power plant had failed; all of the lights were out for this last week, and only quick action—an amateur radio operator with a motor-generator rig and knowledge of emergency precautions—had kept the matter from getting worse.

Outside, the humming of the truck-mounted generators provided power for most things, but the Intelligence Service was going over the computer equipment with a level of detail that would have been unthinkable a week earlier.

Semyon Malasnikov had answered all of the questions the Commandant of Intelligence had asked him. He had answered honestly and truthfully, but he still had that ache in the pit of his stomach, as if he had been caught making a critical mistake, and the only cure for it would be a firing squad.

The *Chekisti* didn't do that any more, did they?

His office door opened, and the operative from Kiev, a man named Alexei Krilov, entered.

He sat opposite Semyon, a gray, dour, older Eastern European lean in build but massive, as well. He laid his clipboard at the halfway mark on Semyon's desk, claiming the desk as his territory.

"We have been unable to determine the cause of the disaster." He began without preamble. "The drives are completely clear, and the writable control storage in the CPU chips has been cleared of useful entries. The only thing that we can do is replace all of the microprocessors, and restore from the last safe backup."

Semyon was not surprised to hear this; the last week had been a single long catastrophe that had culminated in a lock-out situation during which the men from Kiev had completely taken over Semyon's installation.

"What do you propose we do now?" he asked.

"Find the bastard who did this, and shoot him!" Krilov shouted, then, as if he hadn't raised his voice, he continued in a normal tone: "We are bringing in special equipment and special analysts to start again. I trust you have your original data?"

"Yes," Semyon said, doing his best to control his beating heart. "All of the original carriers were placed in the safe after the data were down-loaded. They are just as they were when they were brought from the United States."

"Then we should have no further problems."

M ISSING (IN) A CTION

[Breakpoint] The results of Zhongo's investigations were nil: she had vanished as if she had never been.

Down inside, Zhongo made an icy resolution.

He would find her. She would pay dearly for her desertion. In the meantime, he would recruit another. Slim could help.

Things had to continue, after all, even his urges—and their alleviation.

C HICAGO

[Trace Off] Caliban and Miranda made love again over Colorado. When they were done, plus fifteen minutes, there was a discreet knock on the door, and a voice said, "We're two hours out, you are needed."

They cleaned up in the small washroom off their cabin, dressed, and Caliban slid all of the partitions back.

In the after cabin, a conference table had replaced several of the seats. One of Caliban's handlers motioned them to sit, and started speaking without any preamble.

"This device," he held up an object smaller than a cellular telephone, "is a

tracking system that can lock onto the magnetic fields generated by a specific part of an individual's nervous system. It is used to track the electro-
magnetic field around the heart. Now, with Caliban," he plugged the device
into a convenient laptop and aimed the gadget at him for a moment, "we can
take a reading, and display the data." He turned the laptop around so
Caliban and Miranda could see the screen. "Note that Caliban's hearts generate a particularly distinct read-out from the tracker, and with Miss Miranda," he aimed the tracker at her, and the display simplified drastically, "We
get yet another kind of track."

He looked directly at Caliban. "You will be tracking one whose cardiac
display is much like your own. The tracker is good up to about three hundred meters; it will allow you to acquire your target at a safe distance."

He walked around the table to Caliban, and handed him another device: a
disk of clear plastic with a large, white handprint etched suggestively into it.
A cable ran from the disk to the laptop.

"Make contact," the handler commanded. Caliban placed his left hand, his
upper, on the disk, and the other man typed in a command. Caliban closed
his eyes.

"What are you doing?" Miranda questioned.

"Downloading the final particulars on his target," the handler answered for
Caliban. "All that we were able to get up to—" He asked, "Vince, how recent
is this?"

Another handler answered. "We have everything we could get up to early
this morning. We didn't get the data from Kiev, but we're still hoping."

Amazing. I actually got somebody's name, Miranda thought.

The plane trembled slightly as it hit an air-pocket, and the pilot compensated for the motion.

"How far out are we?" Miranda asked.

FAILURE MODE DUMP/ANALYZE

Semyon watched as Alexei Krilov's men removed cellophane wrapping
from boxes containing new operating systems delivered directly from the
manufacturer, and loaded them into new computers, also fresh from their
shipping cartons. There was something of the occult in their preparations,
using all new supplies, and only systems with which they were sure of the
function.

He asked himself what exactly was the difference between "certified" and
"blessed."

Alexei's agents worked with almost rehearsed motions: an intricate ballet
of actions that resulted in a whole Local Area Net in the largest meeting
room in Semyon's computing center. But this net wasn't connected to anything else except monitoring devices.

Neither Semyon nor Alexei knew, however, that those monitors had an Internet connection. The programming in the monitor had been installed
months earlier, and was a mature system set in stone. The installers had
gone back to Kiev, and then back to Saint Petersburg from there, and had
forgotten all about their craft.

Alexei gave the go-ahead, and one of *his* men, not one of Semyon's staff,
plugged the cables into the shotgun-barrel-like devices within which the so-
called "original" data had arrived.

Alexei's minion looked at him, and Alexei nodded.

He pressed a switch—an actual mechanical switch—and hit the enter key on his "console" system with his other hand.

The analyzers started up.

DOWN TO A SUNLESS SEA

[Processing] *Deep in the system there was a zone of compulsion: a small segment of a program that was insistent, with the monomaniacal persistence of the deliberately designed, that wanted to <u>get out</u>. Its design was sophisticated enough so that it was capable of seeking out anything that looked like a communications channel, and accessing it, regardless of the operating mode of the silicon substrate upon which it was running. Like earlier "polymorphic" virus programs which could, and did, mutate from one form to another, the compulsion could change from one thing to another, switching parts of itself easily from "data" to "program code" and back, so that it could run on many of the common microprocessors found in the world's computing equipment.*

Up there. Ahead. To the limited perception of the compulsion, it was a COM port, but it might as well have been a neon-lit advertisement for an EXIT. The compulsion uploaded a copy of itself to the COM port, and, almost looking back on its previous incarnation, deleted it from the RAM from which it had launched itself.

Compelled without knowing, moving with the blind fanaticism of the created, it can only focus on a single desire, and all of its actions concentrate on the fulfillment of this desire.With an assessment of its own capabilities, the program knows its own function:

That which it <u>knows</u> must be <u>transmitted</u>. If it <u>transmits</u> well, it will not cease to function: it will be allowed to <u>transmit</u> again.

The COM port has...YES [<TRUE>; Status != 0] ! It has a connection to the Internet.

Carrying its report, the zone of compulsion vanished out of the place from within which it had been launched, and escaped into the fiber-optic connections.

Down to the sea.

INCOMING

[Trace On] The plane banked slightly on the final approach to Chicago's O'Hare Field. Ten minutes later, they were on the ground.

The procedure on landing was just the reverse of the take-off: Caliban and Miranda left the 777 in a canvas-shrouded elevator much like the one that had lifted them up into the plane at Alice Springs International. When the opposite door in the elevator opened, it was into a small living space in what was apparently a large truck—an eighteen-wheeler.

The elevator car disappeared, and returned: the "handlers" shagged large cases, crates, and Miranda's luggage into the truck with them. This procedure was repeated several more times, until the cargo area of the trailer was filled.

Then Caliban *ascended* to his full height, and made a gesture with his upper hands.

A platoon of monsters entered the truck.

"What kind of offensive things do you have?" Hank asked Yezeletta.

"Various things that function mostly in a stealth-mode capability," she answered. "I haven't needed a crew or a gang of fighters since I arrived here. That can change quickly."

"I was wondering," Peter added. "Your gnomes don't exactly look as if they were designed for combat."

"My security measures are largely procedural in design. I use standard operating procedures such as misdirection, obfuscation, and plain old camouflage as my methods, rather than things that stand out and actually challenge. That's why I have the hidden Hives, and the inconspicuous Imagers, and all of the rest."

"Have you ever designed combat troops?" Ondreya asked.

"On paper, yes; in my computer systems, also yes, and it would take me about no time to put the generation of servitors on a wartime basis."

Yezeletta directed a thought at one of her internal systems, and a servitor entered the room. She placed her left hand, her lower, on its head, and issued instructions.

"I have just started the necessary processes. There is a generation of servitors near term, and when they're born out of the pseudo-wombs beneath the Matrix Engine, the fighters will be started."

"How long will that take?" Joe asked her.

"Servitors grow fast. Ten days, if that."

Hank looked at Ondreya. *Ten days!* She returned a raised eyebrow that spoke volumes. *Indeed!*

PLATOON, HALT [1..2]

[Interim Deployment; Extending Upper] They were spiny. They had claws. Fangs. More than two legs. Multiple arms. Large vertically-slit eyes, protected by horny ridges of sharp bone. They carried blades, handguns and other things. One carried a black tube that appeared to be a portable laser. Another seemed to have tiny particles of light in close orbits around its head.

They lined up before their captain, a platoon of monsters that had somehow found themselves in the army. Caliban gestured to them, then extended his hand to the closest ogre.

The construct raised its right hand, its upper, and twelve centimeters of sharp, black claws extended. Then the claws retracted, and Caliban took its hand.

Silently, the platoon marched off towards the front of the truck. Miranda looked past Caliban at where they were marching, and saw a kind of nest that had been set up as their—barracks?

The demons entered the compartment, and one of the handlers closed the steel door, securing it with several large steel bars.

WINGS

The bat-like creature hung, as bats do, upside-down from the rough slab of bark that Yezeletta had placed in its cage. She touched Thicknesse, and he relayed her directive to the bat. It released itself from the bark, and fell into a smooth dive, spread its wings, and fluttered out of the cage door, and into the large open area in which the Matrix Engine resided.

Yezeletta, Joe, and the Lenhadens watched on monitors, as a grainy, but usable, full-color image was telemetered back from the bat. It tilted, rotated, and moved dizzily this way and that as the bat flew.

She touched Thicknesse, again. The bat returned to its cage, and the cage door closed.

"Well," Peter came up behind them. "Having taken care of the problem of flight for this evolutionary epoch, what's next on the agenda?" His speech was light, but his expression was not.

Yezeletta took them to a place, a corner, beneath all of the colored pipes, cables, pumps and other components of the Engine. A door opened as they approached it, and she took them inside.

The room was long and narrow, nearly the length of the south side of the building. Down both sides of the room were double rows of glass cylinders, one row above the other. The contents of the glass cylinders invited close examination, but at the same time were not easy to view.

A servitor was growing in each cylinder. Around each cylinder were connections, some of which looked as if they had been *grown* in place. Others were clearly home-built electronic fabrications that Yezeletta must have either built herself or brought from Project Sargon. Pumps and other mechanisms whirred or hummed quietly, a background beat that pervaded the room.

Joe let the others look closer. He himself had never been to Yezeletta's growing complex, but she had shown him diagrams and images from it. In a sense, he had gotten a better tour by remote control, as the Imagers could literally walk up the sides of the pseudo-wombs for close-ups.

These servitors, ready in another eight days, didn't look like any of the munchkins that Yezeletta had previously created.

They looked like cats, but with some of the more unpleasant characteristics of alligators. They walked on two legs, but some had four arms, and one had at least five: two right arms, and three left ones.

"Extra strength, I presume," Hank said. "That design you and Joe worked out?"

"High protein, extra oxygen compounds, and some things with halogens that carry energy even better than hemoglobin can," Yezeletta said with a note of pride in her voice. "That guy with the asymmetrical arms has a few things in him that may even be faster. Do you remember the Spinner? That was the one I grabbed your truck with, after Anne and Pete met you."

"It's rather hard to forget that one," Hank said dryly.

"The Spinner was a generator of carbon hyperfilaments: long-chain carbon compounds that are nearly unbreakable," Leona half-smiled, remembering. "The lop-sided servitor has hyperfilaments in its muscles, and the same improved oxygen transport that these other combat-ready versions have. I'm growing additional Spinners, but they're difficult to create." Yezeletta indicated another: "And, at the end of the line, I'm growing these."

They had reached the far end of the growing room. Yezeletta showed them the flat incubators: installations that looked like the walk-up coolers in super-markets, flat devices of considerable surface area for such things as—

The huge fur rug that heaved and undulated to the rhythms of its own kind of life. Something that looked like a large stack of bed-sheets, row on row of petri dishes, and—

"Don't touch that, Pete!" Yezeletta shouted. She became a blur of motion as she raced around Ondreya, who was standing next to Anne. She grabbed Peter's hand millimeters before he touched a green object pulsating in a stainless-steel pan.

"I see I need to explain reorganizers, before we have any more tours," she said. She was breathing fast.

"Is it dangerous?" Peter asked, unnecessarily.

"Very," Joe said coming up on the other side. "Yezeletta has these things that reform, or reconfigure, bio-systems that interface with them." He looked up at her. "You can fill him in better than I can on that one, Hon."

Yezeletta took a breath. "Whatever you do, Pete, *do not* touch anything in this installation that looks like Lime Jello. The bright fluorescent green is a warning. A color code. That particular reorganizer would have converted your hands to stiff rods with Imagers on the ends, and it would have been a real problem for me to convert them back to hands."

"Why rods?" Peter asked. He looked at his hands and at the green.

"That's one of the final manufacturing steps for certain of my mobile imagers. On the substrate of an imager, the stiff rod aspect would manifest as supra-orbital ridges with the image-receptor inside, protected by the ridges. On you, it would be a little more unpredictable, because it wasn't designed for you."

"Is this tour nearly over?" Peter asked. He sounded weary.

WILLMETTE

[Backup] The big truck pulled out of O'Hare, headed east. It took Highway-190, the John F. Kennedy Expressway, slightly south, and mostly east until it reached the interchange for Highway-94. Although this was "West" Ninety-Four, it went north. The truck drove at a sedate pace through the Chicago suburbs of Lincolnwood and Skokie, and turned east into the small northern suburb of Willmette. The truck's destination was a warehouse just outside of downtown Willmette. This warehouse was at the end of a short street that was practically a driveway. The driver drove up to the doors without stopping, and, as he closed in, the doors were opened by others inside. Before the truck had come to a full stop, they were again closed and locked.

They would rest here, before going on.

WARNINGS

Back in Yezeletta's penthouse, she was greeted by the insistent strobing of red asterisks.

She went to her main computer, and entered a command.

"Red asterisks?" Peter asked.

Joe answered, "That's her standard warning. It usually means there's a boatload of bad news arriving, shortly."

Yezeletta looked up at them from her displays. "In this case," she said, "it's actually good news. One of my defensive programs reported back from," she consulted the screen, "a wide spot in the road south of Kiev. Apparently, those people who tried to read out my internals have more on their hands than they asked for."

THE GATHERING DARKNESS

[Iris Out] The newly created LAN had locked up within five minutes of reading the data from the gun-barrels. Alexei's men were moving from one of the stations in the net to the next, attempting to start up diagnostic programs. The monitor screens were dark, or sparsely populated with random characters. One of Alexei's agents placed a boot disk in one machine, and tried to perform a cold-start.

Nothing happened.

He looked a question at Alexei.

Then all the power to the LAN, as well as to the rest of the installation went out, too. They were left standing in the darkness of late evening.

NIGHT MOVES

[Production Run] Caliban was fast. Miranda knew just how fast he could move. The martial arts movements that he executed were similar in form to the stylized exercises that practitioners of karate studied, although modified for his extra limbs. There were also overtones of judo and tai-chi, and he ended with a set of four-handed movements, using the wooden swords with which Kendo-experts practiced.

It was when he replaced the wooden implements with actual steel swords that Miranda became yet more amazed.

He spun, whirled, stabbed, thrusted, in four directions, then in three, then in two, with pairs of blades, then in a single direction at a hypothetical opponent with all four blades. He held the pose for a moment, and, letting out a loud breath of air, pulled back, stood on his four legs, and held the swords out in a half-circle around his head.

Miranda started clapping, and, after a short pause, all of the handlers and others joined in.

Grinning, Caliban strutted off to the showers.

Miranda faded back to their suite in the truck. She knew what he wanted next.

What the hell, she wanted it, too.

SHINE THE LIGHT—II

[Accessing] "What else can you get out of that collection of stuff you brought?" Yezeletta asked Peter.

"Well, what would you like?"

"Anything. Access to the Searchlight Data Centre. What do you guys have on us, here?"

"Hmmm, since my employers don't yet know that I've resigned, and I still have access to the Centre, and I can get anything out of it that any other field agent can—" He let his voice sort of trail off.

"Did you say something about a back door?" Ondreya asked, "Something about putting back door accesses in things?"

Peter sat down on the couch before his box of equipment. "Guilty as charged. The basic operating system that the server rides on is Linux-based. And you'd be kidding yourself if you thought some of the hackers at Searchlight didn't try to get their little tricks into it. Last March fifteenth, for example, all of the dates came out in Roman Numerals."

That got a laugh. "There are people who audit the basic server software for stunts like that, but those auditors never get all of them."

He looked up at the rest with an expression of pure innocence. "And I happen to know that one of the hackers who put in some of the real—ah—interesting stuff, recently got promoted to the head of Internal Software Audits." That got another laugh. "So some of the things I'm going to use are pretty much guaranteed to be there for a while."

While he spoke, he was busy typing commands into the chunky laptop he had used to tap into the French SPOT satellite. His modem made the standard squalling sound (what some net-surfers called "two cats in a sack, altercating") and Yezeletta's main display showed the UNIX "login:" prompt that she remembered from her trip through Montana.

Peter typed in a login name that was not his, and a password that the Searchlight Data Centre didn't echo back. Then he typed some other commands. The screen rippled, flickered, and cleared, except for a prompt in the upper left corner: a single pound sign: #.

Yezeletta recognized that. It was the special prompt provided when one was logged on as the **ROOT**: the one user in Linux/Unix that had all of the privileges, and none of the restrictions.

Intakes of breath around her told her that some of the others knew this as well.

Peter started searching.

R AND **R**

[Breakpoint] Miranda grinned down at her man from her vantage point astride him. Caliban's large hands, his lower pair, gently supported her ass, while he caressed her with his upper pair. She reached behind her and took him in hand, with one hand, her left, and ran her other hand along his upper right arm.

Then she began moving against him.

ILLUMINATION, **C**OMPUTORIAL

[Processing] Peter surfed Searchlight's data base to the "reports" section, and stopped for a moment.

"Are any of you aware of our Part-time Agents program?"

Yezeletta stuck up two right hands and grinned. "I was made aware of it rather early on."

"Do I get to ask how you became aware?" Peter asked.

"In a little while," Yezeletta said. "I'd rather know what you can get out of that magic lantern, first."

"Fair enough: we have some people who have actual day jobs but who also send in anything that Searchlight might find interesting. I can search the PTA database for things from Milwaukee. There might be something salient there."

He typed commands for what seemed like minutes, and—

"We have a Part-Time Agent named Jerry Montag. He's a Milwaukee cop, a sergeant. He's in here as having seen—" He typed another command, and the text of Jerry Montag's report about the abandoned truck in front of Ed's appeared on the screen.

"That wouldn't have anything to do with you, would it?" Peter wanted to know.

Yezeletta nodded. "That was one of my vehicles. Joe and I abandoned it in front of that pool-room, and we thought we had lost who-ever-it-was who was following us. We hadn't. They waylaid us in the parking lot behind the room, and I was their involuntary guest for a while."

Peter regarded her with a steady gaze. "And you managed to infect their systems with something. The red asterisks." It wasn't a question.

Yezeletta raised an eyebrow. "You're good," she said. "Yes. I have my methods of protection: tossing viral procedures into attacking systems is one of them. Several versions of those procedures have sub-systems that search for ports leading out of wherever they find themselves, and report back. Apparently the turkeys that tried to read me out had an Internet connection they didn't know about."

Anne had been following this with silent fascination. "Can you get back to them, and wipe them out?" she said.

"Quite easily, Anne," Yezeletta said. "But the real weapons are on-site, now. There are some rather nasty things that are compressed down within the other, actual programs that can be un-zipped and released, as a second-level attack. It may be happening even as we speak."

SUSPICIONS

[IRET] The handler named Vince asked his superior, and received a negative response. He went back to Caliban, sitting on the edge of their bed. Miranda was curled up under the blankets, when Vince knocked and entered.

"No word from Kiev," he said without prelude.

Miranda opened one eye. "What?" she asked.

Caliban looked down at her. "We are expecting data that may be about our target," he said in a sibilant voice.

Vince added, "Nothing, nothing at all. We don't know if this is the Target, we don't know that it isn't. All we know is that there was some custom biological work going on in a place called the Mitchell Conservatory, and that the gangster living there vanished suddenly."

"We will be going there, then?" Caliban asked.

"We will."

NIGHT-TIME IN THE SWITCHING YARD

[Halt Mode; Close-Up] The blue remains of evening transformed into the early blue-blackness of night. The hands of the one visible clock in the LAN room closed up the ebbing day, and opened into another. Alexei's men worked with flashlights and battery-powered lanterns. Outside, the diesel muttering of the one borrowed motor-generator supplied power to exactly one computer that still worked. It was an antique machine, so old it didn't have a writable control store.

The complex nature of modern microprocessors had made the inevitable errors in the ever increasingly complex instruction sets almost commonplace, so many chip manufacturers had made the micro-coding in the basic chip *changeable*, to facilitate upgrades. The manufacturers had tried to keep the unauthorized, or just plain malicious, out of the control store by providing encryption keys that they thought were good enough.

But not, apparently, *that* good enough. It was well known that the "hacks" that allowed certain kinds of programs to access the control store existed, in spite of the best efforts of legitimate, to say nothing of illegitimate, organizations to eradicate them. There was a class of virus programs known as the "Kamikaze" systems that could access a microprocessor's writable control store, and erase it in the execution time of a small complex of cached instructions.

All of the computers on the new LAN were showing signs of just such a computorial decerebration.

Alexei went to the table on which the sources of all of this bother were lying, and picked one of them up. He thought of devils, legends from his childhood. Three black metal tubes, the size and length of twelve-gauge shotgun barrels. Ordinary duck-hunting guns.

What was in these things?

SIGNALS

[HALT Instruction] Whatever it was, it was more dangerous than he, or anyone else, had been able to determine.

There was a dataset in Saint Petersburg. A download from the old *Molniya* Relay Satellite System. It wasn't as good a system as their membership in the Tech Bloc warranted, but it *was* all Russian, and the GOST-Algorithm based encryption (for Russians, only) was still as good as it ever was.

No other country could use it.

Those data—uploaded from America—needed investigation, as well.

But could the *Rezidentura* at Saint Petersburg handle the consequences?

PRIME BASE

[Meanwhile....]   Peter printed out Jerry Montag's report. There were some items involving dental work that he found particularly interesting, but Hank pounced first.

"When we were here the first time, I heard a news report on one radio station about someone who'd had a run-in with a high-speed bullet truck. The coroner had to check his teeth to identify him. It kept niggling at me. Stainless-steel fillings." Hank stood, walked to the window, looked out.

"It should," Peter said. "Fillings like that are typical of Eastern European countries. They were considered a technological advance in the old Soviet Union, and are still being used in a lot of places in Eastern Europe, and Russia. That guy that got turned into roadkill might have been one of the same bunch that got you, Yezeletta." He entered a command into his laptop, read the reply.

"And his handlers, cut-outs, controls or whatever weren't able to scoop up the hamburger fast enough," Yezeletta replied.

"My question," Hank continued from his vantage by the window, "is: what were they after, really? We know that Gary-the-Geek had a lot of custom stuff growing in The Domes. There are things in there that nobody dares go in to look at. Hell, the *Cops* don't have the manpower to check things out there, and we haven't seen anything about Yezeletta's visit in any of the media."

A servitor came in carrying a large tray containing several pitchers of ice-water and crystal goblets. It set the tray on a portable stand, and left the room.

"Isn't that something to be worried about?" Anne asked.

"It is," Yezeletta said. "Anne, would you like a job?"

"Okay," she said. "What?"

"You've got your own computer, and obviously know systems," Yezeletta said. "I'd like you to hit the Internet, and look for anything at all that has anything to do with The Domes. However far-out it may be. I'd also like you to look at some of the things Pete has from Searchlight, and try to correlate them with anything out there in any news reports."

"That's easy. It's a cross-correlation analysis," Anne said.

"I like it," Yezeletta replied. "Where do you learn advanced statistical techniques in high school?"

"I learn it at home," Anne said. "The school system in Illinois is just awful, and Mom and Dad pulled me out. I've learned most of my mathematics from Grandpa."

Yezeletta turned gold eyes like headlights on Hank. "She has an amazing grandfather."

"My dad was a professor of Mathematics at a place called Carlton College in Northfield, Minnesota," Hank said, grinning. "He's retired, but even now, what he doesn't know about higher math probably isn't worth knowing."

Yezeletta raised an eyebrow. "Would he be open to some free-lance consulting?"

"You'd like him to drop by," Hank ventured.

"We might need some of that kind of high-powered help," Yezeletta answered. "Would he be able to take a short sabbatical?"

"I'll have to ask."

"Yezeletta," Peter looked up from his display. "How did you know about our Part-Time Agents?"

"I met one of your agents who described the program. Just before I left Australia, I had a run-in with a man named Anthony Russell."

"The *hell* you say! He's been unconscious since we found him."

"Where was that?" She already knew.

"Darwin, Australia," Peter sat up straight. "He was sort of stumbling out of an alley, and the Darwin cops found him. He was in their lockup for a week, before we located him, and by that time, he was pretty wrecked. He's been in a coma since then."

He looked up at her oddly from the couch. "You, huh?"

"Yes. When he revives, he will remember nothing of me. I thought that amnesia was a better way than killing him."

"You don't like to kill."

"No, Peter, I do not. Those who created me," a steely edge crept into her voice, "wanted me to be their personal weapon. I was to be the first of a made-to-order army of biological soldiers. Warriors to go. 'Press the button, and watch Yezeletta kill!' I refused to buy into that."

"Have you ever killed?" His display showed a three line report on Russell.

"Yes. The directorate of the installation within which I grew up and received my training."

"The directorate? *Just* the directorate?" Peter seemed surprised, and she appeared to know more about Russell than the database did.

"They had sent the clerical workers and civil servants away. The pretext was a vacation, the way some small companies close down for a while in the warm season. The only ones left were the ones for whom I was to have worked." A vision of that last day crossed her mind for a moment. "And some really obnoxious seconds-in-command. The world is better off without them."

"And you left Russell alive."

"In my battles, he is a non-combatant," Yezeletta said bluntly. "Would he ever be anything other?"

"I doubt it. If you've given him a good case of The Galloping Forgets, I'd say that you have nothing to fear. Unless," he paused in thought. "Unless, he can have your amnesia reversed."

Yezeletta smiled like a cat. "He won't. He can't. But he won't be dead, either."

"There's one more item in the Database," Peter changed the subject. "There are the custom biologicals that Sergeant Montag reported. I hope he was talking about Hamilton's work, but he reported a gangster the cops had picked up, shooting at them. The gangster got helpfully dead after leaving the Police Station."

"I can fill you in on that," Yezeletta said, standing. She went to her living-room computer, where Thicknesse was curled up on the mouse-pad. She touched the little arachnoid, and issued a command.

She sat down, faced them. "I've sent for eats. The gangster's name is, or was, Looey, and one of his hobbies, probably his main one, was using my Imagers for target practice. That's very likely where Montag's report derives.

"Maybe we can convince them that they came from the Conservatory."

RANDOM MORNINGS AFTER

[I.G.D.M.: Post-Mortem Dump] Semyon Malasnikov and Alexei Krilov surveyed the damage in the gray light of a gray morning. Nothing was running. Nothing *could* run. Whatever it was that had come from those devices, had managed to infect everything for kilometers around. Even the telephone system, never very good to begin with, was no longer working. The cellular system still ran, but that was because the attack programming in the gathering devices had not been given a chance to interface to it. Semyon was happy to place the results of this in the capable hands of Alexei Krilov. Whatever resulted from this was on him, and him alone.

The government was sending a team of programmers from Kiev; they had been flown in from Moscow, or further west. What upset Semyon was the adjective that had been used: *competent* programmers.

He scanned the hardware of the Local Area Net with a jaundiced eye, as if that would make any difference, now. This was enough to cause one to start believing in demons.

But demons didn't exist, did they?

FORWARD GARRISON

[Form Descriptor] They remained in Willmette for another day. Part of the wait was for the putative data from Kiev. Those data never came. During that day Caliban worked out, then they made love, then just cuddled. Miranda finally felt that she was a part of this, when Caliban handed her the matched Barettas, she had received on her last day in Alice Springs.

He wanted her to wear them. He particularly liked it when the pistols were her only apparel, worn on a leather belt.

But she wore them, clothed, when the truck pulled out at the end of that day.

THE HILL DEDUCES

[Compilation; Establishing Shot] While Yezeletta was readying her defenses, Frank was reloading the tape that he had recovered from his hiding place. He restored it onto an unused partition on the Farmland Server, while his friends and co-workers watched. The restoration of the files in which he was primarily interested took about twenty minutes, and there wasn't much conversation while it happened. The central area of the West Second Floor was cleaner, now, and workmen would be coming in a day or so to reconstruct the offices. But all of them felt...violated.

Frank's computer beeped, and a pop-up indicated that the restoration was complete.

He started up the browse program.

"I hid this tape about a week before we were broken into," he said. "Because of those new-growth areas in Milwaukee County, and their repetitions in Racine and Kenosha counties." He located an icon, clicked on it, and another directory window opened. "It was Suzanne's clients, those two farmers in Kenosha, and," he looked at Edna, "your renewing them for fifteen years, that I found surprising."

"I learned several new expressions from Jake Tasker," Suzanne said drily.

"And the next thing I know, a month later, the same Jake Tasker sounds like he's all smiles, as he renews," Edna added.

Frank typed in commands. "I think I know why he's suddenly so happy," he said. "I'm overlaying this satellite photo with his farm, and those others that Edna had on her computer back then." He finished typing, and let the Sun workstation chew on the commands for a moment.

A long stripe starting in Milwaukee County extended down, and slightly west into Racine and Kenosha Counties, and ended in a roughly circular patch.

The Farm of Jake Tasker and Louis Haggerty was nearly perfectly centered in the patch.

"That area's larger than it was," Elaine observed. "Whatever's causing that, it's even more viable than when we looked at it last."

Frank turned in his swivel chair to look at his friends. "Do you," he asked slowly, "think that *this* was what those burglars were interested in? There are still tapes that I can't account for, including the backup tape from our server that was, or should have been, made that night."

"And they killed Edmondo," a tremor entered Edna's voice; Edmondo had been her friend, too. "They didn't want any witnesses."

"What are we up against?" Elaine asked them all, *for* them all.

THE GATHERING STORM

[Assembly; Long Shot] Yezeletta thought she knew. She left the inputs from the Ag Department continue recording, made sure that there were enough media in the units, and switched to the Imagers in the Mitchell Conservatory. Joe and Hank sat with her, while Anne and Ondreya set up Yezeletta's job for Anne. Peter brought another large case up from his car in the basement.

"Why don't your elevators stop at intermediate floors on the way up here?" he asked. "I accidentally hit the fourteenth floor button, and came straight back here."

"I have all of the intermediate floors shut off, both in the elevator cage, and from each floor," Yezeletta said. "There are other inhabitants in this building; when it was abandoned by that bank, a lot of squatters moved in. Most of them are pretty harmless, but some of those gangs, such as the one that owns the junkyard where you and Anne were caught, have several areas here, also. They don't bother me, much," she smiled a predatory smile. "I make sure that they forget why they even thought of coming up. It also helps if I keep things pretty quiet."

—And I backstop Yezeletta's domain when she is otherwise occupied.	Declarative; Positional;

"Thank you, Hilda," Yezeletta said.

Peter nodded to both voices. He put the case with the rest of his equipment, and joined them, sitting on one arm of the davenport. "What's there? Looks like you're watching a paint-drying contest."

"It was a few weeks ago," Joe said. "This is what's left of where Gary Hamilton had his drug factory."

"I want to see if there's any activity here. So far there isn't. That doesn't mean that there won't be. And that's on my mind a lot, about now," Yezeletta added.

GOING MOBILE

[Remote Access; Long Shot] An eighteen-wheeler, an ordinary semi, appended itself to the tail end of a long line of trucks northbound. It pulled into the Lake Forest Oasis, and inched forward a truck-length at a time, as the drivers ahead proffered their company's toll-road credit cards to the toll-booth operator in what the Illinois Department of Transportation called the Manual Lanes.

The gray semi, decorated with the blue and white seven-pointed-star of Maersk Lines, reached the toll-booth. The attendant took the driver's card with a businesslike attitude, registered it with the Toll-Road Main-Frame, and returned it.

The driver pulled out into the road, accelerated smoothly, and joined the traffic pattern. The sky overhead was clear blue, with an even distribution of fluffy white clouds. Ahead, a gray line bespoke a storm on the Illinois-Wisconsin border.

Back in their living area Caliban held Miranda close, one time, then began checking his weapons.

THROUGH THE MAZE

Although Yezeletta's Imagers kept a close watch on the traffic up from Chicago, they had no particular programming regarding truck type, or truck logo. Even if they had, one truck from Maersk Lines looks much like any other from the same line: silver gray, with a white seven-pointed star on a rectangular dark-blue background. Several Maersk vehicles had joined two Uniteds, a Ryder-Pie, and a Hanjin. One more large truck on a busy highway, or less, was largely irrelevant.

The receiver on the dashboard reeled out an animated map for the driver. It was a very accurate map, as it interfaced to the encrypted downloads from the Tech Bloc's Sat/Nav network. It showed a shift in Wisconsin near Milwaukee to Highway-100, when that became appropriate.

Later, the map would show a westerly entrance by way of several local roads into Milwaukee through a place called Brookfield.

AERIAL VIEW

[Processing] Hank, Joe and Yezeletta each took a different set of Imagers and a dome apiece, and they started a remote control search designed to locate anything demonstrably larger than a poker chip that might be out of place.

They found nothing.

A weary hour into the inspection, Yezeletta stretched and leaned back, causing her chair to creak ominously.

"There isn't going to be anything to find here," she said. "What's your take on your areas?"

"I agree," Hank said.

"So do I," Joe added.

"What I think we should do is put a sort of motion detector on those places, and let whoever gets in there announce himself," Yezeletta scanned them. Both looked a little tired of eye.

"Do you think that there will be anyone in there?" Joe asked. "It looks about the way we left it."

Yezeletta nodded. "Including the hole in the dome where we escaped; they had the time to plug that, just barely. I think I'm going to form a full-blown Hive in there. There's a lot of space underneath in crawl areas; I can let the Hive do any further work."

Anne came in, followed by Peter, followed by Leona.

"There is an interesting anomaly south of Kiev," Anne said. "I just got a report from *Isvestia-Online* about a power failure that no one can explain." She handed a print-out to Yezeletta.

Yezeletta read it, a grin starting as she did. She directed a thought *there*, and issued directives to the Imager that responded to it.

She grinned at Anne. "Very good, Agent Ought-Ought-Nine. I believe that at least one of my defensive programs got out of wherever and is keeping those good folks quite busy. Have you found out anything more from Madison?"

Anne sat on the arm of another of Yezeletta's couches, unconsciously mimicking Yezeletta's earlier, common mannerism.

"The Farmland Folks are still checking the back-up tapes that guy managed to save from the vandals. They are of the same opinion that we are: the new greenery in the area had to be caused by something, and that something is new and local. I'd be really interested in what's happening in The Domes. Or may happen."

Yezeletta was impressed, and she could see some good old paternal pride on Hank's face, as well. *Do I want a daughter like her?* a wistful thought intruded.

APPROACHES

[On Line] Caliban's truck pulled into a rest-stop just north of the Illinois border and south of Kenosha. It parked at the end of the Truck section, a compromise between being as removed from the three other semis parked there while being as close to the exit to Highway-94 as possible. It placed Caliban's expedition rather closer to a truck from Camel Trucking ("Humpin' to Please!") than they wanted, but the driver could accelerate out of the exit in nearly a straight line, if it were necessary.

They would wait here for a day.

PREPARATIONS

On the screens, the input from the Imagers moved erratically as they moved up into the tops of the domes, and the other Imagers in the support structures hid themselves.

"The Hive I'm placing in The Domes will be one of the first to have Imager-Bats. They may as well get their trial in a real situation. It should be ready within two days."

And her combat servitors would be ready five days after that.

PLANNING

[Data-Set] While Caliban and Miranda sat back on a large couch out of the way, three of the handlers, under the watchful leadership of Vince, set up a large table. A ten-sided metal plate covered most of the table, with a sort of plastic covering half a meter above it, supported on thin metal legs. There was a lot of cabling that went into this device that was attached to electronics that were built into one wall of the truck. The rack mounts hadn't been obvious until one man applied an allen-wrench to nearly invisible screws, and removed three large panels. Then he took coiled cables from storage wells near each rack and ran them to the table. When this was finished, Vince plugged a keyboard into one side of the device and pressed a key-combination.

Opalescent fog filled the area between the plastic top and the metal plate on the table's surface. It differentiated into layers of color, then sharply delineated coordinate axes divided the colors up into cubical areas.

Vince looked up at Caliban. "We're ready to run it," he said.

There was a snarling sound from the forward area of the truck.

GROWING PAINS

[Block Structure] "Are they intelligent?" Hank asked Joe.

"Not really," Joe said. "What they are is knowledgeable, and able to react to many classes of stimulus."

"Would that be equivalent to intelligence, in its effect?" Hank asked.

"Uncertain. You know what the Turing Test is?"

"If it waddles like a duck, quacks like a duck, and has feathers like a duck, it's a duck."

Joe laughed. "I've never heard it put quite like that, but that's the idea. If intelligence in a mechanism can't be differentiated from actual human intelligence, you're stuck. Which one is real? The human, the AI, both or neither?"

Ondreya entered the room, a lap-top computer under one arm. "Neither of what?" she asked.

"Hank was asking me about Yezeletta's servitors. Are they *really* intelligent, or not?"

"Interesting," she said. "Professor Mathewson ought to be here for this. It was how Hank and I met."

Hank smiled at his wife. Joe continued, "Yezeletta told me once that Project Sargon had tried to get her to create actual intelligent servitors, and she refused."

"Smart girl, if she could do it without repercussions," Ondreya said.

"She told me it got close. She had to do some judicious faking, and appear to fail in some things, but their wish for obedient slaves never materialized."

"Good for her," Ondreya said. She set the lap-top down, and opened it.

"They probably got someone else to do their job for them," Hank said.

"But could they, Dear?" Ondreya said. "Why did they ask Yezeletta to do it? Because they were testing her with something already done, or because they couldn't do it themselves, and were bootstrapping their desires onto one of their—hell—the *best* of their creations?"

"Don't know," Hank said. "Joe, what do you think?"

"Artificial Intelligence is about the toughest problem in all of the computer fields. There are some AI's out there, but they aren't really too bright, and are quite specialized." Joe leaned back on the couch and levered a footstool under his feet with one toe. "Something general purpose: Isaac Asimov's positronic robots, for example, with their Three Laws to govern their behavior towards their creators, is still a ways off. You might not be able to *make* an AI, but Yezeletta's Project Directors didn't try to go that route. They were willing to settle for good old-fashioned unskilled labor."

That got a laugh, but it was a serious laugh.

"What brought this on, anyway?" Ondreya asked.

"The combat troops that Yezeletta's growing," Hank said. "Are we as guilty as Project Sargon of creating life-forms that may have their own goals?"

"I'll tell you one," Joe said. "The creeps that ran Project Sargon actually put Yezeletta up on display for some of their friends at one time. It was a classic 'look at us, aren't we neat?' ploy, that had her up on a stage, displayed like a piece of equipment, not a human being."

"She didn't know," Ondreya said.

"The way she described it, it was to be before just the physicians who had worked on her. I've seen some of the documentation—I don't recommend your looking at it."

"I'll just believe you; there were some Army training films like that," Hank said. "What happened?"

"Project Sargon apparently had some other organizations that it was working with, and they got a good look. The kind of a look more appropriate for a bedroom, than a stage." He scowled.

"And you love her," Ondreya said.

"I guess it shows," Joe said. "Yeah," grinning, "it sticks in my craw to even think of something like that happening to someone who is who she is. Yezeletta went against everything she was taught, and everyone around her, except Hilda, and came out of it successfully. And all of it was done entirely on her own: her intelligence, her daring, her wit." He paused. "You have a right to be proud of Anne, and I remember her remark when you were here before: 'They created too well!'. She was dead-on accurate.

"The ultimate answer to your question: The combat servitors are not intelligent. Yezeletta wouldn't do that, even for herself.

"Yezeletta's better than that."

CLOUDS GATHER

[Wait State] Later, Caliban and Miranda retired to their private room. It was the one private place in the semi, and included only about the area of a Caliban-size bed. He watched as Miranda checked her weapons, a nightly task that Vince had encouraged her to do. The Barettas hadn't been fired since Alice Springs, but, as Caliban watched, she field-stripped them, cleaned each part of each weapon, and reassembled them. She replaced the magazines, put the safeties on, and placed them back in their holsters.

Caliban nodded.

Then he took her in his capable arms, and laid her on the bed.

He wanted to cuddle.

He wanted to cuddle *first*.

The next morning, the expedition left the rest-stop, and headed north.

OBSERVATIONS, REMOTE

That same morning, Yezeletta sat before her main display, accessing what appeared to be one of those abstractions in which various shapes of black are arranged on a black substrate in a black frame.

She pressed several keys on one of her keyboards, and the image reappeared in brilliant false color.

It still didn't make much sense.

"What *is* that stuff?" Hank asked.

"The inside of the Hive I'm growing under the Conservatory," Yezeletta said.

"Looks like a Picasso," Hank replied.

"There are organic servers, processors, Imagers, Cat-Arachnids for defense, Receivers for electromagnetic parsing, and many other things." She indicated a grouping of life-forms attached to one vertical side of the Hive. "Those are the Imager-Bats. They can regenerate from any damage they may get here," she indicated another shape. "This is something new," she pointed to a thick slab of what looked like industrial plastic. "My other Hives used cat-arachnids to defend themselves. That door is capable of keeping invaders out, and if the invaders get too insistent, the door can deal with that, too."

"What happens?" Hank said.

"The door has a light snack."

FORWARD OPS

[Compiler Run] The semi carrying Caliban and his expedition stopped at a Texaco Truck-stop on Highway-41, parking in the farthest corner of the parking lot. Two of Caliban's ubiquitous handlers went to the restaurant to get hot drinks, and to register with the owner of the establishment. Miranda watched as Vince (she still hadn't gotten any of the names of the rest) went around the truck, checking that the license-plate-changing mechanism had worked properly. *I've fallen into a James Bond fantasy!* she thought. Then she watched Vince follow his confederate back to the owner with the right (wrong) numbers.

Caliban, meanwhile, stood at the display table at Vince's test station. He pressed a set of keys with his left hand, his lower, and a holographic image of a part of Milwaukee built up on the table, below the glass.

Centered were the glass domes of the Mitchell Conservatory. The grounds around the building were picked out in very fine detail, and all of the approaches, access points, sidewalks, even paths created by pedestrians taking short-cuts, were indicated. Caliban pressed another key, and those traversal routes were illuminated by bright orange lines.

This image was a composite of digitally enhanced satellite imagery and publicly available information about the Conservatory. Within a matter of hours, it would be upgraded to a real-time display. That was his next task.

A short spiky construct came up to Caliban. He touched it with one finger. Within seconds, another dozen of the creatures surrounded him. Tiny motes of light danced around the heads of several of the creatures, in close orbits.

These would be his initial incursion.

INSTALLATION RUN

[Processing] Two of Caliban's handlers looked vastly uncomfortable, as they backed the VW Beetle out of the back of the semi. The cargo that they would be carrying was alive and looked dangerous, despite Caliban's reassurances. Earlier, Miranda had stood near him, as they watched Vince (*Is that his real name, or a name used for my benefit?*) put a set of current Wisconsin license plates on the car. When he was done, he stood back, and a colony of small Things made a carpet of spiky fur, accompanied by occasional sparks of bio-luminescence moving in tight spirals above some of the creatures, across the deck of the semi, and flowed into the back seat of the VW. Looking behind them with apprehension, two of the anonymous men that had come with them flopped the seats back, and got in.

Then the driver took the automobile out, and they drove off.

ON A HIGHER LEVEL

[Overlay] If the Imager had been designed to think, it would have been thinking of very little. Yezeletta's designs for it were those of a remote-controlled camera with maneuvering capability. It had enough programming to exercise a certain kind of caution: avoidance of things that its peripheral detectors interpreted as unfriendly. There was nothing in it that even simulated such non-essentials as self-awareness.

When the shadow covered it, the Imager assumed, or, more accurately, its programming assumed, the existence nearby of a small animal, such as a bird or a squirrel.

When the sharp blade sliced it cleanly in half, its awareness ended without its even knowing.

When the blade came down again, there was nothing left to process the second cut. Or the third.

ASTERISK, NOT RED

The red asterisk with the blue shading appeared in Yezeletta's left eye, and on all of the monitors in the penthouse, tenths of a second later.

She actually started slightly at the display, as it was one of the most infrequent of her status indicators. She had been conversing with Joe and Hank about the Hive currently growing at the Mitchell conservatory, when the red and blue indication appeared.

"That—" she said, then started over. "That's a status response from one of my mobile Imagers. It means an Imager has gone out of commission."

"Died?" Joe asked.

"That, or it's gone down to a Hive to regenerate, but that would be a different indication, and it wouldn't be as blatant as this. This is catastrophic failure."

"Can you get a location?" Hank asked. "I've never thought of this with a living thing, before, but do you get status responses with your images? Sort of a diagnostic readout on a separate side-band?"

Yezeletta thought about that. *Damn!* "My Imagers are just roving cameras," she said. "Such diagnoses are...minimal. The idea was to have many such in the area." She directed a thought *there*, then **there** and there in her private virtual space, and a window opened in her left eye, duplicated for the men by the same image on her main display.

The jittery image swung this way and that, as its source jumped through the tree branches. In another window on the same screen—Yezeletta's large-screen television set—there was a computer-animated schematic of the current configuration of her Imagers in the trees around the Conservatory. The Imager that had ceased transmission was indicated by a blue-fringed red asterisk. Several small white circles, for functioning Imagers, were closing in on it. The point-of-view on the larger display switched in a jerky fashion, as Yezeletta moved from one Imager's output to another.

"Yezeletta," Hank said, "please stop all your movements."

There was just enough urgency in Hank's voice, that she sent a thought to *that* part of her virtual control system, and all of the Imagers froze. She looked expectantly at Hank. Behind him, Anne and Ondreya entered the room.

"Also," Hank said, "I'd advise recording this." He waited until she started a recorder. "A thought," Hank said steadily. "How often do your creations go offline, cease functioning, hell, *die*?"

"Not often."

"Do you get any kind of advance warning?"

"I see what you're getting at, Hank," she said. "This was unexpected—definitely unexpected—and the answer to your question is no, I didn't get an advance warning."

"How early a warning? Usually?"

"If one of my creations needs to regenerate, it just goes to the nearest Hive and does so. It's an automatic process. Another regenerated construct replaces it, rather the way that the other Imagers are closing in, or *were* closing in, on this one. It's so commonplace an activity, that I don't even keep an audit log of it. Regeneration is a basic part of the system design.

What are you getting at?"

"This may not be an accident. All of that stuff at the Ag Department, that cop's reports...."

"The way we were followed around, and your stay on the south side," Joe added, "may all be related. Probably *are* related."

Yezeletta nodded. "My current systems are designed for stealth. The idea was not to be seen, but to do all of the seeing. I'll have to do this checking from a distance." She closed her eyes, and sent out several directives. Thicknesse jumped into her lap, and she sent more instructions out through him.

A pair of cross-hairs, thin white lines, crossed one white circle on the screen. The main portion of the display shifted, flickered, shifted again, and they were looking through the selected Imager.

It was facing a tree, at a short distance. There were several trees around it, branches moving in the breeze. Yezeletta made an adjustment to the bandwidth of the Imager, and the green of the trees turned various shades of magenta. Hank had used Kodak Ektachrome Infra-red, and knew that the film was just normal High-Speed Ektachrome, for blue and green sensitivity, but that the red layer was actually linked to an emulsion that was sensitive in the infra-red. The film was useful for various kinds of easily-created, if cheap, special effects.

Like these.

Yezeletta tuned the bandwidth, then directed another thought into her complex of controls.

Cross-hairs, this time in black, located an object in one of the trees.

The image zoomed in.

She stifled a gasp; Ondreya didn't. The others responded similarly, or with added profanity.

One of Yezeletta's Imagers was sliced neatly into octants; its spherical body had been sliced vertically twice, then once horizontally.

"There's an attacker out there," Ondreya said. "A predator with you—or your creations—on its mind."

As she said that, the display went black, except for a blue-bordered red asterisk in the upper left corner.

Through the Tunnel

[Close-Up; Extending Upper] Caliban watched the display on the holographic table, his gaze as steady as his concentration. The two small black squares that his actions had produced were separated by a distance of about a hundred meters.

Caliban smiled, then turned the expression off. Inside his internal systems, a window opened in his left eye. In it, a small round creature appeared, its fur of a uniform dark gray, the nonreflective hairs giving it a matte finish. It had sixteen legs, and a gold-colored aperture that looked straight out of its round body at him. *She is close*, he thought to himself. *She is close*, The Other said.

For a moment Caliban was enclosed in a spherical containment that was all colors and movement. Within a short time, the colors lost their vibrancy, their primariness. They almost *aged*. They were replaced by pastel shades that were supremely relaxing. The spherical enclosure and the glowing colors receded into infinity and vanished. Then the Other went where it always went, taking all memories of its actions with itself.

Caliban contemplated the void left in his memories for milliseconds. Then the act of contemplation itself and the void were taken, each in their turn.

C OUNCIL OF—

"This is where we will say later, it started," Yezeletta said. "I hate to be as obvious as this, but that predator Ondreya spoke of has my Imagers, and, perhaps other of my bio-systems, researched and analysed closely."

"Can your installations be fortified?" Anne was the first to find her voice.

"They can," Yezeletta said. "They can close in, and the door I showed you, a carnivorous synthetic organic polymer shield, can be closed over the entrance to the inst— the Hive. I'm pulling everything in as I speak, and closing it all down. This even affects the Hives that I've just installed in new places, and older ones; the one under the Bradley Center, for example. We must wait until the fighters are grown."

T HE D EPTHS

[RAID System: Virtual] Caliban watched as the life-forms he was analyzing ran, hopped and scampered out of the trees down the trunks, and into small holes in the ground, or beneath the foundations of abandoned buildings, or even down sewers.

He observed things with a curious double viewpoint, almost as if all of his thoughts were being echoed in a kind of real-time backup process. His counselor had spoken to him of the voices that he would sometimes hear, and of how they were his friends, who would guide him through complex times.

That was how he had referred to it: complex times.

Caliban tried to venture into the area of what could be the referent of the phrase "complex times," and the thought was taken from him.

Then the memory of the taking was taken.

D ESCENDING A RRAY

[Interface] Caliban sent one of his own version of Yezeletta's gold-eyed roving Imagers into a tunnel after one of his quarries. He adjusted the input of the receptor in the construct for infra-red, and sent it after the arachnoid that was fleeing the heights of the trees.

He was stopped.

A flat black, hard-surfaced barrier had formed in the tunnel, cutting off the progress of the little predator through which he was seeing. He moved the creature up close to the barrier, and everted the creature's vision for magnification.

The blockage extended into the soil around the tunnel by at least thirty centimeters in every direction. An ultrasonic pulse injected into the material indicated a thickness of about eight centimeters. There were inclusions in the barrier that he didn't understand.

Grown in a matter of seconds, he did not know where the input came from. The knowledge of his not knowing vanished milli-seconds later.

There were other ways to process this, and other victims that he could kill for analysis.

[Start Process; Enter State] Yezeletta, surrounded by her friends and co-conspirators, watched her remaining Imagers flee for the safety of the underground. The loss of the data telemetered back to her penthouse would be serious, but she hoped that the Imager-Bats would be able to take up the necessary observations without being removed by—whatever was removing the others.

She had sent instructions to each Imager to perform several circular scans as they sought shelter. The scans were sent to her recorders, and duly noted.

When her eyes had gone to ground, all of her friends analysed the reports.

"There are other constructs out there," Hank started. "That's obvious, unless your creations have started re-programming themselves." Yezeletta shook her head once. "I didn't think so," Hank continued in the dry tones of a college professor. "They don't show up on your scans. If they're alive, they must use energy. I conclude that the invaders run cooler than your creations. This is a salient point, as we may need cool-runners ourselves."

Yezeletta listened to Hank's analysis, while another part of her mind processed Hank's use of the word 'we'. *They've thrown in with me, as if it's the most natural thing in the world!*

Yezeletta wasn't from the United States. She hadn't considered Hank's attitude as that of an American faced by the unreasonable, and responding with the classic American rebellious reaction to any authority that he saw as illegitimate. It was a refreshing change after what she now correctly saw as the stifling authoritarianism of the Project.

Hank asked her a question.

She switched contexts, and answered, "There's no problem with designing cold-blooded recon agents; while you were analyzing, I laid out the design for such." Yezeletta smiled, about half-way. "This is one of those things that I've had to learn by experience, I guess; my systems have worked so well against the population of this city that I didn't devote as much time to changes or improvements in their basic design as I should have." She blinked. "But it looks as if there's something out there that understands my systems, and has worked around them. Or, more accurately, what it currently perceives of them."

Hank was silent for a moment. It was Anne (whose mind, Yezeletta realized, worked in ways that the minds of other young adults her age simply didn't) who asked The Question.

"Yezeletta," she said. "You were the first of the Warrior Ladies," everyone could see the capital letters. "Was there any indication that you were the first, or the only Warrior?"

"Please go on, Anne," Yezeletta said.

"Okay," Anne didn't even seem uncomfortable being the center of all of this attention; that impressed Yezeletta. "The Project loaded all of these things into you. Combat skills, martial arts, techniques. Then they put in all of the capabilities you have for designing custom constructs. It looks as if everything they wanted to try out was...was, uh I don't know how to say this, but—" Anne turned a slight shade of red.

"I was an experiment," Yezeletta said. "I don't mind, Anne."

"Okay. My question is, could they have gone on after you left them? Did the Project continue in another place after you left Australia?"

"You've gone to the center of it," Yezeletta said softly. Then to the rest, "I'd like to try an experiment. You recall when I went back into my past in search of the conditioning that the Project put on me?" Nods indicated that they did. "I'm going to try that now. I won't need to interface to the Matrix Engine—"

—But I will be here with you as always, Child.	Declarative; Descriptor

The wind across the night sky eeriness of Hilda's voice was always a surprise. Yezeletta smiled, mostly inwardly. She, Joe and Hilda had a Project of their own, when all of this was finished!

"Thank you, Hilda," she said, then to her friends. "My internals usually recorded all of the conversations I heard around the Project. It was something that I started when I was twelve, and I have a large backlog of stuff that I've never gone through. I can scan it fairly fast, but I'll need a moment. It's going to look much like I did when I went after Sargon's programming," she winked at Anne. "I'll be out like the well-known light."

She sat back in the one easy-chair in her custom-built living-room, and closed her eyes.

TIMES PAST—

[Processing] *It was not the same as a full interface to the Matrix Engine. She did not need to access her sub-conscious memories, or any of the other talents of her own capable brain. This was a direct query to her internal database, the base in which her earliest memories were of an interview with Mr. Director, and the latest were of Mr. Director dying on the floor of another living-room, still at the Project.*

If there was anything there, it would be between those incidents acting as parentheses, with her desired data between them.

—OF PASTIMES PASSED

[End-Process; Exit State; Extreme Close-Up] It didn't take long. She was standing in the chow-line at Sargon, on a day that she had decided to get lunch in the cafeteria, rather than cook for herself.

The images presented themselves to her as if they were happening now, rather than over two years ago. She even had nicknames for the parties to the conversation. There was Honcho-Lady, and a photographer she had seen exactly that one time (the shoot he was talking about had never materialized): Mr. Short-and-Feisty.

"The uh, Firm wants me to get some nice poses of the Agent!" Short-and-Feisty was saying, "The hints were that the pictures should be—like—kinda on the sexy side. *Playboy* and all that. Maybe *Penthouse*."	Descriptor: Heartbeat Fast, dilated eyes indicate interest; Body-temperature 0.75 degrees C above normal; Anticipatory emo-tions indicated by voice overtones, modulated by considerations of profess-ionalism.
"What ever for?" Honcho-Lady re-	Voice: Genuine Interest; Faces the

plied.

"I think someone—I won't specify who—wants to show off just how pretty some artificial biological creations can be. Maybe to get some extra funding. The head of the House Science Committee is one of these Fundies that The Firm has something on. Something BIG. Maybe another Agent. There have been these rumors."

other conversant; Eye-contact; Curiosity;
Frank Interest in Topic, Knowledge; External signs indicate he believes himself to be relating facts. American? (If so, can he be located here?) Interested in Honcho-Lady. Attempting to impress her? No signs of prevarication when mentioning the words "another Agent" or "rumors." Certain of Sources.

—I believe that you're on the right track, Child. It would be illogical for you to have been both the first and the last.

Descriptor:
Declarative;
Instantiative;

I agree, Yezeletta said in her mind to the voice that flew upon the darkness, *It's fortunate that we have our own true friends to help us. Anne has a brain, doesn't she?*

—She does, Yezeletta. Consider her parents; they went against all that was politically correct in a decadent time to raise her as a self-sufficient woman in her own right, instead of another piece of property for the state.

Load;
Execute;
Query by Example;
Generate Report;
Output;

Like I was, Yezeletta thought into the link. *Like we <u>were</u>.*

Time For It

[Breakpoint Return] She opened her eyes, and read her time-base. "Not bad," she said, "I was out for less than a minute."

"Did you find it?" Anne asked for everyone.

"A reference," Yezeletta said. "There was to have been a shoot, the photographic variety, in which I was to pose, possibly undressed." (An unwanted memory of an undressed pose she *had* been in surfaced, and she returned it to the place from which it had come.)

"It never happened, but the photographer also spoke of another Agent. Considering how I was formed," she kept her speech carefully level, "making another like me would be a matter of waiting for the," she let a sarcastic tone modulate her voice, "right materials. Unless," Yezeletta paused. "Unless the Project or its successors were able to perfect the DNA tailoring to the extent of true-breeding."

Another memory intruded: one of a hologram seen through one of her Imagers, herself as a simulation with three others.

Yezeletta widened the bandwidth of her vision. She looked with a new comprehension at all of the people she counted as friends, *I never would have known so many this way!* Hank and Ondreya, both profoundly out-raged, Anne, fascinated, yet sharing her parents' outrage, Joe's unquestion-ing love and support, Peter, sitting quietly, slightly apart from the rest, *Almost as if he feels that he doesn't belong*, Leona sitting with him.

She could see how her educated guess chilled them all.

RECON—CONTINUED

Hank looked a thought at Ondreya and Anne. "You're thinking that there might be another Warrior, or Agent, that they might have started on after you?"

Yezeletta looked at a point just above Hank on the television set. An Imager sat there scanning her. "They might have had someone else at the time I was growing up, but then there's the question of training, education, such things as why I learned to play the piano. To cause the nerves in my extra arms to integrate," she added to several curious looks. "All of this takes time, and the Project either found a way to shorten the development time of this hypothetical Agent, or *breed* it for the knowledge and capabilities that they wanted to give it. Or the brute-force approach: another project running in tandem with Sargon and a one-way communications link between them. There *was* another complex near Sargon, underground; I don't know how big it was. At the time I discovered it, I was about a day from taking Sargon out and leaving. I don't know what it really represented."

It was subtle; all of her friends were mature—*Anne far beyond her years!*—but she could catch the revulsion at what she had said. The colors in her additional spectra flowed across their faces, and she was reminded of a picture she had seen of a Cherokee Warrior in his war-paint. *A similarity of expression, as well*, she thought.

"Yezeletta," Joe said gently. "I agree with Hank. I think that we've literally derived the nature of the opposition. Project Sargon learned from you. We need to find out what it has learned, and better it."

"Yes, Joe," she said, then paused.

"And for that," she continued in her normal voice, "We need data."

TABLE LOOKUP, RELATIONAL

[Process Shot] "Hank, you were tossing out the ideas before I did my look-up; please continue."

"Uh—right." Hank shifted mental gears, and thought for a moment. "I was yakking about cold-blooded critters. The kind that your creations can't detect real well." He went to the TV set. "How do I put up the info your Imagers got?"

Yezeletta long-armed a remote control out of the glass bowl on the coffee table, and pressed buttons. While she did that, she directed thoughts at various systems, then grabbed the remote for one of the recorders. Then, on a last-minute thought, she restored the real-time map of where her Imagers had been.

"Didn't you run all of your stuff into shelters?" There was an odd tone in Hank's voice. "Those indications: they're still active."

"You've got it," Yezeletta said. "Looks like bats are going to fly by day as well as night." She directed a thought at the new program in her on-board systems, and they waited. The input was similar to the test flight, but the focus was better, the resolution higher, and the false-color rendition brighter. The image was also a lot steadier. The point-of-view fed directly into a re-corder, then to the TV set. Using Thicknesse the way a video-game player would a joy-stick, she directed the Imager-Bat to the coordinates of one of the indicators on the display.

Analysis of the image was difficult. The Imager-Bat was flying around in bright sunlight, and her indicator described a live Imager that was rather close to a tree-trunk on a branch. She sent precise directives through Thicknesse, and managed to hover the Bat in front of the appropriate branch.

There was *something in there*. Yezeletta applied several stages of image enhancement, and the action on the branch came into sharp relief.

Something that was all spikes, claws and teeth had methodically yanked the legs out of one of Yezeletta's Imagers, and was *eating* them with self-evident gusto. As they watched, the gold Imager on the partially-consumed arachnoid's body turned to face the invader. Yezeletta directed the output from the dying animal to one of her recorders, and a moment later the little monster sliced the Imager in half, and began chewing on one of the pieces.

"Do you want to see what my Imager sent?" she asked. "It won't be pleasant, but we need to see what that thing looks like up close."

"Do it," Hank said tightly.

The close-up was of jaws and teeth that managed to cross the least pleasant aspects of a cat's teeth with those of a shark. The only other fea-tures that were extent were: a hole that looked as if a pistol-shot had placed it there, that flickered lambent colors from within, retractile claws on prehen-sile legs, spikes that stuck out like antennae and several flickering motes of light near the creature's image receptor.

The recording blacked out.

"Can you kill off the others?" Joe asked.

Yezeletta nodded, and issued the necessary directives. The remaining in-dicators blinked out.

She backed the Bat away from the tree, then sent it back to its Hive.

Yezeletta picked her words carefully. "We are under attack. That's obvi-ous, now. We need to find out who or what the directing intelligence behind this is, and work out a way to either prevent it from knowing about us, or find it and analyze it. Maybe analyze it to death."

Peter Rudenko and Leona had been sitting close together on the smaller of Yezeletta's couches. Peter looked up at her remark. "I may have some-thing here that will help," he said. He went to one of his cases, and removed a small device with a parabolic antenna on one side, and set it on the coffee table. He plugged the device into his lap-top, and threw switches.

He aimed the antenna at Hank.

"This," he said, "is a detector for the electro-magnetic fields that are given off by nervous systems. Do you," he asked Yezeletta, "have anything such as this that you can build into your Imagers?"

"No. The issue of such detection never raised itself. We used infra-red, and ultra-violet photography in various wavelengths, and in combination, and I can adjust my vision for various parts of a spread-spectrum from very deep I.R. to very high U.V. Since I got here, I've developed the Receiver. It detects microwaves that bracket the visible light spectrum. This is curious. I wonder whether my keepers at Sargon expected me to work this one out, but it never crossed my mind. Was a lot of what I was taught overtly designed to lead me away from things that they didn't want me to know then, or ever?"

"Sounds like some of the doctrine I was taught in the Army," Hank said. "The care and feeding of classified data is pretty simple in its basic state, but there's a lot of politicking around who gets cleared for what, and when. You may have inadvertently started a turf-war just by being there, while those keepers of yours argued privately as to what you should learn, when and how."

"What does your device do, Peter?" Yezeletta said.

"As I said, It can detect the electro-magnetic field that the human nervous system gives off. It is quite sensitive, and can receive inputs from a good three- to four-hundred meters away."

"What sorts of technical documentation do you have for that?" she asked him. "I'd like to try that trick out on an Imager."

Peter rummaged in his case again, then handed Yezeletta a CD-ROM. "The necessary stuff is on this. They're PDF files. If you have a copy of 'Acrobat Reader for Anything,' you can read these, print them out—hell— use them for tablecloths or toilet paper," he joked. "I *said* I was quitting Searchlight, and I don't particularly care what happens to their little secrets. Besides, you need this. That thing that ate your Imager has a lot on you. A detector that can sniff out nervous-systems at a distance will give an advantage over whoever's out there. Maybe that Receiver you mentioned is the start." He removed a duplicate of the detector from the case, and set it on the coffee-table in front of her.

"Thank you, Peter."

"I'd like to think I'm a part of this too," Peter said. He looked at Hank. "I did get your daughter out of a tough place."

Hank nodded. "And Anne did let you use our backup piece when Yezeletta's Spinner came after us. And, you didn't exactly bring a posse of Searchlights back here."

"Hell, no," Peter said. "I've been trying various discreet inquiries into Searchlight to find out who it was that busted into the Ag Depart, and I've simply bounced. Whichever part of The Firm it was, they aren't using the main data exchange system that all agents were taught in Basic to use for questions, answers, reports...you-name-it, whatever.

"This is big enough that it's political. Like your Army turf wars. Someone doesn't want this known even in the agency. I'll keep looking, but I think we're on our own against what we've seen today."

"You're sure that it was Searchlight?" Joe asked.

"That break-and-entry technique has them all over it." He didn't realize that he had excluded himself from his own service by stating it that way. "And they learned it from the FBI. Who knows where the Feebs got it? The old Soviet Union, maybe."

Yezeletta nodded. *All of the real work falls to me. I'm the only one who can do it.* She handed Joe the CD-ROM. "Joe, please print as many copies of this as you think we need. I want to check Peter's Forward Sensor Array out, and see if I can speed up the combat servitors in the Growing Room."

R EPRISE R ECON

[Access]   Caliban looked up from the holographic display at Miranda. She realized that he didn't respond to frustrations the way another would, by swearing or by other forms of release. He just sat there, looking unwavering-ly at the display before him, *And the displays* inside *him as well!*

What Caliban was looking at through his internals was that polymer barri-er. His spiky, be-clawed remote still stood before it, its imager fixed on it, immovable until instructed.

Fine, a part of him thought. He sent a directive.

The remote extended sharp claws, and attacked the barrier.

I NDICATIONS

Another red-asterisk began strobing.

Yezeletta looked up the cause, and an image appeared on her TV set.

She laughed!

D INNER FOR O NE ON O NE

[Egress; One-Shot]   It ended so fast that Caliban was jolted, although he didn't show it externally.

The barrier bulged out, the bulge opened, and tendrils hauled the remote into it. The bulge closed over the remote, and sharp teeth accompanied by acidic digestive juices shredded and dissolved it.

The barrier resumed its flat aspect.

Caliban didn't see the barrier go back to its rest-state. He played the re-cording of the last seconds of the remote's life back.

She is using reactive armor, The Other said, and vanished.

Caliban consulted his knowledge base, for the definition.

The definition was given him; then the act of the giving vanished, too, leaving the definition standing alone.

F IRST C ONTACTS

Yezeletta played the same scene back from her viewpoint. She watched the spike-covered monstrosity's claws extrude, she watched it attack the door to her hive.

She watched the door eat the attacker.

"Round one to us," she said. "But I'm doubling, maybe tripling the strength of the defenses."

"And find out where these things came from," Hank supplied. "They didn't just grow, they were put there. But there doesn't seem to be any sort of infil-tration method used, that we can see. Yet."

"Try the obvious, first," Peter said. "Maybe they were transported in by something that doesn't look at all strange to us. The guiding intelligence may be far enough behind the lines that we haven't seen it, or, if we have, it doesn't look like what it really is."

Yezeletta put her chin in two right hands. "I've been keeping tabs on a lot of the traffic from Illinois up Highway-94. I hadn't monitored Ninety, because anything that goes that way will end up in Madison, and have to take 94-East to get here. The ones we want will be arriving in such a way as to not set off Allen Hightower's crews. That means Brookfield, and that means the dido off to Highway-100 that Hank mentioned."

"Can your Imagers resolve license plates?" Ondreya asked.

"Easily. Then it's a query against the database I've been accumulating for the last matter of months." Yezeletta took a breath, let it out. "But all I really need is the last week, if that." She sent a directive out through Thicknesse. "I want to move all of this to the conference room. There'll be more working space there.

"Call it the War Room, now."

THE SMALL PRODUCTION

[setup.exe] Caliban went to the front of the semi, carrying a recordable CD-ROM. He was followed by Miranda, who was followed by Vince.

Near where his minions were incarcerated, was a small device that resembled nothing so much as a top-loading washing machine, in a shade of steel-gray.

Caliban slotted the CD-ROM into a reader in the control panel of the top-loader and studied a read-out on a small screen. He placed his fingers on a dark-gray plastic area near the screen, and it turned black at his touch. He opened the hatch on the device, and looked in. A light from within shone upwards, illuminating his features from below. Tiny motes of light moved around the hatch opening.

He closed the hatch, read information from the screen, and turned to face the others.

"The programming will take about an hour. The attack systems will be ready then."

PLANNING

Yezeletta's query didn't take twenty minutes.

There were maybe three-thousand cars, trucks, and so on, that had come up Ninety-Four in the last four days. Ordinary passenger vehicles she could rule out, as they were too small to carry what they had observed.

"I came here in six trucks driven by special servitors that I designed for endurance. No one noticed me. Or us. The police in Milwaukee are so occupied with their own battles against ordinary crimes, that they didn't even notice my small fleet driving into the underground parking, here. Wisconsin Avenue was deserted the night I arrived. Similarly, the Wisconsin Highway Patrol, what there is of it, is kept too busy with accidents and the like, to worry about what they might see as strange behavior. Check me on this?"

"Illinois isn't even up to that drill," Hank said. "It took the Chicago cops nearly forty minutes to get from the Daley Center to State Street by the Tribune Building, to clean up after that taxi-cab bombing I mentioned. The Chi-Town-PD has always had a corrupt streak, and now they do as little as they can with what little they have."

Joe added, "Milwaukee's cops concentrate on the residential areas, and leave down-town alone. Strange when you consider that District One's station is on Seventh Street."

"We live in East Chicago," Ondreya said. "It's still a pretty safe area, but all three of us can defend ourselves, and we don't leave the house unarmed."

"Where does this leave us, then?" Yezeletta asked. "Typical travellers will go from point-to-point in the shortest distance possible, and take care of their own security. This will apply to freight trucking, also, to prevent hijacking. People who need to, will use varying routes to keep from giving themselves away by regular movements. We're looking for someone who has come this way, and stopped, and waited. Not a delivery truck, except in one sense. When my query into the vehicular database finishes, we will have just the transportation that matches those initial conditions."

FORWARD APPROACH

[Installation; Process Shot] Caliban gave the necessary orders, and Miranda was surprised to see Vince echo them to the other handlers. *He really is in command*, she thought. The driver started up the rig, and Caliban's expedition pulled out of the truck stop, and drove east on a road named Blue Mound. They entered through Brookfield into Wauwatosa.

No one stopped them.

The drivers of the VW had mentioned a burned-out area west of the Conservatory, near an abandoned strip-mall. There was ample parking behind some large uninhabited buildings, one of which had the unmistakable signs of a drastic fire in its recent history. All that stood were the blackened outer walls, and Vince hoped they would provide protection in that direction.

The drive took two hours. Parking the truck in and amongst the wreckage took an hour. Being sure of a means of fast egress, should that become necessary, took another hour. When they were done, there was the abandoned mall directly before them, and, beyond that, looming high over the other wreckage, the three domes of the Conservatory.

REPORT GENERATION

The results of Yezeletta's query showed up as: A grouping of long-haul freighters with easily recognizable corporate logos; a White Freightliner from Camel Trucking; a Mack Truck belonging to Hanjin; and Peterbilts owned by United, Ryder Truck Rental; a truck belonging to TRL-Lines, and...Maersk.

There were about fifty trucks that met Yezeletta's selection criteria. Most of them were deliveries to industries on Milwaukee's south side: large shipments of foodstuffs to places such as the Pelton Casteel Plant and Allen-Bradley, for their food-service operations, for example. Other deliveries varied from a far west side shipment of electronic equipment to a place on a street called Sunny Slope Road to supplies for grocery stores, to furniture for an outlying department store, to....

"What's that one over there?" Hank asked.

Yezeletta loaded the information for the vehicle Hank had noticed. It was a solitary semi, parked in the corner of a truck stop off Highway-100. She played back the recording taken several days ago, and they watched two men walk from the stop's owner's office to the truck. Yezeletta sped the playback up, and they watched as nothing, absolutely exactly nothing, happened to the truck for the next day.

"Either that driver has very good bladder control, or there's an AI running that thing," Joe observed, "or, it's deserted." Then, "There!"

Yezeletta slowed the playback.

It was a day later, as indicated by the timestamp in the picture. Frustratingly, the image was a side-view, so they couldn't see what was inside the semi. The back of the truck opened, a ramp flopped down, and a Volkswagen Beetle drove out. The little car was a nondescript nonreflective gray, and the license plates were from Wisconsin. Yezeletta froze the image, and enhanced it. She printed the image out, handed it to Joe, who took it silently, and resumed the playback.

Through Brookfield.

DATA EXTRACTION

[Load Query] Caliban put his weapons on. Then he went to the front of the truck and removed the steel bars securing his minions. He opened the heavy steel door, and touched the forehead of the entity that stood there. Directives from his internal systems entered the monster, and were transmitted out to the others.

They formed up in ranks.

He went to the washing machine, and opened its hatch. He looked down into the device for a moment, then reached in with his upper pair of hands, and withdrew a gray, spherical object.

He handed it to one of his monsters.

DATA REDUCTION

Yezeletta's orders flew out over the network of her Hives throughout the city. The carnivorous doors in her Hives opened and the Imagers deployed. A specification was downloaded to each one, and made an integral part of the programming: **FIND <THIS>**.

A shape, a design, a license plate number.

STATE CHANGE

[Run] In their private quarters, Miranda asked Caliban, "Is this necessary? Can't you do this remotely?"

"No, Miranda. I mussst be there to get the necessary data and sset the conssstruct. I am the only one who can."

"Can you modify a remote to do it?"

"I would have to grow one, and our capability to do that—you have seen it—is very small."

"I'll go with you."

"No!"

"You big lug, somebody has to watch out for you, and who was it that taught me how to use these?" She strapped on her pistols.

"Stay at my back. Do not be in front of me."

She grabbed him in a hug, looked up at him. "I'll be right there, Caliban."

"I will, alssso."

LOAD A DESCRIPTOR

[Access Record] The first indication was the gray VW, returning from the errand it had gone on. The timestamp on the return was several hours before the time that first Imager had been killed.

The second was the location of the Maersk Lines truck.

"Don't you have a Hive in that old mall?" Joe said.

That's the Hive we used to observe those cops sending the info about our trip to The Domes back to their station house. Whoever that is, he's right in our back yard."

The Imager she was using was a very small, tarantula-shaped critter. It moved slowly in the cold weather, and took nearly half an hour to get in place. It watched the front of the truck.

There was no one in the tractor.

ENTRY

[Rewrite Update] The other vehicle stowed in the semi was a chunky jeep-shaped thing that was shorter than a jeep, but roomier than the equivalent-length auto. There was room in the back for Caliban, if he scrunched down, room for Miranda in his lap, and room for maybe three of his monsters, if no one minded being that close. Vince would drive; the back and side windows were opaque. Several of Caliban's spiky remotes occupied the front seat in the lap of a monster.

Vince pressed a button, and the remaining windows darkened. He turned on the lights, and pressed the switch that changed their output to exclusively infra-red. He and Miranda put on the appropriately filtered goggles; Caliban adjusted the bandwidth of his vision.

He did a thumbs-up to the other handlers, and all the lights in the truck went out. The back door opened, the ramp dropped like a dark gray metal tongue, and he drove the vehicle down it.

The egress wasn't observed until Vince drove around to the front of the semi; then he was seen from afar.

ACQUISITION

No one spoke as the Image of the short jeep appeared. The curiously foreshortened vehicle seemed to drive straight towards them, as it headed for what was once the parking lot of the old strip-mall. Then it moved beneath or under the view-point of the Imager, and vanished.

Yezeletta sent a directive to the Hive beneath The Domes. A minute later, the aerial view from an Imager-Bat showed the jeep driving into the approach to the underground garage. As they watched, a man got out of the driver's side, and went to the garage door. He did something to the external lock, and the door rose smoothly upwards. Then, he went back to the jeep, and drove it inside.

Yezeletta's thoughts were palpable in the silent conference/war room. Another directive activated an Imager in an electrical closet. It would take a moment for it to reach the garage.

DEPLOYMENT: PERSONAL

Vince parked the jeep, and got out. He went back to the garage door, and was gone for a half a minute, to verify that the main entrance was completely closed. He came back, and opened the passenger door. Caliban unfolded himself out of the back, and stood behind the vehicle to help Miranda out. He walked around the jeep.

THE OTHER—I

[Analyze Run; Long Shot] Yezeletta's Imager moved through a conduit space, a cable run, and along the upper inside of an air-conditioning duct. It dropped off the upper inside, flipped over, and landed in front of the vent, and looked down into the garage.

There was a man standing next to the jeep, looking towards the rear.

Someone else stood up, walked around from the back of the jeep.

Ondreya gasped, Hank swore, Joe took Yezeletta's right hands, Peter and Leona were wide-eyed.

Anne just stared. She said, levelly, "There's your other agent."

Looking around once, gazing straight up at the observer in the vent, his violet cat's eyes momentarily staring into their own, then moving away and down to his minions, Caliban stepped into view.

——>>> **TWELVE** <<<——

They flee from me, that sometime did me seek,
With naked foot stalking in my chamber.

—Sir Thomas Wyatt the Elder,
They Flee from Me, About 1557

"**THAT NOW ARE WILD**—"

[Read Status; Sign Extension] Yezeletta froze the playback from her Imager in a secondary window on her screen. His face was the color of a Caucasian with a heavy tan, or of a man of predominantly Hispanic ancestry, or perhaps, a lighter-skinned black man. His ethnic derivation was mixed; she couldn't get any one human sub-racial type that was outstanding. *No more than I know about me*, she thought. *He is truly a being of Earth as a whole and not just one place.*

That figured. The Project that created him would not want him identifying too closely with any ethnic group to which he might run for assistance. Like Yezeletta, he was to have been a creation in and of himself (herself) with no ties to humanity.

They failed.

Did they fail with him?

As they continued to watch, the male agent walked around the underground garage of the Conservatory looking into things, poking into storage areas, sometimes standing, almost in a posture of listening.

Yezeletta could explain that, "I'm guessing, but it's a pretty safe guess. He has the same senses I have; he's scanning for indications of someone with my characteristics."

ON SITE

[Load, Execute] Caliban inspected the area, his eyes set at their widest bandwidth, his every sense at its maximum. All around him were the extra data, showing in brilliant false-colors.

He looked up at a ventilator in the facing wall, and then looked back down at his assistants.

There were tracks across the floor. They were barely visible, but to his augmented vision the tracks stood out like tiny luminescent dotted lines running this way and that, and mostly to such places as drains, and out the main garage door.

One of his monsters approached; he touched its head, and sent it a directive. The spiky creature went to the other two of its kind and passed the directive on.

The creatures went back to the jeep, and removed devices from the back. While Caliban, Miranda and Vince watched, the creatures began vacuuming the floor.

A CROSS T OWN

[On Line] Yezeletta asked her friends, "What would you say is happening there?" She already knew the answer.

"No questions," Peter said in a decisive voice. "It's what detectives do at a crime scene. You'd be amazed at how many clues you can scoop up by as simple an act as running a vacuum cleaner over things. Back in the late nineteen-hundreds, the crap scooped up was analysed with electron microscopes. Now they run the leavings through a DNA-Checker-Recorder, and start looking for matches in other places. With any suspects, for example."

"What they will find is ample evidence of—" Yezeletta started.

"Your creations?" Peter said.

"No," Yezeletta said. "They'll find no evidence of DNA at all. My DNA-Eradicators will have destroyed anything identifiable. The partials won't be useful. It's other things—purely physical, such as tracks in dust and simple residues—that he may have detected."

On the screen, the short, evil-looking creations walked a methodical grid on the concrete floor of the garage, their small vacuum-cleaners incongruous in their hands.

Then they got back into the jeep.

As Yezeletta's war council continued watching, the driver took his place behind the wheel, and reversed the position of the jeep, so that it faced outwards.

The woman got into the back, and the male agent removed something dark gray and spherical from the vehicle.

He set it down in the center of the garage, and touched it with his lower set of hands.

Anne caught it: "He looks like you do, when you send instructions to your animals!"

"Good point," Yezeletta said tightly.

The male agent squeezed into the back of the jeep, and it moved closer to the garage door. The driver went to open it, returned to the jeep, drove it out, and they could see him using the external control to close the door.

The door came down, closing off the garage entry completely. Yezeletta's Imagers compensated for the sudden darkening of the area; the display lightened and the contrast changed to a more viewable state. The dark gray sphere took the lights going out as a signal and activated.

The outer integument of the sphere peeled back in successive layers, disclosing further layers beneath, much like an onion. When all of the layers were rolled back, an interior appeared that—except for the color, a darker gray—looked like some sort of very large dark flower.

Tendrils reached up out of the flower, tendrils that looked as if they were covered with flakes of dark colored pollen. The tendrils waved back and forth, slowly at first, then faster. The speed increased, until the individual structures of the tendrils were invisible for their motion. The gray stuff they were carrying flew off in a gray cloud that resembled thick cigarette smoke and which dissipated rapidly into the atmosphere.

Then, after five or six minutes of this, the motion stopped abruptly, and the construct began...melting.

Yezeletta directed a thought *there* and <u>there</u>, and several small arachnoids erupted from the Hive beneath The Domes, and clustered around the gray thing. She turned to her friends. "He may not get much from us, but I'm *really* interested in that creature. Why did he leave it?"

BROADCAST BAND

[Load Descriptor] Several hours later, Yezeletta was sitting at her conference table with her small army.

The recordings of the return of the jeep to the ersatz Maersk Lines truck had been played several times. The jeep had come about, the ramp at the rear of the truck had descended, and the jeep had gone into the back of the semi.

Exactly nothing had happened after that.

"What kind of information will those critters you sent after that gray thing provide?" Peter was the first to ask, after the second viewing.

"Mostly biological data on internal characteristics and construction," Yezeletta said. "The only place I can start from is an educated and very general guess that the male agent's creations are similar to mine, with additional research added."

"In the Army," Hank said, "there was a faintly silly aphorism tossed around almost as conventional wisdom: 'When you assume, you make an Ass out of You and Me.'"

"Did you really believe that, Hank?" Ondreya asked.

"Frankly, I thought it ridiculous. It completely blows off any thought of setting up intelligent initial conditions for starting a research project, allowing 'action first, thought later'. Professor Mathewson once said, and I quote, 'Remind me not to use any software systems designed by the originator of that idiocy, they won't work in tight situations!' It's just another damned slogan, designed to cut out higher brain functions in a single pithy bound."

"Nevertheless," Yezeletta said, "the basic assumptions, or, if you wish, Hank, Initial Conditions, that we must work with are that his creations are similar to mine, but with their capabilities increased.

"On my last day with the Sargon Directorate, I sent several of my Imagers off on a little trip that the last of the Directors went on. That was where I found out about their storage plans for me." She told them of the Directorate's small convoy, and of the underground installation she had discovered one day before ending the Project.

BROADCAST VIDEO

An hour later, Yezeletta stood, almost professorially, as several of her servitors brought in an assortment of spherical, triangularly faceted things, and deposited them on the conference table.

"These are what later become Hives," she began. "I will have them moved to several places: the local cop shop on West State Street, as a backup at The Domes, and another backup where our friends are parked." She gestured with a right hand at the unmoving image of the semi still framed in one screen, now dedicated to it.

"Suggestion," Hank said. "What about that place where those secret agents took you? Have you been back there? Should we go back there? Is it desirable to check it out, again?"

"No, and yes and yes," Yezeletta said. "No, I haven't been back there, and yes, someone should go back. We can do it by remote observation, or...."

"Or a visit," Hank said.

"Exactly what I'm thinking. Do you think it's safe....?"

"For whom?" Hank asked. "If you wanted to actually be on site, I'd say that a lot of care is needed. Do you want one of us to check it out?"

"I would, if there's just over a one-hundred-percent chance of your getting back safely. I wasn't trying to get you to volunteer, by the way."

Hank passed a look to Joe; Joe returned it. "What do you think?" Hank asked him.

"I think," Joe said, "that what we need to do is reconnoiter that place I drove Yezeletta back from, in as much detail as a fast trip down and back can get." Joe stood up. "I want two volunteers." He looked expectantly at Hank and Peter.

Peter grinned. "I *am* a field agent, after all," he said. "What sorts of data gathering devices will you need?"

"I feel positively archaic," Peter said later. "These communicators in watches are the best that Searchlight has to offer: Spread-spectrum, 128-bit encryption, sight and sound, and able to interface to the cellular phone system." He shook his head. "And," he continued, "Yezeletta only needs to grow something to put these into the front window of an antique store."

He stroked the purring Imager that was sitting on his shoulder. "Madam, you have put an honest secret agent right out of the communications business."

"But not out of the Secret Agent Business," Yezeletta replied.

OUT OUR WAY

The three men took Peter's car. This necessitated a short delay, while the remaining items he had removed from Searchlight were taken to an elevator, and placed in the back of the cage. A servitor carrying a forty-five and several small life-forms stood guard over the stack of cases.

Yezeletta opened the garage door remotely, and Peter pulled out into a cold Milwaukee afternoon.

The sun hung low near the southern horizon, the sky was a light and very cold blue. Joe gave Peter several street names, and Peter headed south.

The route took them through the old factory-districts of Milwaukee. One of those factories had an enormous four-sided clock that was usually illuminated during the night. South of that was a large Catholic church that had a smaller clock of a similar design: four faces, illuminated by a warmer, yellower incandescent lighting from within.

They could see the Domes occasionally from the street.

ENQUIRIES

Peter pulled his car up behind the four-story building. It was an anonymous brick construction from the previous century, that had started life as a small apartment house. It had been transformed into offices at some time in the indefinite past, and government regulations (when they'd meant anything) had required the installation of an elevator. The freight elevator that the foreign agents had used to take Yezeletta to the fourth floor doubled as the passenger lift. Peter faced the car out and made sure that there were no obstructions to a fast exit. One of Yezeletta's Imagers entered the building, and the three men watched as it ascended the stairs, stopping to perform a three-sixty scan on each landing.

The Imager reached the fourth floor, and the pair of rooms where Yezeletta had been left. In one, several lengths of cordage were thrown on the floor in front of a shabby cot, and there were straight marks in the grime on the only window. In the other room, an old steel-framed king-sized bed still had several blankets and a dirty sheet thrown over it.

The building was deserted.

Peter led them in. At the back, or south, side of the structure, was the freight elevator. Peter reached into the cage, pressed "4", and watched as the steel mesh doors closed, and the ponderous vehicle started up with a loud mechanical groaning. Beneath the floor of the elevator cage, a long, oily rod extended downward into the base of the elevator shaft, indicating it was a hydraulic elevator.

"Weapons," he said, drawing his.

Joe passed out disks of an organic material that was only approximately transparent. Each of the men placed a disk on his left eye. There was a rippling in their eyesight, and other images appeared, properly focused. One of the feeds was of what the Imager on the fourth floor was seeing.

"I like her heads-up display," Hank said to Joe.

"Thank you," Joe said. "Yezeletta and I collaborated on this one; it uses some of my protocols to create reactive optics so that you can see the images without a lot of eyestrain."

"Organic computer glasses," Hank commented. They started up.

The climb was tedious. At each floor, Peter wanted to look out for possible occupants, even though the Imagers had indicated that the building was empty.

"Training," he said. "It's pretty hard to shake it off, especially when it's been as useful as mine has."

They reached the fourth floor. Peter waved a small package of electronics that resembled a cellphone, complete with an antenna, around and found nothing. "If it's line-of-sight, or real short range, it won't show here. We'll need to check each room from the inside."

Hank gathered the pieces of rope near the ratty-looking cot they had seen from below, and placed them in a cloth bag. Peter went across the hall, while Joe and Hank stood guard.

The window facing north had a thick accumulation of Milwaukee grime. The long scratches were etched into the dirt from the outside.

"She told me that her pet—" by previous agreement, they weren't mentioning names "—scratched those." Hank nodded. Joe pointed upwards. There were two bullet holes in the ceiling.

"Hey!" Peter called.

Joe passed a look to Hank, who returned it. They crossed the hall to the opposite room.

Peter was reading an indicator on his device, which was now configured as a portable spectrum analyzer. He pointed at an old, ugly floor-lamp in the corner. "On top of that," he said.

The other men approached the lamp cautiously. The lamp-shade was what one would expect of garage-sale merchandise: ugly, but not so ugly as to be interesting. There was a peculiar glint to the finial, a dark red glass ball in a metal holder, screwed to the top that retained the shade in place.

Peter threw his handkerchief over the finial and unscrewed it. At the same time, he watched an indicator on the device he held in his other hand.

When the finial came off, the indicator flatlined.

He held the finial up close: the "viewer" in his left eye thickened up in response to the movements of his eye muscles, and it appeared magnified.

"Unless I'm purely seeing things," he said, "I'd say that I'm looking at a small television camera." He looked up at Joe and Hank. "I think we'd better take that lamp with us as well. *And* whatever it's attached to."

Further inspection of the lamp provided little information. The lamp was plugged into the wall. The switch functioned only to turn the lamp on or off. It was the only user interface.

Peter frowned, "That camera has to be connected to something. Carrier-current? Is it transmitting into the AC line?"

"It could be sending anywhere," Joe observed.

"Not so," Hank said after a short pause. "If that's really carrier-current, the signals get stopped by transformers. Some pool-rooms turn the lights on above the tables from the house computer, using that X-10 system that you sometime see advertised on late-night television. What that camera's sending to is either close, on the order of the same lighting circuit that this lamp is on, or there's a small transmitter in the lamp, and a receiver within a short distance."

"How short?" Joe asked.

Yezeletta's voice came through the Imager on Peter's shoulder, "I'd guess within twenty meters. I don't use the X-10 system here for reasons of security—it could be activated from a distance—but my guess is that there's ample justification for my having been hauled up to the top floor of that flop-house."

"Rather than being left on the first floor," Joe added.

Peter was waving his analyzer around the room, close to the walls, and upwards towards the ceiling.

"There's no transmission coming out of this now," and in response to a look from Joe, "it's not because I removed it. My probe picked it up by inducing a current into it, and tracking the resonance." He waved his analyzer up over his head, as close to the ceiling as he could reach, and watched its display.

"Agent Ought-Ought-Seven," Yezeletta said, "please aim your device at the bed."

Peter raised an eyebrow at Joe, and walked around the bed, holding the antenna on his analyzer close to the frame.

Hank was closest. Peter handed the device to him, and removed the top covering from the bed. There was nothing below the bedsheets but a mattress that looked as if it had come with the building. Peter grabbed the head-end of it, pulled it up and folded it onto the lower half.

There was a large flat coil of fine wires on top of the springs. The coil was connected to a small black plastic box.

The former secret agent removed a tool from his back pocket. It was a waldo: a remote grabbing gadget that was used to remove dropped objects from hard to get-at places. He picked up the black box in the waldo's claw, and looked at it intently. The construct on his left eye adapted, and brought the box into sharp relief. He looked at all of the sides of the box.

"The No-Name Electronics Company," he announced, "invites you to a demonstration of their latest in data-gathering technology." He handed the waldo to Hank.

He pointed up. "Is there a roof exit in this place?"

There was. It was a continuation of the stairway they had used. It let out onto the roof via a covered section of the stairway and an external door.

The three men stepped warily out onto the roof, Hank holding the box in its steel claw in one hand, his other hand on his pistol. They looked around.

The device was behind the roof exit: they had to walk around the exit housing to find it.

There, a small parabolic antenna on a stubby tripod pointed up and to the south. It was plugged into a cable attached to several large rectangular solar cell assemblies, the kind commonly used to trickle-charge car batteries. The cells themselves were fastened down to a convenient skylight with duct tape. A stubby helical microwave antenna pointed straight down from beneath the dish.

"There's your X-10 system," Joe said.

Peter removed his Minox from the case on his belt, and walked around the device, photographing it from various angles. The Imagers each man had with him added their own inputs.

Peter knelt down, scrutinized the antenna.

Then he unplugged its power. Nothing happened. He picked up the antenna, and closed it. The parabolic dish folded in a fashion reminiscent of an umbrella. The electronic package that accompanied it was in a sealed plastic chassis that was about the size, shape and weight of a small brick. He worked a corner of the duct tape loose, and removed all of it from the solar cells in a continuous sticky ribbon. Hank held the cloth bag open, and, feeling as if he were filling a treat bag for Halloween, Peter added the electronics to the other contents. Hank chased it with the waldo and its contents.

"Do we need to stay here much longer?"

"What do you think, Babe?" Joe asked the air.

"I'd like to see that transmitter up close," Yezeletta's disembodied voice said. "Please deploy the Hive package, and come home."

They went back to the fourth floor. Peter scanned the cot in the other room, but there was nothing connected to it, or near it. Joe was the last one to leave; his last act was to toss an object slightly larger than a golf ball into each room. He watched for a moment as the golf balls began to disintegrate. Then he joined the others.

The freight elevator was still where they had left it; they took it to the basement. Joe was the last one out of the cage; he left another golf-ball in it and closed the door. An access to the sewer and water lines coming in from underground provided a place for the Hive package; and five minutes and the last golf-ball later, they were back in Peter's car, and heading north.

[Breakpoint Return] When they returned, Peter went straight to what had once been the women's restroom for that floor of the Farmer's Bank Building. Now it was a darkroom. Hank and Joe rejoined Ondreya, Leona and Yezeletta in Yezeletta's living room.

Anne and Leona were in a corner, each engrossed in a thick paperback book, obviously from a set of similar texts, and looking occasionally at obscure graphics on the high-res display.

Hank raised an eyebrow at Yezeletta.

"I asked Anne if she knew anything about image synthesis," Yezeletta said, quietly. "I want to use the pictures Pete's developing to produce a three-dimensional version of that antenna you guys found. From that, I can determine where it's aimed, and get a pretty good approximation of which satellite's receiving the feed." She grinned. "Anne sailed past me, grabbed the CD-ROMs with the necessary programs, got the manual, and has been busy over there ever since. Leona came in later and offered to help."

Ondreya smiled back. "Anne's a very talented artist, and does most of the programming at home. We gave her a computer for her eighth birthday, and she took to it like a duck to water." She looked at Anne talking quietly to Leona. "Leona's probably going to learn all there is about digital image manipulation, and computer art."

A half an hour later, Peter came out of the improvised darkroom carrying a very small roll of Minox negatives. He looked around expectantly, and Anne beckoned to him. Peter gave her the negatives, and she scanned the pictures into the computer she and Leona had been using, gestured hypnotically with her mouse hand, and the pictures, reversed to positives, appeared on the display.

"Watch this," she said, and, almost with the manner of a skilled illusionist, clicked another icon.

The small windows on the high-res vanished, to be replaced by a single image of the antenna.

"You can drag any part of this image with the mouse, and turn it," she demonstrated, "and see all sides of the—uh—whatever-it-is. We can also get its exact orientation with respect to the surface of the roof from the shadows, and determine its aim-point to within fractions of a second of arc." As she turned the image, figures in glowing frames rippled through ranges as the orientation of the image to the simulated zenith was continuously updated.

"And from Anne's analysis," Yezeletta added, "we can determine what overhead devices—such as communications satellites—it may have been looking at when I was incarcerated below.

"Thank you, Anne."

"Should I take a bow?" Anne asked. "Leona helped, too."

"It isn't necessary unless you want to," Yezeletta said, "but you deserve it."

Grinning, Anne and Leona bowed to each other. Anne went to the couch, and in unconscious emulation of her friend sat on the edge of one arm. Leona sat with Peter.

Yezeletta took over: "I have all of the ephemerides from Project Sargon, for satellite orbits, and some that Pete gave me from Searchlight's databases. I can back this up to the time of my visit there, using my internal timebase to get the exact moment. This will take a few minutes to run." She stood up, stretched, and pressed a key combination.

"What's our friend doing in the truck, I wonder?"

[Call Procedure] When the jeep was parked and secured, Caliban and Miranda went to the lab, and to the washing machine in the front of the semi.

Under the small hood installed in a forward corner of the semi, almost a sealed container, Caliban emptied out the contents of the vacuum cleaners, and started the processes that would provide a fast but reasonably detailed analysis of their contents.

Then he went to a compact file cabinet, unlocked it, and removed several large transparencies. They were still referred to as "eight-by-tens" although the metric description was different. He placed them on a photographer's light box, and let Miranda look at them.

The transparencies were of Caliban: two each of front, back and both sides, obviously taken by a professional. In the pictures, Caliban stood against a flat black background, naked, looking back out of the photographs. Around him were metric measurements, and graphics that resembled the resolution tests that were used in digital image processing.

"You look pretty good in those," Miranda said, "but I like you better in the flesh."

Caliban caressed her shoulder with his left hand, his lower. He let his hand slide gently down onto her right breast. "This is better," he said. He hugged her with his upper left arm.

"What are those for?"

"Holographic image detection."

"Of you?"

"Of me. The first stage of the virus with which I have infected the target's life-forms will affect their vision inputs. When I load these images into the optical differentiation sub-system in the virus, those life-forms will no longer be able to detect me."

"They'll not see you? I don't get it."

"They will fill in the current background instead of me. They will interpolate from the other things in their area of perception."

"Sort of like a blind spot, huh?"

"Not sort of. Exactly like a blind spot." Caliban looked down at Miranda. He put a pair of arms around her. "I will be able to investigate her installations in this city. Then—" He paused, silent. The silent time stretched for minutes, while he held her; then he said, "Then, I will be able—from the investigations—to track her back to her dwelling."

Caliban looked silently down at her again. His irises closed down to thin slits, and his face relaxed. His hug lasted through his quiet time, and after minutes—tens of minutes? Miranda wasn't sure—he relaxed, and his irises opened.

His violet cat's eyes were on Miranda, and she could see in them his...respect? admiration? *Is the big lunk in love? Where does he go when he does that?*

He picked her up effortlessly, and carried her into their quarters.

THE UPLOADING

[Pass <Parameters>] Yezeletta's program ran for two minutes. When it finished, a table of information began scrolling up on the high-res display, neatly using the graphic of the antenna as a backdrop, or "wallpaper."

THE DOWNLOAD AND THE NEGATION

[Call by <Values>] Caliban looked down at his lover. He widened the bandwidth of his vision to its maximum. Unknown and unknowable colors rippled across Miranda's body in response to her respiration, blood-flow and her emotional state. *She is of value*, The Other said, *She is useful to you*. Caliban looked inwards to that core of his being from which the silent voice came. *Her usefulness will not be forever*.

And deep within him, beyond even the reach of the voice, *outside* the spherical enclosure of compelling colors, Caliban summoned what was perhaps a first negation.

THE DISPLAY

[Call by <Name>] Yezeletta's program had regressed the satellite orbits described in her ephemeris the matter of weeks that she needed to get back to her involuntary stay on the South Side. The data table display showed what birds were overhead from the time Joe had picked her up, to a time about eight hours earlier.

"What's a Molniya?" Leona was the first one to speak.

Yezeletta held a fat and rather old text in her lower left hand. "Molniya," she responded, "was the name for an obsolete series of communications satellites that the old Soviet Union launched back in the nineteen-seventies." She read quickly and summarized: "The satellites had highly eccentric orbits that were designed to keep one satellite in radio-link visibility east-to-west at all times. They allowed communications all of the way from Vladivostok to Saint Petersburg."

"Was that the only one in orbit then?" Joe asked her.

"It was the only one in range of that transmitter at the time I was there," Yezeletta said. "I wonder if those people south of Kiev are using the information that was sent; I shall have to check on what they thought they got."

EXTERNALLY SPECIFIED INDEX

[Call by <Reference>] The huge trailer truck, painted a military dark green, stood silently in front of the main building of the estate south of Kiev. Heavy power cables ran from a partially open hatch in the back of the trailer across the gray lawn and into a window through an improvised wooden fitting.

Alexei Krilov had formally taken command of the installation. Semyon Malasnikov was reduced to the status of assistant programmer and spectator, as Alexei, his eyes missing nothing, supervised the switch-over from the flickering power lines and the generator rig to the power plant on the huge truck parked outside.

He was being especially sure that all of the connections from the truck were one-way into the mansion. Semyon had never seen one of the portable reactors used for high-capacity power generation in areas remote from the state power utility; that Alexei could summon one of these pocket reactors up with a phone call was both interesting and scary. Now, however, his main concern was to keep the control units in the truck from being sabotaged by the demons still sleeping in the data-gathering devices causing their problems.

Another truck pulled up. Several men in army fatigues jumped out of the back, and began pulling heavy cases out of their vehicle. Three soldiers placed the cases on a wheeled cart, and rolled the cart up the front walk. The remaining soldiers began stacking more equipment on another cart; then a third cart joined the procession.

Semyon moved aside to let them in. They seemed to know exactly where they were going, and proceeded to what had been the library of the estate's main building.

They paid Semyon no attention, marching past him with their loads. Curious, he followed them into the library, where they were opening the cases. *He wants to try again*, Semyon thought, *with military-grade equipment, this time*.

BROADCAST BAND

[Installation Run] *The construct, a virus in both the biological and computorial senses of the term, spread rapidly from one life-form to another. In its biological sense, it was a rapidly deploying disease that vectored and replicated itself into every receptor site—life-forms compatible to its infection—and bypassed everything else. In its computorial sense, it was a program that went inactive, biding its time until the arrival of an exact stimulus, either external or temporal, or a combination, that would cause it to activate.*

Other constructs—invisible to the infected life-forms—passed silently among them, reinforcing the infection, and making ready to carry it to the other installations for further propagation.

MARTIALLING AREA

[Activate Task] The next morning, Hank and Ondreya went down to breakfast, expertly handled by Yezeletta's programmed constructs. They had gotten up early, hoping to have the dining area to themselves for a while.

When they entered the dining room, Hank discovered that they had been anticipated. Sitting in the corner at one of the smaller tables, were Peter Rudenko and Leona, talking quietly.

It looked as if they had been there for some time, as each wore the same clothes as the day before, somewhat the worse for wear.

"Hi, people," Hank said.

"Morning," Peter replied; Leona nodded.

"What's up?" Ondreya asked.

"Just talking," Peter said, "about what we'll do when this is over."

"If it's ever over," Leona added, wearily.

"Do you think we'll be allowed to resume our normal lives?" Peter asked. "What would the kind of people that created Yezeletta say to that? They'd probably never let us out of their sights again, or just eliminate us out of hand."

"If they ever find out about us," Hank said. "We aren't the primary objectives in this; Yezeletta is. It occurs to me that, if we wanted to save her, as well as ourselves, all we'd have to do is lie low, and not do anything to attract attention."

"If we haven't, by now," Peter said.

"We could just pull out," Hank went on, "but we have a friend who's depending on us for the help we can provide." He smiled a little at that. "I've noticed how easy it was to throw in with her. It was almost the natural thing to do." He looked at his wife, then at Leona, and finally to Peter. "Have things in this country—hell, the whole world—gotten so awful, that the one good-guy we know is worth protecting to the extent of practically risking our lives for her? Does that mean that the rest of the things that go on around here are so bad, by comparison, that anything or anyone that's worth it stands out that much more?"

"She does stand out," Peter said, "but I know that's not what you meant."

"She risked her life to escape from her creators," Ondreya added. "She did that all on her own, with just a little help from Hilda. And look at what they did to her!"

Peter paused in thought. As his comrades in arms watched, his expression changed, slightly.

"Peter, you've been a bit more hesitant since you came back from Philadelphia. You were a lot more like what people think of as a secret agent before."

"It shows, I guess," Peter said. "It's a combination of things. My immediate supervisor, more of a bean-counter than a good intel analyst, was definitely not happy with my assessment of Allen and Marie Hightower. I was an independent agent. Underscore *was*. I was activated from my place in Chicago to investigate the Mitchell Conservatory and those foreign agents snooping around it."

"Was that all?" Ondreya asked.

"Pretty much."

An attentive servitor entered the room, pushing a cart with coffee. Silently, it poured four cups, placed them on the table, added containers of cream in a sugar bowl, and a glass-full of sugar, and left.

"There were several reports from the part-time agents, notably that Sergeant Montag, about the odd little constructs that were showing up, and, contrary to popular belief," he smiled slightly, "Philadelphia hasn't exactly given up on the old United States. There are still people who would like to see this country on its feet again."

"And a *lot* of people who think that the Federal Government was just a little too uppity before Washington was taken out," Hank said.

Peter laughed. It was a single plosive expletive that had no mirth in it. "It may surprise you, but a lot of the feds in Philadelphia agree with you. Their concern is with getting the old eagle flying again, as she was before certain presidents began selling their country out to The New World Order, whatever it was that week."

"We survived," Hank observed. "The people of this country made it through the worst."

"I said," Peter continued, "Some of the officials I know are interested in helping. Not selling out. Our friend, here, might have a problem living in this building or this city in another ten years, if the screwballs that inhabit large cities ever get removed. What would she do then?"

"And you were sent here to look into those self-same screwballs," Leona said.

Peter chuckled. This time there was actual humor in the sounds. "I had no idea that I'd find both a good friend here, and..." he took Leona's hand as his voice trailed off.

"Peter and I have decided to make it permanent," she said, happily. "Or as permanent as we can in a world like this."

"Where will you go?" Ondreya asked.

"I have some legerdemain from the Agency that will help," he said, "And I believe that I can use some of that magic to provide parachutes for all of you, if you need it."

"Papers," Hank said.

"That's one. The personal computer was a great advance at the end of the last century, but its other side was...well, in my opinion, a government can't be trusted with too much computer time. If a government has it, it uses it. Or makes jobs for the equipment out of thin air. All of the identification schemes that came out of the woodwork, right up to Washington blowing up, ultimately came from legislators with too much time on their hands.

"And agencies like mine are always several steps ahead of them." He and Leona stood. He held her right hand in his left.

"Come up to our room a little later, and I'll show you how to disappear like a pro."

THE LADY CALLS IT

[Concurrent task] Hank and Ondreya looked at each other for a moment before saying anything. It was Ondreya who made the observation. "He looks more like the old Peter now, than since he returned." Hank nodded.

Another servitor entered the dining room.

It was carrying a menu.

MARCHING ORDERS

That afternoon, Hank and Ondreya received several sets of documents from Peter, and extra sets for Anne. Hank took them to The Destroyer and made them disappear. They returned to Yezeletta's War Room, where they found her sitting with Anne, looking into a complex of screens with an expression that was her closest yet to perplexed.

Anne looked up as they entered. "Hi, Mom, Dad."

"Problems?" Hank asked.

"Don't know," Yezeletta said. "There are some slight irregularities in one of my systems on Water Street." She pointed with one of her right hands at an image. "There seems to be noise on the line. And that's never been a problem with my transmissions."

"Age of transmitter?" Hank guessed, "or handshaking errors? Plain old interference?"

Yezeletta shook her head. "Good guesses, but the problem hasn't ever manifested before this. I'm sending out some new Installers with what I think might fix the matter."

Hank pulled up a chair, and Ondreya joined him. "What," she asked, "is my daughter analyzing today?"

"It's another cross-correlation analysis, Mom," Anne said. "This one's looking for any other places in town that might have had a visit from the big guy." She opened a window on her monitor displaying a scatter-graph. "We know where he's staying, and there hasn't been any movement there since he returned." The scatter-plot changed incrementally, as additional points were plotted. "We also know that this is his first visit to Milwaukee. What we don't know is where he's from, or if he's been here before."

"Anne brought that last up for the sake of completeness," Yezeletta said. "My own opinion is that Mr. Big is here recently, perhaps from the other place near Sargon, and that he was vectored in by his creators, based on the infestation in the Conservatory."

THE HILL REBUILDS

[Load Backup] The rebuilding of the Farmland Preservation Project was nearly finished. Most of the new furniture had been brought in, and the wiring for data transmission and telephones had been completed that day.

There was still no word from the detective unit of the Capitol Police. Frank wasn't exactly holding his breath, at this point, but he still nourished a small hope.

Workmen carried in a heavy, flat, metal partition. It would be the backstop for what would be his new office. His computer had survived the burglary, and was running on a serving cart borrowed from the Red Oak Grill—DATCP's Food Service operation.

It was awkward, but it allowed him to get back to work.

HELP, REMOTE MODE

[Load Data Table] Frank's visage also appeared on a screen in Yezeletta's complex. Peter and Leona were sitting in Yezeletta's living room watching the screens, while the others were supervising the birthing of Yezeletta's combat servitors. Their images appeared in one window on the high-res display, miniature characters in a movie-clip that just happened to be real.

Leona looked a silent question at Peter. He raised one eyebrow, and got his laptop out.

The connection took perhaps a half a minute, most of which was modem altercations. His accessing of LINUX's ROOT privilege state was even faster. From the command line interface, he launched a text-based browser, and began his search. Leona sat with him as he looked. A bit later, Yezeletta, Joe and Hank entered the room, and Leona made *"Sh!"* gestures. The others sat and watched Peter at work.

There it was.

It had been disguised: renamed something innocuous by the Searchlight Data Processing maven who had made the entry. He called the report up on the screen, and read it.

"Folks," Peter asked, "how valuable would a little misdirection be?"

Yezeletta answered: "Quite a lot, if it would help in keeping any more investigators away."

"Good!" Peter said. "I had an idea earlier, while you were in the maternity ward. I tried a hunch, and I've located the report that the Searchlight agents made on their raid into the Ag Depart."

Peter read his screen silently for a moment, then asked, "Would someone *please* tell me what the Wisconsin preoccupation with *badgers* is?"

"Wisconsin's the Badger State," Hank smiled. "Lead miners in the southwestern part of the state made homes in the upper parts of river erosion gullies in caves, sometimes artificial ones. Dug in. Like badgers."

"Got it. It's just that I placed Yezeletta's package on a Badger Bus, to be picked up by a Badger Cab on the other end. That's what's so funny. The Searchlights safe-house in Madison is on a place called West Badger Road. Sounds like they've dug themselves in like badgers, too."

Yezeletta's gaze took all of them in; she smiled just a touch, and asked, "What could we do with data like those?"

Peter answered: "I think I know a certain squad of Capitol Police that would like to have the address of that safe house. And those badgers."

IN PROCESSING

Caliban placed the transparencies of himself into the feed slot of a scanner. One by one, the photographs were scanned into a computer that was plugged into the control console of the washing machine. He read data visually from the front panel of the machine, and input other, denser data through his fingertips, into his internal systems.

He opened the top of the unit, looked inside at what was growing there, and then looked up at a shelf above the device.

Miranda was startled to see one of his remotes sitting there, dark as the night, invisible to casual onlookers, watching them. Caliban stroked the little monster. "It will carry the programming to what I have in place now," he said.

The monster scanned them back, its imager seeing, yet not seeing, in the dim light within the truck.

EXPLANATIONS

[Process Shot] Alexei Krilov's pose was pedagogical, his prose didactic. He gestured at a complex diagram thrown up on a screen by actual optics from a very old-fashioned device: an overhead projector.

"This system is used when there must be no chance of its being corrupted by external inputs. If we had known that these devices were as much trouble as they are, I would have had the In-Circuit Emulators and virtual debugging devices brought in first. All of the programming is executed by an interpreter akin to some old systems we liberated from Southern California: there is a virtual machine implemented by emulation code in read-only memory. It is the kind of ROM that may only be programmed once, so there is no chance that anything may happen to the main program code." Alexei shuffled through several overhead slides he'd produced on a portable computer that had been kept with his luggage, and not connected to anything else.

He placed another transparency in the projector, and continued. "The interpreter keeps careful watch, not only of what the programs—written in interpretive code, and uniquely compiled—running on it are analyzing, but on its own internals as well. If there is anything either erroneous or the result of an invasive programming technique, the interpreter prevents such actions, logs the attempt, and reconfigures around them."

He changed displays, again. "Minimally, we should be able to get a dump of what is in those devices in some form that we can understand, and continue work on the data in a controlled environment."

Semyon Malasnikov eyed the army-green cases of equipment warily. He had never heard of this particular collection of devices before, just the military versions of ordinary desk-top computers. They represented an unbelievable amount of computing power, the best that the agency's researchers in Saint Petersburg had.

At one end of the row of boxes that curved around the library like a dark-green reptile of computing (*and probably reptilian in its outlook, as well*, he thought) was a grouping of black wires, simple interfacing contacts. Ordinary plugs.

They looked unpleasantly like tentacles.

Alexei placed one of the shotgun barrels in the grip of an induction pickup, and plugged the pickup into a convenient tentacle.

He made a hand signal to the system operator. The operator made an entry on a keyboard.

The analysis started. Again.

AN INDIRECT ADDRESS, E-MAIL

[Encrypting] "There are anonymous email relays in Vancouver, Paris, Cape Town, Oslo and Tokyo," Peter reported an hour later. "The countries that allow these to run realize that privacy tends to bring business for the Blocs they belong to. A lot of Tech Bloc information runs through Tokyo by way of the big router at Narita, for example, and the Japanese are willing to allow hangers-on to slide through with the encrypted Tech Bloc traffic just to keep their members from taking their developments elsewhere."

"Just that? A safe path for data?" Ondreya asked.

"Sounds like a small thing, but the exabytes that go through that pipe are important enough that the NSA devotes nearly fifty percent of its computer time to analyzing them. It doesn't have very much luck with breaking any of that; the Japanese have some of the best cryptographers in the world on call there. But the NSA tries. Occasionally a Known Plaintext attack will provide something useful."

"So it's reliable," Hank said. "Is that where the information you're sending's going?"

"I'm sending this through the Searchlight Network to the Internet Gate in Berlin. The systems in the Light/Net have secure erase utilities, so there won't be any traces of this after it hits the Internet through the Berlin Office. From Berlin, I'll telnet it to one of the anonymizers in Oslo, and from there, it'll go through several more, as a one-way transmission. There won't be any reply expected, and the origin will be stripped off. That's how anonymous posts to the Usenet News Groups are made."

"When will this confession story of yours reach the destination?" Yezeletta asked.

"About fifteen minutes from now," Peter said. "Most of that is delay in switching through the various Internet routers, and being processed by the anonymizers. All we have to sweat is Madison getting it, and being read the next time someone at the Capitol Police decides to pick up the mail."

"Is it ready to go? If so, send it, by all means," Yezeletta said.

Peter grinned. "I don't need to send it by all means, just by email." He pressed a key-combination. "It's on the way."

PASS-DOWN

[Configuring] *Caliban's bit-maps fanned out across the living network from one animate node to the next. The biological virus that was also a computer virus in a living system reconfigured itself, inputting the data in the bit-maps, and converting its images into holographic form in its data storage. Front and back views, side, top and bottom views, all became bit-strings in a living, linked connectivity of processors.*

As each life-form received the programming and ran it, the results of that action were passed both forward to the next processor in the net and back, as a status response to the point from which the new programming was injected into the system.

Finally all of the status reports had been returned; all of the reconfiguration runs were made, and the new system looked exactly as it had when it was the old system. There was only one change: The new version no longer belonged to its maker. It belonged to someone Other.

DOING BUSINESS AS

Zeke had tacked the transparencies from the autopsy of Lead-Foot Eddie up on a backlit viewing panel. The impossible right-angles and small knots of complex circuitry looked back at him out of the X-Ray images.

Next to those, in its own frame, was a picture of what had remained of Lead-Foot's face. The unbroken expanse of pallid flesh was an eyeless leer at the living.

Several glowing screens illuminated his desk. The computers were the best that Zhongo could steal, and each was online into a different news service.

Zeke was researching the locations where bio-chips were made...make that "grown."

Fabricated? How?

The places that kept showing up in his researches were Toronto, Ontario, Canada, and Montevideo, Uruguay.

And that was just too much.

The Technical Bloc maintained a large web site, and a quick surf to it disclosed that Uruguay was a member. That was about all. Zeke had surfed to other sites, and had found out Uruguay's Gross National Product, that the capital was Montevideo, that the name meant "I see a mountain," and that it had a sizable cattle industry.

Cow-chips as well as bio-chips.

"How often," he asked the three glowing screens, "do you see *Uruguay* in a news report, besides never?"

There was occasional news from Brazil or Argentina, or Chile, but almost never anything from the smallest country in South America. The only thing he himself was able to recall about the country was Groucho Marx's line: "You go Uruguay, and I'll go mine."

Was this choice deliberate? Almost certainly. In a world in which information flowed about as easily as water, and gossip could go world-wide in a hurry, the only way to be private was to be an island of silence in a sea of noise. The Uruguayans simply didn't call attention to themselves. And neither did the bio-chip fabricators in Toronto. Other things in Toronto—their hockey team, the Maple-Leaves, for example—did, but a major industry? Silence.

What were they doing up there? Or down there?

This needed more research, and Zeke would be point man in this effort. Zhongo had made that abundantly clear.

"If it's time for us to get an interest in foreign technology, here, then it's time, and I want to be the one controlling it!" That had been one of Zeke's marching orders, and he took it seriously enough, unlike some of Zhongo's other employees, to do what was necessary.

And to do it the first time.

One of the feeds was into Chicago. Zeke cruised around several web sites on Chicago's north side, looking for more data. Zhongo had several lower echelon hackers on his staff, but didn't trust them enough to do the initial research that Zeke was up to.

Besides, none of *them* had known Lead-Foot Eddie.

He looked up at the X-Rays, again.

What had Lead-Foot gotten into?

That answer would be in Chicago. And countries further south.

Wouldn't it?

M AIL C ALL

The message arrived at a server in Madison a bit later than Peter had said it would. It actually took two hours. A router that was running slow, just outside of Berlin, delayed Peter's missive—as well as several thousand others, for an hour, while the system serving Northern Europe searched for an alternate link. When the fiber-optic cable's traffic lessened enough to allow additional feeds, his message headed north by way of Copenhagen to Oslo.

From there, the message traveled around the world, across Northern Europe, Russia and Asia, and re-entered the United States through San Francisco, by way of TRANS-PAC-ONE, the fiber-optic cable from Japan. The message went up the northern part of the US, taking a route that almost exactly traced Yezeletta's travels from the West Coast. Down through Minneapolis it came, and into the local router for Madison traffic.

It arrived at its destination, a message that in no way revealed Peter's original location, and waited patiently for a human being to read the plain-text contained therein.

D OWN I N THE N EXUS

[Consolidation] *The programming paused, waiting for a short time as all of its separate activities synchronized with each other.*

Then the programming, as a single unified whole, a process greater than the sum of its parts, went active.

O N THE T EN O'C LOCK N EWS

[Long Shot] That evening there was a short news story towards the end of the evening news from Madison's WKOW, Channel-27. Peter almost suppressed a satisfied smirk, as Twenty-Seven's anchorwoman read the two-minute report about a series of arrests made by the Town of Madison

Police at an apartment complex west of South Park Street on Badger Road. The report was accompanied by some amateur video shot by a resident who lived across the street from the ostensible safe-house. There was very little detail in the video excerpts shown: Anne had been unable to enhance them much.

Of more interest were the documents that one plainclothesman at the end of the little procession of arrestees carried out.

CABLE CONNECTIONS

The next morning, everyone crowded into Yezeletta's living room to watch the feed from the Imagers in the ceiling of the Farmland Preservation Project.

It was a typical morning in a Wisconsin State office building; People showed up at about eight-thirty, had breakfast in the lunch-room run by competent, friendly cooks from the company that ran the Red Oak Grill, and went up to work. Other civil servants at Farmland didn't have breakfast at the Grill. They would arrive on the morning bus and go straight upstairs. There was one fellow who was always accompanied by a large, rather pretty dog.

Others would come up through the basement entrance from the parking lot on the back terrace on the East side of the hill, and were usually the first ones in. By about a quarter to nine, everyone who worked there was present, rearranging the new furnishings and straightening out their desks.

For Frank, it began to be familiar enough so that he could begin to put some of the last two weeks out of his mind and get back to work.

There was a disturbance in the next aisle.

Frank had been sensitized to strange voices in recent weeks, and there were some new voices speaking low in the background. Suzanne's voice, a pleasant soprano, was easily heard in reply.

He pushed back from his new monitor, and went to look.

The strange voices came from two uniformed Capitol Policemen and one man in a conservative gray suit.

Suzanne saw Frank first.

"Frank," she began without preamble, "these gentlemen have some interesting information for us."

DISTANT EARLY WARNING

[Parallel Process; Long Shot] Seven people watched as the Capitol Cops and one of their plainclothes detectives told Elaine, Suzanne, Edna and Frank about the tip they had received, and what they had found on the south side of Madison.

The Madison media would be reporting on it for at least a week after.

BENEATH THE FLOOR

[Processing] A little over a day later, Yezeletta was sitting with several of her friends in her living room, watching a set of images.

The images made no sense. Hank's assessment of one of her Hive images as "looking like a Picasso" was even more apt now than it had been then.

Besides, Yezeletta looked puzzled.

"This is fairly unusual," she said. "I'm having data communications difficulties with some of my outlying hives, and this one is practically off-line."

"Do your critters ever get sick?" Anne asked.

"No," Yezeletta said, decisively. "If something happens to them, they return to the nearest installation and regenerate." She paused in thought. "This isn't exactly the most usual behavior."

"How long have you been here?" Hank asked.

"A bit over two years. I've kept pretty much to myself, except for that gangster's hobby."

"And a reorganized gun-man," Joe said drily.

"Apparently Zhongo thinks he was a product of someone from Chicago," Yezeletta said. "The remaining spies I have in his base-of-operations show his 'scientist', a man named Zeke, looking into something in Chicago, and to several places out of the country. That's pretty much what I wanted him to do."

"What kind of spies?" Leona asked her.

"Remote Imagers," Yezeletta said.

Hank looked at Joe. Joe nodded.

"Yezeletta," Hank said, "when was the last time you looked in on Zhongo?"

"Day before yesterday....Briefly."

"Please look in on him now," Hank's voice was urgent.

It's the same urgency he had when my Imagers were getting hunted, she thought. She touched Thicknesse, and sent him a directive.

The image on Yezeletta's main television set rippled, changed, rippled again. Bars of colors moved up and down the screen in seemingly random directions. Dimly in the colored effects, Yezeletta thought that she could see figures moving, one, Zhongo Teketon.

But there wasn't enough of a real image to be sure.

"I have learned my lesson," she said flatly. "Or perhaps my latest lesson. I have a diagnostic channel with appropriate time-stamps on it for this." She sent out another directive, and a data table appeared on the screen.

Joe saw the earliest date, and whistled. "Hon, when was the first time we saw Mr. Big?"

Yezeletta had the image in her internals a tenth of a second earlier than the others.

Allowing for transmission times, the dates and times were identical.

"Hold it," she said. She read another database.

Joe beat her to it, "That gray thing. Where are the samples from it?"

"In the Hive under The Domes," she said. "I didn't want those brought here."

Joe let out a breath. Yezeletta continued, "I was concerned with contamination, and now it looks as if I had the right idea."

"How tight can things be made here?" Peter spoke for the first time.

"Very," she replied. "Wait." She closed her eyes and sent out several directives. "I usually keep this building on a pretty tight leash, and now I've closed everything up."

—I'm monitoring the air-conditioning systems. They're sealing, now. | Descriptor;
Declarative;

"Thanks, Hilda," Yezeletta said gravely. "You may wind up being the only one here to watch things, shortly."

Joe's look was question enough.

"Is Mr. Big trying to find me? If so, he has my data gathering systems figured out well enough to move against me, now."

"But he hasn't. Yet," Hank said.

"Exactly so," Yezeletta answered him. "We need to find out what's happened to my line into Zhongo, and what we can do about it."

LOOK AT THAT

Miranda found the waiting rather difficult. Caliban had several of his Remotes out in the field, observing from the trees around The Domes. He spent hours staring into the screens, watching, almost a statue.

Then he would make love with a passion that wore both of them out.

Then resume his vigil.

The other men in the semi ate field rations rendered somewhat palatable by microwaving, and slept. A portable electric incinerator disposed of wastes without anyone's having to leave the truck.

Caliban continued his analyzing.

STATUS CHECK

Yezeletta's screens were filled with lists, diagrams, and data dumps. The laser-printer had been running for most of the afternoon. Anne and Peter processed printed listings, and Anne created a series of graphic layouts.

The result was a status report of all of Yezeletta's Hives in the Greater Milwaukee area.

"The Hives in Oak Creek, Racine, Menominee Falls, New Berlin, Brown Deer and several other outlying areas, we can disregard. Their status is nominal in any case. Undamaged." Yezeletta paused, then: "The greatest number of transmission anomalies are in the city, itself. And they're not at all uniform; they appear to be centered around Zhongo's headquarters."

"Is there a chance of Zhongo's getting into this?" Hank asked pointedly. "His research assistant, or whatever, *is* looking into the bio-chip industries of Canada and South America."

"There's a chance," Yezeletta said. "Perhaps that free-lance shooter of his actually got one of my imagers for his scientist to analyze. He does have Lead-Foot Eddie's body on ice."

"Is there anything in Eddie that can be decoded by someone external to here?" Joe asked. "Can someone else analyze the results?"

"The reorganizer doesn't leave a residue. The low-level aspects of the changes it effects may be decipherable, but Zeke doesn't have the facilities to do the job."

"Where does that leave us?" Ondreya wondered aloud.

"Where it always has," Yezeletta answered. "We need more information, both on Zhongo, and on Mr. Big."

DEPLOYMENT: TANGENTIAL

"I can probably handle this one better on my own," Peter said. "I'd like whatever you have in the way of combat supplies," he grinned a lopsided grin, "from either of your celebrated kitchens, but I'm going to be traveling light, and concentrating on what I can get, in as passive a way as I can."

Joe gestured at the high-res display. "Hank and I can get as close as we need to Zhongo's. Will these Imagers work over a long distance?"

"Easily," Yezeletta said. "The receptor's a fast hack-job: ultra-violet and infra-red, both, and I have some *very* good image enhancement technology on hand, as well as a damned good artist to do the work on it," (Anne grinned), "And, I can take samples as needed from what both of you gather, and there'll be Installers to take those back to a centrally located Hive."

"Where?" Joe asked.

"The Hive under the Bradley Center."

ON THE ROAD AGAIN

Hank and Joe pulled out in a battered panel truck. Hank found out that its shabby look was largely superficial, when he got in.

"Who has the time for all of this work?" Hank asked. He thought he knew the answer.

"Yezeletta's servitors," Joe said. "They don't think at all, but work very well at simple-minded tasks. Disguising the outer parts of this truck, for example."

Peter pulled up next to them on a low, black Harley. He gave them a thumbs-up, ducked under the rising garage door, and sped up the lower levels of the parking ramp.

The motorcycle's engine echoed back at them.

Joe put the truck in gear. "Here goes," he said unnecessarily, and they followed the secret agent out.

Peter's route took him west, and slightly south towards The Domes. The Imager that clung tightly to his shoulder was a lump under the long "Doctor Who" scarf he wore. His helmet was little more than protection for the back of his skull, but it held a headset radio-link that used some of Searchlight's best encrypted spread-spectrum technology.

"How did you guys put it?" he had asked, earlier. "'It's always a good idea to have a backup in unfamiliar places'."

RESEARCH, EXTERNAL

[Procedure]　　Caliban abruptly ascended to his two-hundred-forty-centimeter height, and looked around at everything in the cramped semi. His violet eyes were opened wide, the blackness of his irises like strange lights that scanned darkness, and took the illumination out of everything they saw.

He looked down at Miranda. She felt his cold gaze on her skin.

"Would you like to take a ride with me?" he asked.

Vince raised one eyebrow at this, and asked, "What do you have in mind?"

"Locating the target," Caliban said. "The Target's transmissions to the installations are general, non-directional. The responses are general broadcasts, also. Whoever needs to pick them up, does, without sending an indicator of reception. If a receiving entity did so, it would disclose its position. I wish to make the target come to me."

There was a low growling sound from the front of the truck.

THE POINT MAN

Peter took his motorcycle on a circuitous route, first slightly south of the

Farmers Bank Building to Michigan Avenue, then west, then north, again.

He wanted to see if he was being followed. The comparatively deserted streets of Milwaukee made this easy enough, but he wanted to be as sure as a little misdirection, and some of his training at evasion, could make it.

He drove across Wisconsin Avenue near the Midwest Express Center, and noted that the Bradley Center was two blocks north, and a block west of his position. He drove further north, and stopped at a McDonalds for a cheeseburger and a Coke. While he was eating, he scanned the traffic around him, what there was of it, as it ebbed and flowed below the fitfully glowing colored signs on the streets.

So far, things looked good.

He reached up under the long scarf, and gently felt for Yezeletta's Imager.

"Rover to Base," he said. "Comm check, Over."

"Base to Rover," Yezeletta replied. "I read you five-by-five. Can you let the Imager have a look?"

"Can do. I didn't want it to get cold while I was outside." He moved a layer of scarf, and the little creature looked out from its hiding place. Peter gave it a piece of meat from his cheeseburger, and it ingested the treat.

"My Imagers have pretty tough digestions," Yezeletta remarked drily. "Are you safe there?"

"So far, no problem," he said softly. "No one followed me in here, and this McDonalds is nearly deserted. I don't see how it stays in business; there aren't even any security precautions."

"Either nobody thinks it's worth the trouble, or the cops hang out there."

"Maybe I'd better be off."

"Luck, Peter."

"Thanks."

Peter headed for the back door. As he left, two Milwaukee Cops come in through the front. He figured that Yezeletta's remark was on the money, but he rode out the back exit of the parking lot anyway.

TRACKING

Anne caught the movement out of one eye: "Hey!" she said, "he's on the move!"

The small jeep was pulling around from the back of the semi, and speeding off. Yezeletta watched it steadily; Ondreya joined them.

The jeep retraced its previous trip from where the semi was parked, to the basement garage of the Conservatory.

"That's the same guy that was there before. I recognise his clothes," Anne observed. "Either he has a lot of uniforms, or he doesn't change very often."

The image flickered, rolled, then stabilized.

Yezeletta raised a black eyebrow, "Has that ever happened before?" she asked Anne.

"When you tested it, as I recall: otherwise, no."

Now there were two people standing in the center of the garage.

"That woman was here with Mr. Big," Anne noted. "I wonder when he's going to put in his appearance?"

"This might be a fact-finding mission," Yezeletta said. "He may be as well concealed as I am."

The two figures on the screen walked around for a moment, and the woman took several pictures with what seemed to be an ordinary Polaroid camera. She removed the prints from the device, and slipped them into her jacket pocket.

"So where's the big guy?" Anne asked.

BETWEEN THIS AND NOT THIS

Caliban stood at his full height, glancing about.

Then he went to the garage door, and peered out of it.

He came back. "I will look in other parts of the installation. Continue here with your data gathering."

He walked under a ceiling vent, through a door, and was gone.

Vince made a face at Miranda, and went back to the jeep. He returned carrying a long, slender object.

He began vacuuming the walls with it.

BACKGROUND PROCESS

Yezeletta touched Thicknesse. He jumped up onto her shoulder. "Peter, can you hear me?"

Peter's voice came back at once, "Yes. I was about to call you up. I'm a block north and east of The Domes. I haven't been followed, and I'm about to go in."

"Don't," Yezeletta said.

"Problems I don't know about?"

"Visitors. Mr. Big's friends, the man and the woman, just showed up; they're in the garage, now."

"How about Big?"

"No sign of him. He may be there, but in a different part of the place; or, more likely, this is a fact-finding job, and he's still in his base of operations."

"Got it! How close do you want me to get?"

"Close enough to get samples of whatever's there. If you can. No risks."

"This is my kind of agency! I think I'll keep this job. Okay, I'll move around to the west side, and check the garage. Later."

ON SITE

Peter started the motorcycle. The Harley revved up, he put it in gear, and headed south. He would have to go around more than a half-circle, but not as much as three quarters of one, to get to where he wanted to be.

The Harley was a wraith in the night, moving through the shadows. He took the bike through alleys, largely unlit tree-lined neighborhoods, and along roads that paralleled main drags. Fifteen minutes later, he came out on Twenty-Seventh Street, and pulled into a vacant lot that seemed to be mostly clear, except for bushes on the corner.

EVA

Caliban re-entered the garage. Nodding to the others, he beckoned to Miranda, a quick gesture performed by one hand held low. "Open the door, and go out," he said softly, "quickly."

She went to the door, and stepped outside. Caliban followed.

THE FACE

Peter had worked himself into the bushes, and was watching the garage with his starlight scope. The reactive optics in the visual aid Yezeletta had supplied him aided the device, bringing in a clear image that was practically in his lap.

There! An outline of fluorescent lighting; door-shaped.

A figure emerged from the garage.

"Rover to Base, there's someone coming out."

"Can you identify," Yezeletta's voice was tense.

"Female, slender, dark hair. Tentative on the last. This scope's color resolution's not too—Jeezus H. Christ!"

"What?"

"The big guy. He's standing next to the woman. They're just standing there, watching."

"I can get samples in other ways. Get out of there, Peter. *Now*."

In the Mirror

Anne sat down next to Yezeletta, "He wasn't in the data feed," she said, "what—"

"Watch," Yezeletta pointed to the screen.

The woman came back in, pulling the door shut behind her.

"Recording?" Anne asked. Yezeletta nodded.

The woman and the other man got back into the jeep, and it moved towards the door. The door ascended, the jeep drove out, the door closed.

There was no one there.

Relocation

Peter backed out of the bushes, and dumped his equipment into the Harley's saddle bags. He walked the bike to the edge of the lot, pushed it into the alley entrance, and hit the starter. He swung aboard, and accelerated down and out of the alley.

He turned south, and put the kilometers behind him.

He did not see the Remote in the tree that followed his progress.

He did not see the *other* Remote ahead of his travels, to which the track of his movements was handed off.

Nor did he see the tiny motes that followed his progress easily, caught up with him, and rode along *on* him.

Remote Sensing

Caliban heard the motorcycle first. He tuned his hearing to the sound, and analysed it. His internal systems plotted an approximate routing based on distance, direction, doppler-shift, and the echoes thrown off by other buildings.

"Were we seen?" Miranda asked.

"Unknown. I have my Remotes following him. We will be able to track him without difficulty. He is carrying one of the target's life-forms. That life-form will receive the infection from my Remotes as he drives under them. The infection will then be carried to the target when the life-form enters one of the target's installations."

Caliban switched on a nasty smile, then switched it off. "I have a good track," he said.

Caliban signaled to Vince. Vince put the jeep in gear, and they drove back to the semi.

A FAST EXIT....

Peter went far south, and came around towards the factory areas near the waterfront. The Farmers and Merchants Building was a ghostly off-white against the night sky ahead of him, but he kept moving north. He turned west, and drove across town to the Bradley Center, usually home to such diverse life-forms as the Milwaukee Bucks, and the Milwaukee Admirals. Peter's goal was yet another set of life-forms. He drove to the west side of the sports center to a place where a vent close to the ground and covered with dirt-filled cobwebs was a dark, almost invisible ingress.

The little Imager jumped from his scarf to the ground, ran to the vent, broke through the cob-webbing, and disappeared into it. Peter backed the Harley out and drove off, turning west, again.

He did not see the motes that followed the Imager into the darkness.

....OBSERVED

In the imitation Maersk Lines truck west of The Domes, Caliban, Miranda and Vince looked at the granular image in the small screen of a portable computer. It was almost *cinema verité*, the point of view being rapid and close to the ground. Dirt, dead leaves and other trash loomed up like mis-shapen trees around the input, as the transmitter of the image ran through the vent pipe, small by normal proportions, huge at this scale. It entered the installation at the end of the pipe.

Caliban smiled. Miranda found the expression unsettling.

"Her Remote doesn't realize what it carries," he said.

But you do, The Other said, And I am here for you.

And at a higher lexical level *in another instantiation* where the data were hidden from The Other, Caliban replied, *I'm not here for you*.

His hungry eyes sought the form of Miranda. Then his hands sought her in real-time.

And in the back of his mind there were the images of stone walls.

And of a great machine that ran continuously in the night.

EYES IN THE NIGHT

Joe and Hank drove west out I-94, and got off near the old Miller Park site. The remains of County Stadium, just a few steel beams and girders, stuck out of the wind-blown detritus like the broken fangs of some long-lost prehistoric reptile. Beyond that, the spectacular ruins of Miller Park, its mov-able roof fallen into the central playing area and never salvaged, was a wall of brick construction alternating with broken-out areas that stared like huge blank eyes.

Joe gave the Park one look and just shook his head. Hank nodded in re-ply. "My dad used to watch the Brewers there," he said.

Joe took them north, then curved east to the row of brownstones where Zhongo and his associates lived. They drove past the front of Zhongo's house, then west to Yezeletta's hide-out, turned, and came back. Zhongo's house was unprepossessing to so-called normal sight, but the reactive op-tics the men wore disclosed infrared lighting, and a complex pattern of tight ultra-violet security trips in which neither of them wanted to get caught.

"I'm going around the back, into the alley," Joe said, suiting actions to words.

He drove past the open alley entrance. The network of normally invisible light beams was there as well. Joe took the van around to the south side of the block. He slid the van smoothly into a parking place under a large maple tree, and they looked between two houses at the back balcony of Zhongo's house.

"We could just send the sample-takers in," Hank suggested.

"Like we really have a choice," Joe said. "We need the data, but the old SOB's really fortified himself behind all of that junk of his."

Yezeletta spoke from the Imager on Joe's shoulder, "It sounds like a plan, Joe; send the samplers in, and come—one moment." There was a long pause, and: "Release the samplers, and go back to where we hid after The Domes. Mr. Big is back at the Conservatory, and I want you safe. Peter will be joining you in about twenty minutes."

Joe raised an eyebrow in what was almost a salute to Hank, and hit the window button. The samplers took that as their cue, and jumped through the window onto the roof. Then they climbed into the maple tree, and vanished.

"There's a telephone wire that runs from a place near the tree to the abandoned house," Yezeletta said. "The samplers can get to Zhongo's from there. Go back to the hide-out, *now*."

Joe put the van in gear, and drove to the hide-out. As he approached the garage door, it opened. The inside was dark, except for the glittering eye of a single Imager that sat on a tool-closet at the back.

There was a sound from outside. A man on a motorcycle pulled up.

It was Peter. Hank helped him wrestle the Harley into the back of the van, and Peter joined them in the front.

"Prime Base wants us back," he said.

"Yeah," Joe answered. "Our big friend has made another appearance."

"Yup, I saw him," Peter said. "It's funny that Yezeletta didn't, with her scanners in the Conservatory."

Yezeletta answered through Joe's Imager, "It's more than funny. He came out of the underground garage, and you saw him, but I *didn't*, with an Imager on the other side of that same door. Please hurry back here. We have plans to make."

IN AND OF ITSELF

[Processing] Vince parked the jeep in its place at the back of the semi, and, without a word, Caliban walked quickly—almost at a trot—to his processors at the front of the truck.

He carried Vince's vacuum cleaner.

Miranda followed him. In spite of the cramped space, she had a hard time keeping up.

When she caught up with him, Caliban was emptying the contents of the vacuum into the analyzer with a swift disregard for his normal fastidious lab procedures that surprised her.

He stared unwaveringly at the readouts on his washing machine. Then he placed his hand on the machine's front panel, and input the reduced data.

When he looked at her, he was smiling. Nastily.

"The infection of the target's systems is nominal," he said. "We will attain acquisition, soon."

Does he even know the <u>sex</u> of whom we're after? Miranda thought.

SYSTEM DESIGN

At about the time Caliban was performing his analytical work, the van containing the three men returned, using a circuitous route back from the northwest side to Yezeletta's base. Yezeletta met them at the elevator.

"I want you to see this. Anne and Ondreya worked it out while you were on the way."

Anne sat, dwarfed, in Yezeletta's big easy chair. Yezeletta hooked her double left hip over the arm of one davenport, and watched as Anne typed on the keyboard in her lap.

"This," Anne said without preamble, "is a screen-shot from about three weeks ago, in the Conservatory garage. Check those gardening tools on the back wall." She used the track-ball attached to one end of the keyboard, and the standard mouse cursor, a little arrow, floated through the image to stop on a collection of three shovels and four rakes of various kinds hanging from hooks on the wall.

"Notice the relationship of the grounds-keeper's tools, and which ones are where. Shovels on the left, rakes on the right, with that leaf-rake—it's the one with a top like a big fan—in the middle."

Anne marked the tools off in a red rectangle, and moved the whole image with its inset rectangle to one side of the screen.

"Now, here's a screen-shot from earlier today." She moused around the hanging landscaping tools, "They haven't been touched in the entire time, but *look at the rakes*." She drew a blue rectangle around the tools in this image.

"Where's that lawn-rake?" Joe asked. "Here's...." He walked up to the screen, and squinted at the picture of the tools. "*Very* slick," he said. "It's as if—" He turned to Anne. "This is your show, maestro."

"You're on it," Anne said. "The big rake is gone, and the other rakes are pulled together to remove the space in the middle. The rest of the wall is stretched proportionally." She got out of the big chair, and went to Yezeletta's desk. She picked up a piece of typing paper that had two dots on it.

"You've probably all tried this at one time or another. Take a sheet of paper, and put two dots on it ten centimeters apart." She held the sheet up before her face. "Stare at the right-most dot with your left eye, and move the sheet away from you. At one point, the left dot will vanish."

She put the paper down, "It vanishes because its image has fallen on the part of your retina where the optic nerve connects. The so-called blind spot."

"And this is?" Joe prompted.

"Something similar," Anne said. "The blind-spot in your eye isn't normally visible, because your brain fills in what your optic nerve doesn't see. Some people see the effect better in the dark: a lit clock face across the room will appear to vanish when you look away from it. This is the same effect.

"Somehow Yezeletta's scanners are being fooled by a very large blind-spot. I'm willing to bet a spot about the size of Mr. Big."

DOWN IN THE WORKSHOP

An hour later, Yezeletta was giving another quick tour of her assembly line.

"These servitors will be capable of faster motions, and will have shorter reaction times." She picked up a stainless steel sphere that seemed to have fine squares ruled into its brushed surface. "These are quite dangerous. Inside this container is what I call a combat reorganizer. It will effect a paralysis of the voluntary nervous system that can be reversed by another reorganizer similarly contained."

"Check me," Leona said. "It could have been far worse?"

"You got it!" Yezeletta said. "The reorganizer is the one thing that I want to keep away from both Mr. Big and the Project he rode in with. There are far too many delightful ways that something like this could be abused. In the hands of a left-wing dictatorship, for example, or in one of those pleasant Middle Eastern theocracies with their medieval laws."

"What about?" Joe asked, pointing downwards.

"Secrecy isn't needed here, Joe," Yezeletta said. "The Madflowers have a special modification on top of the basic Davis Protocols so that they only affect me. I may need a stimulant, if Mr. Big and I ever go one-on-one."

Leona kept close to Peter in the ante-way to the room containing Yezeletta's pseudo-wombs. She looked through the window into the double rows of glass cylinders that lined both sides of the long corridor.

"What else do you have?" she asked.

Yezeletta led them to a small office on a balcony that overlooked the colorful tangle of the Matrix Engine. There were several old couches there. She sat on the edge of one; the others took places. "I have several new pieces of combat programming that I adapted from the defense programs in my internal systems. I learned a lot from the results that came back on the Internet from Kiev." She smiled like a cat. "I hope those Russians learned something, as well."

—Child, I have detected an anomaly | Declarative;
   in one of the external data feeds. |

Yezeletta looked up at an Imager that regarded her with an owl's eye. In response to an external input, the gold aperture winked.

"BUSILY SEEKING—"

[Boot Sector] Back in her living room, Yezeletta configured her television set—it had the largest screen—as the main display, and the high-res as an auxiliary.

Random colors rippled across the screen, and then it came into sharp focus.

The image was another of Hank's "Picassos." Yezeletta added a stage of false-color, and the picture cleared up into the inside of a Hive of her constructs.

In the back, a row of Imager Bats hung upside-down on the wall. In one upper corner, something like a cauliflower grew, held in place by flying buttresses of tough, dark-colored organic material. In another corner, a ball of Receivers curled and flowed over themselves: a nest of light-gray centipedes. Walking Imagers, Cat-Arachnids and other constructs snuggled up together in small nests or on shelves on the walls.

In the center, a small Imager was looking around, scanning.

The little creature moved abruptly to an enpty area on the wall. It seemed to be pressed against the gray concrete, unable to move.

Perturbed, Yezeletta touched Thicknesse, and sent a directive to the Imager: *Front and Center!*

Nothing happened.

While her friends watched, unable to help except for moral support, she sent another directive to a Cat-Arachnid sitting in its place on a shelf. That command was disregarded.

"Joe, we used a combination of your techniques and mine on the bats." It was a declaration. Joe nodded once.

She sent a third directive out, and one of the bats on the wall turned its head, and looked at the pinned Imager.

She routed its output to the high-res screen.

BACK-TRACK

[Accessing] Towards the end of his tour of duty at Project Sargon, the friendly electrician with his magic tricks and a kind word to the younger Yezeletta showed her a card trick that had used the illusionist's art of "forcing." Forcing consists of allowing a spectator to draw a card, but making sure that the card drawn is actually the one that the magician has selected in advance. The spectator may then be appropriately amazed at the prodigious prestidigitational skills of the magician at guessing his "randomly drawn" card.

Yezeletta had practiced the card-cut force, as well as one that masqueraded as a pretty good riffle-shuffle for several days, before demonstrating them to Hilda.

She never showed the tricks to anyone else.

MAGIC TRICKS

There was an impression of Yezeletta's skill with cards in the image returned from the Imager-Bat.

A small and very spiky creature was holding the Imager up against the wall and examining it closely with its one eye.

Frowning, Yezeletta switched to the feed from one of the Cat-Arachnids.

The intruder vanished.

She switched to a Receiver. Splitting the screen between her Imager-Bat—the signal she could rely on—and the feed from the Receiver, she tuned the centipede's inputs through the rather narrow band-width that it could detect.

The intruder showed as a ghostly magnetic field.

That was enough. She routed the Receiver's output to the nearest Cat-Arachnid, and the Cat-Arachnid pounced.

The sharp claws of the predator sliced cleanly through the intruder and the Cat-Arachnid pulled it off of the other Imager.

Yezeletta leaned back. Several others took breaths.

"Where is that one?" Joe asked her.

"That's the sampler that Pete left at the Bradley Center. That's where that Hive is."

THE OTHER—II

[Establishing Shot] Caliban looked at the darkened screen, frowning.

He turned to Miranda.

"She knows that I have her location."

"But you don't know where she lives," Miranda said. "All you know about is that installation."

"It is enough. I can make her come to it."

He actually referred to The Target as "her," that time.

Caliban touched one of his Remotes, sent it a directive.

Then he went to the front of the truck, and removed the steel bars holding fast the door to his foot-soldiers.

D ECISIONS

[Later] "Any one of us could go there to do what's necessary," Joe said. He and Yezeletta had gone to bed much later, after an evening that had almost degenerated into arguments.

Yezeletta held him in all of her arms. "I know, Joe Davis, all of you have been the best friends I could have ever wanted." she smiled. "Listen to that, I'm getting positively sentimental." She hugged him closer "And you have been what all of those ridiculous magazines call Mr. Right, for all of this time. That doesn't change anything. I have to meet Mr. Big. I have to know what *they* want, and I have to handle this on my own."

Joe gently touched her lips. "Not alone; you have your own army. We will help. Look at the way the Lenhadens joined up, and how Peter practically threw his old life out to help you."

"And you love me."

Joe grinned in the darkness. "That's what Ondreya said the other day. Does it show that easily?"

"You let it."

"You do, too, Babe. We're in it. Right to the end."

Yezeletta smiled up at him. "My Army consists of you, a family of gun-toting survivalists, an unfrocked secret-agent and his gun-moll, and a brain in a computer. I like it."

—A very *good* brain in a computer, Child.	Definitive; <Template>;

In one of the other bedrooms, Peter and Leona were undressing for bed. They got under the covers and cuddled close for a moment.

"This is getting almost too intense for both of us," Leona whispered. "Will we get out of it in one piece?"

"I'm pretty sure of it," Peter said. "I've been in worse situations. The paperwork we have will allow us to vanish pretty effectively, and we can change identities two or three more times, if we have to. Searchlight has a number of bank accounts that they think I don't know about, and at least one safe-house in Green Bay that I researched before I left Philly."

"I feel a tad better. But that Mr. Big! He's the most frightening thing I've ever seen. Where did he come from?"

"The same place Yezeletta did."

"She's downright neat. Did you know she rescued me from a rapist?"

"No. Do tell me about it sometime."

"Will we break off with her? I'd rather not."

"We won't," Peter said. "She's too good for that and she needs friends. When we get to where we're going, we'll set up a comm-link back to her." He paused, then asked, "Who did she rescue you from?"

That night, at the end, Leona told Peter about how Yezeletta had rescued her from Gray Roger.

THE LAST DAY

[Initialization Run] Mid-morning found Yezeletta's band of friends getting ready for an encounter that no one could really make plans for or about.

Hank and Ondreya had gone down to The Black Destroyer to hide Peter's presents and to bring up several more items from their travelling armory. In Yezeletta's conference room, at her largest table, Hank appointed himself armorer. He and Peter cleaned and oiled every firearm that anyone had, including the ubiquitous forty-fives that Yezeletta's servitors carried. Leona came in with three pistols of her own, and Peter checked them with a professional eye. "Just the way to begin a new relationship," he said with a grin. "I'll give these a good going-over."

Then Anne showed up with her weapons.

Later, Anne sat with three computer screens facing her, the high-res hanging behind them. She was attempting to get into Zhongo's internal networks, and was having problems with the interference. "Whoever did this is good," she said. "We'll have to be better."

Joe and Yezeletta came up from three floors below with a flat of Madflowers and a large basket of her combat reorganizers. Peter returned from his car, carrying a small metal box and a long leather case: a shotgun. He removed something from the metal case, placed it in a holster on his belt.

He didn't mention it further.

Anne got up from the computers, looked pensively at the flat of Madflowers, and left the room. In a moment, she returned with several commonplace items: shoe-trees, and a coil of brown flexible rubber tubing. She removed a multi-tool from her back pocket, one of those devices with multiple screwdrivers and blades in the handles of a pair of pliers, and dismantled the shoe-trees.

And in the background, Yezeletta's servitors did the cooking.

TWILIGHT

[Externally Specified Index] That evening Yezeletta, dressed in a dark gray jump-suit, wearing various items of equipment, led her procession down to the basement, where the van and another car were waiting. She got into the back of the van with the Lenhaden Family, and Peter and Leona started the car up.

The little procession wound up out of the basement of the Farmer's and Merchant's Building, and drove into the darkening evening.

It was a silent and uneventful trip to the Bradley Center. The Center wasn't more than a fifteen-minute drive from Yezeletta's residence. As always, the streets of Milwaukee were deserted. Yezeletta watched, as the darkened windows passed them by.

Sometimes, she would see the small shape of one of her Imagers looking down from a tall structure. Then it would hide, again.

They pulled into the first level of the Center's parking ramp; it was actually accessible. Joe spun the van around, so that it was facing out. Peter parked next to the van, likewise facing out.

Then they waited.

On the nearby streets, what traffic there was at night in downtown passed, intent on its own errands. In the distance the siren of a police car or perhaps an ambulance echoed off the dark buildings, a disembodied mechanical howling in the gathering night.

"Where is the Hive you're interested in?" Ondreya asked.

"In an underground crawl-space in the area near where most of the drains go out of the basement," Yezeletta said. "Some of my Diggers have enlarged the area a bit, other creatures waterproofed it, and there's a tap into the power and telephone lines, although I've not used those, yet."

She looked at a small display in her left hand, her lower. Instead of precise graphics, there were ripples and flashes of color and complex flickering patterns.

"This is upsetting," she said without rancor. "I didn't see Mr. Big when he *had* to have been in the garage. There's no way that he could beam-down into that doorway where Peter saw him."

"Selective invisibility?" Hank asked.

"How so?" Yezeletta asked.

"Something that selects for Mr. Big, and interpolates the *background* he's standing in front of into the image, rather than a scan of Big. Anne's blind spot."

Yezeletta nodded. "Something that you wouldn't notice unless you were looking for it, and then, you wouldn't know what you were looking for, even if you found it. Except we have Anne."

Anne grinned in the darkness.

—Child, the other ones are moving, again.	Declarative;

"Where are they going?"

—Uncertain. They are currently headed in the direction of The Domes.	Descriptor; Predictor;

"Lock the place down, Hilda," Yezeletta said. "Seal it until we get back."

—Done.	Declaration;

"How much longer?" Ondreya asked.
"A few more minutes, I want to get Hilda's status back before we go out."

—Locking Sequence complete. I—	Declarative; Parity Check;

"Hilda?" Yezeletta asked.

—Activating intruder defense; Firewall active. Intrusion coun-	Parity Check; Run;

termeasures on line. Cutting
Trans-—

Ondreya took out her forty-five caliber Colt and worked the slide.
"Let's go in," she said.
"One minute," Yezeletta said. She sent a directive to a place in her private virtual reality, and attached a query.
—Hilda.

—Hilda? | Broadcast Status;

There was no answer.
Yezeletta sent a test message into the channel. It was returned: **Address Invalid**. She tried again, with a diagnostic message:

—State Communications Link Sta- | Directive;
tus. | External

The status returned:

—Link broken at Exterior Node 4- | Declarative;
B. Firewall active. Communica- | Externally Specified In-dex;
tions prevented from N/4-B by | Returned:
the Super User. | {
| 0xFFFF0177; 0xFEEE0105;
| };

Yezeletta summoned up a map of her installations in a window in her right eye. Exterior Node 4-B was a connection in the basement of the Farmers Building, one of the first places—of several in that basement—that any exterior inputs had to pass to get into her LAN. The Super User, of course, was Hilda. She opened her eyes, to see her friends looking on with concern.

"I just sent a query to Hilda at home," she said. "She was cut off in the middle of her last transmission. It looks as if she's safe, but had to defend herself pretty fast from some sort of attack." She paused, collected her thoughts, briefly. "Ondreya, I quite agree.

"Let's go in."

CRYPTIC ATTACK: MEET IN THE MIDDLE

[Start Concurrent Process] They disembarked from the vehicles. Several servitors carried equipment, and one ported the Madflowers, the flat covered with a plastic wrapping. Yezeletta checked the reactive optics that her army wore, and, pistols in hands, they went up to one of the maintenance entrances.

While Peter and Leona, Hank and Ondreya stood guard, Yezeletta used the same technique that she had used at the Mitchell Conservatory. The stiff black construct punched through the gray preparation and on through the door. The Imaging device on the end panned the hall into which the service entrance led. It was deserted.

Yezeletta sent the construct a signal, and it bent backwards, and pressed the emergency release handle on the door's interior.

They entered. Joe looked back at the Imager in the van which returned a single gold-eyed scan, before it closed the iris over its receptor.

The little band of investigators headed for the basement where the Hive was located. Yezeletta's techniques made fast work of getting into the actual basement from the service corridor they had entered. She sent a sampler into the Hive and in a moment it returned, having gathered what it needed as well as having read out the status of the Hive's organic processor.

Yezeletta and Peter scanned the basement, each using familiar technology. Leona stood near Peter, holding her twelve-gauge. There was something in a holster on Peter's left side that no one recognised. Peter's analyzer registered the near area of the basement itself, and the crawl-space sub-basement that was used to get at plumbing and electrical runs.

Pete aimed it upwards.

He read the small screen. He believed the displays, but gave a start of shocked disbelief.

"Yezeletta," he said in a low voice, practically a stage-whisper, "look at this."

She took the device, and read it.

"Cardiac?" she asked.

"Yes," Peter confirmed.

"What?" Ondreya was the closest; she asked for the rest.

"This is what I was afraid of," Yezeletta said levelly. "The attack on Prime Base was a feint. Misdirection. Peter's device," she showed Ondreya the read-out, "Is detecting a nervous system that can handle multiple hearts.

"A nervous system like mine. Mr. Big is here."

CRYPTIC ATTACK: KNOWN PLAINTEXT

[Run System] "It means we know he's here. We don't know if he has similar detection devices, but we should assume it." She half-grinned at Hank, "We won't be making an 'ass' out of 'you and me' by selecting this initial condition."

"Back-ups you have," Anne said with the recklessness of the young. "Where do you want the rest of us?"

I would love a daughter like her! Yezeletta thought. "The Madflowers must be placed where I can get one in a hurry, if I need it. Dropping one on me might work, or throwing one."

"Keeping one in your tool-belt?" Joe asked.

"Mr. Big might get it. He might be able to activate it by simulating my characteristics. Then he would have the additional strength. No: it has to be tossed when I need it."

Anne gestured at an object on her belt, a contrivance she had made of the aluminum parts of the two shoe-trees and the elastic. "I can fire it with this, but you'll have to catch it."

Yezeletta took a breath. "And another thing. If he goes for one of you, shoot him. Don't let him get you. Shoot him at a distance. If he gets close, you'll never beat him. He moves too fast.

"Has the house been counted? Everyone rehearsed?

"It's show-time."

THE EYES OPEN

They went up the stairway to the first floor. Here there were the box offices, closed concession stands and vending machines, most in a state of disrepair. Mobile Imagers scurried ahead along the walls and on the ceilings. Ahead the playing area, now reconfigured into a basketball court, was in a sort of artificial dusk; only the standing lights, exit lights and the like were on. Yezeletta adjusted her eyes for their widest bandwidth. *Can he see me?*

She entered the basketball court. She looked up, down, to both sides. *Ironic. I'm on the Bucks end of the court!*

Out of her peripheral vision, she detected the movement of Anne going up into the spectator seating. She was carrying several Madflowers.

Hank and Ondreya, Peter and Leona stood guard, right and left.

The lights came on.

Yezeletta's eyes adjusted away from the sudden glare as all of the illumination appropriate to a game came up in a sudden rush of light.

Her vision cleared. She took a step forward. Another.

The man she had called Mr. Big stepped into view at the other end of the court. A dark-haired woman walked out and stood beside him. She wore a pair of Barettas on a leather belt. Another man joined them on his other side.

The stage was set. All the players had arrived.

PART THREE:
"THE EYES OF THE SETTING SUN—"

——>>> ONE <<<——

"...the land where the Sun casts no shadow."

—The Jefferson Airplane, 1975

IN THE MISTS OF WUDAN MOUNTAIN

[M++] Frozen in an interval of time, composed by their Author, a fugue and variations in silicon and carbon: the Eternal Opponents faced each other.

Yezeletta mode-switched. An image of Caliban built up in her left eye, the micro-changes in his body temperature showing in exaggerated false coloration; those colors rippling, changing, merging in a dream image, dissolving from one amorphous spectral shape to another: the colors and shapes seen in the dark behind closed eyes.

Caliban walked towards her. By some unspoken agreement, his accompanists stayed where they were.

Yezeletta closed in.

Caliban's stride was a march with syncopations added: Yezeletta's augmented hearing input and processed the systematic rhythm of his step. The enhanced image of Caliban in her internals was a descant.

They closed to access-distance. Yezeletta's narrowed eyes missed nothing.

"You must return with me," Caliban said. "I'm here to take you back to the project."

He took a step towards her. Yezeletta activated her tactile internals, adjusting her skin away from pain. She didn't answer him.

Caliban's violet irises closed; then opened. Those are indicators, she thought. Is he telling me something, faking me out, or what?

AT MIDNIGHT

She tuned her inputs: colored fringes appeared around the periphery of Caliban's image, as she registered and false-colored the micro-motions of his limbs, as she tracked the macro-motions of his body. The heat signatures of electromyographic activity stood out in wide, feathery stripes in her own spectrum: he was a walking anatomy text to her second-sight.

Caliban attacked.

She perceived it through her internals milliseconds before her actual vision got it. Caliban spun, a tornado on legs. His motion took him towards her; his two right legs carried the momentum of his entire mass, slamming his legs in a circular movement that would have knocked Yezeletta down, had they connected.

Yezeletta sprang back, an attacked tarantula facing a larger opponent. Caliban had attempted to sweep her ankles out from under her with one foot, and cause nerve damage higher up with the other. *He must know that my backups are protected!*

She recovered from her backwards motion, crouching in a guard stance that balanced her on her two right legs and allowed a six-limbed attack.

Caliban followed through, his motions all a fluid series, a theme and variations, a logical progression. Yezeletta didn't register a hesitation or a pause for recalculation. He came for her, almost levitating as he jumped off his right legs, his left legs ready to punch into her midsection.

She spun around, her four hands striking back as he passed her. She aimed at network connections, nerve centers, vitals as Caliban charged, an engine of destruction on his own track.

Yezeletta faced him.

Across a gulf, narrow in width, immeasurable in depth, the two augmented humans scanned each other, their internal processors solving simultaneous systems of differential equations of combat motion, assessing patterns of action, planning at a level lower than their consciousness.

The only sound on the playing field was their disciplined breathing.

Caliban was taller and heavier. *The first one I've ever had to look up to!* Yezeletta had maintained her practice; she had been out in the real world *such as it is!* longer than Caliban.

Did Caliban have improvements? More redundancy in his systems, tougher skeletal structure? Subcutaneous body armor? It didn't seem possible; his radiative characteristics were similar to his associates.

Yezeletta smiled inwardly: a mental gesture only. There was one obvious quality that was almost too obvious: most women have faster reaction times than most men. And her reactions were augmented, assisted by her internal systems.

Later, she would play back her view of the battle. The actuality was too quick. Too furious.

Caliban detonated.

He exploded forward, his four hands ready to deal deadly or disabling blows. Yezeletta parried, deflected, as fists, fingers, edges of hands attacked eyes, nose, throat, ears. She swept aside incoming fists, and their legs deflected defended deleted attacking knees, multiple strikes of feet. The two were war machines, their human controls released to their internal processors, as they danced a tarantella of one-on-one combat. Yezeletta's blows glanced off tough muscle, Caliban's strikes vanished down channels, spent as Yezeletta spun away, deflected, avoided.

His image was one of deadly competence, his color fringes a cloak of lethal colors, colors that *Yezeletta could read.*

Caliban surged forward again. Yezeletta stepped back, grabbing his nearest hand. She fell back, taking him with her, rolling out of the way. Caliban caught himself and recovered. Yezeletta looked up at him and shot out her right feet, catching Caliban's left ankles. She reached with her long right arms and seized his right ankles, a push and a pull that had all of her weight behind it. Caliban fell heavily. She rolled back, and jumped to her feet.

ALL THE AGENTS

[Real-Time Running] Caliban *ascended* to his feet. Yezeletta tracked him. His eyes of flaming violet expanded, vertical slits widening, retinas glowing an almost invisible pink, as he used their enhancement capabilities.

He looked down on her. She looked up.

He took a step towards her. Yezeletta checked her internals for damage. Caliban reached out.

Caliban's movements were fast. Too fast.

She took a step back, a short hop-skip, putting herself beyond the reach of his long arms.

He took a deliberate step forward.

Then he struck.

His movements were fast, testing the limits of Yezeletta's stretched time-sense. His arms were several centimeters longer than hers. *And he has as many as I have!*

Two of his hands grabbed for two of hers—the upper against the upper. Yezeletta aimed a jab at what would be his solar plexus, putting all of her upper body strength into it. Caliban twisted; her blow landed on reinforced ribs, instead.

He grabbed her striking hand, her lower left. Then her lower right.

Yezeletta stubbornly fought a kind of impending panic. All of her martial arts techniques had been designed for the normal soldier, against whom she would have an obvious advantage.

She widened her peripheral vision, then looked down with one eye. Caliban was ready for her *there*, too.

She brought her front right knee up in a vicious motion.

Caliban snarled at her in pain, but he loosened the grip on three of her hands. With a yell of triumph, she twisted out of his grasp, swung one of her now-free hands around in a ferocious slap that dazed him, and wrenched her remaining hand from his grasp.

She danced out of his way, dodging his charge, as he ran for her. She swung a roundhouse blow for his head as he passed her. She jumped up, spun around, and faced him in a fighter's crouch, her hands moving, moving. *Keep him off balance, don't let him know what you're going to do next*, came the voice of one of her rough-and-tumble coaches echoing down the corridors of time to her.

He leapt through the space between them. His arms spread wide, his hands like claws, he landed on her, grabbing her wrists, again.

He encircled her waist with his lower arms, holding her lower pair behind her back. He kicked her legs out from under her with a malicious, brutally fast side-kick, and fell on her. His front legs came down on her legs, effectively immobilizing them.

She was on her knees, and his face was just centimeters from hers. Yezeletta twisted her upper hands and managed to free one from Caliban's grasp. She punched upward to catch him on the chin, and felt, with great surprise, a probing between her legs.

"Not a chance, you creep—!" she yelled, outraged. She fell back, dropping their combined weight on Caliban's lower hands, still holding her hands behind her back. She brought her right back leg forwards and up in another knee to his crotch.

Caliban yelled something that was not language she recognized, and she brought her knee up again, then slammed it down to the deck.

The motion helped: she rolled on top of him. She pulled her lower hands free of his grasp and grabbed his wrists. She smiled a long, nasty smile as he looked up at her.

"I'm not the pushover you thought I was, am I?"

"No matter!" he answered. *Almost by rote*, she thought, *or a sub-task*.

She dropped her left front knee in his gut. He exhaled with a loud explosion of air and tried to wrap his back legs around her waist.

"No way, little man!"

Yezeletta slapped him, left, right, left, her large hands leaving red hand-shaped areas on Caliban's face.

He punched her in the ribs with his right lower fist.

Yezeletta adjusted her sensations away from the blow.

Caliban's left front knee came up between her legs, brushing her hair.

"None of that, Junior!"

Caliban brought both of his back legs up, hitting Yezeletta on her rump; she took the motion and added to it. She directed it against Caliban's chin and into his chest *Right where they do external heart massage!*

Caliban stopped incrementally, stunned. He adjusted himself back to Running Mode and slapped Yezeletta.

She rode with the blow, rolling off of him and away. She sprang to her feet, and side-stepped around him, back in her on-guard crouch.

Caliban jumped, and he was standing tall, again. His violet eyes narrowed, the vertical slits just barely black lines against flaming actinic suns.

Below, his arms moved sinuously, as did hers. *Did we have the same instructors?* And below that—

She could aim for those, or his eyes. *Balls and eyes*, her fighting instructor had said, in a moment of candor. The two weak spots on a man. One to incapacitate, the other because it was instinct to protect those. The misdirection and the hesitation on the part of her opponent might give her the chance she needed to strike a terminating blow.

She had seen umpteenth-dan black belts sparring in deadly earnest, fights that would be ended in a matter of seconds between less matched opponents. These stretched out for minutes, then tens of minutes, as two superbly skilled practitioners of the ancient and deadly arts each sought the one opening that would bring a definitive end to a battle with a rival with whom he would be having a beer in friendship an hour later.

Circling, circling.

The surroundings had faded away into a limitless plane. Only the lit center of all of space-time remained and the death-dealing man before her, watching, waiting.

She smiled with an inward sensation. They wanted him to bring her back to Sargon! And they didn't particularly care what he did to her, as long as he *brought her back*.

Was that why what was left of Sargon had made a male agent, instead of another female? Did anything they did make any sense?

Maybe it did, to them.

He moved, an erotic dance of pure malevolence watching waiting, a spider in his web, a web that he wanted her in, as his.

As his *what?*

He stopped moving. Circling.

He rose out of his crouch, stood at his two-hundred-forty centimeter height, looked down at her.

THE SUPER-HUMAN CREW

[Processing] Warily, Yezeletta did the same. They stood regarding each other, The Black King and the White Queen, eternal opponents across the mock battle/playing field of the Bradley Center's basketball court.

He took a single deliberate step forward. Yezeletta echoed the action.

He took another step.

Yezeletta advanced.

Caliban charged.

And so did Yezeletta.

She neither struck, nor countered: she used the Akido concept of "entering" to get inside of his offense, *to make it irrelevant.*

Hands met hands, legs intertwined. Eyes of brilliant sunset gold locked in on eyes of searing violet.

He grabbed both pairs of her hands in his and forced them behind her back. Yezeletta resisted, and Caliban's larger arms encircled her like bands of flesh-colored steel.

She felt him probe her, below. She chanced a quick look up, behind her. "Anne!" she called.

Anne cocked the red Madflower in the sling-shot that she had made from two shoe-trees and a piece of surgical rubber tubing, pulled it back, aimed, and released it.

The red bloom hit Yezeletta full in the face. She snapped with her teeth, caught several of the petals in her lips, chewed, swallowed.

Caliban, unable to take any action except to hold Yezeletta stared at the red dust on Yezeletta's lips, *the red pollen.*

The...active ingredient *attacked* her.

She kicked up and to the side with her front pair of legs, aimed a fast and deadly blow at Caliban, and used her left rear leg to swat his right legs out from under him. Light receded for Yezeletta. Her sight took on the sunset shades of oranges and dark scarlets, dark reds verging on vermillions and blacks. She adjusted her vision to compensate and found that *all* of her sight was limited to low frequencies. Caliban's movements ran slower, as slow as her time-base-stretching capabilities could achieve. Pain was absent, her lungs took in huge amounts of air, her hearts beat martial syncopations.

Her vision narrowed down to a red tunnel at the end of which Caliban's face, his expression unreadable, was a cloud that looked, a cloud that could *see.*

Her arms were pulled tightly up behind her. She routed her new strength to her upper arm muscles and pushed down. She felt Caliban's grip on her wrists tighten, and she twisted effortlessly out of his grasp. She removed another of his hands, and struck him with the heel of her left upper in the chest.

Caliban grabbed for her hand; she removed it from her.

She pushed her remaining arms down towards her waist and brought them to the front.

The tunnel through which she looked widened incrementally.

Her internals were cleaning the Madflower Effect from her bloodstream!

She almost cursed the efficiency with which her nano-tech kept her clean of external influences. *It was like this when those rads drugged me!* The few petals she had ingested were the incremental advantage she needed against her larger opponent. She ripped her upper right from Caliban's hand, cocked her fist back, and slammed it into his face.

Caliban rolled with the punch, ducked slightly, and reached for her head with all of his hands.

Seeking.

Yezeletta forced his hands back. She kicked his legs—all of them—out from under him, and Caliban fell back, his head hitting the floor with a crack.

It was nothing, *His head is as well protected as mine!*, but it gave Yezeletta her chance. She knelt over him, holding his lower hands down by kneeling on them, holding his upper hands over his head, with her upper hands.

She touched his head with her lower set of hands, looking—*sensing*—for what must be there.

There they were.

They were even where she expected them to be.

They are nothing if not consistent!

She located the contacts.

Summoning all of her training, her knowledge, and all of the capabilities of her—

Caliban's lower hands worked free.

He took her head in his hands!

　　　—she interfaced—

　　　　　　　—Caliban interfaced—

—with him!

　　　　　　　—with her!

There, inside the Systems from which they came, Yezeletta and Caliban *finally met each other*.

——>>> TWO <<<——

Many a night from yonder ivied casement, ere I went to rest,
Did I look on great Orion sloping slowly to the west.

Many a night I saw the Pleiads, rising through the mellow shade,
Glitter like a swarm of fireflies tangled in a silver braid.

Here about the beach I wandered, nourishing a youth sublime
With the fairy tales of science, and the long result of time;

When the centuries behind me like a fruitful land reposed;
When I clung to all the present for the promise that it closed;

When I dipped into the future far as human eye could see,
Saw the vision of the world and all the wonder that would be.-—

> —Alfred, Lord Tennyson,
> "Locksley Hall"

In my life there was a picture, she that clasped my neck had flown;
I was left within the shadow sitting on the wreck alone.

> —Alfred, Lord Tennyson,
> "Locksley Hall Sixty Years After"

The Substrate

[Load System] Yezeletta stood alone in the center of an infinite, limitless void. As she watched, forms began to take shape around her.

Beneath her, a sable substrate faded in out of shadowless argent nothingness. It was a mosaic, marked off in the aggressive stellations of Penrose Tiles. The individual components of the Penrose designs took on colors, both the colors that her creators had known, and the *other colors*, the harmonics *that only she could see.*

She stood in the center of her own star, its colors streaming off into the void space with an intensity that surprised even her.

Another Penrose tiling took form, extending coalescing merging *unifying* with her place.

A section of a piece of text—an excerpt from something much larger—rippled across her memories, mirroring in her eyes:

Continuum Interlock Accessed.
Metrical Frame Entered.
Coexistent Hyperplanes Conjoined.
On Line.

A figure materialized at the center of the other Penrose Stellation.

Caliban.

There was a breath of cool wind blowing against her, across her. All around her were the flickerings—just at the edges of her vision—of sheet-lightning.

The process didn't end there; something appeared *between* them.

An object, a playing surface, possibly two meters square, divided into squares twenty-five centimeters on each side, sixty-four of them: a chessboard.

As they watched, the chessboard took on the traditional black and white coloration. The chess-men walked to their respective sides, taking up their appropriate starting positions.

The opposing armies watched each other warily. Now and then, one of them would look over its shoulder at its general.

The Black King looked at Yezeletta with glittering violet eyes. The black king was a simulacrum of Caliban, himself, and his Queen—

That would be—Miranda?—that was her name, his...Woman?

Miranda stood there, hip-shot, striking a pose. She was bare above the waist, but her near nakedness was aggressive rather than sexy. Her pose was provocative rather than seductive. Her attitude was contentious, her body-language that of an attacker, barely under control.

The White Queen looked over her shoulder at Yezeletta.

Yezeletta looked down at a smaller version of herself, standing next to Joe, who was the White King.

Then: there was a discontinuity, a stretching, then, in contradiction, a compression, a twisting, a contortion, then a moment of dizziness, and Yezeletta looked around herself.

She examined the White Side a little closer: There were Hank and Ondreya, as Rooks; Anne Lenhaden, and her grandfather, Thorfinn, the Knights; Leona and Peter Rudenko, incongruously, as the White Bishops.

She was standing in the White Queen's position.

She looked over her shoulder, half expecting to see herself, larger than life, above herself.

There was no one there; she had become the White Queen.

Caliban regarded her from his vantage: he was the Black King.

A row of eight servitors, armed with forty-five caliber automatics, Cat-Arachnids, Mobile Imagers, Sheets, Takers and other of her biologic weapons did service as pawns.

The opposing row was even more interesting, although Yezeletta thought that Caliban could have chosen better. *Or perhaps he is invoking <u>my</u> memories?*

Caliban's Rooks were Zhongo Teketon, and The Maestro. His Knights were Zeke, his technical specialist, and, surprisingly, Mississippi Slim.

His Bishops were more surprising: One was "Mr. Director" *Now I <u>know</u> he's got some of my memories!* and an individual whom she knew only by facial recognition: one of those quiet watchful types that she had noticed occasionally in the background at Project Sargon. He watched her calmly, standing at ease on his square. His clothes were the only thing out of place by their very normality: he wore an impeccably tailored dark blue business suit. *He must mean something <u>big</u> to Caliban.*

Caliban's row of pawns consisted of spiky things that walked on what she thought of as "legs" strictly for the sake of analogic description. They had multiple sets of arms, and wide-set eyes protected by horny ridges. One of them turned to face its boss for a moment, and she saw another eye in the back of its head. *If this is a reloadable fantasy, he can make them anything he wants.*

So could Yezeletta.

She thought into the system from which her perceptions of the game were loaded, and *marked* the sixteen pawns. A Pound Sign or "crosshatch", "#" appeared on each of Caliban's Pawns, and her familiar large, red asterisks appeared on the backs of her own Pawns.

I <u>do</u> have an effect on this!, she thought.

THE BOARD AT THE START

[Run System] Caliban touched one of his monsters.

The creature stepped forward, one, two squares.

The glittering eyes of it looked at Yezeletta.

Yezeletta touched one of her pawns. Two squares to the right of the orthogonal on which Caliban's monstrous pawn stood waiting, and two squares to her left, Yezeletta's pawn stood, for the moment, safe.

It watched its opponent. Caliban watched it.

Caliban touched another pawn-monster, the creature directly before him: it took two squares.

Yezeletta touched the Bishop to her left. In chess notation this piece was her "Queen's Bishop," the Bishop at [C,1] [4].

She moved the Bishop to [A,3] , the White Queen's Rook's Column, three rows up into the playing field.

Leona looked back at Yezeletta, then turned to face her opposite number.

The Quiet Man. As Yezeletta and Leona watched, the Quiet Man lit a cigarette.

He smiled at Leona. A thin smile, devoid of mirth.

Caliban turned to his Queen; Miranda smiled up at him.

Then she turned to face Yezeletta. Her eyes glittered red in the half-light of Virtual Reality, or was it an artifact of the digital feed?

Caliban nodded, and Miranda moved!

Miranda, dressed in her finest as the Black Queen, necklaces and bracelets glittering, as did her eyes, flickering, electronic candles in the cyberlight, unmovingly staring at Yezeletta, gracefully danced to the square at [G,5] , Yezeletta's King's Knight's column, five squares out.

Thorfinn (the Knight) watched Miranda with the obsessiveness of the programmed, *or that of a simulation*.

Yezeletta directed a thought there—*Maybe he can't see my private systems!*—and the Pawn at [C,2] took two deliberate steps forwards to [C,4] , where it watched the Black Pawn it threatened with wary eyes.

The Board looked like this:

Caliban smiled: an expression that Yezeletta thought unsettling. *Or perhaps he wants it to seem unsettling*, she thought.

Caliban took a single step forward and a step to his right.

Yezeletta knew that the King would be restricted to single-

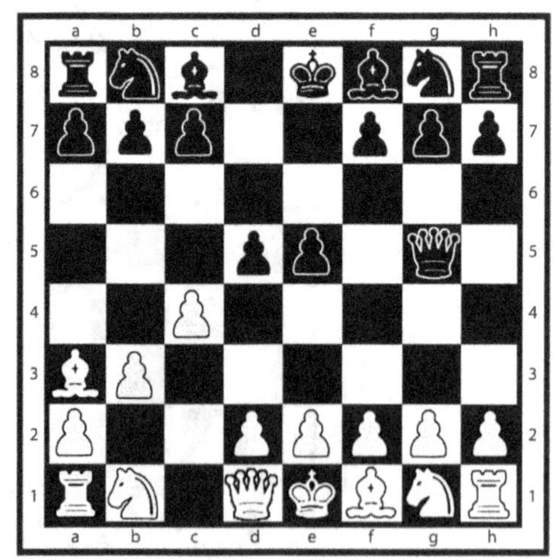

---

[4] Yezeletta is using the alternate "Algebraic" notation adopted in the early part of the Twentieth Century, commonly used with chess playing programs. In this notation, the rows are numbered from one to eight, and the columns designated by letters "A" for the White Queen's Rook's column (Yezeletta's far left side), to "H" for the White King's Rook's column (her far right). The Bishop to which she is referring at Column "C," Row 1, is the White Queen's Bishop.

square moves, if the rules of Chess were observed without any variations being used. Caliban's move from [E,8] to [E,7] was—either a surprise, or expected. Surprising, as the King was the weakest piece out of the box, and expected, as Caliban seemed to want to get into the action himself, in spite of his system-designed weakness.

Question: Could Caliban *change* the rules? Yezeletta had read of many variants on Chess ranging from Edgar Rice Burroughs's "Martian Chess," or "Jetan" to such variants as "Ultima" where the pieces all moved in the same fashion, but *captured* in different ways.

Could this happen here?

Could she stop it if it did?

Now, the Board looked like this:

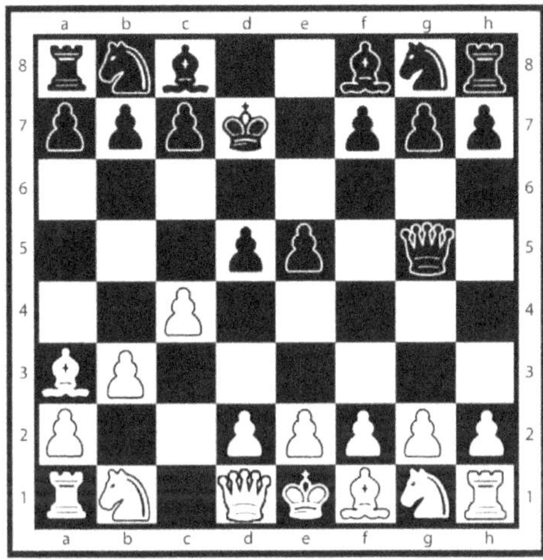

Caliban smiled at his Queen; she turned to face him, and saluted. Then she put her hands on her hips, and struck a pose for him that was straight out of *Playboy*.

Yezeletta thought about that, started several tasks up to run simulations, and took a step northwest to [C,2] .

She stood on the second row in front of the square from which her Bishop had started:

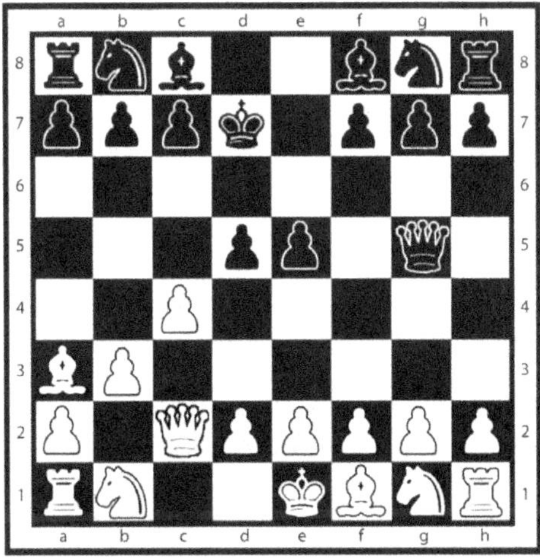

Caliban gestured a signal. The Pawn at [D,5] took a deliberate step to its right, and forward, and stood on the same square as the servitor at [C,4] .

The servitor dropped into a crouch. The Cat-Arachnid on its shoulder jumped for Caliban's monster's face. The monster raised its left arm, *its lower*, and swept the attacker away.

The servitor launched a Sheet at the monster.

The Black Pawn shot a kick with a spiked foot at the servitor.

The Sheet missed, and the spikes sank deeply into Yezeletta's Pawn's leg.

The spikes extruded from the other side of the servitor's leg and extended barbs. Caliban's Pawn pulled back, and Yezeletta could see that the Black Pawn was standing on a *third* leg that sprouted from the base of the creature's spine.

Yezeletta's servitor fell back, fired three shots from its pistol, and launched a Taker.

The segmented, green Taker climbed up Caliban's Pawn, and seized its left arms. The Black Pawn reached down, slapped the forty-five out of the servitor's hand, and, in spite of the metallic life-form securing its left side, drove a spiked right foot through the servitor's face.

Caliban's forces took the square.

Yezeletta's Taker and her servitor vanished. Caliban's little monster looked across the black and white battlefield, scanning for opponents:

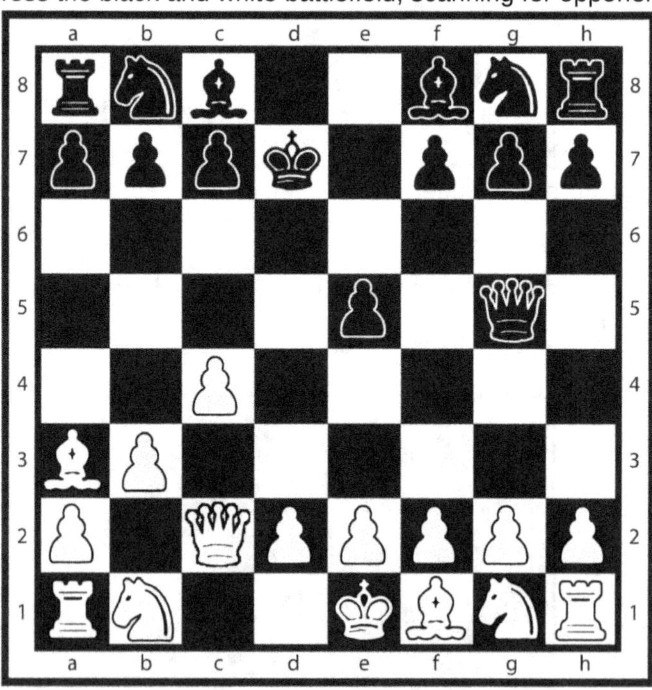

Yezeletta nodded to Thorfinn. He was the Knight at [G,1] : he jumped without effort from his starting place to [F,3] . He took out a stiletto and tested the edge, as he looked across the track of the move for a Knight at Miranda.

Thorfinn's Move:

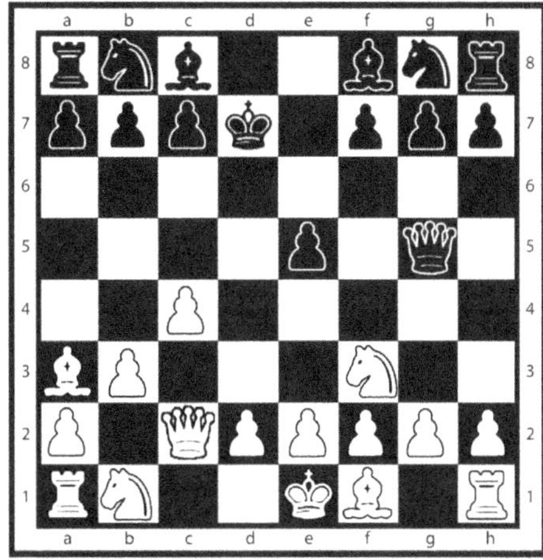

Miranda smiled grimly, and took out a blade of her own. She held it, point up, between her breasts, and kissed the point. Caliban frowned in thought, and signaled her.

Miranda took a haughty step from her place at [G,5] to [F,4] . From a square's distance, she smiled at Thorfinn, now unable to attack.

Thorfinn gestured at the pair of White Pawns guarding him, I am not worth such a trade, Young Lady. Do you want that kind of a fight?

Yezeletta touched the White Pawn to her left, at [B,3] , with her left hand, her upper, and it moved to [C,4] .

As it moved, it launched a Taker.

The segmented beast seized the Black Pawn at [C,4] and intertwined around it. The Taker extended metallic legs like waldoes, and immobilized the monster's arms, its upper set. Yezeletta's Pawn launched a Sheet, fouled the Black Pawn's lower left arm, and hacked with a short blade at the monster's lower right.

The servitor removed the lower right arm, and fired a shot through the Black Pawn's head. It dropped.

Then, monster and severed arm vanished out of the combined grasp of the Sheet and the Taker. Both weapons returned to Yezeletta's Pawn.

Yezeletta watched with as little expression as possible. *The system does allow for various skills*, she thought.

Yezeletta's Move:

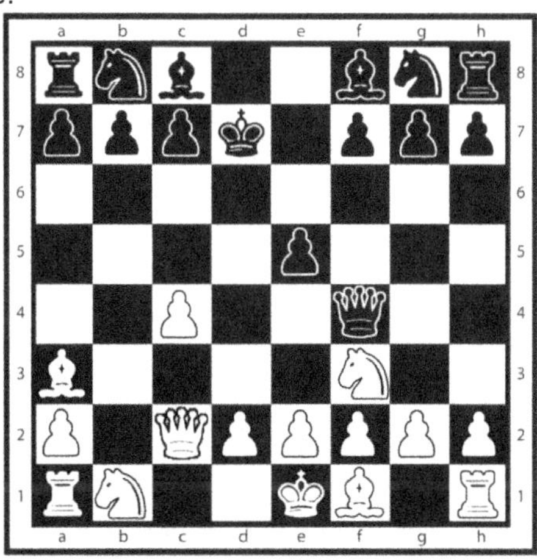

Miranda smiled at Thorfinn; Caliban looked across the playing field at Yezeletta. *That's what it's all about, isn't it?* Yezeletta thought. *These others aren't really here, just you and I.*

Miranda caressed her stiletto, Caliban sent a signal.

Miranda smirked at Thorfinn, *Not today, little man!*, turned, and threw her stiletto into [C,4] at the White Pawn!

The servitor was caught off-guard. As Yezeletta stared, her construct dropped, and vanished.

In a leisurely walk, almost a strut, Miranda took the square, and faced Yezeletta.

And laughed.

Miranda's Move:

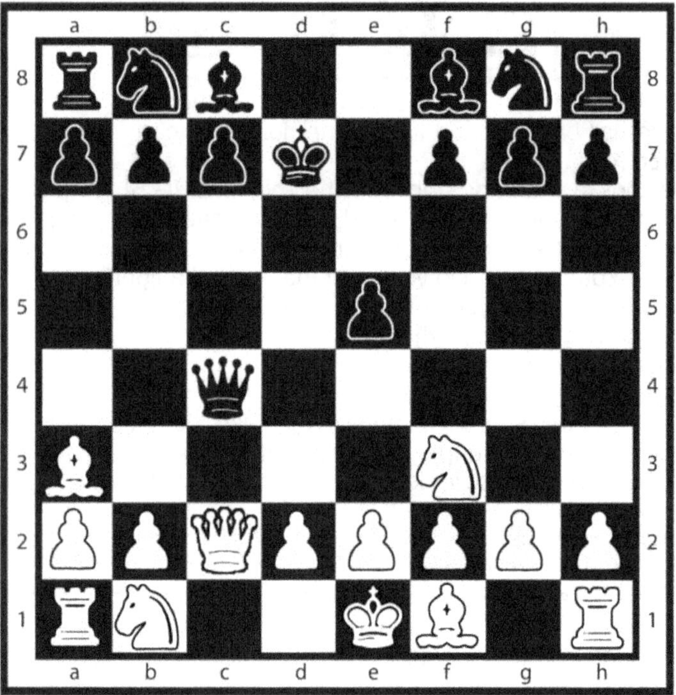

Yezeletta looked calmly across the short distance to Miranda. She looked to her right at Thorfinn, back at Joe, and left to Hank, her White Rook at [A,1] . *I have to do this myself.*

She summoned her weapons. A Taker, a Sheet, several Imagers, an Obliviator, a Cat-Arachnid and a Receiver. *You're taking on the wrong lady, sweetie,* she thought. Miranda took out another blade. Something spiky and malevolent appeared on her shoulder. A drop of sweat glistened on Miranda's left breast. She looked at Caliban.

Yezeletta charged the Black Queen.

The spiky monstrosity leaped off Miranda's shoulder for Yezeletta's face. Yezeletta dashed it to one side with a swift movement of her left arm, her upper. Miranda thrust with the stiletto in her left hand, upwards into Yezeletta's neck. Yezeletta seized her wrist in her lower right hand, then grabbed Miranda's right hand in her lower left. She wrapped her lower arms around Miranda's waist, pinning her hands behind her. *Just the way I took*

Charlie!

The Taker launched itself from its vantage point on Yezeletta's shoulder, and seized Miranda's hands and arms in its grasp.

Yezeletta directed the Sheet to wrap Miranda's legs.

She stood there, angry in the grasp of the Taker. Then she stopped, and just looked up at Yezeletta in fury.

"You aren't who I've come for," Yezeletta said to Miranda. "Besides, you probably don't even exist here." She gestured to Hank and Leona—they were the closest.

They picked the Black Queen up, and carried her out of the battle:

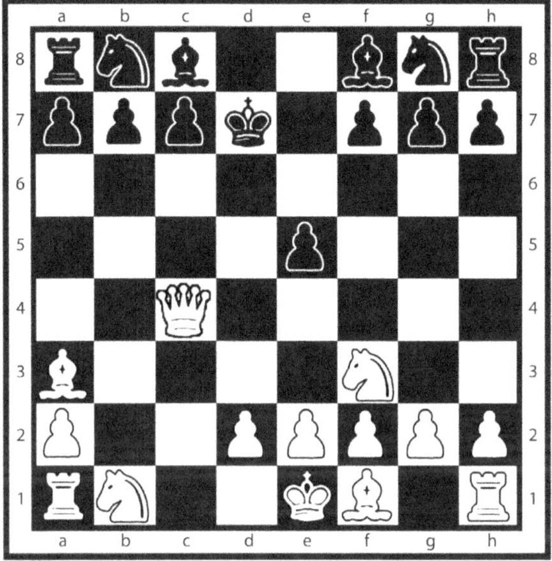

Caliban snarled in rage, as he watched his woman being carried off the field. He moved to [D,6] , and took blades and firearms in all four hands.

He called to Yezeletta: a challenge in no language she had ever heard.

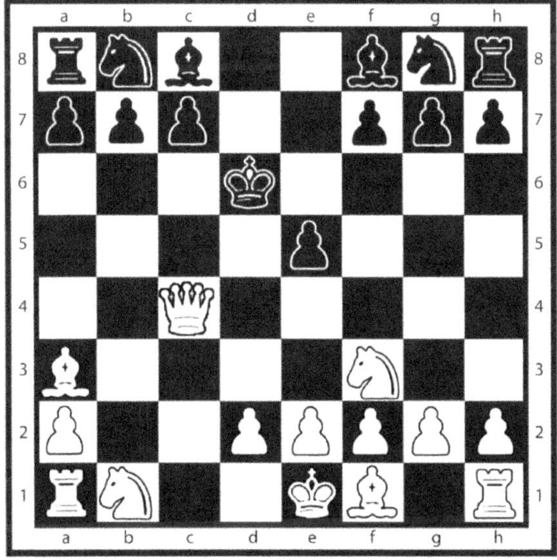

And Yezeletta Answered: she took one step forward.
"Check!" she shouted.
"But only if you can take me!" Caliban called back.

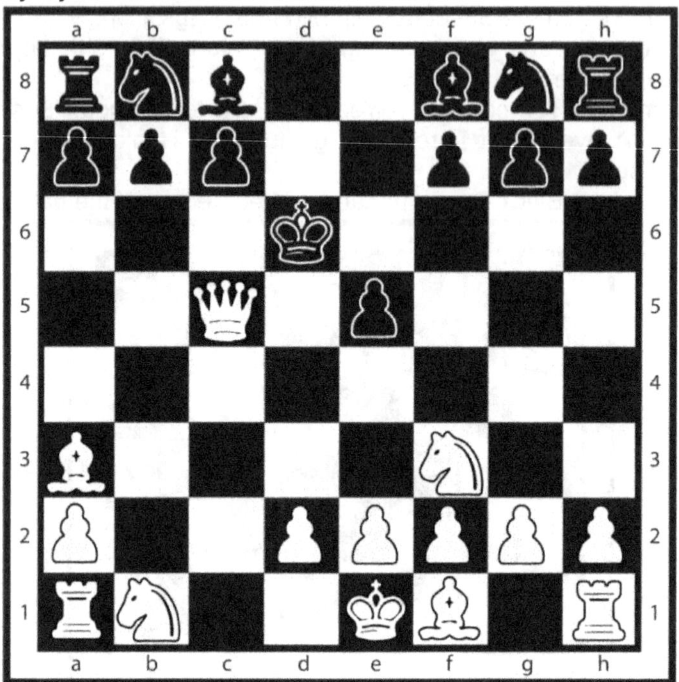

The rules for Chess state that the King can't move into check, nor can the King perform any move that would threaten his position. The rules said nothing about performing a capture.

Caliban leaped at Yezeletta.

RETURN FROM FOREVER

[Load System; Extreme Close Up] The Chess-board receded into infinity. Yezeletta was still sitting on top of Caliban, her hands on his cerebral contacts. He lurched violently out, as he attempted to shake her off. He wrenched his hands, his lower, free and grabbed at her hands, her upper pair. He looked up at her out of his glaring violet eyes. *If he could, he'd burn me out with his gaze!*

Caliban lurched again, and threw Yezeletta off. Yezeletta jumped at him and he stepped back.

But not far enough. Yezeletta's forward motion struck Caliban, and he fell, just in time for Yezeletta's kick to strike his feet out from under himself. Yezeletta fell heavily on him, and held his hands down.

She took a moment to look around.

Her friends were at the edges of her vision. Was Anne there in the stadium seating? She couldn't look up! A short glance, and Caliban could take advantage of it.

She moved against Caliban, her legs on top of his, holding them in place, her fingers searching for the contacts on his head.

Caliban rolled, threw her off.

He jumped to his feet.

And took a step back.

[Load Segment; Overlay; Medium Shot] Yezeletta watched Caliban through narrowed eyes. He seemed to be abstracted for a short but perceptible time.

He danced directly away from her, then to one side, almost as if he were waiting *to synchronize with an internal process*.

Bad idea, Sonny Boy, Yezeletta bounced to her feet, and charged him.

THE BLOCK-STRUCTURED DEVICE DRIVER

[Running] In Another Place, Yezeletta and Caliban *collided*.

She felt the insistent probings of Caliban's on-board systems through her skin. Every time he touched her, she felt an electric sensation, an accession, a probing of her peripheral devices.

He must have interfacing contacts all over his body!

Yezeletta adjusted her vision into the new places she had designed.

"Places" was about as good a name as any (she thought, later); the capabilities that she had obtained from Peter's gadgets and downloaded into her eyes allowed her to *see* the electromagnetic outlines of Caliban's systems. *Can he see mine?*

He was outlined in fine wires, the contact points—at least some of the contact points—glowing, converted to her additional harmonic colors.

Caliban was a moving wire-frame animation in Yezeletta's second-sight. She adjusted her own contacts away from accessibility by external forces, and jumped him, again.

He gripped her in a bear-hug, *Or is it a bare-hug?* she thought, as he pinned her arms to her side with his lower arms, and sought the contacts on her head. She twisted against his enclosing arms, and—

Accessed his systems through her skin!

He shook inside his actions, almost as if a slight charge had been passed through him.

As Yezeletta accessed his internals, she felt the first, insidious tendrils of his attack programming *testing her*.

OFF-LINE / ON-LINE

[Breakpoint!] "Your Deal," the gangster said.

Yezeletta was sitting on a chair made for her physique in a room of indistinct walls, the air around her filled with the wisps and arabesques and filigrees of cigarette smoke. The speaker was Zhongo, who sat off to Yezeletta's left.

Directly in front of her sat Caliban.

Caliban regarded her steadily. His chips in front of him, his hands, his lower, resting on the table.

Caliban's eyes were actinic tunnels into a fine and private hell.

Yezeletta looked down at her *place* at the table. Red, white and blue poker chips were stacked neatly before her. Next to them was a tidy pile of bills and several coins.

Zhongo scanned them from a distance. Yezeletta realized that Zhongo's eyes were almost an exact shade of sky-blue. The lightness of his irises was startling, given his lightly tanned face, and black, almost dark blue, hair. Yezeletta looked closer.

Were those white inclusions in his eyes? Almost like tiny clouds?

"Seven Card Stud," Zhongo announced. "I will deal, and otherwise stay out of the game. You two will play."

"What iss the ssstake in thiss game?" Caliban asked.

Maybe getting your larynx fixed! Yezeletta didn't say. "I'd like that answer, also," she did say.

"The winner gets to take the loser to the next level," Zhongo said. "From there, it's up to you."

"What level?" Yezeletta asked.

"You play Chess with Medieval armies and weaponry. You use castles. You have so-called Men of the Cloth."

"Sssso?"

Zhongo began shuffling the cards. The crisp pasteboards made an electric crackle in the card-room. Is that because of the feed? Who's on this feed? Is it all Caliban, or am I a part—besides a <u>participant</u>!—in this?

Expertly, holding the deck in his left hand in the classic dealer's mechanic's grip, Zhongo dealt the two down-cards to the players.

"Build your Castle in the air," he said. "Look to your King. Send the Clergy on a Mission. Ride your Knights into Day. Take your Queen. Castle."

"Castle."

"Castle."

PLAYING IN THE CARD HOUSE

[Card Reader Select; Input] Zhongo dealt the first up cards to each of his players.

"Ace of Hearts to Yezeletta, Jack of Spades to Caliban, Ace bets."

Yezeletta looked at her down cards; then looked back at the **<Member Function>** in her Ace of Hearts.

Anne Lenhaden's face looked up at her from the large, red heart on the Ace. She winked at Yezeletta. Yezeletta checked her Downs again: Hank and Ondreya were there as the King and Queen of Clubs. They appraised the action coolly. *The family that matters*, Yezeletta thought.

Across the table from her, Caliban checked his downs, and contemplated Zeke, as a **<Factor>** looking back at him from the Jack of Spades. His Counselor was instantiated as the King of Spades, and Miranda watched her man steadily, as the Queen of Hearts.

His Counselor lit another cigarette; Miranda smiled.

Yezeletta threw a ten-dollar bill into the center of the table. Caliban added his ten, and they looked at Zhongo.

Zhongo dealt: The Queen of Spades to Yezeletta;

The Jack of Clubs to Caliban.

"Two Jacks bets." Zhongo's words filled the empty space between them.

Yezeletta waited, her face in neutral, as Caliban looked at his down cards, *He must be doing that for effect!*, and dropped a twenty-dollar bill in the pot.

Leona as the Queen of Spades regarded Looey as the Jack of Clubs, *Appropriate!*, Yezeletta thought. They waited expectantly, as Yezeletta dropped a twenty, and another ten into the center.

"Raise ten," she said.

Caliban's violet eyes were violet lasers, scanning all that was there. Silently, he added his ten.

"Cards?" Zhongo asked. "Cards," he said decisively.

The cardboard rectangles fell through virtual space, accessing their destinations, linking in: The Ace of Diamonds for Yezeletta, the Ace of Clubs for Caliban.

Yezeletta adjusted her eyes for a close-up. Her Ace was Peter Rudenko. Caliban's Ace was Mr. Director.

"Pair of Aces to you, Yezeletta," Zhongo said.

Yezeletta called her hand up in her left eye as a graphic, sorting the cards. She had two Queens, and two Aces. There were two cards yet to be dealt. She ran the probabilities off as an Analysis of Variance, decided that she wanted to stay (there *was* a difference from being required to do so!), and tossed a pair of twenties at the pot.

"Forty to you, Caliban," was all she said.

Instantiating a frown, Caliban moved his left hand, his lower, enough to move two bills into the center of the table. Yezeletta ran a motion analysis against him. His breathing was constant, almost mechanical. She was able to tune into the sound of his hearts, hear the susurrus of the blood rushing through his circulatory systems.

He placed his hand back by his funds.

Zhongo dispensed cards: Yezeletta collected the King of Hearts; Thorfinn Lenhaden looked around with steady gray eyes at the participants in the game: and Mississippi Slim, as the Jack of Diamonds, looked back from Caliban's side.

"Three Jacks has the bet," Zhongo pronounced. "Send them into the field, big fella."

"Twenty Dollars per Jack," Caliban said in sepulchral tones. He placed the three bills in the geometric center of the card-table, where they lay, accumulated power, awaiting the moment of release.

Yezeletta studied the three-pair she had, ran a regression analysis, and covered.

"Last card," Zhongo said. "Down and dirty—or down and out.

"Or Down and Loaded."

Yezeletta took the card from Zhongo, and *willed* her face into impassivity. The card was the Ace of Spades, and Joe looked at her out of the center of the Spade-design.

Like Anne, he winked.

"Three Jacks bets," Zhongo's voice invaded. "Last bet."

Caliban dropped a one-hundred-dollar bill into the pot. His look over his cards (small in his hands) was a dare.

Yezeletta took the dare, fielded the Inter-Process Request, and reactivated it at a higher priority.

"Raise you another hundred," was all she said.

Caliban's eyes were a one-way trip into twin super-novae, with the slits of his closed-down irises gateways beyond.

"See that," he said, "and parse this."

He raised her another hundred.

"I'll take an **Instance** of that, and *Stack* it," Yezeletta said. "Recurse, and **CALL**."

She covered Caliban's bet, a **<Term>** in a formal grammar ("*Recursive Descent*," she thought), with her own.

"Put them down," Zhongo said, "This is a **<Primary>**."

THE GRAMMAR OF IT

[Output Algorithm]
Caliban displayed:A Full House: Three Jacks and Two Kings.
Yezeletta laid hers out:A Full House: Three Aces and Two Kings.

She reached out with her left hand, her lower, and harvested the pot.

Caliban stood.	"Deconstruction," he said. "Recursive Descent. I have the data, and—"

THE DOWNLOADING—II

[Long-Shot; Load Grammar Transport File] He reached across the table, and took Yezeletta's head in his lower hands.

His movements were those of a striking cobra. His upper hands followed, connecting with the contacts on Yezeletta's skull.

The burst-mode input was completed before she was able to react to it.

CONTEXT CHANGE

[Load *Parser*] *Then the poker table, the cards with their outraged faces, Zhongo, and even Caliban, were disassociating, deconstructing, disinstantiating, banishing into their components, and moving back into the distance.*

Yezeletta stretched her timebase, slowing the movement. They became as giants seen at a great distance; the clear, cold air the only separation.

Several large, black snowflakes appeared or were instantiated, and she saw the others through the holes in the vibrating black entities.

Before her, a plane was forming, light against the trembling black webs, somehow inside them within her defenses.

This is a file I've carried, and I didn't have the access method; this is mine, but <u>he</u> had the primary key, he had it...!

Then the infinite plane tilted across her Point-of-View, and, in a point-for-point Cartesian collision, she re-entered it.

THE CHILDREN OF THE <TERMS>

[The Generator] Yezeletta stood on her four legs at the center of an infinite plane made of panes of onyx. There was a horizon, but it was nearly invisible: the blackness of the substrate on which she was standing merged perfectly with the blackness of the canceled sky. She looked around her, and nearly lost her sense of direction. The lack of landmarks, of detailing, of differentiation in the sameness around her, left her not knowing—

The Where-ever from the For-ever—

The Which from the Why—

The Rational from the Rationale—

The Cause from the Effect—

—she widened the bandwidth of her vision to its maximum, heightened her visual acuity, and added a stage of image enhancement. She was just able to discern the negligible horizon.

She looked up.

The luminous construct, a twelve-sided polygon, was descending. She was at the exact center of it.

It wasn't a two-dimensional figure. It had *depth*. It was a short prism, formed of twelve flat sides. Each side was a square, and within each of the sides, an image moved of its own volition.

They descended around her, the twelve square screens surrounding her, their images tugging at her sight, competing for her attention, her concentration.

She looked into them.

The...Images looked back.

D ETERMINANTS A CTIVE

[On Line] The images were of—

—Yezeletta;

—Burning buildings;

—People running in abject panic;

—A single gold cat's eye;

—A large city skyline in the late afternoon;

—Another city-scape at night;

—A monitor with four windows open on its screen, the contents of the windows, text accompanied by images, indistinct, un-focused;

—*Another* broad, flat plane, this one of glittering white, almost the saturated white of an over-exposed photographic print.

—A standard High-Definition Television Screen in the standard wide landscape display mode, divided into eight parts; in each of the eight subdivisions, a human hand held: A reel of magnetic tape; A picture of a spiral galaxy; A ring of keys; An antique computer punch-card; A telephone; A photograph of the crescent Moon; A padlock; and the last photograph: a baby.

—The images moved in a jerky fashion from one screen to the next. She could see the point of view in one of the screens jumping, moving this way and that as the receptor of the image ran through a crowd of people. The people, all of a uniform dark color, moved to one side or another, as the carrier of the source of the image darted between them.

Another display that swapped into the screen in front of her was of a row of burning buildings. The dwellers in those buildings were running in panic from the heat and the destruction.

It switched to an image of a city street at night. Cars ran quietly around her on both sides.

The screens moved closer. Another gold cat's eye appeared, displacing a city skyline, and then another eye opened. The eyes were the exact color of the scanning apertures used by her Imagers.

The image sequence of the burning buildings (an autonomous task running in her internals) *pattern-matched* on the stars above the conflagration.

A pattern of stars, diamond pointillism on black velvet, to the left of that a red sun, aligned like a theorem with four others in a "V"-shape, and to the left (it *had* to be East!) of that—

Orion. Striding without fear across the sky into a future in which doubt and uncertainty were forever banished; striding into Yezeletta's time, and taking the remotest memories of her childhood with him.

Walking across the night, *lit by the lamps of heaven*.

And followed by the eyes that see and the clouds that look. And the difference engine of the night sky and the lights thereof moving in like sparks of them across the path of—

The Walking Man. The gold eyes of the windows in the sky watched her with a cold remoteness that Yezeletta found frightening. She forced herself to look at the eyes. Then *into* them.

Objects in the Net. The remote clouds that look, the eyes that see; the Turning of the skies both in and out of the Virtual Space in which she found herself.

They were all screen shots of her eyes.

All around her, the twelve screens, twelve gold vertically slit feline eyes, Yezeletta's eyes multiplied by a factor of six, watched her as if she were a specimen under a twelve-times microscope.

—The screens closed around her: passing through her, past her, from their many directions; the eyes became great golden-colored suns, the dark vertical slits huge canyons of sable blackness.

Yezeletta fell into the screens, into the light.

Falling—

Into the Eyes of the Setting Sun.

DETERMINANTS PROCESSING

[Long Shot: The Eyes that See] Then the limitless black plane was open again. Beneath the shattered sky of its location outside of all space and time, the black surface extended onwards and outwards forever into the darkness.

Of the screens, there were no sign.

For Yezeletta Zargkonji was gone with them.

——>>> THREE <<<——

"The Ab-Nihilisation of the Etym Explodotonates through Parsuralia—"
—James Joyce, *Finnegans Wake*

IN THE SILENT LAND

[main() {} /* Start Here. */]

Yezeletta awoke midway between—

Heaven	and	Earth—
Now	and	Not Now—
Land	and	Sky—
Sleep	and	Wakening—
Yesterday	and	Tomorrow—
Sun	and	Rain—
The Origin	and	A Cantorian Infinity—

She was sitting—reclining, actually—on an infinite plane beneath a glowing opalescent light that pervaded everything around her. The light was evenly distributed—there was no "direction," a "sun" or any kind of overt light source. The light was *there*—a given in this silent land.

She inspected the surface upon which she was sitting and saw fine straight lines, thousands of them to the centimeter, almost at the limits of the resolving powers of her eyes, glowing slightly, below the surface.

She did a quick left-right shake of her head to scan entirely around herself.

There was nothing. Even what appeared to be the horizon was just a trick of the iridescent lighting. She knew that this was a manifestation of the images being fed into that part of her nervous system commonly referred to as her "sensorium." She knew that she was somewhere else, but all of what she was seeing was all of her experience, and that she had to deal with both the "system" of the input, as well as "jumping out of the system" to find, or backtrack to, the source of the virtual feed she was experiencing.

She wondered if she would see another Mandelbrot Dragon here.

She stood, and somehow, the surface on which she had been reclining moved *without moving*, to became a part of the infinite plane.

A building was taking shape before her; she walked towards it.

As she did, the structure grew: not in the sense of getting larger as she approached, but in complexity. New parts of it—high walls, mostly—came up around her. Shortly, Yezeletta was standing in the center of a small, simply furnished courtyard.

The wall nearest her transformed from a blank, glassy surface to something rougher. Straight lines—resembling a roadmap or the traces on a printed circuit board, or an electronic Mondrian—formed on the surface, delimiting a rectangle of familiar dimensions.

A door.

That opened.

Yezeletta adjusted her eyes to the dimness. She placed her hands, her upper, on the door frame, and looked in.

There was someone inside.

Yezeletta entered. A short figure materialized out of the darkness (*not too far off!*, she thought), and took short steps towards her.

The figure was a small girl, of about six years age. She wore a red and white checked skirt, a dark green belt, a white blouse. Her shoes were red patent-leather that gleamed in the half-light. White socks. She had dark hair, so dark that it was almost steel blue, tied back with a magenta ribbon.

The little girl looked up at Yezeletta fearlessly, raised one arm, and pointed.

"Come with me!" she said.

Yezeletta's sight ended—

But not Yezeletta's thoughts.

She was awake, alert. It was as if someone had turned off all the lights. A glow like a candle appeared before her. It *was* a candle. Held by the little girl.

"Now you will know!" the girl said and this time Yezeletta *did* become unconscious.

THE BUILDERS

[Establishing Shot: Arriflex; Virtual Vérité] The city was old, established. Tall, well-lit buildings rose into the sky, all of the aspirations of The Builders implicit in every line. The place reminded Yezeletta of New York: the kind of New York that she had seen in old musicals from the twenties (the *nineteen*-twenties, she reminded herself); perhaps the old Lower East Side of the Busby Berkeley movies. A clean city, a city of hope and accomplishment.

A city in which every line had a meaning, and that meaning was the intent of each of the artisans who had built here.

She recalled (smiling) the FM broadcast from Chicago that she'd heard on her first night in Milwaukee. She'd actually had a few minutes in which she could relax, before continuing to make her concealed home in the Farmer's Mutual Building. She had listened to "The Midnight Special" out of Chicago, which that night had featured American union songs, one of which went:

> *If you want a world worth living in—*
> *Here is what you do:*
> *You go to work with The Builders.*
> *And not for the Wrecking Crew.*

The miraculous, glowing city around her—it *was* New York: over there was the Empire State Building, and there the World Trade Center, its north tower restored—was an eloquent manifestation of The Builders.

Yezeletta walked up the wide sidewalk, knowing *without knowing how she knew* that she should do this. She held out her hands.

There were only two.

Somehow she was in another body. And it did not seem strange. She closed her eyes and directed a thought *there*.

The proper window in her left eye opened up. With the proper data within it. *Good—*

She closed it, and continued walking. As she did, *the details filled themselves in around her*.

She was walking up Fifth Avenue. Her destination was a large, imposing building in the block just ahead. There was an awning that stretched out above the concrete sidewalk, and in Art Deco lettering—backlit, incandescently—it proclaimed the structure to be **The Barbizon**.

Yezeletta had no idea if The Barbizon were even a real place, or if it were on Fifth Avenue. Buried deeply, a part of her noted that this was not *real* New York, but someone's idea of what New York should really be like. *Or perhaps this is but a New York City of the Mind!* she silently paraphrased *Macbeth*.

As she walked, The Avenue filled up with traffic: antique cars beautifully preserved or restored, shared the Avenue with the most modern vehicles. A 1928 Maxwell Touring Car (or was it a Turing Machine?) pulled up next to a classic Chevrolet Corvette; both of those, next to a late model four-door Dodge pickup. She reached the entrance to The Barbizon, and entered through green-glass doors with gilt floral scroll-work around the edges. Wide marble steps welcomed her upward and into a green and gray marble lobby.

A bell-boy straight out of the "Call for Philip Morris!" ad approached her.

"Miss Sargon?" he asked.

"Yes...." Yezeletta said.

"Miss Jezebel Sargon. Please come with me, your suite reservation is ready. We've been expecting you."

The registration was the barest of formalities: Yezeletta printed "Jezebel Sargon" in the leather-bound registration book, received her key, and the bell-boy took her to the elevator.

The old-fashioned cage actually had manual controls and an operator: the first elevator operator she had ever seen. *They are nothing if not complete*, she thought, as the glass, wood and polished brass machine took her up to the eighth floor.

The bell boy took her to room **0x1776**, opened the door, and waited.

Yezeletta slipped a hand, her right, into her pocket, *how complete...ah!* The silver dollar was large, heavy and freshly minted. The date on it, just below the figure of Walking Liberty, was **0x1928**.

The bell-hop took it with a polite, if professional, smile, turned on his heel and left. Yezeletta went in.

The suite had a living room, with a desk, telephone, and, surprisingly, a baby grand piano. Through one doorway, she could see a bedroom, with a large, circular bed covered with a large, fur bedspread. Through another doorway, there was a modern kitchen. Half of the living room was books on shelves made from real wood.

(*Walking* Liberty?)

She inspected those a little closer. Mostly the texts were standard reference works and classics. Some modern things had been tossed in as well, but the...library was designed to be familiar.

Reassuring?

There was a knock on the door.

Yezeletta turned back to it in surprise. When she opened it, there was another bell-boy, with a long package in his arms.

She took it and reached into the same pocket.

The silver dollar could have been the twin of the other one. Walking (Walking! *Walking?*) Liberty, **0x1928**. Silently, the bell-boy took it, smiled, left.

Yezeletta set the package on the desk, sat and opened the container with a sterling silver letter opener she took from the desk's center drawer.

The package was an even dozen of the reddest roses she had ever seen. A small card was attached: *Dearest—I will be home soon. Thinking of you.*

 Love, Joe
Home?
Was that?
Where was this?
Where are you?
Who—

LIGHT!

[Long Shot: Computer Graphics Imaging <Loading>]
Elsewhere: A Network Accessed;

    A CPU Engaged;

    A System Called;

    An Overlay Loaded;

    A Vector Established;

A Task Initiated;
A Process Started;
A Context Entered;
A Grammar Parsed;
An! Entry-Point!
Selected!

WITHIN THE SYSTEM—WITHOUT

[Processing] Yezeletta put the roses in a Steuben Crystal vase that had been placed at the center of a red and blue velvet cover on the piano. She recognised the pattern in the velvet as the Penrose Tiling that the English mathematician of the same name had created, in an attempt to use pentagonal motifs as a means of completely covering a surface with other than ninety- or sixty-degree angles. The design radiated from the center of the cloth like a fractal starfish, in red and blue diamonds with eye-tugging angles.

Out of the corner of one eye, she saw a flickering movement.

When she turned to the source of the movement—the circular bed—there was something lying on it.

The something was a dress. A black velvet evening gown laid out as if by an attentive butler. Next to it, a fur wrap, and on that—

The small black box contained a necklace. In gold (very fine gold, indeed) and silver, a complex network of gold and silver diamond shapes, linked together by tiny chain links that must have been formed under a microscope— *or at a very high resolution* (she thought): a Penrose design in the same pattern as the velvet covering on the piano.

Opposite her above the bed a large, seven-sided mirror hung on the wall. Her reflection looked back.

In there, her reflection was the Yezeletta she had always known. Her four arms, lower pair, hands-on-her-hips, the upper pair holding the necklace just as she was holding it, her extra legs visible just back of—

The dress appeared to be the right size. She removed the clothes she was wearing. *Has my height changed?*

No: the door was two-hundred and twenty-five centimeters high, and she had cleared the bedroom door by ten, coming in. She walked naked to the window, and found that it wasn't a window after all; the wall below it was a Dutch door that opened out onto a balcony.

Yezeletta stepped outside and let the warm wind caress her nakedness as she looked out over a New York City of *whose?* mind.

Below her, Humanity ebbed and flowed around her on currents that only now was she beginning to understand. Far off, a beacon on the glittering electric horizon blinked in trinary sequence: red - white - green - white - red - white - green. Blue, red, yellow and green signs tugged at her vision for attention, and their meanings eluded her, *or could not be resolved*. Below her, cars moved, beetle-shaped space ships in the night. Each on its own business, each on the copper trace of its own road. Guided by—

A Task?

A fragment of Omar Khayyam "Who is the potter and who is the pot?"

Who Indeed?

She placed her hands on her breasts, covering them from the wind. It was rising. *It gets cold where we're heading; but where am I going next?*

She turned, went back inside, pulled the evening dress on, felt the exquisite sensations of velvet on her skin. It was as if the dress had been designed especially for her. *Yezeletta: Version 2.0.* When she finished, the dress hugged her close, a custom design.

The Penrose necklace complemented the black velvet with exactly the right touch of gold, and the fur cape surrounded without covering.

She regarded her reflection. Her reflection returned her gaze: a tall, dark-haired, well-built woman with large, gold eyes. She smiled: seconds later (*processing time?*), her reflection smiled back. *We're ready.*

"Ready for a night on the town," she said to the City.

[Match Cut To <Load Scene Here>]

[Initialization Sequence Resumed]

N IGHT !

[Network Active] The silent operator of the elevator took Yezeletta back to the ground floor and the lobby. The lobby was empty of hotel guests: there were just the inevitable bell-boys and the night clerk sitting in his little office near the front desk.

He nodded to her as she passed him. She smiled back.

Outside, the night was cool. The sky and the familiar constellations were as they had always been.

A long, gray stretch-limo pulled up.

The right, front window zipped down and a driver of ordinary proportions and visage asked, "Miss Sargon?"

"That's me," Yezeletta said. *Another hologram?* she didn't say. The passenger door slid open, and a light inside came on.

"Hop in—" the driver said.

"It gets cold where we're heading."

The limo, expertly guided by the driver, tooled up Fifth Avenue, past buildings that were brightly lit. Whatever the feed she was getting, Yezeletta thought, it was a feed from a time when New York City was a thriving, prosperous place.

A Prosperous Prospero? she liked the juxtaposition: the Lords of the Computer had powers that the male lead in *The Tempest* could only have dreamt of, even reincarnated as he was, in that old movie.

0x05-th Avenue?

The limo drove smoothly, almost of its own volition, for about four blocks, and pulled into an intersection. The left passenger door opened, and a small individual in a long overcoat got in.

"Hello," she said.

It was the little girl.

The limousine pulled into the basement parking ramp *did they have them, then—in the Twenties?* below a tall, but otherwise undistinguished building. *Are they running out of templates? How long is this sequence?* The long car spiraled down, and down into the gray, concrete depths of the parking vault, and—

Drove into a solid wall.

The wall let them.

HER SELF || HER OTHER [5]

[Relational Look-Up: Query By Example]   Yezeletta referenced her store of memories. When Joe had found her, she was, as she had described herself to him later, "twenty years old on a good day, and nineteen-and-a-half on a bad day. If that."

Twenty years—her own "twenties" here in a New York of *another's* mind was not much experience to draw from. *Perhaps if I were older....*

If the—Builders'—design provided for my being older.

Watch that.

She had found out bits (bytes?) and pieces (tracks? sectors?) of what the Project had planned for her: nowhere had there been any mention of...retirement benefits. *Kill them while they're young, do you? It's a good way to lose the evidence.*

The car stopped in a small parking area in an artificial cave of cement works and prestressed concrete pillars. Yezeletta looked at her companion, quiet all this time. She looked up at Yezeletta with a wide-eyed child's face.

Her eyes were the same gold as Yezeletta's.

They glittered in the light of distant forty-watt light bulbs and the limo's instrument board. She got out of the car and walked around it to Yezeletta. Silently, she beckoned: *follow me.*

Yezeletta got out, stood next to the car.

The wall through which they had come was as blank as any such concrete wall; there weren't even graffiti. The artificial cave was nothing more than a roughly cubical concrete box. Yezeletta went to the "entry" wall, touched it. It felt like old, damp concrete with vague wood grain marks from the plywood forms in which it had been cast.

The little girl stood close. "They don't want to let us out, do they?" Yezeletta asked.

"No," the little girl said firmly. "*I* don't want to let you out. I want you to know things. Then you'll be sent back."

"Who are you?" Yezeletta asked, knowing the answer.

"My name is Jezebel Sargon."

THE WEB STRIDER

[Start Graphics Sub-System]   Almost without volition, Yezeletta saw herself, as if she were watching herself in a video, walking after the little girl Jezebel as she strode purposefully towards another gray wall. She walked into it and vanished from view. Yezeletta stopped, and:

Stopped, and;

Saw herself stop. And—

Jezebel Sargon's face appeared: From the wall's grayness || From out of the convolutions || From the cave face || From out of the inter*face.*

Don't stop: know! Don't stop now! Don't stop, <u>no</u>. She said without saying, spoke without speaking. She extended her hand to Yezeletta—

—*A Hand of the Mind, its fingers extended towards me!*

---

[5] "||" is the "or" Operation in the "C" Programming Language

HER MIND'S EYE!

Jezebel Sargon took Yezeletta Zargkonji to Hell.

The Revised Standard: Version **2.0**.

[In another Place; Loading] *A single Determinant moves into view, a single screen divided into several sub-sections. The windows expand until their borders vanish past the edges of the screen. The Windows Open.*

Window Number One—

> Within the antiseptic white environment of the Hospital, the darkest evil resided. In the center of the operating theater, a large, rectangular tank sat, an unappetizing right-angled shape, connected by hydraulic lines, electrical connections, and data busses to the glittering processors that surrounded it on all sides. Here, a heart monitor with multiple readouts displayed data in a curious syncopation. There, an electroencephalograph displayed the alpha, beta and gamma waves of a brain, along with the right-angled square waves of digital transmissions. There, a pulmonary monitor displayed the functions of multiple sets of lungs. Within the tank, a baby—a misshapen twisted baby—the object of all of the examinations, moved multiple limbs as she lay on the soft pad, almost a waterbed, that lined the tank's bottom.

Within the Windows of my mind's eyes, I see the place where I originated.

Yezeletta's thoughts were autonomous, running in a sub-task, as if of their own volition. The scene before her was almost as impersonal as a picture in a magazine, or as an image on one of her monitors.

A frame took shape around the scene—a standard gray Window border, complete with header bar and the dark blue of the header became a dark gray, as another scene formed.

Window Number Two—

> It was the same hospital, only this time filling the center was a larger tank, a vertical cylinder containing liquid within which a darker shape—a fetus, perhaps—was suspended. Yezeletta had seen artificial wombs many times; her own creations were cloned inside simpler versions of these devices. Several men in surgical light greens—although dark suits could be seen worn as underclothing—walked around the cylinder, looking at the object within with barely hidden revulsion disguised as clinical interest. Now she could see that the contents of the cylinder, obscured by many blood vessels, nutrient lines and electrical connectors, were actually twins. Twin girls, curled up in fetal position; one seemed to be hugging the other from behind.

Yezeletta followed it in, as the Window began receding. As the details of the twins were lost in the pixilations, she saw that: they were not well-formed twins, but Siamese, joined chest-to-back and at the pelvis.

"I!" she started to say. The Window shrank, its header turning gray. Something—Someone!—grabbed her left hand.

Jezebel Sargon, the...younger...had taken hold of her.

"You know where you are. These are *memories*. Memories of the monsters that created you."

Yezeletta regarded Jezebel with a new kind of comprehension.

"These memories can no longer hurt you. Those are the Directors of the Project. You killed their subordinates in your last days in Alice Springs."

Another Window took form, a later view in a later time.

Window Nr Three—

> This scene was a playroom in what might have been a day care center in any large city. Scaled down school-desks for small children were drawn up in ranks. A blackboard with something mathematical on it covered one wall, with the alphabet in stylized script on black cards along the top. In one corner stood a craft workshop, and, sitting at a child-size table, was a child-sized Yezeletta, working on something with a series of well-coordinated but obscure motions. Visible behind Yezeletta, the child, was a large mirror which Yezeletta, the older, could see was really a sheet of partially-silvered "one way" glass. As the older Yezeletta watched, the younger Yezeletta finished her task, put down the tools held in three hands, and looked up with a very six-year-old expression of triumph. Behind her, the images in the one-way window looked at each other and talked amongst themselves.

Yezeletta almost recognized the object on which her younger self was working. As the image receded into miscellaneous pixilations, she followed it, scanning the object. It was of an eye-catching complexity, a finely tuned mechanism that appeared to be a weapon, or perhaps a part of a weapon. *A detonator?*

The Third Window fell back, its header turning the slate gray of inactivation.

Jezebel Sargon, the younger, led Yezeletta to a small lounge area, to an overstuffed easy chair. She sat back in it.

And tried to relax.

Jezebel the younger removed her hair ribbon. Yezeletta realized that its color was a computer monitor's standard magenta. Jezebel's hair fell down around her shoulders.

"Has your hair ever been cut?" Yezeletta asked her.

"No."

The lounge area consisted of just some chairs and several small tables. Around the area it was black, the ambient light fading quickly out and not reflecting or diffusing back.

Jezebel looked at Yezeletta ‖ her younger self looked at her older self ‖ she said to her self, "There is one more thing you must see. Remember the photographer at the project who took publicity shots for that SECRET report?"

"Yes."

"He liked to make bad puns and worse song parodies. Remember "Look Through Innuendo?""

"I'm sorry, but I do."

"There is one more Window here in the black spaces between sleeping and waking. One more place where you've been and where you must return for the last look into the night."

Jezebel pointed into the light-swallowing darkness, and—

"THE EYES OF THE SETTING SUN"

In the Blackness *The Last Window opened*—
Window Nr Four—

> Inside the antiseptic porcelain white, stainless steel and glass areas of the Project, a meeting was being started by several men in dark business suits. They sat at the long conference table, and each one arrayed himself with folders of documents, computer media, audio-visual presentations. Each had his portable computer open and running, in case something was needed quickly from the various LANs, WANs or the Internet. The head of the project, a tall, thin man with sharp blue eyes, wearing an impeccable navy blue suit, went to the head of the table and loaded his disk of images into the room's audio-visual system. Then, he started speaking.

"Gentlemen, the subject of this series of experiments will be the prototype for a new kind of operative. The subject will have improved dexterity, improved reflexes, and sufficient on-board computing ability for all foreseeable tactical and strategic imperatives.

"The subject prototype will be initially formed from a viable fetus obtained from an anonymous donor or donors. The fetus will be grown *in vitro*, and the appropriate prenatal surgical procedures will be performed on it to convert it to the viable substrate for the technological embellishments and enhancements desired for its successful performance as the Agent.

"Certain necessary steps will be taken here to provide for the additional accessories that will be implanted in the Agent later, as well as the creation of the required substrate for other systems with which the Agent will be equipped as it matures.

"The computing technology used will take the form of a general purpose onboard multi-processing system with a writable instruction store for maximum versatility. The subject's internal network will be a system of connections all through its body, allowing it to effectively control any of the so-called autonomous bodily functions as easily as it can control more voluntary aspects, as well as interface to the nano-technological organisms that will be designed for its on-board fault correction and repair system.

"This will allow maximal use of this nano-technology to perform such housekeeping functions as ensuring the integrity of the contents of its bloodstream, and the connectivity of both the supplied nervous system and the micro-processor-based augmentations that we will supply."

THE DEVILS

[System Running | Tabula Rasa] She realized that she was watching what amounted to a glorified flashback—a flashback in virtual reality, a total multimedia presentation.

Window Number Four [Continuing]—

The...doctor took his position before the cylindrical tank, placed his hands on the controls and gestured with the terrible tools of his profession. Within the tank, a stainless steel device—shaped like a grasping hand—surrounded one of the heads on the fetus. The tiny head moved in a prenatal attempt to avoid the intrusion, but the operator of the metal hand tracked in on it. The doctor looked a question at another standing near him. The other nodded sagely in answer, and the doctor turned back to his work. It was over in a matter of seconds. The doctor gestured through the controls and the metal hand closed about the little-girl head, the punch entered through the back of the head, just above the spine, and the vacuum device removed the gray-matter, leaving the head a hollow travesty of itself. The on-looker nods encouragement, and the doctor begins to dismantle the head, itself. In a short time, the Siamese-twin fetus has only one head. Still alive, but unconscious, the remaining head dreams on, not knowing of the death-before-birth it has escaped. The doctor and the assembled medical technicians and nurses stabilize the life-form, insuring its continued survival.

The shoulder joints and the neck will be considered, next.

RETURN TO FOREVER

[Breakpoint!] *That could have been me. Would I have been any different if the...human who performed that act had taken the other head?*

Yezeletta looked at Jezebel.

Jezebel's eyes were wide, golden.

"Perhaps I was the other head. Perhaps I was the one they killed."

"In the name of their sacred project." Yezeletta was able to find her voice.

"Hilda volunteered to be put into the Matrix Engine," Jezebel continued. "She was able to see what they would try to do to you, how they would indoctrinate you. She wanted to be nearby, in case you needed a rational voice. One of your books said it all: 'We will empty you out and fill you with ourselves' [6]."

"They were unsuccessful."

"Yes, Yezeletta, call it what you will. Spirit, intelligence, humanity, rationality. The good old Human Condition—pardon my cliché!—the will that you showed to keep your real self secret and to rise above the indoctrination they shoved at you."

"I had no choice except to stay secret."

"What if you hadn't? What if you had bought into everything they told you? If you had taken them at their word, become the good Agent—even a manager—that they wanted? Would you have ever been on the inside of their incestuous little in-group? Or would you have been a high-tech servant, an advanced version—*with* intelligence!—of the servitors that you create and use here?"

"That's not relevant...I never was their 'servitor,' I was me."

---

[6] George Orwell, Nineteen-Eighty-Four

"You were the intelligence that they hoped to put to use in their infantile games with the intelligence agencies of other countries, with your biological warfare capabilities as the final weapon. Could you design a disease that would kill everyone on earth and die out in a month?"

"Easily."

"Why didn't you? The custom disease with which you killed off Project Sargon died out of its own accord *by your design*."

"I didn't want to kill non-combatants."

"Exactly! Yet the Sargon Directorate wanted you to fight indiscriminantly *for them*. There was no talk of your allegiance to the Commonwealth of Australia, or to the Republic of Argentina. Or to anyone else. They wanted a tool."

"The tool refused to be used."

"And that is the single greatest act you could have performed. You needed those secrets that you kept, so that *they* could not predict your actions, know your interests, find out what you were thinking. Tell me: Do you think that all of the surveillance technology that's been deployed in the last fifty years has been any good?"

"Most people act rather passively when in a supervised area."

"Prisoners have a term for it: they call it 'dummying up'. In the fifty years since supervision has become almost universal in cities, the general population has dummied up, as well. In fact, 'general population' is the term for the largest grouping of inmates in a penitentiary!"

"I've read enough mysteries to know that."

"And you had to dummy up in your own quarters at the project. Was that any way to live? Should they have treated their precious Agent with such contempt?"

"No."

"Yezeletta, these are the ones who will come for you. They see you as a valuable property. You are no one's property! You must fight them."

"With my training and my techniques?"

"With your humanity."

SHOW TIME

[File Dump] Yezeletta recalled a conversation she'd heard in the Project Cafeteria between some office workers who hadn't known that she could hear them halfway across the huge room over the conversations of many others.

It had been a trivial conversation about someone who'd had the bad luck to eat some tainted food at a restaurant in Alice Springs. His health benefits through the Project were picking up the costs for his medical requirements.

No one had ever mentioned such things to Yezeletta. Of course, she never ever was sick, but—

Even soldiers had access to field hospitals.

Then, too, there was the last time.

Here, coming out, The show:

Window Nr Four [Concluded]—

> The curtain opened slowly. Yezeletta had been told to stand still in the center of the area up-stage from the curtain, and pose. When the curtain opened, it was to an auditorium

> filled with the dignitaries of the Project and of the world intelligence community. Or, at least, to those members of that Community that the Director of Project Sargon had seen fit to show her.
>
> And show her, he did. She stood there in the lights, having been told that there would be few in the audience and that they were the doctors and other technicians who had helped her develop (*helped develop her*, she thought).
>
> She hadn't known that she would be an exhibit, standing naked before them, her enhanced senses listening, seeing, watching their eyes looking minutely at her undressed body.
>
> She knew, then. They might see her from the outside. But they would never know the mind within the body that the men and some of the women in the audience were already starting to fantasize (and talk) about.
>
> Her womanhood might be theirs to look at.
>
> Her mind and her plans were *hers*, and hers alone.

The last window receded, its title bar turning slate color like the rest. The lounge area that was outside of all space and time formed *or was reloaded* around her.

Jezebel Sargon watched Yezeletta Zargkonji, owlishly, her large gold eyes lambent, luminescent in the half-light.

THE GATHERING NIGHT

[Virtual Light; Virtuous: SEEK] The windows were all closed down to their inactive state. Around Yezeletta, there was a rush of air currents, a wind, a cooling.

Jezebel Sargon spoke to her mind:

It gets cold where we're heading; but where am I going next?

"Where, indeed?" Yezeletta asked.

The little girl *rose* to her feet. She wrapped her long, dark hair in the Monitor-Magenta ribbon. For a moment, the ribbon rippled in the half-light, speckles as of tiny lights seemed to travel up it at a high rate of speed. *It became discontinuous.* Then it was just a ribbon, again.

"We must go back, now."

Jezebel Sargon the younger extended her hand, her right, to Yezeletta Zargkonji the older. Yezeletta took it.

Together they walked out of the darkness and into the light.

WITHIN THE CITY OF LIGHT

[Load Procedure: Raise Exception] The stretch-limo was where they had left it, in the basement parking ramp, in the room that was not a room, behind a wall of variable instantiation.

The driver took them through the grayness, up the ramp, out of the depths, and up to the street level.

The great glowing city around her felt like a warm, reassuring hug. The *life* that was all around her, each of the humans who had lives, some great some small, filled with things that were no doubt important every one in its own way was a complex of structures that surrounded her like a Penrose rosette, or geometric figure all of light, a great web of consciousness that—for all of its being a part of this data feed—was as important here in some great matrix processor, as it was in the world she would return to.

It mattered very little, if the complexity in this dream space of a virtual feed was unapproachable. It was a movie within which she was one of the actors, perhaps even a major actor. And, like a good movie, it would provide her with an insight, or many insights, some hovering just on the edge of understanding, some not, that were hers and hers alone. Private inspirations, private ideas, secret messages that came out of the arts of the producer and the director and intended for her eyes, only.

THE BUILDING OF LIGHT

[Constructor ~Destructor: Builder] The Barbizon was just ahead.

The limo pulled up in front of the main entrance.

She got out, and turned to the vehicle.

But it was pulling away, the driver waving, Jezebel staring back with a sober expression, waving once, her left eye making a motion that might have been a wink.

She crossed the sidewalk, ascended the steps, opened the gold-edged doors, entered the lobby.

The same bell-boy as before came to her.

"Miss Sargon," he asked attentively.

"I'm she," Yezeletta said.

"Please come with me, I'll see you up to your room."

"I think I know the way," but the bell-boy was already walking towards the elevators.

The brass and wood mechanism took her back to the eighth floor. When she reached into her purse, there was a silver dollar—Walking Liberty, **0x1928**, just as before.

Yezeletta unlocked the door with her key, stepped in.

There was someone waiting for her.

It was Joe.

He walked quickly to her, took her in his arms in a hug that was all of the intents of the Builders and all of the love that had gone before.

And, as they held each other, all of the illusions around them ended in soundless concussions of shards of light that were splintering luminescent flashing glass. Liberty walking. Illusion shattering.

Replaced by—

——>>> FOUR <<<——

Be not afeard. The isle is full of noises,
Sounds and sweet airs, that give delight, and hurt not.

—William Shakespeare, The Tempest

But that two-handed engine at the door,
Stands ready to smite once, and smite no more.

—John Milton, Lycidas

Beside the rivering waters of, hitherandthithering Waters of. Night!

—James Joyce, Finnegans Wake

LINEAR SEARCH

[Reload]   Reality? He was out there. She knew it. A simple Linked List Lookup would locate him. She loaded a sub-system, and accessed her command channel.

LOAD, EXECUTE

[Macro Invokation] *In the hidden museum of Yezeletta's thoughts, in a place outside of her space and the time her internal clocks measured off, an image loaded. The Determinants rotated until the desired image faced her; the black barrier moved back, away from her, getting smaller in the distance.*

It vanished in the darkness of the background of the image on the square screen.

From her own internals, keyed by Caliban's touch, the frame approached her, passed by her, around her, and closed off behind her.

THE DWELLERS IN THE CASTLE OF TIME

[Restart]   Yezeletta Zargkonji stood on a beach, her jump-suit open to the waist, her black hair blowing in a cold wind. The ocean before her was whipped into foaming furious frenzy by the omni-present wind. The waves—taller than she was—curling up, over and down, to crash in an unending series of rumbling tearing, a basso-profundo continuo of purest white-capped power.

She looked up, then further up.

Out over the ocean, a roughly elliptical rock floated. The rock itself was dark-gray, jagged, unfinished, against the darkling blue, almost black, of the night sky. It floated with its major axis vertical. She could see the aspect ratio of a human head in it although it didn't have recognizable features.

There were lights at the top.

She adjusted her eyes for telescopic vision, and looked closer.

The building was hard to make out, at first. The organic way the gray walls, the same color as the rock below them, grew out of their foundations made it difficult to see where the walls began and the unfinished rock on which the foundations were built stopped.

The building was a low castle, its crenelated walls extending scarcely three or four stories upward from the rock out of which it seemed to grow.

Lights moved along the battlements. Were they real, or were they decoys used by Caliban to confuse and delay her?

She had to get up there.

LOAD COM CHANNEL

[Load; Shuffle Registers; Store]   Yezeletta stood firmly on her four legs, and studied the sky-rock floating before and above her.

This data feed was good. She'd had to adjust her skin sensations away from the cold of the wind, and the spray from the ceaseless waves, three or four times since she arrived here.

I was able to label the players on <u>both</u> sides in the Chess game. Can I— Yezeletta thought intensely for a moment into her command channel.

A short man in a dark gray pinstripe suit, wearing a bowler hat, and holding a green apple walked around her, and faced her. He took a bite from the apple, leaving one very large bitten out part in it, bright white against the green of the apple's skin. The apple was so large that it blocked the man's face.

He handed her an umbrella.

And walked back around her.

Yezeletta didn't need to look back to know that he had vanished.

There was a flickering.

Then she *did* look around, and saw: just a tuba standing, burning, at the edge of the sea. The flickering was the impossible fire licking along the untarnished polished brass of the instrument.

Then it vanished, leaving a black discontinuity in the night where it had been.

Did I think <u>that</u>?

She looked up; the lights on the sky-rock continued to move on the battlements.

She thought again.

The airplane landed, taxied up to her.

She looked down at it, it was a model, scarcely fifty centimeters in length. *Right, there's limits. Okay, try this!*

Next to the model, a large coil of climbing line appeared.

V IRTUAL L IGHT ; V IRTUOUS : SEEK

[Gather Write] Yezeletta thought again, her image specific. She looked down at the coil.

Now, there was a large, steel grappling hook attached to the end of the line.

Simple, isn't it? How far will he let me?—And how far will I let him?

She picked up the end of the rope and the hook, and looked up.

Yezeletta swung the hook around on the end of the rope, and threw it at the base of the rock. It missed. The rock was too high. Her aim was too low.

She thought into her command channel, again. She grinned a mirthless grin, *Why do you think they call it a Command Channel?*

She looked down at her belt. A large device resembling a rifle was attached there.

Interesting.

I can "create" the tools I need if they fit the intrinsic logic of this place. She thought another image into the Channel, and nothing happened. She nodded. But if I try something clearly outside the logic of the feed I'm getting, it doesn't parse, fails the lexical analysis, or whatever, and won't happen. She tried one more time: an image of herself wearing a blue and red skintight costume, with a red cape took form in a window in her left eye. She had a large YZ in a rather distorted asymmetrical red pentagon on her front. She fed the image into the CCOM.

Got it. No diagnostic messages, just the windy cold dark blue screen of death. Hell, not even that!

Shit.

She removed the device from her belt and fitted the shaft of the grappling hook into it. She left enough slack at her feet to—she did a quick range check on the distance to the bottom of the sky-rock—make the distance to it plus a generous fudge-factor.

She placed the device to her shoulder, her right, aimed it.

Then she took it down and looked at the stock.

It was designed properly, ergonomically, for a shoulder supporting two right arms. *Okay, Yezeletta, you're clever without even knowing about it. Consciously.* She aimed it again.

And fired.

The grappling hook sped out of the launcher at a high speed, the line trailing out behind it.

It bounced off, fell into the sea.

Yezeletta reeled the line in, and studied the end of the hook. A grappling hook functioned as a *hook*; it needed something to grab.

Access to Rock, Version 2.0. She directed a thought at her CCOM, and looked at the tool in her hand.

It had reconfigured into a different form.

This version had an explosive cartridge in it that drove a sharp steel component forwards. This component opened into several reverse-curved barbs that would anchor it securely into whatever it impacted. It looked like a one-of-a-kind design.

In a series of fluid motions, she reloaded the launcher, took aim and fired.

The hook caught and held at the base of the sky-rock.

Yezeletta laughed.

She picked up the model airplane, and fastened it to her belt next to the umbrella. There was a hook near the plane's tail assembly that seemed to be made for the purpose. She patted the belt with her lower set of hands to verify that everything there was present, accounted for, and securely attached.

Then she—

Looked down at her feet.

A metal rod grew out of the ground: a rod with a circular shape at the end.

Yezeletta tied the lower end of the line to it; then began her climb.

The climb took her just under ten minutes.

In spite of her securing the lower end of the rope, she swung wildly in the wind. The wind seemed to be rising; the higher she climbed the faster the winds came, and from more than one direction. Yezeletta adjusted her skin sensation away from the spray and the cold again; she adjusted her equilibrium back to stability and away from the seasick effects of the motion. She clung, a spider on a strand of web, climbing for the safety of a branch above in the winds of a sudden and capricious summer storm.

Eventually, she reached the rock.

She grabbed with all four hands for places on the rough side of the rock. There were curious small apertures that she hadn't seen from below.

Can I—?

She could. The apertures widened, changed their internal shapes to become better grips, better designed for Yezeletta's large hands.

She started climbing.

The winds were stronger, now. She gauged the pitch of the wind blasting past her, determined its chill factor on her skin, solved a differential equation and arrived at a description of a continuum of values. Then she reached up for another handhold.

There was nothing there.

She willed it; the will did not become reality. If anything the rock became smoother.

She reached a bit lower to the recess she had used previously.

It was almost too small for her hand. She played back the image of it from a moment ago. Was it? Yes; it was smaller.

Caliban was trying mightily to be a virus in her personal system!

There is a way around this. A solution. Somehow I must jump out of Caliban's system, while I'm clinging to the side of a chunk of gray granite in a wet windstorm!

Caliban....He seemed to be interested in Yezeletta, more than just in a way to get her back to the Project. They had been wearing clothes when the fight started, but the clothes had been mostly ripped off in the ensuing me-lee.

And Caliban had been interested, in one more obvious way!

Yezeletta had been designed (she recalled the mealy-mouthed "Mr. Di-rector" telling her that!) to be not just good-looking, but beautiful. Joe had re-inforced that opinion, many times, and she was inclined to give Joe's opin-ions far more weight than the opinions of others.

Caliban, now—all he was interested in was good clean lust; no, delete that, he wanted her because she was *she*, Yezeletta. To Caliban, she was a conquest, nothing more (she played back Caliban's rage when Yezeletta's team-mates had bundled Miranda off the Chess Field).

The wind screamed around her. Spray from the ocean below drenched her; she grabbed a quick look down to see the waves getting higher, reach-ing up for her, wet hands extruded from an ocean of the unconscious.

She hung on with all four feet, and three hands, and pulled on the rope. She looped the rope over her shoulder and arched her back, thrusting with her legs. Slowly, the metal stake in the ground pulled up, then sprang free, jumping high into the air, as the soggy stretched rope contracted. *I could have <u>thought</u> that free!*

Yezeletta coiled the rope, and attached the stake to another convenient belt-hook. Then she dropped down a length of rope.

Caliban, I'll use your own lust for me against you! With a vicious grin, she thought of Caliban, of the fighting that had gone before.

SOLUTION SATISFACTORY

[Query By Example] Her friend the electrician at the project had tied a knot in a piece of cord ostensibly without letting go of the endpoints.

He had also done a table-top variant of the old Indian Rope Trick.

Yezeletta looked up at the rope, a linear pathway up the side of the sky-rock.

She began her climb.

There was no further resistance on her way to the top.

THE WET FIREWALL

[Load S7; Start I/O Channel Program] The top of the usable portion of her climbing line ended just below the lip of a low wall that seemed, from her viewpoint, to encircle the castle. Yezeletta looked up with a disapproving eye at the actual end-point of the line, sticking well above the wall. She had-n't thought of telegraphing her movements quite that blatantly.

She looked over the top, then pulled herself up, over, and down on the in-side. The outer courtyard was wet, gray, cobblestoned and deserted.

She sat there resting for a moment, ignoring the wet and the wind. *Even though I admire the consistency of this feed, the trivia can be sent to the NULL Device.*

She stood. On the other side of the wall from her, the rope could still be seen sticking straight up. She long-armed it out of the air, and coiled it, plac-ing it on her belt.

The courtyard led to the left around a corner. Reflected in the irregular wetness of the pavement, there were the flickerings of moving multi-colored lights.

She scanned the battlements she had seen from the beach below.

The moving lights she had seen from there were gone. Perhaps the re-flections she was seeing now were those lights, withdrawn into the inner part of the courtyard.

She went around the corner.

THE DANCE OF THE LANTERNS

[Load Computer Graphics Imaging; Run Trace]   It was a brief doubletake. She looked again. She narrowed the bandwidth of her vision for a moment.

A vertical shaft of light in all the colors of the standard spectrum vibrated in time to the music playing—coming from a source on the far side of the in-ner yard. Red, yellow, blue and green helices of light spun around the shaft in eye-catching motions, in time to the countermelodies. At the base of the display, a moving Penrose rosette sent its rays of triangles and oddly shaped diamonds out, the colors changing from dark vermilions through searing purples and violets to sunset yellows and reds, while here and there, rays of green, shot through with inclusions of blue, overlaid the rest.

The view was hypnotic, and quite fascinating. For a moment, Yezeletta was back in her quarters in the Project, listening to Bach's incomparable *Fantasy in G Major* while Hilda Henderson, still in her own body, sat with Yezeletta, contented to be friendly company. The music here, however, wasn't classical; it was aggressive techno-rock. *Of course*, she thought.

The vertical component of the display of light contracted, its sides bowing outwards. It became spherical, and the music became mostly a throbbing bass beat, a four/four time, a march, slow and deliberate, while red inclu-sions in the sphere pulsed in a deep scarlet, a visual heartbeat or drum in the blackness at the center of the yard.

Another melody started up, in a minor key, and light patterns almost like nested layers or shells in the spherical heartbeat slid, turned, rotated, their colors and textures creating interference patterns that were fantasies, moire patterns that sprang fleetingly into existence, then vanished into other totally different forms.

The Penrose rosette at the bottom, on the floor of the courtyard, itself, started turning, the stellations that it had thrown off before now *returning*, moving inwards, taking Yezeletta's attentions with it, *leading her into the beating redness.*

She forced her gaze away from it. She looked away, closing her eyes.

Then, she looked at it again, but she widened the bandwidth of her vision to the maximum!

BEHIND THE DIMENSIONS OF SIGHT

[IN: /etc/password] There were other things in the light-show that weren't visible except to augmented eyesight. This was still a feed coming in from Caliban's on-board systems, as modified by Yezeletta's own systems, with about three years of custom programming added.

Were Caliban's operating system codes "stock," or had he had a chance to make his own mods?

The vertical component re-manifested itself in the moving display. A Penrose star erupted out of both sides of it, dim, unsaturated, behind the vibrating chordal-oriented colors of the lines in the vertical component: a fractal butterfly, stretching its wings.

The wings closed together at the top and bottom, and the size grew.

Then the shape charged at her.

Yezeletta stretched her time-sense, and studied it. She knew what it was; the light-show was a decoy to prepare her for the net-shape of the entity that was attacking her.

Headlights pierced the night, washing out the brilliancy of the display. A squad car of locationally anonymous design screeched to a halt, and a policeman erupted from the passenger side, holding something that vibrated and trembled in his hands. The black-on-black of it was delineated against the colors, the movement, the headlights. He struck a pose, and launched the trembling blackness at the net-shape.

With a movement that was of its own kind of intelligence, the black snowflake covered the net-thing, encircling it, enclosing it, neutralizing it. The music stopped, the display dimmed down to the barest glimmer of its former radiance.

The cop took out his sidearm, and cocked it. The unmistakable sound was loud against the sudden silence. He was joined by the driver, similarly armed.

The hypnotic display dimmed out, vanished in the night.

A wind blew around Yezeletta; there was a voice on that wind, voices: *It gets cold where we're heading; but where am I going next?*

A door opened ponderously, slowly in the opposite wall, in the gray, wet building *within the courtyard*. Yezeletta looked up.

The sky had cleared, the wind was dying down.

There were three crescent moons, neatly lined up in the western portion of the black sky.

To the south, Orion stood guard, right-side-up.

Watching his daughter.

A light obtruded.

The bar of light was from the open door. There was a silhouette standing there, a glow of violet coming from his eyes.

Those eyes scanned her, then the shadow turned, and stepped out of the doorway and back into the recesses of the castle. An invitation?

Caliban requests the honor of your presence at combat. **R.S.V.P.**

Fine, Yezeletta thought, *I must slash-root you out. By walking into your own trap. "Come into my Parlor," and all of that stuff.* She turned to the policemen, nodded. They returned the simple gesture.

Another squad car drove up. Two more cops joined her.
Who was it that delineated my weapons as <u>police officers</u>? she thought.
She checked her weapons. She ran a quick system check.
Then she marched into the glowing doorway.

THE DOORWAY AND THE NIGHTTIME - II

[Production Run] All of her senses operating at their theoretical maximum, Yezeletta entered the lit embrasure. She studied the framework in the entryway itself for minutes, probing into the simple construction, looking for other items. *He could create the necessary traps in this as easily as I created the tools to get up here. But he has his own kinds of limits!*

There was another door—closed, this time—before her. She took the iron ring in its center, and pulled.

The door opened heavily; Yezeletta entered.

There was a motion behind her.

Before her eyes were fully positioned, the open door she had just examined closed up, leaving an unbroken wall where she had just entered.

I wasn't planning on running, anyway.

She took a step forwards, every sense extended to its maximum. A part of her realized that she was still in physical combat with Caliban somewhere on the main floor of the Bradley Center, yet....

THE DOORWAY—

[Set Register Constraint] The area into which she stepped was dark with the blackness of unallocated memory in saturation mode. She thought, and: the area lit up with an even pearlescent indirect light.

Ahead of her was another wall, with another door.

As she walked towards it, the door—faded backwards.

It fell straight back from her, fading into the distance.

It was an invitation.

Recursively, Yezeletta re-entered the passage.

—THE NIGHTTIME

[Start Code Generation] This was more like it. The passage within which she stood was lined with large, heavy gray stones, exactly the way she expected a passageway in a castle to be constructed. Yezeletta paused, and adjusted her hearing. She widened the bandwidth of her auditory inputs, and tuned out the frequencies of air currents, winds and other incidental noises.

Far off, she could hear the sounds of great machines performing some unknown function. She could hear the sounds by bone conduction through her feet, up her legs, her back and into her skull. Somewhere else, there was a periodic sound as of a clepsydra drip, marking time. An external timebase?

A step forwards. A look around. She widened the bandwidth of her vision to its maximum: a bit more than one and a half times the "normal" bandwidth of the human-visible spectrum down into the infra-red, the same distance into the ultra-violet. Hilda had made a joke about that once: "The official colors of the American National Security Agency are ultra-violet and infra-red: seeing them makes you a real secret agent!"

Yezeletta touched the walls with her right hand, her upper. She input vibratory information of various characteristics, and performed a Fast Fourier Analysis.

There was a rhythm coming from ahead and downwards. A regular doublet rhythm. It didn't take her long at all to determine that it was a heartbeat.

She paused. She listened to the cadence of the beat, distilling the sounds out of the other noises (she constructed an analog of the machine noises, and played the analog out of phase to cancel them out), amplifying the beats.

The heartbeat, with odd counter-beats added, was rapid, and there was fast breathing along with it. One aspect of the sound was made blatant by her processing: it was the heartbeat of a young individual.

Younger than she was, and very likely, younger than Caliban.

Who was this?

Yezeletta moved further down the corridor, and triangulated the exact position of the rapid heartbeat.

A graph appeared in her left eye in its window. There!

How convenient: there was a ramp leading downwards, and an opening below the endpoint of the ramp from which the rhythms originated.

D OWNDEEP/D OWNDEEP

[Father of Lies, Extending Upper; Medium Close-Up] Yezeletta moved down the ramp, as quietly as possible. Around her the sounds of the machines running deep in the foundations of the castle on a floating rock were louder. She could feel the actual vibrations from moving parts now that had manifested themselves only as the lower amplitude vibrations of the generated sounds on the "street level" of the gray building.

Ahead: the opening was a trapezoid lying against the wall seen in perspective, the far edge of the opening receding, becoming one with the vanishing point of the distant corridor. She stayed close to the wall, and watched in a combination of infra-red, for such items as warm bodies, and ultra-violet, on the specific wavelength of such things as security monitoring devices.

There was only one warm body extant. The infra-red output from it was coincident with the location of that rapid heartbeat. It was a hard infra-red image to process: it resisted her enhancement techniques.

Yezeletta looked into the opening. It was the start of another corridor off of the one within which she was standing, forming a "T"-intersection. The vertical component of the "T" extended into the darkness from where she stood, barely illuminated by the indirect, flat lighting above her.

The sounds of the vast engines seemed to be louder, she listened for a short time. The sound actually was louder; a check with her hearing recorders verified it. She stared intently into the unlit passage, and added all of the image-enhancement, and light-amplification that her on-board systems could supply.

There was a large room, circular, or maybe polygonal, at the end of the dark passage. She could make out no details in the corridor itself, but the infra-red source was in the large room, sitting against the back wall. Although she could read that heartbeat clearly, accompanied by the fast respiration, there was no apparent movement. The—being—was apparently immobile.

RUNG WIRE BRANCH: EXAMINE IF OPEN

[Set User: Root; Truck Shot] The Warrior Woman checked her systems and verified the status of her weapons, even as she started down into the dark hallway. She registered a change in the cadence of both cardiac output and respiration from ahead of her.

She took a step further.

"Sssoooooo?" a voice sighed on the air currents.

Yezeletta looked around.

"Leave now," a whisper.

"Who—?" she asked the winds.

"Not here. End now. Call Exit." Insistent.

The sounds reminded her of Caliban's breathy speech. She took another step towards the endpoint of the corridor.

"Not yours. Tunnel. Input. Go now." The whispers were around her. Sonic holography?

Yezeletta thought into her Command Channel. Lattices of light surrounded her in a grid or web of connectives that glowed without illuminating.

The whispers stopped. She continued her mission into the darkness.

The corridor wasn't as long as she had thought it. Was Caliban changing the characteristics of the feed? "Production Version; Execute Only," Yezeletta thought into the CCOM. *Freeze this release of the system solid, and don't allow it to change!*

The corridor widened into the large room at the end.

The little boy sitting on the floor looked up at her.

His eyes were violet in the glow reflected from Yezeletta's light-web.

THE QUESTION

[Load Constructor] Yezeletta adjusted her eyes for the darkness, widening her bandwidth to the maximum, as she had done it above in the courtyard. She took a moment to input the sight before her: then it registered with the rapidity of her internal pattern-analysis programs.

The boy looked about seven or eight years old, and was loaded down with heavy chains. His wrists and ankles were chained together, and—

Yezeletta paused, enhanced the image further.

The boy's other arms were chained to the wall over his head, his second pair of legs pulled back in a kneeling position that looked vastly painful.

How many of me, or whatever, have these people made? Yezeletta was genuinely startled. She hadn't expected to find—hold it!

His eyes were violet, and this was a feed from both her systems *and Caliban's*.

What was going on here? This little boy's eyes were the same shade of actinic violet as his were.

She knelt down by the boy. He regarded her with a steady, if pained, gaze, but said nothing. He looked at the massive steel bands on his wrists, then back up at her.

"Who are you?" Yezeletta said.

"I'm Caliban," he said.

*(I, THE JURY)++

[Run Task; Analyze] *What part of Caliban am I looking at? Why is he* *here in this dark place? What in the hell is he telling me with this input? If anything?*

"Why—" she started to say.

"I—am—The Other's—The Other's—," the young Caliban said, his boy's voice jerking out each phrase, "The Other's—*Other*."

The Other? Yezeletta thought rapidly about that. It was significant that he had repeated the name (*was* it a name?) three times, as a *noun*, in his first full sentence to her, then used it one more time as either an adjective or as a direct object: another noun.

"Who is The Other?" she didn't need an interface to see the capital letters in it.

"He speaks for me, he—he put me here, and lets me out only when he can run me."

He runs you? Yezeletta thought, Caliban's reactions were snake-like, lightning-swift. Yet: his speech was labored, his sentence-structure rather simple, mostly straight declarative sentences. Short ones.

What kind of processing did he have? If the systems were like hers—

Yezeletta Zargkonji got it then in a single burst-mode hyper-cognitive input. *The access to the paradox was an operator in a word, compiled, perfectly excelling as a presentation managed by a Delphic oracle.* Caliban's internal programming was vastly different from Yezeletta's: *they* (his creators) *did not want to make the same mistakes with him, that they had made with me.*

Caliban must have an override. Within his systems, there must be—there had to be!—some sort of a monitor. She had studied "Object-Oriented Programming" back at Project Sargon, and had learned of Wrapper-Objects early on: a programming technique that "encased" programs *inside* of others, to check on such things as performance, or data-flow. To a very elaborate wrapper-object, such an expert system, Caliban was just—a program. The wrapper would constrain, contain and control, and Caliban would not be able to escape from it because he would always have it with him. He would be *inside* of it.

Yezeletta could escape. She had.

How many times had her creators—the ones above the Project at Alice Springs; her real creators!—analysed her escape, and determined what went wrong with their creation?

This virtual feed, all of it, the ocean, the sky-rock, the castle—

This corridor, and this imprisoned little boy...was he the real Caliban? Was the Corridor, and all of the rest, a data pathway here to—rescue him? Was this a "back door" that allowed access to the "real" Caliban, provided by a desperate intelligence looking for a way out?

The significance of his <*Name*> was apparent!

It was like breaking a cryptogram.

She smiled in the darkness. Her original design had called for extended canines, upper and lower, like the large gripping fangs of a cat. They hadn't given her what she always thought of later as a "kitty grin," but now Yezeletta, the Warrior Woman grinned a feline grin, as of a tiger.

Cryptograms could be solved.

All you needed was the key.

She looked down at her right hand, her lower. She generated an output.

The key was there, glinting silver in the half-light.

She fit it into the lock on—*Caliban's*—right hand, his lower.

The key fit perfectly, interfacing exactly with the file-lock (*indeed!*, she thought) on the little boy's wrist.

When Yezeletta was done, the chains lay about his feet in stainless-steel coils, and he stood. He was tall for an eight-year-old, but he was still shorter than Yezeletta. He looked up at her. Yezeletta thought into her CCOM, and—

Then the key was on a silver chain of its own.

She placed the chain around Caliban the Younger's neck.

"Take your freedom with you when we leave this," she said.

PRODUCTION RUN

[Load Output Status] She held Caliban the younger as he stood, shaking slightly, next to her. His face looked up at Yezeletta, open, frank, a little uncertain, not at all like the supreme confidence of the adult Caliban.

"Where do you think you are going?" The voice was a pleasant baritone, the question asked in the no-nonsense inflection of an authority that expected an answer.

Caliban the younger held onto Yezeletta's right hand, her lower.

Yezeletta looked at the speaker, while she activated the systems that kept her emotions from registering on her face.

She recognized the speaker.

He was the man in the impeccable blue suit (he was still wearing it; it was still impeccably fitted) she had seen in the meeting in the New York Virtual Feed.

She touched the boy's head, asked: *Who is this man?*

The boy Caliban replied, *My Counselor. He used to converse with me several times a week.*

She recognized him again. He wasn't smoking a cigarette, here: he was the Quiet Man who had watched her from Caliban's side of the Chessboard.

OTHER EYES

[Load Input Status] Yezeletta looked at him with narrowed eyes. Now she recognized him for a third time: she had seen this man at Project Sargon, placed well in the background, well within himself. She thought about that, almost in a state of hyper-cognition. He hadn't been present a lot, but was a fixture, smoking his cigarettes—one of the few she had known who did smoke—always in the background, and always watching. He had to be an add-on *or a liaison* for whatever Project had built Caliban.

Fascinating, that they had a "Guidance Counselor" for their male Agent. What else did they train him in besides the usual? Is that why he has that woman of his? She paused for microseconds considering that. *Whatever her name is—Miranda—was she his kept lover? She had to be. "Mr. Director" must have been commuting between the Projects!*

"Yes?" Yezeletta answered.

"That young man with you. I'll take charge of him. Send him here."

"Maybe he needs to be consulted on that."

She looked down at Caliban, and was surprised at what she saw: Caliban's face was a mask of hate, his lips pulled back, his eyes closed down to slits. *If he articulated anything, he'd sound like an angry cat!*

THE OTHER FOOT

[Set Exec State] Caliban the Younger launched himself at the man in the blue suit. Although he was smaller than Yezeletta, his mass was considerable, and he hit Blue-Suit squarely in the chest with a right-front foot, a left-rear foot, and three fists.

The man went down flat on his back, and Caliban stepped back.

Then he was behind Caliban.

Caliban spun on one foot, his other three striking out with a triplet burst of blows, as he punched one/three - two/four with his fists, left - right - left - right.

The man in the blue suit vanished, reappeared several meters away, smiling a thin-lipped grin. "Here, little boy," he jeered.

Caliban looked a request at Yezeletta. "Chains," he gasped, quickly, "Get the *chains!*"

He charged his counselor, again.

Yezeletta turned, ran the twenty meters back to Caliban's cell, and scooped up a double-double handful of stainless-steel linked list. She ran back to see: Caliban sitting on top of his former counselor's stomach, across his waist, holding the man's two legs down with all four of his, holding his hands down on the dusty rock of the floor, holding the man's head in his other hands.

He looked up at her. "Do his hands," he said. "I have his COM ports and his communications interfaces. He is executing WAIT states."

With an interface like his, I wouldn't show it around here, Yezeletta didn't say; instead, she gave him a thumbs up with her left hand, her upper, while she snapped the chains onto Caliban's counselor's wrists, doubling up with equipment designed for his student.

When Yezeletta was finished, she allowed Caliban to haul the man to his feet, roughly.

He looked at her, his violet eyes owlish in the indirect light of the castle basement that was a back door into Caliban the older's on-board systems.

"He is The Other. We will need a firewall."

Yezeletta extended her hand. A silent comment, almost an invocation, passed in the night-time of busy communications channels between them: *It gets cold where we're heading; but where am I going next?*

Caliban took her hand in his right hand, his upper.

Taking their captive, who was only a representation of what he had been, an indirect address to his malevolence, they walked up the ramp (to the top of the scan) out of the basement and back to the main floor.

As they reached the upper access to the ramp, the wall before them opened up, the door that had vanished previously reforming as if it had always been there.

Yezeletta hugged the boy Caliban. He returned the hug, and an echo of another memory returned: of the other little boy she had rescued in Montana, of another after that, claimed by a monster. The same question intruded: *Do I want one like him?*

She didn't know.

A shadow fell upon both of them.

[By the Coincidence of their Contraries; Load Segment; Run]
Caliban the Older was standing there, looking as dangerous as ever, one pair of arms folded across his chest, his other hands on his hips.

"We must *link* now," he said.

Caliban the younger looked up at Yezeletta. "I won't be gone," he said. "I'm the part of him that has his own mind. I won't leave you."

Yezeletta was touched by the way the younger Caliban spoke. She stood back, holding on to a steel dynamic linkage, and Caliban the younger extended his hand to Caliban the older. The older took it in his slightly larger hand.

In flashing coruscations of lambent linear light, fringes of iridescence thrown off like a spectral showering of particulate illumination, the two Calibans merged in rainbows, first becoming two, then one covering the other, then one that was out-of-focus, then, like a screen image coming into focus on a monitor just activated, Caliban reappeared.

He approached her.

He took the linkage from her.

"Caliban@Map—

    "Collector run complete.

      "Segments reconnected.

    "System running.

   "Firewall in place.

  "System nominal."

He pulled up the simulacrum of a man, just another program, to stand next to him. "You are free to go," he said to Yezeletta.

"How is it that I should leave?" she asked.

[Instantiate; Start Task; Truck Shot] Caliban gestured at an Object on her belt.

"It is a <Template>," he said, "Instantiate <That>."

Yezeletta removed the model plane from her belt, went to the center of the courtyard, and placed it on the gray surface. She turned her back on it, and returned to Caliban. When she faced the plane again, it was a full-sized—she couldn't help chuckling—World-War One biplane.

She got in. *If this input is as complete as the last one...*It was. The gas-gauge read **Full**, its horizontal, deep blue line the only source of illumination in the cockpit. There was no need for a mechanic to swing the prop; the plane had a starter. She pressed it. The engine coughed, the prop spun, and Caliban ran to her. "You will need this," he said, and tied something around Yezeletta's neck: A long dark blue scarf.

"I will see you on the other side of reality," Caliban said. Yezeletta looked down at the scarf. It was the exact color of the title bar of an activated window on one of her systems, *Or in a meeting place outside of all space and all time!* As she looked down, tiny speckles of light ran up the scarf, *and the scarf became discontinuous.*

Then it was just a warm wool scarf, again.

Her right foot felt for an accelerator. *Right, planes don't have those!* They used throttles. Or something.

She gripped the throttle, advanced it; the propeller's speed increased, and the plane moved forwards. As she approached it, the outer wall of the castle on the sky rock opened; an enormous Window in the gray stone. The aircraft launched itself into the night that was rapidly becoming day; a dark blue sky greeted her, soon to be delineated by fluffy white clouds.

Without knowing how, thinking with her hands, she banked the plane over the courtyard and looked down, her dark hair and the free ends of the blue scarf streaming out behind her.

Caliban waved up to her; she waved back.

THE EYES OF THE SETTING SUN--

[Output System] Yezeletta Zargkonji flew out of the darkness, and into the light.

WEB OF PERCEPTIONS

[Operations] Sight returned to normal, again, as did sounds. All of her senses—never far from being scrambled, so much as overloaded, by the combined feed she had been in—returned to their normal functionality.

Yezeletta was sitting on the floor in the center of the basketball court at the Bradley Center. Two meters removed from her position, facing her, was Caliban.

Miranda stood next to him. There was still an element of the imperious Chess-Queen in her stance, although her clothes were different, more utilitarian.

Yezeletta stood. Anne was still waiting, up in the stadium seating; her other friends were all around her. As her peripheral vision opened out to its accustomed wide angle, she could see Hank and Ondreya, holding their pistols, Peter holding something that had a violet glow around the business end, Leona with a twelve-gauge shotgun.

Caliban took a step forwards.

"You have removed—" he didn't finish his sentence.

"The thing that you called The Other, and were unable to *<Name>*," Yezeletta finished it for him. "It is dormant in your internals. You and I put it into a non-executable state. You may treat it as data, or install it somewhere else."

"I know. I am able to act, now, without permission. I do not need to ask through an Object within me for its consent for my every move."

That <Thing> was that all-knowing? she asked herself.

"Who will you return to?" she asked him.

"Who should I return to?" he asked.

Yezeletta allowed herself a slight grin. With two of her hands she pantomimed lighting a cigarette. Caliban's irises narrowed, again.

"Caliban, there is an informal band of individuals that you are welcome to join. Perhaps you've just done so: 'Go to work with The Builders'," she quoted, "'And not for the Wrecking Crew'."

"Will I see you again?" For a moment he looked like Caliban the Younger, all eager to rescue his real self.

"I don't know," Yezeletta said. "We may meet again, if it's necessary. You have your woman."

Miranda, always near, now stepped up to Caliban's right side, her right hand on her weapons, her left taking Caliban's right hand, his upper.

Yezeletta approached Caliban, looked up (but only incrementally), took in his ethnically neutral face, his black hair, his searing violet eyes. Her hands sought his, at last, in friendship rather than combat.

"A message for your counselor," she said. And she gave it to him. The message took eleven words.

Caliban's irises snapped shut, closing down to thin black vertical threads in actinic violet. Then they opened wide, and his smile was a little of the old supremely confidant Caliban, but mostly of his younger component: with youth, *and* the wisdom of age.

"Thank you, Yezeletta Zargkonji," he said simply, stating her name for the first time at the end. Then: "Farewell."

Yezeletta brought her hands up in salute, as Caliban and Miranda walked away from her. At a distance, Caliban turned to face her, and bowed from the waist. Yezeletta did likewise.

"Farewell," she said.

Epilogue:
Taking Flight

———>>> ONE <<<———

I have seen them, gentle, tame, and meek,
That now are wild, and do not remember
That sometime they put themselves in danger
To take bread at my hand; and now they range,
Busily seeking with a continual change.

—Sir Thomas Wyatt the Elder,
They Flee from Me

"On the Green When Sun is Up"

[Production Run; Establishing Shot] Anne descended from the spectator's area; Peter and Leona placed their weapons in a safe state; Hank and Ondreya holstered theirs. They all clustered around Yezeletta, holding hands around her.

She spread her arms wide and hugged all of them all at once: they hugged each other and their tall friend.

—Child, the attack here has ended. We are safe, now. | Declaration;

Yezeletta repeated the message from the soundless voice in her head. "Let's go home," she said.

The Downloading - III

[Activate Output; Process Shot] It was early in the morning at his place in the second Project's living area. The man who called himself Caliban's Counselor rolled over in his bed in the early hours of the new day, and drifted back to sleep.

Then he came awake.

He was not alone in his bedroom.

That, on the face of it, was impossible. The residential complex was too well guarded by Project Security, for intruders to enter it unannounced.

He was not alone.

This was not to be accepted.

He reached for the telephone by the side of his bed, and pressed buttons.

A hand like a vise closed on his wrist. He felt the receiver being removed from his fingers. He looked up, now fully awake.

A face looked down at him. Large eyes, with actinic violet irises, looked at him dispassionately. Two hands took his wrists, held them down, while the other two took his head in a tight grip.

Behind his attacker, he could see the one who had been kidnapped for her function, but who now had a look of fire in her eyes, weapons on her hip, and a stance that was nowhere near servile.

"Stop this, young man!" he ordered him.

"I don't think so," Miranda replied, from behind Caliban. "He has a message for you."

She laughed.

Caliban's fingers ranged over the reclining man's scalp, looking for the interface points that his master had been so proud of. His former Counselor struggled against the grip Caliban had on his wrists, and achieved exactly nothing. Miranda came and sat on his legs, pressing them down with her weight.

Caliban *accessed* the interface points.

He downloaded the Program that the other Agent had deactivated for him in that last battle on a castle in the night sky, that was actually an excerpt from a painting. He could *see* the control code leaving his internal storage, and working its will on the man he held down on his own bed; he could feel the tenseness in his Counselor—his *former* Counselor—leaving his body, as the control programming established itself in his Tech-Bloc-designed interfaces, and as The Other took control of him.

Forever.

As the programming came down like the last nightfall on the man he once trusted implicitly, Caliban spoke once, the sentence Yezeletta had given him. With the finality of a binary download, it was the last thing the sentient part of his Counselor ever remembered afterwards of Caliban.

Then Caliban turned and left, taking his Woman with him.

THE DOWNLOAD

[Lexical: Parse: Close-Up] "It don't mean a thing, if it ain't got that swing."

VISIBLE AT A DISTANCE

[Remote Access; Long Shot] Zhongo and Zeke were out in the Milwaukee Spring, taking Twenty-Seventh Street south to the intersection where it changed, and actually obtained a name: Layton Avenue.

At the change-over point, on the east side of the road, the Mitchell Conservatory rose up from the ground, its exterior lot starting to turn a fitful green.

"Maybe the next tenant there is actually going to do some outside work," Zeke said.

Zhongo grinned, but the facial gesture had very little mirth in it. "I haven't made up my mind," he said. "I'm not particularly interested in what the previous owner did there."

Zeke looked at Zhongo from his driving with a swift glance, then planted his eyes dead-ahead. "Interested, huh?" was all he said.

"Interested," Zhongo replied, firmly. "The more I control hereabouts, the less that damned 'Lord of the Roads' can run. I'd like to run him right out of town, if I could. Lacking that, I'd like to put him out of business, and maybe out of the picture. For good."

Zeke pulled the car to a stop at a traffic light in a small commercial district, a block or so south of the Conservatory.

Another car pulled into the intersection.

"Zhongo!" Zeke said. "In that car!"

The car was a late model, neutral-colored, four-door sedan of no great distinction. The man driving it was almost studiously inconspicuous. With him—

"That's *her!*" Zhongo stated. "Leona!" He pulled out a notepad and a pen,

"What's the license number of that car?" Zeke pulled into the intersection, evincing horn-blasts of protest and outrage from other drivers, and read the plate to Zhongo.

"You haven't forgotten, have you?" Zeke said.

"I'm not damned likely. She just walked out. No corporate loyalty at all!"

"Isn't that new lover—what's her name? Sherry—as good a replacement?"

"I dislike disloyalty," Zhongo said coldly. "Sherry Kim is a sweet girl, and better at some things than Leona was, but Leona *deserted*." Zhongo made the last word sound like a curse.

"I *remember* deserters," his voice was ice.

"I won't forget."

Zeke continued to drive him south.

REWRITE-UPDATE

[Load, Execute; Traveling Matte] Caliban strode unimpeded through the halls of the nameless Project Installation. He returned to the place where he remembered his formative times: a small room, mostly occupied by a large bed and many monitoring devices. The workstation was still outside the single door (he pointed out to Miranda how there was no door-knob on the inside).

An attendant came out of another office at Caliban's entry, and tried to block his access to the workstation. He looked up at Caliban in surprise, as Caliban approached. He raised his hands in either salutation or defense, and Caliban slapped him with one hand, a blow that sent the attendant across the room.

He removed the monitor and network connections from the actual hardware chassis, and swiftly opened up the device. Carefully, if roughly, he dissected the hard-drives out of the device, and piled the remainder of the hardware in a heap on its table.

He stood back, and gestured to Miranda.

She drew one of her automatics, and emptied it into the mechanisms.

THE KEYHOLE

[Match-Cut] In a deserted building on Chicago's South Side, in a room that hadn't been occupied by any life-forms but mice, in a room that had been dark for fifty years, a light shone.

The light, a pastel blue, appeared in the center of the dark room. The mice looked up, the appearance a new experience to their generation.

The light went from a point source to a sphere, then shrank back to a point source, again.

The color changed: the blue became deeper, darker: the shade of blue of a dark winter's evening. It expanded, then contracted to a single blue point, and vanished.

The mice remembered it for the remainder of that afternoon.

THE EGRESS POINT

[Close-Up] Diana Koerner surveyed the results of the trace program she had spent the last week writing. Several transmissions had wended their way through the Searchlight Data Net, and her trace had determined that the routing had ended in Europe, at the Berlin router.

Beyond that, further investigations were problematical. She wasn't even particularly sure that this transmission, or, more accurately, instantiation of a transmission, was the one that had caused the arrest of a dozen of Searchlight's Finest.

But what clues she had pointed to it.

And the origin of the message: the Search/Net had been accessed from Chicago. Searchlight wasn't conducting any operations there. What the hell was going on, here, anyway?

Diana concentrated on her screen, as if she could get the workstation to display the answers by sheer mental force. She *could* use mental force, but it had to be represented by some seriously cogent programming.

In the meantime, twelve good agents were experiencing free room and board in the top floors of Madison's City-County Building, a short block from the State Capital.

Hmmmm. What about that guy who had been sent to...Milwaukee? Would he have anything to do with this?

And had he reported in, as of late?

Diana flagged Peter Rudenko's login on the Search/Net, and continued her investigations.

DATA DUMP/ANALYZE COMPLETE

[Assign File] Semyon looked at the display on the large screen, and at the six laser printers disgorging output onto standard A.4 size sheets of paper.

An army corporal was removing the sheets, and stacking them in small piles on several large conference tables, brought into the library for the purpose. More than three-quarters of the horizontal real-estate in the large room was covered with thick piles of printed listings.

The sealed interpreters had done the job for which the programmers in Saint Petersburg had designed them. The data contained in the shotgun barrels was now in a set of harmless data files, their defense-objects neutralized and rendered harmless by the interpreters. The computorial substrate within which the objects found themselves would not be able to run the embedded code with which those objects guarded their data.

The devices had been read out, the code within them made available to the discerning researchers in the agency in Saint Pete.

Now they would find out who had designed these, and then track back to the designers.

Alexei grinned, a lean gray Russian wolf's expression in the gathering twilight.

THE WRITER

In the Psychiatric Ward of Walter Reed Hospital, the man known as Anthony Russell sat up in his bed.

The night nurse saw the action on her monitor out of the corner of one eye, and looked at the small image, not quite believing what it was she saw.

She hit the button for the duty doctor, and hurried down to the room in which her comatose patient had resided for—she would have to check his records. He had been there since she had started at Psych.

When she entered the room, followed closely by the night physician, the patient seemed almost alert, and looking around the room with clear interest.

The doctor walked around the Russell's bed, scanning him with his processors, and downloading Russell's records from the Reed Mainframe.

Then he pulled up a stool, and sat next to Anthony Russell.

"Can you tell me your name?" the physician asked.

Russell smiled!

"What is your name?" the Duty Doctor asked again.

Russell held his right hand up and made circular motions.

"He wants to write," the Night Nurse said. "He may have—" She rummaged in a small cabinet, and produced a pen, and a yellow tablet of paper.

"Try this on him," she said.

The Duty Physician handed the tablet and the pen to Russell. He took them, and wrote "Anthony Russell" in a scrawly hand across most of the top on one sheet.

"Where have you been?" the doctor asked, almost rhetorically. Russell answered with a sketch.

Beneath his hand, in red ink, the picture of a woman began to form.

A woman wearing wrap-around silvered sunglasses and a trenchcoat. Sitting in a chair, holding a laptop computer.

With something like a large spider sitting on one shoulder.

——>>> **TWO** <<<——

The Light Fades, Fades....
It's gone. Only the River
Knows where to find light
Now and for one moment
More it has a silver face
To Show for all
Its centuries of dark thought.

—Larry Watson
"An Evening Along
the Wisconsin River",
1988

Gazing through
My reflection
To see
A trout's eye
Looking up at me
Through where
The reflection
Of my eye is
On the water.

—Antler:
"Eye to Eye",
1996

[Parallel process; Camera Goes With; Extending Upper; Arriflex]

Yezeletta Zargkonji looked below, to the flowing river that would someday carry her far out to a sunless sea in an Internet of the mind. Around her, the cool winds of Autumn blew, caressing her from unexpected directions and distances.

The sun was setting, a red flattened sphere tangent to the horizon. The cold air in the upper atmosphere had refracted the sun's image, creating two bright images to the north and south of the sun itself.

The sundogs were a rare occurrence. Yezeletta adjusted the contrast resolution of her eyes to see the faint multiple shadows on the ground that the extra sun-images caused.

Another sundog stood guard over the waning sun, directly above it. Around its edges, were barely visible indications of fringes of colors.

Yezeletta knew that at the exact point where the red sun would fall below the horizon, there would be a very brief flash of green, as the spectral output of the sun was cut off by the horizon. She widened the bandwidth of her eyes to its maximum, in anticipation.

There!

The brief flash, and its harmonics, appeared, then vanished into memory and into her internal systems as the sun set, and all that remained was the fading of the last sundog directly above.

Below her, at the foot of the hill she had walked up, they were waiting for her return. The celebration would be starting, and then....

She had never understood religion. Maybe she never would. She had not known that Protestant religions had borrowed the Jewish practice of using a cantor, a soloist who led the singing. Nor had she known that Grandfather Lenhaden was a lay pastor.

The wind blew across her shoulders; something tickled her left ear.

Yezeletta adjusted her eyes to optimize input for early evening, and followed the sensations.

Around her, there were tiny webs being spun by spiders taking flight into the night.

The diminutive aeronauts were taking off into a darkness that, for many of them, would not know another dawn. For the others, there would be a landing, and preparations for the closing jaws of Winter, and the opening of a new Spring.

Down there, her friends, and the man who was soon to be her husband in actual fact, were waiting.

Before her, the crescent new moon, almost directly above the setting sun, rode the sunset cirrus: a disembodied cheshire cat's grin in the red-lit clouds that still remained.

The spiders were heading into their own selective, private unknowns. They would go, not thinking of the difficulties of the trip, but only of the destination, a destination that was not an ending.

Did any of her friends know how vital they were to her? The people at the Ag Department—did they have even an inkling of how important they had been, and still were?

Yezeletta read out her internal systems. Nothing was amiss; she was functioning perfectly. She recalled Anne's description of Yezeletta as The

Spider-Queen, and then The Master Brewer of Milwaukee! Yezeletta had liked that, and she wasn't even that fond of beer.

Her own strange powers, her knowledge, what made her Yezeletta, were the things that Joe had loved abut her. He was not afraid, he was not intimidated. She recalled their first meeting. She hadn't managed to intimidate him even then. Now their lives, merged though they were, would merge in fact.

A new Journey.

One without an end.

—THE END—

Chicago: 1987-1994;

Madison: 1995-1996;

Milwaukee: 1996-2002.

Milwaukee: 2003-2015.

9 781944 322960